Using the pseudonym **J.D. Robb**, **Nora Roberts** published her first Robb novel in 1995 and introduced readers to her tough as nails, but emotionally damaged homicide cop Eve Dallas and billionaire Irish rogue Roarke.

With the In Death series, Robb has become one of the biggest thriller writers on earth, with each new novel reaching number one on the bestseller charts all over the world.

For more information, visit www.jd-robb.co.uk

J. D. ROBB OMNIBUS

Creation in Death
Strangers in Death

J. D. Robb

piatkus

PIATKUS

This omnibus edition first published in Great Britain in 2011 by Piatkus

Copyright © 2011 by Nora Roberts

Previously published separately:
Creation in Death first published in the United States in 2007 by G. P Putnam's Sons,
A division of Penguin Group (USA) Inc., New York
First published in Great Britain in 2007 by Piatkus Books
Paperback edition published in 2007 by Piatkus Books
Reprinted 2008, 2009, 2010
Copyright © 2007 by Nora Roberts
Strangers in Death first published in the United States in 2008 by G. P Putnam's Sons,
A division of Penguin Group (USA) Inc., New York
First published in Great Britain in 2008 by Piatkus Books
Paperback edition published in 2008 by Piatkus Books
Reprinted 2008 (twice), 2009
Copyright © 2008 by Nora Roberts

The moral right of the author has been asserted.

A CIP catalogue record for this book
is available from the British Library.

ISBN 978-0-7499-5665-3

Typeset in Granjon by Phoenix Photosetting, Chatham, Kent
Printed and bound in Great Britain by CPI Mackays, Chatham ME5 8TD

Papers used by Piatkus are natural, renewable and recyclable
products sourced from well-managed forests and certified
in accordance with the rules of the Forest Stewardship Council.

Mixed Sources
Product group from well-managed
forests and other controlled sources
www.fsc.org Cert no. SGS-COC-004081
© 1996 Forest Stewardship Council

Piatkus
An imprint of
Little, Brown Book Group
100 Victoria Embankment
London EC4Y 0DY

An Hachette UK Company
www.hachette.co.uk

www.piatkus.co.uk

Creation in Death

Ah! The Clock is always slow;
It is later than you think.
—ROBERT W. SERVICE

And music pours on mortals
Her magnificent disdain.
—RALPH WALDO EMERSON

Creation in Death

PROLOGUE

FOR HIM, DEATH WAS A VOCATION. KILLING WAS NOT MERELY an act, nor a means to an end. It certainly was not an impulse of the moment or a path to gain and glory.

Death was, in and of itself, the all.

He considered himself a late bloomer, and often bemoaned the years before he'd found his raison d'être. All that time lost, all those opportunities missed. But still, he had bloomed, and was forever grateful that he had finally looked inside himself and seen what he was. What he was meant for.

He was a maestro in the art of death. The keeper of time. The bringer of destiny.

It had taken time, of course, and experimentation. His mentor's time had run out long before he himself had become the master. And even at his prime, his teacher had not envisioned the full scope, the full power. He was proud that he had learned, had not only honed his skills but had expanded them while perfecting his techniques.

He'd learned, and learned quickly, that he preferred women as his partners in the duet. In the grand opera he wrote, and rewrote, they outperformed the men.

His requirements were few, but very specific.

He didn't rape them. He'd experimented there, as well, but had found rape distasteful and demeaning to both parties.

There was nothing elegant about rape.

As with any vocation, any art that required great skill and concentration, he'd learned he required holidays—what he thought of as his dormant periods.

During them he would entertain himself as anyone might on a holiday. He would travel, explore, eat fine meals. He might ski or scuba dive, or simply sit under an umbrella on a lovely beach and while away the time reading and drinking mai tais.

He would plan, he would prepare, he would make *arrangements*.

By the time he went back to work, he was refreshed and eager.

As he was now, he thought as he readied his tools. More, so much more . . . with his latest dormant period had come the understanding of his own destiny. So he'd gone back to his roots. And there, where he had first seriously plied his trade, he would re-form and remake connections before the curtain came down.

It added so many interesting layers, he mused, as he tested the edge on an antique switchblade with a horn handle he'd purchased while touring Italy. He turned the steel blade to the light, admired it. Circa nineteen fifty-three, he thought.

It was a classic for a reason.

He enjoyed using tools from long ago, though he also employed more modern pieces. The laser, for instance—so very excellent for applying the element of heat.

There must be a variety—sharp, dull, cold, heat—a series of elements in various forms, in various cycles. It took a great deal of skill, and patience and concentration to spin those cycles out to the absolute zenith of his partner's aptitude.

Then, and only then, would he complete the project and know he'd done his best work.

This one had been an excellent choice. He could congratulate himself on that. For three days and four nights, she'd survived—and there was life in her yet. It was so satisfying.

He'd started out slowly, naturally. It was vital, absolutely vital, to build and build *and build* to that ultimate crescendo.

He knew, as a master of his craft knew such things, that they were approaching that peak.

"Music on," he ordered, then stood, eyes closed as he absorbed the opening strains of Puccini's *Madame Butterfly*.

He understood the central character's choice of death for love. Hadn't it been that choice, so many years before, that had sent him on this path?

He slipped the protective cover over his tailored white suit.

He turned. He looked at her.

Such a lovely thing, he thought now. He remembered, as he always did, her precursor. Her mother, he supposed.

The Eve of all the others.

All that pretty white skin covered with burns and bruises, with narrow slices and meticulous little punctures. They showed his restraint, his patience, his thoroughness.

Her face was untouched—as yet. He always saved the face for last. Her eyes were fixed on his—wide, but yes, a bit dull. She had experienced nearly all she was capable of experiencing. Well, the timing worked well. Very well, because he'd anticipated, he'd prepared.

He'd already secured the next.

He glanced, almost absently, at the second woman across the room, peacefully sleeping under the drug he'd administered. Perhaps tomorrow, he thought, they could begin.

But for now . . .

He approached his partner.

He never gagged his partners, believing they should be free to scream, to beg, to weep, even to curse him. To express all emotion.

"Please," she said. Only, "Please."

"Good morning! I hope you rested well. We have a lot of work to do today." He smiled as he laid the edge of the knife between her first and second ribs. "So let's get started, shall we?"

Her screams were like music.

IEVERY ONCE IN A WHILE, EVE THOUGHT, LIFE was really worth living. Here she was, stretched out in a double-wide sleep chair watching a vid. There was plenty of action in the vid—she liked watching stuff blow up—and the "plotline" meant she didn't have to actually think.

She could just watch.

She had popcorn, drowned in butter and salt, the fat cat stretched across her feet keeping them nice and warm. She had the next day off, which meant she could sleep until she woke up, then veg until she grew mold.

Best of all, she had Roarke cozied up in the chair beside her. And since her husband had complained after one handful that the popcorn was disgusting, she had the whole bowl to herself.

Really, it didn't get any better.

Then again, maybe it did—would—as she planned to nail her husband like an airjack when the vid was over. Her version of a double feature.

"Iced," she said after a midair collision of a tourist tram and an ad blimp. "Seriously iced."

"I thought this storyline would appeal to you."

"There *is* no storyline." She took another handful of popcorn. "That's what appeals to me. It's just some dialogue stitching explosions together."

"There was brief full-frontal nudity."

"Yeah, but that was for you, and those of your ilk." She flicked a glance up at him, as on screen pedestrians ran screaming from falling wreckage.

He was so damn gorgeous—in anyone's ilk. A face sculpted by talented gods on a really good day. Strong bones laying the excellent foundation under that Irish white skin, the mouth that made her think of poets, until he used it on her so she couldn't think at all. Those wild Celt's eyes that saw just who she was.

Then you topped it off with all that black silky hair, added that long, lean body, the sexy Irish accent, tossed in brains, wit, temper, and street smarts and you had yourself a hell of a package.

And he was all hers.

She intended to make really good use of what was hers for the next thirty-six hours or so.

On screen a street battle erupted among the rubble with hurled miniboomers and whooshing blasters. The hero—distinguished by the fact he'd kicked the most ass thus far—burst through the mêlée on the back of a jet-bike.

Obviously caught up, Roarke dug into the popcorn. Then immediately pulled his hand out again and scowled at his own fingers. "Why don't you just dump salt into melted butter and eat that?"

"The corn makes a nice vehicle for it. Aw, what's the matter? You get your pretty hands messy?"

He wiped his fingers down her face, smiled. "Clean now."

"Hey!" She laughed, set the bowl aside. It would be safe, she knew, as even Galahad, the cat, wouldn't eat it her way. She poked a finger hard into Roarke's ribs, rolled until she was on top of him.

Maybe they'd just have a sneak preview of tonight's second feature.

"Going to pay for that one, pal."

"How much?"

"It's going to be the installment plan. I figure we'll start with . . ." She lowered her mouth to his, nipped that excellent bottom lip. She felt his hand move over her. Lifting her head, she narrowed her eyes at him. "Are you feeling my ass or wiping the rest of the butter and salt off your fingers?"

"Two birds, one ass. About that first payment."

"The interest is going to be—ha-ha—stiff." She went for the mouth again, started to sink in.

And her communicator signaled.

"Goddamn it." She pulled up. "This is crap. I'm not on call."

"Why is it in your pocket?"

"Habit. Stupid. Damn it," she spurted as she dragged the communicator out, checked the display. "It's Whitney." Sighing, she shoved a hand through her hair. "I have to take it."

"Pause vid," Roarke ordered, then rubbed the butter off her cheek. "Lights on, seventy percent."

"Thanks." Eve clicked on. "Dallas."

"Lieutenant, report to East River Park, at Second Street and Avenue D, as primary."

"Commander—"

"I understand you were neither on duty nor on call," he interrupted. "Now you are."

The word *why* went through her head, but she was too well-trained to verbalize it. "Yes, sir. I'll contact Detective Peabody en route."

"I'll see you at Central."

He clicked off.

"Unusual," Roarke commented. He'd already turned off the vid. "For the commander to contact you personally, and to yank you in this way."

"Something hot," Eve replied and shoved the communicator back in her pocket. "I've got nothing hot open. Not that it would have him tagging me directly when I'm not on the roll. Sorry." She glanced over. "Screws vid night."

"It'll keep. But as my evening is now open, I believe I'll go with you. I know how to keep out of the way," he reminded her before she could object.

He did, she admitted. And since she knew he'd changed his own schedule, possibly postponing acquiring a small country or planetoid, it seemed only fair.

"Then let's get moving."

He knew how to stay out of the way when it suited him. He also knew how to observe. What Roarke saw when they arrived at the park were a number of black-and-whites, a small army of uniforms and crime scene techs.

The media people who had a nose for this sort of thing were there, firmly blocked by part of that army. The barricades had been erected, and like the media and the civilian gawkers, he would have to make his observations from behind them.

"If you get bored," Eve told him, "just take off. I'll make my own way back."

"I'm not easily bored."

He watched her now, observed her now. His cop. The wind kicked at her long black coat, one she'd need as this first day of March was proving as brutal as the rest of 2060 had been. She hooked her badge on her belt, though he wondered how anyone could mistake her for anything other than a cop, and one with authority.

Tall and rangy, she moved to the barricades in strong strides. Her hair, short and brown, fluttered a little in that same wind—a wind that carried the scent of the river.

He watched her face, the way those whiskey-colored eyes tracked, the way her mouth—that had been so soft and warm on his—firmed. The lights played over her face, shifting those angles and planes.

She looked back at him, very briefly. Then she moved on, moved through the barricades to do what, he supposed, she'd been born to do.

She strode through the uniforms and techs. Some recognized her; some simply recognized what Roarke had. Authority. When she was approached by one of the uniforms, she stopped, brushed her coat back to tap her badge.

"Sir. I was ordered to look out for you, to escort you. My partner and I were first on scene."

"Okay." She gave him a quick once-over. On the young side, cut as clean as a military band. His cheeks were pink from the cold. His voice said native New Yorker, heading toward Brooklyn. "What have we got?"

"Sir. I was ordered to let you see for yourself."

"That so?" She scanned the badge on his thick uniform coat. "All right, Newkirk, let's go see for myself."

She gauged the ground covered, studied the line of trees and shrubs. It appeared the scene was well secured, locked tight. Not only from the land side, she noted as she glimpsed the river. The water cops were out, barricading the riverbank.

She felt a cold line of anticipation up her spine. Whatever this was, it was major.

The lights the techs had set up washed white over the shadows. Through them, she saw Morris coming toward her. Major, she thought again, for the chief medical examiner to be called on scene. And she saw it in his face, the tightness of concern.

"Dallas. They said you were on scene."

"They didn't say you were."

"I was nearby, out with friends. A little blues club over on Bleecker."

Which explained the boots, she supposed. The black and silver pattern she assumed had once belonged to some reptile wasn't the sort of thing a man would normally sport on a crime scene. Not even the stylish Morris.

His long black coat blew back to reveal a cherry-red lining. Under it, he wore black pants, black turtleneck—extreme casual wear for him. His long, dark hair was slicked back into a tail, bound top and tip with silver bands.

"The commander called you in," she said.

"He did. I haven't touched the body yet—visual only. I was waiting for you."

She didn't ask why. She understood she was meant to form her own conclusions without any outside data. "With us, Newkirk," she ordered, and walked toward the lights.

It might have been a sheet of ice or snow. From a distance, it might appear to be. And from a distance, the body arranged on it might appear to be artful—a model for some edgy shoot.

But she knew what it was, even from a distance, and the line of cold up her spine took on teeth.

Her eyes met Morris's. But they said nothing.

It wasn't ice, or snow. She wasn't a model or a piece of art.

Eve took a can of Seal-It from her kit, set the kit down.

"You're still wearing your gloves," Morris told her. "That stuff's hell on gloves."

"Right." With her gaze steady on the body, she pulled the gloves off, stuffed them in her pocket. Sealed up. She hooked her recorder to her coat. "Record on." The techs would be running one, as would Morris. She'd have her own.

"Victim is female, Caucasian. Did you ID her?" she asked Morris.

"No."

"As yet unidentified. Mid- to late twenties, brown and blue. Small tat of a blue and yellow butterfly on left hip. The body is naked, posed on a white cloth, arms spread, palms up. There's a silver ring on the third finger of her left hand. Various visible wounds indicating torture. Lacerations, bruising, punctures, burns. Crosshatch of slash wounds on both wrists, probable cause of death." She looked at Morris.

"Yes. Probable."

"There's carving in the torso, reading eighty-five hours, twelve minutes, thirty-eight seconds."

Eve let out a long, long breath. "He's back."

"Yes," Morris agreed. "Yes, he is."

"Let's get an ID, TOD." She glanced around. "Could have brought her in through the park, or by water. Ground's rock hard, and it's a public park. We may get some footprints, but they won't do us much good."

She reached in her kit again, paused when Peabody hustled up. "Sorry it took me so long. Had to come crosstown and there was a jam on the subway. Hey, Morris!" Peabody, a red cap pulled low over her dark hair, rubbed her nose, looked at the body. "Oh, man. Someone put her through it."

In her sturdy winter boots, Peabody sidestepped for a better view. "The message. There's something about that. Dim bell." She tapped at her temple. "Something."

"Get her ID," Eve ordered, then turned to Newkirk. "What do you know?"

He'd been standing at attention, but went even stiffer, even straighter. "My partner and I were on patrol, and observed what appeared to be a robbery in progress. We pursued a male individual into the park. The suspect headed in an easterly direction. We were unable to apprehend, the suspect had a considerable lead. My partner and I split up, intending to cut off the suspect. At which time, I discovered the victim. I called for my partner, then notified Commander Whitney."

"Notifying the commander isn't procedure, Officer Newkirk."

"No, sir. I felt, in these circumstances, that the notification was not only warranted but necessary."

"Why?"

"Sir, I recognized the signature. Lieutenant, my father's on the job. Nine years ago he was part of a task force formed to investigate a series of torture murders." Newkirk's gaze shifted to the body, back to Eve's. "With this signature."

"Your father's Gil Newkirk?"

"Yes, sir, Lieutenant." His shoulders relaxed a fraction at her question. "I followed the case back then, as much as I could. Over the years since, particularly since I've been on the job, my father and I have discussed it. The way you do. So I recognized the signature. Sir, I felt, in this case, breaking standard and notifying the commander directly was correct."

"You'd be right. Good call, Officer. Stand by."

She turned to Peabody.

"Vic is ID'd as Sarifina York, age twenty-eight. Address is on West Twenty-first. Single. Employed at Starlight. That's a retro club in Chelsea."

Eve crouched down. "She wasn't killed here, and she wasn't wrapped in this cloth when she was brought here. He likes the stage clean. TOD, Morris."

"Eleven this morning."

"Eighty-five hours. So he took her sometime Monday, or earlier if he didn't start the clock. Historically, he starts on the first very shortly after he makes the snatch."

"Starting the clock when he begins to work on them," Morris confirmed.

"Oh, shit. Oh, crap, I remember this." Peabody sat back on her heels. Her cheeks were reddened by the wind, and her eyes had widened with memory. "The media tagged him The Groom."

"Because of the ring," Eve told her. "We let the ring leak."

"It was, like, ten years ago."

"Nine," Eve corrected. "Nine years, two weeks, and . . . three days since we found the first body."

"Copycat," Peabody suggested.

"No, this is him. The message, the time—we didn't let that leak to the media. We closed that data up tight. But we never closed the case. We never closed him. Four women in fifteen days. All brunettes, the youngest twenty-eight, the oldest thirty-three. All tortured, between a period of twenty-three and fifty-two hours."

Eve looked at the carving again. "He's gotten better at his work."

Morris nodded as he made his study. "It appears the more superficial wounds were inflicted first, as before. I'll confirm when I get her home."

"Ligature marks, ankles, wrists—just above the slashes." Eve lifted one of the hands. "She didn't just lie there and take it, not from the looks of this. He used drugs on the others."

"Yes, I'll check."

Eve remembered it all, every detail of it, and all the frustration and fury that rode with it. "He'll have washed her, washed her clean—hair and body—with high-end products. Wrapped her up, probably in plastic, for transport. We never got so much as a speck of lint off any of the others. Bag the ring, Peabody. You take her, Morris."

She straightened. "Officer Newkirk, I'm going to need a full and detailed written report, asap."

"Yes, sir."

"Who's your LT?"

"Grohman, sir. I'm out of the one-seven."

"Your father still there?"

"He is, yes, sir."

"Okay, Newkirk, get me that report. Peabody, check Missing Persons, see if the vic was reported. I need to contact the commander."

By the time she exited the park, the wind had died down. Small mercy. The crowd of gawkers had thinned out, but the media hounds were more dogged. The only way to control the situation, she knew, was to meet it head on.

"I won't answer questions." She had to shout to be heard over the questions already being hurled at her. "I will make a brief statement. And if you keep shouting at me, you won't get that either. Earlier this evening"—she continued through the shouts and the noise level dropped—"officers of the NYPSD discovered the body of a woman in East River Park."

"Has she been identified?"

"How was she killed?"

Eve simply stared holes into the reporters who attempted to break rank. "Did you guys just drop into the city out of a puffy cloud, or are you just running your mouths to hear your own voice? As anyone with half a brain knows, the woman's identity will not be given out until after notification of next of kin. Cause of death will be determined by the medical examiner. And anyone stupid enough to ask me if we have any leads is going to be blocked from receiving any ensuing data on this matter. Clear? Now stop wasting my time."

She stalked off, and was halfway to her own vehicle when she spotted Roarke leaning against the hood. She'd completely forgotten about him.

"Why aren't you home?"

"What? And miss the entertainment? Hello, Peabody."

"Hey." She managed to smile even though her cheeks felt like a couple of slabs of ice. "You've been here the whole time?"

"Nearly. I did wander off." He opened the car door, took out a couple of insulated takeout cups. "To get you presents."

"It's coffee," Peabody said, reverently. "It's hot coffee."

"Should thaw you out a bit. Bad?" he said to Eve.

"Very. Peabody, track down contact info on the vic's next of kin."

"York, Sarifina. On it."

"I'll get myself home," Roarke began, then stopped. "What was that name?"

"York," Eve repeated, "Sarifina." Something sank in her belly. "You're going to tell me you knew her."

"Late twenties, attractive brunette?" He leaned back against the car again when Eve nodded. "I hired her a few months ago to manage a club in Chelsea. I can't say I knew her other than I found her bright, energetic, capable. How did she die?"

Before she could answer, Peabody stepped back up. "Mother in Reno—that's Nevada—father in Hawaii. Bet it's warm there. She has a sister in the city. Murray Hill. And the Missing Person's data came through. The sister reported her missing yesterday."

"Let's take the vic's apartment first, then the club, then the next of kin."

Roarke laid a hand on Eve's arm. "You haven't told me how she died."

"Badly. This isn't the place for the details. I can arrange for transpo for you or—"

"I'm going with you. She was one of mine," he said before she could object. "I'm going with you."

She didn't argue. Not only would it waste time and energy, she understood. And since she had him, she'd use him.

"If an employee—especially one in a managerial position—didn't show for work a few days running, would you be notified?"

"Not necessarily." He did what he could to make himself comfortable in the back of the police issue. "And I certainly wouldn't know her schedule off the top of my head, but I will find out about that. If she missed work, it's likely someone covered for her, and—or—that her absence was reported to a supervisor in that particular arm of the Entertainment Division."

"I need a name on that."

"You'll have it."

"Reported missing yesterday. Whoever was assigned to that case would have, or damn well should have, interviewed coworkers at the club, neighbors, friends. We need to connect to that, Peabody."

"I'll run it down."

"Tell me," Roarke repeated, "how she died."

"Morris will determine cause of death."

"Eve."

She flipped a glance in the rearview mirror, met his eyes. "Okay, I can tell you how it went down or close to it. She was stalked. The killer would take all the time he needed to observe and note her habits, her routines, her mode of traveling, her vulnerabilities—i.e., when she would most likely be alone and accessible. When he was ready, he'd make the grab. Most likely off the street. He'd have his own vehicle for this purpose. He'd drug her and take her to his . . ."

They'd called it his workshop, Eve remembered.

". . . to the location he'd prepared, most likely a private home. Once there he would either keep her drugged until he was ready, or—if she was the first—he'd begin."

"The first?"

"That's right. And when he was ready, he'd start the clock. He'd remove her clothes; he would bind her. His preferred method of binding is rope—a good hemp. It chafes during struggle. He would use four methods of torture—physically, we can't speak to psychologically—which are heat, cold, sharp implements, and dull implements. He would employ these methods at increasing severity. He'd continue until, you could speculate, the victim no longer provides him with enough stimulation or pleasure or interest. Then he ends it by slitting their wrists and letting them bleed out. Postmortem, he carves into their torsos, the time—in hours, minutes, and seconds—they survived."

There was a long moment of absolute silence. "How long?" Roarke asked.

"She was strong. He washes them afterward. Scrubs them down using a high-end soap and shampoo. We think he wraps them in plastic, then transports them to a location he'd have already scouted out and selected. He lays them out there, on a clean white cloth. He puts a silver band on their ring finger, left hand."

"Aye." Roarke murmured it as he stared out the window. "I remember some of this. I've heard some of this."

"Between February eleventh and February twenty-sixth, 2051, he abducted, tortured, and killed four women in this manner. Then he stopped. Just stopped. Into the wind, into the fucking ether. I'd hoped into Hell."

Roarke understood now why she'd been called in, off the roll, by the commander. "You worked these murders."

"With Feeney. He was primary. I was a detective, just made second grade, and we worked it. We had a task force by the second murder. And we never got him."

Four women, Eve thought, who had never gotten justice.

"He's surfaced again, here and there," she continued. "Two weeks, two and a half—four or five women. Then he goes under. A year, a year and a half. Now he's come back to New York, where we think he started. Back to where he started, and this time, we'll finish it."

I n his well-appointed living room, with the split of champagne he traditionally opened to celebrate the end of a successful project, the man the media had long ago dubbed The Groom settled down in front of his entertainment screen.

It was too early, he knew, most likely too early for any reports. It would be morning before his latest creation was discovered. But he couldn't resist checking.

A few moments, just to see, he told himself, then he'd enjoy his champagne with some music. Puccini, perhaps, in honor of . . . he had to pause and think before he remembered her name. Sarifina, yes. Such a lovely name. Puccini for Sarifina. He really believed she'd responded to Puccini best.

He surfed the channels, and was rewarded almost immediately. Delighted, he sat up, crossed his ankles, and prepared to listen to his latest reviews.

Identification is not being released in order for the woman's next of kin to be notified. While there is no confirmation at this time that the woman was murdered, the participation of Lieutenant Eve Dallas on the scene indicates foul play is being considered.

He applauded, lightly, when Eve's face came on screen. "There you are," he said. "Hello, again! So nice, so very nice to see old friends. And this time, this time we're going to get to know each other so very much better."

He lifted his glass, held it out in a toast. "I know you're going to be my very finest work."

2

SARIFINA'S APARTMENT WAS URBAN HIP. STRONG colors dominated in paint and fabric, with glossy black as counterpoint in tables, shelves. Sleek and vibrant, Eve thought. And low-maintenance, which made her think of a woman who didn't have the time or the inclination to fuss.

Her bed was made, covered with a stoplight-red spread and boldly patterned pillows. In the closet was a collection of vintage gowns. Sleek again, simple, and still vibrant in color. Shoes Eve thought might be vintage as well were in clear protective boxes.

She took care of what was hers.

"Is this the sort of gear she'd wear at the club?" Eve asked Roarke.

"Yes, exactly. It's retro—1940s theme. She'd be expected to mingle, to recognize and greet regulars, to table hop. And to look the part."

"Guess she would have. Some more up-to-date street clothes, two business-type suits. We'll tag her electronics," she added glancing at the bedside 'link. "See if he contacted her. Not his usual style, but things change. Tag her 'links, her comp. Did she have an office at the club?"

"Yes."

"We'll tag the e-stuff there, too." She pulled open a drawer on the little desk under the window. "No date book, no planner, no pocket 'link. She would have had them on her. Big-ass purse in the closet, and one of those—what do you call them—city bags. Go with the suit and the street clothes. A few evening bags. We'll see if the sister knows what's missing."

"A pint of soy milk in the fridge," Peabody reported as she entered. "Expired Wednesday. Some leftover Chinese, which by my gauge has been in there near to a week. Found a memo cube."

Peabody held it up. "Shopping list—market stuff and a few other things. Also a fridge photo of her and a guy, but it wasn't on the fridge. It was facedown in the kitchen drawer, which says recently *ex*-boyfriend to me."

"All right, let's bag and tag." Eve glanced at her wrist unit. It was nearly one in the morning. If they started to knock on doors and woke up neighbors at this hour, it would only piss people off.

Pissed people were less willing to talk to cops.

"We'll hit the club next."

With Roarke's fondness for old vids, particularly the moody black-and-whites produced in the middle of the last century, Eve knew something about the fashions and music, the cadence of the 1940s. At least as depicted in the Hollywood of that day.

Walking into Starlight at two in the morning, she felt she now also knew what it might be like to take a spin in a time machine.

The club was a wide and sparkling space divided into three levels. Each was accessed by a short set of wide, white stairs. And each, even at this hour, was filled with people who sat at white-clothed tables or silver-cushioned booths.

The waitstaff, men in formal white suits, women in short, full-skirted black dresses, moved from table to table serving drinks from trays. The patrons were decked out in black tie, retro suits, sleek gowns of the type that had been in Sarifina's closet, or elaborate and frothy ones.

Elegance and sophistication were the bywords, and Eve was mildly surprised to see tables of people in their twenties, straight through to those who had, no doubt, celebrated their centennial.

Music pumped out from the band on the glossy black stage. Or maybe "orchestra" was the term, she thought, as there were at least twenty of them with strings, horns, a piano, drums. And the swinging beat had couples massing over what was the centerpiece of the club. The dance floor.

Black and silver, the large pattern of squares gleamed and sparkled under the shimmering lights of slowly revolving mirror balls.

"This is, like, ultimately uptown," Peabody commented. "Extreme."

"Everything old is new again," Roarke said, scanning the club. "You'll want the assistant manager here, a Zela Wood."

"You have all your employees' names at the tips of your fingers?" Eve asked.

"No, actually. I looked up the file. Name, schedule, ID photo. And . . ." He zeroed in. "Ah, yes, that would be Zela."

Eve followed his direction. The striking woman wore pale gold that glowed against skin the color of good, strong coffee. Her hair was worn in long, loose waves that tumbled around her shoulders, down her back. She covered a lot of ground quickly, Eve noted, and still managed to glide as if she had all the time in the world.

It was obvious she'd seen and recognized the big boss as her eyes— nearly the same color as her dress—were fixed on him. Her fingers skimmed the silver rail as she climbed the steps toward him.

"Ms. Wood."

"How lovely." She offered him a hand and a dazzling smile. "I'll have a table arranged right away for you and your party."

"We don't want a table." Eve drew Zela's eyes to hers. "Let's see your office."

"Of course," Zela said without missing a beat. "If you'll just come with me."

"My wife," Roarke said and got an automatic scowl from Eve, "Lieutenant Dallas, and her partner, Detective Peabody. We need to talk, Zela."

"Yes, all right." Her voice remained as smooth as the cream that might be poured in that strong, black coffee. But worry came into her eyes.

She led the way past the coat check, the silver doors of rest rooms, then used a code to access a private elevator.

Moments later, they stepped out into the twenty-first century.

The room was simply and efficiently furnished, and reflected business. All business. Wall screens displayed the club, various areas—which included the kitchen, wine cellar, and liquor storage area. The desk held a multi-link, a computer, and a tray of disc files.

"Can I offer you anything to drink?" Zela began.

"No, thanks. You know Sarifina York?"

"Yes, of course." The worry deepened. "Is something wrong?"

"When did you last see her?"

"Monday. We have our Monday teas geared toward our older patrons. Sarifina runs those, she has such a knack for it. She's on from one to seven on Mondays, and I take the evening shift. She left about eight, a little before eight, I think. I asked because she didn't show on Wednesday."

Zela glanced at Roarke, pushed at her hair. "Tuesdays are her night off, but she didn't come in Wednesday. I covered. I just thought . . ."

Zela began to fiddle with the necklace she wore, running her fingers over the sparkling, clear stones. "She had a breakup with the man she's been seeing, and she was down about it. I thought they might have picked things up again."

"Has she missed work without notice before?" Eve asked.

"No."

"Are you saying that to cover?"

"No. No. Sari's never missed." Now Zela's gaze latched onto Roarke's face. "Never missed, and that's why I covered for her initially. She loves working here, and she's wonderful at her job."

"I understand and appreciate that you'd cover a night for a friend and coworker, Zela," Roarke told her.

"Thank you. When she didn't show Thursday, and I couldn't reach her, well, I'm not sure if I was annoyed or worried. A combination of both, really, so I contacted her sister. Sari had her sister listed as contact person. I didn't contact your office, sir. I didn't want to get her in trouble."

Zela's breath trembled as she drew it in. "But she is in trouble, isn't she? You're here because she's in trouble."

It was going to be a kick in the face, Eve knew. It was always a kick in the face. "I'm sorry to tell you, but Sarifina is dead."

"She's . . . what? What did you say?"

"You should sit down, Zela." Taking her arm, Roarke nudged her gently into a chair.

"You said . . . she's dead? There was an accident? How . . ." Those pale gold eyes gleamed with wet and shock.

"She was murdered. I'm sorry. You were friends?"

"Oh, God. Oh, God. When? How? I don't understand."

"We're looking into that, Ms. Wood." Eve let her gaze drift briefly to Roarke as he walked to a wall panel, and opening it chose a bottle of brandy from the selection of liquors. "Can you tell me if anyone bothered her or seemed unusually interested in her?"

"No. No. I mean, a lot of people were interested in her. She's the sort of person who interests people. I don't understand."

"Did she complain about anyone bothering her, or making her uncomfortable?"

"No."

"Drink a bit of this." Roarke pressed a glass of brandy into Zela's hand.

"Has anyone come in, asking questions about her?"

"Just tonight, a few hours ago, a police detective. He said, he told me that Sari's sister had reported her missing. And I thought . . ." Tears spilled now. "I honestly thought Sari's sister was overreacting. I was a little worried, a little, because I thought she'd gone back to the ex, and he'd talked her into blowing off this job. That was the problem," Zela continued as she rubbed a tear from her cheek. "He didn't like her working here because it took up most of her nights."

Now those damp eyes widened. "Did he hurt her? Oh, my God."

"Did he strike you as the type who would?"

"No. No, no. A whiner, that's what I thought. Passive-aggressive, and kind of a jerk. I'd never have believed he'd hurt her. Not like this."

"We have no reason to believe he has, at this time. Can you give me his name, his address?"

"Yes. All right."

"Would you still have your security discs from Monday?"

"Yes. Yes, we keep them for a week."

"I'm going to need those. I'll take the discs from last Saturday and Sunday as well. On Monday, did she leave alone?"

"I didn't see her leave. What I mean is, I came in here at about quarter to eight, and she was just putting on her coat. I said something like, 'So you can't get enough of this place?' and she laughed. Just wanted to finish up some paperwork. We talked for a few minutes, just shop talk mostly. She said she'd see me Wednesday, and I said . . . I said, 'Have a good day off.' Then she went out of the office, and I sat down to do a quick check on the late reservations. As I assumed, she'd gone straight out. She never mentioned being with anyone."

"All right. I'd appreciate it if you could get me those discs, and that information on the man she'd been seeing."

"Yes." Zela got to her feet. "Is there something I can do? I don't know what I should do. Her sister? Should I contact her sister?"

"We'll be taking care of that."

When there was a knock on the door in the middle of the night, most people knew, in the gut, it wasn't going to be good news.

When Jaycee York opened her door, Eve could already see the dread. Even as she stared into Eve's eyes, before a word was spoken, Eve saw grief rise up through that dread.

"Sari. Oh, no. Oh, no."

"Ms. York, may we come in?"

"You found her. But . . ."

"We should go inside, Ms. York." Peabody took Jaycee's arm, eased her around. "We should go sit down."

"It's going to be bad. It's going to be very, very bad. Will you please say it quickly? Would you please tell me fast?"

"Your sister's dead, Ms. York." With her hand still on Jaycee's arm, Peabody felt the shudder. "We're very sorry for your loss."

"I knew, I think. I knew as soon as they called from the club. I knew something awful had happened to her."

Peabody guided Jaycee to a chair in the living area. Lots of clutter, Eve noted, the kind that shouted a family lived there. There were photographs of young boys, of a laughing man, of the victim.

There were several colorful throws, a lot of big floor pillows that looked as if they'd had a great deal of use.

"Is your husband at home, Ms. York?" Eve asked. "Would you like us to get him for you?"

"He's not . . . Clint took the boys to Arizona. To . . . to Sedona. A week. It's a school camp." Jaycee looked around the room as if expecting to see them. "They went to camp, and I didn't. I didn't want to camp, and I had work. And wouldn't it be nice, I thought, wouldn't it be nice to have a week at home by myself. I didn't call them. I didn't tell them because they'd worry. Why worry them when everything's going to be fine? I kept telling myself everything was going to be fine.

"But it's not. It's not."

She covered her face with her hands and began to weep.

Eve put her at a decade older than her sister. Her hair was short and blond, her devastated eyes a summer blue.

"I called the police." She sobbed out the words. "When they said she hadn't come into work, I called the police. I went to her apartment, but she wasn't there, so I called. And they said to file a report. A missing person's report."

She closed her eyes. "What happened to Sari? What happened to my sister?"

There was an ottoman in front of the chair. Eve sat on it so they would be face to face. "I'm sorry. She was murdered."

The splotchy color weeping painted in her cheeks died away to shock-white. "They said—I heard—they said there was a woman found tonight, in East River Park. Identification withheld, they said, until notification of next of kin. I'm next of kin."

Jaycee pressed a hand to her lips. "I thought, 'No, no, that's not Sari. Sari doesn't live on the East Side.' But I kept waiting for someone to knock on the door. And you did."

"You were close, you and your sister."

"I . . . I can't. I can't."

"I'm going to get you some water, Ms. York." Peabody touched a hand to Jaycee's shoulder. "Is it all right if I go into the kitchen and get you some water?"

Jaycee only nodded as she stared at Eve. "She was my babydoll. My mother died when I was little, and a few years later, my father remarried. They had Sari. Sarifina. She was so pretty, like a doll. I loved her."

"Would she have told you if anyone was bothering her? If she was disturbed or uneasy about anything?"

"Yes. We talked all the time. She loved her job. She was so good at it, and it made her so happy. But it was a problem for Cal. The man she'd been seeing for the last few months. The fact that she worked at night and couldn't spend that time with him. She was angry and hurt that he'd given her an ultimatum. That she had to quit her job or he'd break things off. So they broke up. She was better off."

"Because?"

"He isn't good enough for her. That's not just sister talk." She paused, took the water Peabody offered her. "Thank you. Thanks. He just wasn't good enough—selfish streak, and he didn't like the fact she was making more money that he was. She knew it, recognized it, and was ready to move on. Still, she was sad about it. Sari doesn't like to lose. You don't think . . . Do you think Cal hurt her?"

"Do you?"

"No." Jaycee drank, breathed carefully, took another small sip. "I wouldn't have thought it. It never crossed my mind. Why would he? He didn't love her," Jaycee said dully. "And he was much too interested in himself to get worked up enough to . . . I need to see her. I need to see Sari."

"We'll arrange for that. When did you see her last?"

"Last Sunday afternoon. Before Clint and the boys left. She came by to say good-bye. She was so full of life, of energy. We made plans to shop on Saturday—tomorrow. My guys aren't coming home until Sunday, they're taking a play day before they come home. Sari and I are going shopping, and out for lunch. Oh, God. Oh, God. How did she die? How did my baby die?"

"We're still investigating, Ms. York. As soon as I can give you details, I will." She would not, Eve thought, tell this poor woman, not while there was no one to lean on, what had happened to her sister. "We can contact your husband. You want him and your sons home now?"

"Yes. Yes, I want them to come home. I want them home."

"Meanwhile is there someone we can call, a neighbor, a friend, to stay with you?"

"I don't know. I don't . . ."

"Ms. York." Peabody spoke gently. "You don't have to be alone now. Let us call a friend to come be with you."

"Lib. Could you call Lib? She'll come."

When they were outside, Roarke took a long breath. "I often wonder how you do what you do, standing over death, looking so unflinchingly into the minds of those who bring it. But I think of all you do, taking what's been done to those left behind, feeling—as you'd have to—their pain—is more wrenching than all the rest of it."

He brushed his hand over Eve's. "You didn't tell her what happened to her sister. You're giving her time to get through the first of the pain."

"I don't know if I did her any favors. It's going to break her to pieces. Might've been better to do it now when she's already broken."

"You did it right," Peabody said. "She's got her friend, but she'll need her family. They're going to need each other to get through that end of it."

"Well. We'll go see what Morris can tell us. Listen." She turned to Roarke. "I'll get in touch as soon as I can."

"I'd like to go with you."

"It's already, what, after four in the morning. You don't want to go to the morgue."

"A moment," he murmured to Peabody, and taking Eve's hand drew her aside. "I'd like to see this through. I'd like you to let me."

"I can tell you whatever we get from Morris, and you can grab some sleep. But," she continued before he could speak, "that's not the same thing. I want you to tell me you don't feel responsible for this."

He looked back toward the sister's apartment, thought of the grief that lived there now. "She's not dead because I hired her. I'm not quite that egotistical. All the same, I want to see it through."

"Okay. You drive. We're going to need to make a stop on the way. I need to talk to Feeney."

He'd been her trainer, her teacher, her partner. He was, though neither of them spoke of it, the man who stood as her father in the ways that mattered.

He had plucked her out of the pack when she'd still been in uniform, and made her his. She'd never asked Feeney what he'd seen that persuaded him to take on a green uniform. She'd only known that by doing so, he'd made all the difference.

She'd have been a good cop without him. She'd have made detective through her own need, dedication, and aptitude. And maybe, eventually, she'd have held the rank she held now.

But she wouldn't have been the same cop without him.

When he'd earned his bars, he'd requested EDD. E-work had always been his specialty, and his passion, so his request for the Electronic Detective Division was a natural.

She remembered she'd been just a little annoyed he'd moved out of Homicide. And for the first few months, she'd missed him, seeing him, working with him, talking to him every day, like she might've missed her own hand.

She could've left this for morning—at least a decent hour of the morning. But she knew, had their positions been reversed, she'd want this knock on the door.

She'd have been damn pissed if she didn't get the knock.

When he answered his face was sleep rumpled, making it more lived-in than usual. His hair, a gingery scrubbing brush mixed with silver, was standing straight out. As if the air around him had been suddenly ionized.

And while he might've been wearing a tattered robe in the surprising color choice of purple, his eyes were all cop.

"Who died?"

"Need to talk to you about that," Eve told him. "But more how than who."

"Well." He scratched his jaw, and Eve could hear the rasp of his fingers on the night's growth of beard. "Better come on in. Wife's asleep. Let's go on in the kitchen. Need coffee."

It was a homey place. Lived in, Eve thought, like Jaycee's had been, if you added another decade or two. Feeney's kids had grown up, and there were grandkids now. Eve was never quite sure of the number. But there was a good-sized eating area off the kitchen, with a long table to accommodate the lot of them at family dinners.

Feeney brought in coffee, scuffing along in slippers Eve would bet a month's pay were a Christmas gift.

On the middle of the table was a strangely shaped vase in streaky colors of red and orange. Mrs. Feeney's work, Eve determined. The wife had a penchant for hobbies and crafts, and was always making things. Often unidentifiable things.

"Caught a case," Eve began. "Vic is female, brunette, late twenties, found naked in East River Park."

"Yeah, I caught the report on screen."

"Found nude. She'd been tortured. Burns, bruising, cuts, punctures. Her wrists were slashed."

"Fuck."

Yeah, he had it already, Eve noted. "Vic was wearing a silver band on the third finger of her left hand."

"How long?" Feeney demanded. "How long did she last? What was the time he carved into her?"

"Eighty-five hours, twelve minutes, thirty-eight seconds."

"Fuck," he said again. "Motherfucker." Feeney's hand balled into a fist to rap, light and steady, on the table. "He's not walking again, Dallas. He's not walking away from us again. He'll have number two already."

"Yeah." Eve nodded. "I figure he's got number two."

Feeney braced his elbows on the table, scooped his fingers through his hair. "We've got to go through everything we had nine years back, what data there is on him from the other times he went to work. Put a task force together now, at the get. We don't wait for the second body to show up. You get anything from the scene?"

"So far, just the body, the ring, the sheet. I'll get you a copy of the records. Right now, I'm heading to the morgue to see what Morris can tell us. You're going to need to get dressed, unless you're wearing purple terry cloth to work these days."

He glanced down, shook his head. "If you saw the one the wife got me for Christmas, you'd understand why I'm still wearing this one." He pushed to his feet. "Look, you go on, and I'll meet you at the morgue. Going to need my own ride anyway."

"All right."

"Dallas."

In that moment, Roarke realized neither he nor Peabody existed. They simply weren't a part of the reality between the other two.

"We have to find what we missed," Feeney said to Eve. "What everybody's missed. There's always something. One piece, one step, one thought. We can't miss it this time."

"We won't."

Roarke had been to the morgue before. He wondered if the white tiles through the tunnels of the place were meant to replace natural light. Or if they had merely been chosen as an acceptance of the stark.

There were echoes throughout as well—the repeat and repeat of bootsteps as they walked. More silence, he supposed, as the staff would be on graveyard shift. So to speak.

It was still shy of dawn, and he could see the long night was wearing on Peabody a bit, with a heaviness under her dark eyes. But not on Eve, not yet. The fatigue would rush up and choke her—it always did. But for now she was running on duty and purpose, and an underlying anger he wasn't sure she recognized as vital fuel.

Eve paused outside the double doors of an autopsy room. "Do you need to see her?" she asked him.

"I do. I want to be of some help in this, and if I'm to be of any help, I need to understand. I've seen death before."

"Not like this." She pushed through.

Morris was inside. He'd changed, she noted, into gray sweats and black and silver skids she imagined he kept on the premises for working out. He sat, and continued to sit for a moment, in a steel chair drinking something thick and brown out of a tall glass.

"Ah, company. Protein smoothy?"

"So absolutely not," Eve said.

"Tastes marginally better than it looks. And does its job. Roarke, good to see you, even though."

"And you."

"Vic worked for Roarke," Eve said.

"I'm very sorry."

"I barely knew her. But . . ."

"Yes, but . . ." Morris set the smoothy aside before he pushed to his feet. "I regret that we'll all come to know her quite well now."

"She managed one of Roarke's clubs. The Starlight down in Chelsea?"

"Is that yours?" Morris smiled a little. "I took a friend there a few weeks ago. It's an entertaining trip back to an intriguing time."

"Feeney's on his way in."

Morris shifted his gaze to Eve. "I see. It was the three of us over the first of them the last time. Do you remember?"

"Yeah, I remember."

"Her name was Corrine, Corrine Dagby."

"Age twenty-nine," Eve confirmed. "Sold shoes in a boutique downtown. Liked to party. She lasted twenty-six hours, ten minutes, fifty-eight seconds."

Morris nodded. "Do you remember what you said when we stood here then?"

"No, not exactly."

"I do. You said: 'He'll want more than that.' And you were right. We learned he wanted more than that. Should we wait for Feeney?"

"He'll catch up."

"All right." Morris crossed the room.

Roarke looked, then he stepped over.

He'd seen death, bloody, vicious, violent, useless, and terrible death. But he saw, once more, Eve was right.

He'd never seen the likes of this.

SO MANY WOUNDS, HE THOUGHT, AND ALL washed clean. Somehow it might have been less horrid if there had been blood. Blood would be proof, wouldn't it, that life had once been there.

But this . . . this woman he remembered as vital and brimming with energy looked like some poor doll, mangled and sliced by a vicious child.

"Tidy work," Eve stated, and had Roarke's gaze whipping toward her.

He started to speak, to let loose some of the horror he felt. But he saw her face, saw the anger was closer to the surface now however calm her voice. Saw, too, the pity. She had such pity inside her he often wondered how she could bear the weight of it.

So he said nothing.

"He's very methodical." Morris engaged the computer before offering Eve microgoggles. "You see these wounds on the limbs? Long, thin, shallow."

"Scalpel maybe, or the tip of a sharp blade." Though the wounds were displayed, optimized, on screen, Eve leaned down to study them through the goggles. "Precise, too. Either she was drugged or he had her restrained in such a way she couldn't struggle enough to make a difference."

"Which gets your vote?" Morris asked.

"Restraints. What's the fun if she's out of it, can't feel fully? Burns are small along here." Eve turned the victim's left arm. "Here in the bend of the elbow, precise again, but the skin's charred some at the edges. Flame? Not a laser, but live fire?"

"I would agree. Some of the other burns look like laser to me. And there, on the inner thigh where it's mottled? Extreme cold."

"Yeah. The bruising—no laceration, no scraping. Smooth implement."

"Sap." Roarke studied the bruising himself. "An old-fashioned sap would bruise like that. Leather's effective if you can afford the cost. Filled with ordinary sand, it does its job."

"Again, agree. And we have the punctures," Morris continued. "Which are in circular patterns here, here, here." The screen flashed with close-ups of the back of the right hand, the heel of the left foot, the left buttocks. "Twenty minute punctures, in this precise pattern."

"Like needles," Eve mused. "Some kind of tool . . . He could . . ." She curved her right hand, laid it on the heel of the body, pressed. "That's new. We don't have this wound pattern on record."

"He's an inventive bastard," Peabody added. "Morris, can I get a bottle of water?"

"Help yourself."

"You need air," Eve said without looking at her, "go get some."

"Just the water."

"This pattern might be new," Eve continued, "but the rest is consistent. More creative, maybe, a little more patient. You do what you do long enough, you get better at it. Longer, deeper wounds along the rib cage, over the breasts. Wider burn areas, deeper bruising up the calves.

"Increases the pain, gradually. Wants it to last. Cuts and burns on her face. No bruising there. Sap her and she might lose consciousness. Don't want that."

The doors swished open. Feeney walked in, came straight to the table. He looked down. "Ah, hell," was all he said.

"We've got one new wound type. Circular pattern of punctures. See what you think of it."

Eve bent close to the ruined face, her eyes behind the goggles unflinching. "No bruising here that would indicate he gagged her—or not tightly. Nothing that would mar the skin. He has to have a place, a very, very private place. So she can scream. Tox back?"

"Yes, just before you came. There were small traces of a standard sedative in her bloodstream. Barely registered. She'd have been awake and aware at TOD."

"Same MO. Puts her to sleep when he's busy with other business."

"There were traces, too, of water and protein in her system. The lab will confirm, but . . ."

"He likes to give them enough nutrients to keep them going," Feeney said.

Eve nodded. "I remember. Then ends it this way." She lifted the victim's hand, turned the wrist up. "Crosshatches, but not too deep. She'll bleed out, but it'll take time. Adds to his clock."

"I expect, given the prior blood loss, trauma, two hours. Three at the most. She would have lost consciousness before the end of it."

"Any trace of what he used to wash her down?"

"Yes. In the scalp wounds, and the punctures under the nails. I sent it to the lab."

"Send over some skin scrapings, some hair. I want to see what kind of water. City water? Suburbs?"

"I'll take care of it."

"He'll be starting on the second." Feeney looked at Eve as she took off the goggles. "Probably has the third picked out."

"Yeah. I'm going to see the commander. For now, you tag a couple of your best men. I want them running and analyzing data as we get it, running probabilities. First on scene was Gil Newkirk's son."

"Son of a bitch."

"Yeah, you reach out to Newkirk, senior? He's out of the one-seven, so's his kid. I'm bringing the son in on the uniform end of the task force, if his lieutenant doesn't have a problem with it."

"Who's the LT?"

"Grohman."

"I know him," Feeney told her. "I'll handle it."

"Good." Eve checked the time, calculated. "Peabody, book us a conference room, and I want it for the duration. They give you any lip about it, toss them to Whitney. We'll meet there for the first briefing at oh-nine-hundred."

As they headed out, Eve shot a look at Roarke. "I take it you want to stick for the briefing."

"You trust correctly."

"I'm going to need to clear that with Whitney."

"All right."

"Take the wheel. I'll see what I can do."

She put the call through, unsurprised to find Whitney already at his desk. "Sir, we're heading into Central now from the morgue. We're booking a conference room."

"Locked in A," Peabody said from the backseat.

"Conference room A," Eve relayed. "And I'm scheduling the first briefing at oh-nine-hundred."

"I'll be there. So will Chief Tibble."

"Yes, sir. I've brought in Captain Feeney as we worked together on the previous investigation. I've asked him for two additional e-men to run data. I would like to put Officer Newkirk on the uniform part of the task force as he was first on scene, and is the son of an officer who was involved in the previous investigation."

"I'll clear that for you."

"Sir, Feeney's on that. I want four additional men. Baxter, Trueheart, Jenkinson, and Powell. I'll reassign whatever caseloads they're currently carrying. I need them clear for this."

"It's your call, Lieutenant, but Trueheart's an aide, not a detective, and doesn't have extensive experience."

"He's tireless, sir, and has an excellent eye. Baxter's given him some seasoning."

"I'll trust your judgment."

"Thank you. I'll need Dr. Mira to review and possibly update the profile, and could make use of an expert consultant, civilian."

Whitney said nothing for five long seconds. "You want to bring Roarke in on this, Dallas?"

"The victim was an employee. The connection can clear some roads in the investigation and interviews. In addition, Commander, he has access to better equipment than the NYPSD. We may have use for it."

"Again, your call, your judgment."

"Yes, sir."

Dawn was breaking as Roarke swung into the garage at Central. "We're in the house, sir. I'll be set up by nine hundred."

"I'll contact Dr. Mira and the chief."

Eve sat for a moment when Roarke pulled into her slot. In the back, Peabody snored in quiet, almost ladylike snorts. "You know something about torture," she said at length.

"I do, yes."

"And you know people who know people."

"True."

"That's what I want you to think about. And if you have a contact that can add to the data, I want you to use it. He has tools, and he has a workshop. It would be well set up, well equipped. I think he'd have e-toys, too. Monitor the vic's pulse rate, maybe brain wave patterns. Cameras, audio. It seems to me he'd want to watch, and you can't watch and work. Not when you're that focused."

"Whatever you need from me."

She nodded, then turned and shoved Peabody's knee.

"Huh? What?" Peabody jerked upright, blinked. "I was thinking."

"Yeah, I always drool and snore when I'm lost in thought."

"Drool?" Mortified, Peabody wiped at her mouth. "I wasn't drooling."

"You've got one hour in the crib."

"No, I'm okay." Peabody climbed out, blinked her eyes wide as if to show she was alert. "Just nodded off for a minute."

"An hour." Eve strode toward the elevator. "Take it, then report to the conference room. I'll need you to help me set up."

"You don't have to get pissed just because I dropped out for a couple minutes."

"If I was pissed I'd be kicking your ass instead of giving you an hour down. And you don't want to argue with me when I'm jonesing for coffee. Take the hour. You're going to need it."

When the doors opened, Eve stepped off with Roarke, then turned, jabbed a finger at Peabody's sulky face. "That hour starts now."

Roarke waited until the doors closed. "You could use an hour yourself."

"I could use coffee more."

"And food."

She slid her eyes up to his. "If you start nagging me about eating and sleeping, I'm booting you off my team."

"If I didn't nag you about eating and sleeping, you'd do precious little of either. What's in your office AutoChef?"

"Coffee," she said, and yearned for it.

"I'll meet you there shortly." When he turned and headed in the opposite direction, she only scowled after him.

Still, if he was off doing whatever, it would be easier for her to write her initial report, call in the members of her team.

She passed through the bullpen. It was nearly change of shift. In her office, she went straight for the coffee, then stood where she was and drank the first half of the first cup.

There hadn't been real coffee to wake up her blood the first time around, she remembered. Instead of a cramped office, she'd had a cramped desk in the bullpen. She hadn't been in charge then; Feeney had. She knew that was weighing on him, knew he was remembering all the steps, all the fizzled leads, the dead ends. All the bodies.

It needed to be remembered. It all needed to be remembered, so it didn't happen again.

She sat at her desk, shot out transmissions to Baxter and to Jenkinson, with orders for them to notify their respective aides and partners, and report.

She mercilessly dumped their caseloads on other detectives.

There would, she knew, be some extensive bitching and moaning in the bullpen, very shortly.

She ordered up the cold-case files from nine years before—including Mira's initial profile—sent out the request for the files and reports on the other cases, yet unsolved, that matched the MO.

She contacted the lab and pushed for any and all results, left a clipped voice mail for the chief lab tech, Dick Berenski.

And with a second cup of coffee on her desk, began to write her report.

She was fine-tuning it when Roarke came in. He set an insulated bowl on her desk, handed her a toss-away spoon. "Eat."

Cautious, Eve pried up the lid of the bowl and peeked. "Damn it. If you were going to go to the trouble to get food, why did you get oatmeal?"

"Because it's good for you." He sat in her single visitor chair with his own bowl. "Are you aware that the Eatery here serves nothing that could be considered remotely palatable?"

"The eggs aren't that bad. If you put a lot of salt on them."

Roarke simply angled his head. "You put a lot of salt on everything, but it doesn't make it palatable."

Because it was there, she spooned up some oatmeal. It would fill the hole. "Cop food's what you get around here." She ate, frowned. As

CREATION IN DEATH 41

oatmeal went, it wasn't completely disgusting. "And this isn't cop food."

"No. I got it from the deli around the corner."

For a moment, her face rivaled Peabody's for full sulk. "They have bagels there, and danishes."

"So they do." He smiled at her. "You'll do better with the oatmeal."

Maybe, she thought, but she wouldn't be as happy about it. "I want to say something before this really gets started. If you feel, at any time, you want to step out, you step out."

"I won't, but understood."

She took another spoonful of oatmeal, then swiveled in her chair so they were face-to-face. "Understand, too, that if I feel your involvement is doing more harm—on a personal level—than it's adding to the investigation, I'll have to cut you loose."

"Personally or professionally?"

"Roarke."

He set his bowl aside to get up and program coffee for himself. She could attempt to cut him loose, he thought, but they both knew she wouldn't shake him off the line. And that, he acknowledged, would be a problem indeed.

"Our personal life has, and will, weather the bumps and bruises it takes when we work together, or more accurately, when I contribute to your work."

"This one's different."

"Yes, I understand that as well." He turned with his coffee, met her eyes. "You couldn't stop him once before."

"Didn't stop him," Eve corrected.

"You'd think that, and so it's personal. However much you try to keep it otherwise, it's personal. It's harder for you, and it may be harder for us. But things have changed in nine years, a great many things."

"I didn't have anybody pushing oatmeal on me nine years ago."

"There." His lips curved. "That's one."

"It's unlikely we'll save the second one, Roarke. Barring a miracle, we won't save her."

"And so, you're already afraid you won't save the next. I know how that weighs on you, and eats at you, and pushes you. You have someone who understands you, who loves you, and who has considerable resources."

He crossed over, just to touch a hand to her face. "*His* pattern may have changed little in all this time, Eve. But *yours* has. And I believe, completely, that it will stop here. You'll stop it."

"I need to believe that, too. Okay, then." She took one more spoonful of oatmeal. "Peabody's crib time's up. I need to finish this report, have copies made for the team. I've ordered copies of the old reports, and put in requests for files from other murders attributed to him. Find Peabody, tell her I need her to pick up the cold files, and then the two of you can start setting up. I need another ten minutes here."

"All right. But unless you have something other than the usual drudge around here in that conference room, I'm taking coffee with me."

True to her word, Eve walked into the conference room ten minutes later. Behind her, a pair of uniforms hauled in a second board. She carted a boxful of file copies.

"I want the current case up first," she told Peabody. "Then we'll have our history lesson." She pulled the files out, set them on the conference table. "I generated stills of the scene and the body. Use the second board for those."

"On it."

She walked over to a white data board on the wall and began to print.

Her printing always surprised Roarke. It was so precise, so perfect, while her handwriting tended toward scrawl. He saw she was printing out the victim's name, and the timeline from the moment she'd been reported leaving the club, through her death, and the discovery of her body.

After drawing a line down the center of the wide board, she began printing out the others, beginning with Corrine Dagby.

Not just data, Roarke thought. A kind of memorial to the dead. They were not to be forgotten. More, he thought, she wrote them out for herself because she stood for all of them now.

Feeney walked in. "The kid's cleared for this. The Newkirk kid." His gaze moved to the board, stayed there. "His old man's going to dig out his own notes from before. Said he'll put in any OT you want, or take his own personal time on this."

"Good."

"I pulled in McNab and Callendar. McNab knows your rhythm and won't bitch about the drone work. Callendar's good. She doesn't miss details."

"I've got Baxter, Trueheart, Jenkinson, and Powell."

"Powell?"

"Transferred in from the six-five about three months ago. Got twenty years in. Chips away at a case until he gets to the bones. I've got Harris and Darnell in uniform. They're solid. But I'm giving Newkirk the lead there. He was first on scene and he knows the previous investigation."

"If he's like his old man, he's a solid cop."

"Yeah, I'm thinking. Tibble, Whitney, and Mira should be on their way down."

She stepped back from the board. "I'm going to brief on the current first. Do you want to brief on the prior investigation?"

Feeney shook his head. "You take it. Might help me see it from a different angle." He pulled a book out of his pocket, handed it to her. "My original notes. I made a copy for myself."

She knew he wasn't only passing her his notebook, but passing her the command as well. The gesture had something tightening just under her heart. "Is this how you want it?"

"It's the way it is. The way it's supposed to be." He turned away as cops began to come into the room.

She snagged one of the uniforms, ordered him to distribute the files, then studied the boards Peabody and Roarke had set up.

All those faces, she thought. All that pain.

What did she look like, the one he had now? What was her name? Was anyone looking for her?

How long would she last?

When Whitney walked in with Mira, Eve started over. It struck her what a contrast they made. The big-shouldered man with the dark skin, the years of command etched on his face, and the woman, so quietly lovely in the elegant pale pink suit.

"Lieutenant. The chief is on his way."

"Yes, sir. The full team's assembled and present. Dr. Mira, there are copies of your original profile in each packet, but if there's anything you want to add verbally, feel free."

"I'd like to reread the original murder books."

"I'll make them available. Sir, do you wish to speak?"

"Lead it off, Dallas." He stepped to the side as Tibble entered.

The chief of police was a tall man and—Eve always thought—a contained one. Not an easy man to read, but she doubted he'd have climbed the ranks as he had if he'd been otherwise. He played politics—a necessary evil—but to her mind he found a way so that the department came out on top.

Dark skin, dark eyes, dark suit—part of his presence, she decided. Along with a strong voice, and a strong will.

"Chief Tibble."

"Lieutenant. I apologize if I delayed the briefing."

"No, sir, we're on schedule. If you're ready now."

He only nodded, then moved to the back of the room. He didn't sit, but stood. An observer.

Eve gave Peabody a nod, then walked to the front of the room. Behind her, the wall screen flashed on.

"Sarifina York," Eve began. "Age twenty-eight at TOD."

She was putting the victim first, Roarke realized. Putting that image, that name into the mind of every cop in the room. So that every cop in the room would think of her, remember her as they were buried in routine, in data, in the long hours and the frustrations.

Just as they would remember what had been done to her as those next images came up.

She went through them all, every victim. The names, the faces, the ages, the images of their suffering and death. It took a long time, but there were no interruptions, no signs of restlessness.

"We believe all of these women, twenty-three women, were abducted, tortured, and murdered by one individual. We believe there are likely more than these twenty-three who have not been connected or reported, whose bodies may not have been found or who were not killed in the same manner. Earlier victims, we believe, before Corrine Dagby, when he decided on his particular method."

She paused, just a moment, to insure, Roarke understood, that all eyes, all attention focused on the image of that first victim.

"The method deviates very little from vic to vic, as you'll see in your copy of the case file from nine years ago. Copies of case files, in full, from murders attributed to the unsub will be forthcoming."

Her eyes scanned the room, and Roarke thought, saw everything.

"His methodology is, initially, typical of a serial. We believe he stalks and selects his victims—all within a certain age group, race, gender, and coloring—learning their routines, habits. He knows where they live, where they work, where they shop, who they sleep with."

She paused again, shifting. Roarke saw the light slanting through the privacy screens on the window glint on her sidearm.

"Twenty-three women, known. They were specific targets. No connection was found between any of the victims other than age and basic appearance. None of the victims ever reported a stalker, never mentioned to a friend, coworker, relative that she had been approached or troubled. In each case, the victim left a location and was not seen again until her body was discovered.

"He must have private transportation of some kind, and using it takes the victim to a preplanned location. It, too, must be private as he takes—as with Sarifina York—several days to kill them. In all prior investigations, it was learned through time lines and forensics that he always selects and abducts his second victim before finishing with the first, and so selects and abducts the third before killing the second."

She outlined the investigator's on-scene reports, the ME's reports, taking them through the process of the torture, the method of death.

Roarke heard the e-cop, Callendar, breathe out a soft "Jesus," as Eve outlined the specifics.

"Here, he may deviate slightly," Eve continued, "adjusting his method to suit the specific victim. According to Dr. Mira's profile, this is tailored to the victim's stamina, tolerance for pain, will to live. He's careful, he's methodical, patient. Most likely a mature male of high intelligence. He lives alone, and has some steady method of income. Probably upper bracket. Though he selects females, there is no evidence he abuses them sexually."

"Small blessing," Callendar murmured, and if Eve heard she gave no sign.

"Sex, the control and power gained from them doesn't interest him. They aren't sexual beings. By carving the time spent on them into their torsos—postmortem—he labels them. The ring he puts on them is another kind of branding.

"It's ownership." She glanced at Mira for confirmation.

"Yes," Mira agreed, and the lovely woman with the soft waves of sable hair spoke in her calm voice. "The killings are a ritual, though not specifically ritualistic in the standard sense. They are *his* ritual, from the selection and the stalking, through the abduction and the torture, the attention to detail, which includes the time elapsed, to the way he tends to them after death. The use of the rings indicates an intimacy and a proprietary interest. They belong to him. Most likely they represent a female who was important to him."

"He washes them, body, hair," Eve continued. "While this removes most trace evidence, we were able to determine the brand of soap and shampoo on previous vics. It's high end, indicating their presentation matters to him."

"Yes," Mira agreed when Eve glanced at her again. "Very much."

"It matters, as does the dumping method. He lays them on a white sheet, habitually leaving them in a park or green area. Legs together, as you see—again, not a sexual pose—but arms spread."

"A kind of opening," Mira commented. "Or embrace. Even acceptance of what was done."

"While he follows the traditional path of the signature serial killer to this point, he then deviates. Full timeline up, Peabody," Eve ordered, then turned when it flashed on screen. "He does not escalate in violence, the time between killings doesn't appreciably narrow. He spends two to three weeks at his work, then he stops. In a year, or two, he cycles again, in another location. His signature has been identified in New York, in Wales, in Florida, in Romania, in Bolivia, and now again in New York.

"Twenty-three women, nine years, four countries. The arrogant son of a bitch is back here, and here's where it stops."

And here, Roarke noted, was the fierceness she'd held back during the relaying of data, of names and methods and evidence. Here was the hint of the anger, of the avenger.

"Right now, there's a woman between the ages of twenty-eight and thirty-three. She has brown hair, light skin, a medium to slender build, and she's already been taken. We find him. We get her back.

"I'm going to give you your individual assignments. If you have any questions, any problems, wait until I'm done. But I'm going to tell you one more thing. We're going to nail him. We're going to nail him here, in New York, with a case so tight he'll feel it choking him every hour of every day of every year he spends in a cage."

Not just anger, Roarke noted, but pride. And she was pushing that anger and pride into them so they'd work until they dropped.

She was magnificent.

"He doesn't walk, run, fly, or crawl out of this city," Eve told them. "He doesn't slither out in court because one of us gave his lawyer an opening the size of a flea's ass.

"He pays, we're going to make goddamn sure he pays for every one of these twenty-three women."

4   AS EVE WRAPPED UP, TIBBLE WALKED TO THE front of the room. Automatically, she stopped, stepped to the side to give him the floor.

"This team will have the full resources of the NYPSD at its disposal. Any necessary overtime will be cleared. If the primary determines more manpower is needed, and the commander agrees, that manpower will be assigned. All leave, other than hardship and medical, is canceled for this team until this case is closed."

He paused, gauging the reactions, and obviously satisfied with them, continued. "I have every confidence that each and every member of this team will work his or her respective ass off until this son of a bitch is identified, apprehended, and locked in a cage for the rest of his unnatural life. You're not only the ones who'll stop him, but who'll build a case that will lock that cage. I don't want any fuckups here, and trust Lieutenant Dallas to flay you bloody if you come close to fucking up."

Since he looked directly at her as he made the statement, Eve simply nodded. "Yes, sir."

"The media will pounce like wolves. A Code Blue status has been considered, and rejected. The public requires protection and should be made aware that a specific type of female is being targeted. However, they will be made aware by one voice, and one voice only, which represents this task force, and, in fact, this department. Lieutenant Dallas will be that voice. Understood?" he said, looking directly at her again.

"Yes, sir," she said, with considerably less enthusiasm.

"The rest of you will not comment, will not engage reporters, will not so much as give them the current time and temperature should they ask. You will refer them to the lieutenant. There will be no leaks unless they are departmentally sanctioned leaks. If there are, and the source of that leak is discovered—and it damn well will be—that individual can expect to be transferred to Records in the Bowery.

"Shut him down. Shut him down hard, clean, and fast. Lieutenant."

"Sir. All right, you all know your primary assignments. Let's get to work."

Tibble signaled to Eve as feet and chairs shuffled. "Media conference, noon." He held up a finger as if anticipating her reaction. "You'll make a statement—short, to the point. You'll answer questions for five minutes. No longer. These things are necessary, Lieutenant."

"Understood, sir. Chief, we held back the numbers carved into the victims in the previous investigations."

"Continue to do so. Copy me on all reports, requests, and requisitions." He looked over at the boards, at the faces. "What does he see when he looks at them?" Tibble asked.

"Potential." Eve spoke without thinking.

"Potential?" Tibble repeated, shifting his gaze to hers.

"Yes, sir, that's what I think he sees. Respectfully, sir, I need to get started."

"Yes. Yes. Dismissed."

She walked over to Feeney. "This space work okay for the e-end of things?"

"It'll do. We're bringing down the equipment we need. It'll be set up inside of thirty. He comes back, he comes back here, you gotta wonder does he use the same place he did before? Does he have a place? Maybe even lives here when he's not working."

"Private home, untenanted warehouse. Lots of that in the city, the outlying boroughs," Eve speculated. "Bastard could be working across the river in Jersey, then using New York as a dump site. But if it is the same place—and he strikes me as a creature of habit, right?—then it narrows it some. We check ownership of buildings that fit the bill for ones in the same name for the last nine years. Ten," she corrected. "Give him some prep time."

"Narrows it some." Feeney pulled on his nose. "Like looking for an ant hill in the desert. We'll work it."

"You okay with taking the Missing Persons search?"

He blew out a breath, dipped his hands into his saggy pockets. "Are you going to ask me if I'm okay with every assignment or step in this?"

Eve moved her shoulders, and her hands found her own pockets. "It feels weird."

"I've run the e-end of your cases and ops before this."

"It's not like that, Feeney." She waited until their eyes locked, until she was certain they understood each other. "We both know this one's different. So if it bugs you, I want to know."

He glanced around the room as uniforms and team members carried in equipment and tables. Then cocked his head, gesturing Eve to a corner of the room with him.

"It bugs me, but not like you mean. It burns my ass that we didn't get this guy, that he slipped out and on my watch."

"I worked it with you, and we had a team on it. It's on all of us."

His eyes, baggy as a hound's, met hers. "You know better. You know how it is."

She did, of course she did. He'd taught her the responsibility and weight of command. "Yeah." She dragged a hand through her hair. "Yeah, I know."

"This time it's on you. You're going to take some hits because we both know there's going to be another name, another face on the board before we get him. You'll live with that; can't do anything else but live with it. It bugs me," he repeated. "It would bug me a hell of a lot more if anyone else was standing as primary on this. We clear?"

"Yeah, we're clear."

"I'll start the Missing Person's run." He cocked his head toward Roarke. "Our civilian would be a good one to handle the real estate search."

"He would. Why don't you get him on that? I'm going to swing over to the lab, bribe and/or threaten Dickhead to push on reports." She glanced over, saw that Roarke was already working with McNab to set up data and communication centers. "I'm just going to have a word with the civilian first."

She crossed to Roarke, tapped his shoulder. He'd tied his hair back as he often did before getting down to serious e-business, and still wore the sweater and jeans he'd put on—had it only been that morning?—when they'd left the house for the crime scene.

She realized he looked more like a member of the team than the emperor of the business world.

"Need a minute," she told him, then stepped a few feet away.

"What can I do for you, Lieutenant?"

"Feeney's got work for you. He'll fill you in. I'm heading out with Peabody. I just want . . . look, don't go buying stuff."

He lifted his eyebrows, and the amusement showed clearly on his face. "Such as?"

"E-toys, new furniture, catered lunches, dancing girls. Whatever," she said with a distracted wave of her hand. "You're not here to supply the NYPSD."

"What if I get hungry, then feel the urge to dance?"

"Suppress it." She gave him a little poke in the chest that he interpreted—correctly—as both affection and warning. "And don't expect me to kiss you good-bye, hello, and like that when we're on the clock. It makes us look—"

"Married?" At her stony stare he grinned. "Very well, Lieutenant, I'll try my best to suppress all my urges."

Fat chance of that, she thought, but had to be satisfied. "Peabody," she called out, "with me."

On the way out, Peabody hit Vending for a Diet Pepsi for herself, a regular tube for Eve. "Gotta keep the caffeine pumping. I've never been on something like this, not when you catch a case and a few hours later you've got a task force, a war room, and a pep talk from the chief."

"We work the case."

"Well, it's this case, and the ones from nine years ago, and even the ones between that went down elsewhere. That's a lot of balls in the air."

"It's all one," Eve said as they got into the car. "One case with a lot of pieces."

"Arms," Peabody said after a minute. "It's more like arms. It's like an octopus."

"The case is an octopus."

"It's got all these tentacles, all these arms, but there's only one head. You get the head, you get it all."

"Okay," Eve decided, "that's not bad. The case is an octopus."

"And say, okay, maybe you can't get to the head, not at first, but you get a good hold on one of those tentacles, then—"

"I get it, Peabody." Because she now had an image of a giant octopus swimming in her head, Eve was relieved when her dash 'link signaled. "Dallas."

"So, what's up?"

"Nadine." Eve let her glance shift down to the screen where Nadine Furst, a very hot property in media circles, beamed out at her.

"Media conference, you as the department's spokesperson—I know you love that one."

"I'm primary."

"I got that." On screen, Nadine's cat eyes were sharp and searching. "But what gives this one enough juice? A dead woman in the park, identity yet to be given."

"We'll give her name at the conference."

"Give me a hint. Celebrity?"

"No hints."

"Come on, be a pal."

The trouble was, they were pals. Moreover, Nadine could be trusted. And at the moment, Nadine had plenty of juice of her own. She could, Eve mused, be useful.

"You're going to want to come to the media conference, Nadine."

"I've got a conflict. Just —"

"You're going to want to be there, and when it wraps, you're going to want to find your way to my office."

"Offering me a one-on-one after a media announcement takes off the shine, Dallas."

"You're not getting a one-on-one. Just you, just me. No camera. You're going to want to do this, Nadine."

"I'll be there."

"That was smart," Peabody said when Eve clicked off. "That was really smart. Bring her in, bargain, and get her resources and contacts."

"She'll keep a lid on what I ask her to keep a lid on," Eve agreed. "And she's the perfect funnel for any departmentally sanctioned leaks." She parked, rolled her shoulders. "Let's go harass Dickhead."

Dick Berenski had earned his nickname. Not only did he have a head like an egg covered with slick black hair, his personality was oilier than a tin of sardines. He was slippery, sleazy, and not just open to bribes—he expected them.

But despite being a dickhead, he ran a top-flight lab and knew his business as well as he knew the exact location of the dimples on the ass of this month's centerfold.

Eve strode in, moving by the long white counters and stations, the clear-walled cubes. She spotted Berenski scooting back and forth on his stool in front of his counter, tapping his spider-leg fingers on keyboards or tapping them to screens.

For a dickhead, she thought, he was hell at multitasking.

"Where's my report?" she demanded.

He didn't bother to look up. "Back up, Dallas. You want it fast or you want it right?"

"I want it fast and right. Don't fuck with me on this one . . . Dick."

"I said, 'Back up.'"

She narrowed her eyes because when he swung around on the stool, there was fury on his face. Not his usual reaction to anything.

"You think I'm screwing with this?" he snapped out. "You think I'm jerking off here?"

"Wouldn't be the first time."

"This isn't the first time either, is it?"

She flipped back through her memory. "You weren't chief nine years back."

"Senior tech. I did the skin and hair on those four vics. Harte took the bows for it, but I did the work. Goddamn it."

Harte, Eve remembered, had also had a nickname: Blowharte.

"So you did the work. Applause, applause. I need an analysis of *this* vic's hair and skin."

"I did the work," he repeated, bitterly now. "I analyzed and researched and identified what was barely any trace. I gave you the damn brand names of the soap, the shampoo. You're the one who didn't catch the bastard."

"You did your job, I didn't do mine?" She leaned down, nose-to-nose. "*You*'d better back up, Dick."

"Ah, excuse me. Don't clock the referee." Courageously—from her point of view—Peabody eased between the chief tech and the primary. "Everyone who was involved nine years ago feels this one more now."

"How would you know?" Dick rounded on Peabody. "You were in some Free Ager commune sitting in a circle chanting at the frigging moon nine years ago."

"Hey."

"That's it." Eve kept her voice low, and the tone stinging. "You can't handle this one, Berenski, I'll request another tech."

"I'm chief here. This isn't your shop. I say who works what." Then he held up his hand. "Just back off a minute, back off a minute. Goddamn it."

Because it wasn't his usual style, Eve kept silent while he stared down at his own long, mobile fingers.

"Some of them stick with you, you know? They stick in your gut. Other shit comes in and you work that, and it seems like you put it away. Then it comes back and kicks you in the balls."

He drew a breath, looked up at Eve. It wasn't just fury, she saw now, but the bitter frustration that on the job could push perilously close to grief.

"You know how when it stopped, just stopped cold, everybody figured he got dead, or he got tossed in a cage for something else? We didn't get him, and that was a bitch, but it stopped." Berenski heaved out a breath. "But it didn't. He didn't get dead or tossed in a cage. He was just bopping around Planet Earth having his high old time. Now he's back on my desk, and it pisses me off."

"I'm serving as President of the Pissed-off Club. I'll take your application for membership under advisement."

He snorted out a laugh, and the crisis passed.

"I got the results. I was just rerunning the data. Triple check. It's not the same brands as before."

"The old brands still available?"

"Yeah, yeah, here's the thing. He used shea butter soap with olive and palm oils, oils of rose and chamomile on the four prior vics. Handmade soap, imported from France. Brand name L'Essence or however the frogs say that. Cake style, about fifteen bucks a pop nine years back. Shampoo, same manufacturer, same name, caviar and fennel extracts."

"They put caviar in shampoo?" Peabody demanded. "What a waste."

"Just fish eggs, and disgusting if you ask me. Tech in Wales was good enough to work the trace, got the same deal as me. Same for Florida. They didn't get anything in Romania or in Bolivia. But now he's switched brands."

"To?"

"Okay, what we got is still handmade soap, got your shea butter—cocoa butter addition, olive oil, and oil from grapefruit and apricot. Specifically—and this took a little finessing—your pink grapefruit. It's made in Italy, exclusively, and get this, it's going to run you fifty smacks a bar."

"So he upgraded."

"Yeah, that's the thing. I took a look at the Internet site, check these out." He brought the images of the soaps up. Each was a deep almost jewel-like color, with various flowers or herbs studding the edges. "Only one store in the city carries them. The shampoo's from the same place. White truffle oil, running one-fifty for an eight-ounce bottle."

He sniffed, he snorted. "I wouldn't pay that for a bottle of prime liquor."

"You don't have to pay," Eve said absently. "You get your booze in bribes."

"Yeah, but just the same."

Pricey, exclusive products. Prestige, Eve thought. The best of the best? "What's the outlet in the city?"

"Place called Scentual. Got a store midtown on Madison and Fifty-third, and one down in the West Village on Christopher."

"Good. How about the sheet?"

"Irish linen, thread count of seven hundred. That's another change. First time he used Egyptian cotton, five hundred thread count. Manufacturer's in Ireland and Scotland. Buncha outlets around. Your higher-end department stores and bedding places carry the brand. Fáilte."

He massacred the Irish, Eve knew, as she'd heard the word before.

"Okay, send copies to me, to Whitney, to Tibble, and to Feeney. You finish with the water?"

"Still working it. At a guess, and I mean guess, it's city water, but filtered. May be out of the tap, but with a filtration system that purifies. We got good water in New York. This guy, I'm thinking, is a fanatic for pure."

"For something. Okay, thanks. Peabody, let's go shopping."

"Hot dog!"

"Dallas." Berenski swiveled on his stool again. "Bring me something more this time. Get me something."

"Working on it."

She hit the downtown boutique first, and was assaulted with fragrance the moment they walked in. Like falling into some big-ass bouquet, Eve thought.

The clerks all wore strong colors. To mirror the products, Eve supposed, and the products were displayed as if they were priceless pieces of art in a small, intimate museum.

There were a number of customers, browsing, buying, which, given the price tag on a bar of soap, made Eve wonder what the hell was wrong with them.

She and Peabody were approached by a blonde who must have hit six-two in her heeled boots. The boots, like the skinny skirt and rib-bruising jacket, were the color of unripe bananas.

"Welcome to Scentual. How can I help you today?"

"Information." Eve pulled out her badge.

"Of what sort?"

"Soap with cocoa and shea butter, olive oil, pink grapefruit—"

"From our citrus line. Yes, please, this way."

"I don't want the soap, I want your customer list for sales of that soap, and for the truffle oil shampoo. Customers who purchased both products."

"That's a little difficult as—"

"I'll make it easy. Customer data or warrant for same, which will tie up the shop for a number of hours. Maybe days."

The blonde cleared her throat. "You should probably speak to the manager."

"Fine."

She glanced around as the blonde hurried off, and saw Peabody sniffing at minute slivers of soap that were set out as samples. "Cut it out."

"I'll never be able to afford so much as a scraping of this kind of thing. I'm just smelling. I like this one—gardenia. Old-fashioned, but sexy. 'Female,' as my guy would say. Did you see the bottles? The bath oil?"

Her dazzled eyes tracked along the jewel-toned and delicate pastels of fancy bottles in display shelves. "They're so mag."

"So you pay a couple hundred for packaging for stuff that eventually goes down the drain. Anything in a bottle costs that much, I want to be able to drink it."

She turned back as another woman came over, this one petite and redheaded in a sapphire suit. "I'm Chessie, the manager. There's a problem?"

"Not for me. I need your customer list for purchases of two specific products as said products are related to a police investigation."

"So I understand. Could I see some identification, please?"

Eve pulled out her badge again. Chessie took it, studied it, then lifted her gaze to Eve's. "Lieutenant Dallas?"

"That's right."

"I'll be happy to help you in any way I can. The specific products?"

Eve told her, nodded as the woman asked for a moment, then watched her walk away. "Peabody—" When she looked around, her partner was testing out an elf-sized sample bottle of body cream on her hands.

"It's like silk," Peabody said, reverently. "Like liquid silk. I've got a cousin who makes soaps and body creams and all, and they're really nice. But this . . ."

"Stop rubbing stuff all over yourself. I have to ride with you, and you're going to make the ride smell like some big, creepy meadow."

"Meadows are pastoral."

"Exactly. Creepy. He could've bought the stuff here," she said, thinking out loud. "Or at the midtown store, off the Net. Hell, he could've bought the stuff in Italy or wherever the hell else it's sold and brought it with him. But it's something."

Chessie came back with some printouts. "We haven't had any sales—cash or credit—of both products at the same time. Nor has our Madison Avenue store. I contacted them. As a precaution, I've generated all the sales for each product, from each of our stores. Obviously, we don't have customer names for the cash sales. I went back thirty days. I can go back further if that would be helpful."

"This should do for now. Thanks." Eve took the printouts. "Did you get a memo about me?"

"Yes, certainly. Is there anything more I can do for you?"

"Not right now."

"If she got the 'Cooperate with Lieutenant Dallas' memo, Roarke owns that place," Peabody said when they were back on the street. "You can *swim* in that bath oil if you want. How come you—"

"Hold on." She flipped out her 'link, contacted Roarke.

"Lieutenant."

"Do you manufacture bedding—sheets and linens—under the brand name Fáilte?"

"I do. Why?"

"I'll let you know." She ended transmission. "I'm not buying coincidence here, Peabody."

"Oh. Just caught up. First vic worked for him, was washed down in products from a store he owns, was laid out on a sheet he manufactures. No, I'm not buying that today either, thanks. But I don't know what the hell it means."

"Let's go. You drive." Eve pulled out her 'link again, and tagged Feeney. "Missing persons, add in a new piece of data. Look for a woman who's employed by Roarke. Don't say anything to him as yet. Just look for anyone reported missing in the last few days who fits our vic profile and who works for one of Roarke's interests in the city."

"Got that. I've got three potentials from MP from the tristate. Give me a minute on this. Aren't you due at the media blather?"

"I'm on my way there."

"Okay, okay," he grumbled, "takes time. He's got a lot of layers on some of his . . . son of a bitch. Rossi, Gia, age thirty-one, works as a personal trainer and instructor at BodyWorks, a subsidiary of Health Conscience, which is a division of Roarke Enterprises. She was reported missing last night."

"Take one of the uniforms, get to her place of employment, her residence, talk to the person who reported her missing, to—"

"I know the drill, Dallas."

"Right. Move on it, Feeney." She clicked off. "Goddamn media."

"You have to tell him, Dallas. You've got to tell Roarke about this."

"I know, I know. I've got to get through this media crap first, and *think*. I have to think. Roarke will deal. He'll have to deal with it."

She'd think about that part later. At the moment, she could only think that it might be too late for Gia Rossi. She could only wonder what might have been done to her already.

He cleansed her to *Falstaff*. It always put him in a happy mood—this music, this little chore. His partner needed to be absolutely clean before the work began. He particularly enjoyed washing her hair—all that lovely brown hair.

He enjoyed the scents, of course—that hint of citrus, the feminine fragrance mixed with the smell of her fear.

She wept as he washed her, blubbered a bit, which concerned him just a little. He preferred the screams, the curses, the prayers, the pleas, to incoherent weeping.

But it was early days yet, he thought.

The water he hosed her off with was icy, which turned the weeping to harsh gasps and small shrieks. That was better.

"Well now, that was refreshing, wasn't it? Bracing. You have excellent muscle tone, I must say. A strong, healthy body makes such a difference."

She was shivering now, violently, her teeth chattering, her lips pale blue. It might be interesting, he decided, to follow up the cold with heat.

"Please," she choked out when he turned away to study his tools. "What do you want? What do you want?"

"Everything you can give me," he replied. He chose his smallest torch, flicked on the flame, then narrowed it to the point of a pin.

When he turned, when her eyes wheeled toward that flame, she rewarded him with those wild, wild screams.

"Let's get started, shall we?"

He moved to the base of the table, smiled in delight at the high, elegant arch of her feet.

5 SHE HATED MEDIA CONFERENCES, BUT NEARLY always hated the media liaison more. It was suggested, by same, that Eve might prep for fifteen minutes with the media coach, and make use of the provided enhancements in order to present a more pleasant image on screen.

"Murder isn't pleasant," Eve snapped back as she strode toward the main doors of Cop Central.

"No, of course not." The liaison jogged to keep up. "But we're going to avoid words like murder. The prepared statement—"

"Isn't going to be tasty when I stuff it down your throat. I'm not your mouthpiece, and this isn't a political spin."

"No, but there are ways to be informative and tactful."

"Tact's just bullshit with spit polish over it."

Eve pushed through the doors. Tibble had opted for the steps of Central not only to show the sturdy symbol of the building, but, Eve guessed, to insure the briefing would remain short.

The March wind wasn't being tactful.

She stepped up to the podium, and waited for the noise level to drop off. She picked Nadine out immediately. The bright red coat stood out like a beacon.

"I have a statement, then I'll take a few brief questions. The body of a twenty-eight-year-old woman identified as Sarifina York was found early this morning in East River Park. It has been determined that Ms. York was most likely abducted last Monday evening, held against her will for several days. The method in which she was murdered and the evidence gathered so far indicates Ms. York was killed by the same individual who took the lives of four women in a fifteen-day period in this city, nine years ago."

That caused an eruption, and she ignored it. She stood still and silent while questions and demands were hurled out. Stood still and silent until they ceased.

"The NYPSD has authorized and formed a task force. Its soul purpose will be to investigate this crime, and to apprehend and incarcerate the perpetrator. We will use every resource, every man-hour, and all the experience at our disposal to do so. Questions."

They flew like missiles. But the fact that there were so many allowed her to cherry pick.

"How was she killed?" Eve repeated. "Ms. York was tortured over a period of days, and died as a result of blood loss. No, we do not have any suspects at this time, and yes, we are, and will continue to follow any and all leads."

She fielded a few more, grateful her time was nearly up. She noted Nadine tossed out no questions, and had in fact moved out of the pack to talk on her 'link.

"You said she was tortured," someone called out. "Can you give us details?"

"I neither can nor will. Those details are confidential to this investigation. If they weren't, I wouldn't give them to you so you could broadcast her suffering and cause yet more pain for her family and friends. Her life was taken. And that's more than enough for outrage."

She stepped back, turned, and walked through the doors of Central.

It would take Nadine a few minutes to get up to Homicide and charm her way through any potential roadblocks to Eve's office.

Besides, Eve thought, she could wait. Just wait.

First, Eve needed to speak to Roarke.

She caught the scent as soon as she stepped into the conference room, and much preferred it to the olfactory bombardment at Scentual.

Somebody, she thought, brought in gyros.

She made her way over to Roarke's workstation, noted he'd gone for the cold-cut sub. He paused in his work long enough to pick up half the sub, hand it to her. "Eat something."

She peered between the slabs of roll. "What is it?"

"No substance in nature, I can promise you. That's why I said eat *something*."

More to please him than out of appetite, she took a bite. "I need to talk to you."

"If you're after some answers on this chore you gave me, you won't get any as yet. There are, literally, countless homes, private residences, warehouses, and other potential structures in New York, the boroughs, into New Jersey, that have been owned by the same person or persons or organization for the last decade."

"How are you handling it?"

"Dividing into sections—quadrants, you could say. Subdividing by types of structure, then by types of ownership. It's bloody tedious work."

"You asked for it."

"So I did." Watching her, he picked up a bottle of water, drank.

"There's something else. The lab's identified the soap and shampoo used to wash down the vic."

"Quick work."

"Yeah, Dickhead's got his teeth in it. He worked the case before."

"Ah."

"He uses extremely high-end products. Very exclusive. Only one outlet in New York, two locations. It's yours."

"Mine?" He sat back, eyes cold and hard on her face. "And so was the sheet he used."

"That's right." Now, simply because it was there and so was she, Eve took another bite of mystery-meat sub. "Someone less cynical might think coincidence, particularly since you manufacture or own big, fat chunks of everything."

"But you and I aren't less cynical."

"No, and so I tagged Feeney and put you into the Missing Persons search he was running. You're not going to like it."

"Who is she?"

"Gia Rossi." She picked up his water, took a gulp. "She's a trainer and instructor at BodyWorks. Do you know her?"

"No." He pressed his fingers to his eyes a moment, then dropped them. "No, I don't believe so. Were there any of these connects, any of these overlaps in the previous investigation to me or mine?"

"No, not that I know of, and I started a check on the way back. He changed the products with this one. If you're part of the reason, we need to figure out why. A competitor maybe, a former employee. We need to work that angle."

"When did he take the second one?"

"She was reported missing yesterday. I don't have the details yet— Feeney's on it. I've got to go pull another chain now, but we're going to dig into this. I know this is a kick in the ass, but it's also a mistake. His mistake. There was nothing connecting the victims in any of the other cases. Now there is."

"Yes. Now there is."

"I'm sorry, I have to go do this."

"Go on. I'll stick with this for now."

She didn't kiss him, though part of her wanted to, just to give comfort. Instead she laid her hand over his, squeezed gently. Then left him.

She started back toward her office and crossed paths with Baxter. "Got nothing," he told her. "Reinterviewed the sister, went to the club, talked to the vic's neighbors. Big zero."

"Ex?"

"Out of town for the weekend. Neighbor said he went snowboarding out in Colorado."

"Why would anybody deliberately jump and flop around in the snow, on a mountain?" she wondered.

"Beats me. I like summer sports, where the women are very, very scantily clad. Snow and ice? No skin."

"You're such a pig, Baxter."

"And proud of it. Do you want me to run down the ex? The neighbor thought he knew where the guy was staying. He'll be back tomorrow night."

"We'll hit him once he gets back. Check with Jenkinson. See how far he and Powell have gotten going down the list of people interviewed in the other cases. You and Trueheart can help them run through it. Media's out with this now, which means by tomorrow we'll be buried in looney leads. We'll have to follow up on them, so let's clear this first plate today."

Nadine was waiting, sitting in the visitor's chair, legs crossed, examining her nails as she talked on her headset.

"You have to reschedule or cancel," she said. "No. No. We agreed in writing when I took this that if and when I had something hot, something I felt it was necessary to pursue personally, it would take precedence over everything else. That was the deal."

She looked over at Eve, rolled her clever green eyes. "That's what assistants are for, and assistants to assistants. And as far as the piece, the reporter can reschedule. I know. I'm a goddamn reporter."

She yanked off the headset.

"Heavy is the price of fame," Eve said.

"Tell me, but I wear it so very well. Can I have coffee?"

Obligingly, Eve moved to the AutoChef. Her own system kept begging to sag. Coffee would put it back on alert. Nadine sat, saying nothing.

She did wear fame well, Eve supposed. The streaky and stylish hair, the sharp features, the camera-ready suit. But Eve knew: Though Nadine might have her own show, though *Now*'s ratings were reputedly higher than a souped-up chemi-head, the woman was exactly what she'd claimed—a goddamn reporter.

"Who were you talking to during the briefing?"

"Who do you think?" Nadine countered.

Eve turned, offered the coffee. "Your research people to give you the pertinent details of the case from nine years ago."

Nadine smiled, sipped. "Look who's wearing her thinking cap today."

"Some of the details on that investigation leaked."

"Some," Nadine agreed and the smile faded. "Some of the details on how the victims were tortured. I imagine there was a lot more, a lot worse, that didn't leak."

"There was more. There was worse."

"You worked it."

"Feeney was primary, I was his partner."

"I wasn't in New York nine years ago. I was fighting my way out of a second-rate network affiliate in South Philly. But I remember this case. I remember these murders. I bullied my way into doing a series of reports on them. That's part of what got me out of South Philly hell."

"Small world."

Nadine nodded, sipped more coffee. "What do you want?"

"You've got that research department at your fingertips now, being you're a big shot." Eve eased a hip down on the corner of her desk. "I want everything, anything you can dig up on the murders. All the murders. Here, Europe, Florida, South America."

Nadine blinked. "What? Where?"

"I'm going to explain it all to you, off the record, then you can put your researchers and your own honed skills on the scent. He's already got the second one, Nadine."

"Oh, God."

"Can't help her. Odds are slim we'll track him fast enough to save her. I need to know everything I can know. Maybe we can save the one he's hunting now."

"Let me think." Closing her eyes, Nadine sat back. She drank more coffee. "I've got a couple of smart people I can bully and bribe to keep the work and the results off the radar. I'm pretty damn smart myself, so that's three." Nodding, she sat up again. "You know I'd do this because I believe a life is worth more than a story. Marginally," she said with a smile. "I'd do it because you and I are friends who also happen to respect each other to play it straight. No payback required."

"I know that. Just like you know I'm going to pay you back."

Nadine cocked a brow. "Being pretty damn smart, I'm not going to say no. A one-on-one exclusive with you."

"After he's bagged, not before."

"Deal. A live appearance on *Now*."

"Don't push it."

Nadine laughed. "By any member of your team you choose—with portions of that exclusive—and did I mention extensive—interview by you to run during the show. Recorded prior."

Eve thought it through. "I can work with that."

"Okay. To get details, I need details." Nadine pulled out her recorder, cocked her head. "All right?"

"All right."

There was something unnerving on some visceral level about working in a cop shop. It was an interesting experience, Roarke thought, but very, very strange for someone with his . . . colorful background.

He'd worked *with* cops—in addition to his own—a number of times now, had had cops in his home professionally and socially. But working in a war room in the core of Cop Central for the best part of a day, well, that was a different kettle.

They came and went, he noted. Clipping into the room, clipping out again, communicating for the most part in that cop speak that was oddly formal, as clipped as their footsteps and somehow colorful all at the same time.

He was flanked by McNab whom he had great fondness for, and the dark, curvy, and sloe-eyed Callendar. They might sit, or stand and walk—almost dance—around as they worked. Slogging through data, searching for just one vital byte. Busy bees in their busy hive.

As for colorful, well, excepting their captain, it appeared the e-division went for the flashy. McNab with his bright yellow jeans, the turquoise shirt with what appeared to be flying turtles winging across it. He had his long blond hair sleeked back in a tail and secured with a thick yellow band. On either side of his thin, pretty face, his earlobes were weighted down with a complex series of hoops and studs.

Roarke wondered why, honestly, anyone would wish to have that many holes punched into his flesh.

But the boy had a way about him, and was damn clever at this job.

The girl, for she looked barely twenty, was an unknown. She had burnt honey skin, masses and masses of black curly hair pinned in a multitude of hanks with a neon rainbow of clips. Silver hoops he could have punched his fists through hung at her ears. She wore baggy, multipocketed pants in bleeding colors of lavender and pink with a snug green sweater that exclaimed E-GODS! across her rather impressive breasts.

She had long, emerald-colored nails, and when she went to manual they clicked against the keys like mad castanets.

She, like McNab, appeared to be tireless—brightly wrapped bundles of energy barely contained so that something on them constantly jiggled or bounced. A foot, a head, shoulders, ass.

Fascinating.

"Yo, Blondie-Boy," she called out and McNab glanced over his shoulder.

"You talking to me, D-Cup?"

"You're up. Liquid."

"Can do. You want?" he said to Roarke. "Something to drink."

"Yes, thanks."

"Buzz or no buzz?"

It took Roarke a moment to translate, and in that moment he felt very old. "Could use the buzz."

"On it." As McNab bounced out of the room, Callendar sent Roarke a quick and pretty smile.

"So, you're like absolutely packed, right? Doing the backstroke in the megawealth. What's that like?"

"Satisfying," he decided.

"Betcha." With a push of her feet, she sent her chair skidding over so she could see his screen. "Wow. Multitudinous data with simo searches and cross. You got secondary recog going, too?"

This, he could easily translate. "I do. Checking like names, anagrams, cross dates. Lay it down for a spread, go deep for ancestry and other potential connects."

"Smart. McNab said you were frosty in there. Serious mining." She looked back at her own station. "All around."

She slid back to her work, and jiggling her shoulders to some internal tune, went back to the task at hand.

Amused, he turned back to his own work, then stopped when Eve and Feeney came in.

Gia Rossi, he thought, as the name, the idea of her that he'd made himself set aside, pushed once again into the forefront of his mind.

His eyes met Eve's, so he pushed back from the work to walk to her.

"We need to update the team regarding Rossi," Eve said. "Those in the field will be briefed via 'link. We need to factor your connection in."

"Understood."

"Okay, then."

Peabody came in, sent Roarke a quiet, sympathetic look. She crossed over to insert a new data disc.

"We have an update," Eve announced, and the clacking, the bouncing, the voices, and shuffling ceased. "We have reason to believe a woman reported as missing since Thursday night was abducted by our unsub. Rossi, Gia."

Peabody ordered the image and data on screen. "Age thirty-one, brown and brown, height five feet, five inches, one hundred and twenty-two pounds. She was last seen leaving her place of employment, a fitness center called BodyWorks on West Forty-sixth. Captain Feeney."

"Rossi's ex-husband," Feeney began, "one Riley, Jaymes, notified the police at oh-eight-hundred Friday morning. Per procedure, she wasn't formally listed as missing until the twenty-four-hour time limit had passed. The subject did not return home as expected on Thursday night where she was scheduled to meet her ex who, according to his statement, was there to drop off the dog they had joint custody of."

There were a few of the expected smirks at this, and Feeney just eyeballed the smirkers until they faded away.

"Neighbors confirm the arrangement. Nor was Riley able to reach her via her pocket 'link. We've confirmed that he did, in fact, attempt to ascertain her whereabouts by contacting her coworkers, her friends. The statements given to the responding officer and to me have been corroborated. He is not considered involved in her disappearance.

"Habitually the subject exited the building on Forty-sixth and walked west to Broadway, then north to the Forty-ninth Street subway. We'll canvass for witnesses in that area. Transit Authority security discs do not show the subject entering that station on Thursday evening, nor has her Metro pass been used since Thursday morning. Witnesses do verify the subject left the building at approximately seventeen-thirty on the night in question. She was wearing a black coat, black sweatpants, a gray sweatshirt with the BodyWorks logo, and a gray watch cap."

He stepped back, looked at Eve. "Lieutenant."

"The subject fits the established pattern. Probability runs exceed ninety-six percent that she was taken and is being held by the unsub. Her disappearance and other information gathered today add another element to the pattern. Both York and Rossi were employed by an arm of Roarke Enterprises. Given the breadth of that organization, that factor alone scores low on the probability scale for a connect. However, the soap and shampoo identified by brand by the lab has been determined to be manufactured and sold through subsidiaries of that organization, as was the sheet used with York."

Roarke felt the eyes on him, and the speculation. Accepted them.

"The probability is high," Eve continued, "that there's a connection on some level between the unsub and Roarke Enterprises. To this point, no connection, no central point has ever been determined. Now we have one, and we're going to use it. The hair and body products are extreme high-end and have limited outlets. He bought them somewhere. McNab, find out where."

"On it."

"Callendar, take the sheet, cross-reference purchases with McNab's data. Roarke."

"Lieutenant."

"Employee lists. Find and pull out individuals who fit the pattern and work or live in the city. He takes them from the city. He will, in all likelihood, move on number three within a matter of days. We need names."

"You'll have them."

"Jenkinson, I want a full and detailed report from you and Powell by nineteen hundred. Baxter, the same from you and Trueheart. I'll be available twenty-four/seven, and expect to be notified immediately should any new data come to light. We'll brief again at oh-eight-hundred. That's it."

She pulled off her headset. "Peabody."

"Yes, sir."

"Log and copy, then go home and get some sleep. Feeney, can you look over the e-work to date, send me a basic rundown?"

"Can and will," Feeney confirmed.

"Roarke, go ahead and log and copy what you've got so far, then shoot additionals to my unit here and at home. When you're done, I need you in my office."

Eve walked out, contacting Mira's office on the way. "Put me through to her," she ordered Mira's overprotective admin. "Don't give me any crap."

"Right away."

"Eve." Mira's face swam on, and instantly her eyes registered concern. "You look exhausted."

"Second wind blew out, I'm waiting for the third to blow in. I need a sit-down with you."

"Yes, I know. I'll clear any time that works for you."

"I want to say now, but I need that wind before I start digging through the psychology of this. And there's more data that needs to be factored in from your end. Peabody's sending you a copy of the update right about now."

"Tomorrow, then."

"After the eight-o'clock briefing."

"I'll come to you. Get some sleep, Eve."

"I'm going to factor that in, somewhere."

She went into her office, programmed more coffee, and considered popping one of the departmentally approved energy pills. But they always made her jittery.

She drank, standing at her narrow office window, looking out at her slice of the city. Commuter trams were crisscrossing the sky, lights beaming against the growing dark.

Time to go home, time to have dinner and kick back, watch a little screen.

Below, the street was thick with traffic, with people thinking just the same as those who chugged along above their heads.

And somewhere out there was a man who really enjoyed his work. He wasn't thinking about kicking back.

Did he take a dinner break? she wondered. Have a nice, hearty meal before he went back to the business at hand? When had he started on Gia Rossi? When did he start the clock?

Forty-seven hours missing, Eve thought. But he wouldn't start it ticking until he got down to it. Number two always started after number one was finished.

She didn't hear Roarke come in, he had a skill for silence. But she sensed him. "Maybe we'll get lucky," she said. "Maybe he won't start on her until tomorrow. We've got another angle to work this time, so we could get lucky."

"She's gone. You know it."

Eve turned. He looked angry, she thought, which was probably a good thing, and just a little worn around the edges, which was a rare one. "I don't know it until I'm standing over her body. That's the way I'm dealing with it. We're going home. We can work from home."

He closed the door behind him. "I looked her up. She's worked for me for nearly four years. Her parents are divorced. She has a younger brother, a half brother, a stepsister. She went to college in Baltimore, where her mother and younger brother still live. Her employee evaluations have been, consistently, excellent. She was given a raise three weeks ago."

"You know this isn't your fault."

"Fault?" He could be faulted for a great deal, he knew and accepted that. But not for this. "No. But somewhere in it, I may very well be the reason these particular women die at this particular time."

"Reason has nothing to do with it. You're no good to me if you screw yourself up with misplaced guilt. You do that, you're out."

"You can't push me out," he countered, with considerable heat. "With or without your bleeding task force, your sodding procedure, I'm bloody well in this."

"Fine. Waste time pissing on me then." She grabbed her coat. "That's helpful."

She started to shove by him, but he grabbed her arm, swung her around. For an instant the rage was carved into his face. Then he yanked her against him, banded his arms around her.

"I have to piss on someone. You're handy."

"Maybe." She let herself relax against him. "Okay, maybe. But you have to think in a clear line with this. I need your brain, as well as your resources. It's another advantage we didn't have nine years ago."

"Knowing you're right doesn't make it easier to swallow. I've got to get out of this place," he said as he eased back. "That's God's shining truth. I can only breathe in cop for so long without choking."

"Hey."

He tapped his finger on her chin. "Excepting one."

She hauled up the file bag she wanted to take with her. "Let's go."

She drove primarily because she knew the battle uptown would keep her awake. A hot shower, she thought, something quick and solid in her stomach, and she'd be good to go for a few more hours.

"Summerset would be useful," Roarke considered.

"As what, a hockey stick?"

"The employee files, Eve. He can run those, generate a list of women who fit this pattern who work for me. It would free my time up for other things."

"All right, as long as he understands he answers to me. And that I get to debase him and ream him out as is often necessary with those under my command. And adds some entertainment to my day."

"Because you're so good at it."

"Yeah, I've got a knack." She scanned the army of vehicles heading north, the throngs of pedestrians hustling along on the sidewalk, the glides, or bullying their way on the crosswalks. "Nobody notices things—other people. Sure, if somebody jumps out of a building and lands on their head, it gives them a moment's pause, but they don't click to a woman being forced into a car or a van or Christ knows unless she puts up one hell of a stink about it. Mostly, they just keep their heads down and keep going."

"Cynicism is another of your finely tuned skills. It's not always so, not with everyone."

She shrugged. "No, not always. He's slick about it, or has some cover, something people don't register. If she kicked up enough fuss, yeah, somebody would notice. They might not do anything about it, but they'd notice. So no overt struggle on the street. One of the working theories is he drugs them somehow rather than overpowers them.

"Quick jab," she added. "Wraps an arm around her. 'Hey, Sari, how you doing?' Just a guy walking along with some zoned-out woman, helping her into his ride. Ride would need to be close to wherever he picks her up. Going to hit lots and garages tomorrow."

When she drove through the gates of home, she couldn't remember ever being more grateful to see the jut and spread of the gorgeous house, to see the lights in the windows.

"Going to grab a shower, grab something to eat in my office."

"You're going to grab some sleep," he corrected. "You're burnt, Eve."

No question she was, but it annoyed her to have it pointed out. "I got some left."

"Bollocks. You haven't slept in more than thirty-six hours. Neither have I, come to that. We both need some sleep."

"I'll take a couple hours after I set up a board here, review some notes."

Rather than argue—he was too bloody tired to bother—he said nothing. He'd just dump her into bed bodily, and he imagined once she was horizontal for thirty seconds, she'd be unconscious.

She parked in front of the house, grabbed her file bag.

She knew Summerset would be in the foyer, and he didn't disappoint. "Fill your personal cadaver in," Eve said before Summerset could speak. "I'm hitting the showers before I get started on this."

She headed straight up, neglecting to take off her coat and sling it over the newel as was her habit. And which, she knew, irritated Summerset's bony ass. Once she was out of sight, she rubbed at her gritty eyes, and allowed the yawn that had been barely suppressed to escape.

The shower was going to feel like a miracle.

She dumped the bag in the bedroom, shrugged out of her coat. As she hit the release on her weapon harness, her gaze landed on the bed. Maybe five minutes down, she considered. Five off her feet, then she could shower without risking drowning herself.

Tossing the harness aside, she climbed the platform where the bed spread like the silk clouds of heaven. She slid onto it, stretching out across it, facedown.

And beat Roarke's guess by being out in ten seconds flat.

He came in five minutes later, saw her on the bed, with the cat slung across her ass. "Well, then," Roarke addressed Galahad. "At least we won't have to fight about it. But for Christ's sake, couldn't she have pulled off her boots? How can she sleep well like that?"

He pulled them off himself—and she didn't stir a bit—pulled off his own. Then he simply stretched out beside her, draped an arm around her waist.

He dropped out nearly as quickly as she had.

6 IN THE DREAM THERE WAS A WHITE SHEET OVER the dark ground, and the ruined body that lay on it. Bitter with cold, dawn carved its first light, etching the eastern spires into sharpened silhouettes.

She stood with her hands in the pockets of a black peacoat, a black watch cap pulled low on her forehead.

The body lay between her and a big black clock with a big white face. The seconds ticked away on it, and every strike was like thunder that sent the air to quaking.

And in the dream Feeney stood beside her. The harsh crime scene lights washed over them and what they studied. There was no silver in his hair to glint in those lights, and the lines in his face didn't ride so deep.

I trained you for this, so you could see what needs to be seen, and find what's under it.

She crouched down, opened her kit.

She doesn't look peaceful, Eve thought, as people so often said about the repose of the dead. They really never do.

But death isn't sleep. It's something else again.

The body opened its eyes.

I'm Corrine Dagby. I was twenty-nine. I was born in Danville, Illinois, and came to New York to be an actress. So I waited tables because that's what we do. I had a boyfriend, and he'll cry when you tell him I'm dead. So will the others, my family, my friends. I bought new shoes the day before he took me. I'll never wear them now. He hurt me, he just kept hurting me until I was dead.

Didn't you hear me screaming?

She stood in the morgue, and Morris's bloody hand held a scalpel. His hair was shorter, worn in a neat and tidy queue at the nape of his neck. Over the body, he looked at Eve.

She used to be healthy, and had a pretty face until he ruined her. She sang in the shower and danced in the street. We all do until we come here. And in the end, we all come here.

In the corner, the big clock ticked the time so every second echoed.

They won't come if it stops, she thought. Not if I stop it. They'll sing in the shower and dance in the street, they'll eat cupcakes and ride the train if I stop it.

But you haven't. Corrine opened her eyes again. *Do you see?*

The faces and bodies changed, one melding into the next while the clock hammered the time. Hammered until her head pounded with it, until she pressed her hands to her ears to block it out.

Faster, faster, the faces flashed and merged while the seconds raced. So many voices, all the voices calling, coalescing into one, and the one cried out.

Can't you hear us screaming?

She woke with a gasp, with that awful cry echoing in her head. The light was dim, warm with the fire simmering low in the hearth. The cat butted against her shoulder as if telling her, "Wake up, for God's sake."

"Yeah, I'm up. I'm awake. Jesus." She rolled over, stared up at the ceiling as she got her breath back. With one hand she scratched

Galahad between the ears, and checked the time on her wrist unit. "Oh, crap."

She'd been out nearly three hours. Shoving off sleep, Eve pressed the heels of her hands to her eyes and began to push off the bed. She heard it then, the sizzle and pulse of the shower.

She laid a hand on the spread beside her, felt his warmth lingering there. So they'd both slept, she realized. Good for them.

Stripping as she went, she headed for the shower.

She wanted to wash away the fatigue, the grit, the ugliness of the past twenty-four hours. She wanted the beat of the water to push away the vague headache she'd woken with, and flood out the remnants of the dream.

Then, when she stepped to the wide opening of the glass that enclosed the generous shower, she knew she wanted more.

She wanted him.

He was facing away from her, his hands braced on the glass, letting the water from the multiple jets beat over him. His hair was seal-sleek with wet, his skin gleaming with it. Long back, she mused, a taut, bitable ass, and all those tough, toned muscles.

He hadn't been up for long, she thought, and was likely as worn down as she.

The water would be too cold, she knew. But she'd fix that.

They'd fix each other.

She slipped in, wrapped her arms around his waist, pressed her body to his back. Nipped lightly at his shoulder. "Look what I found. Better than the toy surprise in the cereal box. Increase water temp to one hundred and one degrees."

"Must you boil us?"

"I must. Anyway, you won't notice in a minute." To prove it, she glided her hands down, found him. "See?"

"Is this how you behave with all the members of your task force?"

"They only wish."

He turned, caught her face in his hands. "And look how my wishes come true." He kissed her softly, brow, cheeks, lips. "I thought you might sleep a bit more."

"I already took more than I meant to." She pressed to him again, laying her head on his shoulder as the water flooded them. "This is better than sleep."

As the steam began to rise she tipped her head back. She found his mouth with hers, soft again, soft so they could both sink deep.

His fingers skimmed up into her hair, combing through the sleek cap of it as he murmured something that tasted sweet against her lips. Even through the sweetness she recognized need.

Yes, they would fix each other.

She tore her lips from his to press them to his throat, to feel his pulse beat while her hands stroked up his back. As he held her, as he turned her so the water sluiced over them, more than the day washed away.

Now his hands moved over her, creamy with soap, gliding over skin that all but hummed at the pleasure. Again he turned her, drew her back against him. And those hands circled her breasts, slid over them while his mouth sampled the side of her throat, her shoulder.

She moaned once, lifted an arm to hook around him, and quivered as his hands circled down.

He could feel her giving, opening, awaiting. The way her body moved, the way her breath caught. He could hear it in the quick cry that escaped her when he slipped his hands between her legs to cup her. How she trembled, her arm tightened when he used his fingers to tease and to pleasure. And the shock of her release when he dipped them into that hot, wet velvet.

"Take more." He had to give more.

Her trembles went to shudders, her breath to sobbing.

Her surrender, to him, to herself, aroused him beyond imagining. And the fatigue and sorrow that sleep and shower hadn't washed away drowned in his love for her.

He spun her around, pressed her back against the wall. Her breath was short, but her eyes stayed on his.

"You take more now," she told him.

Gripping her hips, he fought for control, to hold the moment. And so slipped slowly inside her.

Steam smoked around them; the water streamed. They watched each other, moved together.

More than pleasure, he thought. Somehow even more than love. At a time they each needed it most, they gave each other that essential human gift of hope.

Even as her breath caught, caught again, he saw her smile. Undone, he captured those curved lips. Surrounded by her, drowning in her, he let himself take the pleasure, take the love. Take the hope.

Well, that set me up." Eve stretched her neck after she dragged on her old and favored NYPSD sweatshirt. "Sleep and shower sex. I ought to make the combo required for the team."

"I'm afraid I don't have the time to sleep and play in the shower with Peabody and Callendar. Even for the good of the team."

"Ha-ha. Funny." She sat on the arm of the sofa in the sitting area to pull on thick socks. "I'll just keep you as my personal energy booster. Gotta get back to it."

"Food," Roarke said.

"Yeah, I figured on—"

"I know what you figured on." He took her hand to walk out of the bedroom with her. "But disappointment is what you're doomed for as it's not going to be pizza."

"I think you have prejudice against the pie."

"I have no pie prejudice. However, I insist on another element to your energy boost. In addition to sleep and shower sex, we're having steak."

"Red meat's hard to argue with, but I'm having fries with it."

"Mmm-hmm."

She knew that *mmm-hmm*. It meant vegetables. She also knew that fussing over getting decent food into her would keep his mind off what was happening to Gia Rossi.

She let him order up whatever he considered proper nutrition while she fed the cat. The vegetables turned out to be some sort of medley he called *niçoise*. At least they had the crunch going for them.

She read over her detectives' reports while they ate. "People remember the details," she said. "Such as they were. The people who were close to the prior vics remember the details."

"I imagine so. For them—each of them," Roarke commented, "it was likely a once-in-a-lifetime shock and loss."

"If they're lucky. But even so, they don't tell us anything new. No new people in their lives, no comments or complaints about being bothered or worried. Each one had a basic routine—with some variations, sure. But each walked to and from work or transportation at basically the same time frame every day. No viable witnesses came forward claiming they saw them with anyone at the time they disappeared."

"Viable."

She shrugged, ate a fry. "You get the loonies and the attention-grabbers. Nothing panned. Still you check them out, every one. End up wasting time following false leads. People are a pain in the ass."

"You said you were going to check lots and garages. I assume you did then as well."

"Yeah. Watched hours of security vids, questioned dozens of attendants, droid and human, checked ticket records. We got nothing. Which means he could've used street parking, an unsecured lot, or just got lucky."

Roarke lifted his eyebrows as he ate. "Four times lucky?"

"Yeah, exactly. I don't think it was luck. He's not lucky, he's precise and prepared."

"Did you consider he might use an official vehicle? A black-and-white, a city official, a cab?"

"Yeah, we pushed that angle, and got nowhere. And we'll push it again. I've got Newkirk sifting through the records, looking for any private purchase of that kind of ride. They go up for auction a couple times a year. Checking the stolen vehicles records. I've got McNab searching the city and transportation employee records to see what we see there. We'll cross all that with the other case files. Even if he changed his name and appearance, prints are required on all ID for that kind of thing. Nothing's popped yet."

"What about medical equipment and supplies? He drugs them, restrains them, and certainly must have some equipment to deal with the blood."

"Went there, going there again. Countless clinics, hospitals, health care centers, doctors, MTs. Doctors and MTs and aides and so on who lost their licenses. Toss in funeral parlors and bereavement centers, even body sculpting salons. You've got hours and hours of leg and drone work."

"Yes. Yes, you would. You're covering every possible area."

"Maybe. We worked it for weeks, even after the murders stopped. Then Feeney and I worked it weeks more, every time we could squeeze it in. No sleep and shower sex and steak in those days."

She pushed up to pace a little. Maybe by looking back she'd see something she hadn't seen before. "We'd work around the clock sometimes, pushing and prodding at this on our own time. Sitting over a beer at three in the morning in some cop bar, talking it through all over again. And I know damn well, he'd go home, pick through it. I did."

She glanced back at Roarke, sitting at her desk with the remnants of the meal they had shared, with data on death on her comp screen, on the wall screen. "Mrs. Feeney, she's one of the ones who gets it. She understands the cop, the job, the life. Probably why she has all those weird hobbies."

"To keep her from sitting, worrying, wondering when it's three in the morning and he hasn't come home."

"Yeah. Sucks for you guys."

He smiled a little. "We manage."

"He loves her a lot. You know how he'll talk in that long-suffering way about 'the wife.' He'd be lost without her. I know how that is. I know how he's working this right now while she's probably knitting a small compact car. How he's seeing all those faces, the ones from then, the ones from now."

Can't you hear us screaming?

"And he knows it's on him."

"How can you say that?" Roarke demanded. "He did everything that could be done."

"No, because there's always something else. You missed it, or you didn't look at it from just the right angle, or ask just the right question at exactly the right time. And maybe someone else would have. Doesn't make them better or mean they worked harder at it. It just means they . . ." She lifted a hand, swiveled it like a door. "Means they turned something, opened something, and you didn't. He was in command, so it's on him."

"And now it's on you?"

"Now it's on me. And that hurts him because, well, he brought me up. As far as being a cop goes, he brought me up. I didn't want to bring him into this," she said and sat again. "And I couldn't leave him out."

"He's tough and he's hardheaded," Roarke reminded her. "Just like the cop he brought up. He'll handle it, Eve."

"Yeah." She sighed, looked back at the wall screen. "How does he pick them? We know, this time, part of his requirement is that they work for you in some capacity. He's so fucking smart he had to figure we'd click to that. So he wants us to know that much. He gives us the information he wants us to have. The type he prefers, how long he worked on them. He doesn't mind if we know what products he used to clean them up. But this time, he's given us a little more. Here's a new piece, what do you make of that?"

She looked back at Roarke. "Does he know you? Personally, professionally? Has he done business with you? Did you buy him out, and maybe he didn't want to be bought out? Did you underbid him on some contract? Did you fire him, or overlook him for promotion? Nothing's random with him, so his choice here is deliberate."

He'd inched all those same questions through his mind, turning them over from every angle. "If he works for me, I can find out. The travel," Roarke said. "Whether it was business-related or personal time, I can search files for employees who were sent to the locations of the other murders in that time period, or who took personal leave."

"How many employees would you figure you have?"

His lips curved again. "I honestly couldn't say."

"Exactly. But using Mira's profile—and we'll have an updated one tomorrow—we can cut that back considerably."

Following the usual arrangement when he dealt with the meal, Eve rose to clear the dishes. "I'll run a probability, but I think there's a low percentage he works for you. He doesn't strike me as a disgruntled employee."

"Agreed. I can check the same information on major competitors and subcontractors. Using my private equipment."

She said nothing at first, just carted the dishes into the kitchen, loaded them into the machine. His private office, with its unregistered equipment, would allow him to evade CompuGuard and the privacy laws.

Whatever he found, she couldn't use it in court, couldn't reveal where she'd gotten the data. Illegal means, she thought, crossing the line. Such maneuvers gave a defense attorney that flea-ass opening.

Can't you hear us screaming?

She walked back into the office. "Run it."

"All right. It'll take considerable time."

"Then you'd better get started."

Alone, she began to set up her murder board while her computer read off the progress reports from her team.

Board's too small, she thought. Too small to hold all the faces, all the data. All the death.

"Lieutenant."

"Computer pause," she ordered, then turned to Summerset. "What? I'm working."

"As I can see. Roarke asked I bring you this data." He held out a disc. "The employee search he asked I run."

"Good." She took it, walked over to put it on her desk. Glanced back. "You still here? Go away."

Ignoring her, he stood in his funereal black suit, his back stiff as a poker. "I remember this. I remember the media reports on these women. But there was nothing about these numbers carved into them."

"Civilians don't need to know everything."

"He takes great care in how he forms them, each number, each letter so precise. I've seen this before."

Her eyes sharpened. "What do you mean?"

"Not this, not exactly this, but something similar. During the Urban Wars."

"The torture methods?"

"No, no. Though, of course, there was plenty of that. Torture's a classic means of eliciting information or dealing out punishment. Though it's rarely so . . . tidy as this."

"Tell me something I don't know."

He looked over at her. "You're too young to have experienced the Urbans, or to remember the dregs of them that settled in some parts of Europe after they ended here. In any case, there were elements there, too, that civilians—so to speak—didn't need to know."

He had her full attention now. "Such as?"

"When I served as a medic, the injured and the dead would be brought in. Sometimes in piles, in pieces. We'd hold the dead, or those who succumbed to their injuries—for family members if such existed, and if the body could be identified. Or for burial or cremation. Those who didn't have identification, or were beyond being identified, would be listed by number until disposal. We kept logs, listing them by any description possible, any personal effects, the location where they'd been killed, and so on. And we would write the number on them, and the date of their death, or as close as we could come to it."

"Was that SOP?"

"It was what we did when I worked in London. There were other methods in other areas, and in some of the worst areas only mass burials and cremations without any record."

She walked back over to the board, studied the carving. It wasn't the same, she thought. But it was an angle.

"He knows their names," she said. "The name's not an issue. But the data's important. It has to be recorded. The data's what identifies them. The time is what names them for him. I need another board."

"Excuse me?"

"I need another board. I don't have enough room with one. We got anything around here that'll work?"

"I imagine I can find what you need."

"Good. Go do that."

When he left, she went to her desk, added the Urban Wars data to her notes, then continued to jot down her speculations.

Soldier, medic, doctor. Maybe someone who lost a family member or lover . . . No, no, she didn't like that one. Why would he torture and desecrate the symbol, you could say, of anyone who'd mattered to him? Then again, if a loved one had been tortured, killed, identified in that manner, this just might be payback or some twisted re-creation.

Maybe he'd been tortured, survived it. Tortured by a female with brown hair, within the age span.

Or maybe he'd been the torturer.

She rose, paced. Then why wait decades to re-create? Did some event trigger it? Or had he been experimenting all along, until he found the method that suited him?

And maybe he was just a fucking lunatic.

But the Urbans were an angle, yes they were. Mira's profile had indicated he was mature, even nine years back. Male, likely Caucasian, she remembered, between the ages of thirty-five and sixty.

So go high-end, and yeah, he could've seen some of the wars as a young man.

She sat again and, adding in new speculations, ran probabilities.

While they ran, she plugged in the disc Summerset had brought in. "Computer, display results, wall screen two."

Acknowledged. Working . . .

As they began to scroll, her jaw simply dropped. "Well, Jesus. Jesus." There were hundreds of names. Maybe hundreds of hundreds.

She couldn't complain that Summerset wasn't efficient. The names were grouped according to where they worked, where they lived. Apparently, there were just one hell of a lot of women with brown hair between twenty-eight and thirty-three who worked in some capacity for Roarke Enterprises.

"Talk about a big, honking octopus."

She was going to need a whole bunch of coffee.

Roarke's private office was streamlined and spacious, with a dazzling view of the city through privacy screens. The wide U-shaped console commanded equipment as sophisticated and extensive as any the government could claim.

He should know, he held several government contracts.

And he knew, however artful the equipment, successful hacking depended on the operator's skill. And patience.

He ran his own employee files first. However numerous they were, it was still a simple matter. As was the search he implemented to locate any male employees who worked or had worked for him who had traveled to the other murder locations or taken personal leave during that time frame.

As it ran he generated a list of major competitors. He would, subsequently, search through those companies he didn't consider genuine competition. But he'd start at the top.

Any company, organization, or individual who was, in actuality, competitive would have—as he did—layers and layers of security on their internal files. And each would need to be peeled back with considerable care.

He sat at the console where the controls shimmered or flashed like jewels. His sleeves were pushed up, his hair tied back.

He started with companies with offices or interests in one or more of the locations.

And began to peel.

As he worked, he talked to himself, to the machines, to the layers that tried to foil him. As time passed, his curses became more Irish, his accent more pronounced, and layers melted away.

He took a break for coffee and to scan the results of his initial search.

He had no employee who fit all the requirements. But, he noted, there were some who'd been in at least two of the locations or on leave during the time of the murders.

They'd be worth a closer look.

He shifted back and forth between tasks, to keep himself sharp. He wormed his way through security blocks, picked his way through data. Ordered search, cross match, analysis so his equipment hummed in a dozen voices.

At some point he got up for yet another pot of coffee, and glanced at the time.

Four-sixteen a.m.

Cursing, he sat back, scrubbed his hands over his face. Hardly a wonder he was losing his edge. And Eve, he knew, would be asleep at her desk. If she'd decided to call it a night, she would have come by to check his progress first.

Instead, she'd work herself into the ground, and as he was doing exactly the same, he had no room to fight with her about it.

Nearly half-four, he thought. Gia Rossi might already be dead, or praying to all the gods death would come soon.

Roarke closed his eyes a moment, and though he knew the guilt was useless, let it run through him. He was too tired for the anger.

"Copy document C to disc, save all data. Ah, continue current run, copy and save when complete. Operator will be off-line."

Acknowledged.

Before he left, he put in a call to Dublin.

"Good morning to you, Brian."

His old mate's wide face creased with a surprised smile. "Well now, if it isn't the man himself. Which side of the pond would you be on?"

"The Yank side. It's a bit early on your side of it for me to be calling a publican. I hope I didn't wake you."

"You didn't, no. I'm just having my tea. How is our Lieutenant Darling?"

"She's well, thanks. Would you be alone there?"

"I would be, more's the pity. I've no enchanting woman to warm the sheets with me at the moment, as you do."

"I'm sorry for that. Brian, I'm looking for a torturer."

"Is that so?" Only the mildest surprise showed in Brian's eyes. "And are you too delicate these days to be after taking care of such matters yourself?"

"I was always too delicate for this, and so were you. He's done over twenty women in the last decade, late twenties, early thirties, all of them. And all of them with brown hair, light skin. The last was found only yesterday. She worked for me."

"Ah," Brian said. "Well."

"Another is missing—that's part of his method—and she was mine as well."

Brian sucked air through his nose. "Were you diddling with them, on the side, like?"

"No. He'd be older than we are, that's how they're profiling him. At least a decade older if not more. He's very skilled. He travels. He must have enough of the ready to afford a place, a private place, to do this work. If he's a professional, he takes this busman's holiday every year or two. There's no sex involved. No rape. He takes, binds, tortures, kills, cleanses. And he times how long each lasts under it."

"I haven't heard of anyone like this. Nasty business." Brian pulled on his ear. "I can make some inquiries, tap a few shoulders."

"I'd be grateful if you would."

"I'll be in touch if and when," Brian told him. "Meanwhile, give Lieutenant Darling a sweet kiss from me, and tell her I'm only waiting for her to throw your worthless ass aside and come into my waiting embrace."

"I'll be sure to do that."

After he'd ended the transmission, Roarke took the discs he'd generated and, with the machines still humming, left the office.

He found Eve where he'd expected to. Her head was on her desk, pillowed on her forearm. He noted the murder boards, the pair of them, the discs, the handwritten notes, the comp-generated ones.

The half cup of coffee, not quite cold—and the cat curled in her sleep chair.

He moved to Eve, lifted her out of the chair. She muttered some complaint, stirred, and shifted.

"What?"

"Bed," he said as he carried her toward the elevator.

"Time is it? Jeez." She rubbed at her eyes. "I must've conked."

"Not for long, your coffee was still warm. We need to shut down, both of us."

"Briefing at eight." Her voice slurred with fatigue. "Need to be up by six. Need to organize first. I didn't—"

"Fine, fine." He stepped out of the elevator into the bedroom. "Go back to sleep, six will come soon enough."

"You get anything?"

"Still running." He set her on the bed, seeing no reason she couldn't sleep in her sweats. Apparently neither did she as she crawled under the duvet as she was.

"Is there any data I can use? Anything I can work in?"

"We'll see in the morning." He stripped off his shirt, his pants, slid into bed with her.

"If there's any—"

"Quiet." He drew her against him, brushed her lips with his. "Sleep."

He heard her sigh once—it might've been annoyance. But by the time the sigh was done, she was under.

7 IT WAS SO UNUSUAL FOR HIM NOT TO BE UP before her that Eve just stared into the Celtic blue eyes when he woke her by stroking her hair.

"You think of something?"

"Apparently, I inevitably think of something when I'm in bed with my wife."

"Being a man—and you—you probably think of sex when you're crossing the street."

"And aren't you lucky that's true?" He kissed the tip of her nose. "But thinking's as far as we'll get this morning. You wanted to be up at six."

"Oh, yeah. Shit. Okay." She rolled onto her back and willed her body clock to accept morning. "Can't you invent something that pours coffee into the system just by the power of mind?"

"I'll get right on that."

She climbed out of bed, stumbled her way over to the AutoChef. "I'm going to go down, swim a few laps. I think that'll wake me up and work out the kinks."

"Good idea. I'll do the same. Give me some of that."

She thought, crankily, he could easily get his own damn coffee, but she passed the mug to him, along with a scowl. "No water polo."

"If that's a euphemism for pool sex, you're safe. All I want's a swim." He passed her back the coffee.

They rode down together, she bleary-eyed, him thoughtful.

The pool house was lush with plants, sparkling with blue water. Tropical blooms scented the warm, moist air. She would have liked to indulge herself with a strong twenty-minute swim, followed by more coffee and a soak in the bubbling curve of the hot tub.

And hell, since he was there, maybe just one quick match of water polo.

But it wasn't the time for indulgence. She dove in, surfaced, then pushed off in a full-out freestyle. The dullness in her brain and body began to fade with the effort, the cool water, the simple repetition.

After ten minutes, she felt loose again, reasonably alert. She might have thought wistfully about lounging for just a couple of minutes in the hot, jetting water of the hot tub, but acknowledged the comfort of it might put her back to sleep.

Instead, she pulled on a robe. "Do you want to go downtown with me, or work from here?"

He considered as he scooped back his dripping hair. "I think I'll stick with the unregistered, at least for the time being. If I manage to finish or find anything, I'll contact you or just come down on my own."

"Works." She crossed to the elevator with him. "Any progress?"

"Considerable, but as of four a.m., nothing really useful."

"Is that when we finished up?"

"A bit later, actually. And darling Eve, you haven't had enough rest." He touched her cheek. "You get so pale."

"I'm okay."

"And did you find anything useful?"

"I'm not sure yet."

She told him about Summerset's observation while they readied for the day.

"So you think it's possible he was in one of the medical centers, in some capacity, during the Urbans."

"It's a thought. I did some research," she added as she strapped on her weapon harness. "Not a whole lot of detail about it, that I've found so far anyway. But there were other facilities that used that same basic method. A handful here in New York."

"Where he started this."

"I'm thinking," she agreed with a nod. "Something here in particular that matters. He starts here, he comes back here. There's a wide, wide world out there and he's used some of it. But now he repeats location."

"Not just location. You and Feeney. Morris, Whitney, Mira. There are others as well."

"Yeah, and I'm mulling on that. More usually if a repeat killer has a thing about cops, he likes to thumb his nose at us. Send us messages, leave cryptic clues so he can feel superior. We're not getting that. But I'm mulling it."

She took one last, life-affirming glug of coffee. "I've got to get started, or I won't have myself lined up for the briefing."

"Oh, I'm to tell you Brian's waiting for you with open arms when you're done with me."

"Huh? Brian? Irish Brian?"

"That would be the one. I contacted him, asked him to look for torturers. He has connections," Roarke continued. "And knows how to ferret out information."

"Huh." It struck her she'd married a man with a lot of unusual associates. Came in handy now and then. "Okay. I'll see you later."

He moved to her, ran a hand over her hair again. "Take care of my cop."

"That's the plan." She met his lips with hers, stepped back. "I'll be in touch."

In briefing the team, Eve had everyone give their own orals on progress or lack of same. She listened to theories, arguments for or against, ideas for approaching different angles, or for pursuing old ones from a new perspective.

"If the Urbans are an angle," Baxter put in, "and we look at it like this fucker was a medical, or he got his torture training back then, we could be looking for a guy pushing eighty, or better. That gives him a half-century or more on his vics. How's a guy starting to creak pull this off?"

"Horny Dog's missing the fact that a lot of guys past middle age keep up." Jenkinson pointed a finger at Baxter. "Eighty's the new sixty."

"Sick Bastard has a point," Baxter acknowledged. "And as a border-line creaker himself, he's got some insight on it. But I'm saying it takes some muscle and agility to bag a thirty-year-old woman—especially since he goes for the physically tuned ones—off the street."

"He could've been a kid during the Urbans." As if in apology for speaking out, Trueheart cleared his throat. "Not that eighty's old, but—"

"You shave yet, Baby Face?" Jenkinson asked.

"While it's sad and true that Officer Baby Face doesn't have as much hair on his chin as Sick Bastard does in his ears, there were a lot of kids kicked around, orphaned, beat to shit during the Urbans. Or so I hear," Baxter added with a wide grin for Jenkinson. "Before my time."

She accepted the bullshit and insults cops tossed around with other cops. She let it go for another few minutes. And when she deemed all current data had been relayed, all ideas explored and the stress relieved, she handed out the day's assignments and dismissed.

"Peabody, locate York's ex. We need to have a word. I'm taking Mira into my office for a few minutes. Doctor?"

"So many avenues," Mira commented as they started out.

"One of them will lead us to him." Eventually, Eve thought.

"His consistency is both his advantage and disadvantage. It'll be a step on the avenue that leads you to him. His inflexibility is going to undermine him at some point."

"Inflexibility."

"His refusal to deviate," Mira confirmed. "Or his inability to deviate from a set pattern allows you to know a great deal about him. So you can anticipate."

"I anticipated he'd have taken number two. That isn't helping Gia Rossi."

Mira shook her head. "That's not relevant. You couldn't have helped Rossi as she was already taken before you knew, or could know, he was back in business."

"That's what it is?" Eve led the way to her office, gestured toward the visitor's chair while she sat on the corner of her desk. "Business."

"His pattern is businesslike, a kind of perfected routine. Or ritual, as I said before. He's very proud of his work, which is why he shares it. Displays it, but only when it's completed."

"When he's finished with them, he wants to show them off, wants to claim them. That's why he arranges them on a white sheet. That's the ring he puts on them. I get that. During the Urbans—if we head down that avenue—bodies were laid out, piled up, stacked up, depending on the facilities. And covered. Sheet, drop cloth, plastic, whatever was available. Usually, their clothes, shoes, personal effects were taken. Mostly these were recycled to other people. It's 'waste not and want not' in wartime. So he takes their clothes, their personal effects, but he reverses, leaving them uncovered."

"Pride. I believe, to him, they're beautiful. In death, they're beautiful to him." Mira shifted, crossed her legs. She'd pinned her hair up into a soft roll at the nape of her neck, and wore a pale, pale yellow suit that seemed to whisper a promise of spring. "His choice of victim type indicates, as I said in the briefing, some prior connection with a woman of this basic age and coloring. She symbolizes something to him. Mother, lover, sister, unattained love."

"Unattained."

"He couldn't control this person, couldn't make her see him as he wanted to be seen, not in her life or in her death. Now he does, again and again."

"He doesn't rape or molest them sexually. If it was a lover, wouldn't he see her as sexual?"

"Love, not lover. Women are Madonnas or whores to him, so he fears and respects them."

"Punishes and kills the whore," Eve considered, "and creates the Madonna, who he cleanses and displays."

"Yes. It's their womanhood, not their sexuality, he's obsessed with. He may be impotent. In fact, I believe we'll find this to be the case when you catch him. But sex isn't important to him. It doesn't drive him or, again if impotent, he would mutilate the genitals or sexually abuse them with objects. This hasn't been the case in any of the victims.

"It's possible he gains sexual release or satisfaction from their pain," Mira added. "But it's secondary, we could say a by-product. It's the pain that drives him, and the endurance of the subject, and the result. The death."

Eve pushed up, wandered to the AutoChef, absently programmed coffee for both of them. "You said 'businesslike,' and I don't disagree. But it seems like a kind of science to me. Regular and specific experiments. Artful science, I guess."

"We don't disagree." Mira accepted the coffee. "He's focused and he's dedicated. Control—his own, and his ability to control others—is vital to him. His ability to step away, to step outside of the active work for long periods, indicates great control and willpower. I don't believe, even with this, it's possible for him to maintain personal or intimate relationships for any length of time. Most certainly not with women. Business relationships? I believe he could maintain those to some extent. He must have income. He invests in his victims."

"The high-end products, the silver rings. The travel to select them from different locations. The cost of obtaining or maintaining the place where he works on them."

"Yes, and given the nature of the products, he's used to a certain level of lifestyle. Cleansing them is part of the ritual, yes, but he could do so with more ordinary means. More mainstream products."

"Nothing but the best," Eve agreed. "But it also leads me down the avenue that he may be a competitor of Roarke's, or an employee in a top-level position."

"Both would be logical." Mira drank her coffee, quietly pleased Eve remembered how she preferred it. "He's chosen to make this connection. Just as he chose to come back to New York to work at this time. But there was a connection for him to make, Eve."

She set her cup aside now, and her gaze was sober when she looked at Eve. "There was you. These women are, in a sense, Roarke's. You are his in every sense."

Testing the idea, Eve frowned. "So he opts for this specific pattern because of me? I wasn't primary on the initial investigation."

"You were a female on the initial investigation, a brunette. Too young at that time to meet his requirements. You aren't now."

"You're looking at me as a target?"

"I am. Yes, I am."

"Huh." Drinking coffee, Eve considered it more carefully. Mira's theories weren't to be casually dismissed. "Usually goes for long hair."

"There have been exceptions."

"Yeah, yeah, a couple of them. He's been smart. This wouldn't be smart." Eve tipped the angle of it in her mind, shifted the pattern. "It's a lot tougher to take down a cop than it is a civilian."

"You would be a great prize, from his viewpoint. It would be a challenge, and a coup. And if he knows anything about you, which I promise you he does, he would be assured you would endure a long time."

"Tough to stalk me. First, I'd click to it. Second, I don't have regular routines, not like the others. They clocked in and out at fairly uniform times, had regular haunts. I don't."

"Which, again, would add to the challenge," Mira argued, "and his ultimate satisfaction. You're considering that he may have added Roarke as an element because he's in competition with him. That may very well be true. But what he does isn't payback, not on a conscious level. Everything he does is for a specific purpose. I believe, in this, you're a specific purpose."

"It'd be helpful."

"Yes." Mira sighed. "I imagined you'd see it that way."

Eyes narrowed, Eve tipped the angle again, explored the fresh pattern. "If we go with this, and I could find a way to bait him in—to nudge him into making a move on me before he grabs another one—we could shut him down. Shut him down, take him out."

"You won't bait him." Watching Eve, Mira picked up her coffee. "I can promise you he has his timetable already set. The only variable in it is the length of time his victims last. He has the third selected. Unless he planned only three—which would be less than he's ever taken before—the next won't be you."

"Then we have to find her first. Let's keep your theory between us, just for now. I want to think about it."

"I want you to think about it," Mira said as she got to her feet. "As a member of this team, as a profiler, and as someone who cares a great deal about you, I want you to think about it very carefully."

"I will."

"This is a hard one for you, for Feeney. For me, the commander. We've been here before, and in a very real sense, we failed. Failing again—"

"Isn't an option," Eve finished. "Do me a favor. I know it's a tough process, but take a look at the list Summerset generated. The female employees. Just see if any of them strike you as more his type. We can't put eyes on all those women, but if there's a way to whittle it down . . ."

"I'll start on that right away."

"I've got to get going."

"Yes." Mira passed her empty cup to Eve, brushed her fingers lightly over the back of Eve's hand. "Don't just think carefully. Be careful."

Even as Mira left, Eve's desk 'link beeped. Scanning the readout, she picked up. "Nadine."

"Dallas. Any word on Rossi?"

"We're looking. If you're interrupting my day looking for an update—"

"Actually, I'm interrupting mine to give you one. One of my eager little researchers plucked out an interesting nugget. From Romania."

Automatically Eve pulled up on her computer screen what she had on the Romanian investigation. "I should have the full case files from that investigation later today. What have you got?"

"Tessa Bolvak, a Romany—gypsy? Had her own show on screen. Psychic hour—or twenty minutes, to be accurate."

"You're interrupting both of our days with a psychic?"

"A renowned one in Romanian circles during the time in question. She was a regularly consulted sensitive, often consulting for the police."

"Those wacky Romanians."

"Other police authorities make use of sensitives," Nadine reminded her. "You did, not that long ago."

"Yeah, and look how well that worked out for everybody."

"However," Nadine continued, "we're not here to debate that issue. The amazing Tessa—as both she and her producers recognized the value of a big, juicy case—ran a special on the murders there, and her part in the investigation. She claimed your guy was a master of death, and its servant."

"Oh, jeez."

"*And*. That death sought him, provided for him. A pale man," Nadine said, shifting to read off her own comp screen. "A black soul. Death is housed in him as he is housed in it. Music soars as the blood runs. It plays for her—diva and divine—who sang for him. He seeks them out, flowers for his bouquet, his bouquet for her altar."

"Nadine, give me a—"

"Wait, wait. A pale man," she continued, "who bears the tree of life and lives by death. Tessa got a lot of play out of the program."

"Did I mention wacky Romanians?"

"And here's more wacky for you. Two days after the program aired, her body was found—throat slit—floating in the Danube."

"Too bad she didn't see that one coming."

"Ha. The authorities deemed it a robbery-homicide. Her jewelry and purse were never found. But I wonder if those in charge of such things over there lack my sense of irony or your innate cynicism."

"How come you get the irony?" Eve complained. "I've got plenty of irony. Maybe, maybe she's so busy looking through the crystal ball she doesn't notice some guy who wants her baubles."

Just a little too much coincidence, Eve mused, to pass the bullshit barrier. "And maybe our guy took her out because something in the overdone woo-woo speak hit a little too close."

"It occurred to me," Nadine agreed. "Doesn't fit his pattern, but—"

"He doesn't give her the . . . status, we'll say, he affords his chosen victims. She just annoyed him, so he took her out. You got a copy of the program she did?"

"I do."

"Send me a copy. I'll reach out to Romania again, see if they'll get me the juice on her case. You got anything else?"

"A lot of screaming tabloid headlines, screen and print. My busy bees will pick through them, see if there's anything worth looking at twice."

"Let me know."

When she clicked off, Eve noted down: Pale man. Music. Tree of life. Death house.

Then she went to snag Peabody.

I think it's getting warmer." Peabody hunched her shoulders and tried to lever her body so the wild March wind didn't blow straight into her marrow.

"Are you standing on the same side of the equator as I am?"

"No, really. I think it's a couple of degrees up from yesterday. And seeing as it's March, it's practically April. So it's almost summer if you think about it."

"The frigid wind has obviously damaged your brain." Eve pulled out her badge for the security scanner on Cal Marshall's building. "That being the case, I need to rethink the fact that I was about to tell you to take the lead on this guy."

"No! I can do it. It's freezing, okay. The wind's so freaking cold it's drilling right through my corneas into my retinas. But it hasn't yet entered the brain."

When they were cleared, Peabody stepped in, yanked off her earflap cap. "Do I have hat hair? You can't effectively interview with hat hair."

"You have hair. Be satisfied with that."

"Hat hair," Peabody muttered, raking her hands through it, shaking her head, fluffing and pushing as they got in the elevator.

"Stop! Stop being a girl. Jesus, that's annoying. If I had a partner without tits, there would be no hair obsessing."

"Baxter would combat hat hair before an interview."

Because it was inarguably true, Eve only scowled. "He doesn't count."

"And there's Miniki. He—"

"Keep it up, and I'll tie you down and shave you bald. You won't ever suffer the pain and embarrassment of hat hair again."

Eve strode out of the elevator, followed the numbers to Cal Marshall's apartment.

"Do I still take the lead?" Peabody asked, meekly.

Eve sent her a withering look, then knocked. When the door opened, she shifted slightly to the side so that Peabody had the front ground.

"Mr. Marshall? I'm Detective Peabody. We spoke earlier. This is my partner, Lieutenant Dallas. May we come in?"

"Yeah. Sure. Yeah."

He was blond, tanned, fit, with eyes the blue of an arctic lake. They looked a little hollow now, a little dull, and his voice held the same tone. "About Sari. It's about Sari."

"Why don't we sit down?"

"What? Yeah, we should sit."

Through an open door, Eve spotted the bed—made—with a large duffle tossed on it. There was a snowboard tipped against the wall. In the living area, a heavy ski coat was draped over a chair, the lift pass still clipped on it.

On the molded black table in front of the dark blue gel sofa were several empty bottles of beer.

Came in, Eve mused, tossed down his gear, checked his 'link messages. Got the word. Sat here and drank most of the night.

"I heard. I got home and heard—" He rubbed at his eyes. "Um, Bale—he heard from Zela. She works with Sari at the club. She told him . . . he told me."

"It must've been a shock," Peabody said. "That was the first you heard of her death? You didn't have your pocket 'link, or see any reports while you were gone?"

"I shut down my 'link. Just wanted to board. It was all about boarding. Me and Bale went out to Colorado. Incommunicado Colorado. Big joke," he said. "Shuttled back last night. Bale, he's closer to the station, got home first. Zela left him a message. Zela talked to him. He called. I got home, and he . . ."

"You and Sarifina were involved."

"We were . . . we were together until a couple of weeks ago." He scrubbed both hands over his face. "A couple of weeks . . . We broke up."

"Why did you break up?"

"She was always too busy. She was always . . ." He trailed off, lifted his gaze to Peabody's. "I wanted more, okay? I wanted her more available, more interested in what I wanted to do when I wanted to do it. It wasn't working out, not the way I wanted it. So I said I was done with it. With her."

"You argued."

"Yeah. We both got pretty harsh. She said I was selfish, immature, self-involved. I said something like, 'Right back at you.' Shit, shit, shit. She's dead. Bale said . . . I was snowboarding and trashing her to Bale. And she was dead. You think I hurt her? I wanted to hurt her. Here," he said, thumping a fist to his heart. "I wanted her to feel crappy that I flipped her, you know? I wanted her to be lonely and miserable while I found somebody—lots of somebodies—who knew how to have a good time. Christ."

He dropped his head in his hands. "Oh, my Christ."

"We don't think you hurt her, Mr. Marshall. Before you broke up, did she stay here with you?"

"Less and less. Things were disintegrating. We barely saw each other. Once or twice a week maybe."

"Did she ever mention anyone bothering her? Anyone that made her uncomfortable?"

"We weren't doing a lot of talking lately." He said it quietly while he looked down at his hands. "I don't remember her saying anything like that. She liked the old guys who came into the club. Especially the old guys. Smooth, she said. They got smooth with age, like whiskey or something. Some hit on her now and then, and she got a kick out of it. At least I didn't get twisted about that. I thought it was funny."

"Anyone specifically?"

"I don't know. I didn't pay much attention. I'm not into that retro crap. Bored me senseless, you know? She looked good though, when she dressed up for work? Man, she looked good."

Not much of a well to pump there," Peabody commented as they rode down.

"I don't know. She liked older men, older men liked her. It's high probability the killer is an older man."

"And?"

"I bet he chatted her up somewhere along the line. A week or two before he grabbed her, he makes contact in the club. That'd be a big thrill for him, having a conversation, maybe a dance with his intended victim. A good way to get another sense of her, a gauge, a rhythm."

"Yeah." Peabody hissed in her breath as they started outside. "And . . . If he did, and she saw him later—on the street, wherever he made the grab, she'd be friendly, at ease. It's Mr. Smooth from Starlight."

"So, if he made contact with her . . . maybe he made contact with Gia Rossi."

"The fitness center."

"Place to start."

He knew how to blend. He knew how to make himself inconspicuous, so that eyes passed over him without notice. It was a skill he put to good use during the research phase of any project.

He used it now as he watched her—Eve Dallas—stride out of the apartment building, down the street. Ground-eating strides. Loose and busy. Strong.

He very much approved of strong women—physically and mentally.

She'd been strong. The Eve of all the others. The mother. She'd been very strong, he remembered, but he believed this Eve—this last Eve—would be stronger than any who had come before.

Not time for you yet, he thought as he watched her, watched the way she moved. Not quite time for this Eve. But when it was, oh . . .

He believed she would be his finest work to date. A new level of excellence. And the pinnacle of all he'd accomplished.

But for now, there was another who required his attention.

He really should get home to her.

The manager of BodyWorks was a six-foot Asian with a body like molded steel. He went by the name of Pi. He wore a black skin-suit and a small, trim goatee.

"Like I told the other cops, it was just another day. Gia had her classes, her clients. I gave them the client list. Do you need—"

"No, they have it. Thanks for cooperating."

He dropped down into a chair in his office, a glass box that allowed him to view all the areas on that level of the center. Outside it, people pumped, sweated, trotted, flexed, and twisted.

"We're pals, you know? I can't get through the idea something may have happened to her. But I'm telling you, she can take care of herself. That's what I think. She's tough."

"Anybody ask for her specifically in the last few weeks?" Eve asked him.

"Yeah, like I told the other guys. She'd get referrals from clients. Word of mouth. She's good at what she does, gets results, but doesn't drill sergeant the client into it."

"How about older guys, say over sixty?"

"Sure. Sure. Fitness isn't just for kids, you know. She has some clients like that, and we get them in for classes. She runs a tai chi class twice a week, a yoga class every other morning geared for the over-sixty group. Twice a week she has classes geared for the centennials."

"She pick up anybody new in any of those in the last few weeks?"

"Like I told the others, if you're a member you don't have to sign up for any of the classes. You just come in, take whichever you want."

"How about anybody who joined in, say, the last thirty days. Male, over fifty, let's say."

"I can get you that. But you don't have to have joined at this location. If you hold a membership from any of our clubs—that's global—you just key in."

"You have a record of who's keyed in? You keep track of how your members use the facilities, how often they use them, who pays the fee for a trainer?"

"Sure. Sure. That kind of data goes straight to the main offices. But I can—"

"I can get that," Eve told him. "No problem. Did she take outside clients?"

"That's against policy," he began.

"We're not worried about policy, Pi. She's not going to get jammed up if she pulled in some extra on the side. We want to find her."

"Yeah, well, maybe she did." He puffed out his cheeks, blew out the air. "Somebody's willing to pay you stiff for going to their house for an hour a couple times a week, it's hard to flip it. We're pals, but I'm management. She knows I know, and like that, but we don't talk about it. Not really."

"How about a sense, since you were pals, if she took on a private client recently?"

He puffed out his cheeks again. "She sprang for Knicks tickets—courtside. We're going to the game next week. My birthday. Son of a bitch." He smoothed his hands over his shaved head. "Pretty much out of her range. She joked, said she'd hit a little jackpot. I figured she'd gotten a side fee, a couple of them maybe."

"When did she get the tickets?"

"A few weeks ago. Look, you need to find her, okay? You just need to find her."

8

OUTSIDE, EVE WALKED THE ROUTE GIA HABIT-
ually took to the subway. The woman was a New
Yorker, Eve mused. Which meant she'd move along
at a brisk pace, and though her radar would be on, she'd be inside
her own thoughts.

Might be a window-shopper, Eve thought. Might stop and study a
display, even go inside a shop. But . . .

"Baxter and Trueheart checked out the stores and markets along the
route," she said to Peabody. "Nobody remembers seeing her that day.
Some clerks recognized her picture. Previous visits. But not on the day
she poofed."

"She didn't make it to the station."

"No. Maybe she wasn't going to the station." Eve turned, sidestepping toward the buildings as New York bustled by. "Had extra dough,
enough for a pair of courtsides. She takes an outside client. Maybe the
client's address is within walking distance. Or he provided cab fare or
transportation."

And considering this, she factored in Baxter's point about the potential age difference, and the fact that Gia Rossi had been a trainer, in peak physical condition.

"Maybe she walked right into it. Maybe she walked right into his nest."

"He doesn't grab her. He just opens the door."

"Slick," Eve said softly. "Yeah, that would be slick. Contact Newkirk. I want him and the other uniforms canvassing this area. All directions, five blocks." Eve headed toward the car. "I want her picture shown to every clerk, waitperson, sidewalk sleeper, doorman, and droid. Get McNab," she added as she climbed behind the wheel. "I want him to send her picture to every cab company and private transpo service. Bus companies, air trams. Hit them all. Then the Transit Authority. Check the run for that night on other stations. She didn't use her pass, but maybe she took a ride anyway."

Peabody was already relaying to Newkirk.

"She went to him," Eve said before she swung out into traffic. "That's what I think. She went right to him."

Following the hunch, she contacted Zela at home.

"Yes?" Obviously half asleep, Zela stifled a yawn. "Lieutenant? What—"

"Did Sarifina ever give private lessons?"

"Private lessons? I'm sorry, I'm a little foggy."

"Dance lessons. Did she ever give private dance lessons?"

"Now and again, sure. People want to be able to do the moves for special occasions. Weddings, bar or bat mitzvahs, reunions. That sort of thing."

"At the club, or at the client's home?"

"Generally at the club. Mornings when we're closed."

"Generally," Eve pressed, "but there were exceptions."

"Give me a second." Zela moved as she spoke, and Eve heard the beep of an AutoChef. "I worked until nearly three last night, then took a pill. I haven't been sleeping well since . . . I need to clear my head."

"Zela." Impatience ground through Eve's voice. "I need to know if Sarifina went to clients' homes."

"Every once in a while, particularly for the older clients. Or the kids. Sometimes parents want their kids to learn. Or an older couple wants to swing it a little—for an occasion, or a cruise. But usually, we do that sort of thing here, through the club."

"Had she taken on any personal clients in the last few weeks?"

"Just let me think, okay? Let me think." Zela gulped down what Eve assumed was coffee. "She may have. She was an easy touch, you know? Liked to do favors for people. We didn't check that kind of thing off with each other all the time. But if it was through the club, I mean if she was going to instruct someone here, she'd have noted in down. The club gets a cut of the fee, and Sari was religious about keeping good records on that."

"No cut if she went to them?"

"Well, that's a gray area. Like I said, she liked to do favors. She might go give someone an hour or two, cutting her rate, doing it off the books. On her own time, before or after work, on her day off. What's the harm?"

What's the harm? Eve thought as she clicked off.

"We figured he grabbed them off the street. But they went to him. These two, at least, my money says they went right to him. How'd they get there?"

"York's image has been out since yesterday. Weekend, though," Peabody added. "If she took a cab, the driver might not have paid any attention, or might not have seen the reports on her yet."

"No. No. We have to run it down, but that would be sloppy, and he isn't sloppy. Why take a chance like that? Leave a record, a possible wit? Cab driver dumps the vic right at his door? Doesn't play."

"Well, the same thing applies to private transpo."

"Not if he's providing it. Personally. We check anyway, we check all the transits. All the pickups in the area the vics were last seen."

Man hours, wasted hours, Eve thought. And still it had to be done. "He's not going to chance something like that. Lures them in, that's what he does. Nice, harmless guy, nice older gentleman who wants to learn to tango, wants to get fit. There's a nice, sweet fee for the personal service. Provides transportation for them."

"Nobody sees them on the street because they're not on the street that long." Peabody nodded as the theory solidified for her. "They come out of work, get into a waiting vehicle. Nobody's going to notice. But . . ."

"But?"

"How can he be sure they're not going to tell somebody? What I mean is, neither of these women seems stupid. How could he be sure they're not going to tell a friend, a coworker, they've got this private gig. Here's where I'm going to be, and with whom."

Eve pulled over in front of Gia Rossi's apartment building, then just sat, tapping her fingers on the wheel. "Good point. We know they didn't tell anyone, or anyone who's passed on that information. So the why, the how can he be sure. Gotta play the percentages." She got out, drawing her master to deal with the door. "First he's going to give them a bogus name and address. Now, if they're smart, or concerned in any way, they're going to check that out, make sure it's legit. Not hard to pull that off if you've got enough money and know-how. But that's another area for EDD to look into."

They stepped inside the three-story walk-up, where Rossi's apartment was on ground level. "Next, think of his profile. Intelligent, mature, controlled."

She used the master again to break the seal Baxter had activated, and uncode the locks. "We know he travels, so we're looking at someone who's likely sophisticated, and I'm just going to bet charming. He *knows* his victims."

When they stepped in, Eve paused to look around the cramped living area. Big wall screen, she noted, small couch, a couple of chairs, tables holding decorative bits and pieces. Tossed socks, shoes—mostly of the athletic variety. The electronics had already been taken in.

"Knows what they like," she continued, "what appeals to them. Plays that. Gets familiar with them face-to-face, dropping into their respective clubs, chatting them up. But not too much, not so anyone pays particular attention. He blends, and he blends. Mr. Smooth, Mr. Nice Guy, Mr. Harmless."

She walked over to the window, studied the street, the sidewalk, the neighboring buildings. "He gains their trust. Maybe he talks about his wife or his daughter, something that paints a picture in their heads. Normality. Takes time, sure, but he likes to take time. Then he brings up the private work—or smarter, he maneuvers them into mentioning it or suggesting it."

She turned, walked into the tiny, equally cramped bedroom. "Then he's got them. She's got privacy screens, but they're old and cheap. Right equipment, you could watch her in here. You know when she gets up, how long it takes her to get ready for work, what time she leaves, her route. Bet you keep it all documented. Scientific, that's what it is. I wonder how many he's picked, watched, documented, and rejected. How many women are alive because they didn't quite fit his precise requirements."

"Creepy."

"Yeah." Dipping her hands into her pockets, Eve rocked back on her heels. "Maybe he's always worked this way, or worked this way before. The prior personal contact, the maneuvering the target to go to him. We'll go back over the old cases with that angle. And we'll look at the projected targets in this one with that in mind."

"Dallas? What are we looking for here? I mean, here in her place."

"Her. Gia Rossi. He knows the pieces of her, or thinks he does. Let's see what we find."

It was what they didn't find that added weight to Eve's theory. However cramped and messy the living space, Gia Rossi kept her exercise and music discs meticulously organized.

"Two slots empty in her workout disc tree, three empty in her music disc tree. The way she's got them alphabetized, I'm guessing cardio and yoga on the fitness end. We'll check the personal effects Baxter took from her gym locker."

"She's got a lot of personal equipment. Hand weights, ankle and wrist weights, mats, medicine balls, running track." Peabody gestured inside the closet that Rossi had outfitted for equipment storage. "I'm guessing some's missing. Lightest and heaviest ankle weights, light and heavy resistance ropes."

"Light for him, heavy for her. Takes some basic equipment, some music, the demo vids. You ever work with a PT?"

"No." Peabody flexed her butt muscles, wondering if that was the way to reduce the square footage of her ass. "You?"

"No, but I'm betting a good one would outline a program for a client—something specifically created for his body type, age, weight, goals, and so on. If she did it here, EDD can find it. Let's go."

Roarke walked into a war room full of chatter of both the human and electronic varieties. Cops on 'links, on headsets, on comps. Cops sitting, pacing, dancing.

But his cop was nowhere to be seen.

He crossed paths with McNab, who was outfitted in silver jeans and a casual Sunday sweatshirt of searing orange. "Is the lieutenant in the house?"

"In the field. Heading in, though. Working some fresh angles. You want?"

"I want."

Tapping the toes of his silver airboots, McNab swiveled in his chair. "Just covered all public and private transpo with pictures of York and Rossi. Dallas is working the idea that our guy provided transpo."

"And they just hopped in?"

"Yeah. Need liquid. Walk and talk."

McNab filled Roarke in as he headed out to Vending, debated his choices, and opted for an orange fizzy—perhaps to match his shirt.

"A home lesson or consultation," Roarke mused. "Interesting, and it would eliminate the risk of any sort of public abduction. Still, the method has its own risks and problems."

"Yeah, what if they change their minds, don't show, decide to bring a pal along. Lots of possibles." He sucked in fizzy. "But she wants it worked, so we work it. She said if you popped in, you should take a look at your employee list with this angle in mind. Women who fit the parameters who might do a house call on the side."

"Yes, I can do that."

"Lots of possibles," McNab repeated, "considering all the pies you've got fingers in. Anything moving on the real estate angle?"

"Nothing that stands out from the crowd, no."

"Sometimes you've got to toss it up, you know. Let it fall in a different pattern. You keep working it, it gets so it's just data. Maybe I could take that for a while when you work the new business."

"Fresh eyes. Yes, that's a good idea."

"Icy, then . . . Hey, here come our ladies. Just looking at them gives you the *uh*, doesn't it?" McNab gave the sound a push that was unmistakably sexual as he grinned down the long corridor where Peabody got off the glide with Eve.

Then he shot Roarke a quick look. "I mean the *uh* me for mine, you for yours. It's not like I get the *uh* for the lieutenant, for which she would kick my ass, then leave you to turn what was left of it into bloody dust. Which She-Body would then grind into the earth before she set it on fire. I was just saying."

"I know what you were saying." McNab could, invariably, entertain him. "And I couldn't agree more, with everything including the bloody dust. They are compelling women. Lieutenant," Roarke said as her long stride brought her to him.

"So glad you two have time for fizzy breaks."

"Sir. I've been bringing Roarke up to date, and relaying your orders."

"Looked like slurping and ogling to me."

"Ah . . . those may have been minor factors, but neither overshadowed the update or relay. Vic's images are broadcasted, Lieutenant. I set up another line for responses from those sources. We've been fielding tips and inquiries on the investigations, and I figured if we got something out of this, we didn't want it to get bogged down in the general dump."

"Good. That's good thinking. I want you to pass off whatever you're doing and take Rossi's equipment. Her comp. I'm looking for personalized fitness programs. Find me one that matches our unsub."

"On that."

"Feeney?"

"Roving mode," McNab told her. "Gives a look and a buzz to whatever everyone's working. Tightens it up or opens it out. He was playing the medical equipment angle when I came out to get—when I stepped out to update Roarke."

"Tell him I need somebody to go down to BodyWorks. Rossi used a couple of comps there routinely. The manager's been contacted and is cooperating. Get them brought in and gone through. Same search."

"Yes, sir."

"Roarke, with me."

Roarke fell into step beside her. "Formidable."

"What?"

"You. I'd used compelling, but formidable suits as well. Very sexy."

"Don't say 'sexy' on the job."

"You just did."

Okay, she admitted, he made her laugh. Which was obviously the point and intent. And it did relieve some of the tension at the base of her skull. "Got your smarty pants on, I see."

She moved into the bullpen, stopped her forward motion when one of the men called her name. "Got a DB in a flop off Avenue D," he began. "Licensed companion over there . . ."

He jerked his head toward the skinny woman in a bloody shirt seated at his desk. "She says the guy wanted to party, the party was had. He refused to pay the bill and popped her two good ones when she objected to getting stiffed. Pulled out her sticker, which she claims he ran into. Six times."

"Clumsy of him."

"Yeah. Thing is, Lieutenant, she called it in. Didn't try to rabbit, and she's sticking to the story. Claims he laughed like a looney bird every time the knife went in. Got a couple of wits saw them make the deal, another who heard them yelling in the flop. You can see she's got herself a pretty good shiner working there."

"Yeah. Got priors?"

"Couple little bumps, nothing violent. Had her LC ticket for three years."

"And the DB?"

"Oh, he had a nice long sheet. Assaults, assaults with deadlies, illegals—possession and intent. Just got out of the cage for an attempted robbery—beat hell out of a clerk at a twenty-four/seven. On the Zeus."

Eve studied the LC. The woman looked more annoyed than worried. And her face was sporting a sick rainbow of bruises. "Guy on Zeus could run into a knife multiple times. Wait for the tox screen on the DB, run her through again, see if she stands on the story, then put her in holding."

"Guy was juiced up, a lime green PD's going to get a self-defense. Could slap her for the sticker, as it was over legal limit."

"What's the point?"

"Yeah, that's what I was thinking. Wanted to run it by you first."

"She ask for a PD or a rep?"

"Not yet. Pissed is what she is." He nodded over to her desk. "Knows the incident means an automatic thirty-day suspension of her license. So she's out the fee and a month's work, got a fist in the face, and ruined what she says is a new shirt."

"That's the life. Get the tox, wrap it up. Reach out to Illegals on the DB if anything looks shaky," Eve added. "Somebody over there probably has a take on him."

She walked into her office, shut the door.

"She'll walk," Roarke commented.

"Likely. Smart not to run, to come in voluntarily. Less smart to party with a guy on Zeus, if that was the case. And if she's worked that sector for a couple, three years, she'd know if he was pumped."

"A girl's got to make a living."

"That's what they tell me. So, anything from the unregistered?"

"Nothing that gels, not at this point. I have Summerset running more searches and crosses. He knows what to look for, and how to find it."

Her brows drew together. "Am I going to have to be grateful to him?"

"I'll take care of that."

"Good." She pulled off her coat, went for coffee. "Did McNab actually give you an update?"

"He did, yes. I'll go through the employee list, cull out any who might take a home appointment or consultation. Do you think now this has been his pattern all along?"

"I don't know, can't say." Eve rubbed at her eyes, then scratched her head furiously as if to wake up the brain under her scalp. "But we're talking more than twenty women. How likely is it that not one of them ever told anyone where they were going? Bogus name, sure, but if they had the location in advance, made this appointment, how likely is it none of them told anyone, or left any sort of record of the appointment?"

"Low. Yes, I see. But . . . There may have been more than the twenty. And I see you've considered that as well," he added when he studied her face. "He picked them, made the arrangements, and if he sensed or learned they'd mentioned it, he'd simply follow through with the cover. Take his fucking dance lesson."

"Yeah, I think he could pull that off. And I think he could grab or lure them later in his schedule. So we go back over the prior cases, find out if any of the vics took a house call in the week or two before they were killed. He's focused," Eve continued, "careful enough to make sure he's clear, but focused. I can see him postponing the grab, or switching vics. If so, it's something we didn't have before. A mistake we missed."

Roarke drank his coffee. The office seemed ridiculously confining to him all at once. The piss-poor light barely seeping through her excuse for a window, the tight box formed by the walls.

"Haven't you ever considered asking for a bigger office?"

"What for?"

"A little breathing room might be a plus."

"I can breathe fine. You can't take this in, Roarke."

"And how would you suggest I avoid that?" he demanded. "I'm his springboard, aren't I? There's a woman dead because she worked for me. Another who, even now, is being tortured. It's too late for Gia Rossi."

"It's not too late until it's too late." Still, she knew she owed him the straight line, and that he had to be able to deal with it. "The probability is low that we'll find her in time. It's not impossible, but at this point, it's not likely."

"And the next, she'd already be in his sights."

"He'd have stalked her, selected her, worked her by now. But we've got more time there. He's not infallible, and there's only one of him. I've put the best I've got on this. It ends here."

Her eyes went flat, cop flat. "It's going to end here. But you're no good to me if you can't set the emotional connection aside."

"Well, I can't. But I can use it. I can do what I need to do."

"Okay."

"Which includes getting right pissed from time to time."

"Fine. But get this in your head. The responsibility for this is his. Totally, completely, absolutely. No portion of it's yours. He owns it. If his mother used him as her butt monkey when he was a kid, he still owns it. He made the choice. If his father, uncle, aunt, cousin from Toledo kicked his ass every Tuesday, it's still his. You and I know that. We know about the choice. We know, whenever we take a life, whatever the circumstances, whatever the reasons, it's still our choice. Right or wrong, we own it."

Roarke considered his coffee, set it aside. And his eyes met hers. "I love you, for so many reasons."

"Maybe you can give me a few of them later."

"I'll give you one now. That unfailing moral center of yours. So very solid and true." He laid his hands on her shoulders, drew her in. Kissed her softly. "And then there's the sex."

"Figured you'd work that in."

"As often as humanly possible. Well then." He gave her shoulders a rub, stepped back. "There's one thing I can do now, and that's order in lunch for the team. Don't," he continued, lifting a warning finger, "give me any lip."

"I thought you like my lip—the set of them. Look, I don't want you to—"

"I was thinking pizza."

Her eyes slitted; she huffed out a breath. "That's hitting below the belt, pal."

"I know your every weakness, Lieutenant. And this one's topped with pepperoni."

"Just don't make a habit of it. The food. They'll get greedy."

"I think your team's steady enough to handle a few slices. I'll take care of it, and start on the employee list."

When he left, she closed the door behind him. She wanted to work in the quiet for a while, with minimal interruption. To think and theorize before she went back to the noise and pressures of the war room.

She brought up the files on the first investigation.

She knew these women. Their names, their faces, where they'd come from, where they'd lived, where they'd worked or studied.

A diverse group, in all but general appearance. And now she would look for one more point of origin.

Corrine, would-be actress working as a waitress, who'd squeezed in acting, dance, and vocal lessons when she could afford them. He could have played her, yes, he could have in several ways. Come to this location to audition for a part—what hungry young actress wouldn't bite? Or come to this address on this date and time to help serve at a party. Pick up some extra cash. Possibilities.

She went down the list of names. A secretary, a grad student working on her master's in foreign studies, a clerk in a gift shop who dabbled in pottery.

Following the string, she began to make calls, questioning people she'd interviewed nine years before.

There was a quick knock, then Peabody stuck her head in. She had a slice of pizza, half eaten, in her hand. "Pizza's here. They're pouncing on it like wolves. You'd better get out there if you want any."

"Minute."

Peabody took another bite. "You got something?"

"Maybe. Maybe." Eve wished the scent of pizza wasn't so damn distracting. "I'll bring it in. Get whoever's in the field on a headset. I want to brief everyone at once."

"You got it."

"Get the vics from the first investigation up on screen, with data."

Eve gathered her notes, her discs, then tagged Mira. "I need you in the war room."

"Ten minutes."

"Sooner," Eve said and clicked off.

When Eve strode into the war room, she noted that two pizzas had been demolished along with most of a third. After setting down her notes, she marched over, grabbed a slice.

"Got Jenkinson, Powell, Newkirk, and Harris on the line," Peabody told her. "Everyone else is here."

"Mira's on her way. I want her take on this." Even as Eve bit in, Feeney was coming toward her.

"You've got something. I can see it."

"Might. A possible link, possible method. I'm going to lay it out as soon as Mira's in the room." She glanced over, then handily caught the tube of Pepsi that Roarke tossed her. "Progress?" she asked him.

"I have fifty-six most possible, given their vocations or avocations. Still coming."

"Okay. Peabody, get the screen up, backed with the disc I brought in." She nodded when Mira came in. After taking a long sip, Eve put on the headset.

"Listen up, people. I need your full attention. If you can't eat pizza and think—"

"You got pizza?" was Jenkinson's complaint in her ear.

"We're working on a new theory," Eve said, and began to lay it out.

9 "ONE OF CORRINE DAGBY'S COWORKERS AT THE time of her death remembers—or more accurately thinks she remembers—the vic mentioning she was up for a part in a play. Off-off Broadway. If she spoke of this to anyone else, family, friends, other students in her classes, they don't recall.

"Melissa Congress, second vic, secretarial position. Last seen leaving a club Lower West, well lubricated. This remains, most probably, a grab. A moment of opportunity. She was, however, known to complain with some consistency about her level of employment, her pay, her hours. There remains a possibility that she was approached about interviewing for another position and therefore knew or recognized her abductor.

"Anise Waters," Eve continued. "Grad student at Columbia. Fluent in Mandarin Chinese and Russian, and working on a master's in political science. She sometimes supplemented her income by tutoring, most usually on campus. Last seen leaving the university's main library. Wits stated that she took a pass on joining a group for drinks, claiming she had work. As she was a serious and dedicated student, it was assumed she was heading home to study. She didn't mention, to anyone's recollection, an outside tutoring job. The language discs she checked out from the library were never recovered. The vic did have a scheduled tutoring job, on campus, the next day. It was assumed she'd checked out the discs for that purpose.

"Last, Joley Weitz. Last seen leaving Arts A Fact, a shop where she was employed, at approximately seventeen hundred. The vic did pottery, and had sold a few pieces she had on consignment at her place of employment. Her employer stated that the vic mentioned she had an important stop to make before she got ready for a date with a new boyfriend. The boyfriend was identified and cleared. As the vic had a dress on hold at a boutique she frequented, it was thought picking that item up for her date was her stop. She never reached the boutique, if indeed that was her intended destination."

She waited a moment, let it soak. "New theory. The vics were approached by the unsub at some time. York gave dance instruction, Rossi moonlights as a personal trainer off-site. It's a reasonable assumption all or most of these women were offered a private job, and went to their killer. I've begun examining the other cases, outside of New York, and believe this possibility extends. We have an assistant chef, a photographer, a nurse, a decorator, a data cruncher, a freelance writer, two health care aides, two artists, a clerk in a nursery—plants, the owner of a small flower shop, a librarian, a hair and skin consultant, a hotel maid. A music instructor, an herbalist, a caterer's assistant.

"No link but physical appearance was ever found between these women. But if we factor in this possibility. An opportunity to head the kitchen for a private dinner party, to do a photo shoot, private nursing care, write an article, so on."

"Why didn't anyone know they were going off for a private job, an audition?" Baxter asked.

"Good question. Some of them are likely grabs, as we assumed all along. It's also possible he took the time once they were inside the location to engage them in casual conversation, determine if they had told anyone. In some cases, outside jobs would be against their rules of employment. Cop moonlights as a security guard, a bouncer, a body guard, he keeps it to himself. Dr. Mira? Any thoughts on this?"

"It could be another form of control and enjoyment. Inviting his victims in, having them willingly enter, would be yet more proof to him of his superiority over them. It may indeed be another part of the ritual he's created. The lack of violence on the bodies—and by that I mean the fact there's no evidence he used his fists, his hands to strike, to throttle, that there is no sexual molestation—indicates he isn't physical in that way. The violence is through implements and tools. A method such as you're theorizing would fall within the structure of his profile."

"I like it," Baxter commented. "Makes more sense to me, if he's hitting on sixty or over, he'd use deception instead of force to bag them."

"Agreed," Eve said. "If this holds, it indicates he's aware they're physically stronger than he is, or might be," Eve put in. "All these women were in good physical shape, a number of them in exceptional physical shape. He targets young, strong women. We believe he isn't young, maybe he isn't particularly strong."

"Which may be one of the reasons he needs to subdue, humiliate, and control them." Mira nodded. "Yes, by luring them into a location he has secured, he's dominated them intellectually, and then he proceeds to dominate them physically up to and including the point of their death. He not only masters them, but makes them other than they were. And by doing so, makes them his own."

"What does that tell us?" Eve scanned the room. "It tells us one thing we didn't know about him before."

"He's a coward," Peabody said, and gave Eve a quick, inner glow of pride.

"Exactly. He doesn't, as we believed, confront his victims, doesn't risk a public struggle, even with the aid of a drug. He uses guile and lies, the lure of money or advancement or the achievement of a personal goal. He has to know them well enough to use what works, or has the greatest potential of working. He may have spent more time observing and stalking each vic than we previously supposed. And the more time he spent, the more chance there is that someone, somewhere, saw him with one or more of the victims."

"We've been shooting blanks there," Baxter reminded her.

"We go back, interview again, and ask about men the vics spent time with at work, who may have taken one of their classes or talked about doing so. A month ago, two months ago. He wouldn't have been back since he abducted them. He's done with them; he's moved on from that stage. Who used to hang out at these locations, or frequent them who hasn't been there in the last week for York, the last three days for Rossi.

"McNab, dig into Rossi's comps, find me a new outside client. Roarke, names, addys, place of employment on everyone on your list who feels like she fits. Feeney, keep at the Urban War angle. Body identification, comments, commentaries, names of medics officially assigned, of volunteers where you can find them. I want photos, horror stories, war stories, editorials, every scrap you can dig up. Baxter, you and Trueheart hit the street. Jenkinson, you and Powell stay out there, find somebody whose memory can be jogged.

"Write it up, Peabody."

"Yes, sir."

She started out, and Feeney caught up with her. "Need a minute," he said.

"Sure. Got something?"

"Your office."

With an easy shrug, she kept going. "Heading back there. I want to go through the cases between the first and this one more carefully, start calling names on the original interview lists. We just need one break, one goddamn crack, and we can bust it. I know it."

He said nothing as they wound through the bullpen, into her office. "Want coffee?" she asked, then frowned as he closed the door. "Problem?"

"How come you didn't come to me with this?"

"With what?"

"This new theory."

"Well, I—" Sincerely baffled, she shook her head. "I just did."

"Bullshit. What you did was come out as primary, as team leader, you briefed and assigned. You didn't run this by me. My case, you remember? It's my case you were using out there."

"It just popped. Something York's boyfriend said clicked on a new angle for me. I started working it and—"

"*You* started working it," he interrupted. "Going back over my case. A case where I was primary. I was in charge. I made the calls."

Because the muscles in her belly were starting to twist, Eve took a long, steady breath. "Yeah, like I'm going to go back over the others. They're all part of the same whole, and if this is an opening—"

"One I didn't see?" His tired, baggy eyes were hard and bright now. "A call I didn't make while the bodies were piling up?"

"No. Jesus, Feeney. Nobody's saying that or thinking that. It just turned for me. You're the one who taught me when it turns for you, you push. I'm pushing."

"So." He nodded slowly. "You remember who taught you anyway. Who made a cop out of you."

Now her throat was drying up on her. "I remember. I was there, Feeney, from the beginning when you pulled me out of uniform. And I was there for this case. Right there, and it didn't turn for us."

"You owe me the respect of cluing me in when you're going to pick my work apart. Instead you roll this out, roll it over me, and you push me off on some bullshit Urban Wars research. I lived and breathed this case, day and night."

"I know it. I—"

"You don't know how many times I've dug it out since and lived and breathed it again," he interrupted furiously. "So now you figure it's turned for you and you can rip my work to pieces without so much as a heads-up."

"That wasn't my intent or my purpose. The investigation is my priority—"

"It's fucking well mine."

"Is it?" Temper and distress bubbled a nasty stew in her belly. "Fine, then, because I handled this the best I know how—fast. The faster we work it, the better Rossi's chances are, and right now they're about as good as a snowball's in hell. Your work wasn't the issue. Her life is."

"Don't tell me about her life." He jabbed his finger in the air toward her. "Or York's, or Dagby's, or Congress's, Waters's, or Weitz's. You think you're the only one who knows their names?" Bitterness crackled in his tone. "Who carries the weight of them around? Don't you stand there and lecture me about your priorities. *Lieutenant*."

"You've made your viewpoint and your feelings on this matter clear. *Captain*. Now, as primary, I'm telling you, you need to back off. You need to take a break."

"Fuck that."

"Take an hour in the crib, or go home and crash until you can shake this off."

"Or what? You'll boot me off the investigation?"

"Don't bring it down to that," she said quietly. "Don't put either of us there."

"You put us here. You better think about that." He stormed out, slamming the door hard enough to make the glass shudder.

Eve's breath whistled out as she braced a hand on her desk, as she lowered herself into her chair. Her legs felt like water, her gut like a storm inside a violent sea.

They'd had words before. It wasn't possible to know someone, work with someone, especially under circumstances that were so often tense and harsh, and not have words. But these had been so biting and vicious, she felt as if her skin was flayed from them.

She wanted water—just a gallon or two—to ease the burning of her throat, but didn't think she was steady enough to get up and get it.

So she sat until she got her wind back, until the tremor in her hands ceased. And with a headache raging from the base of her skull up to her crown, she called up the next file, prepared to make the next call.

She stuck with it for two hours solid, with translators when necessary. Needing air, she rose, muscled her window open. And just stood, breathing in the cold. A couple more hours, she thought. In a couple more, she'd finish with this step, run more probabilities, write up the report.

Organizing data and hunches, statements and hearsay, writing it all down in clear, factual language always helped you see it better, feel it better.

Feeney had taught her that, too.

Goddamn it.

When her communicator signaled, she wanted to ignore it. Just let it beep while she stood, breathing in the cold.

But she pulled it out. "Dallas."

"I think I've got something." The excitement in McNab's voice cut through the fog in her brain.

"On my way."

When she walked into the war room, she could almost see the ripple of energy and could see Feeney wasn't there.

"Her home unit," McNab began.

"Fell into your lap, Blondie," Callendar commented.

"Was retrieved due to my exceptional e-skills, Tits."

The way they grinned at each other spoke of teamwork and giddy pride.

"Save it," Eve ordered. "What've you got?"

"I'll put it on the wall screen. I found it under 'Gravy.' I'd been picking through docs labeled 'PT,' 'PP,' 'Instruction,' and well, anyway. I hit the more obvious, figuring gravy was like nutrition or, I dunno, recipes. What she means is extra—the gravy."

"Private clients."

"Yeah, like she couldn't have doc'd it that way? So, she's had a bunch. Works with someone until they don't want anymore, or does monthly follow-ups. Before she starts she does this basic analysis—sort of like a proposal, I think. Tons of them in there. But this one . . ."

McNab tapped one of his fingers on the comp screen. "She created sixteen days ago, and she's finessed and updated it here and there since. Up to the night before she poofed. She made a disc copy of it, which isn't anywhere in her files."

"Took it with her," Eve concluded as she studied the wall screen. "Took the proposal to the client. TED."

"His name, or the name he gave her. She has all her private clients listed by first name on the individualized programs she worked up."

"Height, weight, body type, measurements, age." Eve felt a little giddy herself. "Medical history, at least as he gave it to her. Goals, suggested equipment and training programs, nutrition program. Thorough. Boys and girls," Eve announced. "We've got our first description. Unsub is five feet, six and a quarter inches, at a weight of a hundred and sixty-three pounds. A little paunchy, aren't you, you son of a bitch? Age seventy-one. Carries some weight around the middle, according to these measurements."

She kept her eyes on the screen. "Peabody, contact all officers in the field, relay this description. McNab, go through the comps from BodyWorks, find us Ted. Callendar, do a search on York's electronics for this name, for any instruction program she might have written that includes body type, age. Anything that coordinates or adds to this data."

She turned. "Roarke, give me anything you've got. You and I will start contacting the women on your list, find out if they've been contacted or approached by anyone requesting a home visit. Uniforms, back to canvass, making inquiries about a man of this description. Baxter, Trueheart, you're back to the club, back to the fitness center. Jog somebody's memory. I need a station, a d and c. We've got a hole. Let's pull this bastard out of it."

He sighed as he stepped back from his worktable. "You're a disappointment to me Gia. I had such high hopes for you."

He'd hoped the rousing chorus from *Aida* would snap her back, at least a bit, but she simply lay there, eyes open and fixed.

Not dead—her heart still beat, her lungs still worked. Catatonic. Which was, he admitted as he moved over to wash and sterilize his tools, interesting. He could slice and burn, gouge and snip without any reaction from her.

And that was the problem, of course. This was a partnership, and his current partner was very much absent from the performance.

"We'll try again later," he assured her. "I hate to see you fail this way. Physically you're one of the best of all my girls, but it appears you lack the mental and emotional wherewithal."

He glanced at the clock. "Only twenty-six hours. Yes, that's quite a step back. I don't believe you'll be breaking Sarifina's record."

He replaced his tools, walked back to the table where his partner lay, bleeding from the fresh cuts, her torso mottled with bruising, cross-hatched with thin slices.

"I'll just leave the music on for you. See if it reaches inside that head of yours." He tapped her temple. "We'll see what we see, dear. But I'm expecting a guest shortly. Now, I don't want you to think of her as a replacement, or even a successor."

He leaned down, kissed her as yet unmarred cheek as kindly as a father might kiss a child. "You just rest awhile, then we'll try again."

It was time—time, time, time—to go upstairs. To cleanse and change. Later he would brew the tea, and set out the pretty cookies. Company was coming.

Company was such a treat!

He unlocked the laboratory door, relocked it behind him. In his office, he glanced at the wall screen, tsked at the image of Gia as she lay comatose. He was afraid he would have to end things very soon.

In his spotless white suit he sat at his desk to enter the most current data. She was simply not responding to any stimuli, he mused as he noted down her vital signs, the methods and music used in the last thirty minutes of their session. He'd believed the dry ice would bring her back, or the laser, the needles, the drugs he'd managed to secure.

But it was time to admit, to accept. Gia's clock was running down. Ah, well.

When his log was completed, he made his way through the basement labyrinth, past the storage drawers that were no longer in use, past the old work area where his grandfather had forged his art once upon a time.

Family traditions, he thought, were the bedrock of a civilized society. He eschewed the elevator for the stairs. Gia had been quite right, he thought. He would benefit from more regular exercise.

He'd let himself go just a little, he admitted as he patted his plump belly, during his last dormant stage. The wine, the food, the quiet contemplation, and of course, the medication. When this work period was finished, he would take a trip to a spa, concentrate on his physical and mental health. That would be just the ticket.

Perhaps he would travel off planet this time. He'd yet to explore anything beyond his own terra firma. It might be amusing, and certainly beneficial, to spend some time in Roarke's extra-planetary playground, the Olympus Resort.

Doing so would be a kind of delicious topping after he'd completed his current goal.

Eve Dallas, Lieutenant, NYPSD. She would not disappoint as Gia had, he was sure. Still a few kinks to work out in securing her, he admitted. Yes, yes, that was true. But he would find the way.

He unlocked the steel-core basement door using code and key, stepped into the spacious and spotless kitchen. Relocked it.

He would spend some quality time the next day studying the data he'd accumulated on his final Eve. She wasn't as predictable as the ones he usually selected. But then again, that was one of the elements that would make her so special.

He was looking forward to getting reacquainted with her, after so many years.

He moved through the lovely old house, glancing around to make certain all was in order. Past the formal dining room, where he always took his meals, and the library, where he would often sit and read or simply listen to music.

The parlor, his favorite, where he had a pretty little fire burning in the rose granite hearth, and Asian lilies, blushed with pink, rising glamorously out of a wide crystal vase.

There was a grand piano in the corner, and he could still see her there, creating, re-creating such beautiful music. He could see her trying to teach his unfortunately stubby fingers to master the keys.

He'd never mastered them, nor had his voice ever mastered the demands and beauty of the notes, but his love for music was deep and true.

The double doors across from the parlor were closed, were locked. As he'd kept them for many years now. Such business as had been done there was carried on in other places.

His home was his home. And hers, he thought. It would always be hers.

He went up the curve of stairs. He still used the room he'd had as a boy. He couldn't bring himself to use the bedroom where his parents had slept. Where she had slept.

He kept it preserved. He kept it perfect, as she had once been.

Pausing, he studied her portrait, one painted while she had glowed, simply glowed, with the bloom of youth and vibrancy. She wore white—he believed she should always have worn it. For purity. If only she'd remained pure.

The gown swept down her body, that slim and strong body, and the glittery necklace, her symbol of life, lay around her neck. Swept up, her hair was like a crown, and indeed the very first time he'd seen her he'd thought her a princess.

She smiled down at him, so sweetly, so kindly, so lovingly.

Death had been his gift to her, he thought. And death was his homage to her through all the daughters he lay at her feet.

He kissed the silver ring he wore on his finger, one that matched the ring he'd had painted onto the portrait. Symbols of their eternal bond.

He removed his suit. Put the jacket, the vest, the trousers, the shirt in the bin for cleaning. He showered, he always showered. Baths could be relaxing, might be soothing, but how unsanitary was it to lounge in your own dirt?

He scrubbed vigorously, using various brushes on his body, his nails, his feet, his hair. They, too, would be sanitized, then replaced monthly.

He used a drying tube. Towels were, in his opinion, as unsanitary as bathwater.

He cleaned his teeth, applied deodorant, creams.

In his robe he went back to the bedroom to peruse his closet. A dozen white suits, shirts ranged on one side. But he never greeted company in his work clothes.

He chose a dark gray suit, matching it with a pale gray shirt, a tone-on-tone gray tie. He dressed meticulously, carefully brushed his snow-white hair before adding the trim little beard and mustache.

Then he replaced the necklace—her necklace—that he'd removed before his shower.

The symbol of a tree with many branches gleamed in gold. The tree of life.

Satisfied with his appearance, he traveled down to the kitchen, moved through it to the garage where he kept his black sedan. It was a pleasant drive across town, with Verdi playing quietly.

He parked, as arranged, in a small, ill-tended lot three blocks from Your Affair, where his potential partner worked. If she was timely, she would be walking his way right now, she would be thinking about the opportunity he'd put in her hands.

Her steps would be quick, and she would be wearing the dark blue coat, the multicolored scarf.

He left the car, strolling in the direction of the store. He'd found her there, in the bakery section, and had been struck immediately by her looks, her grace, her skill.

Two months had passed since that first sighting. Soon, all the time, the work, the care he'd put into this selection would bear fruit.

He saw her from a block away, slowed his pace. He carried the two small shopping bags from nearby stores he'd brought along with him. He would be, to anyone glancing his way, just a man doing a little casual Sunday shopping.

No one noticed, no one paid any mind. He smiled when she saw him, lifted his hand in a wave.

"Ms. Greenfeld. I'd hoped to make it down and escort you all the way. I'm so sorry to make you walk so far in the cold."

"It's fine." She tossed back the pretty brown hair she wore nearly to her shoulders. "It's so nice of you to pick me up. I could have taken a cab, or the subway."

"Nonsense." He didn't touch her as they walked, in fact moved aside as a pedestrian, chattering on a pocket 'link, clipped between them. "Here you are, giving me your time on a Sunday afternoon." He gestured toward the lot. "And this gave me an opportunity to do a little shopping."

He opened the car door for her, and estimated they'd been together no more than three minutes on the street.

When he got in, he started the car, smiled. "You smell of vanilla and cinnamon."

"Occupational hazard."

"It's lovely."

"I'm looking forward to meeting your granddaughter."

"She's very excited. Wedding plans." He laughed, shook his head, the indulgent grandfather. "Nothing but wedding plans these days. We both appreciate you meeting with us, on the QT, we'll say. My darling is very choosy. No wedding planners, no coordinators. Has to do it all herself. No companies, no organizations."

"A woman who knows her own mind."

"Indeed. And when I saw some of your work, I knew she'd want to meet with you. Even though you worked at Your Affair, and she refuses to so much as go through the doors." With a little laugh, he shook his head. "Over a year now since she had trouble with the manager. But that's my girl. Her mother, God rest her, was the same. Stubborn and headstrong."

"I know Frieda can be temperamental. If she found out I was doing a proposal like this on the side, she'd wig. So, well, keeping this between us is best for everyone."

"It certainly is."

When he pulled off the street, she gaped at the house. "What a beautiful home! Is it yours? I mean, do you own the whole building?"

"Yes, indeed. It's been in the family for generations. I wanted us to meet here, particularly, so you could see it, the wedding and reception venue."

He turned off the engine and led the way into the house. "Let me take you into the parlor—you can make yourself at home."

"It's gorgeous, Mr. Gaines."

"Thank you. Please, call me Edward. I hope I can call you Ariel."

"Yes, please."

"Here, let me have your coat."

He hung her things in the foyer closet. He would, of course, dispose of the coat, the scarf, her clothing. But he enjoyed this part of the pretense.

He stepped back into the parlor, sighed. "I see my granddaughter isn't here yet. She's rarely prompt. I'm just going to make us some tea. Be at home."

"Thanks."

In the kitchen, he switched his security screen to the parlor, so he could watch her as he prepared.

He had house droids, of course, and replaced their memory drives routinely. But for the most part he preferred doing for himself.

He selected Earl Grey, and his grandmother's Meissen tea set. He brewed it as he'd been taught—heating the pot, boiling the water fully, measuring precisely.

Using tongs, he added the precious and pricey sugar cubes to the bowl. She would add sugar, he knew. He'd observed her adding the revolting chemical sweetener to her tea. She would think the cubes a treat, and never notice they were spiked with the tranq until it was already swimming in her system.

After setting a lacy doily on a plate, he arranged the thin, frosted cookies he'd bought especially for this little tête-à-tête. And on the tray he set a single pink rose in a pale green bud vase.

Perfect.

He carried the tea tray—with the three cups to maintain the granddaughter fantasy—into the parlor where Ariel wandered, looking at some of his treasures.

"I love this room. Will you use this for the wedding?"

"We will. It's my favorite room in the house, so welcoming." He set the tray down between the two wing chairs that faced the fire. "We'll have some tea while we wait for the bride. Oh, these cookies are some of her favorites. I thought it might be nice if you re-created them for the reception."

"I'm sure I can." Ariel sat, angling herself so she could face him. "I brought a disc with images of some of the cakes I've done, and some I've assisted in making."

"Excellent." He smiled, held up the sugar bowl. "One lump or two?"

"I'll live dangerously, and go for two."

"Perfect." He sat back, nibbling on a cookie while she chattered about her plans and ideas. While her eyes began to droop, her voice began to slur.

He dusted the crumbs from his fingers when she tried to push out of the chair. "Something's wrong," she managed. "Something's wrong with me."

"No." He sighed and sipped his tea when she slumped into unconsciousness. "Everything's just as it should be."

10 IN ORDER TO WORK WITHOUT GOING MAD, Roarke erected a mental wall of silence. He simply put himself behind that wall and filtered out the ringing, the clacking, the voices, and electronic beeps and buzzes.

Initially, he'd taken the names A through M, with Eve working on the second half of the alphabet. How could he possibly employ so many brunettes with names beginning with A? Aaronson, Abbott, Abercrombie, Abrams, and down to Azula.

It hadn't taken long before it had been monumentally clear two people weren't enough to handle the contacts.

Eve pulled in more cops, and the noise level increased exponentially.

He tried not to think about the time dripping away while he sat, contacting employees he didn't even know, had never met, would unlikely ever meet. Women who depended on him for their livelihoods, who performed tasks he, or someone else who worked for him, created and assigned to them.

Each contact took time. A housekeeper at a hotel wasn't accustomed to receiving a call at home, at work, on her pocket 'link from the owner of that hotel. From the man in the suit, in the towering office. Each call was tedious, repetitious, and he was forced to admit, annoyingly *clerical*.

Routine, Eve would have called it, and he wondered how she could stand the sheer volume of monotony.

"Yo, Irish." Callendar broke through Roarke's wall, poking him in the arm. "You need to get up, move around, pour in some fuel."

"Sorry?" For a moment, her voice was nothing more than a buzz within the buzz. "What?"

"This kind of work, the energy bottoms if you don't keep it pumped. Take a break, get something to power up from Vending. Use a headset for a while."

"I'm not even through the bloody B's."

"Long haul." She nodded, offered him a soy chip from the open bag at her station. "Take it from me, move around some. Blood ends up in your ass this way, not that yours isn't prime. But you want to get the blood back up in your head or your brain's going to stall."

She was right, he knew it himself. And still there was a part of him that wanted to snarl at her to mind her own and let him be. Instead he pushed back from the station. "Want something from Vending, then?"

"Surprise me, as long as it's wet and bubbly."

It did feel good to be on his feet, to move, to step away from the work and the noise.

When he walked out, he noted cops breezing along, others in confabs in front of vending machines. A man, laughing wildly, was quick-marched along by a couple of burly uniforms. He didn't rate even a glance from the others in the corridors.

The place smelled of very bad coffee, he thought, old sweat, and someone's overly powerful and very cheap perfume.

Christ Jesus, he could've used a single gulp of fresh air.

He selected a jumbo fizzy for Callendar, then just stood, staring at his choices. There was absolutely nothing there he wanted. He bought a water, then took out his 'link and made a call.

When he turned, he saw Mira walking toward him. There, he decided, was the closest thing to fresh air he was likely to experience inside the cop maze of Central.

"I didn't realize you were still here," he said.

"I went home, couldn't settle. I sent Dennis off to have dinner with our daughter, and came back to do some paperwork." She glanced down at the enormous fizzy in his hand, smiled a little. "That doesn't strike me as your usual choice of beverage."

"It's for one of the e-cops."

"Ah. This is difficult for you."

"Bloody tedious. I'd sooner sweat a year running an airjack than work a week as a cop."

"That, yes, not at all the natural order for you. But I meant being used this way, and not knowing why, or by whom."

"It's maddening," he admitted. "I was thinking a bit ago that I don't know the bulk of these women we're trying to contact. They're just cogs in the wheel, aren't they?"

"If that's all they were to you, you wouldn't be here. I could tell you that you're responsible for none of what's happened, or may happen to someone else. But you know that already. Feeling it, that's a different matter."

"It is," he agreed. "That it is. What I want is a target, and there isn't one. Yet."

"You're used to having the controls, and taking the actions, or certainly directing them." She touched a sympathetic hand to his arm. "Which is exactly what you're doing now, though it may seem otherwise. And that's why I'm here, too. Hoping Eve will give me some job to do."

"Want a fizzy?"

She laughed. "No, but thanks."

They walked in together, then separated as Roarke went back to his station and Mira crossed to Eve.

"Give me an assignment," Mira said. "Anything."

"We're contacting these women." Eve explained the list, the approach, then gave Mira a list of names.

Wearing black-tie, he settled into his box in the Grand Tier of the Metropolitan Opera House. He richly anticipated the performance of *Rigoletto*. His newest partner was secured and sleeping. As for Gia . . . well, he didn't want to spoil his evening dwelling on that disappointment.

He would end that project tomorrow, and he would move on.

But tonight was for the music, the voices, the lights, and the drama. He knew he would take all of that home with him, relive it, re-experience it while he sipped a brandy in front of the fire.

Tomorrow, he would stop the clock.

But now, he would sit, tingling with pleasure, while the orchestra tuned up.

He *ordered a freaking deli,* was all Eve could think when the food began to roll in. There were trays and trays of meats, bread, cheese, side salads, sweets. Added to it, she saw two huge bags—distinctly gold—of the coffee (real coffee) he produced.

She caught his eye, and hers was distinctly hairy. He only shook his head.

"No lip," he said.

She pushed her way through the schoolyard rush to his station. "A word."

She moved out of the room, and when he joined her the din from the war room was a clear indicator no one else objected to the possibility of corned beef on rye.

"Listen, I went along with the pizza parlor, but—"

"I have to do something," he interrupted. "It's little enough, but at least it's something. It's positive. It's tangible."

"Cops can spring for their own eats, and if I clear an order in, I've got a budget. There are procedures."

He turned away from her, turned back again with frustration simply rolling off of him. "Christ Jesus, we're buried in shagging procedures already. Why would you possibly care if I buy some fucking sandwiches?"

She stopped herself when she felt the teeth of her own temper in her throat. "Because it's tangible." She pressed her fingers into her eyes, rubbed hard. "It's something to kick at."

"Can't you take an hour? Look at me. Look at me," he repeated, laying his hands on her shoulders. "You're exhausted. You need an hour to stretch out, to turn off."

"Not going to happen, and by the way, you're not looking so perky yourself."

"I feel like my brain's been used as a punching bag. It's not the time, or even the lack of sleep so much. It's the unholy tedium."

That made her frown—and put her back up again, a little. "You've done cop work before."

"Bits and pieces it comes clear to me now, and that with some challenge and a clear end goal."

"Challenge? Like risking your life and getting bloody."

Calmer, he circled his head on his neck and wondered how many years it might take to get the last of the kinks out. "A lot more appealing, sad to say, than sitting in front of a screen or on a 'link for hours on end."

"Yeah. I know just what you mean. But this is part of it, a big part of it. It's not all land to air chases and busting in doors. Listen, you can take an hour in the crib. Probably should. I'll clear it."

He flicked a finger along the dent in her chin. "Not only does that sound extremely unappealing, but if you're on, I'm on. That's the new rule until we've finished this."

Arguing took energy she didn't have to spare. "Okay. All right."

"Something else is wrong." He put a hand under her chin, left it there even when she winced and tried to knock it off. "Shows what happens when your brain's used as a punching bag that I didn't see it before. What is it?"

"I figure having some murdering bastard who slipped by us before back torturing and killing women under our noses is pretty much enough."

"No, something else in there." It was the "slipped by us" that clicked for him. "Where's Feeney?"

For an answer, she shifted, and kicked the vending machine so viciously it sent off its security alarm.

Warning! Warning! Vandalizing or damaging this unit is a crime, and punishable by a maximum of thirty days incarceration and a fine not to exceed one thousand dollars per offense. Warning! Warning!

"All right, then," Roarke said mildly, and taking her arm, pulled her down the corridor. "Let's just take this to your office before we're both arrested for attempting to steal fizzies."

"I don't have time to—"

"I think making time is in everyone's best interest."

He took her straight through, so the scatter of cops on weekend evening shift barely glanced over.

Inside her office, he closed the door, leaned back against it while she kicked her desk. "When you're done abusing inanimate objects, tell me what happened."

"I screwed up, that's what happened. Fuck, fuck, and shit. I messed up."

"How?"

"What would it have taken me? Ten minutes? Five? Five minutes to give him the rundown before the briefing. But I didn't think of it, never crossed my mind." Obviously at wit's end, she fisted her hands on either side of her head and squeezed in. "What the hell's wrong with me that it never crossed my mind?"

"Once more," Roarke suggested, "with clarity."

"Feeney, I didn't feed him the new data, tell him about the new angle we'd work. That the suspect had contacted the target, lured her to him rather than doing the grab on the street. The way we'd worked the first case. Damn it!"

Her desk took another slam with her boot. "I just lumped him in with everyone else, didn't take into account that he'd led the first investigation. All I had to do was pull him aside, tell him, 'Hey, we've got something fresh.' Give him a little time to take it in."

"He didn't react well, I take it?"

"Who could blame him?" she tossed back. Her tired eyes were dark with regret. "Jumped on me with both feet. And what do I do? I get my back up, that's what I do. Can't just say, hey, I'm sorry, I got caught up in the roll and didn't think it through. No, can't say that. Oh well, shit!"

She covered her face a moment, heeled away the tears that got away from her. "This isn't good."

"Baby, you're so tired."

"So the fuck what? So I'm tired, that's the job, that's the way it is. Tired means nothing. I bitch slapped him, Roarke. I told him to take a break, to go home. Why didn't I just knock him down and rub his face in it while I was at it?"

"Did he need a break, Eve?"

"That's not the point."

"It certainly is."

Now she sighed. "Just because it was the right call doesn't mean it was right. He said I didn't respect him, and that's not true. That's so far from any truth, but I didn't show him respect. I told you before, the other one was on him—that's command. All I did by handling it this way was add to that weight."

"Sit down. Oh, for Christ's sake, sit for five minutes." He strode over, all but lifted her bodily into her chair. "I know something about command, and it's often not pretty, nor comfortable, and very often it's not fair. But someone had to make the calls, the decisions. Maybe you didn't account for his feelings, and you can regret that if it helps you. But the simple fact is, you had a great deal more on your mind than coddling Feeney."

"It's not coddling."

"And he had a great deal on his, and obviously needed to vent some of the pressure," Roarke continued as if she hadn't spoken. "Which he did, quite handily, I'd say, on you. Now you're both feeling sorry for yourselves."

Her mouth dropped open in sheer shock for two seconds, then twisted into a snarl. "Bite me."

"I hope to have the energy for that at some point in the near future. You told him to go home because you understood, even if you were angry and hurt, you understood he needed to step away for a time. He went because he understood, even being angry and hurt, that he needed to. So, mission accomplished, and I imagine sometime tomorrow, you'll both clean up the fallout and forget it. Correct?"

She sniffled, scowled. "Well, if you want to be all insightful and reasonable about it."

"He loves you."

"Oh, jeez."

Roarke had to laugh. "And you love him. If you were just cops to each other, it might still be a bit tricky. Add love, and it's a very thorny path the two of you walk when you're entrenched in something like this."

From where she sat she could still kick her desk. She did so, but lightly this time. "You sound like Mira 101."

"I'll take that as a compliment. Any better?"

"I don't know. Maybe." She pressed her hands to her temples. "My head's killing me."

He merely reached into his pocket, took out a tiny case. Thumbing it open, he held it out to her. She frowned down at the little blue pills. Standard blocker, she knew, just as she knew he'd nag her to take one if she balked—which would only make the headache worse. Or he'd just force one down her throat, which was a humiliation she didn't want to risk so close on the heels of pity tears.

She took one, popped it.

"There's a good girl."

"I repeat: Bite me."

He pulled her up, pulled her in. Nipped her bottom lip. "Just a preview of things to come."

Since it was there, she touched his face. "You looked a little worn and down before, too."

"I was feeling that way. Worn and down." He rested his brow on hers a moment. "Let's go have a sandwich and some decent coffee."

McNab signaled the minute they walked back in.

"Getting some beeps here."

"Wipe the mustard off your face, Detective."

"Oh, sorry." He swiped at it with the back of his hands. "Started the Ted search at the branch where Rossi works," he began. "Got guys that fit the height and weight, but not the age, fit the age, but not otherwise. Fanned out to other branches. This Pi's being really trim about it. But still nothing that really rings the bell. So I moved out to the boroughs."

"Bottom-line it, McNab."

"Okay, I've got a few—nobody named Ted—but a few who fall into the description you may want to have checked out. But they don't fit the profile. We got married guys, with kids, grandkids, and no property like we're thinking listed under their name or names of family members I've dug up so far."

"And those are my beeps."

"No. I started thinking, hey, let's try the locales of the other murders. Hit Florida first, and got us a beep."

He called the data on screen. "Membership in the name of Edward Nave. DOB June 8, 1989—down on the age—and the membership required a workup, so we've got his height—down with that—weight— a few pounds lighter, but you gotta figure on some flux. Oh, and Peabody says that Ted's a nickname for Edward, so—"

"Address."

"Yeah, that's a problem. Address is bogus. He lists a Florida addy that would have him setting up in Miami's Grand Opera House. I checked it out."

"Bring up his ID."

"Okay." McNab pulled at his heavily decorated ear. "Problem number two. I can give you a fistful of Edward Naves, but none of their ID data matches the membership data."

"Copy me on them anyway. We'll run them down. How long has he held the membership? When did he pick it up in Florida?"

"Five years. About three months before the first murder there. It's him, Dallas." Conviction pushed through McNab's voice, hardened his face. "Gotta go with the gut on it, but he's covered it."

"We're going to uncover it." She looked at Roarke. "This franchise in Europe?"

"It is."

"Start searching the memberships in the other target cities. Maybe, just maybe, this was one of his trolling tools."

She started to go to her own station. She'd dig into Florida again, she decided, see if she could find any connection between the fitness center and any of the victims there. A member, one of the staff, cleaning crew.

"Eve." Mira stood up, and the look in her eyes had Eve's stomach sinking. "I've been trying to contact an Ariel Greenfeld. She's a baker at a place called Your Affair downtown. She doesn't answer the 'link numbers listed on her information. I've just spoken with her emergency contact, a neighbor. Greenfeld hasn't been back to her apartment since she left for work this morning."

"Get me the address." She started to tell Peabody to get moving, then stopped. She'd made a mistake with Feeney, there was no point in giving out another personal slap. "Roarke and I will check it out. Unless notified, all team members are to go the hell home by twenty-three hundred or hit the crib. Report back at oh-eight-hundred for first briefing. Anything, absolutely anything pops meanwhile, I'm the first to know."

As they headed toward Ariel's apartment, Eve glanced at Roarke. His face was unreadable, but she understood it. Guilt, worry, questions.

"What's Your Affair?"

"An event shop. Ah . . . upscale, everything you might need under one roof. A variety of specialty boutiques—attire, floral and planting, bakery, catering, decor, event planners. It was something I thought of when we were dealing with our wedding. Why go to all these places, all these people, if you can go to one location and find effectively every thing you'd need. And if you want something else, there are consultants who'll find that something else for you."

Eve thought she might actually shop in a place like that. If she fell out of a three-story window, cracked her head on the sidewalk, and suffered severe brain damage. But she said, "Handy."

"So I thought, yes. It's doing quite well. She's worked there eight months. Ariel Greenfeld."

"And right now, she could be boinking some guy she picked up in a bar."

He turned his head to look at her. "You don't think that. I should contact her supervisor, find out what time she left work."

"Let's wait on that. Let's check out her place, talk to her neighbor. Look, do you know why I'm keeping the team on another two hours? She might not be the one. We pull off, push everything into this, maybe somebody else gets taken. First, we get a clearer view of the situation."

"Yes, a clearer view. How's the headache?"

"Sulking behind the blocker. I know it's there, but it's pretty easy to ignore."

When they'd parked, he laid a hand over hers. "Where are your gloves?"

"Somewhere. Else."

He kept her hand in his, opened the glove box. And took out the spare pair he'd bought her on a recent shopping trip. "Wear these. It's cold."

She pulled them on, and was grateful for them as they hiked a block to the apartment building. "You never got that sandwich," she pointed out.

"Neither did you."

"At least I didn't shell out hundreds of dollars and not even end up with a pickle chip or a splat of veggie hash."

"I've never understood the appeal of anything referred to as 'hash.' " Appreciating her, he draped an arm over her shoulders as they walked.

Rather than wait to be buzzed in, she used her master on the front entrance door.

Decent building, she noted. What she thought of as solid working class. Tenants with steady employment and middle-class income. Tidy entranceway, standard security cams, single elevator.

"Third floor," she requested. "She could walk to work from here, if she didn't mind a good hike. Catch the subway and save five blocks in crappy weather or if she's running late. Bakers, they start early, right? What time does the store open?"

"Seven-thirty for the bakery, the café. Ten to six for most of the re-tail, with extended hours to eight on Saturdays. But yes, I'd think the bakery section would start work before opening hours."

"Couple hours maybe. So if she had to be there by six . . ." She trailed off as they reached the third floor. "Neighbor's 305."

She walked to it, had just lifted a fist to knock when the door opened. The man who answered was late-twenties, sporting spikey hair of streaked black and bronze. He wore a baggy sweater and old jeans, and an expression of barely controlled worry.

"Hey, heard the elevator. You the cops?"

"Lieutenant Dallas." Eve held up her badge. "Erik Pastor?"

"Yeah, come on in. Ari's not home yet. I've been calling people, to see if anybody's seen her."

"When did you see her last?"

"This morning. Early this morning. She came in to bring me a couple of muffins. We went out last night, a group of us. Ari went home before midnight, because she had to be at work at six this morning. And she figured—correctly—I'd be hungover."

He lowered to the arm of the couch. The area reflected the debris of a man who'd spent the bulk of the day nursing a long night. Soy chips, soft-drink tubes, a bottle of blockers, a blanket, a couple of pillows were scattered around.

"I only made it as far as the couch," he continued. "So I heard her come in, groaned at her. She razzed me a little, and said she'd see me later. If I wasn't dead, she'd pick up a few things on her way home and fix me some dinner. Has something happened to her? They wouldn't tell me anything on the 'link."

"You're tight? You and Ariel?"

"Yeah. Not, you know, that way. We're friends. We hang."

"Could she be out with someone she's more than friendly with?"

"There's a couple of guys—casual, nothing serious. I checked with them, hell, with every damn body. Plus, she'd have told me." His voice shook a little, telling Eve he was struggling with that control. "If she says she's going to come back and fix dinner, that's what she does. I was starting to worry before you guys called."

"What time did she get off work today?"

"Ah . . . give me a minute. Four? Yeah, I think four. It's her long Sunday, so it's four. Usually she heads straight back. Short Sundays she might do some shopping, or some of us would meet up for lunch or something."

"We'd like to look in her apartment."

"Okay, sure. She wouldn't mind. I'll get the key. We've got keys to each other's places."

"Did she say anything about having an appointment today? About meeting someone?"

"No. Or, God, I don't know. I had my head buried under the pillow and was praying for a quick, merciful death when she popped in this morning. I didn't pay attention." He dug a set of keys out of a drawer. "I don't understand why she's not answering her pocket 'link. I don't understand why you're asking all these questions."

"Let's take a look at her place," Eve suggested. "Go from there."

It smelled of cookies, Eve realized. Though the kitchen was small, it was organized and equipped by someone who knew what they were doing.

"Some women buy earrings or shoes," Erik said. "Ari, she buys ingredients and baking tools. There's a specialty shop in the meatpacking district called Baker's Dozen? She'll have an orgasm just walking in there."

"Is there anything missing that would normally be here if she was just going to work?"

"Uh, I don't know. I don't think so. Should I look around?"

"Why don't you?"

While he did, Eve studied the little computer on a table just outside the kitchen. Couldn't touch it, she thought, not until there was an official report.

Bending the line of probable cause.

"He might be on there," Roarke murmured. "Something to do with this might be on there."

"And she could walk in the door in the next thirty seconds, and I'd have invaded her privacy, illegally."

"Bollocks to that." He started to move past Eve to open the computer himself.

"Wait, damn it. Just wait."

"Her shoes." Erik stepped out of the bedroom, his face radiating both confusion and concern.

"What about them?"

"Her good black shoes aren't here. She wears skids to work. She walks. It's eight blocks, two of them crosstown, and she's on her feet all day. Her work skids aren't here, either. She'd take a change if she was going somewhere after. She'd take other shoes."

His face cleared. "She took her good black shoes. She must've had a date or something, just forgot to tell me, or I was so out of it. . . . That's all it is. She hooked up with somebody after work."

Eve turned back to Roarke. "Open it."

II

EVE RELAYED THE NEW DATA TO THE TEAM AT Central, and ordered Ariel's electronics picked up. Riding on the fresh spurt of adrenaline, she turned to Roarke.

"We've got a jump on him."

Roarke continued to study the little screen with its images of wedding cakes and cost projections. "From the glass-half-empty side, it seems he's gotten the jump on us."

"That's wrong thinking. We're moving on a lead we didn't have before this investigation. And we're moving in the right direction. Otherwise, we wouldn't have known, not for hours—potentially days—that Greenfeld was missing. We wouldn't know how he pulled her in."

"And how does that help her, Eve?"

"Everything we know gives her a better chance of making it through. We know he's had her about five hours. We have to assume he's frequented the store where she worked, and contacted her by some method. Five hours, Roarke," she repeated. "He hasn't done anything to her yet. Probably has her sedated. He won't start on her until he's . . ."

He looked up then, eyes frigid. "Until he's finished with Gia Rossi. Until he's done cutting and carving on her."

"That's right." No way to soften it, Eve thought. No point in trying. "And until we find Rossi's body, she's alive. Until we find her body, she's got a chance. Now, with this, she has a better one. We canvass, we check parking lots, we check public transpo. We talk to her coworkers, her other friends. We have his age, his body type. We didn't have any of that twenty-four hours ago."

She stepped to him, touched his arm. "Make a copy of that program, will you? We'll work this from home. Maybe something will shake loose on the search Summerset's been running, or on the real estate angle. Something's going to click into place."

"All right. But neither of us is working on this until we've stepped back for a couple hours. I mean it, Eve," he said before she could protest. "You ordered your team to take some downtime for good reason."

"I could use a shower," she said after a moment. "An hour. Compromise." She held up a hand, held him off. "You've got to admit it beats fighting about it for half that downtime."

"Agreed." He copied the data, handed her the disc.

Since she didn't consider the drive home part of the break, she let Roarke take the wheel and shuffled through her notes, the timelines, the names, the statements.

He'd taken the third target sooner than projected, Eve mused. Two reasons she could think of for that. Either the earlier snatch suited his personal schedule or the target's. Or Gia Rossi wasn't holding up well.

She could already be dead—a possibility Eve saw no reason to share with Roarke.

Hours, she thought. If the contact had been made hours sooner, they would have found Ariel Greenfeld before he had her. The right question, the right time. Not only would the woman have been safe, but they'd have had solid data on the suspect.

Off at four, she noted. Planned to make dinner for her neighbor. So, she'd planned to be home from this outside appointment in two or three hours, most likely.

"How long would you budget for a meeting?" Eve asked. "For going over a proposal for wedding cakes and desserts, that sort of thing?"

"From her end?" Roarke considered. "She put together a lot of images, a number of variations of style and type, flavors. A great deal of trouble. I'd guess she'd prepared for a couple of hours. If she assumed—correctly—that many people take every detail of a wedding very seriously, she would have been prepared to give the potential client all the time he needed or wanted."

"Okay, let's say two, so that makes it eighteen hundred not including travel time. She tells the guy across the hall she's going to pick up a few things on the way home to make—actually cook—a meal. That's got to take some time. The shopping part, the cooking part. Probably, what, an hour?"

"Your guess." Roarke shrugged. "Summerset would know better."

"Yeah, well, until we consult His Boniness, I'm figuring an hour. Which puts it at nineteen hundred, again without travel. Late night Saturday, long day Sunday, early to work on Monday. I don't figure she was prepping a late meal."

"And what does that tell you?"

"It tells me that, most likely, as far as she knew, she wasn't going that far for this meeting. Not across the river into Jersey, probably not across the bridge into Brooklyn or Queens. Too much bridge-and-tunnel traffic. Probability is higher he's in Manhattan. Narrows the search."

Eve shifted. "She's tossing a meal together for a friend, not planning a fancy deal for a lover. Just a pal, one she's hoping she can share this good news with if she copped the job. Picking up a few things on the way home. That says she planned to get herself home. Public transportation or on foot. So she can stop by the market. Decent chance he's downtown, at least not above midtown."

She sat back. "Focus there to start. Fan out, sure, but we start there, focus there."

She worked the problem the rest of the way home, adding in factors, playing with angles. Urban Wars, body ID method, Lower West or East Side clinics.

He almost certainly had some sort of transportation, but it would also serve if he could stalk any or all of his victims on foot.

People tended to shop and frequent restaurants in their comfort-zone. The soap and shampoo—downtown store was very likely the source unless he web-shopped or brought it into New York with him. Starlight was in Chelsea, the bakery downtown, the first dumping spot in this round on the Lower East. Gia Rossi worked midtown.

Maybe he wasn't traveling far from home this time around.

Maybe.

She plugged her knowns and unknowns into her PPC, intending to transfer the information to her desk unit and run probabilities.

"I want whatever Summerset's worked up on disc and on my unit," she began as they drove through the gates. "We can get his take on the timing as far as shopping/cooking, but I want to check out what markets and stores Greenfeld most usually frequented. And other specialty places below Fiftieth. The way her neighbor talked, she'd have gotten a charge out of wandering some new food place. We'll interview the others she went out with Saturday night. Maybe she let something slip about her Sunday plans."

They got out on opposite sides of the car, but Roarke put a hand on her arm when they reached the base of the steps of home. "You never thought there was a chance for Rossi."

"I never said that, and there's always a chance."

"Slim to none. It didn't stop you pushing—hard and in every way you could push, but you knew her chances were all but nil, and on some level accepted it."

"Listen—"

"No, don't misunderstand me. That's not a criticism. It's a small, personal revelation that came to me on the way home. Watching you work, listening to you even when you weren't speaking. Your mind says volumes. You don't feel the same way about Ariel Greenfeld."

He slid his hand down her arm until he found hers, linked fingers. "You believe there's a real chance now. Not only in finding him, stopping him. That you have to believe every minute or you'd never be able to do what you do. But you believe you'll find him, stop him before it's too late for this woman, and because of it Gia Rossi's chances have gone up from slim to none to slim. It has to energize you, and at the same time, it must weigh all the heavier. They have a chance. You're their chance."

"We," Eve corrected. "Everyone working the case is their chance. And we'd better not let her down."

She expected Summerset to materialize in the foyer and intended to have Roarke take point with him. But the minute they stepped in, she heard laughter in the parlor, and the bubbling sound of it was unmistakable.

"Mavis is here."

"There's your hour of downtime." Roarke slipped Eve's coat from her shoulders. "Difficult to find a more entertaining or distracting way to rest the brain cells than a portion of Mavis Freestone."

It was tough to argue the point. But when Eve stepped to the parlor doorway, she saw Mavis had brought Trina along. If that wasn't scary enough, they'd hauled the baby out for the evening.

Most terrifying, at the moment, the infant Belle was being held by Summerset, and having her chin chucked by his skeletal fingers.

"I'm traumatized," Eve stated. "He's not supposed to smile like that. It's against the laws of man and nature."

"Don't be such a hard-ass." Roarke gave her a little poke in the ribs. "Ladies," he said in normal tones, and had the group looking over.

"Hey!" Mavis's already glowing face brightened. "You're back! We were about to head out, but Bella wanted another Summerset smoochie."

Which, to Eve's mind, confirmed the innate oddity of babies and kids.

Mavis bounced over, sending the short, flirty skirt she wore swirling over polka-dot tights. The skirt was candy pink, the tights pink on brilliant blue. She'd gone for the blue in her hair, too, Eve noted, in a few wild streaks against silvery blond.

She grabbed one of Roarke's hands, one of Eve's, and pulled them into the room. "Leonardo had to shoot out to New L.A. for a client, so Trina and Belle and I had a total girl day. Ended it with some Summerset time. Look who's here, Belle. Look who came to see you."

With little choice Eve looked down at the baby still tucked in Summerset's arms. Most, Eve supposed, would say the kid looked like a doll. But to Eve's way of thinking, dolls were just creepy.

The fact was, the baby was a knockout—if you discounted the drool—pink, pretty, and plump. A lacy white ribbon was tied around her hair, as if she'd been wrapped like a gift. The dark blue eyes were lively, maybe a little too lively. They made Eve wonder just what went on inside the brain of a human the size of a teacup poodle.

She wore some sort of outfit with feet and a kind of sweater deal over it that may have been trimmed in actual fur. Over it all there was a bib—due, Eve supposed, to drool—that proclaimed:

MY DADDY IS ICED!

"Cute," Eve said and would have stepped back, but Roarke blocked her as he studied the baby over Eve's shoulder.

"I think gorgeous is more accurate. What nice work you do, Mavis."

"Thanks." The former street urchin and current music vid sensation stared down at her daughter with sparkling eyes of unearthly blue. "Sometimes I look at her and just can't believe she came out of me."

"Do you have to bring up that part of it?" Eve asked and made Mavis laugh again.

"Maybe we could hang a little while more, unless you're too tired. You guys look pretty whipped."

"Could use a treatment," Trina commented.

"Stay away from me." Eve jabbed a finger in the consultant's direction.

"We could use a meal." Roarke smiled at their guests. "Why don't you join us?"

"Summerset already fed us until we popped, but we could stick, keep you company. It's off knowing our big daddy won't be home when we get there, isn't it, Bellarama?"

"I'll prepare something right away."

Eve saw Summerset shift and—anticipating—was quick and cowardly. She sidestepped, hip-bumped Roarke, leaving him in the line of fire.

She loved her man, would unquestionably risk her life for his. But when it came to babies, he could sink. She was swimming.

His arms came out instinctively, as a man's might when something fragile or potentially explosive was about to be dropped into them. "I don't. . . I should . . . Oh, well then," he muttered as Summerset deftly made the transfer.

"Is there anything in particular you'd like?" The faintest wisp of a smile touched Summerset's lips as Roarke's eyes burned a hole through him. "For supper?"

"Something quick," Roarke managed. He'd once diffused a bomb with seconds to spare, and had felt less panic.

"I was hoping to see you." Mavis beamed at him, then dropped into a chair, leaving Roarke standing on what felt like very unsteady ground. "Just about dropped all the belly weight now, and got the full-steam from the docs. I've got a boat of new material, so I thought I could get in the studio, rock it out, cut some vids."

"Yes. That sounds . . . all right."

"Mag. I figured to bring Bella in with me. She's completely about music. If it doesn't work, Leonardo and I'll figure something."

"Doesn't want a nanny," Trina commented.

"Not yet anyway. I just want her to be all mine right now. Mine and her daddy's. But I've got the itch to get back to work, so I want to see if I can do it on my own."

"I'm sure you'll do fine." Roarke glanced down at the baby and saw Belle's eyes were drooping. As if the thick, dark lashes were too heavy for the delicate lids to hold. "She's going to sleep." His own lips curved as what he held went from being mildly terrifying to quietly sweet. "Worn out from all the partying, are you now? Is there something I should do?"

"You're doing it," Mavis told him. "But we'll put her down. There's a monitor in her travel bed." Mavis rose. "Receiver right here." She tapped a flamingo-shaped pin just above her right ear. "Just lay her right in here. If she wakes up a little, you just pat her belly for a minute. She conks."

It was something like a small, portable sleep chair, Roarke noted, well padded in Mavis's—or Bella's, he supposed—signature rainbow hue. Though setting her down in it seemed fairly straightforward, he actually felt sweat pool at the base of his spine.

When she was down, and he straightened, the relief and satisfaction was very nearly orgasmic.

Mavis crouched, fussed with the blanket. "She'll be fine right here, won't you, my baby girl?"

"The cat. Isn't there something about cats and babies?"

Mavis smiled up at Roarke. "I think it's bogus, but anyway, Galahad's scared of her. He took one look and lit. If he comes snooping around her, I'll hear it. I can actually hear her breathing through the receiver."

After giving the blanket one last fiddle, Mavis stood. "You should eat in the dining room like we did. There's a nice fire in there, too. You'll relax more. You guys really do look wrung. We won't stay long."

"We're taking an hour down." Now that all danger of being expected to hold the baby had passed, Eve moved back to Roarke. "Let's go eat."

They settled in the dining room where the fire roared and a dozen candles were lit. To give Summerset his due, he'd managed quick and tasty. There were thin slices of roast chicken in some sort of fragrant sauce, fancy potatoes, and something that might have been squash but was prepared so it wasn't really objectionable.

He served Trina a glass of wine, and Mavis something rose-colored and frothy with a plate of thin cookies and fancy chocolates.

"I come around here too often, I'll be back to belly weight." Mavis picked up a chocolate. "Nursing makes me nearly as hungry as pregnancy did."

"No breast milk at the table," Eve warned her. "So to speak."

"I sort of carry it everywhere." But Mavis grinned. "You can talk about the case. You're going to think about it anyway. We heard about it on screen. I remember when this guy was around before. I was on the grift then. All the girls on the street were scared all the time."

"You were too young for him then."

"Maybe, but it was scary. Trina and I both went way far from brunette last night during our hair party. Just, you know, in case."

Eve eyed Mavis's silver and blue streaks, then Trina's flame red tower of curls. "Yeah, you're not his type."

"Glad to hear. How's it going, anyway? Everything's dire on screen."

"We've got some buttons to push."

"I was doing hair at Channel Seventy-five yesterday." Trina studied the cookies narrowly, picked one. "On-air reporter was trying to make my celeb, you know? Spouting and such. He gave her some gory on the case to impress her, and said the police were stymied."

"Reporters are mostly assholes."

"Lot of them say the same about cops." Trina smiled. "I think it's pretty much fifty-fifty. Anyway, it was the buzz in the salon yesterday, and we had the chairs full of women ditching their brunette."

Eve forked up some chicken. "You're still working the salon route?" she considered. "I thought you were on Nadine's show, and working private."

"You get private through the salon if you know how to play it. Plus, Roarke set me up pretty."

"To what?"

"Trina manages the salon section of Bliss, the downtown spa," Roarke explained. "An excellent choice on my part."

"You got that." Trina toasted him. "Business is up seven percent since I took over."

"Your operators take private?" Eve asked her.

"It's against policy." Trina wiggled her dramatic eyebrows at Roarke as she sipped her wine. "Private means they don't come in, the salon and spa don't get the business. And they don't drop impulse dough. But let's get real. A customer asks—they're called consultants, by the way—to do a house gig, they're not going to say no unless they don't want the job."

"I'm looking for a man about seventy, short, pudgy."

"We get that type, sure. Policy is to tactfully steer the pudge part into our spa or the body sculpting section. Barring, we talk up the fitness centers, and—"

"I'm talking specifically," Eve interrupted. "A man of that basic type coming in, feeling out one of the consultants for a private. Within the last, let's say, two months."

"Lotta room, Dallas," Trina said. "We get a lot of traffic, and being manager, most of the consultants aren't going to mention a private to me, unless it's sanctioned."

"Sanctioned how?"

"Like we send teams or a solo in for special occasions, and the salon takes the big cut."

"Long shot," Eve muttered.

"But come to think of it, I had somebody like that. I guess."

Eve set down her fork. "You guess or you had one?"

"Look, like I said, we get a lot of traffic. People tap me for private most every day. What's the big . . . Oh, hey, hey!" Her wine sloshed toward the rim as she hastily set the glass down. "Is this the guy? Is this the fucking guy? Holy shit storm."

"Just tell me what you remember."

"Okay, Jesus, let me clear the decks." Trina closed her eyes, sucked air through her nose several times. "This guy . . . walk-in. Manicure, I'm thinking. Don't remember who had him. I'm thinking it was a Saturday afternoon, and we're busting on Saturday afternoons. He waited a long time for the nail job, wandered over into the retail section. I think. I was busy. I just remember catching sight of him a few times. Then I took my break, went into the bar for a smoothie. Maybe a fizzy. No, it was a smoothie."

"Trina, I don't care what you had to drink."

"I'm getting the picture." Her eyes flashed open. "You want the picture, I need to get it first. So it was a smoothie. A banana-almond smoothie. We make killers. And he comes up, real polite. 'Excuse me, Miss,' like that. He noticed I was in charge, and since he'd had to wait awhile he'd noticed, too, how skilled I was."

She smiled to herself. "So I didn't tell him to flip, that I was on a break. He wanted to know how to arrange an at-home appointment. Not for him, though, not for him, wait a minute."

Frowning, she picked up her wine, sipped again while Eve struggled not to just leap up and pound the rest of the details out of her.

"His wife? Yeah, yeah, yeah, at-home for his wife. She wasn't well, and how he thought it would make her feel better to have her hair done, maybe a facial, a mani, pedi, like that. A package treatment."

"Trina—"

"Wait a damn minute. Let me get a fix on it. I'm telling him how we arrange this, the fees, and so on, and he's wondering if I'd consider doing this on my day off. So I wouldn't have to rush back to work, but could give his wife as much time as she wanted. Whenever it suited me. He even showed me a picture of the wife. He'd be happy to pay whatever I think appropriate."

"Did he give you an address?"

"You keep interrupting." Obviously annoyed, Trina opened her eyes again. "No. I said how I'd need to check my book. So I did, taking my time, thinking it over. Even the older guys can be stringing you, you know? I was booked up for a while. I think I gave him a couple possible dates. A couple of weeks down the road. He said he'd check the dates out with his wife's nurse, see which she thought would work best. He asked if I had a card, so he could contact me. I gave him one. And that was it."

"He didn't get back to you?"

"Nope. I thought maybe I saw him about a week later. Somewhere. Where was it? Oh, yeah, in this bar where I was having drinks with this guy I was thinking of doing. But I figured, nah. Not the kind of joint you see a suit with a sick wife."

"He give you a name?"

"Maybe. I don't remember. If I can pin down the mani he got, we'd have it on the books. First name anyhow. Is this the guy?"

Don't rush it, Eve thought. Dot the *i*'s. "What color was your hair?"

"You gotta be kidding. It was, like, a month ago. Yeah, a month, like the first Saturday in February, because I remember thinking if we did business like that through the month, I was going to ask for a raise. We did, I did. And hey, thanks again," she said to Roarke.

"Caramel Mocha," Mavis murmured. "With Starfish highlights."

"Yeah?" Trina turned to her. "You sure?"

"You did me Starfish with Candyland tips." Mavis's hand trembled a little as she reached for her glass. "I've got a memory for this stuff. Oh, wow. Oh, wow. I think I feel a little sick."

"You? I'm the one he was planning to torture and kill. I think I feel . . ." Trina pressed a hand to her belly, then squinted out of slitted eyes. "Pissed. That's what I feel. That son of a bitch. Sick wife? Pay me whatever. He was going to *kill* me." She picked up her wine, guzzled it. "Why didn't he?"

"You changed it." Mavis took slow, deep breaths. "You didn't stick with that shade even a week. You went straight to Wild Raven with Snow Cap streaks."

"Just back up," Eve demanded. "This mocha bit? Does that translate to brunette?"

"On a basic level," Trina confirmed. "Of course, the way I work it's way beyond anything basic."

"Can you describe him?"

"Yeah, yeah, I think. But he was wearing a hair enhancer."

"Meaning wig?"

"A good one, too, but you're talking to the expert. Hey, hey, that's why I didn't think it was him in the bar. He wasn't. I mean he was, the hair enhancer wasn't. At least not the same one. I didn't get a close or long enough look to tell if it was hair or enhancer."

"I want you to describe him. I want you to give me every detail you can remember about him. Appearance, voice, body type, gestures, any distinguishing marks. Everything. Tomorrow morning, you'll work with a police artist."

"Really? No shit? I'm like an eyewitness. Frosty."

"Let's take this up to my office. Think. Get him in your head."

She pulled out her 'link. "Peabody. I need you to contact Yancy. I want him ready to work with a witness tomorrow. Seven sharp."

"Is that *morning*?" Trina demanded.

"Stow it." Eve simply shot out a finger. "Got that, Peabody?"

"Got it. Is that . . . Is that Trina?"

"Yeah. She's our wit. Small freaking world. I want Yancy, Peabody. I'm taking down her description now, and I'll relay it to the team. Tell McNab I want him and the e-geeks ready to run with the description, then with the image as soon as Yancy's got one."

She was walking as she talked, moving briskly out of the dining room, through the corridor, the foyer, up the stairs. As orders and instructions rolled out of her, Trina glanced over at Roarke.

"She's a little scary when she's on the scent."

"She can be a lot scarier. You go up. I'll be along." He turned back, brushed a hand over Mavis's shoulder. "Why don't you and Bella and Trina plan to stay here tonight?"

"Really? It's okay?"

"Absolutely. I'll have Summerset take care of whatever you think you'll need."

"Thanks. Boy. Thanks. I know it's silly. Nobody's going to bother us, but . . ."

"We'll all feel better, under the circumstances, if you're tucked in here. Why don't you get in touch with Leonardo, let him know?"

"Okay. Good. Thanks. Roarke?"

"Hmmm?"

"If Trina hadn't changed her hair . . ."

"I know." He kissed the top of her head now. "We're all very glad mocha didn't suit her."

EVE WENT STRAIGHT TO HER DESK, POINTED
TO a chair. "Sit. Let's get this down. Start with height,
weight, build."

"I thought you had that already." Trina glanced around. She'd been
in Eve's office before, but not in eyewitness capacity. "How come you
don't fix this place up, like the rest of the house?"

"It's not the rest of the house. Trina, concentrate."

"I just wondered why you'd want to work in the low rent section of
the Taj Mahal or whatever."

"I'm a sentimental fool. Height."

"Okay, ummm. On the short side. Under five-eight. More than five-
four. See, I was sitting at the counter at the bar, and he stood, and . . ."
She pursed her lips, used the flat of her hand to measure the air. "Yeah.
Like five-six or -seven? That's best guess."

"Weight."

"I don't know. When I do bodywork, people are naked. I don't
gauge when they've got clothes on. I'm going to say he was, like, solid,
but not the R-and-P type."

"R-and-P?"

"Roly and poly. He was . . ." She curved her hands over her stomach, rolled them up her chest. "Carrying it in the front, like some guys do. Not a waddler, but not Mr. Health and Fitness Club either. Poochy, like your uncle Carmine."

"If I had one. Okay. How about coloring?"

"He had this pewter brushback, thick on top and short on the sides. But that was the enhancer."

"Dark gray, short and thick."

"Dark gray's dull, you ask me. Pewter's got a soft gleam. But anyway, yeah. It was white when I saw him at the bar the other time. If it was him, which I pretty much think it was. Fluffy and white. Nice. Don't know why he'd go for pewter when he has the Snow Cap going."

"White hair. You're saying that wasn't a wig."

"It was a glimpse—a quick 'Oh, hey, I know that guy.' But yeah, at a glimpse it looked like his own topper. Not a hundred percent on that one."

"Eyes?"

"Jeez. Look, Dallas, I don't know for sure. I'm thinking light. On the light side, but I'm not sure if we're talking blue or green or gray, hazel. But I'm almost sure they weren't dark. You know, the hair enhancer looked off to me from the get, because it *was* dark, and the rest of him wasn't. He had really good skin."

"How so?"

"Pale, soft-looking. Some lines, sure, but not dug in. He takes care of his skin. No jowly stuff going on either, so he's maybe had a little work. He had a nice smooth texture to his skin."

"Pale," Eve mumbled. Pale hair, pale eyes, pale skin. A pale man. Maybe the Romanian psychic hadn't been completely full of shit.

"Yeah, yeah. He colored his eyebrows to match the enhancer. It was off, just a little. Mostly you wouldn't notice, but it's my business to notice. White in the bar when I was figuring to give this guy I was drinking with the ride of his life."

"You said he was a suit. Was that literal or just because he looked like a suit?"

"Both. He was wearing one—I think gray, like the hair and eyebrows. Probably. And he looked like the kind of guy who had a closetful of suits. Three-piece," she added. "Yeah, yeah, vest, pants, jacket. Little pocket accent and tie. Spiffed, you know? Same in the bar. Dark suit. Nice contrast with the white hair."

She paused, then rubbed the back of her neck. "It's just really hitting me. I'd've taken the gig. If he'd tagged me back, I'd've taken it. Personal day, a nice chunk of change. No harm."

Her breath trembled out as the color slid out of her cheeks. "He seemed so nice and . . . I want to say 'safe.' Some sweet older guy who wanted to do something special for his sick wife. I'd've charged him through the nose, but I'd have taken the job."

"You didn't take it," Eve reminded her. "And he made a mistake trying for you. You pay attention, you notice details and you remember. Listen to me."

She leaned forward because she could see it was, indeed, just hitting Trina. Not only had she lost color, she was beginning to shake a little. "Look at me and listen to what I'm telling you. He took someone today. Another one today. She's got some time before he starts on her. He takes time. Are you hearing me?"

"Yeah." Trina moistened her lips. "Yeah."

"He made a mistake with you," Eve repeated. "And what you're telling me, what you're going to do tomorrow with the police artist is going to help us get to him. You're going to help us save her life, Trina. Maybe more than hers. You get that?"

Trina nodded. "Can I get some water, maybe? I just went so dry."

"Sure. Hold on a minute."

As Eve went into the kitchen, Roarke stepped into the room. "You're doing fine," he said to Trina.

"Got the shakes," Trina admitted. "Whacked, really. Here I am in the Fortress of Roarke in the Chamber of Dallas. Can't get any safer than that. And I've got the shakes. Mavis?"

"She's contacting Leonardo. You'll all stay here tonight, if that suits you."

"Right down to the ground. Classy place like Bliss. You just don't expect crazy killers to come in for a manicure. You know?"

"This one likes to work with tidy nails," Eve commented as she came back with a chilled bottle of water. "I'm going to need that appointment book," she said to Roarke.

"I'll see to it. And," he told Trina, "I'll make sure you're covered for tomorrow. Don't worry about it."

"Thanks." She gulped down water. "Okay."

Eve waited while Trina drank. "Tell me about his voice."

"Um . . . Soft, I guess. Quiet. Um . . . Refined? I think that's the word. Like somebody educated, and who had the money behind him for a really good one. Kind of culture but not poofy. It was another thing that made him seem nice and safe, now that I think about it."

"Any accent?"

"Not really. I mean, educated, yeah. Not like an accent though."

"Distinguishing marks, tats, scars."

"Nope." Her voice was steadying, her color coming back. "Not showing."

"Okay." It was enough, Eve thought. If she pushed too hard now, it could diminish what Yancy could draw out of Trina the next day. "Anything else you remember, you let me know. I'm going to need the names of everyone who was working the day he came in, who was working the counter where you talked to him, who might have tried to sell him anything in the retail section. I can get most of that from Roarke. I want you to try to get a good night's sleep."

"Yeah, so do I. I think I'll go down and stick with Mavis and Belle for a little while, till I smooth it out a little more."

"Summerset will show you where you'll stay tonight. If you need anything," Roarke added, "just ask."

"Will do. This is so . . . complete." Trina shook her head as she rose. "I'm just going to . . ." She started out, stopped. "He smelled good."

"How?"

"Good product—and not smothered in it. Some people don't know how to be subtle with a product. It was like . . ." She squeezed her eyes shut again. "Just a hint of rosemary, undertones of vanilla. Nice." She shrugged, then continued out of the room.

"Major break."

"For you." Roarke walked over to sit on the corner of her desk. "And, I'd say, for Trina."

"Yeah, being a hair-color slut paid off big-time for her. I need to get this description out. I want to run it through IRCCA. I don't think we'll hit there. I don't think he's been in the system, but it's worth the shot. You need to work it with the results from the unregistered. See if you've got a competitor who fits the bill."

"All right."

"Skipped over Trina, went for York instead."

"Christ. Don't tell her that."

Eve arrowed a glare at him. "Give me some credit."

"Sorry. Of course. I'll take another look at the real estate, focusing below Fiftieth. Check in when I'm done."

"Good enough. Odds are shifting. Tide's turning."

"I believe you." He reached out, rubbed a thumb along the shadows under her eye. "Try not to drink too much coffee."

She decided that trying didn't mean she had to succeed. Besides, how much coffee was, in actuality, too much? She sent out the description, then keyed it into IRCCA.

She'd get countless hits with a description that general, and have to take a great deal of time to cull through them. But she couldn't leave out the step.

She began to run various probabilities. The suspect lived, worked, had ties to downtown Manhattan. The suspect frequented shops, restaurants, businesses in that sector in order to scout out targets. The suspect used various enhancements to alter his appearance during his meets with potential victims.

She ran a search of public and private parking lots and garages downtown, then began to contact owners, managers, attendants on duty.

She fought her way through a search of buildings—still standing or subsequently razed, that had housed bodies or had been used as clinics during the Urbans.

When it came through she read Newkirk's report on the first canvass of Greenfeld's apartment building.

Zip.

Still, she had to give Newkirk a nod for being thorough. She had names, addresses, and a detailed rundown of every conversation.

And thinking he may have come by it naturally, she flipped through her files and came up with Gil Newkirk's contact number.

He answered swiftly, on full alert, and with a blocked video that reminded her, abruptly, of the time.

"Officer Newkirk, Lieutenant Dallas. I apologize for disturbing you so late."

"No problem, Lieutenant. One minute."

She waited on blue-screen hold for thirty seconds less than that. Video popped on, and she saw a square-jawed, slightly grizzled version of the young cop she'd first met on scene. "What can I do for you?"

"I'm pursuing a new line, and should tell you beforehand that your son is a solid asset to the task force. You must be proud."

"Every day," he agreed. "Thank you, Lieutenant."

"I wonder if you can stretch your memory back, over your canvasses during the investigation nine years ago. I'm interested in a specific individual."

She related the description.

"Nine years ago."

"I know it's a stretch. He may be carrying some extra weight now, and we may be looking for darker hair. But I think the white may be consistent. He may have lived or worked or had a business in the area of one or more of the incidents."

"Talked to a lot of people back then, Lieutenant. And I wasn't pulled in until the second murder. But if you'll give me some time, I can look through my notes."

"Your notes are as concise and detailed as your son's reports?"

Gil grinned. "Taught him, didn't I?"

"Then I'd appreciate any time you can give me on this. I'll be at Central by oh-seven-hundred. You can reach me there, or any of my 'links, anytime. I'll give you my contact numbers."

He nodded. "Go ahead." When he had them down, he nodded again. "I've been going over some of my notes anyway. Captain Feeney and I have had some conversations about this."

"Yeah, I know. Feel free to contact him in lieu of me on this. Sorry to wake you."

"Been a cop thirty-three years. Used to it."

Another long shot, Eve thought when she ended transmission. But they were starting to pay off.

When Roarke walked in she had to struggle to focus. Her eyes wanted to give up. "Anything?"

"Nothing on the competitor search, nothing that fits cleanly."

"How about messily?"

"A handful of men who somewhat fit the description who are, in some way, involved in the upper echelons of competitors. No real hits. And a portion of those are out of the country, or off planet. When I take them through the other locations and times, none of them coordinates. I've gone down a few levels—supposing one of the lower-rung employees has a hard-on against me or my organization. I'm not finding anything there. And while I was running that, I realized that's chasing the wild goose."

"You gotta chase it to catch it."

"Eve, it's not my business. It's not even me that's the root. It's you."

She blinked twice. "I—"

"No, I can see it in your face." Temper whipped out in the words. "You're too damn tired to pull it off. This is no surprise to you. Goddamn it to bloody hell. You've had this in mind for some time now, and you've been fobbing me off with busywork."

"Whoa. Wait."

He simply strode over, lifted her right out of the chair. "You've no right. None. You knew or you believe that he's using me because I'm connected to you. You, who connect to him, his first spree, the first investigation."

"Ease off."

"I damn well won't."

His wrath, hot or cold, was dangerous at the best of times. Add emotional turmoil and brittle fatigue and it was deadly.

"You'd be a target. The biggest jewel in his bloody crown. You've had that in your head, and never said, never gave me the courtesy of telling me."

"Don't. I've had about enough of people telling me I didn't give them courtesy. This is a murder investigation and I left my etiquette disc at the office. Ease off!"

He just drew her up until she was on her toes. "If I hadn't been so guilty and distracted, thinking it was something I did, or was, or had that was causing him to take my people, I'd have come to this myself long before. You let me think it."

"I don't know if it's me or if it's you, but I did know—and boy are you proving it out—that if I told you this possibility, you'd go off."

"So you lied to me."

Her fury bloomed, so ripe and real at the accusation she had to fight, viciously, to stop herself from punching him. "I did not lie to you."

"By omission." He dropped her back on her feet. "I thought we trusted each other more than this."

"Fuck it. Just fuck it." She sat down, pressed her hands to her head. "Maybe I'm screwing up, right, left, back, forth. Feeney, you. I *do* trust you, and if I haven't shown you that by now with every goddamn thing I have, I don't know how else to do it."

"Mentioning this bloody business might've done the job."

"I needed to think it through. It never really occurred to me until Mira brought it up. And that was just today. I haven't had time to *think*, goddamn it. I haven't even run the probability yet."

"Run it now."

She dropped her hands, looked up at him. Her own temper had fizzled like a wet fuse, and all that was left were the soggy dregs.

"I can't take it. You've got to know, however spineless it is, I can't take it if you slap me back, too. I can't take it from both of you in one day. I wasn't trying to hurt either of you. I was just doing my job the best I know how. I wasn't keeping this from you, I just hadn't . . . assimilated it yet."

"Or figured out how to use it, if your assimilation indicated it had merit."

"Yes. If it has merit, I will use it. You know that if you know me."

"I know that, yes." He turned away, walked to her windows.

"There was a time I wouldn't have had anyone to consult on a decision. There was a time," she continued, "I wouldn't have considered it necessary to take anyone's thoughts or feelings into account in any decision I made. That's not true anymore. When I'd thought it through, when I'd come up with ideas or options, I would have told you. I wouldn't have moved forward without telling you."

True enough, he told himself as he mastered his own fury and fear. That was all true enough, for both of them. And small, hard comfort.

"Still, you'll move forward, if you believe you must, regardless of my thoughts and feelings."

"Yes."

He turned back. "I probably wouldn't love you so much it all but chokes me if you were otherwise."

She let out a breath. "I probably wouldn't love you, et cetera, et cetera, if you didn't understand I can't be otherwise."

"Well, then."

"I'm sorry. I know it's hard for you."

"You do." He crossed back. "Aye, you do, but you don't understand the whole of it. How could you? Why should you?" He touched her cheek. "I wouldn't have been so angry if it hadn't taken me so bloody long to realize it wasn't about me, but about you."

"Not everything's about you, ace."

He smiled, as she'd meant him to, but his eyes stayed intense. "We'll talk through, thoroughly, any plans you make to try to use this angle. To use yourself as bait."

"Yes. My word on that."

"All right, then. We need to go to bed. I'll have my way on that, Lieutenant. It's nearly two in the morning, and you'll want to be up around five, I'd guess."

"Yeah, okay. We'll catch some sleep."

She walked with him, but couldn't stop the ball he'd launched from bouncing around in her mind. "It was shuffling around in my head," she began. "The idea of me being a target. A lot of information and supposition was shuffling around in my head."

"As I've marched along with you on this one for the past two days and three nights, I have a good understanding of how much is crowded in your head on this."

"Yeah, but see—God, I'm becoming a woman even before the words come out of my mouth."

"Please, you must be stopped."

"I'm serious." Mildly embarrassed by it, she shoved her hands in her pockets. "The way women just nibble and gnaw at something, just can't let it alone. Any minute I'm going to start wondering which color lip dye works best with my complexion. Or my shoes."

He laughed, shook his head. "I think we're safe from that."

"If I ever start going that way, put me down. Okay?"

"My pleasure."

"But what I have to say, which is annoying, is that I don't even know if it's a viable angle. I'm not going to drop over to some guy's house to plan a party for him or teach him the samba."

"You often go to strangers' houses to interview them or take statements."

"Okay, yeah." She pushed at her hair as they entered the bedroom. "But I'm rarely solo, and I'm logged, and Jesus, Roarke, I'm a cop. It wouldn't be a snap for some old guy to get the drop on me."

"Which makes you quite the challenge. That would be an added appeal."

"And that's shuffling around, too. But—"

"He might have targeted you instead of Ariel Greenfeld. If you've been in his sights the last few days—weeks, come to that—it could've been you he took today."

"No, it couldn't." And this, she realized as she undressed, was why she was gnawing at this. He had to see, accept, and relax. "Think about it. I've barely had an hour alone in my own office since Friday night. Outside this house or Central, I've been with you or Peabody. Maybe you think he can get the drop on me, but is he going to get the drop on both of us, or on two cops?"

He stopped, studied her. The clenched fist in his gut relaxed fractionally. "You have a point. But you're considering changing that."

"Considering. If we go that route, and that's still a major *if*, I'll be wired, I'll be protected. I'll be armed."

"I want a homing beacon on your vehicle."

"There will be."

"No, I want one on before we leave the grounds in the morning. I'll see to it."

Give and take, she reminded herself. Even when—maybe especially when—give and take was a pain in the ass. "Okay. But there go my plans to slip off and meet Pablo the pool boy for an hour of hot, sticky sex."

"We all have to make sacrifices. Myself, I've had to reschedule my liaison with Vivien the French maid three times in the last couple of days."

"Blows," Eve said as they slipped into bed.

"She certainly does."

She snorted, jabbed her elbow back lightly as he drew her back against him. "Perv."

"There you go, stirring me up when we need our sleep." His fingers brushed lightly over her breast, trailed down her torso, teased, trailed lightly up again.

On a sigh, she laid her hand over his, encouraging the caress. This was better, she thought, this was the way to end a long, hard day. Body to body, sliding away in the dark.

When his lips found the nape of her neck, she stretched like a lazy cat. "Sleep's only one way to recharge."

"So it seems. Just as it seems I can't keep my hands off you."

She felt him harden against her, and heat. "Funny place for a hand. You ought to see a doctor about that. It could . . . Oh." She shuddered, seemed to shimmer when he slipped into her.

"There's a better place." Now his hand glided down, pressed against her as he pleasured them both with long, slow strokes.

She went soft, breath catching, body fluid as wine. His hands were free to touch, to take, to tease. Breasts, torso, belly, that glorious heat where they joined.

He could feel every quiver and quake that passed through her even as she surrounded him.

She breathed out his name as she rolled up and over, rolled through the climax. In the utter dark he knew all of her: body, heart, mind. Steeped in the moment, he murmured to her in the language of his shattered childhood. With her, he was complete.

So easy, so exquisite and simple, this merging, this melding. No empty spaces when he was with her, no haunting images of blood and death. Just peace, she knew only peace and pleasure. Those hands, so skilled, so patient. The whispers she knew were love dipped from a deep and turbulent well.

Here she could be pliant, here she could yield. So she rose up, and up, trembling as she clung, one moment, just one moment more to that breathless peak. Holding as she felt him climb with her, hold with her.

And so she slid down again, wrapped with him.

In the dark, she smiled, clutched his hand to bring it between her breasts. "*Buenas noches*, Pablo."

"*Bonne nuit*, Vivien."

She dropped, grinning, into sleep.

It was a shame. A true shame. But he could do nothing more with Gia. Nothing in his research of her had indicated she would have a mind so easily broken. Honestly, he felt as if they'd barely begun, and now he had to end it.

He'd risen early, hoping against hope that she'd revived sometime in the night. He'd given her dopamine, tried lorazepam—which weren't easy to come by, but he felt the trouble he'd gone to was necessary.

He'd tried electric shock, and that he could admit had been very interesting. But nothing—not music, not pain, not drugs, not the systemic jolts—had been able to reach in and find the lock to the door her mind had hidden behind.

After the truly rousing success with Sarifina, this was a crushing disappointment. But still, he reminded himself, it took two to make a partnership.

"I don't want you to blame yourself, Gia." He laid her arms in the channels that ran the length of the table so the blood would drain. "Perhaps I rushed things with you, approached the process poorly. After all, we each have our own unique tolerance for pain, for stress, for fear. Our minds and bodies are built to withstand only so much. Now, it's true," he continued as he made the first cut on her wrist, "that training, exercise, diet, education can and do increase those levels. But I want you to know I understand you did your very best."

When he'd opened the veins on her right wrist, he walked around the table, took her left. "I've enjoyed our time together, even though it was brief. It's simply your time, that's all. As my grandfather taught me, every living thing is merely a clock that begins winding down with the very first breath. It's how we use that time that counts, isn't it?"

When he was done, he moved away to wash and sterilize the scalpel, to scrub the blood off his hands. He dried them thoroughly under the warm air of his blower.

"Well now," he said cheerfully, "we'll have some music. I often play 'Celeste Aida' for my girls when it's time for them to go. It's exquisite. I know you'll enjoy it."

He ordered the aria and, as the music filled the room, sat, eyes dreamy, his memory stretching back decades, to her.

And watched the last moments of Gia Rossi's life drain away.

13 EVE SHUFFLED INTO THE SHOWER AS ROARKE was drying off from his. Her voice was rusty when she ordered the jets on, and her eyes felt as if someone had coated a thin adhesive inside her lids during the night.

The hot blast helped, but she knew it was going to take considerably more to get all engines firing. She considered the departmentally approved energy pill, then opted to hold that in reserve. It would boost her, no question, and it would leave her feeling overwired and jumpy all day.

She'd stick with caffeine. Lots and lots of caffeine.

When she came out, Roarke was wearing trousers. Just trousers, she noted—all bare-chested, bare-footed, with all that gorgeous black hair still a little damp from the shower.

There were other things that gave the system a good jolt, and he was certainly top of her personal list.

And when he crossed to her, offering a mug of black coffee, her love knew no bounds.

The sound she made was as much in appreciation of him as that first life-giving gulp.

"Thanks."

"Food's next. We didn't quite make it through dinner, and you're not going through the day on coffee and attitude."

"I like my attitude." But she went to the closet, pulled out what looked warm and comfortable. "How come you can look sexy and rested after a couple hours' sleep, and I feel like my brain's been used for Arena Ball practice?"

"Enormous strength of will and lucky metabolism." He selected a shirt, slipped it on, but didn't bother to button it. He studied her as she pulled on stone gray trousers. "I could order up an energy drink."

"No. They always have a crappy aftertaste and make me feel like my eyes are crossing and uncrossing. Weirds me." She pulled on a long-sleeved white tee, dragged a black sweater over it. "I'm just going to—"

She stopped, frowned at the knock on the bedroom door. "Who else in their right mind would be up at this hour?"

"Let's find out." Roarke walked to the door, and opened it to Mavis and Belle.

"I saw the light under the door."

"Is something wrong with the baby?" Roarke asked. "Is she sick?"

"Bella? No, she's trip T's—Totally Tip-Top. Just needed her morning change and snuggle. But I peeked out, saw the light. Okay if we come in a minute?"

"Of course. I was just about to deal with breakfast. Would you like something?"

"No, just too early for me to fuel up. Well, maybe some juice. Papaya maybe?"

"Have a seat."

"Everything okay?" Eve asked her.

"Yeah, well, you know. When Belle sent out the morning call, I just didn't want to cuddle in. Restless."

Mavis stood, in red-and-white–striped pajamas Summerset must have unearthed from somewhere. They were too big for her, and way too conservative.

They made her look, to Eve's eyes, tiny and fragile.

"Everything's fine, going to be fine. You've got nothing to worry about."

"I guess I just wanted to see if you were okay, and if there was something I could do."

"It's under control." Since Mavis was standing, swaying gently side to side in a way that was making Eve vaguely seasick, Eve gestured to a chair in the sitting area. "Sit down."

"I was thinking Trina and I could look over the appointment books, and maybe we could try to find the hair enhancement." Mavis shrugged. "And Trina was telling me she thinks the guy was using one of a couple of product lines—face and body creams and lotions. I could maybe track down where they're available, and—I don't know. Maybe it would help."

"Maybe it would."

Roarke set down a tall glass of juice, some fresh fruit, and a basket of muffins. Mavis glanced at them, then up at Roarke. "If I wasn't gone squared over my huggie bear, I'd fight Dallas for you."

"I'd squash you like a bug," Eve told her.

"Yeah, but you'd limp awhile after. Would it be all right if we stayed here—Belle and me—until . . . Leonardo's going to be back this afternoon. I thought—"

"You can stay as long as you like," Roarke told her as he brought over two plates from the AutoChef.

"Thanks. He's just worried. He started thinking what if Belle and I had been with Trina, and this guy had made a move on her. I know it's fetched, but you have a kid and you start winding through the crazed meadow."

"All meadows are crazed," Eve commented. "You and Belle relax and hang."

On cue, Belle began to fuss and whimper. Mavis shifted, smoothly unbuttoning the pajama top. "I thought maybe if Trina was finished before—"

"Sure, sure." Instinctively Eve averted her eyes, grabbed her coffee. "I'll have her brought back here when she's done. No problem."

"Mag. Big relief. So—"

"Oh, well then." Roarke pushed to his feet as Mavis's breast popped out and Belle's eager mouth popped on. "I'll just . . ." Go anywhere else.

His reaction had Mavis's face clearing, and her laughter bubbling. "She wants her breakfast, too. Mostly everyone's seen my boobies before."

"And, as I believe I've said, they're absolutely charming. I wonder if I shouldn't—"

"No, sit." Giggling now, Mavis picked up the juice, rose, easily balancing the glass and the baby at her breast. "You'll get used to it before long, but right now, we'll go on back. Usually we both want a little nap after breakfast. If I find anything on the hair enhancement, the products, I'll tag you."

"Do that."

When they were alone again, Roarke stared down at his plate. "Why do you suppose I chose this morning to want my eggs sunny-side up?"

"They do look like a pair of nice, shiny yellow breasts." Grinning, Eve plucked up a piece of bacon. "And Mavis has been known to paint hers yellow on occasion."

"Every time she feeds the baby, I feel so . . . rude."

"I thought it was freaked."

"A bit of that, but more intrusive. It seems so intimate."

"I'd say we're both going to have to get over it. We've got to get moving. Eat your boobies."

They separated at Central, Eve leading Trina through to where Yancy would work on the composite.

"You know, if cops put more thought and creativity into fashion and grooming, it might improve public relations."

Eve hopped on an up glide and watched a trio she recognized from Illegals troop onto a down. Stubbled faces, scarred shoes, and a sag at the side of each jacket where the sidearm rested.

They looked fine to her.

"Yeah, we're putting together a seminar on that. Defensive Fashion."

"That's not out there," Trina insisted. "Clothes can be like a defense, or an offense—"

"Tell me."

"Or a statement or a reflection. Yours say you're not only in charge but more than willing to kick ass."

"My pants say I'm in charge?" Eve didn't need Mira's various degrees to recognize babbling nerves.

"The whole deal. Dark colors, but not somber. Good fabrics, clean lines. Could power things up now and again, strong reds or greens, sharp blues."

"I'll keep that in mind."

"You should wear sunshades."

"I lose them."

"Well, stop. What are you, twelve? Sunshades would totally complete the package. Is this going to take long? Do you think this is going to take long? What if I can't do it? What if I get it wrong? What if—"

"Stop. What are you, twelve?" At Trina's nervous laugh, Eve stepped off the glide. "It takes as long as it takes. You need to stop, you stop. Yancy's the best I've got, best I've worked with. And if you get it wrong we'll just toss you in a cage for a few hours, until you get it right."

"You're rocking on this."

"Some." She pushed through doors.

Yancy was already there, setting up at his workstation. He rose, shot out his quick, easy smile. "Lieutenant."

"Detective. Appreciate you coming in early for this."

"No big. Trina?" He offered a hand. "How you doing?"

"A little tipped, I guess. I never did this before."

"Just relax. I'll steer you through it. How about something to drink? Something cold?"

"Uh, maybe. Maybe like a lemon fizz? Diet."

"I'll get that for you. Just have a seat."

Trina watched him walk out. "Whoa, daddy. He's a yummy one."

"You're not here to nibble on him."

"He's got to go off-duty sometime." Trina craned her neck to get a better view of Yancy's ass before he rounded the corner. "Did you ever bump with that?"

"No. Jesus, Trina."

"Bet that was your loss. Build like that, I bet he can hammer it all night."

"Thank you. Thanks so much for putting that into my head. It'll certainly enhance my working relationship with Detective Yancy."

"I'd like to enhance his working relationship." Trina blew out a breath. "Hey, thinking about sex makes me feel not so nervous. Good to know. Plus, it won't be a hardship to work with Detective Hot Ass."

"Don't screw around." Eve raked a hand through her hair as Yancy came back with Trina's drink and one for himself. "You know how to reach me," she told him.

"Yep. Trina and I . . ." He sent Trina a wink. "We'll get this guy's face for you. So, Trina, how long have you been in the business of beauty?"

Eve knew that was the way he worked, getting the witness to relax, talking small, easing them in. She fought back the need to tell him to push it, and simply stepped back. Walked away.

She had enough time to get to her office, organize the data—and her own thoughts—for the briefing. Pull in Peabody, Eve mused, as she aimed for Homicide. Get said data set up.

Do the briefing, then move out for the stupid, annoying morning media briefing. She needed to run the probabilities on herself as a target, work in some time during the day to discuss that with Mira. But she needed to get out in the field, needed to be out on the streets.

If this bastard was watching her, she might spot the tag.

She beelined for her office, then pulled up short when she saw Feeney sitting in her visitor's chair, brooding over a mug of her coffee.

He got to his feet. Worse for wear, she thought. That's how he looked, a hell of a lot worse for wear. Her back went up even as her stomach churned.

His eyes, baggy and shadowed, stayed on hers. "Got a minute?"

"Yeah." She stepped in, closed the door. And for once wished her office was bigger. There wasn't enough room for them to maneuver around each other, she thought, or to give each other enough space for whatever was coming.

Then it popped out of her, simply popped out without thought or plan. "I want to apologize for—"

"Stop." He tossed it out so quickly her head nearly snapped back as from a blow. "Just stop right there. Bad enough, this is bad enough without that. I was off. Out of line. You're primary of this investigation, and you're heading up this task force. I was off, questioning you and your authority. And I was out of line with what I said to you. So." He paused, took a good slug of coffee. "That's it."

"That's it," she repeated. "That's how it's going to be?"

"It's your call on how it's going to be. You want me off the team, you got cause. You got my notes, and I'll get you a replacement."

At that moment she wished he had popped her one instead of handed her these hurtful insults. "Why would you say that to me? Why would you think I'd want you off?"

"In your shoes, I'd think about it. Seriously."

"Bullshit. That's bullshit." She didn't kick her desk. Instead she kicked the desk chair, sending it careening into the visitor's chair, then bouncing off to slam against the wall. "And you're not in my shoes. Stupid son of a bitch."

His droopy eyes went huge. "What did you say to me?"

"You heard me. You're too tight-assed, too stubborn, too *stupid* to put your hurt feelings aside and do the job with me, you're going to have to get the fuck over it. I can't afford to lose a key member at this stage of the investigation. You know that. You *know* that, so don't come in here and tell me I've got cause to boot you."

"You're the one who's going to get a boot, right straight up your ass."

"You couldn't take me ten years ago," she shot back, "you sure as hell can't take me now."

"Want to test that out, kid?"

"You want a round, you got one. When this case is closed. And if you're still carrying that stick up your ass, I'll yank it out and knock you cold with it. What the hell's wrong with you?"

Her voice broke, just a little, making them both miserable. "You come in here, stiff and snarly, and won't even let me apologize. You start spouting off, won't even let me apologize for fucking up."

"You didn't, goddamn it. *I* fucked up."

"Great. Fine. We're a couple of fuckups."

He sank down in the chair as if the wind had gone out of him. "Maybe we are, but I got more years at it than you."

"Now you want to pull rank on fuckup status? Great. Fine," she repeated. "You get the salute. Feel better?"

"No, I don't feel any goddamn better." He let out a tired sigh that smothered the leading edge of her temper.

"What do you want, Feeney? What do you want me to say?"

"I want you to listen. I let it eat at me. This one got away from me and I let it eat at me. Taught you, didn't I, that you can't get them all, and you can't beat yourself up when you can't put the pieces together, not when you gave it your best."

"Yeah, you taught me."

"Didn't listen to myself this time. And that bile just kept rising up out of my belly into my throat over it." His lips tightened as he shook his head. "You find a fresh angle, and instead of jumping on that, grabbing hold and pushing on that, I jump on you. Part of me's thinking, 'Did I miss that? Did I miss that before, and did all those women die hard because I did?' "

"You know better than that, Feeney. And yeah, I get knowing better isn't always enough. How good was I nine years ago?"

"Needed seasoning."

"That wasn't the question. How good was I?"

He drank again, then looked up at her. "You were the best I ever worked with, even then."

"And I worked that case with you, minute by minute, step by step. We didn't miss it, Feeney. It wasn't *there*. The evidence, the statements, the pattern. If he got them that way, or some of them that way, the evidence wasn't there to show us."

"I spent a lot of time yesterday going over the files. I know what you're saying. What I'm saying is that's the reason I jumped on you."

He thought of what his wife had said the night before. That he'd railed at Dallas because she was his family. That she'd let him rail because he was her family. Nobody, according to his Sheila, beat each other up as regularly or as thoughtlessly as family.

"Didn't like you telling me I needed a break either," he muttered. "Basically telling me I needed a damn nap, like somebody's grandfather."

"You are somebody's grandfather."

His eyes flashed at her, but there was some amusement in the heat. "Watch your step, kid."

"I should've run the new angle by you before the briefing. No, I should have," she insisted when he shook his head. "Like you should've known I would have if everything hadn't been moving so fast. There's nobody on the job, nobody with a badge I respect more than you."

It took him a moment to clear his throat. "Same goes. I got one more thing, then this is closed." He rose again. "I didn't put you here. You never were a rookie," he told her in a voice roughened with emotion. "So I saw good, solid cop the minute I laid eyes on you. I gave you a hell of a foundation, kid, a lot of seasoning and pushed you hard because I knew you could take it. But I didn't put you here, and saying that, well, that was stupid. You put yourself here. And I'm proud. So that's it."

She only nodded. Neither of them would handle it well if she blubbered.

As he went out, he gave her two awkward pats on the shoulder, then closed the door behind him.

She had to stand where she was a minute until she was sure she had herself under control. After a few steadying breaths she turned, started to sit at her desk. Someone knocked on the door.

"What?" She wanted to snarl, then did just that when Nadine poked a head in. "Media conference at nine."

"I know. Are you okay?"

"Peachy. Go away."

Nadine just sidled in, shut the door at her back. "I came by a little while ago, and . . . well, let's say overheard a few choice words in raised voices. The reporter in me fought with the reasonably well-mannered individual. It was a pitched battle, and did take a couple of minutes. Then I wandered off until I thought the coast was clear. So again, are you okay?"

"That was a private conversation."

"You shouldn't have private conversations in public facilities at the top of your lungs."

Point well taken, Eve was forced to admit. "I'm fine. We're fine. Just something we had to work out."

"It made me think it might be interesting to do a segment on tension in the workplace, and how cops handle it."

"You're going to want to leave this one alone."

"This particular one, yes. Price of friendship."

"If that's all—"

"It's not. I know you didn't think much of the Romanian psychic, but—"

"Actually, there may have been a nugget there. Got another?"

"Really? I expect to be fully filled in on that. And, yes, I may just." In her slim-skirted suit the color of raspberry jam, Nadine managed to ease a hip down on the corner of Eve's desk.

"Bolivia," she began. "We've been digging through the tabloids. You'd be surprised what nuggets can be found there that you cops disdain."

"Yeah, those alien babies are a menace to society."

"A classic for a reason. But we found an interesting story about the Moor of Venice."

"Last time I checked, Venice was in Italy."

"No, Othello—Shakespeare? And Verdi. Othello was this black dude, important guy, married to a gorgeous white women—mixed race marriages were not common back then in . . . whenever the hell it was."

"Nine years ago?"

"No." Nadine laughed. "More like centuries. Anyway, Othello ends up being manipulated by this other guy into believing his wife's been cheating on him. Othello strangles her. And ends up in song and story."

"I'm not following this, Nadine."

"Just giving you some background. There was a big costume ball at the opera house in—"

"Opera?"

"Yeah." Nadine's eyes narrowed. "That means something."

"Just keep going."

"A woman in La Paz claimed she was attacked by a guy dressed like Othello. Black mask, cape, gloves. Claimed he tried to drag her off, tried to rape her. Since she didn't have a mark on her, and witnesses stated that she was seen chatting amiably with a guy in that costume earlier in the evening, and she was skunk drunk when she started shrieking, her claims were dismissed by the police. But the tabs played it up. She was thirty-one, brunette, and the alleged incident occurred between the discovery of the second and third bodies. Had The Groom tried to claim another bride? Was the Moor of Venice seeking Desdemona? She played it up, too."

Nadine shifted on the desk. "Or maybe she was giving some of it straight. She claimed he spoke exceptional Spanish, but with an American accent, was knowledgeable about music and literature, and was well-traveled. Now, with a little more research we learned she was a party girl—and that several were peppered through the guests to . . . entertain."

"An LC?" Eve pursed her lips thoughtfully. "He hasn't targeted any pros. Doesn't fit his profile."

"The party girls at functions like this don't advertise. They're frosting."

"Okay, so it's possible he didn't make her as a pro."

"Exactly, and you can read between the lines and assume she smelled money and played it up with this guy. He suggested they go out for some air, which they did. Then that they go for a drive—which she couldn't do or lose her event fee. In any case, she said she started feeling off—dizzy, woozy. She also claimed she hadn't been drinking, which, of course, she had. But I'm betting she knew her limit when she was working, and they mistook drugged for skunk drunk."

"Could be." Eve nodded. "Yeah, that could be."

"When she realized he was leading her away from the opera house, she resisted. Here's where I think she embellished or there would have been marks, tears, something. Figure when she started to struggle, to scream, he cut his losses. She tears back to the party. He slides off."

"You gotta have more than that."

"Yeah, I do. The third victim was a waitress, worked for the caterer who did this party. She worked the party. And a week later, she's dead. So—"

"He cherry-picks potentials at the event," Eve concluded. "Weeds it down to two. The first doesn't work out for him. So he goes for the second. Where was she last seen?" Eve turned to boot up the file.

"Leaving her apartment four days before her body was found. She'd been scheduled to work that evening, called in sick. She wasn't reported missing for two days because—"

"She's the one who took an overnight bag, clothes. Good clothes."

"Good memory. Yeah. It was assumed she'd gone off with some guy. Which, I guess she did. First woman said Othello had a voice like silk—soft and smooth. Wore heeled boots and a high headdress—compensating."

"Short guy, we got that."

Nadine's brows lifted. "Oh, do you?"

"You'll get everything when you get it. Anything else?"

"She said he talked about music—opera particularly—like it was a god. She said a lot of bullshit, actually. His eyes were burning red, his hands like steel as they closed around her throat. Blah, blah. But there was one more interesting thing that sounded true. She said she asked about his work, and he said he studied life and death. In a twisted way, that could be what he's doing, or thinks he's doing."

"Okay. That's okay."

"Worth any inside info?"

"I leak anything at this point, it's my ass. Don't bother with the media briefing. Send a drone. When I'm clear, you'll get it all."

"Off the record. Are you close?"

"Off the record. I'm getting closer."

Since the two conversations had eaten away her prep time, Eve just gathered everything up. She'd organize on the fly. Lining it up in her head, she headed out, reminding herself there was now—courtesy of Roarke—decent coffee in the conference room.

She glanced over at raised voices, saw one of her detectives and a couple of uniforms dwarfed by a man about the size of the vending machine they'd gathered in front of.

"I want to see my brother!" the giant shouted. "Now!"

Carmichael, generally unflappable in Eve's estimation, kept her voice low and soothing. "Now, Billy, we explained that your brother's giving a statement. As soon as he's done—"

"You've got him in a cage! You're beating him up!"

"No, Billy. Jerry's helping us. We're trying to find the bad man who hurt his boss. Remember how somebody hurt Mr. Kolbecki?"

"They killed him dead. Now you're going to kill Jerry. Where's Jerry?"

"Let's go sit over—"

Billy screamed his brother's name loudly enough that cops stopped, turned, slipped out of doorways.

Eve changed direction, headed toward the trouble. "Problem here?"

"Lieutenant." The unflappable Carmichael sent Eve a look of utter frustration. "Billy's upset. Somebody killed the nice man he and his brother work for. We're talking to Billy's brother now. We're just going to get Billy a nice drink before we talk to him, too. Mr. Kolbecki was your boss, too, right, Billy? You liked Mr. Kolbecki."

"I sweep the floors and wash the windows. I can have a soda when I'm thirsty."

"Yeah, Mr. Kolbecki let you have sodas. This is Lieutenant Dallas. She's my boss. So now I have to do my job, and we're all going to sit down and—"

"You'd better not hurt my brother." Going for the top of the authority ladder, Billy plucked Eve right off her feet, shook her like a rag doll. "You'll be sorry if you hurt Jerry."

Cops grabbed for stunners. Shouts rang in Eve's ears as her bones knocked together. She judged her mark, estimated the ratio of his face and her fist. Then spared her knuckles and kicked him solidly in the balls.

She was airborne. She had a split second to think: *Oh, shit.*

She landed hard on her ass, skidded, then her head rapped hard enough against a vending machine to have a few stars dancing in front of her eyes.

Warning! Warning! the machine announced.

As Eve reached for her weapon, someone took her arm. Roarke managed to block the fist aimed at his face before it landed. "Easy," he soothed. "He's down. And how are you?"

"He rang my bell. Damn it." She reached around, rubbed the back of her head as she glared at the huge man now sitting on the floor, holding his crotch and sobbing. "Carmichael!"

"Sir." Carmichael clipped over, leaving the uniforms to restrain Billy. "Lieutenant. Jesus, Dallas, I'm sorry about that. You okay?"

"What the fuck?"

"Vic was found by this guy and his brother this morning when they reported for work. Vic owned a little market on Washington. It appears the vic was attacked before closing last night, robbed and beaten to death. We brought the brothers in for questioning—we're looking for the night guy. We don't believe, at this time, the brothers here were involved, but that they may have pertinent information regarding the whereabouts of the night clerk."

Carmichael blew out a breath. "This guy, Billy? He was fine coming in. Crying a little about the dead guy. He's, you know, a little slow. The brother, Jerry, told him it was okay, to go on with us to get a drink, to talk to us. But he got worked up once we separated them. Man, Dallas, I never thought he'd go for you. You need an MT?"

"No, I don't need a damn MT." Eve shoved to her feet. "Take him into Observation. Let him see his brother's not being beaten with our vast supply of rubber hoses and saps."

"Yes, sir. Ah, you want us to slap Billy with assaulting an officer?"

"No. Forget it." Eve walked over, crouched down in front of the sobbing man. "Hey, Billy. Look at me. You're going to go see Jerry now."

He sniffled, swiped at his runny nose with the back of his hand. "Now?"

"Yeah."

"There was blood all over, and Mr. Kolbecki wouldn't wake up. It made Jerry cry, and he said I couldn't look, and couldn't touch. Then they took Jerry away. He takes care of me, and I take care of him. You can't take Jerry away. If somebody hurts him like Mr. Kolbecki—"

"Nobody's going to do that. What kind of soda does Jerry like best?"

"He likes cream soda. Mr. Kolbecki lets us have cream sodas."

"Why don't you get one for Jerry out of the machine? This officer will take it to him, and you can watch through the window, see Jerry talking to the detective. Then you can talk to the detective."

"I'm going to see Jerry now?"

"Yeah."

"Okay." He smiled, sweet as a baby. "My nuts sure are sore."

"I bet."

She straightened, stepped back. Roarke had retrieved her disc bag, and the discs that had gone flying as she had. He held it out now. "You're late for your briefing, Lieutenant."

She snatched the bag, suppressed a smirk. "Bite me."

14

IT WAS FASCINATING, ROARKE THOUGHT, IN SO many ways to watch her work.

He'd wandered out of the conference room when he'd heard the commotion, in time to see the erupting mountain of a man lift her a foot off the ground. His instinct had been, naturally, to rush forward, to protect his wife. And he'd been quick.

She'd been quicker.

He'd actually seen her calculate in those bare seconds her head had been snapping back and forth on her neck. Punch, gouge, or kick, he remembered. Just as he'd seen more irritation than shock on her face when she'd gone flying.

Took a hell of a knock, he thought now, but temper had been riper than pain. He'd seen that, too. Just as he'd seen her compassion for the distress and confusion of a scared little boy inside a man's body.

And here she was, moments later, taking charge of the room, putting all that behind her.

It was hardly a wonder that it had been her, essentially from the first minute he'd seen her. That it would be her until his last breath. And very likely well beyond that.

She hadn't worn her jacket for the briefing, he noted. She looked lean and not a little dangerous with her weapon strapped over her sweater. He'd seen her drape the diamond he'd once given her over her neck before she'd put on the sweater that morning.

The priceless Giant's Tear and the police-issue. That combination, he thought, said something about their merging lives.

As he listened to her brisk update, he toyed with the gray button— her button—he always carried in his pocket.

"I expect to have a face within the next couple of hours," she continued. "Until that time, these are the lines we pursue. Urban Wars connection. Captain Feeney?"

"Slow going there," he said, "due to the lack of records. The Home Force did have documented billets and clinics in the city, and I'm working with those. But there were any number of unofficial locations used, and used temporarily. More that were destroyed or subsequently razed. I've interviewed and am set to interview individuals who were involved militarily, paramilitarily, or as civilians. I'm going to focus on body disposal."

"Do you need more men?"

"I've got a couple I can put on it."

"Do that. Knocking on doors. Newkirk, you and your team will recanvass this sector." She turned, aiming her laser pointer to highlight a five-block area around the bakery where Ariel Greenfeld worked. "Every apartment, every business, every street LC, sidewalk sleeper, and panhandler. Somebody saw Greenfeld Sunday afternoon. Make them remember. Baxter, you and Trueheart take this sector around Greenfeld's residence. He watched her. From the street, from another building, from a vehicle. In order to familiarize himself with her routine, he staked her out more than once. Jenkinson and Powell, recanvass the area of York's and Rossi's residences. Peabody and I will take the gym and the club."

She paused, and Roarke could see her going through her mental checklist. "The real estate angle. Roarke."

"There are a significant number of private residences," he began, "and businesses with residences on site that have been owned and operated by the same individual or individuals for the time frame. Even reducing this search area to below Fiftieth in Manhattan, the number is considerable. I believe, if I cross with Feeney, do a search for private buildings that were in existence during the Urbans, whether as residences or otherwise, we'll cut that down."

"Good." She thought a moment. "That's good. Do that. Connecting cases. McNab."

"It's been like trying to pick the right flea off a gorilla."

"My line," Callendar muttered beside him, and he grinned.

"Her line, but I think we may have a good possible. First vic in Florida, housekeeper at a swank resort, last seen after leaving the Sunshine Casino at approximately oh-one-hundred. She habitually spent a few hours on her night off playing the poker slots. Going on the theory that her killer had made earlier contact, may have been known by her, I did a run on the resort's register for the thirty days prior to her death. Investigators at that time took a pass through it after the second body was discovered, but as it appeared the vic had been grabbed outside the casino, focused their efforts there. But a copy of the register was in the case file. Tits here and I went though it."

"And you got lucky," Callendar mumbled.

"And I'm so good," McNab said smoothly, "that I hit on a guest registered three weeks before the vic was snatched, with a four-day stay. Name of Cicero Edwards. Resort requires an address, to which Edwards listed one in London. I ran the name with said address and came up with zip. No Edwards, Cicero, at that address at that time. And better, the address was bogus. It's the address for—"

"An opera house," Eve said and had McNab's pretty face moving into a pout.

"Wind, sails, sucked out," he commented. "The Royal Opera House, to be exact. Leading your crack e-team to deduce this was our guy, and that our guy has a thing for fat women singing in really high voices."

"I have information that may add further weight to that." She encapsulated Nadine's information. "Good work." She nodded at McNab and Callendar. "Find more. Roarke, see if you can dig up any buildings that were used as opera houses or theaters that held operas during the Urbans. And—"

"He'll have season tickets," Roarke said. "If he's a serious buff, and is able to afford the luxury, he'd indulge it. Box seats, most likely. Here at the Met, very likely at the Royal and other opera houses of repute."

"We can work that," she replied. "Dig, cross-check. He likes to vary his name. Punch on any variation of Edward." She glanced at her wrist unit, cursed. "I'm late for the damn media. Get started."

She turned, studied the name she'd added to the white board. Ariel Greenfeld.

"Let's find her," she said, and went out.

She got through the media without actually grinding her teeth down to nubs. She considered that progress. Whitney was waiting for her outside the briefing room.

"I'd hoped to make it to your morning briefing," he told her. "I was detained."

"We do have some new leads since my report. Sir, I'd like to check on Detective Yancy's progress with the witness if I could update you on the way."

He nodded, fell into step beside her.

"An opera lover," he said when she'd brought him up to speed. "My wife enjoys the opera."

"Yes, sir."

He smiled a little. "I actually enjoy some opera myself. He may have gotten too clever with his fake addresses, using opera houses."

"Houses may be one of the keys, Commander. I don't know much about opera, but I take it they deal with death a lot of the time. The psychic in Romania talked about his house of death. Psychics are often cryptic or their visions symbolic."

"And we should consider he might have, or have had, some more direct connection with opera. A performer, or backer, a crew member, musician."

"It's a possibility."

"*Phantom of the Opera*. A story about a disfigured man who haunts an opera house, and kills," Whitney explained. "His killing place may be a former opera house or theater."

"We're pursuing that. There are other areas we may pursue. I'd like to discuss them with you and Mira at some point, if those areas seem relevant."

"We'll work around you."

He went with her to Yancy's division. Eve wondered if he registered the fact that wherever he passed, cops came to attention . . . or if it was something he no longer noticed.

Eve saw first that Yancy was alone at his workstation, and second that his eyes were closed, and he was wearing a headset. Though she'd have preferred the commander had been elsewhere when she was forced to berate a detective, it didn't stop her from giving Yancy's desk chair a good, solid kick.

He jerked up. "Hey, watch where you're—Lieutenant." Annoyance cleared when he saw Eve, then shifted over into something closer to anxiety when he spotted Whitney. "Commander."

He came out of the chair.

"Where the hell is my witness?" Eve demanded. "And just how often do you take a little nap on the department's time?"

"I wasn't napping. Sir. It's a ten-minute meditation program," he explained as he pulled off the headset. "Trina needed a break, so I suggested she go down to the Eatery or take a short walk around. At this point in the work, it's easy to stop guiding and start directing. Meditating for a few minutes clears my head."

"Your methods generally produce results," Whitney commented. "But in this case, ten minutes is an indulgence we can't afford."

"Understood, sir, but, respectfully, I know when a wit needs a breather. She's good." Yancy glanced at Dallas. "She's really good. She knows faces because it's her business to evaluate them. She's already given me more than most wits manage, and in my opinion, after this break she's going to nail it solid. Take a look."

He'd used both a sketch pad and the computer. Eve stepped around to get a closer look at both. "That's good," she agreed.

"It'll be better. She keeps changing the eyes and the mouth, and that's because she's second- and third-guessing. She can't pull out the eye color, but the shape? The shape of the eyes, the face, even the way the ears lie, she doesn't deviate."

The face was rounded, the ears lying neatly, and on the small side. The eyes were slightly hooded and held a pleasant expression. The mouth, a little thin on top, was curved in a hint of a smile. Short-necked, Eve noted, so that the head sat low on the shoulders.

All in all, it struck her as a bland, nondescript kind of face. The sort that would be easily overlooked. "Nothing stands out about him," she commented. "Except his absolute ordinariness."

"Exactly. And that makes it harder for the wit. Harder to remember details about somebody who doesn't really have anything about him that catches the eye. She was more into how he dressed, how he spoke, how he smelled, that sort of thing. They made the impression. Took her a while to start building the face beyond that. But she's good."

"So are you," Eve complimented. "Give me a copy of this for now. Get me the finished when you have it."

"Some of these details are going to change." Still, Yancy ordered a print. "I think the nose is going to be shorter, and—" He held up a hand as if signaling himself to stop. "And that's why we needed a break from each other. I'm projecting."

"This gives us a base. When you're done with Trina, I'd like you to arrange for her to be taken back to my residence. She's expected."

"Will do."

"Nice work, Detective."

"Thank you, Commander."

As they left, Whitney glanced at Eve. "Check with him in an hour. If there isn't any change, we'll release this image. We need it made public as soon as possible."

"Yes, sir."

"Contact me when you want to meet with me and Dr. Mira," he added, then peeled off to go his own way.

Eve didn't care how cold it was, it was good to be back on the street. She'd had enough, for the time being, of desk work and comp work and briefings. It was true enough she needed some thinking time, just her and her murder board, but right now, she needed to move.

"It's hard to believe we've only been on this since Friday night." Peabody hunched her shoulders as they walked to BodyWorks. "It feels like we've been working this one for a month."

"Time's relative." Ariel Greenfeld, Eve thought, missing for approximately eighteen hours.

"McNab humped on this until nearly three this morning. I fizzled just past midnight, but he was revved. Something about e-juice, I guess. Of course, when he's really humping the comp, he doesn't have any left to, you know, hump yours truly. This is the longest we've gone since cohabbing not using the bed—or some other surface—for recreational purposes."

"One day," Eve said as she cast her eyes to heaven, "one fine day you'll be able to go a full week without inserting an image of you and McNab having sex into my head."

"Well, see, that's what I'm worried about." They passed into the lobby of the center, flashed badges on the way to the elevator. "You think maybe the bloom's wearing off? That we're losing the spark? It's actually been since Wednesday night that we—"

"Go no further with that sentence." Eve ordered the elevator to take them to the main gym. "You can't go, what, four days without worrying about blooms and sparks?"

"I don't know. I guess. Well, no," Peabody decided, "because four days is basically a work week if you're not a cop. If you and Roarke went a week, wouldn't you wonder?"

Eve wasn't sure this had ever been an issue. She only shook her head and stepped off the elevator.

"So you and Roarke haven't gotten snuggly since we caught this?"

Eve stopped, turned. Stared. "Detective Peabody, are you actually standing there asking me if I've had sex in the last few days?"

"Well. Yes."

"Pull yourself together, Peabody."

"You *have!*" Peabody trotted after Eve. "I knew it. I *knew* it! You're practically working around the clock, and you still get laid. And we're younger. I mean, not that you're old," Peabody said quickly when Eve shifted very cool eyes in her direction. "You're young and fit, the picture of youth and vitality. I'm just going to stop talking now."

"That would be best." Eve went straight to the manager's office.

Pi got up from his desk. "You have news."

"We're pursuing a number of leads. We'd like to talk to the staff again, and make inquiries among some of your members."

"Whatever you need."

Though Yancy had a little time left on his clock, Eve drew out the sketch. "Take a look at this, tell me if you know this man, or have seen him."

Pi took the sketch, studied it carefully. "He doesn't look familiar. We have a lot of members, a lot of them casual, others who are transient, using this facility while they're in town for business or pleasure. I know a lot of the regulars on sight, but I don't recognize him."

He lowered this sketch. "Is this the man who has Gia?"

"At this time, he's a person of interest."

They spent an hour at it, without a single hit. As they stepped outside, Eve's 'link signaled. "Dallas."

"Yancy. Got it. Good as it's going to get."

"Show me."

He flipped the image on screen. Eve saw it was a bit more defined than the sketch she was carrying. The eyebrows were slightly higher, the mouth less sharply shaped. And the nose was, in fact, a little shorter. "Good. Let's get it out. Notify Whitney, and tell him I requested Nadine Furst get a five-minute bump over the rest of the media."

"Got that."

"Good work, Yancy."

"He looks like somebody's nice, comfortable grandfather," Peabody commented. "The kind that passes out peppermint candy to all the kids. I don't know why that makes it worse."

Safe, Trina had said. She'd said he looked safe. "He's going to see himself on screen. He'll see it at some point in the next few hours, the next day. And he'll know we're closer than we've ever been before."

"That worries you." Peabody nodded. "He might kill Rossi and Greenfeld out of panic and preservation, and go under again."

"He might. But we've got to air the image. If he's targeted another woman, if he's contacted her, and she sees it, it's not only going to save her life, it may lead us right to his door. No choice. Got no choice."

But she thought of Rossi. Eighty-six hours missing, and counting.

Considering the sketch she had was closer than most, Eve used it while they talked to other businesses, to residences, to a couple of panhandlers and the glide-cart operators on the corners.

"He's, like, invisible." Peabody rubbed her chilled hands together as they headed toward the club. "We know he's been around there, been inside the gym, but nobody sees him."

"Nobody pays attention to him and maybe that's part of his pathology. He's been ignored or overlooked. This is his way of being important. The women he takes, tortures, kills, they won't forget him."

"Yeah, but dead."

"Not the point. They see him. When you give somebody pain, when you restrain them, hold them captive and isolated, hurt them, you're their world." It had been that way for her, she remembered. Her father had been the world, the terrifying and brutal world the first eight years of her life.

His face, his voice, every detail of him was exact and indelible in her mind. In her nightmares.

"He's the last thing they see," she added. "That must give him a hell of a rush."

Inside Starlight it was colored lights and dreamy music. Couples circled the dance floor while Zela, in a waist-cinching red suit Eve had to assume was retro, stood on the sidelines.

"Very smooth, Mr. Harrow. Ms. Yo, relax your shoulders. That's the way."

"Dance class," Peabody said as Zela continued to call out instructions or encouragement. "They're pretty good. Oops," she added when one of the men wearing a natty bow tie stepped on his partner's foot. "Kinda cute, too."

"Adorable, especially considering one of them might dance on home after class and torture his latest brunette."

"You think . . . one of them." Peabody eyed Natty Bow Tie suspiciously.

"No. He's done with this place. He's never been known to fish from the same pool twice. But I'm damn sure he fox-trotted or whatever on that floor within the last few weeks."

"Why do they call it a fox-trot?" Peabody wondered. "Foxes do trot, but it doesn't look like dancing."

"I'll put an investigative team right on that. Let's go."

They headed down the silver stairs, catching Zela's eye. She nodded, then applauded when the music ended. "That was terrific! Now that you're warmed up, Loni's going to take you through the rhumba."

Zela gestured Eve and Peabody over to the bar while the young redhead led Natty Bow Tie to the center of the floor. The redhead beamed enthusiastically. "All right! Positions, everyone."

There was a single bartender. He wore black-tie, and set a glass of bubbly water with a slice of lemon in front of Zela without asking her preference. "What can I get you, ladies?"

"Could I have a virgin cherry foam?" Peabody asked before Eve could glare at her.

"I'm good," Eve told him, then drew out the sketch, laid it on the counter. "Do you recognize this man?"

Zela stared at it. "Is this . . ." She shook her head. She lifted her water, drank deeply, set it down again. Then, picking up the sketch, she angled it toward the lights. "I'm sorry. He just doesn't look familiar. We get so many men of a certain age through here. I think if I'd worked with him—in a class—I'd remember."

"How about you?" Eve took the sketch, nudged it across the bar.

The bartender stopped mixing Peabody's drink to frown over the sketch. "Is this the fucker—sorry, Zela." She only shook her head, waved the obscenity away. "This the one who killed Sari?"

"He's a guy we want to talk to."

"I'm good with faces, part of the trade. I don't remember him sitting at my bar."

"You work days?"

"Yeah. We—me and my lady—had a kid six months ago. Sari switched me to days so I could be home with my family at night. She was good about things like that. Her memorial's tomorrow." He looked over at Zela. "It's not right."

"No." Zela laid a hand over his for a moment. "It's not right."

There was grief in his eyes when he moved away to finish mixing the drink.

"We're all taking it pretty hard," Zela said quietly. "Trying to work through it, because what can you do? But it's hard, like trying to swallow past something that's stuck in your throat."

"It says a lot about her," Peabody offered, "that she mattered to so many people."

"Yeah. Yeah, it does. I talked to Sari's sister yesterday," Zela continued. "She asked if I'd pick the music. What Sari liked. It's hard. Harder than anything I imagined."

"I'm sure it is. What about her?" Eve glanced toward the redhead. "Did she work with Sari on any of the classes?"

"No. Actually, this is Loni's first class. We've had to do some . . . well, some internal shuffling. Loni worked coat check and revolving hostessing. I just bumped her up to hostess/instructor."

"I'd like to talk to her."

"Sure, I'll send her over." Zela rose, smiled wanly. "Pity my feet. Mr. Buttons is as cute as, well, a button, but he's a complete klutz."

The dancers made the switch with Loni giving her klutzy partner a quick peck on the cheek before she dashed over to the bar on three-inch heels.

"Hi! I'm Loni."

"Lieutenant Dallas, Detective Peabody."

Peabody swallowed her slurp of cherry foam and tried to look more official.

"I talked to those other detectives? I have to say *mmmm* on both. I guess they're not coming back?"

"Couldn't say. Do you recognize this man?"

Loni looked at the sketch as the bartender set down beside her something pink and fizzy with a cherry garnish. "I don't know. Hmmm. Not really. Sort of. I don't know."

"Which is it, Loni? Sort of or not really?"

"He kind of looks like this one guy, but that guy had dark hair, slicked back dark hair and a really thin mustache."

"Short, tall, average? This one guy."

"Ummm, let me think. On the short side. 'Cause Sari had an inch or two on him. Of course, she was wearing heels, so—"

"Hold on. You saw this man with Sari?"

"This one guy, yeah. Well, lots of the men liked to dance with Sari when she was working the floor. It's probably not this guy because—"

"Hold on." Eve pulled out her 'link, tagged Yancy. "I need you to alter the sketch. Give him dark hair, slicked back, a thin mustache. Send it to this 'link."

"Give me a minute."

"When did you see this man with Sari?" Eve asked Loni.

"I'm not sure. A few weeks ago, I guess. It's hard to remember exactly. I only remember at all because I was working the floor, and I asked this guy to dance. We're supposed to ask the singles to dance. He was sort of shy and sweet, and said how he'd just come in for the music, but thank you. Then just a little while later, I saw him dancing with Sari. It sort of frosted me, you know? Silly." She shrugged. "But I was, like, I guess he goes for brunettes instead of . . . Oh." She went a little pale. "Oh, God. *This* guy?"

"You tell me." Eve turned her 'link around so that Loni could view the screen with the adjusted sketch.

"Oh God, oh God. I think, I really think that's the guy. Brett."

"It's okay." The bartender took her hand. "Take it easy." He angled his head to look at the screen. Shook his head. "He didn't come to the bar. I don't remember him sitting at the bar."

"Where was he sitting, Loni?"

"Okay. Okay." She took long breaths as she swiveled around to study the club. "Second tier—I'm pretty sure—toward the back over there."

"I need to talk to whoever waits tables in that section. Can you pinpoint the night, Loni?"

"I don't know. It was a couple weeks ago. Maybe three? You know, I checked his coat once. I remember checking his coat, and that's why I zeroed on him that night. I'd checked his coat before, and he'd been alone. So when I was working the floor, I spotted him and thought, 'Oh yeah, that guy's a solo.' But he didn't want to dance with me."

A single tear slid down her cheek. "He wanted Sari."

15 "UNOBTRUSIVE," EVE SAID, PUSHING HER WAY through traffic as a thick, heavy snow began to fall. "Limits contact with anyone other than the target."

"None of the waitstaff could make him, none of the valets. Could live or work within walking distance of the club," Peabody ventured.

"Yeah, or he parks elsewhere on his own. Or he's using public transportation for this part of his game. What cabbie's going to remember picking up or dropping off a fare days later, or in this case weeks? We're spitting into the wind there. Loni only remembered him because he'd spanked her vanity. Otherwise he'd have just been another forgotten face. He'd have been smarter to dance with her. She wouldn't have remembered him for five minutes after."

Eve glanced in the sideview, changed lanes. "He comes in, slides into the crowd, stays out of the main play, keeps to the back. Probably tips the waiter smack on the going percentage. Later, they don't think, 'Oh yeah, this guy stiffed me,' or 'This guy seriously flashed me.' Just ordinary and average. Steady as she goes."

"The confirmation's good to have. Loni verifying he'd been in the club, made contact there with York. But it doesn't tell us much."

"It tells us he likes to alter his appearance. Slight alterations, nothing flashy. Dark hair, little mustache, gray wig. It tells us it's unlikely he frequents or revisits the point of contact after he's got the target. We know that he doesn't lose control, that he can and does maintain whatever role he's chosen to play during the stalking phase."

She turned, headed west for a block, then veered south. "He danced with York, had his hands on her. They're eye to eye, talking. It would be part of her job to talk to her partner. Everything we know about her says she was smart, self-aware, and knew how to deal with people. But she doesn't get any signals, nothing that puts a hitch in her step, that this guy is trouble.

"Check the side view," Eve told Peabody. "See that black sedan, six cars back?"

Peabody shifted, trained her gaze on the mirror. "Yeah. Barely. This snow is pretty thick. Why?"

"He's been tailing us. Five, six, seven back, since we left the club. Not close enough for me to make out the plate. Since, as was recently pointed out, you're younger than me, maybe your eyes are sharper."

Peabody hunched her shoulders. "No. Can't make it. He's too close to the car in front of him. Maybe if he drops back a little, or comes around."

"Let's see what we can do about that." Eve gauged an opening, started to switch lanes.

The blast of a horn, the wet squeal of brakes on sloppy pavement had her tapping her own. One lane over a limo fishtailed wildly in an attempt to miss hitting some idiot who dashed into the street.

She heard the thud, saw the boy fall and roll. There was a nasty crunch as the limo laid into the massive all-terrain in front of her.

"Son of a bitch."

Even as she flipped on her On Duty light, she looked in the rearview again. The sedan was gone.

She slammed out of her vehicle in time to see the boy scramble up, start a limping run. And to hear the scream of: "Stop him! He's got my bag!" over the urban symphony of horns and curses.

"Son of a bitch," she said again. "Handle it, Peabody." And set off in pursuit of the street thief.

He got his rhythm back quickly, proving—she supposed—someone else was younger than she. He dashed, darted, skidded, all but flew across the street, down the sidewalk.

He may have been younger, but her legs were longer, and she began to close the distance. He glanced back over his shoulder, his eyes showing both alarm and annoyance. As he ran he yanked the big brown bag out from under his bulky coat and began to swing it like a stylish pendulum.

He knocked over pedestrians like bowling pins so that Eve had to leap, dodge, swerve.

When he spun, swung the bag at her head, she ducked, snagged the strap, and simply yanked it to send him tumbling to the sidewalk.

Annoyed, she crouched. "You're just stupid," she muttered, and shoved him over on his back.

"Hey! Hey!" Some good Samaritan stopped. "What are you doing to that boy? What's the matter with you?"

Eve planted her boot on the boy's chest to keep him down, flipped out her badge. "You want to keep moving, pal?"

"Bitch," the boy said as the Samaritan frowned at Eve's badge. Then, like an angry terrier, bit her.

Human bites are more dangerous than animal bites." Peabody had the wheel now as Eve sat in the passenger seat dragging up her pants leg to see the damage. "And he broke the skin," Peabody noted with a sympathetic wince. "Gee, he really clamped down on you."

"Little bastard son of a bitch. Let's see how he likes the assaulting-an-officer strike on top of the robberies. Biting Boy had a dozen wallets in his coat pockets."

"You need to disinfect that."

"Made me lose the sedan. Could've kicked him bloody for that." Setting her teeth, Eve used the clean rag Peabody had unearthed from somewhere to staunch the wound. "Turned on the cross street as soon as there was a commotion. That's what he did, that's what he does. Avoids crowds and confrontations. Fucking fucker."

"Bet that really hurts. You're sure it was the guy?"

"I know a tail when I see one."

"No question. I'm just wondering why he'd tail us. Trying to find out what we know, I guess. But what's the point? All he can get is where we go—and where we've gone is pretty standard for an investigation."

"He's trying to get my rhythm, my pace, my moves. Trying to find a routine."

"Why would . . ." It hit, and had Peabody jerking in her seat. "Holy shit. He's stalking you."

"Thinks I won't make a tail?" She jerked her pants leg back down because looking at the teeth marks only made it hurt more. "Thinks he can figure me. Fat chance. He doesn't know his target this time, he—ha—bit off more than he's going to be able to chew."

"How long have you known he was looking at you?"

"Know? Since about a half hour ago. Toyed with the possibility for a while, but having him tail us pretty much nailed it down."

"You could have mentioned the idea to your partner."

"Don't start. It was one of God knows how many possibles. Now I'm giving it a high probable, and you're the first to know. Black sedan, nothing flashy—which fits right in—round headlights, no hood ornamentation. It looked like a five-bar grill. We should be able to get a model from that."

She all but sighed with relief when Peabody turned into the garage at Central. She wanted to ice down the damn leg. "New York plate was all I could make. Just a quick glimpse on the plate color. Too much distance, too much snow to get any number."

"You need to take standard precautions with that injury."

"Yeah, yeah."

"One of them should be an hour in the crib. You're wiped out."

"I hate the crib." Eve climbed, somewhat achily, out of the car. "If I need to shut down for an hour, I'll use the floor in my office. It works for me. Do me a favor," she added as she hobbled to the elevator. "Set up a meet with Whitney and Mira, asap. I'm going to go steal some disinfectant and a bandage from the infirmary."

"You don't have to steal it. They'll fix you up."

"I don't want them to fix me up," Eve grumbled. "I hate them. I'll just palm what I need and take care of it myself."

E ve swung through the infirmary, committed—if you wanted to be absolutely technical—some basic shoplifting by pocketing what she needed without logging it in.

But if she logged it, they'd insist on seeing the wound. If she showed them the wound, they'd start badgering her to have it treated there. She just needed to clean it up, slap a bandage on it. And, okay, maybe take a blocker.

When she stepped into her office, Roarke was already there.

"Let's see it."

"See what?"

He merely lifted his eyebrows.

"Damn Peabody. She's got a mouth on her." Eve pulled the lifted items out of her coat pocket, tossed them on her desk. She hung her coat on the rack, then sat and propped her injured leg on the desk.

Roarke studied the wound when she tugged up her pants leg, and hissed a little. "Bit nasty, that."

"I've had worse than a nip from some half-assed sissy street thief."

"True enough." Still, he cleaned, treated, and bandaged the bite himself. Then leaned over and pressed a quick kiss to the neat white square. "There, that's better."

"He tailed me."

Roarke straightened now, and the quiet amusement in his eyes faded. "We're not talking about the half-assed sissy street thief."

"I made him—black sedan, couldn't get the plate, but I think we can pop on the model, maybe the year. I might've been able to get more, maybe even have managed to box him in if that asshole hadn't run out in the street. I had to control the vehicle or else crash into the limo that bumped the asshole and crashed into an ATV in front of me. A few seconds, and he was gone."

"He wouldn't know you made him."

"Don't see how, no. He's just cautious. There's trouble up ahead, so he slithers off and avoids it. If he's been out and about shadowing me, he might not have seen the media reports with his face on them. But he will."

She shifted to try to ease the throbbing in her calf. "Be a pal, would you? Get me coffee."

He went to her AutoChef. "And your next step?"

"Meet with Whitney and Mira to discuss the possibilities of baiting a trap. Check in with the team members, input any new data. At some point I need an hour or two just to think. I need to work it through in my head, play with it."

He brought the coffee back to her. "As a party with vested interest in the bait, I'd like to attend this meeting."

"Just can't get enough of meetings, can you? You'll have to leave your buttons outside the room."

"Sorry?"

"If your buttons aren't there, they can't be pushed." She let her head lean back for just a minute, let the coffee work its magic on her system. "And to remember I'm not just bait, I'm an experienced and kick-ass cop."

"With a sissy bite on her tightly muscled calf."

"Well . . . yeah."

"Dallas." Peabody stepped to the door. "How's the leg?"

"Fine, and as of now, removed from all discussion."

"The commander and Dr. Mira will take us in the commander's office in twenty."

"Good enough."

"Meanwhile, Officer Gil Newkirk's come in. He's in the war room."

"On my way."

Gil Newkirk wore his uniform well. He had a rock-solid look about him, indicating to Eve he knew how to handle himself on the street. His face bore the same sort of toughness, what she supposed Feeney might call "seasoning."

She'd met him a handful of times over the years, and considered him to be sensible and straightforward.

"Officer Newkirk."

"Lieutenant." He took the hand she offered with a firm, brisk shake. "Looks like you've got an efficient setup here."

"It's a good team. We're narrowing the field."

"I'm glad to hear it, and wish I'd brought you something substantial. If you've got some time . . ."

"Have a seat." She gestured, joined him at the conference table.

"You've got his face." Newkirk nodded to the sketch pinned to one of the four case boards. "I've been studying that face, trying to put it in front of me nine years back during one of the knock-on-doors. There were so many of them, Lieutenant. That face isn't coming up for me."

"It was a long shot."

"I went through my notes again, and I went over to Ken Colby's place, he was on this. He went down five years ago."

"I'm sorry."

"He was a good man. His widow, she let me dig out his files and notes on the old investigation. I brought them in." He tapped the box he'd carried in with him. "Thought they might add something."

"I appreciate that."

"There were a couple of guys that popped for me when I was going through it again this morning—going off what you gave me last night. But the face, it doesn't match."

"What popped about them?"

"The body type and coloring. And my boy and I, we've talked this through some." He cocked a brow.

"I've got no problem with that."

"I know you're working the Urban Wars angle, and I remembered one of these guys told us he used to ride along in a dead wagon in the Urbans, with his old man. Pick up bodies. Worked as an MT, then kicked that when he went to some convention in Vegas and hit a jackpot. I remember him because it was a hell of a story. The other was this rich guy, third-generation money. He did taxidermy for a hobby. Place was full of dead animals.

"I pulled them out." He passed her a disc. "In case you wanted to check them out again."

"We'll do that. Are you on duty, Officer Newkirk?"

"Day off," he said.

"If you got the time and the interest, maybe you could run these through with Feeney, for current data. I'd be grateful."

"No problem. I'm happy to assist in any way."

Eve got to her feet, offered her hand again. "Thanks. I've got a meeting. I'll check back as soon as I can. Peabody, Roarke, with me."

She had to concentrate not to limp, and giving into her throbbing leg, headed for the small and often odorous confines of the elevator.

"Remember," she said to Roarke, "you're a civilian, and this is a NYPSD op."

"That's expert civilian to you, copper."

She didn't smirk—very much—then squeezed herself onto an elevator. "And don't call the commander Jack. It negates the serious and official tone, and . . . it's just wrong."

"Yo, Dallas!"

She turned her head to see one of the detectives from Anti-Crime grinning at her. "Renicki."

"Heard some mope took a chunk out of you, and now he's got himself a case of rabies."

"Yeah? I heard some LC got a taste of you, and now she's got herself a case of the clap."

"And that," Roarke murmured as a number of cops hooted, "is serious and official."

In his office, Whitney stood behind his desk, and Mira beside a visitor's chair. "Lieutenant," he said. "Detective. Roarke."

"Sir, as I believe the expert consultant may be able to assist with the content of this meeting, I've asked him to be included."

"Your call. Please, sit."

While Roarke, Peabody, and Mira took seats, Eve remained standing. "With permission, Commander, to first update you and Dr. Mira."

She ran it through, quick and spare.

"You were shadowed?" Whitney didn't question her statement. "Any thoughts on why?"

"Yes, sir. Dr. Mira broached the possibility that I may be a target. That rather than the springboard for these particular women being Roarke, the springboard for any connection with Roarke may be me."

"You didn't mention this theory to me, Doctor."

"I asked Dr. Mira to give me time to evaluate," Eve said before Mira could speak. "To consider, and to run probabilities before we shifted the focus on this area of the investigation. Having done so, I believe it's a viable theory. I was a detective on the first investigation, partner to the primary. I fall within the parameters of his choice of victim. I may have crossed paths with him nine years ago, or walked a parallel line.

"I think he came back to New York for specific reasons. And I think one of them is his intention to bag me."

"He'll be disappointed," Whitney commented.

"Yes, sir, he will."

"How strongly do you support this theory, Mira?"

"I've run my own probabilities, and I believe, given his pathology, he would consider capturing the lieutenant, a woman with considerable training and authority, a woman married to a man with considerable power, to be his finest achievement. However, it leads me to another question. How will he top it?"

"He can't," Roarke stated. "And knows that he won't. She's the last, isn't she? The best, the most challenging, his ultimate."

"Yes." Mira nodded. "I agree. He's willing to alter, even slightly, his victim profile. This is not a woman who can be pinned to a specific routine, to a pattern of habits and haunts. Nor one he could approach, face-to-face, as we believe he has with many if not all in the past, and lure her. It must be worth it to him to take this great risk, to devise a way to pull her in. He's circled back," Mira continued. "Come back to what we could call his roots. Because this will finish his work."

"He's stopped before," Peabody put in. "A year or two. But how can he just decide he's finished? This kind of killer doesn't stop unless he's captured or killed."

"No, he doesn't."

"You think he's dying," Eve said to Mira. "Or that he's decided to self-terminate after he finishes me."

"I do. Yes, I believe exactly that. I also believe he doesn't fear it. Death is an accomplishment to him, and a timed cycle, which he has, for nearly a decade we know of, controlled. He doesn't fear his own death, and that only makes him more dangerous."

"We need to give him an opening." Eve narrowed her eyes. "And soon."

"If it's too easy, he won't bite." Roarke met Eve's gaze when she turned. "I know something about challenges. If it comes too easy, it's not worth the trouble. He'll want to work for it. At the very least he'll want to believe that he outwitted you. And he's had much longer to plan, to devise and study the problem than you have."

"I agree." Mira leaned forward. "If what we believe is true, you're the finish to his work. You complete it. The fact that you're pursuing him even as he pursues you not only ups the stakes but adds a particular shine. You would be, quite literally, his masterpiece. With his need for control, he must feel he's manipulated the outcome. Lured you, despite your training and advantages, as he's lured the others."

"So we let him believe it," Eve said, "right up to the moment we take him down. He has to be aware by now that we know his face. My take, from the profile, from what we know, is that it will only add to his excitement, his enjoyment. No one's ever gotten this close before. And while he's never overtly sought attention from the killing, his method indicates pride in it. In the end, if that's what this is, won't he want to be known?"

"And remembered," Mira confirmed.

"We don't know where or when, but we know who the target is, and we know why. Big advantages. We have his face, body type, age range. We know more about him than we did nine years ago."

She wanted to pace, to move while she talked it through, but Eve considered that inappropriate in Whitney's office. "He probably has a connection with the Urban Wars, he likes opera, rather than physical means, he uses manipulation and deceit to obtain his victims, and often makes personal contact with them before the abduction. Unlike nine years ago, his victims lived or worked from midtown down. That's purposeful."

"He wanted us to get closer this time." Whitney nodded. "And by using Roarke's people, he made it personal."

"But he doesn't know how much we know," Peabody put in. "He doesn't know we've concluded Dallas is his end game. That's another advantage. As long as he thinks she's looking ahead—I mean that she's focused on the pursuit, he'll think he can ease around behind her, bag the prize."

"Back to an opening. One he can believe he helped make," Eve said to Roarke. "You're going to need to go back to work."

"Back to?"

"To the buying-controlling-interest-of-the-known-universe-one-sector-at-a-time work. He's not going to move on me if I'm in lockstep with you, or you," she said to Peabody, "or anyone else. We have to give him a little room. If he knows my routines, then he knows I generally travel to and from Central solo, that I might do a follow-up after shift on my own. We need to crack the window for him."

"Giving the appearance I've gone back to business, so to speak, is easy enough," Roarke replied. His tone was even, almost casual. But Eve heard the steel under it. "But as long as that window's cracked I'll be an active member of this team. This is not," he continued, and addressed himself to the commander now, "simply a matter of me insisting on having some part in protecting the lieutenant. This man has taken three of my people, and one is already dead. It won't be back to business for me until he's apprehended—or as dead as Sarifina York."

"Understood. Lieutenant, it was your choice to bring the civilian on board. Unless you feel his particular talents and expertise are no longer useful, I believe he should remain active."

"You can't stick too close," Eve began. "If he senses you're concerned for my safety, he could pull back. So make the appearance a good one."

"Not a problem."

"We keep working it, no dramatic shifts in the routine. But we split some of the legwork and interviews."

"And you go, wherever you go," Whitney ordered, "wired."

"Yes, sir. I'm going to set that up with Feeney. I'll need a homer for my vehicle, and—"

"Already done," Roarke said, then smiled serenely when she turned on him. "You agreed to that action earlier."

True, she thought, but she hadn't expected him to take it on himself before she'd officially cleared it. Which, she had to admit, was stupid. That's exactly what she should've expected. "Yeah, I did."

"You'll wear a vest," Mira told her.

"A woman after my own heart," Roarke murmured, and his smile spread at the annoyance on Eve's face.

"A vest's overkill. His pattern—"

"He's breaking pattern with you," Mira reminded her. "A vest ensures your safety and success, should he try to stun or injure you in order to incapacitate you. He's intelligent enough to know he needs a physical advantage with you."

"Wear the vest." Whitney's voice was clipped. "Set up the electronics with Feeney. I want to know where you are, from this point on, at all times. When you're in the field, in your vehicle, on the street for any reason, so is a shadow team. It's not just a matter of keeping one of my people safe, Lieutenant," he told her, "it's a matter of slamming that window shut, the minute he comes through it. Work it out, relay the details."

"Yes, sir."

"Dismissed."

Roarke ran his fingers down her arm as they headed for the glide down. "A vest isn't a punishment, darling."

"You wear one for a couple hours, then say that. And no 'darling' on shift."

"You can call me darling anytime," Peabody told him, and made him grin.

"I've a few arrangements to make. I'll see you back in the war room." He started to split off from them. "Later, darling. I was talking to Peabody," he said when Eve bared her teeth.

16 IT DIDN'T TAKE LONG FOR ROARKE TO MAKE arrangements. In the end, however, it would be more than the appearance he was tending to his own organization. He'd have to put in some time on just that, once he could get to his home office, juggling deals and finance with murder.

But for now he headed back to the war room to keep the various balls of his e-work in the air. He caught sight of Eve coming from the direction of her office. With a few yards between them, he watched her—long, quick strides. Places to go, he thought, murderers to catch.

He stopped off, grabbing a bottle of water for both of them, then walked in.

She'd gone to Feeney's station. The cop Feeney was working with— the detail-minded young Newkirk's father, Roarke remembered— nodded, and gathering a few discs, shifted to another area.

So she wanted a direct with Feeney, Roarke concluded. He went to his own station to work on a problem, and to study their dynamics.

He could see Feeney absorb the information, see Feeney's eyes narrow in consideration. And the faintest frown of concern. There was some back-and-forth, rapid-fire on Feeney's part, then he scratched his ear, dipped into his pocket. Out came a bag.

It would be nuts, Roarke knew, as Feeney dipped into it, then held it out to Eve.

Taking that as a signal they were now at the thinking through and strategy stage, Roarke rose to walk over and join them.

"Raised his sights considerably," Feeney said to Roarke.

"So it would seem."

Feeney swiveled idly left to right, right to left, in his chair as he spoke. "We can wire her up, no problem there. Could put a camera on her, too. Give us eyes if and when we need them."

"I don't want him spotting a camera," Eve began.

"I have something." Roarke looked at Feeney. "The new generation of the HD Mole. XT-Micro. Most often used lapel-style, but as she's not known for accessorizing it can be easily reconfigured into a button— shirt or jacket. Voice print option. She can activate or deactivate it with any choice of keyword or phrase."

"She's standing right here," Eve pointed out.

"There were a couple bugs in the last generation," Feeney pointed out, easily ignoring Eve.

"Exterminated," Roarke assured him. "It would take care of audio and video, and with the XT model—unless she's going up against top-level security—it wouldn't be detected."

Feeney nodded and munched. "We can go with that. Like to have a look at it first."

"I've got one coming in now. I used a multitrack homer on her vehicle, military grade."

In appreciation of the high-level equipment, Feeney let out a low whistle, along with a quick grin. "We sure as hell won't lose her, even if she decides to drive down to Argentina. We'll set up receivers here, and in the mobile. Shadow team can give her five or six blocks."

"What about air?"

"We can mobilize if we have to."

"It's not a bloody coup," Eve muttered. "It's one homicidal old man."

"Who's captured, tortured, and killed twenty-four women."

Eve merely scowled at Roarke. "I think if he goes through the god-damn window, I can take him. You two go ahead and set up all the e-toys you want. But let's remember, it's not just smoking him out. It's getting in. For Rossi and Greenfeld to have a chance, we have to get to them. I have to get inside, let him think he's lured me in. We take him outside his place, there's no guarantee we'll nail down where he's keeping them."

She had their attention now, waited a beat. "I'm not having these two women bleed or starve to death because we're so worried about keeping my skin in place we take him down or put him down before we know where they are. Their safety is paramount. That's a directive from the primary."

Feeney rattled his bag of nuts, held it out to Roarke. "Gil and I boxed in a few locations and individuals worth checking out."

"Peabody and I will take that. That's SOP if he's watching. Give me what you've got. How long before your shiny new toy gets here?" she asked Roarke.

"Should be along in ten or fifteen minutes now."

"Good enough. I'll go dig out the stupid vests." She signaled to Peabody. "Roarke, you're going to have to arrange your own transpo home."

"Understood. Lieutenant, a moment." Roarke walked with her to the door. "I want those women back, safe, as much as you. I also like your skin exactly where it is. We're going to find a way to make all of that work. And that's a directive from the man who loves you. So watch your ass, or I'll be first in line to kick it."

He knew she wouldn't like it, but he needed it, so caught her chin in his hand and kissed her, hard and brief, before walking away.

"Awww." Peabody sighed a little as she hustled out of the war room behind Eve. "That's so sweet."

"Yeah, ass-kickings are sugar in our house. Locker room. Vests."

"Vests? That would be more than one?"

"I wear one, you wear one."

"Aw," Peabody repeated, but in an entirely different tone.

In under forty minutes they were in the garage, vested and wired. Peabody tugged on her jacket. "This makes me look fat, doesn't it? I know it makes me look fat, and I'm still carrying a couple pounds of winter weight."

"We're not trying to distract the son of a bitch with your frosty figure, Peabody."

"Easy for you to say." Shifting, she tried to get a look at her reflection in a side-view mirror. "This damn thing thickens my entire middle, which doesn't need any help in that area. I look like a stump. A tree stump."

"Stumps don't have arms and legs."

"They have branches. But I guess if they have branches, they aren't technically stumps. So what I look like is a stunted tree." She dropped into the passenger seat. "I now have extra motivation for taking this bastard down. He's made me look like a stunted tree."

"Yeah, we're going to fry his ass for that one." Eve pulled out. "Watch for a tail. Activate, Dallas," she said to test the recorder. "You copy?"

"Eyes and ears five-by-five," Feeney responded. "Shadow will hang back, minimum of three blocks."

"Copy that, remaining open while in the field."

They took the former dead wagon rider first. He'd done well for himself, Eve mused. Had a dignified old brownstone all to himself in a quiet West Village neighborhood.

A droid answered the door—a stupendously designed female Eve would have gauged as more usual in the sexual gratification department than the domestic. Smoky eyes, smoky voice, smoky hair, all in a snug black skin-suit.

"If you'd like to wait in the foyer, I'll tell Mr. Dobbins you're here." She walked off—more slinked off, Eve thought, like a lithe and predatory feline.

"If all she does is vacuum around here," Peabody commented, "I'm a size two."

"She may vacuum, after she polishes the old man's brass."

"Women are so crude," Roarke said in her ear.

"Mute the chatter." Eve studied the foyer.

More of a wide hallway, she noted, with the light coming in through the front door's ornate glass panel. Doors on either side, kitchen area probably in the back. Bedrooms upstairs.

A lot of room for a man to shuffle around in.

He did just that, shuffled in on bunged-up slippers. He wore baggy sweats, and had his near-shoulder-length hair combed back and dyed a hard and improbable black.

His face was too thin, his mouth too full, his body too slight to be the man both Trina and Loni had spoken with.

"Mr. Dobbins."

"That's right. I want to see some identification, or you're both turning right back around."

He studied Eve's badge, then Peabody's, his mouth moving silently as he read. "All right then, what's this about?"

"We're investigating the murder of a woman in Chelsea," Eve began.

"That Groom business." Dobbins wagged a finger. "I read the papers, I watch the news, don't I? If you people did your jobs and protected people you wouldn't have to come around here asking me questions. Cops come around here years ago when that girl across the street was murdered."

"Did you know her, Mr. Dobbins? The girl who was murdered nine years ago?"

"Saw her coming and going, didn't I? Never spoke to her. Saw this new one's picture on screen. Never spoke to her, either."

"Did you ever see this new girl?" Eve asked.

"On the screen, didn't I just say? Don't get up to Chelsea. Got what I need right here, don't I?"

"I'm sure you do. Mr. Dobbins, your father drove a morgue truck during the Urban Wars?"

"Dead wagon. I rode with him most days. Loaded up corpses right, left, and sideways. Got a live one now and again somebody took for dead. I want to sit down."

He simply turned around and shuffled through the doorway to the right. After exchanging glances, Eve and Peabody followed.

The living area was stuffed with worn furniture. The walls might once have been some variation of white, but were now the dingy yellow of bad teeth.

Dobbins sat, took a cigarette from a tarnished silver tray, and lighted it. "A man can still smoke in his own damn house. You people haven't taken that away. A man's home is his damn castle."

"You have a lovely home, Mr. Dobbins," Peabody commented. "I love the brownstones in this area. We're lucky so many of them survived the Urbans. That must've been a terrible time."

"Not so bad. Got through it. Toughened me up, too." He jabbed the air with the cigarette as if to prove it. "Seen more by the time I was twenty than most see in a hundred twenty."

"I can't even imagine. Is it true that there were so many dead in some areas, the only way to keep a record of them was to write an identification number right on the bodies?"

"That's the way it was." He blew out a stream of smoke, shook his finger. "Looters get to them first, they'd take everything, strip them right down. I'd write the sector we found them on the body so we could keep track. Haul them in, and the dead house doc would write the number after that, record it in a book. Waste of time mostly. Just meat by then anyway."

"Do you keep in touch with anybody from back then? People who worked like you did, or the doctors, the medics?"

"What for? They find out you've got a little money, they just want a handout." He shrugged it off. "Saw Earl Wallace a few years back. He'd ride shotgun on the wagon sometimes. Stirred myself to go to Doc Yumecki's funeral, I guess five, six years back. Paid my respects. He was worth respecting, and there aren't many. Gave him a nice send-off. Grandson did it. Waked him in the parlor instead of the main house, but it was a nice send-off all the same."

"Would you know how to reach Mr. Wallace, or Dr. Yumecki's grandson?"

"How the hell should I know? I check the obits. I see somebody I know who's worth the time, I go to their send-off. Said we would back then, so I do."

"What did you say back then?" Eve prompted.

"Dead everywhere." His eyes blurred, and Eve imagined he could see it—still see it. "No send-off. Ya burned them up, or you buried them, and mostly with company, you could say. So, those of us that carted them in, ID'd and disposed, we said how when it was our time, we'd have a send-off, and those of us still living and able would come. So that's what I do."

"Who else does it? From the Urbans?"

Dobbins took one more drag. "Don't remember names. See a few now and again."

"How about this one?" Eve took out the sketch. "Have you seen this man?"

"No. Looks a little bit like Taker maybe. A little."

"Taker?"

"We picked up the bodies, dropped them off. He took them, so he was Taker. Went to his send-off twenty years back, maybe more. Big one for Taker." He sucked wetly on the cigarette. "Good food. Long time dead."

Out in the car again, Eve sat a moment to think. "Could be an act—bitter, slightly tipped old man. But that's reaching."

"He could've worn a disguise when Trina saw him."

"Could've," Eve agreed, "but I'd say Trina would have spotted any major face work. It's what she does. Let's run down the two names he remembered."

Her next stop was a Hugh Klok off Washington Square Park. The victim Dobbins had seen "coming and going" had been dumped there. Gil Newkirk's notes stated that Klok had been questioned, as were the other neighbors. Klok was listed as an antiquities dealer who had purchased and renovated the property several years before the murders.

He was listed as cooperative and unilluminating.

Antiquities turned a good profit if you knew what you were doing. Eve assumed Klok did as the property was impressive. What had originally been a pair of town houses had been merged into one large home, set back from the street by a wide courtyard.

"Pretty spruce," Peabody commented as they approached the courtyard's ornamental iron gate.

Eve pressed the button on the gate and was momentarily ordered by a computerized voice to state her business.

"Police. We'd like to speak with Mr. Hugh Klok." She held up her badge for scanning.

Mr. Klok is not in residence at this time. You may leave your message at this security point or—if you choose—pass through and leave same with a member of the household staff.

"Option two. Might as well get a closer look," she said to Peabody.

The gate chinked open. They crossed the bricked courtyard, climbed a short flight of steps to the main level. The door opened immediately. This, too, was a droid, but fashioned to represent a dignified middle-aged man.

"I'm authorized to take your message for Mr. Klok."

"Where's Mr. Klok?"

"Mr. Klok is away on business."

"Where?"

"I'm not authorized to relay that information. If this is an emergency or the business you have with him of great import, I will contact Mr. Klok immediately so that he can, in turn, contact you. He is, however, expected home within the next day or two."

Behind the dignified droid was a large, dignified entrance hall. And surrounding it Eve sensed a great deal of uninhabited space. "Tell Mr. Klok to contact Lieutenant Eve Dallas, NYPSD, Cop Central, upon his return."

"Of course."

"How long has he been gone?"

"Mr. Klok has been out of residence these past two weeks."

"Does Mr. Klok live alone?"

"He does."

"Any houseguests in his absence?"

"There are no guests in residence."

"Okay." She'd have preferred to get inside, snoop around a little. But without warrant or cause, there was no legal way past the threshold.

She left the Klok house for a bustling section of Little Italy.

One of the victims had been a waitress in a restaurant owned by Tomas Pella. Pella had served on the Home Force during the Urbans, and in them had lost a brother, a sister, and his bride of two months. His young, doomed wife had served as a medic.

He'd never remarried, had instead opened and owned three successful restaurants before selling out eight years before.

"Reclusive, according to Newkirk's notes," Eve said. "Also listed as hot-tempered and angry."

He lived in a trim whitewashed home within shouting distance of bakeries, markets, cafés.

When she was greeted for the third time by a droid—female again, but of the comfortable domestic style—Eve concluded that men of that generation preferred electronic to human.

"Lieutenant Dallas, Detective Peabody. We'd like to speak to Mr. Tomas Pella."

"I'm sorry, Mr. Pella is very ill."

"Oh, yeah? How's that?"

"I'm afraid I can't discuss his medical condition with you without his authorization. Is there any other way I can be of help?"

"Is he lucid? Conscious? Able to speak?"

"Yes, but he requires rest and quiet."

Droids were tougher than humans on some levels, but could still be bullied and intimidated. "I require an interview with him." Eve tapped her badge, kept her eyes keen and level. "I think it would disturb his rest and quiet a great deal more if I had to get a warrant and bring police medicals in here to evaluate his condition. Is there a medical with him?"

"Yes. There's a medical with him at all times."

"Then inform the medical that if Mr. Pella is awake and lucid, we need to speak with him. Got that?"

"Yes, of course." She stepped back, shutting the door behind them before going to a house 'link. "If Mr. Pella is able, there are two police officers here who insist on speaking to him. Yes, I'll wait."

The domestic glanced back at Eve and looked as intimidated as a droid could manage.

The entrance boasted soaring ceilings, and was elegantly if sparely furnished. The staircase was directly to the left, a straight, sleek line, the treads were highly polished wood with a faded red runner climbing their center. The chandelier was three tiers of blown glass in shades of pale, delicate blue.

She wandered a few feet farther to glance to the right, into a formal parlor. Photographs lined the creamy white mantel, and from the style of dress worn in them, she judged them to be a gallery of Pella's dead. Parents, siblings, the pretty and forever young face of his wife.

Third man on the list, she thought, and it could be said—in this case—that Pella occupied a house of the dead.

"If you'd come with me?" The droid folded her hands neatly at her waist. "Mr. Pella will see you, but his medical requests you make your visit as brief as possible."

When Eve didn't answer, the droid simply turned and started up the steps. They creaked softly, Eve noted. Little moans and groans of age. At the top was a landing, which split right and left. The droid walked to the right, and stopped at the first door.

It would, Eve thought, overlook the street and the bustle of life outside.

It wasn't life she sensed when they stepped inside. If this was a house of the dead, this was its master chamber.

The bed was enormous, canopied, with head- and footboards deeply carved with what she supposed were cherubs on the wing. The light was dim, drapes drawn fully across the tall windows.

The man in bed was ghostly pale, propped against white pillows. An oxygen breather was fixed over his face, and above it his eyes were almost colorless and full of bitter rage.

"What do you want?"

For a sick man, his voice was strong enough, though the breather made it raspy. Fueled, perhaps, by what Eve saw in his eyes.

"Sir." The medical was female, sturdy and competent. "You mustn't upset yourself."

"Go to hell." He tossed it off like a shrug. "And get out."

"Sir."

"Out. I'm still in charge around here. You get out. And you." He pointed a finger that shook slightly at Eve. "What do you want?"

"We're investigating the murder of a woman whose body was found in East River Park."

"The Groom. Back again. I was a groom once."

"So I hear." She stepped closer to the bed. She couldn't insist he remove the breather, and with that and the poor light, his features were difficult to distinguish. But she saw his hair was white, his face round. She would have said somewhat doughy—and thought: steroids. "You're aware she was killed in the same way Anise Waters, who worked for you, was killed nine years ago."

"Nine years. A fingersnap of time, or a life sentence. Depends, doesn't it?"

"Time's relative?" she asked, watching those eyes.

"Time's a son of a bitch. You'll find out."

"Eventually."

"You cops looked me over nine years ago. Now you're back to do the same? Well, take a look."

"When's the last time you were out of bed?"

"I can get up whenever I damn well please." There was frustrated insult in his voice as he shifted to sit up straighter. "Can't get very far, but I can damn well get up. You thinking I got up and killed that girl. Grabbed myself a couple others?"

"You're well informed, Mr. Pella."

"What the hell else do I have to do all damn day but watch the screen." He jerked his chin toward the one on the wall opposite the bed. "I know who you are. Roarke's cop."

"Is that a problem for you?"

He grinned, his teeth showing through the breather.

"How about him." Eve pulled out the sketch. "Do you know who he is?"

He glanced toward the sketch in a way that told Eve he was ready to dismiss it all. Then she saw something come into his eyes, saw something pass in and out in that beat where he really looked at the face. "Who is he?"

"Guy who likes to kill women, be my guess." That hard resistance was back on his face, the *screw you* expression. "From where I'm sitting, that would be your problem, not mine."

"I can do a lot to make it your problem, too. Do you like brunettes, Mr. Pella?"

"I don't have time for women. They don't listen to you. Die on you."

"You served on the Home Force during the Urbans."

"Killed men, women, too. But they called it heroic. She was busy saving lives when they killed her. Somebody probably said that was heroic. None of it was. Killing's killing, and you never get it out of your head."

"Did you identify her body?"

"I'm not talking about that anymore. You don't talk about Therese anymore."

"Are you dying, Mr. Pella?"

"Everyone's dying." He grinned again. "Some of us are just closer to finishing it than others."

"What's finishing you?"

"Tumor. Beat it back, been beating it back for ten years. This time they say it's going to beat me. We'll see about that."

"Any objection to my partner and me looking around while we're here?"

"You want to run tame in my house?" He pushed himself up a little. "This isn't the Urbans, Roarke's Cop, where your kind can do as they damn please. And this is still the United States of goddamn America. You want to search my house? You get a warrant. Now get out."

E ve stood outside, hands on hips, studying Pella's house. In moments she saw the bedroom drapes twitch, then quickly settle.

"Tough son of a bitch," Eve commented.

"Yeah, but is he tough enough?"

"I bet he is. If killing's what he wanted, killing's what he'd do. There's the groom angle, the lost love. Why should these women live, be happy, young, when he lost his wife? Soldier during the Urbans. Knows how to kill, and he strikes me as a man with plenty of anger, and a lot of control—when he wants to use it."

"The sick room, the breather," Peabody considered. "Could be an act."

"Could be, but he has to know we could find that out. Of course, if he is dying, that's just one more check in the plus column. And no judge is going to give us a warrant with what we have to search the home of a dying, bedridden old man.

"Dallas, mute off. Feeney, you copy?"

"Read you."

"Let's put a couple of uniforms on this place. Surveillance goggles. Pella doesn't give me the full buzz, but there's a minor tingle happening. He knows something about something, and the face in that sketch triggered it."

"Done."

"Shadow pick up on any tail?"

"Nada."

"Yeah, me either. I'm going to drop Peabody by her place, head home myself. I'll be working from there. Dallas out."

"Home sweet home?"

"Home where you can start digging up data on Pella's dead wife. Details, all you can find. I can wrangle clearance to search his medicals. Take a closer look at Dobbins, too."

"Looks like I'm not getting laid again tonight."

Eve ignored her. "I'll take another glance at the currently unavailable Hugh Klok. Guy's into antiquities and that says travel to me. Let's see if any of these guys frequents the opera. Roarke can take a closer look at their real estate. Maybe the houses mean something. I want blueprints in any case."

She pulled away from the curb, hoping to sense someone watching, someone sliding through the traffic behind her. But all she felt was the crowded streets, and the sluggish push of vehicles that had turned the earlier snow into dismal mush.

17

"LOCKED IN," EVE SAID WHEN THE GATES OF home closed behind her. "Eyes and ears off. Dallas out."

No ugly mush and slush here, she thought. The snow spread, pure and pristine, over the grounds, draped heavy as wet fur on the trees so that the great house rose like the powerful focal point of a winter painting. And like a painting, now that the frigid March wind had died, it all stood utterly still.

She left the car, and even moving through winter's irritable bite, she had the thought that maybe Peabody was right. Maybe spring was edging closer.

As she entered the house Summerset oozed into the foyer with the fat Galahad shadowing him.

"I'm to tell you that Roarke will be somewhat late. It seems he has considerable business of his own to deal with as he's been spending so much of his time entrenched in yours."

"His choice, Scarecrow." She tossed her coat over the newel.

"There's blood on your pants."

She glanced down. She'd nearly forgotten the bite. Little thieving bastard. "It's dry."

"Then you won't drip on the floor," he said equably. "Mavis wishes you to know she wasn't able to pinpoint the hairpiece, but she and Trina believe they may have narrowed the brand of body cream down to three choices. The information is on your desk."

Eve climbed two steps, partly because she just wanted to get the hell upstairs, and partly because it allowed her to look down on him. "They're gone?"

"Since midday. Leonardo returned. I arranged for their transportation home, where Trina will be staying with them until this matter is resolved."

"Good. Fine." She went up two more stairs, then stopped. He was a righteous pain in her ass most of the time, but she'd heard the concern in his voice. Whatever his numerous flaws—and don't get her started—he had a big, gooey soft spot for Mavis.

"They've got nothing to worry about," she said, looking straight into his eyes. "They're clear of this."

He only nodded, and Eve continued upstairs. Galahad trotted up after her.

She went to the bedroom, but only glanced at the big, gorgeous bed. If she went down, she knew she'd stay down, and that wasn't the answer. Instead, she stripped, placing her weapon—and the clutch piece she'd strapped onto her ankle that afternoon—her badge, electronics on the dresser, then pulled on a tank and shorts.

She started to pick at the bandage on her calf, then ordered herself to stop. If she looked at the wound, the stupid thing would start hurting again.

What she needed was a good, strong workout where she could empty her mind and push her body awake.

Galahad obviously had other ideas on how to use his time and was already curled up dead center of the bed. "See, that's why you're fat," she told him. "Eat, sleep, maybe prowl around a little, then eat and sleep some more. I oughta get Roarke to put a pet treadmill downstairs. Work some of that pudge off you."

To show his opinion of the suggestion, Galahad yawned hugely, then closed his eyes.

"Sure, go ahead. Ignore me." She stepped into the elevator, went down to the gym.

She did a two-mile run, using her favored shoreline setting. She had the texture of sand under her feet, the smell of the sea around her, the sight and sound of waves rolling, receding.

Between the effort and the ambiance, she finished the run in a kind of trance, then switched to weights. Sweaty, satisfied, she ended the session with some flexibility training before she hit the shower.

Okay, maybe the bite on her leg throbbed a little in protest, but it was still better than a nap, she assured herself. Though she had to admit the cat snoring on the bed looked pretty damn happy. She pulled on loose pants, a black sweatshirt she noticed with baffled surprise was cashmere, thick socks. With her file bag in tow, she went from bedroom to office.

She programmed a full pot of coffee, and drank the first cup while updating, then circling and studying her murder boards. She paused, looked into the eyes of the killer Yancy had sketched.

"Did you come home to die? Ted, Ed, Edward, Edwin? Is it all about timing and circles and death? Has it all been your own personal opera?"

She circled again, studying each victim's face. "You chose them, used them. Cast them away. But they all represent someone. Who is that? Who was she to you? Mother, lover, sister, daughter? Did she betray you? Leave you? Reject you?"

She remembered something Pella had said, and frowned.

"Die on you? More than that? Was she taken, killed? Is this a re-creation of her death?"

She studied her own face, the ID print she'd pinned up. And what did he see when he looked at it? she wondered. Not just another victim this time, but an opponent. That was new, wasn't it? Hunting the hunter.

The grand finale. Yes, Mira could be right about that. The twist at the end of the show. Applause, applause, and curtain.

She poured out a second cup of coffee, sat to prop her feet on her desk. Maybe not just an opera fan. A performer? Frustrated performer or composer . . .

The performer didn't fit profile, she decided. It would involve a lot of training, a lot of teamwork. Taking direction. No, that wasn't his style.

A composer, could be. Most people who wrote anything worked alone a lot of the time. Taking charge of the words or the music.

"Computer, working with all current data, run probability series as follows. What is the probability the perpetrator has returned to New York, has targeted Dallas, Lieutenant Eve, in a desire to complete what he may consider his work?

"What is the probability that desire is fostered by his knowledge of his own death, or plans to self-terminate?

"What is the probability, given his use of opera houses for false addresses, he is or was involved in opera as a profession?

"What is the probability, given the timelines of the perpetrator's sprees and subsequent rest periods, he utilizes chemicals to suppress or release his urge to kill?"

Acknowledged.

"Hold it. I'm still thinking. What is the probability the victims represent a person connected to the perpetrator who was, at some time, tortured and killed by methods he now employs? Begin run."

Acknowledged. Working . . .

"You do that." Leaning back, Eve sipped coffee, closed her eyes.

She let it filter in, chewed on it awhile, used the results to formulate other runs. Then she simply sat and let it all simmer in her head.

When Roarke stepped in, she had her boots on the desk, ankles crossed. There was a coffee mug in her hand. Her eyes were closed, her face blank. The cat padded in behind him and arrowed straight for the sleep chair, lest someone get there first. Then he sprawled out, as if exhausted by the walk from nap to nap.

Roarke started across the room, then stopped dead in front of the murder board. If someone had slammed a steel bat into his chest it would've been less of a jolt than seeing Eve's face on that board, among the dead and missing.

He lost his breath. It simply left his body as he imagined life would if he lost her. Then it came back, blown through him by sheer rage. His hands clenched at his sides, hard balls of violence. He could see them punching through the face of the man who saw Eve as a victim, as some sort of grand prize in his collection. What he felt, literally, was the connection of those fists to flesh, to bone and blood, not to empty paper and ink.

And he reveled in the raw phantom pain in his knuckles.

She didn't belong there. Would *never* belong there, in that hideous gallery of death.

Yet she had put herself there, he realized. Had put her image among the others. Steely-minded, he thought now. His cop, his wife, his world. Coolheadedly, cool-bloodedly aligning the facts and data, even when her own life was part of them.

He ordered himself to calm, to understand why she'd put herself there. She needed to see the whole picture, and seeing the whole picture would shut it down.

He looked away from the board and over to her. She was exactly as she'd been when he entered. Kicked back, still—and safe.

He went to her, realized some of the rage and fear was still with him when he wanted to simply pluck her up, wrap himself around her, and hold on. And on. Instead he reached down to take the mug out of her hand.

"Get your own coffee," she muttered, and opened her eyes.

Not asleep, he realized, but in the zone. "My mistake. I thought you were sleeping on the job."

"Thinking time, pal. Didn't hear you come in. How's it going?"

"Well enough. I grabbed a swim and a shower to delude myself that I was still feeling human."

"Yeah, I went the beach run and iron pumping route. Mostly works. I've been doing probabilities and some data juggling. I need to write up a report, then do some runs. When—"

"I want ten minutes," he interrupted.

"Huh?"

"Ten minutes." He took the coffee now, set it aside, then captured her hand to pull her out of the chair. "Where it's just you, just me."

She cocked up her eyebrows as he drew her away from the desk. "Ten minutes isn't anything to brag about, ace."

"I'm not meaning sex." He slid his arms around her, kept moving in what she now understood was a slow and easy dance. "Or not precisely that. I want ten minutes of you," he repeated, lowering his brow to hers. "Just that, without anything or anyone."

She drew in a breath, and smelled the shower on him. That lingering scent of soap on his skin. "It already feels good." She touched her lips to his, angled her head. "Tastes good, too."

He skimmed a finger down the dent in her chin, brushed his lips on hers. "So it does. And there's this spot I know." He used his finger to turn her head slightly, then laid his lips along her jawline, just below her ear. "Just exactly there. It's perfect."

"That one spot?"

"Well now, there are others, but that's a particular favorite of mine."

She smiled, then rested her head on his shoulder—a favorite spot of hers—and let him guide her through the easy dance. "Roarke."

"Mmm?"

"Nothing. It just feels good to say it."

His hand stroked up and down her back. "Eve," he said. "You're right again. It does. I love you. There's nothing that feels more perfect than that."

"Hearing it's not bad. Knowing it's the best." She lifted her head, met his lips again. "I love you."

They held on, and they ended the dance as they'd begun. With his brow resting against hers. "There, now," he murmured. "That's better." He drew back, then lifted her hands to his lips.

He had a way, just that way, of making her insides curl. His lips warm on her skin, and those wild blue eyes looking over their joined hands into hers made her wish she had a hundred ten minutes just to be. As long as he could just be along with her.

"It's pretty damn good," she told him.

"Why don't I get us a meal," he suggested, "and you can tell me about those probabilities."

"I'll get it. It's got to be my turn by now. You can go ahead and look them over if you want."

She stepped back, turned. And saw, as she realized now he would have seen, her photo on the board. "Oh, Jesus. Jesus." Appalled, she gripped a handful of her own hair and tugged. "Listen, this was stupid. I'm stupid. I only put this up there to—"

"Don't call yourself stupid, for you're far from it most of the time." His tone was cool and even. "I'm more than happy to let you know when you are stupid. It's not a problem for me."

"Yeah, you've made that clear in the past. But this was just so—"

She broke off again when he held up a hand. "You put yourself there because you have to be objective, and more—you have to be able to see yourself as he does. Not only as you are, but as he sees you. If you don't, you may be careless."

"Okay, yeah." She slid her hands into her pockets. "Got it in one. Are you okay with this?"

"Does it help you if I'm not okay with it? Obviously not. So I'll deal with it. And I'll kill him if he hurts you."

"Hey, hey."

"I'm not meaning the garden variety of bumps, bruises, and occasional bites," he added with a glance at her leg, "you seem to incur on an alarmingly regular basis."

"I hold my own," she snapped back, oddly insulted. "And you've taken some hits yourself, pal." Her eyes narrowed when he held up a finger. "Oh, I really hate when you do that."

"Pity. If he manages to get past your guard, past me, and all the rest, and causes you real harm, I'll do him with my own hands and in my own way. You'll have to be okay with that, as that's as much who and what I am and it's who and what you are that put your own face up there."

"He won't get past my guard."

"Then we won't have a problem, will we? What's for dinner?"

She wanted to argue, but she couldn't find any room to maneuver. So she shrugged and stalked off toward the kitchen. "I want carbs."

The man was exasperating. One minute he was kissing her hand in the sort of quietly romantic gesture that turned her to putty, and the next he was telling her he'd do murder in that calm, cool voice that was scarier than a blaster to the temple.

And the hell of it was, she thought as the cat bumped his head against her leg, he meant both those things absolutely. Hell, he *was* both of those things absolutely.

She ordered spaghetti and meatballs, leaned back on the counter, and sighed. He might be exasperating, complicated, dangerous, and difficult, but she loved every piece of the puzzle that made him.

She gave the now desperate Galahad a portion from each plate—fair was fair—before carrying them back into the office. She saw he'd correctly interpreted her carbs as spaghetti, and had opened a bottle of red. He sat, sipping, and scanning her comp screen.

"Maybe he'll cause you real harm." Eve set the plates on her desk. "Then I'll kill him."

"Works for me. Interesting questions posed here, Lieutenant." As if it were any casual meal—and for them perhaps it was—Roarke expertly wound noodles around his fork. "Interesting percentages."

"Probability's high Mira hit it with the reasons he's come back to New York, and the reason he's targeted me. Also in the high range he's connected to opera professionally. I'm not sure I agree."

"Why?"

"Has to be a lot of work, right? Focus, energy, dedication. And in most cases, a lot of interaction with others. Factor it in, sure," she said, studying the display on-screen, "but when I rolled it around during my thinking time, it doesn't fit for me. He's no team player. My gauge is he likes his quiet time. You could, on some level, call his killings performances, but that's not how I see them. They're more intimate. Just between him and the vic until he's done."

"A duet."

"A duet. Hmm." She rolled that around, too. "Yeah, okay, a duet, I can see that. One man, one woman, the dynamics there, extremely personal. A performance, okay, without an audience, too intimate to share. Because, I think, at some time he was intimately connected to the woman all the rest represent. Yeah. They were a duet."

"And his partner was killed."

"Derailed his train. That's why I think he uses chemicals to rein himself in for long periods—or conversely to free himself for short ones. There, the computer and I agree. So, I look for types of medications that can suppress homicidal urges. And if he's sick, as we're theorizing, he may be taking meds for whatever his condition might be. Do you know Tomas Pella?"

"The name's not familiar, no."

"He seemed to know you."

"I know a great many people."

"And a great many more know you, I get that. He used to own some restaurants in Little Italy. Sold them shortly after the time all this started nine years ago."

"I might have bought them, or one of them. I'll check the records."

"How about Hugh Klok, antiquities dealer. You buy a lot of old stuff."

"Doesn't ring."

"I'll do a run on him. One of the others Newkirk remembered from the prior was this guy who did taxidermy. You know, stuffed dead animals."

"Which always begs the question: Why in the bloody hell?"

"Yeah, what's with that?" Eve slanted her gaze over to Galahad, who'd wandered back in to sit and wash up after his meal. "I mean, would you want . . . you know, when he uses up his nine?"

"Good God, no. Not only, well, creepy would be the word, wouldn't it, for us, but bloody humiliating for him."

"Yeah, that's what I think. I liked the idea of the taxidermy guy for the symbolism. House of death and blah. But he's clear. Lives on Vegas II, and has for four years. Checked out. So anyway, you want the background on these other two, and the third I questioned today, Dobbins?"

"I'm sure it's as much sparkling dinner conversation as the philosophy of taxidermy and dead cats. Go ahead."

Downtown in their apartment, Peabody and McNab worked on dueling computers. Because he worked better with noise and she didn't care, the air blasted with trash rock and revisionist rap. She sat, hunched over, tuning most of it out and picking her way through a complicated search.

He was up and down like a restless puppy, alternately snapping out directives and singing lyrics. She didn't know how anyone could get any work done that way. But she also knew he not only could, he had to.

The remnants of the Chinese delivery they'd ordered were scattered around both their workstations. Peabody was already wishing she'd resisted that last egg roll.

When she finally found the data she was after, tears blurred her eyes. The hot prick of tears warned her she was overtired and her resistance was bottoming out.

"Hey, hey, She-Body!" McNab caught the look on her face. "Music off. Computer, save and pause. What's wrong, honey?"

"It's so sad. It just makes me so sad."

"What does?" He'd already come behind her to pat and rub her shoulders.

It was a pretty good deal, she thought, to have somebody there to pet you when you were shaky. "I found Therese—Therese Di Vecchio Pella. Tomas Pella's wife, one of the guys Dallas and I talked to today."

"Yeah, from Old Newkirk's notes, from the first go-round."

"They got married in April. They were with the Home Force. He was a corporal, she was a medic. And see, look." She tapped the comp screen. "In July she was dispatched to this area, on the edge of SoHo and Tribeca. An explosion, mostly civilian casualties. There was still firing in the sector, but she went in. She was wearing the red cross—the medic symbol. But she got hit by sniper fire when she tried to reach the wounded. She was only twenty. She was trying to help wounded civilians, and they killed her."

She sat back, knuckled away the tears. "I don't know. It just rips me, I guess. You've got to have hope, right, to stop long enough to get married in the middle of all that. And then, you're gone. Trying to help people, and you're gone. She was only twenty."

McNab leaned down, pressed a kiss to the top of her head. "Want me to take this for a while?"

"No. We talked to that old man today. Well, not that old, really, but it seemed like he was older than Moses in that bed, with the breather on. And then I read this, and think how he'd been so young, and he'd loved this girl. Then . . . she's too young."

"I know it's tough, baby, but—"

"No, no. I mean, yeah, it's tough, but she's too young to be the source of the pattern." Tears—and some still clung to her lashes—were forgotten. "She was only twenty, and the youngest vic was twenty-eight. Twenty-eight to thirty-three, that's been his span. So Therese Pella died too young, it most likely eliminates Pella as a suspect."

"You were seriously looking at this guy?"

"He's the right age, the basic type, connection with the Urbans, private home—and can you spell bitter? Got a tumor—or he says—Dallas is checking that. Lost his bride—bride and groom—who was a pretty brunette. But after that it doesn't follow."

Peabody sat back, shaking her head at the data on screen. "Doesn't follow pattern. She's hit by sniper fire, not tortured. She's eight years younger than his youngest vic when she was killed. Misses the profile. But there was something. A tingle, Dallas called it. There was a tingle when we talked to him."

"Maybe he knows something. Maybe he's connected."

"Yeah, maybe. I need to get this to Dallas, then try for deeper data on Pella."

"I'll give you a hand." McNab gave her shoulders another rub, then toyed with the ends of her hair. "Okay now?"

"Yeah. I guess it's not enough sleep and too much on the brain."

"You need to take a break."

"Maybe I do." She knuckled her eyes again, but this time to clear fatigue instead of tears. "If it wasn't so cold out, I'd take a walk, get some air, some exercise."

"I don't know about the air," he said as she rose. "But I can help with the exercise." Grinning, he laid a hand on her ass, gave it a squeeze.

"Yeah?" Her eyes danced; her libido boogied. "You wanna?"

"Let me answer that question by ripping your clothes off."

She let out a laughing squeal as they tumbled to the floor. "I thought, you know, you weren't feeling the bloom and spark."

"Something's blooming just fine," he said as he dragged off her sweater.

She tugged his pants down over his hips to check for herself. Looking down, she said, "I'll say."

"And as for sparkage." He crushed his mouth to hers in a kiss hot enough she envisioned smoke coming out of her ears. "Any more, and we'd torch the place."

She saw his eyes go dreamy when his hand cupped her breast, felt her stomach muscles tighten in response.

"Mmmm, She-body, the most female of females. Let's see what we can light up."

Later, considerably later, Eve studied the data Peabody had sent to her office unit. "She's right," Eve mumbled. "Too young, wrong method. Dobbins hits me as just too sloppy, just too disinterested. Klok's coming across as straight and narrow. But there's something here. I just can't see it yet."

"Maybe you would if you got a decent night's sleep."

Instead, she walked around her boards again. "Opera. What about the opera-tickets angle?"

"I've got the list for season ticket holders for the Met. Nothing on the first cross-check. I'll try others."

"He jumps names, jumps names and ID data. Covert stuff. Smooth, under radar. Where'd he learn how? Torture methods. Covert operations have been known to employ torture methods."

"I can tell you my sources on the matter of torturers isn't popping anyone of this generation still living and in business, or anyone who moonlights by targeting young brunettes."

"It was worth a shot," Eve mused. "Covert might change that. Someone who was in military ops, or paramilitary at one time. He learned the methods somewhere, and developed the skill to manipulate his data."

"Or has the connections or the funds to hire someone to manipulate it," Roarke reminded her.

"Yeah, there's that. So. Why do we torture someone?"

"For information."

"Yeah, at least ostensibly. Why else do you torture? Kicks, sexual deviation, ritual sacrifice."

"Experimentation. Another tried and true rationale for inflicting pain."

She looked at him. "We eliminate the need or desire for information, and the sexual deviation. No doubt in my mind he gets personal gratification from inflicting pain, but it has to be more. Ritual's part of it, but this isn't some sick religious deal or cult. So, experimentation," she repeated. "Fits. Factor in that he's very good at it. Torture skills are specialized. He isn't messy about it, he's precise. Again, where did he learn?"

"And you're back to the Urbans."

"It keeps crossing there. Someone taught him, or he studied. Experimented before the experimentation. But not here, not in New York."

Circling her board, she studied, considered angles. "We ran searches for others before. I did a Missing Persons run on the victim type. But what if he experimented elsewhere? If he purposefully mutilated the bodies to eliminate the correlation, or disposed of them altogether?"

"You're going to do a global search on mutilations and missing persons involving the victim type."

"He might not have been as careful. If we find something . . . he might have left something behind." She stopped, stared at the sketch of the man she hunted. "Still honing his craft, still finding his way. We did globals, but maybe we didn't go back far enough."

"I'll set it up. I can do it faster," he said before she could argue. "Then it'll take a good long while for any results you can actually work with. I'll set it up, then we're getting some sleep."

"All right. Okay."

The dreams came in blurry spurts, as if she were swimming through fog that tore and re-formed, tore and re-formed. The clock ticked incessantly.

Over that endless, echoing tick, she heard the sounds of a battle raging. A firefight, she thought. Blasts and bullets and the wild shouts and calls of the men and women who fought.

She could smell the blood, the smoke, the burning flesh before she could see it. Carnage carried a sickly sweet aroma.

As vision cleared, focused, she saw the battle was on a stage, and the stage was dressed to depict the city in a strange, stylized form. Buildings, all black and silver, were tipped and tilted above hard white streets that jagged into impossible angles or inexplicable dead ends.

And the players on stage were dressed in bright, elaborate costumes that flowed through bloody pools and swirled in dirty smoke as they murdered each other.

She looked down on it all with interest, from her gilded box seat. Below, in a pit where bodies lay twisted, she could see the orchestra madly playing their instruments. Their fingers ran with blood from razor-sharp strings.

On stage, the shouts and calls were songs, she realized, fierce, violent. Vicious.

War could never be otherwise.

"The third act is nearly over."

She turned, looked into the face of the killer as he took a huge stopwatch out of the pocket of his formal black.

"I don't understand. It's all death. Who writes these things?"

"Death, yes. Passion and strength and life. Everything leads to death, doesn't it? Who would know that better than you?"

"Murder's different."

"Oh, yes, it's artful and it's deliberate. It takes it out of the hands of fate and puts the power into the one who creates death. Who makes a gift of it."

"What gift? How is murder a gift?"

"This . . ." He gestured to the stage as a woman, brown hair bloody, face and body battered, was borne in on a stretcher. "This is about immortality."

"Immortality's for the dead. Who was she when she was alive?"

He only smiled. "Time's up." He clicked the stopwatch, and the stage went black.

Eve came rearing up in bed, sucking for air. Caught between the dream and reality, she closed her hands over her ears to muffle the ticking. "Why won't it stop?"

"Eve. Eve. It's your 'link." Roarke curled his fingers over her wrists, gently tugged her hands down. "It's your 'link."

"Jesus. Wait." She shook her head, pulled herself into the now. "Block video," she ordered, then answered. "Dallas."

Dispatch, Dallas, Lieutenant Eve. Report to Union Square Park off Park Avenue. Body of unidentified female, evidence of torture.

Eve turned her head, met Roarke's eyes. "Acknowledged. Notify Peabody, Detective Delia, request Medical Examiner Morris. As per procedure on this matter, relay notification to Commander Whitney and Dr. Mira. I'm on my way. Dallas out."

"I'll be going with you. I know," Roarke said as he rose, "you don't make prime bait with me along, but that'll be Gia Rossi left on the ground. And I'm going with you."

"I'm sorry."

"Ah, Eve." His tone changed, softened. "So am I."

18

AS EVE HAD SEEN THEIR HOME IN ITS SNOWY
landscape as a painting, Roarke saw the crime scene as
a play. A dark play with constant movement and great
noise, all centered around the single focal character.

The white sheet on the white snow, the white body laid over it, with
deep brown hair shining in the hard lights. He thought the wounds
stood out against the pale flesh like screams.

And there his wife stood in her long black coat, gloveless, of course.
They'd both forgotten her gloves this time around. Hatless and hard-
eyed. The stage manager, he thought, and a major player as well.
Director and author of this final act.

There would be pity in her, this he knew, and there would be anger,
a ribbon of guilt to tie them all together. But that complicated emotional package was tucked deep inside, walled in behind that cool,
calculating mind.

He watched her speak to the sweepers, to the uniforms, to the others who walked on and off that winter stage. Then Peabody, the de-
pendable, in her turtle-shell of a coat and colorful scarf, crossed the

stage on cue. Together, she and Eve lowered to that lifeless focal point that held the dispassionate spotlight of center stage.

"Not close enough," McNab said from beside him.

Roarke shifted his attention, very briefly, from the scene to McNab. "What?"

"Just couldn't get close enough." McNab's hands were deep in two of the many pockets of his bright green coat, with the long tails of a boldly striped scarf fluttering down his back. "Moving in on a dozen roads from a dozen damn directions. Moving in, you can feel we're getting closer. But not close enough to help Gia Rossi. It's hard. This one hits hard."

"It does."

Had he really believed, Roarke wondered, a lifetime ago, had he honestly assumed that the nature of the cop was to feel nothing? He'd learned different since Eve. He'd learned very different. And now, he stood silent, listening to the lines as the players played their parts.

"TOD oh-one-thirty. Early Monday morning," Peabody said. "She's been dead a little over twenty-six hours."

"He kept her for a day." Eve studied the carving in the torso. Thirty-nine hours, eight minutes, forty-five seconds. "Kept her a day after he was finished. She didn't last for him. The wounds are less severe, less plentiful than on York. Something went wrong for him this time. He wasn't able to sustain the work."

Less severe, yes, Peabody could see that was true. And still the cuts, the burns and bruising spoke of terrible suffering. "Maybe he got impatient this time. Maybe he needed to go for the kill."

"I don't think so." With her sealed fingers, Eve picked up the victim's arm, turned it to study the ligature marks from the binding. Then turned it back to examine more closely the killing wounds on the wrist. "She didn't fight like York, not as much damage from the ropes, wrists and ankles. And the killing strokes here? Just as clean and precise as all the others. He's still in control. And he still wants them to last."

She laid the arm down again, on the white, white sheet. "It's a matter of pride in his skill—torture, create the pain, but keep them alive. Increasing the level of pain, fear, injury, all while keeping them breathing. But Rossi, she wound down on him ahead of his schedule, ahead of his goal."

"Before he'd have been able to see the media bulletins with his image," Peabody pointed out. "It's not because he panicked, or took his anger out on her."

Eve glanced up. "No. But if he had, she'd still be dead. If he had, we still did what we had to do. Put that away. He started on her Saturday morning, finished early Monday. York Friday night. So he had a little celebration, maybe, or just gets a good night's sleep before he rewinds the clock for Rossi."

Takes time out to shadow me, Eve thought. Another tried and true torture method. Rest and revisit. Time out again to lure and secure Greenfeld. Need your next vic in the goddamn bullpen.

"Cleans her up, takes his time. No rush, no hurry. Already got the dump spot picked out, already surveyed the area. Set up a canvass."

From her crouched position, Eve surveyed the area. "This kind of weather, there aren't going to be a lot of people hanging out in the park. Bides his time," she continued. "Loads her up, transports her here. Carries her in."

"Sweepers have a lot of footprints to work with. The snow was pretty fresh and soft. They'll make the treads, give us a size, a brand."

"Yeah. But he's not worried about that. Smart enough, he's smart enough to wear something oversized, try to throw us off. To wear something common that's next to impossible to pin. When we get him, we'll find them, help hang him with them, but they won't lead us to him."

As dispassionate now as those harsh crime scene lights, Eve examined the body. "She was strong, in top shape." Good specimen? she wondered. Had he thought he'd had a prime candidate for his nasty duet? "She struggled, but not as much as York. Not nearly as hard as York, not as long. Gave out, that's what she did. Physically strong, but something in her shut down. Must've been a big disappointment to him."

"I'm glad she didn't suffer as much. I know," Peabody said when Eve lifted her head. "But if we couldn't save her, I'm glad she didn't suffer as much."

"If she could've held out longer, maybe we could've saved her. And either way you look at it, Peabody, doesn't mean a fucking thing."

She straightened as she spotted Morris coming toward them. In his eyes she saw something that was in her, some of what was in Peabody. She would, Eve thought, see that same complicated mix of anger, despair, guilt, and sorrow in the eyes of every cop involved.

"Gia Rossi," was all Morris said.

"Yes. She's been dead a little more than twenty-six hours by our gauge. A group of kids cutting through the park found her. Mucked up the scene some, but for the most part then just cut and ran. One of them called it in.

"Something went wrong for him with her." Eve looked down at the body again. "He didn't get a lot of time out of her. Maybe she just shut down, or maybe he used something—experimenting—some chemical that shut her down."

"I'll flag the tox as priority. She isn't as damaged as the others."

"No."

"Can she be moved yet?"

"I was about to roll her."

With a nod, he bent to help, and together they rolled the body.

"No injuries on her back," Morris said.

"Most of them don't. He likes face-to-face. It has to be personal. It has to be intimate."

"Some bruising, lacerations, burns, punctures on the back of the shoulders, the calves. Less than the others." Gently, he brushed the hair aside, examined the back of the neck, the scalp, the ears. "In comparison, I'd say he barely got to stage two in this case. Yes, yes, something went wrong. I'll take her in now."

He straightened, met Eve's eyes. "Will there be family?"

He never asked, or so rarely she'd never registered it. "She has a mother in Queens, a father and stepmother out in Illinois. We'll be contacting them."

"Let me know if and when they want to see her. I'll take them through it personally."

"All right."

He looked away, past the lights into the cold dark. "I wish it were spring," he said.

"Yeah, people still end up dead, but it's a nicer atmosphere for the rest of us. And, you know, flowers. They're a nice touch."

He grinned, and some of the shadows around him seemed to lift. "I like daffodils myself. I always think of the trumpet as a really long mouth, and imagine they chatter away at each other in a language we can't hear."

"That's a little scary," she decided.

"Then you don't want to get me started on pansies."

"Really don't. I'll check in with you later. Peabody, get that canvass started." She left Morris, heard him murmur, *All right now, Gia*, then stepped up to Roarke.

"I'm nearly done here," she began. "You should—"

"I won't be going home," Roarke told her. "I'll go in, start working in the war room. I'll take care of getting myself there."

"I'll go on in with you." McNab looked at Eve. "If that's all right with you, Lieutenant."

"Go ahead, and contact the rest of the team. No reason for them to lay around in bed when we're not. This is a twenty-four/seven op now. I'll work out subteams, twelve-hour shifts. The clock's about to start on Ariel Greenfeld. We're not going to find her like this."

She looked back. "I'm goddamned if we're going to find her like this."

It was still shy of dawn when she got to Central. Before she went to her office, she walked into the war room. As the lights flicked on she looked around. It was quiet now, empty of people. It wouldn't be so again, she thought. Not until they'd closed this down.

She was adding more men, more eyes, ears, legs, hands. More to work the streets, flash the killer's picture, talk to neighbors, street people, cabbies, chemi-heads. More to knock on the doors of the far too numerous buildings Roarke had thus far listed in his search.

More people to push, push, push, to track down every thread no matter how thin and knotted.

Until this was done there was only one investigation, only one killer, only one purpose for her and every cop under her.

She walked to the white board and in her own hand wrote out the time it had taken for Gia Rossi to die after Rossi's name.

Then she looked down at the next name she'd written. Ariel Greenfeld.

"You hold the hell on. It's not over, and it's not going to be over, so you hold the hell on."

She turned, saw Roarke watching her from the doorway. "You made good time," he told her. "McNab and I detoured up to EDD, to requisition more equipment. Feeney's on his way in."

"Good."

He crossed over to stand, as she was, in front of the whiteboard. "It depends, on some level, on her now. On you, on us, certainly on him, but on some level, on her."

"Every hour she holds on, we get closer."

"And every hour she holds on, is another hour he may move on you. You want that. You'd will it to happen if you could."

No bullshit, she decided. No evasions. "That's right."

"When they killed Marlena, all those years ago, broke her to pieces to prove a point to me, I wanted them to come at me."

Eve thought of Summerset's daughter, how she'd been taken, tortured, and killed by rivals of the young, enterprising criminal Roarke had been. "If they had, the whole of them, you'd have ended up in the ground with her."

"That may be. That very likely may be." He shifted his gaze from the board to meet hers. "But I wanted it, and would have willed it if I could have. But since that wasn't to be, I found another way to end every one of them."

"He's only one man. And there may not be another way."

Thinking of those who were lost, he looked at the board again. Only one man, and perhaps only one way. "That's all very true. Here's what I know, here's what I understood out there in the cold and the dark with you tending to what he'd made of Gia Rossi. He thinks he knows you."

He turned his head now, and those brilliant blue eyes fired into hers. "He thinks he understands what you are, knows who you are. But he's wrong. He doesn't know or understand the likes of you. If it comes to the two of you, even for a moment, if it comes to the two of you, he may get a glimmer of who and what you are. And if he does, he'll know something of fear."

"Well." A little shaken, a little mystified, she blew out a breath. "That's not what I was expecting out of you."

"When I looked at her, at what he'd done to her, I thought I would envision you there. Your face with her face, as it is on your board."

"Roarke—"

"But I didn't," he continued, and lifted her hand to brush his fingers to her cheek. "Couldn't. Not, I think, because it was more than I could stand. Not because of that, but because he'll never have that power or control over you. You won't allow it. And that, Darling Eve, is of considerable comfort to me."

"It's a nice bolster for me, too." She aimed a glance toward the door, just to make sure they were still alone. Then she leaned in, kissed him. "Thanks. I've got to go."

"And if he kills you," Roarke added as she strode to the door, "I'm going to be extremely pissed off."

"Who could blame you?"

She started back to her office, stopped when Peabody hailed her. "Baxter and Trueheart are notifying the mother, as ordered. I just spoke with the father."

"All right. When Baxter reports in, we'll clear it for her name to be released to the media."

"Speaking of the media, I poked into your office in case you were there. There's about a half a million messages from various reporters."

"I'll take care of it. Let me know when everyone's in the house. We'll do the briefing asap."

"Will do. Dallas, do you want me to update the boards?"

"I've already done it." She turned away to go to her office.

She flicked through the source readout on the messages, transferring them to the liaison. Only when she came to one from Nadine did she pause, then order playback.

"Dallas, the lines are buzzing you've got another one. It's going to get ugly, so this is a heads up. The spit's already flying and most of it's going to splatter on you and the NYPSD. If you've got anything I can use, get back to me."

Eve considered, then ordered the callback. Nadine picked up on the first beep.

"I thought media darlings slept till noon."

"Sure, just like cops. I'm already in my office," Nadine told her. "Working on some copy. I'm going on at eight. Special report. If you've got anything, now's the time to share."

"A source from the NYPSD stated this morning that new and salient information regarding the individual the media has dubbed The Groom has come to light."

"What new and salient information?"

"However, the source would not divulge any details of this information due to the need to confine any and all such data within the investigation. It was also stated by the same source that the task force formed to pursue the investigation is working around the clock to identify and apprehend the individual responsible for the deaths of Sarifina York and Gia Rossi. As well as to seek justice for them and for the twenty-three other women whose deaths are attributed to this same individual."

"Nice, but there's a lot of spin in there. The media's going to come at you hard. You're going to take hits."

"You really think I give a rat's ass about a few publicity bruises right now, Nadine? Air the statement. What I want is for him to know we're coming, and to worry about what we might have. Don't release Rossi's name until the eight o'clock airing."

"How about this? Will the NYPSD source confirm or deny that the investigation is focused on a specific suspect?"

"The source won't confirm or deny, but stated that members of the task force are seeking or have located and interviewed persons of interest."

"Okay." Nadine nodded as she scribbled. "Still doesn't really say anything, but it sounds like it says something."

"Do you still have your researchers on tap?"

"Sure."

"I may have something for them to play with later. That's it, Nadine. You want the official department statement, go to the liaison."

Eve clicked off, got coffee. Though it annoyed her, she used it to chase an energy pill. Better jumpy than sluggish, she decided, then called up the results from the global search she'd done from home.

As the names began rolling on, she sat back, closed her eyes. Thousands, she thought. Well, what had she expected given the search elements she'd had Roarke input.

So she had to narrow them, refine it.

Her 'link beeped. "Yeah, yeah."

"Team's in the house," Peabody told her.

"I'll be there."

Tired cops, Eve thought when she stepped into the war room. Her team now consisted of tired, frustrated, and pissed off cops. Sometimes, she thought, cops did their best work that way. They'd be running on adrenaline and irritation—and in a lot of cases the boost of energy pills.

No bullshit, she thought again. No evasions.

"We lost her." The room fell instantly silent. "We've got the full resources of the top police and security departments in the country behind us. We've got the experience, the brains, the bullheadedness of every cop in this room. But we lost her. You've got thirty seconds to brood about that, to feel crappy about it, to shoulder the guilt. Then that's done."

She set down her file bag, walked over to get more coffee. When she came back, she took out the copy she'd made of Ariel Greenfeld's photo, pinned it in the center of a fresh board.

"We're not losing her. As of now we're round the clock for the duration. As of now, she's the only victim in this city. As of now, she is the single most important person in our lives. Officer Newkirk?"

"Sir."

"You and the officers you've been working with will take this first twelve-hour shift. You'll be relieved by officers I've assigned at . . ." She checked her wrist unit. "Nineteen hundred. Captain Feeney, I'll use your recommendation for another pair of e-men to take the second shift. Field detectives, I'll have your relief lined up shortly."

"Lieutenant." Trueheart cleared his throat, and Eve could see him fighting the urge to raise his hand. "Detective Baxter and I have worked out a crib rotation. I mean to say we discussed same on the way back from notifying next of kin. With your permission, we'd prefer not to be relieved, but to handle the twenty-four-hour cycle ourselves."

"You need more men," Baxter added, "you get more men. But we don't go off the clock. How about you, Sick Bastard?" He used Jenkinson's nickname.

"We'll sleep when we get him."

"All right," Eve agreed. "We'll try it that way. I've done a global search for mutilations, murders, and missings meeting the targets' descriptions. We concluded in the first investigation that it was likely the killer had killed before, practiced before. I widened the search," she told Feeney, "went global and back five years, and netted thousands of results."

She held up the disc copy of the run, tossed it to Feeney. "We need to whittle it down, refine it. And we need to find one or more that could be his—and find his mistakes.

"Item second," she continued, and worked through her list.

As Eve briefed her team, listened to their reports and coordinated the duties, Ariel Greenfeld came awake. She'd surfaced twice before, barely registering her surroundings before he'd come in. Small room, glass walls, medical equipment? Was she in the hospital?

She struggled to see him clearly, but everything was so blurry. As if her eyes, and her mind, had been smeared with oil. She thought she heard music, high trilling voices. Angels? Was she dead?

Then she'd gone under again, sliding down and down to nothing.

This time when she awoke, the room was larger. It seemed larger to her. The lights were very bright, almost painful to her eyes. She felt weak and queasy, as though she'd been sick a very long time, and again thought, "Hospital."

Had she been in an accident? She couldn't remember, and as she lay still to take stock, felt no pain. She ordered herself to think back, to think back to the last thing she *could* remember.

"Wedding cakes," she murmured.

Mr. Gaines. Mr. Gaines's granddaughter's wedding. She had a chance for the job, a good job, designing and baking the cake, standing as dessert chef for the reception.

Mr. Gaines's house—big, beautiful old house, pretty parlor with a fireplace. Warm and cozy. Yes! She remembered. He'd picked her up, driven her to his house for a meeting with his granddaughter. And then . . .

It wanted to fade on her, but she pushed the fog away. When it cleared, her heart began to hammer. Tea and cookies. The tea, something in the tea. Something in his eyes when she'd tried to stand.

Not the hospital. God, oh God no, she wasn't in the hospital. He'd drugged her tea, and he'd taken her somewhere. She had to get away, had to get away now.

She tried to sit up, but her arms, her legs were pinned. Panicked, sucking back a scream, she pushed up as far as she could. And felt terror run through her like a river.

She was naked, tied, hands and feet, to a table. Some sort of metal table with rope restraints that looped through openings and bit into her skin when she strained against them. As her eyes wheeled around the room she saw monitors, screens, cameras, and tables holding metal trays.

There were sharp things on the trays. Sharp, terrifying things.

As her body began to shake, her mind wanted to deny, to reject. Tears leaked when she twisted and writhed in a desperate attempt to free herself.

The woman in the park. Another woman missing. She'd seen the media reports. Horrible, that's what she'd thought. Isn't that horrible. But then she'd gone off to work without another thought. It didn't have anything to do with her. Just another horrible thing that happened to someone else.

It always happened to someone else.

Until now.

She dragged in her breath, let it out in a scream. She screamed for help until her lungs burned and her throat felt scorched. Then she screamed some more.

Someone had to hear, someone had to come.

But when someone heard, when someone came, fear choked off her screams like a throttling hand.

"Ah, you're awake," he said, and smiled at her.

E ve input the names on the list Roarke had generated of season ticket holders. Her first search requested highlighting males between sixty and eighty years of age.

She'd expand that, if necessary, she thought. He may have created a bogus company for this particular purpose, or any type of persona.

No guarantee he sprang for season tickets, she mused. He could cherry pick the performances that appealed to him rather than just blanket the whole season.

When the amended list came up, she followed through with a standard run on each name.

She was over three-quarters through when she zeroed in.

"There you are," she murmured. "There you are, you bastard. Stewart E. Pierpont this time? 'E' for some form of Edward. Who's Edward to you?"

His hair was salt-and-pepper in the ID photo, worn in a long, dramatic mane. He claimed to be a British citizen, with residences in London, New York, and Monte Carlo. And a widower this time around, Eve noted. That was new.

The deceased wife was listed as Carmen DeWinter, also British, who died at the age of thirty-two.

Eve narrowed her eyes at the date of death. "Urban War era. Maybe you got too damn clever this time, Eddie."

She did a run on DeWinter, Carmen, but found none who matched the data given on the Pierpont ID. "Okay, okay. But there was a woman, wasn't there? She died, was killed, or hey, you took her out yourself. But she existed."

She went back to Pierpont, checked the listed addresses. An opera house in Monte Carlo, a concert hall in London, and Carnegie Hall in New York.

Sticks with his pattern, she thought. But the season tickets were either delivered somewhere, or were picked up.

She grabbed what she had, hustled to the war room, and Roarke's station. "Who do you know at the Metropolitan Opera, and how much grease can you use to clear the way for me?"

"I know a few people. What do you need?"

"Anything and everything on him." She tossed down the printout on Pierpont. "That's him, season-ticket-holder style. Nice call on that, by the way."

"We do what we can."

"Do more. There isn't time for bureaucracy and red tape. I want a clear path to whoever can give me the juice on this guy."

"Give me five minutes," he said, and pulled out his personal 'link.

She stepped away to give him room as her own 'link signaled. "Dallas."

"Might have something," Baxter announced. "On the rings. We've been working it, and I think we've nailed where he bought them. Tiffany's—gotta go with the classic."

"I thought we checked there before."

"Did, nobody remembered, no rings of that specific style carried. We decided to give it another push. Classic style, classic store. And while they're not flashy, they are sterling. We're trolling the clerks, batting zero, then this woman overhears. A customer. She remembers being in there right before Christmas and noticing this guy buying four sterling bands. Commented on it, and the guy gives her a line about his four granddaughters. She thought it was charming, so she remembers it. Turns out, when we get the manager to dig a little, they carried a limited supply of that style late last year."

"Record of the sale."

"Cash, four sterling accent bands, purchased December eighteenth. The wit's a peach, Dallas. Said she 'engaged him in conversation.' I get the feeling she was trying to hit on him, and she said she complimented him on his scent, asked what it was. Alimar Botanicals."

"Trina's got a damn good nose. That's one of her picks."

"Better yet, he mentioned he'd first discovered it in Paris, and had been pleased to find it was carried here in New York, in a spa boutique on Madison, with a downtown branch. Place called Bliss. He scoped Trina in the downtown salon."

"Yeah, that's the spot. See if your wit will work with Yancy."

"Already asked and answered. She'd be, quote, 'tickled pink.' A peach, Dallas, with eyes like a hawk. She saw a photo in his wallet when he took out the cash. She said it was an old photo, took her back to her own youth. A lovely brunette. She thinks she can give Yancy something to work with there, too."

"That's good work, Baxter. That's damn good work. Bring your peach in. Dallas out. It's moving for us." Her eyes were hard and bright as she turned back to Roarke. "It's moving now."

"Jessica Forman Rice Abercrombie Charters." Roarke tossed Eve a memo cube. "Chairman of the Board. She'll be happy to speak with you. She's at home this morning. If she can't help you, she'll find the person who can."

"You're a handy guy."

"In many, many ways."

The smile felt good on her face. It felt powerful. "Peabody, with me."

19 JESSICA WITH THE MANY LAST NAMES LIVED in a three-story apartment the size of Hoboken. The sprawling living area was highlighted by a window wall that afforded a panoramic view of the East River.

On a clear day, Eve calculated, you could stand at the clear wall and see clear to Rikers.

The lady had furnished the place to suit herself, mixing the very old with the ultra-new, with the result an eclectic and surprisingly appealing style. Eve and Peabody sat on the thick cushions of a sofa done in murderous red while their hostess poured tea from a white pot scattered with pink rosebuds into distressingly delicate cups.

The tea and a plate of paper-thin cookies had been brought in by a smartly dressed woman with the build of a toothpick.

"We have met a time or two," Jessica began.

"Yes, I remember." Now that she had the face, Eve did remember. The woman was a trim and carefully turned-out eighty-something with short, softly waved hair of deep gold around a sharp-featured face. Her mouth, long and animated, was painted petal pink, and her eyes—thickly lashed—a deep river green.

"You wear Leonardo."

"Only if he washes up first."

Jessica giggled, an appealing sound of eternal youth. "One of my granddaughters is mad for his designs. Won't wear anyone else. He suits her, as he does you. I believe people should always choose what suits them."

When she passed Eve the tea, Eve had to resist commenting that coffee in a good, sturdy mug suited her.

"We appreciate you giving us your time, Ms. Charters."

"Jessica, please." She offered Peabody a cup and a flashing smile. "Indulge me just one moment. Could I ask, when the two of you interrogate—oh, wait, the term's 'interview' these days—when you interview a suspect, do you ever rough them up?"

"We don't have to," Peabody told her. "The lieutenant scares confessions out of them."

The giggle rang again. "What I wouldn't give to watch that! I just love police dramas. I'm always trying to imagine myself the culprit, and how I'd stand up under interviews. I desperately wanted to kill my third husband, you see."

"It's a good impulse to resist," Eve commented.

"Yes." Jessica smiled her flower petal smile. "It would've been satisfying, but messy. Then again, divorce is rarely much tidier. Now, I'm wasting your time. How can I help you?"

"Stewart E. Pierpont."

Jessica's eyebrows quirked. "Yes, yes, I know that name. Has he done something murderous?"

"We're very interested in speaking to him. We're having a little trouble locating him."

Though mild confusion was evident on Jessica's face, her tone remained absolutely pleasant. "His address would be on file. I'll have Lyle look it up for you."

"The address he's listed doesn't jibe. Unless they're taking tenants at the Royal Opera House or Carnegie Hall."

"*Really?*" Jessica drew out the word, and now came a quick and avid light to her eyes. "Well, well, well. I should have known."

"How and what should you have known?"

"A very odd duck, Mr. Pierpont. He's attended a few galas and events over the years. Not particularly sociable and not at all philanthropic. I could never wheedle donations out of him, and I am the world record holder for wheedling."

"Galas and events are by invitation, aren't they?"

"Of course. It's important to— Ah! I see. How did he receive invitations if his address is not his address? Give me one moment."

She rose, crossed the polished tiles, the thick Turkish rug, and went out of the room.

"I like her." Peabody helped herself to a cookie. "She kind of reminds me of my grandmother. Not the way she looks, or lives," Peabody continued with a glance around the room. "But she's got that snap to her. Not just that she knows what's what, but like she's *always* known.

"Hey, these cookies are mag. And so thin you can practically see through them." She took another. "See-through food can't have many calories. Eat one, or I'm going to feel like an oinker."

Absently, Eve took a cookie. "He doesn't donate to the Met. Goes to a function now and then, but doesn't lay out any real bucks. Tickets cost, events cost, but he's getting something out of those. There's the control again. If you donate, you can't direct, not precisely, where your scratch is going."

She looked over as Jessica returned.

"The mystery's solved, but remains mysterious. Lyle reports that our Mr. Pierpont requested all tickets, all correspondence, invitations, begging letters, and so on, be held for him at the box office."

"Is that usual?" Eve asked.

"It's not." Jessica sat, picked up her tea. "In fact, it's very unusual. But we try to accommodate our patrons, even those we have to squeeze funds out of."

"When was the last time you saw or spoke with him?"

"Let me see. Oh, yes, he attended our winter gala. Second Saturday in December. I remember I tried, again, to convince him to join the Guild. It's a hefty membership fee, but has lovely benefits. He's the type who enjoys the opera, who knows and appreciates it, but isn't interested in funding. Tight-fisted. I've seen him come or go to performances over time. Always on foot. Doesn't even spring for a car. And always alone."

"Did he ever speak to you at all about his personal life?"

"Let me think." Crossing her legs, she swung one foot back and forth. "Drawing on the personal is an essential tool of the wheedle. A longtime widower, travels a great deal. He claims to have attended performances in all the great opera houses of the world. Prefers Italian operas. Oh!"

She held up a finger, closed her eyes just a moment as if to pull together a thought. "I remember, some years ago, pumping him a bit—as he'd had a couple of glasses of wine, I thought I might slide that membership fee out of him. I had him discussing whether true appreciation for art and music is inherent or learned. He told me he'd learned his appreciation from his mother when he was a boy. I said that was, arguably, inherent. But no, he said, though she had been the only mother he'd known, she had been his father's second wife. She had been a soprano."

"A performer."

"I asked him just that. What did he say? It was a bit odd. She had been, but circumstances had denied her, and time had run out. I'm sure that's what he said. I asked him what had happened, but he excused himself and abruptly walked away."

"Would Lyle know when Pierpont last picked up anything from the box office?"

"He would, and I asked him, anticipating you. Just last week."

"How does he pay?"

"Cash, Lyle tells me. Always, and yes, that's unusual. But we don't quibble about eccentricities. He always wears black-tie to the theater, which is also a bit eccentric, I suppose. So do his guests."

"You said he's always alone."

"Yes. I meant whenever he gives his performance ticket to a guest." An obliging hostess, she lifted the pot to pour more tea into Peabody's cup. "I've occasionally seen other men in his box. In fact, there was a guest in his seat at the opening of *Rigoletto* last week."

"Can you describe him?"

"Ah, black and white. That's how I thought of him, actually. Black-tie—very formal—white hair, white skin. I remember wondering if he might be a relation of Mr. Pierpont. There was a resemblance, or it seemed to me there was. I didn't see him before or after the performance, or at intermission. Or I didn't notice."

"Can you dig up the names of those who have been in the same box with Pierpont?"

"There never is anyone when Pierpont or one of his guests attend." Jessica smiled as she held out the plate of cookies. "That's rather odd, isn't it?"

Buys up the other tickets in the box," Eve said when they were in the car. "Doesn't want anyone else nearby, disturbing him, or getting too close."

"We'll stake out the opera." Peabody pulled out her book to key in some notes. "Maybe he'll need another fix."

"Yeah, we'll set that up. His stepmother. That's who the women represent. That's whose picture he carries in his wallet. Idealizes and demonizes her at the same time."

"You sound like Mira."

"It's what plays. He kills her, again and again—probably re-creating her actual death. Then he washes her, lays her on white linen. Her time ran out, so he sees that time runs out for the ones he picks to represent her. That's the core of it, with the cross in the Urbans. She clocked out in the Urbans, and I'm betting on the date he's used for his fake wife in the Pierpont data."

"The wife thing—the wedding band. His stepmother, but also his fantasy woman," Peabody theorized. "His bride. He doesn't rape her, that would shatter the fantasy. Not sexual, but romantic. Pathologically romantic."

"Now who's Mira? We start searching for women of her description who died on or about the date in the Pierpont data."

"A lot of deaths weren't recorded during the Urbans."

"Hers will be." Eve whipped the wheel to change lanes and shoehorn herself into a minute opening in the clog of traffic. "He'd have seen to it. It would've been here in New York. New York's the beginning and the end for him. We find her, and she'll lead us to him."

Eve heard the internal clock in her head ticking, ticking, ticking away the time. And thought of Ariel Greenfeld.

S he didn't know it was possible to experience such pain, to survive it. Even when he stopped—she'd thought he would never stop—her body burned and bled.

She'd wept and she'd screamed. In some part of Ariel's mind, she'd understood he'd enjoyed that. He'd been entertained by her helpless shrieks, wild sobs, and desperate struggles.

She lay now, shivering in shock while voices twined through the air in a language she didn't understand. Italian? she wondered, fighting to focus, to stay conscious. It was probably Italian. He'd played music while he'd hurt her, and her screams had cut through the voices then as his nasty little knives had cut through her flesh.

Ariel imagined using them on him. She'd never been violent. In fact, she'd been a pitiful failure in the basic defense classes she'd taken with a couple friends. *Weakfeld*, they'd called her, she remembered. And they'd all laughed because they'd never believed, not really, that any of them would ever have to use the punches and kicks they'd tried to learn.

She was a baker, that's all. She liked to cook and create cakes and cookies and pastries that made people smile. She was a good person, wasn't she? She couldn't remember ever hurting anyone.

Maybe she'd toked a little Zoner in her teens, and that was wrong. Technically. But she hadn't caused anyone any harm.

But she found the idea of causing him harm dulled the pain. When she imagined herself breaking free, grabbing one of the knives and just plunging it into his soft belly, she didn't feel so cold.

She didn't want to die this way, this horrible way. Someone would come, she told herself. She had to hold on, had to survive until someone came and saved her.

But when he came back, everything inside her cringed. Tears flooded her throat and her eyes so that even her whimpers were drowned.

"That was a nice break, wasn't it?" he said in that hideously pleasant voice. "But we have to get back to work. Now then, let's see. What's it to be?"

"Mr. Gaines?" Don't scream, she ordered herself. Don't beg. He likes that.

"Yes, my dear?"

"Why did you pick me?"

"You have a pleasing face and lovely hair. Good muscle tone in your arms and legs." He picked up a small torch. She had to bite back a moan as he turned it on with a low hiss, narrowed the flame to a pinpoint.

"Is that all? I mean, did I do anything?"

"Do?" he said absently.

"Did I do something to upset you, or make you mad at me?"

"Not at all." He turned, smiled kindly as the narrow flame hissed.

"It's just, Mr. Gaines, I know you're going to hurt me. I can't stop you. But can you tell me why? I just want to understand why you're going to hurt me."

"Isn't this interesting?" He cocked his head and studied her. "She asks, always she asks why. But she screams it. She doesn't ever ask so politely."

"She only wants to understand."

"Well. Well, well, well." He turned the torch off, and Ariel's chest heaved with relief. "This is different. I enjoy variety. She was lovely, you know."

"Was she?" Ariel moistened her lips as he pulled up a stool and sat so he could speak face-to-face. How could he look so *ordinary*? she wondered. How could he look so nice, and be so vicious?

"You're very pretty, but she was almost exquisite. And when she sang, she was glorious."

"What . . . what did she sing?"

"Soprano. She had a multiple voice."

"I . . . I don't know what that means."

"Her brilliance was so bright. She was *allegra*—those high, clear notes seeming to simply lift out of her. And the color, the texture of *lirica* with the intensity and depth of the *drammatica*. Her range . . ."

Moisture sheened his eyes as he pressed his fingers to his lips, kissed the tips. "I could, and did, listen to her for hours. She would accompany herself on the piano when at home. She tried to teach me, but . . ." He smiled wistfully as he held up his hands. "I had no talent for music, only a vast appreciation for it."

If he was talking he wasn't hurting her, Ariel thought. She had to keep him talking. "Is it opera? I don't know anything about opera."

"You think it's stuffy, boring, old-fashioned."

"I think it's beautiful," she said carefully. "I've just never really listened to it before. She sang opera?" Questions, Ariel thought desperately. Ask questions so he'll spend time answering. "And—and was a soprano? With, um, multiple voice like—like ranges?"

"Indeed, yes, indeed, that's very good. I have many of her recordings. I don't play them here." He glanced around the room. "It wouldn't be appropriate."

"I'd love to hear her sing. I'd love to hear her multiple voice."

"Would you?" His eyes turned sly. "Aren't you clever? She was clever, too." He rose now, picked up the torch.

"Wait! Wait! Couldn't I hear her sing? Maybe I'd understand if I could hear her sing? Who was she? Who was— Oh, God, God, *please!*" She tried to shrink away from the tip of the flame he traced, almost teasingly, along her arm.

"We'll have to chat later. We really must get to work."

Eve went directly to Feeney when she reached Central. "Female brunettes between the ages of twenty-eight and thirty-three who died on this date in New York. We need names, last known addresses, cause of death."

"Records around that time are sketchy," he told her. "A lot of deaths went unrecorded, a lot of people were unidentified, or misidentified."

"Dig. She's what's going to open locks on this. I'm going to check with Yancy, see if he's got any sort of an image on the wallet photo."

To give Yancy more time, she went first to Whitney and asked for more men to form a stakeout team at the Met.

"Done. I need you for a media briefing at noon."

"Commander—"

"If you think I don't know how pressed and pressured you are, you're mistaken." And he looked just as irritated as she did. "Thirty minutes. I'll cut it off at thirty, but unless you're on your way to arrest this son of a bitch, I need you there. We have to hold back the flood."

"Yes, sir."

"Confirm the new and salient you fed Nadine this morning, and the twenty-four-hour shifts. I want you to express confidence that Ariel Greenfeld will be found alive."

"I will, Commander. I believe she will be."

"Let them see you do. Dismissed. Oh, Lieutenant, if I learn you've stepped foot outside this building without your vest or your wires, I'll skin you. Personally."

"Understood."

It was a little annoying to realize he'd sensed she was considering *forgetting* the vest. She hated the damn thing. But she had to respect a man who knew his subordinates.

She strode into Yancy's section and saw him working with Baxter's peach. He caught Eve's eye before she wound her way through the stations. He rose, smiled, and said something to the witness before heading Eve off.

"I think we're making progress here. She's got him nailed, but she only got a quick look at the photo. We're working on it, Dallas. You've got to give me more time, more room."

"Can you give me him?"

"Already sent it to your office unit. Subtle differences in the facial structure from Trina's image, different hair, eyebrows. My eye says same guy."

"Your eye's good enough for me. When you get the woman's image, send it to me, and to Feeney. Make it work, Yancy. This one could be the money shot."

By the time Eve reached her own division, Peabody was heading out of the war room. "Tried Morris, as ordered. He's on his way here with the tox results. Jenkinson and Powell reported in. They're at the spa boutique. There's a clerk who thinks maybe she saw our guy in there sometime."

"There's a fresh image on my unit. Send it to them, have them show it around the store and the salon."

"Got it."

"Lieutenant Dallas?"

Both she and Peabody turned. Ariel's hungover neighbor, Eve realized. "Erik, right?"

"Yeah. I have to talk to you. I have to find out what's going on. That woman, Gia Rossi, she's dead. Ariel . . ."

"I'll take him," Peabody told Eve.

"No, I got it. Get the image to Jenkinson. Let's sit down, Erik." She didn't have time to take him to the lounge, didn't have the heart to boot him out. Instead, she led him to one of the benches outside her own bullpen.

"You're worried and you're upset," Eve began.

"Worried? Upset? I'm scared out of my goddamn mind. He's got her. That maniac has Ariel. They said he tortures them. He's hurting her, and we're just sitting here."

"No, we're not. Every cop assigned to this case is working it."

"She's not a *case!*" His voice rose, threatened to crack. "Goddamn it, she's a human being. She's Ariel."

"You want this prettied up for you?" Her voice was sharp, deliberately so to cut off any risk of hysteria. "You want pats and strokes, you've come to the wrong place, and you've come to the wrong person. I'm telling you that everything I've got is on this, is in this, just like every cop working it. If you think we don't know who she is, you're wrong. If you think her face isn't in everyone's head, you're wrong."

"I don't know what to do." His hands fisted on his thighs, pounded against them. "I can't stand not knowing what to do, how to help. She must be so scared."

"Yeah, she must be scared. I'm not going to bullshit you, Erik. She's scared, and she's probably hurting. But we're going to find her. When we do, I'll make sure you're contacted. I'll make sure you know we've got her safe."

"I love her. I never told her. Never told me either," he managed on a long, shaky breath. "I'm in love with her, and she doesn't know."

"You can tell her when we've got her back. Go home. Better, go be with a friend."

When she'd nudged him along, she went back to the war room, straight to Roarke's station. She picked up his bottle of water and guzzled.

"Help yourself," he commented.

"Popped a buzz a couple hours ago. Always makes me thirsty. And . . ." She rolled her shoulders. "Wired. Location, location, location," she added and made him smile.

"I have some others for you, and I'm working on trimming the number of them down. Any help on the opera connection?"

"Pieces, bits and pieces of him—and I'm getting a handle on the women he's re-creating, we'll say. Once we ID her, we're going to have more data on him. I've got to go flap lips with the media."

She started out, nearly ran headlong into Morris. "Sorry. Sorry." The damn booster made her feel as if she were jumping out of her own skin. "What have you got? Tell me while we walk. I've got to get to the media room."

"Energy pill?"

"It shows?"

"Generally, on you. He used dopamine and lorazepam on her. We haven't detected those substances before."

"What do they do?" She wished she'd copped Roarke's water. "Would they have turned her off?"

"I'd say he was hoping for the opposite result. They're sometimes used on catatonics."

"Okay, so she turned off on him, and he tried to bring her around, keep the clock going."

"I agree. Still, if she went into true and deep catatonia, he could have, potentially, kept that clock going for hours more. If not days."

"But what fun is that?" Eve countered. "Not getting any reaction. She's not participating."

"Yes, again I agree. It holds with the fact she didn't sustain as many injuries as the others. He couldn't bring her around, so he gave up."

"I don't imagine you can pick up dopamine or whatzit?"

"Lorazepam."

"Yeah, those. Probably didn't pick them up at his local drug store."

"No. And a doctor isn't going to prescribe either for home use. It's something that would be administered, by a licensed professional, under controlled conditions."

"Maybe he's a doctor, or some sort of medical. Or managed to pose as one." Good at posing, she thought. Good at his roles. "Could be he scored it from a hospital or medical facility. But he's never used it before, so why would he have had it on hand? Wouldn't," she said before Morris could speak. "If he scored it, he scored it over the weekend, and in New York."

"Psychiatrics, primarily, would be the most logical source."

"Give this to Peabody, okay? I want a search on facilities in New York that carry those meds. Tell her to use Mira if she needs grease or an expert. Meds like that have to be, by law, under lock and fully accounted for."

"By law," Morris agreed, "but not always strictly by practice."

"We track it down. Start by getting full accountings from those facilities of these drugs. Any deviation, we take another push."

"I can do this. A doctor for the dead's still a doctor," he added when she frowned at him. "I think I could help on this."

"Take it to Peabody," Eve repeated. "Work with her. I'll check back with you when I'm done in here."

In the war room Roarke saved, copied, and printed out the real estate list. Curious, he took out his PPC to access the last few minutes of Eve's briefing while he wandered out for another bottle of water. She looked, he thought, rough and tough—and if you knew her as he did, a little ragged around the edges.

She'd make herself ill if this wasn't over soon, he concluded. Push herself until she, very literally, collapsed.

There was absolutely no point in nagging or browbeating her this time as he was in it too deeply himself. He switched off as she was finishing up, then shifted to communications.

He thought if he ordered a dozen pizzas, she'd at least end up eating something. And he could damn well do with some food himself at this point.

After returning to his station, he took a fresh look at his list. Lowell's Funeral Home, Lower East location, he mused. Sarifina York's memorial was being held there. Today, he remembered. He should go, pay his respects.

He called up the funeral home on his comp to check the time of the service. If he couldn't get away from the work—and the living took precedence over the dead—he could and would at least send flowers.

He noted down the time, the address, the specific room where the memorial was scheduled to be held. Cleverly, he thought, the page linked to a local florist. Handy and quick, he decided, but he preferred to trust Caro for the floral tribute.

Thoughtfully, he glanced at the link labeled "History," and tapped it. It might tell him more than the standard data he'd already unearthed from the records.

Moments later his eyes went cool, his blood went hot. Roarke glanced over at Feeney, who was pushing at his own search.

"Feeney. I believe I have something."

20

EVE STOOD, HANDS FISTED ON HER HIPS, STUDYing the data Roarke ordered on wall screen.

"The property didn't pop in the initial searches as it's been retitled a number of times, and not officially owned by the same person, persons, or company for the time period you asked I check. But with a deeper search, the ownership is—buried under some clever cover—held by the Lowell Family Trust."

"Funeral parlor. Death house."

"Indeed. As you see from the website history, the building first belonged to the Lowell family in the early nineteen-twenties, used both as a residence and as a funeral home. James Lowell established his business there, and lived in residence with his wife, two sons, and one daughter. The older son was killed in the Second World War, and the younger, Robert Lowell, joined the business, taking it over at his father's death. He expanded, opening other locations in New York and New Jersey."

"Death's a profitable business," Eve commented.

"So it is. And more so during wartime. Robert Lowell's eldest son, another James, joined in the business, residing in their Lower West

Side location—they had a second by that time. During the Urbans, this location, the original, was used as a clinic and base camp for the Home Force. Many of the dead were brought there, and tended to by the Lowells, who were reputed to be staunch supporters of the HF."

"The second James Lowell is too old." With her hands on her hips, Eve studied the data. "There are some spry centurians, but not spry enough for this."

"Agreed. But he, in turn, had a son. Only one child, from his first marriage. He was widowed when his wife died from complications in childbirth. And he subsequently remarried six years later."

"Pop," Eve said quietly. "Have we got the second wife? The son?"

"There's no record of the second wife that we've found as yet. A lot of records were destroyed during the Urbans. And the databases were far from complete in any case."

"It's one of the reasons these clowns—the Lowells," Feeney said, "were able to manipulate the records."

"Likely for tax purposes at one time," Roarke continued. "Changed the name from Lowell's to Manhattan Mortuary during the Urbans— with a bogus sale of the building. Then to Sunset Bereavement Center, another sale, roughly twenty years ago, with a return—five years ago—to the original name, with another deed transfer in the officials."

"Just kept switching."

"With a bit of creative bookkeeping, I imagine," Roarke confirmed. "It caught my interest when I read that a Lowell has been at the helm of the business for four generations. Interested enough, I scraped away a bit."

"The man's got a golden e-shovel," Feeney commented, and gave Roarke a slap on the back.

"Well, digging in, it turns out that the Lowell Family Trust owned companies that owned companies, and so on, which included the ones who ostensibly purchased the building."

"Meaning they've been there all along."

"Exactly so. And on the last generation, Robert—named for his grandfather—we have this."

He pulled up the ID shot and data. Eve stepped closer to the screen, frowned. "He doesn't look like Yancy's sketch. The eyes, yes, maybe the mouth, but he doesn't look like the sketch. Age is right, professional data, okay. Address in London."

"Which is the English National Opera," Feeney put in. "We ran it." He tapped the image on screen. "Could Yancy have been this far off?"

"Never known him to be. And we have two wits verifying. That's not him." Eve shoved her fingers through her hair. Time to move. "Print it out. I want a team of five: Feeney, Roarke, Peabody, McNab, Newkirk. We'll pay a visit to a funeral home. I want the team ten minutes behind me."

"Ten?" Roarke repeated.

"That's right. It's time to open that window a little wider. Time's moving for Ariel Greenfeld. And this might be when he makes his move on me, either en route to this place or when I'm inside it."

She held up a hand as Yancy came in. "Feeney, get us a warrant. I don't want any trouble going through that building. Yancy, give me a face."

"Here she is."

A strong face, Eve thought. Strong and very feminine, almond-shaped eyes, slim nose, a wide, full mouth, and a cascade of dark hair. She was smiling, looking directly out. Her shoulders were bare but for two slim, sparkling straps. Around her neck was a glittering chain holding a pendant in the shape of a tree.

Tree of Life, Eve remembered. "Well, son of a bitch." Another point for the Romanian psychic.

"Callendar, get a copy of this face. Find her. Run a data match for her picture. Search the newspapers, the magazines, the media reports from 1980 through 2015. Cross-check her with opera."

"Yes, sir."

"Yancy." Eve jerked her chin at the image still on screen. "That's what his official ID has him looking like."

"No." Yancy just shook his head. "No way. Trina had him. This is a relative, maybe. Brother, cousin. But that's not the guy Trina gave me, or the one Ms. Pruitt described from Tiffany's."

"Okay. Morris, you all right working on the meds alone?"

"I can handle it."

"You get a hit, I get the buzz. Let's move it, people. Ten minutes at my back. And nobody comes inside until I give the signal."

"Sarifina York's memorial is being held there," Roarke reminded her. "It would be completely appropriate for me to pay my respects."

Eve gave it a moment's thought. "Ten minutes at my back," she repeated. "Unless I signal sooner, you come on in to pay your respects. Get us that warrant, Feeney."

"Vest and wire," Roarke said, firmly.

"Yeah, yeah. In the garage. In five." She strode out to prep.

When she pulled out of the garage, Eve's instincts were tuned for a tail. And her mind was on Ariel.

She prayed to pass out, but the pain wouldn't allow the escape. Even when he stopped, finally stopped, agony kept her above the surface. She tried to think of her friends, her family, of the life she'd led before, but it all seemed so distant, so separate. Nothing that had been would come clearly into focus.

There was only now, only the pain, only him.

And the time ticking away on the wall screen. Seven hours, twenty-three minutes, and the seconds clicking by.

So Ariel thought of how she would make him pay for taking away everything she had. Her life, her sense of order, her pleasures, her hopes. If only she could get free, she would make him pay for stripping her bare.

Talk, she reminded herself. Find a way to make him talk again.

Make him talk, and live.

Eve didn't spot a tail, and found that it pissed her off. What if he'd changed his mind about trying for her? If she'd somehow scared him off, and even now he was moving in on another innocent woman?

"At location," she said. "And heading in. Feeney, make me smile."

"Warrant's coming through."

"All right. Keep the chatter down. Ten minutes, on the mark."

Studying the building, she crossed the sidewalk. Three floors, including basement. Riot bars, solid security. Solid, if faded, red brick. Two entrances in the front, and two in the back, with emergency exits front and back, top floor.

If Ariel was inside, odds were on the basement. Main level was public, third level public and staff.

She climbed the steps, pressed the buzzer.

The door was opened moments later by a dark-skinned woman in dignified black. "Good afternoon. How can I help you?"

Eve held up her badge. "Sarifina York."

"Yes, we're gathering in the Tranquility Room. Please come in."

Eve stepped in, scanned the area. The wide central hallway split the main floor in two parts. The air smelled of flowers and polish. She could see through the open double pocket doors to her left that several people had already arrived to memorialize Sarifina.

"I'll need to speak to whoever's in charge."

"Of the service?"

"Of the business."

"Oh. Of course. Mr. Travers is with a client just at the moment, but—"

"What about Mr. Lowell?"

"Mr. Lowell isn't in residence. He lives in Europe. But Mr. Travers is head of operations."

"When's the last time Mr. Lowell's been here?"

"I couldn't really say. I've been with Lowell's for two years, and haven't met him. I believe you could say he's essentially retired. Would you like to speak with Mr. Travers?"

"Yeah. You'll have to interrupt him. This is official police business."

"Of course." As if she heard the phrase "official police business" every day, the woman smiled serenely as she gestured. "If you'll come with me, I'll take you to one of the waiting rooms upstairs."

Eve looked into the Tranquility Room as she passed. There were photographs of Sarifina, the flowers were plentiful, and the music was the retro big band sound the deceased had loved.

"What's in the basement?" Eve asked as they went upstairs.

"It's a work area. Preparation areas. Many of the bereaved request or require viewings of those they've lost."

"Embalming? Cosmetics?"

"Yes."

"How many work down there, routinely?"

"We have a mortician, a technician, and a stylist on staff."

Stylist, Eve thought. No point in being unfashionably dead.

The woman led her to a small waiting room full of quiet, flowers, and soft-cushioned furniture. "I'll tell Mr. Travers you're waiting. Please be comfortable."

Alone, Eve wandered the room. Not here, she thought. It didn't make sense for him to have brought Ariel and the others here, where work went on throughout the building. Too many people. Too much business.

He wasn't part of a troupe, but a solo act.

But this was a conduit, she was sure of it. Just as she was damn sure Robert Lowell, or whatever he was currently calling himself, wasn't in London.

Travers came in. He was tall, reed thin, with a comfortable if somber face. If Eve had been casting funeral directors, he'd have been her top pick.

"Officer?"

"Lieutenant. Dallas."

"Kenneth Travers." Since he offered his hand as he crossed to her, Eve took it. "I'm director here. How may I help you?"

"I'm looking for Robert Lowell."

"Yes, so Marlee indicated. Mr. Lowell lives in Europe, and has for some years now. While he retains ownership of the organization, he has very little actual involvement with the day-to-day operations."

"How do you get in touch with him?"

"Through his solicitors in London."

"I'll need the name of the firm, and a contact number."

"Yes, of course." Travers folded his hands at his waist. "I'm sorry, may I ask what this is in reference to?"

"We believe he's connected to an ongoing investigation."

"You're investigating the murders of the two women who were found recently. Is that correct?"

"That would be right."

"But Mr. Lowell is in London." He repeated the information slowly, and with what seemed to be a wealth of patience. "Or traveling. He travels quite extensively, I understand."

"When did you see him last?"

"Five, perhaps six years ago. Yes, I believe it would be six."

Eve pulled out the ID print. "Is this Robert Lowell?"

"Why yes, yes it is. I'm very confused, Lieutenant. This is Robert Lowell, the first. He's been dead for, my goodness, nearly forty years. His portrait hangs in my office."

"Is that so?" Smart, Eve decided. Some smart son of a bitch. "How about this man?" She took out Yancy's sketch.

"Yes, that's the current Mr. Lowell, or a close likeness." His color receded a bit as he looked from the sketch to Eve. "I saw this displayed on screen, on media reports. I honestly never connected it. I—as I said—I haven't seen Mr. Lowell in several years, and I never . . . I simply didn't *see* him in this until you asked just now.

"But you see, there has to be some mistake. Mr. Lowell is a very quiet and solitary man. He couldn't possibly—"

"That's what they all say. I have a team arriving momentarily, with a warrant. We need to go through this building."

"But Lieutenant Dallas, I assure you he's not here."

"It happens I believe you, but we still go through the building. Where does he stay when he comes to New York?"

"I don't honestly know. It's so rare . . . and it wasn't my place to ask." Travers's fingers moved up to the knot of his somber tie, brushed there twice.

"There was a second location on the Lower West Side during the Urbans."

"Yes, yes, I believe so. But we've been the only location downtown for as long as I've been associated with the company."

"How long would that be?"

"Lieutenant, I've been director here for almost fifteen years. I've only had direct contact with Mr. Lowell a handful of times at best. He's made it clear he doesn't like to be disturbed."

"I bet. I need the lawyers, Mr. Travers, and any other information on Robert Lowell you have. What do you know about his stepmother?"

"His . . . I think she was killed during the Urban Wars. As she wasn't, to my knowledge, involved with the business, the information I have on her is very minimal."

"Name?"

"I'm so sorry, I don't know it offhand. It might be in our records. Well, this is—this is all very disturbing."

"Yeah," Eve said dryly. "Murder can just ruin a perfectly good funeral."

"I only meant—" Color came into his cheeks, then died away. "I understand you must do your job. But, Lieutenant, we have a memorial in progress for one of the women who was killed. I have to ask you and your men to be discreet. This is an extremely difficult and delicate time for Ms. York's friends and family."

"I'm going to make sure Ariel Greenfeld's friends and family don't end up in your Tranquility Room anytime soon."

They were as discreet as a half a dozen cops could be, with Feeney and McNab tackling the electronics for any data. Eve stood in the basement prep room with Roarke.

"Not much different from the morgue. Smaller," she noted, scanning the steel worktables, the gullies on the sides, the hoses and tubes and tools. "I guess he got some of his knowledge of anatomy working here. Might have had some of his early practice sessions on corpses."

"Charming thought."

"Yeah, well, being as they were already dead—hopefully—it probably didn't upset them too much. Oh, and FYI? When my time comes, I don't want the preservatives and the stylist. You can just build a big fire, slide me in. Then you can throw yourself on the pyre to show your wild grief and constant devotion."

"I'll make a note of it."

"Nothing down here for us. I want the second location that was up and running during the Urbans. Any other properties owned by Lowell, in any of his guises or fronts."

"I'll get to it," Roarke told her.

She drew out her communicator, scowled at the buzzing static. "Reception's crappy down here. Let's go up. I want to see if Callendar had any luck with the stepmother.

"She could have had property in her name," Eve continued as they started out. "Maybe he uses that. Lawyers are dragging their feet, as the breed's prone to do. Between Whitney and Tibble they'll cut through that bullshit quickly enough."

"If he continues to be smart," Roarke commented, "the lawyers would only lead you to a numbered account and message service. He covers himself well."

"Then we'll tackle the account and the service. Fucker's in New York. He has a bolt-hole here, a work space, transportation. And one of these lines we're yanking is going to bring us down on him."

Eve had no more than reached the main level when her communicator beeped. "Dallas."

"Found her!" Callendar all but sang it. "Edwina Spring. Found her in the music and entertainment section of an old *Times*. Opera sensation, if you believe the hype. Prodigy. Barely eighteen when she bowled over New York at the Met. I've got more coming up now that I've got her name."

"Run a multitask. See if you can find any property in the city listed under her name."

"On it."

"Get it all together, Callendar. I've got a stop to make, then I'm heading in."

"What stop?" Roarke wanted to know.

"Pella. He knows something. His medicals confirm he's clocking out, and is barely able to walk across the room. But he knows something, and I'm not dicking around with him."

"You weren't tailed here."

"That's right."

"Then it's unlikely you'll be tailed from here. As Peabody's busy, I'll go with you to see this Pella."

"I can handle myself."

"You certainly can. But do you want to pull any part of the team here off to run your wire? Simpler, quicker, if I go with you, then the rest of them meet us back at Central."

"Maybe." And for the sake of expediency, she shrugged. "Fine."

When they arrived at Pella's, there was a great deal of objecting and hand-fluttering from both the housekeeping and medical droids. Eve just pushed through it.

"If you've got a complaint, report it to the chief of police. Or the mayor. Yeah, the mayor loves to get complaints from droids."

"We're obliged to look after Mr. Pella, to see to his health and comfort."

Obviously, some joker had programmed the housekeeping droid to whine. "None of you are going to feel very healthy or comfortable if I haul you into Central. So move aside or I'll cite you for obstructing justice."

Eve elbowed the medical away, shoved open the bedroom door. "Stay back, out of eyeline," she said quietly to Roarke. "He might not talk if he sees I've brought company."

It was dim, as it had been before, and she could hear the steady rasps of Pella sucking air through the breather.

"I said I didn't want to be disturbed until I called for you." His voice was testy, and sounded years older than it had the day before. "I'll have you broken down into circuits and limbs if you don't give me some damn *peace*."

"That would be tough to manage from where you are," Eve commented.

He stirred, his eyes opened to latch on to hers. "What do you want? I don't have to talk to you. I spoke with my lawyer."

"Fine, speak with him again and tell him to meet you at Central. He'll explain that I can hold you there for twenty-four hours as a material witness to homicide."

"What kind of bullshit is this! I haven't witnessed anything but those damn droids hovering like vultures for the past six months."

"You're going to tell me what you know, Pella, or a good chunk of the time you've got left is going to be spent with me. Robert Lowell. Edwina Spring. Tell me."

He shifted restlessly in the bed, plucked at the sheet. "If you know so much, why do you need me?"

"Look, you son of a bitch." She leaned over him. "Twenty-five women are dead, and another is in dire straits. She may be dying."

"I *am* dying! I fought for this city. I bled for it. I lost the only thing in the world that mattered, and nothing has mattered since. What do I care about some women?"

"Her name's Ariel. She bakes for a living. She has a neighbor across the hall from her pretty little apartment. Seems like a nice guy. She doesn't know he's in love with her, doesn't know he came to me today desperate and scared, pleading with me to find her. Her name is Ariel, and you're going to tell me what you know."

Pella turned his head away, stared toward the draped windows. "I don't know anything."

"You lying fucker." She grabbed hold of his breather, saw his eyes go wide. She wouldn't actually rip it off—probably wouldn't—but he didn't know that. "You want to take another breath?"

"The droids know you're in here. If anything happens to me—"

"What? Like you just—oops—fall over dead when I happen to be talking to you? An officer of the law, sworn to protect and serve. And with a witness to back me up?"

"What witness?"

Eve glanced over, jerked her head so that Roarke stepped into Pella's view. "If this fucker just happened to kick it when I was duly questioning him about his knowledge of a suspect, it would be an accident, right?"

"Absolutely." Roarke smiled, cold and calm. "An unforeseen event."

"You know who he is," Eve said when Pella's eyes wheeled. "And who I am. Roarke's cop, that's what you called me. Believe me when I tell you if you happen to stop breathing, and I lie about how that might've happened, he'll swear to it."

"On a bloody stack of Bibles," Roarke confirmed.

"But you're not ready to die yet, are you, Pella?" Her hand stayed firm on the breather when he batted at it. "It shows in the eyes when someone's not ready to die yet. So, if you want that next breath, then the one that comes after, you tell me the goddamn truth. You know Robert Lowell. You knew Edwina Spring."

"Let go of it." He wheezed in air. "I'll have you up on charges."

"You'll be dead, and the dead don't scare me. You knew them. Next breath, Pella, say yes."

"Yes, yes." He shoved his hand at Eve's, and the harsh sound of his labored breath eased when she lifted it. "Yes, I knew them. But not to speak to. They were the elite. I was only a soldier. Get the hell away from me."

"Not a chance. Tell me what you know."

Pella's eyes ticked over to Roarke, back to Eve. Then, for a moment, he simply closed them. "He was about my age—a few years younger—but he didn't serve. Soft." Pella's hand trembled a little as it came up, stroked over the breather to be sure it was in the correct position. "Soft look about him, and he had his family money at his back, of course. His type never got dirty, never risked their own skin. She . . . I need water."

Eve glanced over, saw the cup with a straw on the bedside table. She picked it up, held it out.

"I can't hold the damn thing. It's bad today. Worse since you got here."

Saying nothing, she angled it down so he could guide the straw with a trembling hand to the opening in the breather.

"What about her?"

"Beautiful. Young, elegant, a voice like an angel. She would come to the base sometimes, sing for us. Opera, almost always Italian opera. She'd break your heart with every note."

"You have a thing for her, Pella?"

"Bitch," he muttered. "What would you know of real love? Therese was everything. But I loved what Edwina was, what she brought us. Hope and beauty."

"She came to the base on Broome?"

"Yes, on Broome."

"They lived there, didn't they?"

"No. Before I think, but not during the fighting, not while soldiers were based there. After, who the hell knows, who the hell cares? But when I was assigned there, they didn't live in the base on Broome. They had another place, another place on the West Side."

"Where?"

"It was a long time ago. I was never there, not a foot soldier like me. Some of the others went, officers, and you heard things. Yeah, some of the officers, and the Stealths."

She felt the next click. "The coverts?"

"Yes. You'd hear things. I heard things." He closed his eyes. "It hurts to go back there." For the first time, his voice sounded weak. "And I can't stop going back there."

"I'm sorry for all you lost, Mr. Pella." And in that moment she was. "But Ariel Greenfeld is alive, and she needs help. What did you hear back then that might help her?"

"How the hell do I know?"

"It would have to do with her, with Edwina Spring. She died, did she?"

"Everyone dies." But his hand came to his breather again, and his eyes watched Eve warily over it. "I heard her—Edwina—talking to a soldier I knew. Young first lieutenant, sent down from upstate. Can't remember his name. They'd slip off when she'd come to sing. Or you could see the way they looked at each other. The way Therese and I looked at each other."

"They were lovers?"

"Probably. Or wanted to be. She was young, a lot younger than Taker."

"Who? Taker?"

"That's what they called Lowell—James Lowell."

"Because he took the bodies the dead wagon brought in," Eve said, remembering Dobbins's comment.

"That's right. She was half his age, vital, beautiful. He was too damn old for her, and . . . and there was something in his eyes. In the old man's, too, his father. Something in their eyes that brought the hair up on the back of the neck."

"They found out about her and the soldier."

"Yes. I think they were going to run away. He wouldn't have been the first to desert, or the last. It was summer. We had the sector secured, temporarily in any case. I went out, just to walk, to remind myself what we were fighting for. I heard them talking, behind one of the supply tents. Her voice, you couldn't mistake it for anyone else's. They were talking about going north, up into the mountains. A lot of people had fled the city for the mountains, the country, and he still had family up that way."

"She was going to leave her husband, run off with this soldier." And Robert Lowell, Eve calculated, would have been around twenty.

"I didn't let them know I was there. I wouldn't have turned him in. I knew what it was to love someone, and be afraid for her.

"I backtracked a little, then crossed the street so they wouldn't know I'd been close. Give them privacy, you know. Fucking little privacy back then. And I saw him, on the other side of the tent, listening to them."

"Lowell," Eve realized. "The younger one."

"He looked like he was in a trance. I'd heard he had a mental condition. There were whispers, but I thought it was just the excuse they used to keep him out of the fight. But when I looked across the street, when I looked at him, there was something not right. No, not right at all. I need water."

Once again, Eve lifted the cup and straw to his mouth.

"He turned them in."

"He must have. There was nothing I could do, not with him there. I was going to warn them later, warn the lieutenant about the kid. But I never got the chance. I went up the block, debating with myself on what I should or shouldn't do—wanted to talk to Therese about it first. They were gone when I came back. The soldier off on assignment, and Edwina back home. I never saw either of them alive again."

"What happened to them?"

"It was more than a week later." His voice was tiring, genuinely, she judged. She wouldn't get much more. "The soldier was listed as

AWOL, and she hadn't been back. I thought they'd gotten away. Then one night, I went out for sentry duty. She was on the sidewalk. No one would ever say how whoever had tossed her there had gotten through the posts. She was dead."

A tear slid out of his eye, tracked around the side of the breather. "I'd seen bodies like that before, I knew how they came to be like that."

"Torture?"

"They'd done despicable things to her, then tossed her, naked and mangled, on the street like garbage. They'd shorn off her hair, and had ripped up her face, but I knew who she was. They'd left her wearing the Tree of Life necklace she always wore. As if to make certain there would be no mistake."

"You thought the Lowells did it? Her husband, father-in-law, stepson."

"They said she'd been taken and tortured by the enemy, but it was a lie. I'd seen that kind of work before, and it had been on the enemy. The old man was a torturer. Everyone knew it, and everyone was careful not to speak of it too loudly. If they believed a prisoner had information, they took him to Robert Lowell—the old one.

"When they came to get her, he wept like a baby, the one you're looking for now." Pella's eyes opened, and they were fierce despite his flagging voice. "When he saw her under the sheet we covered her with, he wept like a woman. Two days later, I lost Therese. Nothing mattered after that."

"Why didn't you tell the police this nine years ago when these murders started?"

"I didn't think of a dead woman from a lifetime ago. I never thought of it, nor of her. Why would I? Then, I saw that sketch. A long time ago, but I thought there was something familiar. When you came yesterday, I knew who he was."

"If you'd given me this yesterday, given me his name, you might have spared Ariel twenty-four hours of pain."

Pella just turned his head away and closed his eyes. "We all have pain."

Riding on disgust, Eve stormed out of Pella's town house. "Miserable bastard. I need any and all properties owned by the Lowells, or Edwina Spring, during the Urbans. Get out that damn golden shovel and dig."

"You drive, and you'll have it," Roarke told her, already working with his PPC.

She got behind the wheel, then tagged Callendar at Central. "Any more data?"

"Data, yes, property, no. I can tell you Spring retired—with great lamentations from opera buffs, at the age of twenty when she married the wealthy and prominent James Lowell. There's society stuff after that. This gala, that party, then interest in her seemed to fade out some.

"But I found her death record. She's listed as Edwina Roberti. Data reads opera singer, and that she was survived by her spouse, Lowell, Robert. COD is listed as suicide. There's no image, Lieutenant, but it's got to be her."

"It's her."

"And, Lieutenant, Morris has something."

"Put me through."

"Dallas, the Manhattan Family Center on First. There's a children's psychiatric wing that was funded by the Lowells in the late twentieth. Endowment continues through a trust. I've spoken with the chief of staff. Saturday they received an unexpected visit from the Lowell Family Trust's representative. A Mr. Edward Singer. At his request, he was taken through the facility. Their drug count's off."

She calculated the distance. "I'll send somebody over to get a statement."

"Dallas, they keep their security discs, in full, for seven days. They have him on disc."

"We'll pick 'em up. We'll have sweepers go over the drug cabinet. Maybe we'll keep getting lucky. Nice going, Morris."

"Felt good."

"Know what you mean. Out." She clicked off, looked over at Roarke as she switched over to Peabody's communicator. "We're building the cage. All we have to do is throw the bastard in it."

21 SHE WAS BUILDING A GOOD CASE, LINING UP her connections, her motives, her pathology. She had no doubt that when they found and arrested Robert Lowell, they'd be handing the prosecuting attorney a slam dunk.

But that didn't help Ariel Greenfeld.

"Get me something," she said to Roarke as they stepped into the elevator at Central's garage.

"Do you know what the records are like from that era?" he snapped. "What there are of them? I'm putting together a puzzle where half the major pieces are missing or scattered about. And I need better equipment than my bloody PPC."

"Okay, all right." She pressed her fingers to the center of her forehead. The damn energy pill was wearing off, and she could feel the system crash waiting to happen. "Let me think."

"I don't know how you can at this stage. You're going to fall flat on your face, Eve, if you don't take a bit of downtime."

"Ariel Greenfeld doesn't have any downtime." She swept out of the elevator. "We need the locations of all Lowell's businesses and documented properties—worldwide. Anything current's going to pop straight out, and we work from there. Talk to the director, put the strong arm on these damn Brit lawyers, the financial institutions where he has his numbered accounts."

"I can tell you it would take weeks—at the very best—to pry anything out of the financials. Their lawyers will have lawyers, who will run you around. And if he was careful, and I imagine he was, in setting these up, those accounts would simply feed into others, and so on. I could cut through that, at home, but it would take considerable time."

Would it help find Ariel? Eve asked herself. "I can't spare you for that. We'll push on the properties and the lawyers first. Got to have a bank box, too. Or boxes. Uses cash, so why wouldn't he store cash in a bank box at the different locations where he has homes, or plans to work? Downtown bank's best bet."

She walked into the war room, and up to Callendar. "Search for downtown banks. I want you to send every one of them every sketch and description we have on Robert Lowell, along with the various known aliases. And I want a search for any and all relations on Lowell, living or dead. Names, last known locations, property deeded in their name.

"Roarke, if you need any help on the property search, pull in any of the EDD team. Heads up," she said, boosting her voice over the chatter and clacking. "When Captain Feeney isn't in the house, and I'm not in the war room, the civilian's in charge of electronics. Questions on that? Go to him."

"Lieutenant's pet," Callendar said just loud enough for Roarke to hear, and in a mock sulk that made him smile a little.

"I'll wager ten I hit on the property before you hit on the banks."

"You're on, Prime Buns."

Eve left them for her office to update her notes, to take another pass through them. While she worked she tried Feeney.

"Anything for me?"

"There's nothing on the records here. The business passed to our guy when his old man died. These records list the same bogus London address. Director said there were some paper records, some disc files in storage, but Lowell took them years ago. Sorry, kid."

"Tidy son of a bitch. Anyone still working there who was employed when Lowell was still in residence?"

"No, checked that. I'm bringing in what records there are. We'll pick through them. On my way in now."

"I'll see you in the war room."

She pushed up, wanting to be on her feet. Her system was bottoming out, she could feel it, and if she didn't keep moving, she'd drop.

He was in New York, she thought. And wherever he lived and worked, wherever he was holding Ariel would be in New York, in a building that survived, or at least partially survived, the Urbans. It would have a connection to him, to her, to that time.

Nothing else would do for him, she was sure of it.

Death was his business. Body preparation or disposal, echoes of the Urban Wars, profit and science. He lived by death.

By killing he re-created the death of one woman, over and over again, while feeding his own need to control, to give pain. To study pain and death.

The torture devices were, in the opinions of the ME and the lab, tools and implements used during the Urbans with a few modern devices worked in. Same with the drugs found in the victims. He had to keep the connection.

Opera. The drama, the scope, the tragedy, and again the connection to Edwina Spring. The disguises were really costumes, the aliases simply roles to play.

Weren't the victims the same? Just another element of his role-playing.

How much longer before he gave Eve her cue to come onstage? And why the hell was she waiting?

She got herself some coffee, took out another energy pill. Technically she wasn't supposed to take a second one within the same twenty-four-hour period. But if she was going to push for her entrance in the play, she wasn't going out so blurry she couldn't remember her lines.

She popped it, and with the coffee in hand went back to the war room. She opened communications so anyone in the field could hear and participate. "Updates. EDD first. Feeney?"

"We're about to run searches through the discs taken from Lowell's Funeral Home. We'll go through the paper records as well, looking for any pertinent data on Robert Lowell and/or Edwina Spring. Secondary unit has a list of prior open homicides and Missings that may be his earlier work. We're requesting case files, moving from the highest probability down."

"Anything sing for you?"

"Two. Both in Italy, one fifteen years back, one twelve. Both missing females that bull's-eye our vic profile. One from Florence, one from Milan."

"Roarke, does Lowell have business operations in Italy, either of those cities?"

"Milan, established just prior to Lowell's inheriting the business."

"I want every detail of the Milan case first. Baxter, I want you to reach out to the investigating officer or his superior. Get a translator if necessary. Roarke, put the other Lowell operation locations on screen.

"We hit these," she said as he complied. "Blanket warrant—Feeney, make that happen. Three-man teams at each location, communication open throughout. Hit private and/or employee-only areas first. Get statements, get data, get every fucking thing."

"I have two prior business locations," Roarke put in. "Buildings that were sold. One was severely damaged during the war, torn down and rebuilt as an apartment building. The second was intact, but sold by this Lowell's father twenty-three years ago. He bought it shortly after the Urbans."

"I'll take those two. Fire up my eyes and ears, Feeney. Peabody and two uniforms can shadow me. Ten-block minimum. I move out in five."

Roarke got up to follow her out, and after scratching his head, Feeney went after both.

"Three-man teams," Roarke commented. "Except for you."

"You know why."

"I don't have to like it. You can spare a uniform. I'll shadow with Peabody."

She shook her head. "I need you here. Out there, you're just weight. In here, you may make the difference."

"That's a hell of a thing."

"Can't be helped." She swung into her office for her coat, spotted Feeney when she started to pull it on.

"Let's check you out, kid."

"Oh. Right." She depressed and turned the button on her jacket to activate. "System's a go?"

He glanced at his hand monitor. "That's affirmative." Then he looked up at her. "We're closing in. You get that, too?"

"Yeah. Another twenty-four, maybe thirty-six, we'll pin him. I don't want it to go that long, Feeney. He probably started on her this morning, bright and fucking early this morning. Been at her now ten or twelve hours, I'd say. Maybe she can make another twenty-four or thirty-six. Maybe she can't. I can't make him go for me, but I'm going to be out there the next few hours, giving him the chance to try."

Feeney's glance drifted to Roarke, then back to her. "Not enough for him to try."

"No. I've got to get inside, got to get him to take me where she is. I know how to handle it. I know how to handle it," she repeated, looking directly at Roarke. "If he gives me the chance. If he doesn't, I need the two of you here, digging out the next piece that brings us to him. If we had this much nine years ago, if we believed he might move on me then, Feeney, what would you have done?"

He puffed out his cheeks. "I'd've sent you out."

"Then I'd better get going."

Roarke watched her go, and when he was back at his station, split his work screen with her camera. He could see what she saw, hear through his ear bud what she heard.

That would have to be enough.

She took the second location he'd given her first. Private home, higher probability. While his searches ran he focused all his attention on the building she approached. Urban and attractive, he decided, tucked in among other urban and attractive buildings.

When the door was opened by a woman with a dog yapping at her feet and a toddler on her hip, he relaxed. The probability had just dipped very low.

Still he kept her on split screen as she went inside, sidestepping the dog the woman shooed away.

He let bits of the conversation wind through his head as he put the bulk of his concentration on the work. Everything the woman said to Eve confirmed the official data on the property. A family home owned by a junior exec and his wife, professional mother, who lived there with their two children and a very irritable terrier.

"Nothing here," Eve said as she moved back outside toward her vehicle. "Heading to second location. No tails spotted."

She was cold. She was so awfully cold. It was probably shock, Ariel told herself. In vids when somebody went into shock, they put a blanket over them. Didn't they?

Parts of her had gone numb, and she didn't know if that was a blessing or if it meant those pieces of her had died. She knew she'd lost consciousness the second—or had it been the third?—time he'd hurt her.

But then he'd done something, something that had shot her back into the nightmare. Something that had jolted her like a hot blue electric current.

Sooner or later, he wouldn't be able to bring her back. A part of her wanted to pray for that, so she buried that part, that weeping, yielding part.

Someone would come. She would stay alive, then someone would come.

When he came back, she wanted to scream. She wanted to scream and scream until the force of the sound shattered all those glass walls. Until it shattered him. She could imagine it, how that kind and quiet face of his would shatter into pieces like the walls of glass.

"Could I . . . May I please have some water?"

"I'm sorry, but that's not allowed. You're getting fluids through the IV."

"But my throat's so dry, and I was hoping we could talk some more."

"Were you?" He wandered over to his tray. She wouldn't let herself look, didn't dare look at what he picked up this time.

"Yes. About music. What's the music that's playing now?"

"Ah, that would be Verdi. *La Traviata*."

He closed his eyes a moment, and his hands began to move like a conductor's. "Brilliant, isn't it? Stirring and passionate."

"Did—did your mother sing this one?"

"Yes, of course. It was a favorite of hers."

"It must have been so hard for you when she died. I had a friend whose mother self-terminated. It was terrible for her. It's . . . it's hard to understand how anyone could be so sad or so lost that it seems to them death is the answer."

"But of course, it is, just that. It's the answer for all of us in the end." He stepped closer. "It's what we all ask for when our time comes. She did. You will."

"I don't want to die."

"You will," he said again. "Just as she did. But don't worry, I'll give you that answer, and that gift, just as I did for her."

Other chatter came and went as teams reported in from their destinations. Roarke drank coffee and painstakingly scraped layers off old records, pried out ragged bits of data, and tried to sew them together into answers.

The second building had a basement. Though Eve knew the chances were small, she did a walk-through.

Not his kind of place, she decided. Too modern, too ugly, too crowded, and with too much security. A guy couldn't comfortably drag a terrified or unconscious woman inside without annoying the neighbors.

Still she questioned a few, showed Lowell's picture.

What if she was off, she wondered, about him working out of the city? Maybe he'd bought a damn house in the suburbs, and used Manhattan for hunting and dumping. How much time would she have wasted looking for the right building among thousands if he was killing women in some ranch in White Plains or Newark?

She got back in the car. She'd go back to the bakery, back to Greenfeld's apartment. Maybe she'd missed something. Maybe they all had. She'd do another sweep of each victim's home and place of employment.

Swinging out into traffic, she relayed her intentions back to base. "It'll keep me out on the street a couple more hours, keep me in the open. And it'll look like what it is. Like I'm chasing my goddamn tail."

"I've got another possibility," Roarke told her. "It was a sewing machine factory, regentrified into lofts in NoHo late in the twentieth. I've got a bit about it being used for barracks during the Urbans, taking some considerable hits. It was repaired and sold for lofts again in the early thirties."

"Okay, I'll check that one. Give me the location." She pursed her lips when he gave her the address. She'd gone from west to east, and now would cross west again, head north. "Peabody, you copy that?"

"Affirmative."

"Heading west."

She made her turn, then answered the signal of her in-dash 'link. "Dallas."

"Lieutenant Dallas? I'm calling for Mr. Klok. You requested that he contact you when he returned home. He arrived today, and would be happy to speak with you if you still wish it."

"Yeah, I still wish it."

"Mr. Klok is able to meet with you at your convenience. However, it would be helpful if you could come to his residence as he's injured himself in a fall. His doctors prefer he remain at home for the next forty-eight hours."

"Yeah? What happened?"

"Mr. Klok slipped on some ice on the sidewalk upon his return. He suffered a mild concussion and a wrenched knee. If it's not convenient for you, Mr. Klok wishes for me to relate to you that he will come to your office as soon as his doctors allow."

"I can come to him. Actually, I'm in the area now. I can be there in a few minutes."

"Very well. I'll inform Mr. Klok."

Eve ended the transmission, and said, "Hmmm."

"Got a smell to it," Feeney commented in her ear.

"Yeah, awfully well timed and convenient. It's also pretty stupid for our guy to invite me into his home to make his move. No tail on me. As far as he knows I've got my partner here."

She tapped her fingers on the wheel as she thought it through. "Klok ran clean—and no, I'm not discounting that could be another fabrication. Either way, I want to talk to him. And if this actually turns out to be his move on me, he's giving me free entry."

"Into a trap," Roarke pointed out.

"It's only a trap if I let him spring it. I've got three men at my back, I've got eyes and ears. I'm going in, and you can dig deeper on his house while I'm in transit. If I see or feel anything off, you'll know it. Peabody move in, secure the van three blocks from destination."

"Copy," Peabody acknowledged. "We're about ten blocks back now, got a little snag in traffic. We'll route around it and move in."

"Go ahead and do another run on Klok. Let's see if he arrived in New York today as advertised. Search public and private shuttles and transports. If you get those results while I'm in, relay. Otherwise, cut all chatter now. I'm only a couple blocks away."

Jumpy, Eve thought, rolling her shoulders. Damn chemicals from the energy pills were bouncing around inside her like little springy balls.

"Transmission's going a little fuzzy on the homer," Feeney commented, then glanced over at Roarke. "You getting that?"

"I am. A little interference. Could be some stray transmission that bled onto the frequency. Can you clean it up?"

"Working on that. Peabody, you still have her?"

"Yeah. McNab says the beacon's jumping a little."

"It's interference," Roarke repeated as the signal went in and out. "It's another transmission, crossing ours. Bloody hell." He shoved back from his station. "It's another homer. Another homer on her vehicle. It's crossed ours now because she's near or at the base point. He's tracked her, that's how he knew to call her in. He knew she was close."

"Dallas, Dallas, you copy?" Feeney shouted into the receiver. "Dallas, goddamn it. Peabody, move in, move the fuck in." He leaped up, rushed after Roarke as Roarke ran out of the room. "She knows what she's doing," Feeney said as they shoved onto an elevator.

"So does he."

Eve parked, then moved across the sidewalk. The courtyard gate opened for her. Awfully damn accommodating, she mused, and shifted her shoulders just to feel the weight of her weapon.

"At the door," she murmured into her receiver and pressed the bell.

The droid opened it. "Lieutenant, thank you for coming. Mr. Klok is in the parlor. May I take your coat?"

"No. Lead the way."

She'd keep the droid where she could see him, just in case.

The curtains were drawn, the lights low. She could see the figure of a man in a chair near a quiet fire, his foot wrapped with a soft cast and resting on a padded stool.

He had a short brown beard, short brown hair, some bruising around his left eye. "Corpulent" would have been the polite word for him, Eve supposed. Hers would have been "really fat."

"Lieutenant Dallas?" He had the slightest Germanic accent. "Please pardon me for not getting up. I was clumsy, banged myself up a bit this morning. Please sit down. Can I offer you something? Tea? Coffee?"

"No."

He offered his hand as he spoke. She moved in to take it. The common gesture would bring her closer, close enough, she judged for her to determine if he was Robert Lowell.

And as she angled herself to look into his eyes, she knew. She shifted, pulling her right hand back to reach for her weapon. "Hello, Bob."

He only smiled. "No one has ever called me Bob. You saw right through me."

"Get up. You." She gestured toward the hovering droid. "If you don't want your circuits fried, stay exactly where you are."

"I'm a little hampered," Lowell said pleasantly. "All this padding, and the cast."

Eve kicked the footstool away, so his foot thudded on the floor. "On the floor, on your face, hands behind your back. Now."

"I'll do my best." He slid and humped his way off the chair, huffing as he struggled to roll onto his belly.

When she reached down to grab his wrist, to pull his arm behind his back, he turned his hand, closed it over hers.

She felt the prick, cursed. "Son of a bitch tranq'd me." She aimed her weapon mid-body, fired a stream. Then her legs buckled and sent her to her knees.

"An old method," Lowell said as he effortfully rolled over. "Often used in assassinations at one time. Just a tranquilizer now, as you said." He smiled as she slid the rest of the way to the floor. "Very quick acting, of course."

He sat where he was until he'd unbuttoned the padded suit, pulled it aside. Underneath he wore standard body armor. "I thought, as you're very skilled, you might fire your weapon. It's always wise to take precautions. Carry her down to my workroom," he ordered the droid.

His duplicate droid was already taking her car away, very far away.

"Yes, sir."

Plenty of time, Lowell thought. When he was certain all was well, he'd call the droid home, replace his hard drive as he would replace this house droid's memory. As he'd done many times before.

Clean slate.

For now, he gathered the suit, the cast, picked up the weapon Eve had dropped. It was possible she'd called in her intention to stop there. Someone would come, be that the case. But there would be no sign she'd been there.

Her vehicle would be found miles away.

He would have all her communication devices, and all would be shut down.

He would have her, Lowell thought as he started down the steps to his work area. And complete his life's work.

Outside the house, Peabody stood sick with frustration and dread. She'd called for a battering ram for the door they couldn't budge, and for laser torches to cut through the riot bars on every window.

Eve was inside, and she couldn't find a way in.

"You've got to override the security."

"I'm working on it," McNab said between his teeth as he pulled out every trick he knew. "It's got backups on its backups. I've never seen anything like it."

They both whirled as a car squealed to a halt in the street. Some of her dread lessened when she saw Roarke and Feeney jump out.

"We can't get past the system. The place is locked down like a fort."

"Move aside." Roarke shoved McNab away, pulled out his own tools.

"Tried the master, tried the override, got my comp to spit out codes. But when you input, they shift to another sequence."

"It was a Stealth base during the Urbans," Feeney told Peabody as sweat rolled down his back. "The minute she walked in, all comms were useless. We got the data on the way over. First Robert Lowell had it titled in his wife's maiden name, ran a branch of the business out of here. More a front during the Urbans.

"Get that damn system down," he ordered Roarke.

"Quiet and let me work."

"You don't get that down, get us inside before he puts hands on her, I'll be kicking your ass for the rest of my natural life."

Ariel's eyes tracked to him as he came in behind the droid. "Who is she? Who is she?"

"You could say the last of her breed." He leaned over the table where the droid laid Eve, went through her pockets for her 'link, her communicator, her PPC. He removed her wrist unit. "Take these and put them into the recycler. Go upstairs, shut down," he told the droid.

"Well, now." Gently Lowell brushed a hand through Eve's hair. "You'll need to be washed and prepared. Best to do that while you're sleeping. We're going to spend some time together, you and I. I've been looking forward to it."

"Are you going to kill me now?" Ariel asked.

"No, no, indeed, your time's still running. But I am going to do something very special." He turned to Ariel as if pleased to be able to discuss it. "I've never taken the opportunity to work with two partners at the same time. And you're proving to be so much more than I anticipated. I really believe you're going to exceed most, if not all who came before you. But she?" He glanced back at Eve. "I've set the bar very high for her. The last Eve."

"She . . . she looks familiar."

"Hmm?" Absently, he looked at Ariel again. "Yes, I suppose you might have seen her on some of the media reports. Now—"

"Mr. Gaines!"

He stopped his pivot back to Eve, frowned down at Ariel. "Yes, yes? What's so urgent? I have work."

"What . . . what is the most time? I mean, how long is the longest anyone—any of the women you've brought here—has lasted?"

His eyes brightened. "You're such a delightful surprise to me! Are you challenged? Have I tapped your competitive streak?"

"I can't . . . if I don't know how long, I can't try to last longer. Will you tell me how long?"

"I can." With her clutch piece in her hand, Eve sat up on the steel table. "Eighty-five hours, twelve minutes, thirty-eight seconds."

"No." He looked baffled first, then red-faced and furious. "No, no. This is *not* allowed."

"You don't like that, you're going to hate this."

Eve shot out a stun, on a setting a little higher than was considered proper procedure, and dropped him like a stone. "Fuckhead," she muttered, and prayed she wasn't going to pass out or vomit.

"I knew you'd come." Tears swam in Ariel's eyes. "I knew someone would come, and when I saw them bring you in, I knew it was going to be okay."

"Yeah, hold on." She had to slide to her feet, give herself a moment to balance. "You did good. You did real good keeping his attention on you so I could get to my piece."

"I wanted to kill him. I imagined killing him. It helped."

"I bet it did. Listen, I'm a little off center. I don't think I'd better try cutting those ropes just yet. You've got to hang in there a little bit longer. I know you hurt, but you've got to hang in."

"I'm so cold."

"Okay." Eve managed to pull off her coat, then draped it over Ariel's bleeding and battered body. "I'm going to secure him, okay? I'm going to secure him, then go call for backup."

"Would you bring me back some water?"

Eve laid a hand on Ariel's cheek. "Sure."

"And maybe a whole bunch of drugs." While the tears spilled out, Ariel struggled to smile. "This is a really nice coat."

"Yeah. I like it."

22 TWO ENERGY BOOSTS WITH A TRANQ CHASER, Eve thought. The combination had her feeling stupid, shaky, and not a little sick. But she not only had to stay on her feet, she had to do the job.

Reaching around, she fumbled at her back for her restraints. Either they weren't there, or she'd lost all sensation in her left hand. "Crap. I've got to restrain this son of a bitch, but my cuffs . . . I must've dropped them upstairs when he tranq'd me. Let me just . . . okay."

She turned, saw the ropes looped through the side holes in the table. "Here we go. Okay."

"You don't look so good," Ariel commented. "I probably look a whole lot worse, but you don't look so good."

"Been putting in a lot of hours looking for you, Ariel." Eve fought the knots on the rope, cursing under her breath as her fingers felt as agile as limp soy dogs.

"Thanks."

"No problem. Bloody buggering hell! Was this son of a bitch a Youth Guide or something?"

"I always thought they were little psychos."

Unsteady fingers slick with sweat, Eve tugged and dragged. "Almost got this bitch. Just hold on."

"I'm not going anywhere."

Eve muscled one rope free, then bent over from the waist, blowing out breath as her stomach tried to heave. "Little sick to my stomach. Don't be alarmed if I boot."

Ariel managed a smile through gritted teeth. "If you do, boot on him. Bastard."

On an appreciative and slightly drunk laugh, Eve crouched down to tie Lowell's hands. "You're a stand-up, Ariel. A goddamn Amazon. I can see why Erik's in love with you."

"What? Erik? Erik loves me?"

Eve swiped at her sweaty brow, glanced up and over at Ariel's pale face. "That was probably something I was supposed to keep to myself. Crossed the line. Blame the tranq. But listen," she continued as she tied the rope around Lowell's wrists just a little tighter than strictly necessary. "If you don't go for him, you know? If you don't, take it easy on him, okay? 'Cause he's really gone over you."

Eve stood, ignoring the way her head swam, to release the second rope for Lowell's feet. And saw tears sliding down Ariel's cheeks. "Oh, man, I know you're hurt. I know this sucks out loud, but just hang on a few minutes more."

"I've loved that dumbass almost since he moved in across the hall. Dumbass never made one move."

"Oh." God, people were strange, Eve thought. The woman had stood up under unspeakable pain, but she was leaking because some guy was soft on her. "He probably will now. Jesus, music off!" she ordered as she bound Lowell's feet. But the voices continued to soar. "You know how he shut that shit off?"

"Not really. I've been kind of tied up since I got here."

Eve plopped down on her ass and laughed like a loon. "You ever think of giving up baking and going into police work, Ariel—I swear you've got the spine and the nasty streak for it."

"I like baking. I'm going to bake you the most incredible cake. It's going to be a goddamn work of art. Oh, God, God, do you think someone's coming with drugs soon?"

"It won't be long. I'm going to see if I can get the doors open, or break the glass."

"But . . . don't leave me."

"Listen." Eve gained her feet, stepped over so she and Ariel were face-to-face. "I'm not going anywhere without you. On my word."

"What's your name? I'm sorry, did you tell me your name already?"

"It's Dallas. Eve Dallas."

"If I give Erik a break and we get married, I'm naming the first kid after you."

"There's a lot of that going around."

"Get us the hell out of here, Dallas."

Eve moved to the door, yanked, shoved, pulled, kicked, rammed. Cursed. Turning again, she pulled the coat over Ariel's face. "Just for a minute, in case the glass flies around." And taking out her weapon again, she upped the stream and blasted at the door.

The glass held, but she saw it shake. She hit it again, aiming for the same spot, then a third time. On the forth, the glass erupted into a wild spiderweb of cracks.

"Nearly through, Ariel." Eve holstered her weapon, picked up the stool and slammed it into the damaged door. She beat at it until the ground sparkled and the opening was clear.

After heaving the stool aside, Eve went back to uncover Ariel's face. Paler now, Eve noted, shaking a little more. Had to get moving, had to get gone. "Found a way out. I'm going to cut these ropes now."

"Try not to let the knife slip. I'm pretty tired of getting cut."

Eve picked up one of Lowell's tools, nudged the coat away from Ariel's arm. It was patterned with cuts, punctures, burns. Eve set the blade on the rope, looked up into Ariel's eyes. "He's going to pay. He's going to pay for every minute you spent in here. I swear it."

She had to saw through the rope, leaving bracelets of it around Ariel's abraded wrists. And she had to turn her mind, her rage away from the wounds she saw.

As she freed Ariel's feet, she heard Lowell give a soft groan.

"He's waking up, he's waking up." Voice pitched in panic and pain, Ariel struggled to sit. "He can't get loose, can he?"

"No. He's not getting up on his own. And look, if he tries, we have this." Eve drew her weapon again.

"Why don't you stun him again? While I watch."

"Appreciate the sentiment, but I think it's time to get you out of here. Here, let's get this coat on you." As Eve slid the sleeves on, Ariel hissed. "Sorry."

"It's okay." She kept her eyes trained on Lowell. "I'm okay. Can you help me down so I can kick him? In the face. That's what I imagined doing. I want to kick him in the face."

"Again, kudos on the sentiment. But here's what we're going to do. I want you to wrap your arms around my neck. Glass everywhere, and I don't have a spare pair of shoes on me. I just need you to hold onto me, and I'm going to carry you out. You hold onto me, Ariel. I'll get you out."

"Like . . . Like piggyback," Ariel managed between shaky breaths when Eve backed up to the table.

"Yeah, that's the way. You get a little piggyback ride, and I'm hoping you don't sample a lot of your products."

Ariel managed a watery laugh, then collapsed against Eve's neck and shoulders.

"Ready? Here we go." With her own legs wobbly from the drugs, Eve bent to take the weight. She focused on the door. Five feet to get through, she calculated as she put one foot in front of the other. Another two, maybe three to get past the broken glass on the floor.

There was communication equipment out there, she reminded herself as sweat slid over her skin and Ariel bit back whimpers. She'd tag her backup, the MTs.

She heard something crash, then the rush of feet. And tightened her grip on the weapon in her hand. She let out the breath she was holding when she heard Roarke shout her name.

"Back here! Call the MTs! That's the cavalry, Ariel."

"No." Ariel's head slumped on Eve's shoulder. "You are."

Roarke flew through the maze of the basement toward the echo of Eve's voice. The sound of it had stabbed through the music, blown through him like breath.

He saw her, pale, face gleaming with sweat, her weapon in her hand, and a quietly weeping woman on her back.

He lowered his own weapon, let the tremor in his belly come and go. "We've come to save you."

She worked up a grin for him. "About damn time."

He was to her in the single beat of a heart, and despite the flood of cops pouring down, gripped her exhausted face in his hands and kissed her.

"Here." He shifted to lift Ariel from Eve's back. "Let me help you."

"Is he yours?" Ariel asked.

"Yeah. He's mine."

Ariel stared up into Roarke's face. "Wow." She let out a deep, deep breath, then just closed her eyes.

"MTs, now." Eve bent, bracing her hands on her knees. "Peabody, you here?"

"Present and accounted for."

"I want this place secured. I want a team of sweepers in here, going over every inch, documenting everything."

"Dallas, you look a little green."

"Tranq'd me. Fucker got by me for a half a second. Energy pills, tranqs, I'm a chemical stew." She stayed as she was, snorting out a laugh. "Damn it. All electronics seized. Droid somewhere upstairs deactivated. And Jesus, somebody get that music off before my head explodes."

She pushed herself up, swayed, and might have tumbled if Feeney hadn't gripped her arm. "Head rush. I'm okay, just a little queasy. Lowell's in there, secured. You need to haul his ass in. Your collar."

"No, it's not." Feeney gave her arm a squeeze. "But I'll haul his ass in for you. McNab, help the lieutenant upstairs, then get your butt back down here and start on the electronics."

"I don't need help," Eve protested.

"You fall on your face," Feeney murmured in her ear, "you'll ruin your exit."

"Yeah. Yeah."

"Just lean on me, Lieutenant." McNab wrapped an arm around her waist.

"You try to cop a feel, I can still put you down."

"Whatever your condition, Dallas, you still scare me."

"Aw." Touched, she slung an arm around his shoulders. "That's so sweet."

Taking her weight, he led her through the maze of rooms, up the stairs. "We couldn't get in," he told her. "We were maybe ten minutes behind you—traffic snarl—then we couldn't get in the damn house. Your car wasn't there, but we knew you'd gone in. I couldn't get through the security. Roarke did. We had battering rams and laser torches coming, but he got through."

"Nothing much keeps him out."

"It took time, even for him. Place is like the frigging Pentagon or something. Then we had to get through the next level on the basement."

"How long was I in there?"

"Twenty minutes, half an hour, maybe."

"Not too bad."

"I'll take her from here," Roarke said.

"Don't—aw, no picking me up." But she was already cradled in his arms.

"I have to, for a minute anyway." He simply buried his face against the side of her neck as cops and techs swarmed by. "I couldn't get to you."

"Yeah, you did. Besides, I told you I could handle myself."

"So you did, so you always do. Are you hurt?"

"No. Feel like I guzzled a bottle of wine, and not the good stuff. But it's passing some. Gee, your hair smells good." She sniffed at it, caught herself, and winced. "Damn tranqs. You gotta put me down. This is undermining my rep and authority."

He eased her onto her feet, but kept his arm around her waist for support. "You need to lie down."

"Really don't. You lie down and everything starts spinning around. Just need to walk it off."

"Lieutenant?" Newkirk walked up with her coat. "Ms. Greenfeld asked that this get back to you."

"Thanks. Where is she?"

"MTs are working on her, in the hall—the foyer, I guess it is."

"All right. Officer Newkirk? You did good work."

"Thank you, Lieutenant. Right now it feels like good work."

"I want to take a look at her before they transport her," Eve said to Roarke, and let him help her to the foyer.

Ariel was on a stretcher, covered with a blanket, a pair of MTs preparing to roll her out.

"Give me a minute. Hey," she said to Ariel, "how you doing?"

"They gave me some really mag drugs. I feel *sooooo* good. You saved my life." Ariel reached up to grip Eve's hand.

"I had a part in it. So did the cops crowding into this place, and this civilian here, too. But mostly, Ariel? You saved yourself. We're going to need to talk to you some more, when you're feeling a little better."

"So he pays."

"That's right."

"Anytime, anyplace."

"Okay. One more second," she told the MTs, and held out a hand to Roarke. "Let me have your pocket 'link." She took it, keyed in a number. "Hey, Erik. Hey," she repeated when he began to spew out questions. "Quiet down. I've got someone here who wants to talk to you." She put the 'link into Ariel's hand. "Say hi, Ariel."

"Erik? Erik?" She began to cry, to laugh, and beamed up at Eve with drug-hazed eyes. "He's crying. Don't cry, Erik. I'm okay now. Everything's okay."

"Go ahead," Eve said to the MTs, "and tell the guy on the 'link where you're taking her. He'll want to be there."

"Nice job, Lieutenant," Roarke murmured as they wheeled Ariel out.

"Yeah. And you can always get another 'link. I have to go in, finish this up."

"We have to go in, finish this up," Roarke corrected.

She was steadier when she got to Central, and forced down some of the Eatery's fake eggs in the hopes of smoothing out her system. She forked them up in the war room, chasing them with all the water she could stand.

She wanted a shower, she wanted a bed. But more than she wanted anything, she wanted a turn with Lowell in the box.

She set the food aside, rose, and walked over to stare at all the names on the board. "For all of them," she said quietly. "What we did, what we do now, it's for all of them. That's the point that has to be made. In the box, in the courts, in the media. It's important."

"No one who worked in this room these last days will forget them," Roarke told her.

She nodded. "This is going to take some time. I know you're not leaving until it's done, so I won't bother suggesting it. You can stand in Observation, or be more comfortable and watch from one of the monitors."

"I like Observation."

"Okay then. I'm going to have him brought up, so go pick your spot. I need to talk to Peabody."

She headed toward the bullpen. It was buzzing, and as she stepped inside, applause broke out. Eve held up a hand. "Save it," she ordered. "It's not done yet. Peabody."

Peabody shoved up from her desk, turned, and took a quick bow before going out after Eve. "We're pumped."

"Yeah, I know. Peabody, I have to ask you for a solid."

"Sure."

"You earned a turn in Interview with this bastard, and you're secondary on the investigation. It's your right. I need to ask you to step aside for Feeney on this."

"Can I stand in Observation and give Lowell the finger?"

"Absolutely. I owe you."

"No. Not on this one. Nobody owes anybody on this one."

"Okay. Bring him up for us, will you? Interview A."

"Oh, my sincere pleasure. Dallas? I've just gotta dance." And she did so, a kind of tap/shuffle as she walked away.

Eve went into her office, tagged Feeney. "Interview A, he's coming up."

"Burn his ass."

"Then get yours down here and help me fry him, ace."

"Peabody—"

"Is observing, like half the cops in this place. Come on, Feeney, this one's ours. Let's wrap it up."

"I'm on my way."

When it was time, she walked into Interview A with Feeney. Lowell sat quietly alone, an ordinary-looking man past middle age with a pleasant if somewhat quizzical smile on his face.

"Lieutenant Dallas, this is very unexpected."

"Record on, Dallas, Lieutenant Eve, and Feeney, Captain Ryan, in interview with subject Lowell, Robert." She fed in the case numbers—all of them, then read off the Revised Miranda. "Robert Lowell do you understand your rights and obligations in this matter?"

"Of course. You were very clear."

"You understand you're being charged with the abductions, assaults, forced imprisonments, and murders of six women, the abduction and forced imprisonment of Ariel Greenfeld, and will subsequently be questioned by Global authorities on the abductions, assaults, illegal captivity, and murders of others."

"Yes, I do." He continued to smile genially, folded his plump hands. "Should we save time by my acknowledging all those charges. Confessing to them? Or would that be anticlimactic?"

"You're awful damn chipper," Feeney commented, "for a man who's going to spend the rest of his miserable, murdering life in a cement cage."

"Well, actually, I won't be. I will be quietly ending my time within the next twenty-four hours as per my requested and granted self-termination contract. It will stand," he said pleasantly, "as my doctors have certified my terminal condition and my application. My lawyers have assured me that the certification will override even criminal charges. Neither the State nor Global will supersede an individual's right to die. And, of course, it saves considerable expense. So . . ." He lifted his shoulders.

"You think you can get off, get out, by swallowing a few pills?" Feeney demanded.

"Indeed I do. It's not what I hoped for, believe me. I haven't finished my work, not completely. You were to be my ultimate," he said to Eve. "The culmination of everything. When you were finished, then I would have approached my own death with all fully realized. Still, I have accomplished a great deal."

"Well." Eve leaned back in her chair, nodded. "You sure covered the bases. I have to say—Bob—you thought of everything. I admire that. It's not nearly as satisfying to pull in a sloppy killer."

"Order is one of my bywords."

"Yeah, I noticed. I appreciate you saving us time by being willing to confess to everything, but after all the work we put in, we'd really like the details. You could call it our culmination. So . . . this is going to take a while," she said with an easy smile. "You want something to drink?

I'm still a little off from the tranq you got into me. I'm going to go get myself some cold caffeine. You want?"

"That's very nice of you. I wouldn't mind a soft drink."

"You got it. Feeney, why don't you step out while I hit Vending. Pause record."

"What the hell," Feeney began when they were outside Interview.

Everything about her hardened: face, eyes, voice. "I've got a way around this. I don't want you to ask me about it. Ever. When we go back in, we play along. We get the details, and we sew him up. Give me your 'link, will you? I haven't replaced mine yet. And wait for me."

She took Feeney's 'link, wandered down to Vending. And beeped Peabody on privacy mode. "Tell Roarke—quietly—to step out for a minute. Don't say anything to me. We haven't spoken." She clicked off, then stared at the machine.

Moments later, Roarke walked up behind her. "Lieutenant?"

"Get me a Pepsi, a ginger ale, and a cream soda. I need you to make this go away," she said under her breath. "Can you make his self-termination clearance disappear? No trace of it, anywhere?"

"Yes," he said simply as he ordered the tubes.

"It crosses the line, what I'm asking you. I gave her my word he'd pay. And in the war room before I came out, I gave them all my word. So I'm crossing the line."

He retrieved the tubes, passed them to her. His eyes, meeting hers, spoke volumes. "I have to get on," he said in a clear voice. "I wish I could stay, wait for you, but I'm expecting some calls and transmissions, and you gave Ariel my 'link. I'll try to come back once I've taken care of this. Otherwise, I'll see you at home."

"Yeah. Okay. Thanks."

They parted ways with her heading back to Feeney. "I got you cream soda."

"For Christ's sake—"

"Hey, if you wanted something else you should've said so. It's going away," she whispered. "Don't ask me about it, just take my word. He's not going out the way he wants. We'll let him think he is, until we have everything we need."

Feeney stared into her eyes for a long moment, then nodded. "Okay, let's get it down."

It took hours, but Lowell never requested a break. He was, Eve realized, basking. After all the time, all the effort, he was finally able to share his obsession.

He gave them meticulous details on every murder.

Eve and Feeney worked in tandem, an old and easy rhythm.

"You got yourself a good memory," Feeney commented.

"I do. You'll find every project documented—keeping records, and we could say *amending* them, was one of my tasks during the wars. I'm sure you've collected all the records from my lab and office. I'd hoped, before I learned I was dying, to arrange for my work to be published. It will have to be posthumously, but I believe that's appropriate."

"So, your work," Eve began, "what got you started? We understand the women—"

"Partners. I considered them partners."

"I bet they didn't see it your way, but fine. Your partners represented to you your stepmother."

"They *became* her, which is entirely different. She was the first, you see. The Eve." He smiled brilliantly. "So you can see why I knew you were to be the last."

"Yeah, too bad about your luck on that."

"I always knew I could fail, but if I succeeded it would have been perfection. As she was. She was magnificent. You'll also find many recording discs of her performances. She gave up a great career for me."

"For you?"

"Yes. We were, well, the term would be 'soul mates.' While I could never play—she was an accomplished pianist—nor did I have a voice to offer, it was through her I gained my great love and admiration for music. It was by her I was saved."

"How so?"

"My father considered me imperfect. Some difficulties with my birth, which caused, well, you could call it a defect. I had some trouble with controlling my impulses, and there were mood swings. He institutionalized me briefly, over my grandfather's objections, when I was quite young. Then Edwina came into my life. She was patient and loving, and used music to help me remain calm or entertained. She was my mother and my partner, and my great love."

"She was killed during the Urbans," Eve prompted.

"Her time came during the Urbans. The human cycle is about time, you see, and will and individual acceptance."

"But you turned her in," Eve said. "You heard her talking with the man, the soldier she was in love with. Heard that she was planning to leave you. You couldn't let her go, could you?"

Irritation flickered over his face. "How do you know anything about that?"

"You're a smart guy, Bob. We're smart guys, too. What did you do when you found out she was going to leave you?"

"She couldn't leave me, she had no right. We belonged together. It was a terrible betrayal, unforgivable. There was no choice, none at all, in what had to be done."

"What had to be done?" Feeney asked him.

"I had to go to my father, and my grandfather, and tell them that she'd betrayed us. That I'd overheard her planning betrayals with one of the men. That she was a traitor."

"You made them think she was a spy. Betraying the cause."

He spread his hands, all reason. "It was all the same, and a great tragedy for us all. She was taken, as the soldier was, down to my grandfather's laboratory."

"In the house where you took the women, here in New York. Down where you worked, where your grandfather tortured prisoners during the Urbans."

"I learned a great deal from my grandfather. I watched as he worked with Edwina—he insisted on it. I understood so much as I watched. It made me strong and aware. Days, it took. Longer than it took for the soldier."

He moistened his lips, took a small, tidy drink. "Men are weaker, my grandfather taught me. So often weaker than women. In the end, she asked for death. I looked into her eyes, and I saw all the answers, all the love, all the beauty that comes when the body and mind are stripped down to the core. I stopped time for her myself, my gift to her. She was my first, and all who've come after have only been reflections of her."

"Why did you wait so long to look for those reflections?"

"The medication. My father was very insistent about my medication, and monitored me quite closely. The understanding, the clarity of mind needed for the work dulls with the medication."

"But Corrine Dagby, here in New York nine years ago, she wasn't your first." Eve shook her head. "Not nearly. You had to practice, to perfect. How many were there before Corrine?"

"I learned from my grandfather, continued my education, and worked in the family business. I practiced on the dead under my grandfather's tutelage. And I traveled. I first began serious practice nearly twenty years ago, after my father's death. I had a great deal to learn and experience first. It took me another decade before I felt ready to begin the projects. I did document all the others, the failures, the near successes. You'll find all that in my records."

"Handy." Eve glanced over at the knock on the door. Peabody poked her head in.

"Excuse me, Lieutenant. Can I see you just for a minute?"

"Yeah. Keep going," she said to Feeney, then stepped outside.

"Roarke just tagged me. He asked if I'd tell you that he was able to finish the work he needed to deal with, and since it's cleaned up, he was heading back down. He said he hoped to see you finish the interview."

"Okay. I need you and McNab to check on this bastard's ST. No point in taking his word that he's got the go to clock out. Check all his personal data taken from the scene, wake up his lawyers in London. His doctors, if you find their data. I want confirmation he's not stringing us on it."

"Why would he—"

"Just get me confirmation, Peabody."

"Yes, sir."

Eve went back in, slid into a chair as Feeney pried more details out of Lowell.

"I meant to ask you," she inserted, "how long Edwina Spring lasted. Her time."

"My grandfather employed different methods, with longer rest periods than I've found necessary. Regardless, she was very strong, and had a high survival instinct. It was ninety-seven hours, forty-one minutes, and eight seconds. No one has ever reached her capacity. I believe you may have done so, which is why I wanted to end with you as I'd begun with her."

"I wonder how long you'd last," Eve commented, and rose as Peabody appeared at the door again.

Eve stepped out and eased the door closed behind them. "And?"

"I don't get it. There's no documentation supporting his claim. Nothing in his records, nothing in the official data banks, and McNab searched through them twice. I contacted the London lawyer—head of the firm, who was not pleased to be disturbed at home."

"Aw."

"Yeah. He did the privacy dance. I explained that his client was under arrest for multiple murders, and hauling out this ST claim to avoid trial and incarceration. Pulled the commander into it. Legal guy claimed Lowell had secured certification, but he couldn't produce the documentation either. Went a little nuts about it. He's spouting about holding interviews and so on, but he doesn't have any pull in the U.S. of A."

"That's all I need."

"But—"

"Going to wrap this up now, Peabody. Good job."

Eve walked back in, closed the door in Peabody's face. "Just to summarize," Eve began. "You have confessed, with full understanding of your rights and obligations, having waived any counsel or representation, to the crimes heretofore documented?"

" 'Crimes' is your word, but yes, I have."

"How long did the medicals estimate you had left?"

"No more than two years, with the last several months extremely painful, unpleasant, and demeaning even with medication. I prefer a quiet and controlled end to my time."

"I bet you do. But you know, you're not going to get it. You don't have any ST certification on record. Bob."

"I certainly do."

"Nope—and your fancy Brit lawyers can't produce one either." She laid her palms on the table, leaned over into his face. "No record means we're under no obligation to take your word for it, under no obligation to accommodate your easy out. A couple of years isn't as much as I'd like, but you'll be spending it in a box. You'll be spending some of it in pain, in distress, in despair."

"No." He shook his head slowly. "I have certification."

"You've got nothing. And you are no longer free to apply for ST. You've been charged and you have willingly confessed to multiple homicides. Your out just slammed shut."

"You're lying." His lips trembled. "You're trying to upset me, to trick me."

"You go ahead and think that. You go on thinking that for the next two years. You get to live, and every second you get to live, you're going to suffer."

"I want . . . I want my lawyers."

"Sure. You can have an army of goddamn lawyers. They're not going to help you." Her eyes were fierce now, not the flat, objective eyes of the cop, but the fierce, burning eyes of justice. "You're going to know pain. You're going to choke out your last breath in pain."

"No. No. It's my time, it's all worked out. I need my music, my pills."

"Bob, you need to die a long, slow, agonizing death." She straightened. "Why don't you haul him down, Feeney. He can go cry to his lawyers before he starts learning what it's like to live in a cage."

"I've been waiting for nine years to do this." Feeney hauled Lowell to his feet. "I'm betting on medical science," he said as he dragged Lowell to the door. "Couple of years? They might find a fix. That would be sweet." He glanced over his shoulder, sent Eve a strong smile. "That would be goddamn sweet."

EPILOGUE

WHEN EVE STEPPED OUT, COPS POURED OUT OF OBSERVATION, out of the conference room where the monitors had been set up. She saw Roarke with them before Baxter elbowed through, and shocked her speechless by hauling her off her feet and planting a noisy kiss on her mouth.

"Jesus Christ, are you out of your tiny mind?"

"Somebody had to do it, and he always gets to." He jerked his thumb at Roarke. "I'm already punchy so don't hit me. You either," he said to Eve as he dropped her back on her feet. "Call me a sucker, but I get emotional at happy endings."

"I'm going to be calling you in the nearest hospital if you try anything like that again. All of you who aren't on regular shift, go home. Dismissed, get the hell . . . Commander."

"Excellent job, all of you. I suggest you follow the lieutenant's orders. Go home, get some sleep. The department is goddamn proud of every one of you. Lieutenant."

"Sir. I'll have the paperwork finished and filed within the hour."

"No, you'll get the hell out. You'll go home. I'll see the paperwork is dealt with."

"Sir—"

"That's an order." He took her hand, shook it. "And consider that I'm going to give you a very large break and handle the media."

"Yes, sir."

She didn't object when Roarke slung an arm around her shoulders. "Why don't I drive you home, Lieutenant."

"Yeah, you could do that. Peabody, I don't want to see you here before ten tomorrow."

"I am so all over that. Dallas—"

"Don't even think about hugging me. Is there no end to the humiliation my men dole out?"

"Aw," Peabody said, but was grinning as Eve walked away.

She dropped off like a stone the minute she was in the car. Roarke drove with one hand on the wheel, one hand over hers. Halfway home, he switched to auto and let his own exhausted mind rest.

The lights of home were like stars, shining. He took his hand from hers to press his own fingers to his eyes, then climbed out to go around and open her door. But when he reached down to lift her, she batted a hand at his arm.

"No. I can walk."

"Thank Christ, because I think trying to haul you up at this point would have both of us on our asses in the bloody driveway. Here." He gripped her hand, gave her a tug. And the two of them stood a moment in the cold, bleary with fatigue.

"We just have to get inside, get upstairs, and fall into bed," she decided. "We can do that."

"All right then. Here we go."

They wrapped arms around each other's waists, held each other up as they walked to the front door, and through.

"Look at the pair of you." Summerset stood like a black cloud in the foyer. "Stumbling in like drunks, and I'd say in need of a good wash and a decent meal."

"Up yours, fuckface."

"As always, such a command of the language."

"Have to stand with my wife on this one," Roarke said. "Or fall, as may very well be the case any moment. Though the fuckface was a bit harsh. Let's take the elevator, darling. I'm too bleeding tired for the stairs."

Summerset shook his finger at Galahad, who stood up to follow as they passed. "I think not," he said quietly to the cat. "Let's leave it just the two of them, shall we? And now that the children are home safe and sound, we'll have a little snack before bed."

"Bed," Eve said as they stumbled out of the elevator. "I think I can actually smell bed—but in a good way." She began to let things fall— her coat, then her jacket, her weapon—on her way to the bed, as Roarke did exactly the same.

"I have something to say."

"Better make it quick," she warned, "because I think I'm already asleep."

"I've worked with you before, watched, understood—to some extent—what you do. But I haven't really gone the gamut, as with this time. Beginning to end, and most of the steps between." He fell into bed with her. "You're an amazing woman, Lieutenant, my darling Eve."

"You're not so shabby yourself." She turned to him, and with the lights still on looked into his eyes. "I'm not going to ask how you pulled off what I asked you to pull off."

"It's a bit complicated to explain at the moment in any case."

"We had him, we stopped him, and Ariel Greenfeld's safe. But there wouldn't have been justice, not even a shadow of real justice, if you hadn't done it." She laid her hand on his cheek. "We did good work."

"So we did." Their lips pressed together briefly. "Now let's have ourselves an eight-hour vacation."

"To quote Peabody," she said, voice already slurring, " 'I'm so all over that.' "

"Lights off," he ordered.

In the dark, with her hand on his cheek, they slid into sleep.

Strangers in Death

I MURDER HARBORED NO BIGOTRY, NO BIAS. IT subscribed to no class system. In its gleeful, deadly, and terminally judicious way, murder turned a blind eye on race, creed, gender, and social stratum. As Lieutenant Eve Dallas stood in the sumptuous bedroom of the recently departed Thomas A. Anders, she considered that.

Only the night before she'd caught—and closed—a case dealing with the homicide of a twenty-year-old woman who'd been throttled, beaten, then chucked out the window of her nine-story flop.

The rent-by-the week flop, Eve mused, where the victim's boyfriend claimed to have slept through her demise, smelled of stale sex, stale zoner, and really bad Chinese food. Anders? His Park Avenue bedroom smelled of candy-colored tulips, cool, clean wealth, and dead body. Death had come to him on the luxurious sheets of his massive, silk-canopied bed. And to Tisha Brown it had come on the stained mattress tossed on the floor of a junkie's flop. The header to the sidewalk had just been the flourish.

The point was, Eve supposed, no matter who you were—sex, race, tax bracket—death leveled it all out. As a murder cop going on a dozen years for the NYPSD, she'd seen it all before.

It was barely seven in the morning, and she was alone with the dead. She had the first officers on scene downstairs with the housekeeper who'd called in the nine-one-one. With her hands and boots sealed, she walked around the edges of the room while her recorder documented.

"Victim is identified as Anders, Thomas Aurelious, of this address. Male, caucasian, age sixty-one. Vic is married. Spouse is reported to be out of town, and has been notified by Horowitz, Greta, domestic who discovered the body at approximately oh-six-hundred and placed the nine-one-one at oh-six-twelve."

Eve cocked her head. Her hair was a short, somewhat shaggy brown around a face of angles and planes. Her eyes, a few shades lighter than her hair, were all cop—sharp, cynical, and cool as they studied the dead man in the big, fancy bed.

"Anders was reputed to be alone in the house. There are two domestic droids, both of which were shut down. On cursory exam, there are no signs of forced entry, no signs of burglary, no signs of struggle."

On long legs, she crossed to the bed. Over her lean body she wore rough trousers, a plain cotton shirt, and a long coat of black leather. Behind her, over a gas fireplace where flames simmered gold and red, the view screen popped on.

Good morning, Mr. Anders!

Narrow-eyed, Eve turned to stare at the screen. The computerized female voice struck her as annoyingly perky, and the sunrise colors bleeding onto the screen wouldn't have been her choice of wake-up call.

It's now seven-fifteen on Tuesday, March eighteenth, twenty-sixty. You have a ten o'clock tee time at the club, with Edmond Luce.

As the computer chirpily reminded Anders what he'd ordered for breakfast, Eve thought: *No egg-white omelette for you this morning, Tom.*

Across the room in an ornate sitting area, a miniAutoChef with bright brass fittings beeped twice.

Your coffee's ready! Enjoy your day!

"Not so much," Eve murmured.

The screen flipped to the morning's headline news, anchored by a woman only slightly less perky than the computer. Eve tuned her out.

The headboard gleamed brass, too—all of its sleek, shiny rungs. Black velvet ropes tied Anders's wrists to two of them, while two more ropes bound his ankles by a length to the footboard. The four matching ropes were joined by the fifth that wrapped around Anders's throat, pulling his head off the pillows. His eyes were wide, and his mouth hung open as if he was very surprised to find himself in his current position.

Several sex toys sat on the table beside the bed. Anal probe, vibrator, colorful cock rings, gliding and warming lotions, and lubricants. The usual suspects, Eve thought. Leaning down, she studied, sniffed Anders's thin, bare chest. Kiwi, she thought, and angled her head to read labels on the lotions.

Definitely the kiwi. It took all kinds.

As she'd noticed something else, she lifted the duvet from where it pooled at Anders's waist. Under it, three neon (possibly glow-in-the-dark) cock rings rode on an impressive erection.

"Not bad for a dead man."

Eve eased open the drawer in the nightstand. Inside, as she'd suspected, was an economy pack of the top-selling erection enhancer, Stay-Up. "Hell of a product endorsement."

She started to open her field kit, then stopped when she heard approaching footsteps. She recognized the clomp of boots as her partner's shit-kickers. Whatever the calendar said about the approach of spring, in New York that was a big, fat lie. As if to prove the point, Detective Delia Peabody stepped through the door in an enormous—and puffy—purple coat, with a long, striped scarf that appeared to be wrapped around her neck three times. Between that and the cap pulled over her ears, only her eyes and the bridge of her nose were visible.

"It's freaking five degrees," somebody who might have been Peabody said against the muffle of scarf.

"I know."

"With the windchill, they said it's, like, freaking minus ten."

"I heard that."

"It's freaking March, three days before spring. It's not right."

"Take it up with them."

"Who?"

"The *they* who have to go mouthing off about it being freaking minus ten. You're colder and pissier because they have to blabber about it. Take some of that shit off. You look ridiculous."

"Even my teeth are frozen."

But Peabody began to peel off the multiple layers covering her sturdy body. Scarf, coat, gloves, insulated zippy. Eve wondered how the hell she managed to walk with all of it weighing her down. With the hat discarded, Peabody's dark hair with its sassy little flip at the nape appeared to frame her square face. She still sported a pink-from-cold-tipped nose.

"Cop on the door said it looked like sex games gone bad."

"Could be. Wife's out of town."

"Bad boy." Down to her street clothes, sealed up, Peabody carted her field kit to the bed. Scanned the nightstand. "Very bad boy."

"Let's verify ID, get TOD." Eve examined one of the limp hands. "Looks like he had a nice manicure recently. Nails are short, clean, and buffed." She angled her head. "No scratches, no bruises, no apparent trauma other than the throat. And . . ." She lifted the duvet again.

Peabody's dark brown eyes popped. "Wowzer!"

"Yeah, fully loaded. Place like this has to have good security, so we'll check that. Two domestic droids—we'll check their replay. Take a look at his house 'links, pocket 'links, memo, date, address books. Tom had company. He didn't hoist himself up like this."

"*Cherchez la femme.* It's French for—"

"I know it's French. We could also be *cherching* the . . . whatever 'guy' is in French."

"Oh. Yeah."

"Finish with the body," Eve ordered. "I'll take the room."

It was a hell of a room, if you went for a lot of gold accent, shiny bits, curlicues. Besides the big bed in which Anders had apparently died, a sofa, a couple of oversized scoop chairs, and a full-service sleep chair offered other places to stretch out. In addition to the AutoChef, the bedroom boasted a brass friggie, wet bar, and an entertainment unit. The his and hers bathrooms both held jet tubs, showers, drying tubes, entertainment and communication centers within their impressive acreage. The space continued with two tri-level closets with attached dressing areas.

Eve wondered why they needed the rest of the house.

She should talk, she admitted. Living with Roarke meant living in enough space to house a small city—with all the bells and whistles big, fat fists of money could buy. He had better taste—thank God—than the Anderses. She wasn't entirely sure she could've fallen for him, much less married him, if he'd surrounded himself with gold and glitter and tassels, and Christ knew.

But as much *stuff* as there was jammed into the space, it all looked . . . in place, she decided. No sign or sense anything had been riffled through. She found a safe in each closet, concealed so a child of ten with dirt in both eyes could have found them. She'd check with the wife on those, but she wasn't smelling theft or burglary.

Walking out into the main bedroom again, she took another, hard look around.

"Prints verify ID as Anders, Thomas A., of this address," Peabody began. "Gauge gives me three-thirty-two as time of death. That's really late or really early to be playing tie-me-up, tie-me-down games."

"If killer and vic came up here together, where are his clothes?"

Peabody turned toward her lieutenant, pursed her lips. "Considering you're married to the hottest guy on or off planet, I shouldn't have to tell you that the point in the tie-me-wherever game is to be naked while you're doing it."

"One of the other points is to get each other naked. If they came in here together," Eve considered, "if they came up here for games, is he going to strip down, *then* hang up his clothes or dump his shorts in the hamper? You got that on the menu—" She gestured to the sex toys. "—you're not thinking about tidy. Clothes get pulled, tugged, torn, yanked off—fall on the floor. Even if this is an old game with a usual playmate, wouldn't you just toss your shirt over the chair?"

"I hang up my clothes. Sometimes." Peabody shrugged now. She angled her head to study the scene again, absently tossed back the hair that fell over her cheek. "But, yeah, that's going to be when I'm not thinking about jumping McNab, or he's not already jumping me. Everything looks pretty tidy in here, and in the rest of the house I got a look at on the way up. Vic could've been a neat freak."

"Could. The killer could've come in when he was already in bed. Three in the morning, surprise, surprise. Then things got out of hand—accidentally or on purpose. Killer comes in—the probability's high the vic or another household member knew the killer. No sign of break-in, and there's a high-end security system. Maybe this is another part of the game. Comes in after he's asleep. Surprises him. Wake me up. Trusses him up, works him up. Toys and games."

"And went too far."

Eve shook her head. "It went as far as he or she meant it to go. The erotic asphyxiation oops doesn't play."

"But . . ." Peabody studied the body again, the scene, and wished she could see whatever Eve could. "Why?"

"If it was all in fun, and went wrong, why did the killer leave the noose around Anders's neck? An accident, but you don't loosen it, try to revive when he starts choking, convulsing?"

"Maybe in the throes . . . Okay, that's a stretch, but if it happened fast, and she or he panicked . . ."

"Either way, we've got a corpse, we've got a case. We'll see what the ME thinks about accidental. We'll go interview the housekeeper, let the sweepers in here."

Greta Horowitz was a sturdy-looking woman with a long rectangle of a face and a no-nonsense 'tude Eve appreciated. She offered coffee in the big silver and black kitchen, then served it with steady hands and dry eyes. With her strong, German-accented voice, direct blue eyes, and Valkyrie build, Eve assumed Greta handled what came her way,

"How long have you been here, Ms. Horowitz?"

"I am nine years in this employment, and in this country."

"You came to the U.S. from . . ."

"Berlin."

"How did you come to be employed by the Anderses?"

"Through an employment agency. You want to know how I came here and why. This is simple, and then we can speak of what is important. My husband was in the military. He was killed twelve years ago. We had no children. I am accomplished in running households, and to work I signed with an agency in Germany. I came to wish to come here. A soldier's wife sees much of the world, but I had never seen New York. I applied for this position, and after several interviews via 'link and holo, was hired."

"Thank you. Before we get to what's important, do you know why the Anderses wanted a German housekeeper, particularly?"

"I am House Manager."

"House Manager."

"Mr. Anders's grandmother was from Germany, and as a boy he had a German nanny."

"Okay. What time did you arrive this morning?"

"Six. Precisely. I arrive at six precisely every morning but Sunday, which is my full day off. I leave at four, precisely, but for Tuesdays and Thursdays when I leave at one. My schedule can be adjusted as needed, and with sufficient notice."

"When you arrived at precisely six this morning, what did you do? Precisely?"

Greta's lips twitched, very slightly. It might have been humor. "Precisely, I removed my coat, hat, scarf, gloves, and stored them in the closet. Then I engaged the in-house security cameras. Mr. Anders disengages them every night prior to retiring. He dislikes the sensation of being watched, even if no one is in the house. My first duty in the morning is to turn them on again. After doing so, I came in here. I turned on the news, as is my habit, then checked the communication system. My employers most usually leave their breakfast orders the night before. They prefer I prepare them, rather than using the AutoChef. Mr. Anders ordered sliced melon, an egg-white omelette with dill, and two slices of wheat toast, with butter and orange marmalade. Coffee—he takes his with cream and one sugar—and a glass of tomato juice."

"Do you know what time he put the order in?"

"Yes. At twenty-two-seventeen."

"So you started breakfast?"

"I did not. Mr. Anders would have breakfasted today at eight-fifteen. My next morning duty would have been to re-engage the two domestic droids, as these are shut down every evening before Mr. and Mrs. Anders retire, and to give them the day's work schedule. The droids are kept in the security room, there." She gestured. "I went in to deal with them, but I noticed the security screens—the in-house. I saw Mr. Anders's bedroom door was open. Mr. Anders *never* leaves his door open. If he's inside the room, or has left the room, the door is closed. If I'm required to be in the room, I'm to leave the door open while I'm inside, then close it again when I leave. It's the same for the domestics."

"Why?"

"It's not my place to ask."

It's my place, Eve thought. "You saw the door was open, but you didn't notice the dead man in bed?"

"The bedroom camera screens only the sitting area. Mr. Anders programmed it that way."

"A little phobic, maybe?"

"Perhaps. I will say he's a very private man."

"So his door was open."

"Nine years," Greta continued. "The door has never been open when I arrive in the morning, unless my employers are not in residence. I was concerned, so I went upstairs without booting up the droids. When I got to the bedroom, I saw the fire in the hearth. Mr. Anders will not allow the fire when he sleeps or when he is out of the room. I was more concerned, so I went into the room. I saw him immediately. I went to the bedside, and I saw that I couldn't help him. I went downstairs again, very quickly, and called nine-one-one."

"Why downstairs?"

Greta looked puzzled. "I thought, from books and plays and vids, that I was not to touch anything in the room. Is that wrong?"

"No, it's exactly right. You did exactly the right thing."

"Good." Greta gave a brisk, self-congratulatory nod. "Then I contacted Mrs. Anders, and waited for the police to come. They came in, perhaps, five or six minutes. I took the two officers upstairs, then one brought me back down to the kitchen, and waited here with me until you stepped in."

"I appreciate the details. Can you tell me who has the security codes to the house?"

"Mr. and Mrs. Anders and myself. The codes are changed every ten days."

"No one else has the codes? A good friend, another employee, a relative?"

Greta shook her head, decisively. "No one else has the codes."

"Mrs. Anders is away."

"Yes. She left on Friday for a week in St. Lucia with some female friends. This is an annual trip, though they don't go to the same place necessarily."

"You contacted her."

"Yes." Greta shifted slightly. "I realize, after thinking more clearly, I should have waited, and the police would have notified Mrs. Anders. But . . . they're my employers."

"How did you contact her?"

"Through the resort. When she goes on holiday, she often shuts off her pocket 'link."

"And her reaction?"

"I told her there had been an accident, that Mr. Anders was dead. I don't think she believed me, or understood me initially. I had to repeat it, twice and I felt, under the circumstances, I couldn't tell her when she asked what kind of accident. She said she would come home immediately."

"Okay, Greta. You have a good relationship with the Anderses?"

"They are very good employers. Very fair, very correct."

"How about their relationship, with each other? It's not gossip," Eve said, reading Greta perfectly. "It's very fair, and it's very 'correct' for you to tell me any and everything you can that may help me find out what happened to Mr. Anders."

"They seemed very content to me, very well suited. It would be my impression that they enjoyed each other, and their life together."

Enjoying each other wasn't what the crime scene transmitted, Eve thought. "Did either, or both of them, have relationships outside the marriage?"

"You mean sexual. I couldn't say. I manage the house. I've never seen anything in the house, that would lead me to believe either, or both, engaged in adulterous affairs."

"Can you think of anyone who'd want him dead?"

"No." Greta eased back slowly. "I thought—I assumed—that someone had broken in to steal, and that Mr. Anders was killed by the thief."

"Have you noticed anything missing or out of place?"

"No. No. But I haven't looked."

"I'm going to have you do that now. One of the officers will take you around." She glanced over as Peabody came in. "Peabody, get one of the uniforms. I want Mrs. Horowitz escorted while she looks around the house. You're free to go afterward," Eve told Greta. "If you'd give my partner or me the contact information where you'll be."

"I prefer to stay, until Mrs. Anders arrives, if this is allowed. She may need me."

"All right then." Eve rose, signaling the end to the initial interview. "Thanks for your cooperation."

As Greta went out, Eve walked to the room off the kitchen. Inside two droids, disengaged, stood. One male, one female, both uniformed and dignified in appearance. The security screens Greta had spoken of ranged over a wall and, as she'd stated, the master bedroom camera showed only the sitting area.

"Dallas?"

"Huh?"

"House security was disengaged at 2:28, re-engaged at 3:26."

Eve turned to frown at Peabody. "Re-engaged before TOD?"

"Yeah. All security discs for the twenty-four-hour period before the security was reset are gone."

"Why, I'm shocked. We'll get EDD in here to see if they can dig something out. So Anders's night visitor left him hanging and still alive. That doesn't sound like sex games gone wrong."

"No," Peabody agreed. "Sounds like murder."

Eve pulled out her communicator when it signaled. "Dallas."

"Sir, Mrs. Anders just got here. Should I bring her in?"

"Bring her straight back to the kitchen." Eve switched off. "Okay, let's see what the widow has to say."

Turning back to the screens, she watched Ava Anders sweep through the front door, her sable coat swinging back from a slim body dressed in deep blue. Her hair, a delicate blond, was pulled severely back from a face of high planes. Fat pear drops swung at her ears, shaded glasses masked her eyes as she crossed the wide, marble foyer, through ornate archways, in skinny-heeled boots with the uniform at her side.

Eve stepped back into the kitchen, took her seat at the sunny breakfast nook seconds before Ava strode in. "You're in charge?" She pointed a finger at Eve. "You're the one in charge? I demand to know what's going on. Who the hell *are* you?"

"Lieutenant Dallas, NYPSD. Homicide."

"Homicide? What do you mean 'Homicide?'" She pulled off her sunglasses, revealing eyes as blue and deep as her suit, tossed them onto the counter. "Greta said there'd been an accident. Tommy was in an accident. Where's my husband? Where's Greta?"

Eve got to her feet. "Mrs. Anders, I'm sorry to tell you your husband was killed this morning."

Ava stood where she was, her eyebrows drawing together, her breath coming in short little bursts. "Killed. Greta said . . . but I thought." She braced a hand on the counter, then slowly walked over to sit. "How? Did he . . . did he fall? Did he get sick, or . . ."

Always best to stab quick and clean, Eve thought. "He was strangled in his bed."

Ava lifted a hand, pressed it to her mouth. Lifted the other to cross it over the first. Those deep-blue eyes filled, and the tears spilled as she shook her head.

"I'm sorry, but I need to ask you some questions."

"Where's Tommy?"

"We're taking care of him now, Mrs. Anders." Peabody stepped over, offered a glass of water.

She took the water and, when one hand shook, gripped the glass with both. "Someone broke in? I don't see how that can be. We're secure, we're very secure here. Fifteen years. We've been here for fifteen years. We've never had a break-in."

"There weren't any signs of a break-in."

"I don't understand."

"Whoever killed your husband either knew the security code, or was given access to the house."

"That can't be." Ava waved a hand in quick dismissal. "No one other than Tommy and myself and Greta has the code. Surely you're not suggesting Greta—"

"I'm not, no." Though she'd be doing a thorough check on the house manager. "There wasn't a break-in, Mrs. Anders. Thus far there's no sign anything in the house was taken, or disturbed."

Ava laid a hand between her breasts where a rope of luminous pearls rested. "You're saying Tommy let someone in, and they killed him. But that doesn't make sense."

"Mrs. Anders, was your husband involved with someone, sexually or romantically?"

She turned away immediately, first her face, then her body. "I don't want to talk about this now. I'm not going to talk about this now. My husband is dead."

"If you know anyone who could gain access to the house, to his bedroom—while you were out of the country—it could tell us who killed your husband, and why."

"I don't know. I don't. And I can't *think* about something like that." The anger slapped out at Eve. "I want you to leave me alone. I want you out of my house."

"That's not going to happen. Until we clear it, this house is part of a homicide investigation. Your husband's bedroom is a crime scene. I suggest you make arrangements to stay elsewhere for the time being, and to stay available. If you don't want to finish this now, we'll finish it later."

"I want to see my husband. I want to see Tommy."

"We'll arrange that as soon as possible. Do you want us to contact anyone for you?"

"No." Ava looked out the sunny window. "I don't want anyone. I don't want anyone now."

Outside, Eve climbed behind the wheel while Peabody sat shotgun. "Rough," Peabody commented. "You're soaking up tropical drinks and rays one minute, and the next, your husband's dead."

"She knows he was screwing around. She knows something about it."

"I guess they probably always do. The spouse, I mean, of the screwing-arounder. And I think a lot of times they can just block it out, pretend it's not happening hard enough so they start to believe it."

"Would you be shedding tears for McNab's dead body if he'd been screwing around on you?"

Peabody pursed her lips. "Well, since I'd've been the one who killed him, I'd probably be shedding tears for me because you'd be arresting me. And that would really make me sad. Easy enough to verify Ava Anders was out of the country when Anders died."

"Yeah, do that. And we'll check her financials. They've got plenty of dough to roll. Maybe she cut off some to hire somebody to kill him. Paid his playmate to do it."

"Man, how cold would *that* be?"

"We'll run friends, business associates, golf partners—"

"Golf?"

"He had a golf game scheduled this morning with an Edmond Luce. Maybe we'll shake loose something on who he played other games with when the wife was off with the girls."

"Wouldn't you like to do that? Have a girl trip?"

"No."

"Ah, come on, Dallas." The very idea brightened Peabody's voice. "Go somewhere with girlfriends, hang, drink lots of wine or fussy drinks, get facials and spa treatments, or lie on the beach, and talk about stuff half the night."

Eve glanced over. "I'd rather be dragged naked over jagged glass."

"Well, I think we should do it some time. You, me, Mavis, maybe Nadine and Louise. And Trina—she could do our hair and—"

"If Trina comes on this mythical nightmare, I get to drag *her* naked over jagged glass. That's my bottom line."

"You'd have fun," Peabody muttered.

"I would, I probably would. I'd feel bad about dragging her over jagged glass ten or twenty years later, but at the time, I'd have fun."

Giving up, Peabody huffed out a breath, took out her PPC and began to do the checks and runs.

2 IT WAS INTERESTING, BUT NOT SURPRISING, THAT
Anders Worldwide's New York headquarters
were housed in the sleek black tower on Fifth

Roarke Enterprises New York headquarters also housed its
base there and owned every inch of that sleek black tower.

"Do you want to stop by and see—"

"No."

Peabody rolled her eyes at Eve's back as they stepped into
the huge, glossy lobby with its rivers of flowers, its moving
maps, its busy shops. "I just figured since we were right
here—"

"Why are we right here, Peabody? And if you roll your eyes
behind me again, I'm going to poke them out with a stick."

"You don't have a stick."

"There's a tree right over there. I'll get one."

Peabody sighed. "We're right here because we're
investigating a murder."

"And do we think Roarke killed Anders?"

"No."

Eve stopped at Security, started to badge the guard on duty. And he smiled toothily. "Lieutenant Dallas. You can go right up."

"I'm not going there. Anders Worldwide."

He tapped his computer screen. "Twenty-first and -second floors. Reception on twenty-one. You'll want the first bank of elevators. Do you want me to call up?"

"No, thanks."

Eve called the car, stepped on, ordered the twenty-first floor.

"Do you think Roarke knew Anders?"

"Probably."

"Could be handy."

"Maybe." Eve had nearly reached the point where having Roarke know so many damn people wasn't completely annoying. "The run said Anders is worth about half a billion including his controlling interest in Anders Worldwide." Hooking her thumbs in her pockets, Eve tapped her fingers on her thighs. "That's a lot of motives for murder. Add sex, you've pretty much got it all. Greed, jealousy, gain, revenge."

"The guy was practically asking for it."

Eve grinned. "Let's find out." Her face sober again, she walked through the open elevator doors.

Behind a long red counter, three receptionists wore headsets and appeared very busy. Even so, the center one, a dark-skinned brunette, offered a beaming smile. "Good morning! How can I help you?"

"I need to see whoever's in charge."

"Which department are you— Oh." She broke off, blinking rapidly at Eve's badge when it slapped on the slick red counter.

"All of them. Who's the top dog under Thomas A. Anders?"

"This is my first week. I don't know what I'm supposed to do. Frankie!"

"What is it, Syl?" The man at her left glanced over, then down at the badge. "Is there something I can help you with, ah . . ."

"Lieutenant. I need to speak with Thomas Anders's second-in-command, or whoever's highest in the pecking order and in house now."

"That would be Mr. Forrest. Benedict Forrest. He's in a meeting, but—"

"Not anymore."

"Right. If you could give me a minute to contact his admin. He'll come down and escort you upstairs."

"I can get upstairs myself. Tell the admin to get Forrest out of the meeting." Eve got back in the elevator, rolled her shoulders. "That was fun."

"Pretty bitchy."

"That's what was fun about it."

As Eve stepped off again, a stick-thin woman in high, stick-thin heels came bolting through a set of glass doors. "Ah, officers! If you'd come with me."

"You're the admin?"

"No, I'm the AA. Assistant administrator. I'll take you to Mr. Walsh's office."

"Who would be the administrative assistant, rather than the assistant administrator."

"Exactly."

"How does anybody get business done when they have to translate all these titles?"

"Ah, Mr. Walsh is letting Mr. Forrest know you're here. Apparently Reception didn't get the nature of the business you're here to discuss."

"No, they didn't."

The AA opened her mouth, obviously thought better of it, and closed it again. They wound their way through a busy hive of offices and cubes, then made a forty-five degree turn into the efficient space of—as his name was

STRANGERS IN DEATH   19

engraved on a small onyx plaque beside the door—Leopold Walsh.

His workstation was a long, free-standing counter in sleek black holding the usual necessities of comp, data and communication unit, and little else. A second counter ran along the wall to support a laser fax, a secondary computer. A third counter served as a refreshment center with AutoChef and friggie. A trio of visitors' chairs ranged together, backless cubes in pristine white.

The only color in the room came from the showy plant with its vivid red blossoms spearing up from the middle windowsill of the generous triple glass.

Supplies, she supposed, and any necessary paperwork would be tucked away in the cabinetry built in to the wall.

Altogether she preferred the miserly space and tattered style of her office at Central.

"If you'd like to have a seat, Mr. Walsh should be—" The AA glanced at the door with obvious relief lighting her face. "Mr. Walsh."

"Thank you, Delly." He stepped in, an imposing man with dark chocolate skin in a pin-striped suit. His hair formed a skullcap that set off a striking face of sharp angles. Deep-set eyes, the color of good, strong coffee, flicked over Peabody, fastened on Eve. "Leopold Walsh. Lieutenant . . ."

"Dallas." For form, Eve presented her badge again. "And Detective Peabody. We're here to see Benedict Forrest."

"So I'm told." He handed her badge back to her. "As you were told, Mr. Forrest is in a meeting."

"Badge trumps meeting."

"It would be helpful if you told me what this is in regards to."

"It would be helpful if I told Mr. Forrest what this is in regards to."

He wanted to stonewall—she could see it. And couldn't blame him as she'd have wanted to do the same.

"Mr. Forrest—" He broke off, holding up a hand as the ear-com he wore blinked blue. "Yes, sir. Of course. Mr. Forrest," he began again, "is available. This way, please."

Benedict Forrest's office was only steps away from his admin's—but a world away from it in style. Here, the workstation held the necessary and the efficient, crowded together with what Eve thought of as guy toys—an autographed baseball on a pedestal, a handheld golf game, a couple of trophies, a sponge-weight toy football. Photographs and posters of sports figures or sports products juggled for space along the wall.

Chairs were leather, deep, and looked comfortably worn.

Forrest himself stood about three inches under his admin's height. He wore a shirt open at the collar, casual khakis, and trendy gel-skids. There was a friendly, just-one-of-the-guys look about him with his tousled sandy hair, easy smile, cheerful hazel eyes.

"You've been waiting. Sorry. I had to wrap things up. Ben Forrest." He crossed the office as he spoke, shot out his hand. Eve shook, studying him as he offered his hand to Peabody.

"Lieutenant Dallas, Detective Peabody."

"Have a seat. What can we get you? Coffee, bottled water, a sports drink?"

"We're fine. We're hear to speak with you about Thomas Anders."

Humor danced over Forrest's expressive face. "Don't tell me Uncle Tommy's in trouble."

"Uncle?"

"My mother's brother. Please, sit." He gestured, then dropped down into a chair. "More, really, as he basically raised me after my mother died."

"How did she die?"

"Eaten by a shark."

Intrigued, Eve sat. "Really?"

His grin flashed. "Yeah, really. I was about six, and don't remember her that well, so it's more interesting than tragic for me. Scuba diving off the coast of Madagascar. Anyway, what about my uncle?"

Sticky now, Eve thought. "I'm sorry to have to tell you Mr. Anders was killed this morning."

Amusement snapped into shock that leached the healthy color out of his face. "What? Killed? How? Are you sure? Wait." He rose, dug a 'link out of his pocket.

"Mr. Forrest, we've just left your uncle's home, and his widow."

"But . . . we're going to the Knicks game tonight. We—we played golf on Sunday. He . . ."

"Ben." Leopold moved across the room. After taking the 'link out of Ben's hand, he laid a hand on Ben's shoulder, eased him down into the chair. "I'm very sorry. So very sorry. I'm going to cancel the rest of your appointments for the day." He walked to a cabinet, tapped the door. When it opened, he took out a chilled bottle of water, unscrewed the top. "Drink some water."

Like a puppet, Ben obeyed. Eve made no objection when Leopold ranged himself like a guard behind Ben's chair.

"What happened?"

"He was strangled."

"That can't be right." Ben shook his head slowly from side to side. "That just can't be right."

"Do you know anyone who wished him harm?"

"No. No."

"Where were you this morning between one and four a.m.?"

"Jesus. Home. Home in bed."

"Alone?"

"No. I had . . . a friend." He rubbed the cold bottle over his face. "Gatch Brooks. She was there all night. We got up about six, worked out together. She left—we both left around eight. You can check. Just check. I wouldn't hurt Uncle Tommy. He's like a father to me."

"You were close. How would you describe Mr. Anders's relationship with his wife?"

"Great. Good. Ava's . . . you said you'd talked to her. Told her. God. Leopold, get the number where she's staying. I need to—"

"She's home, Mr. Forrest," Peabody told him.

"She . . . Oh, she came home. She came home when you told her . . ." Ben pressed his fingers to his eyes. "I can't think straight. I need to get over to the house, to Ava. I need to—Where is he? Is he still home, or . . ."

"He's been taken to the morgue." He didn't bother to fight tears, Eve noted. He let them come. "You—your family— will be able to make arrangements as soon as we finish our examination."

"Okay." Now he pressed the heels of his hands to his eyes, leaning forward to brace his elbows on his thighs. "Okay."

"Who was your uncle sexually involved with?"

"Huh." Ben's eyes, already rimmed with red, lifted to Eve's face. "Well, Jesus, Ava. I mean they were married for Christ's sake."

"Outside of marriage."

"Nobody." Anger and insult snapped through the grief, brought color back to Ben's face. "That's a hell of a thing to say. He didn't cheat. He wasn't a cheater. You don't know the kind of man he was. He believed in honesty, in good sportsmanship, in playing to win, but playing it straight."

"Who stands to gain from his death?"

"Nobody," Ben replied. "His death diminishes all of us. You mean financially. I would, Ava would." He let out a long breath. "I don't know how things were set up. There are probably charitable organizations, there'd be something for Greta—the house manager. But what you're talking about, that would be me and Ava. I need to get over there."

Even as he rose the 'link Leopold still held signaled. After a glance at the display, Leopold offered it. "It's Mrs. Anders."

Ben grabbed the 'link, turned his back. "Privacy mode," he ordered. "Ava. God, Ava, I just heard . . . I know. I know. It's all right. Yes, the police are here. Yes, that's right. I'm coming right over. I—" His voice cracked, then firmed again. "I can't believe he's gone. I can't take it in. I'll be there as soon as I can."

After ending the transmission, Ben turned back to Eve. His expression was simply shattered. "She needs family. I have to go now."

"We'll need to see Mr. Anders's office," Eve told him. "And we'll need to access his electronics."

"All right. Yes, all right. I have to go. Leo, whatever they need."

Eve waited until they were heading down. "Funny, isn't it, how Anders's office—like his nephew's—is all casual guy, even a little toward man cave with the trophies and the sports equipment everywhere. Nothing polished, fashionable or edgy. Nothing like where he lives."

"Well, he sells the sports stuff. And lots of houses more reflect the woman's taste than the guy's. Or one partner's taste over the other's."

She thought of herself and Roarke. When it came to decor, she . . . never gave it a thought, she admitted. Yet, she had her home office, her somewhat shabby by comparison to the rest home office that fit what could be called her style.

"Didn't notice a man cave at the house," she commented, and shrugged. "How'd Forrest play for you, Peabody?"

"Forrest wins actor of the century award, or he was sincerely shocked when you told him his uncle was dead, and was sincerely and deeply broken up. There just wasn't a false note. I believe him."

"Seemed straight enough. We'll verify his alibi. If Anders stood as daddy since Forrest was six, that's twenty-five years or so. Funny that Ava said they didn't have any children."

"Well, *they* didn't."

"She didn't even mention him, and doesn't call to tell him for hours after the house manager notified her. Maybe a false note," Eve speculated, "maybe just shock and confusion. Forrest comes off as a nice guy—and a nice, well-off kind of guy. Now he's a really rich kind of guy."

"I'll start a run on him. You didn't mention really cute kind of guy," Peabody added as they rode down to the underground garage. "He had that easygoing, athletic thing happening. But the admin?" Peabody hissed air in between her teeth. "*Sizzling.*"

"Sure, if you're another guy."

"Huh?"

"Gay, Peabody."

"Uh-uh. Why?"

"Could be bi." With another shrug Eve leaned against the wall. "Either way, he's got a serious man crush on his boss."

"I didn't get that. I did not get that."

"Because you were too busy being sizzled. Myself, I was practically buried in the unrequited love/lust vibes. Sizzling Leopold had them in check, until Forrest fell apart. Must be tough."

"Maybe the love/lust isn't unrequited?"

Eve shook her head. "Forrest is clueless to that part of it. Didn't even notice Leopold's quick flinch when he mentioned sleeping with the alibi. Let's run the sizzler, too." She pushed off the wall as the doors slid open. "Love makes you do the wacky."

Yes, indeed it did, she thought a moment later when she saw Roarke leaning casually on her we're-on-a-budget police vehicle. Tall, lean, with a mane of black hair framing a face blessed by the gods, he shifted those killer blue eyes toward her. It was ridiculous, she thought, to feel that burn in the belly, that thump of the heart over a look—but no more ridiculous than a man who owned a fat chunk of the known universe passing the time on his PPC while he loitered in a parking garage.

He slipped the PPC into his pocket, smiled. "Lieutenant. Hello, Peabody."

"Shouldn't you be upstairs buying Alaska?"

"I did that last week. I got wind cops were in the house. What can I do for the NYPSD that I haven't already done?"

Oh yeah, she thought, the voice was another killer, hinting of Ireland's misty green hills. And she supposed she should have known he'd *get wind*. Nothing got by Roarke.

"This one isn't on you, since you're alibied for the time in question."

"Pretty solid," Peabody put in, "sleeping with the primary." At Eve's cool stare, Peabody hunched. "Just saying."

Roarke grinned at her. "And the primary was up and out early as duty called." He looked back at Eve. "So who's dead then?"

"Thomas A. Anders of Anders Worldwide."

The grin faded. "Is he? Well, that's a shame."

"You knew him?"

"A bit. Liked what I knew well enough. You've been up to his office then, seen Ben—Benedict Forrest."

"Points for you. How well do you know Forrest?"

"Casually. He's a casual sort of man. Agreeable, and smarter than a lot take him for."

"How about the widow?"

Roarke cocked his head. "Seems we're having ourselves an interview after all. You should've come up, and we'd have done this in more pleasant surroundings."

"I have to get to the morgue."

"How many men are married to women who say that routinely, I wonder? Well." He glanced at his wrist unit. "As it happens I have some business downtown. You could give me a lift, and question me ruthlessly along the way."

The idea had its merits. Eve uncoded the car. "You can ride as far as the morgue, then you're on your own."

"Again, how many are as blessed as I?" He opened the door for Peabody, but she waved him on.

"I'll take the back. I've got work anyway."

"Track down Forrest's alibi first," Eve ordered, then took the wheel.

"How was Anders killed?" Roarke asked her.

"Give me impressions first. The vic, the widow, anyone else who applies."

"Anders would've been the second generation of the company—taking it over from his father, who I believe died a year or so ago. A bit longer maybe. It does quite well, good quality products at a reasonable price point."

"Not the business," Eve said as she wound through the garage. "Not for now."

"One influences the other. Lived fairly quietly, I believe. Sports mad—both him and Ben—which fits with the fact they sell and develop sports equipment. He enjoyed golf, particularly, I believe, and various other games that feature whacking or hurling a ball about. I gather he preferred, when possible, to conduct his business on some court or green rather than in the office. My impression would be he enjoyed his work, and was good at it."

Eve streamed through traffic, cutting around a maxibus, then began to hack her way across town. "How about the spouse?"

"Attractive, well-spoken. Ah, involved in some charity work, it seems to me. Anders sponsors sports camps for underprivileged children. I believe she beats the drum for funding. I can't say I've seen them out and about together more than a handful of times, but he had a reputation for avoiding the social scene . . . as some do."

She slid her eyes in his direction. "I go to stuff. Impressions of their relationship?"

"Hard do say, as we weren't chummy. They struck me as a team, appeared affectionate. In synch, I suppose I'd say."

"Any mumbles about him screwing around on her?"

Roarke's brows lifted. "None I've heard, though I don't know as I would, either way. Is that basic cop cynicism, or is there reason for you to believe he cheated on his wife?"

"At the time of death, the wife was out of town. That's verified. Anders's housekeeper—house *manager*," Eve corrected, "found him this morning just after six. Naked, hands and feet bound with black velvet rope. The kind the bondage shops sell by the yard. Another length was wrapped around his neck in what would appear to be an erotic scarfing session gone bad. There were numerous sex aids and toys on the nightstand, and the corpse still sported an impressive hard-on when the primary began her investigation. There was no sign of forced entry, no sign of struggle, no additional visible signs of trauma or violence on the body."

Roarke was silent a moment. "People have their secrets, and the appetites they hide from the rest. Still, I wouldn't have thought him the sort for sport of that nature. It's the kind of salacious details the media will salivate over. Difficult for the family he leaves."

"Anybody you can think of who might want to do him, and set it up so the media salivates?"

"For what point? If you're thinking a competitor, killing Anders doesn't kill, or damage, the company. And a scandal like this? It wouldn't hurt stock or sales—not appreciably. In fact, it might give them a temporary boost. People are odd creatures. I need a new pair of track shoes, one might say. I think I'll buy some by that guy who died with a boner."

"If he lasted, so will they."

"Exactly. They could use it as a bloody slogan."

"Forrest's alibi checks," Peabody said from the backseat. "I tagged EDD, and they've got a geek squad on scene. Another will be transporting Anders's office electronics. First report verifies my findings. Security shut down at 2:28, rebooted at 3:36. Security was dark for more than an hour."

"Had to be remote." Eve glanced at Roarke. "Have to have the passcode or system specs to avoid the auto alarm."

"There are ways. There are always ways."

"You wouldn't need ways unless it was premeditated. Randy Tom's going to entertain, he doesn't need to shut down his security. His wife's out of the country, and for several days yet. So he lets them in, or he gives them the passcode. This way? It's too elaborate, it's too fucking *careful*."

"With a side of mean," Roarke added. "There are ways, always ways, to kill a man. Why choose to kill this way? Intimately, and in a manner that smears the victim and his family?"

"We'll find out. First stop." Eve pulled over to double park in front of the morgue. "Peabody, I'll take this. Head back to Central, start the runs. See if you can locate the vic's golf partner, and run him. I want EDD to start evaluations on what type of remote was used. Let's start a time line on the vic's day yesterday."

Ignoring the furious blast of horns, she shifted to Roarke. "This is your stop, ace."

He glanced through the window at the morgue. "Not for some time, I hope. Good luck, Peabody," he added as he slipped out of the car to join Eve on the sidewalk. "I could make some inquiries. I know people who knew him, people who did business with him."

"You could." Considering that, Eve stuck her hands in her pockets, and surprised herself by finding gloves in them. "Word's spreading by now, so it couldn't hurt. Do you really have business downtown?"

"I do. But even if I didn't, it would've been worth the trip."

She looked at him in the stubbornly frigid, blowing wind. "Murder talk makes it worth the trip?"

"As entertaining as that invariably is, no. This would make it worth the trip."

He grabbed her—she should've seen it coming—and his mouth covered hers. The instant blast of heat slammed right through such matters as late winter freezes and windchill factors. The sudden power and punch of the kiss rocked her back on her heels, and made her wonder if little beams of sunlight were shooting out of her fingertips.

He caught her chin in his hand, smiled down at her. "Definitely worth it."

"Cut it out."

"Nice work, stud."

They both glanced over at the sidewalk sleeper huddled in a nearby doorway. The woman—or Eve thought it was a woman as she was bundled in so many mixing layers she resembled a small, patchwork mountain—offered a grin and a thumbs-up.

Eve jammed a finger into Roarke's chest to dismiss any notion of an encore. "Go away now."

"Absolutely worth the trip. Good hunting, Lieutenant."

He strolled off, and she peeled away to the entrance of the morgue. But when she couldn't resist a glance back at him, she saw him stop and crouch down to speak to the sidewalk sleeper. Curious, she slowed her pace to keep him in view a moment longer, and wasn't surprised to see him dig something out of his pocket and pass it over.

Credits, she supposed, and probably more than the sleeper generally pulled in over the course of a week. She'd probably buy brew with it instead of a bed out of the cold, Eve thought. He had to know that, and still . . .

And still, she thought, pleased to love a man who'd toss a handful of credits into the void, just in case. Thinking of that, she walked into the house where death always had a room.

IN A ROOM OF WHITE TILE AND BRIGHT STEEL, Chief Medical Examiner Morris stood unruffled and stylish over Thomas Anders's corpse. He'd teamed a rust-colored shirt with a dull gold shirt, and mirrored those tones with the thin rope worked through his long, dark braid. His clever face with its long eyes and hard planes was half covered with goggles while his skilled fingers gently lifted out the liver Anders no longer had any use for.

He set the organ aside on the scale, then offered Eve a welcoming smile. "A traveler stops by a farmhouse to ask for shelter for the night."

"Why?"

Morris wagged a bloody finger. "The farmer tells the traveler he can share a room with the farmer's daughter, if he keeps his hands to himself. The traveler agrees, goes into the room, and in the dark slips into bed beside the farmer's daughter. And, of course, breaks his word. In the morning, guilty, the traveler offers to pay the farmer for the hospitality, but the farmer waves this off. So the traveler says he hopes he didn't disturb the daughter in the night. 'Unlikely,' the farmer replies, 'as we're burying her today.'"

Eve let out a snort. "Sick death humor."

"A specialty of the house. And it seemed apt under the circumstances." He gestured toward Anders's stubborn erection.

"Yeah, how about that?"

"Somehow sad and enviable at the same time. I'm running tox, but unless your dead is a medical marvel, we can presuppose he was loaded with happy cock aids. Then after he achieved liftoff, the strategically placed rings trapped the blood supply at the—sticking point."

"Gee, Morris, I'm just a cop. You're confusing me with all these complicated medical terms."

He laughed, then removed a thin section of the liver. "We see death erections fairly routinely, particularly in strangling or hangings as the blood in the torso tries to obey the laws of gravity and travel down. The erectile tissue fills with it, and expands. But once the body's moved, as our friend's here was, it dissipates."

"Yeah, and people noticed guys got boners when they were publicly hanged, back in the good old days, and thought: Hey, maybe if I choke myself during sex I'll make really good wood. People are really stupid."

"Difficult to argue that point, as you and I often see them at their most terminally stupid. So, as to our current guest: Erotic—or autoerotic if you're going solo—asphyxiation decreases oxygen, and pumps up the endorphins to heighten sexual pleasure. It's responsible for a considerable number of accidental deaths annually, and many deaths that are officially termed suicide."

"This wasn't suicide."

"No, indeed." Morris looked down on Anders. "I believe it took him between fifteen and twenty minutes to die, slowly choking. Yet, there's no bruising on his wrists or ankles.

However cushioned the rope, when a man slowly chokes to death he'll fight, he'll struggle, and velvet restraints or not, there would be ligature marks. Even here." He gestured again, then offered Eve a pair of microgoggles. "Here, where the rope tightened, cut in, cut off his oxygen, there's no evidence he fought against it, writhed, strained. The bruising here is almost uniform."

"So he just lay there and died."

"Essentially."

"Even if a guy wants to self-terminate, the body fights it."

"Exactly so. Unless—"

"It can't. How long for the tox?"

"I flagged it. But I can give you something now. Look here."

She bent over Anders again, scanning the bruising under the right ear until she saw it. The faint, circular mark was nearly obscured by the more traumatic bruising. "Pressure syringe."

"Yes, my bright young student. An odd place for self-medicating—especially by a right-hander—which he was."

Shoving up the goggles, Eve put herself back in Anders's bedroom. "Killer comes in, crosses to the bed. Sealed up, all sealed up, booties over the feet to muffle any sound. Lots of thick carpet anyway. Tranqs Anders while he's sleeping. Quick, clean. Guy could've slept right through that—even if he started to wake up, a good tranq would take him under in seconds. Then you truss him up, set the scene, walk out, and leave him to die. Pick up the security discs. You've already shut down the system, but you take the discs. You're either anal or hoping we're just incredibly stupid and that'll throw us off and make us think it was an accident."

"Incredibly stupid we aren't."

"Either way, he's dead." She paced away, among the steel and comps, back again. "If you're going there to do the guy, why just tranq him? Why not load him up so he ODs? Okay, you don't slit his throat or beat him to death with a bat because maybe you're squeamish, or you prefer more passive methods. But why the elaborate and demeaning when a lethal dose of barbs or poison or any number of substances would've done the job?"

"It was too personal for that."

She nodded, appreciating a like mind, and her grin was fierce. "See? Incredibly stupid we aren't. As soon as you get the tox back, Morris."

"As soon as."

When she strode into the Homicide bullpen at Cop Central, Eve saw Peabody sucking down something from a mug the size of the Indian Ocean while she worked at her desk. It reminded Eve that she was probably about a quart low on coffee. She signaled her partner, jerked a thumb toward her office and, turning, nearly plowed into one of her detectives.

"Make a hole, Baxter."

"Need a sec."

"Then fall in line." She moved through to her office with its single, stingy window, battered desk, and sagging visitor's chair. And hit the AutoChef for coffee.

Taking the first slug, she studied Baxter over the rim. He was slick, savvy, and smart enough to wait to have his say until she'd kicked in some caffeine. "What's your deal?"

"Case I caught about a couple months ago, it's stalled."

"Refresh me."

"Guy gets his throat slashed and his works sliced off in a rent-by-the-hour flop down on Avenue D."

"Yeah." She flipped through the files in her head. "Came in with a woman nobody remembers, and nobody remembers seeing said woman leaving."

"Maid service, and I use the term loosely, found him the next morning. Custer, Ned, age thirty-eight, worked in building maintenance for an office building downtown. Guy left a wife and two kids."

"*Cherchez la femme*," Eve said, thinking of Peabody's comment that morning.

"I've been *cherchezing* the damn femme. Got zip. Nobody remembers her—not clearly. We dug, found the bar—using *that* term loosely, too, where they hooked up, but other than her being a redhead with a sense she was a pro, nobody can paint her picture. Guy was a player. A little pushing with his friends and associates got that much. He screwed around regular, cruised bars and clubs once or twice a week to score—usually paying for it. The kid and I," he continued, speaking of his aide, Officer Troy Trueheart, "we've put in hours trolling dumps, dives, and dens of iniquity. We're stalled, Dallas. It's going stone-cold."

"What about the wife? Did she know he was dipping strange?"

"Yeah." Baxter blew out a breath. "It didn't take more than a poke to get her to cop to it. And to admit they fought about it. He tuned her up now and then, too. She copped to that, and neighbors verified."

"Maybe *she* should've cut his dick off."

"Yeah, yeah, women always go for the jewels. She didn't though. When he didn't come home by midnight, she tried his 'link, left messages until nearly three. TOD was about one-thirty, and we've got her tagging him from her home unit at one-fifteen, again at one-forty. Pissed off, crying, and nowhere near Avenue D. She's better off, seems to me. But I hate to lose one."

"Hit the flop again, push the street LCs who use it, or work the bars in the neighborhood. How about transpo?"

"No cabs letting off fares on that block, and nothing popped on the underground surveillance. We figured they hoofed it, and that's how we zeroed in on the bar."

"Make the rounds again, get meaner. Any chance he was into something nastier than banging strange?"

"Nothing's popped. Blue collar asshole, pissing it away on cheap brew and loose women with a nice wife and a couple of cute kids at home. The thing is, Dallas, it was a cold kill. One slice." Baxter mimed cutting his own throat. "From behind. Then the bastard drops, but he's still alive according to the ME when she cuts off his dick. She had to be freaking covered with blood, but there's no trail, not out the door, not out the window and fire escape. Not a drop."

"Cleaned up after."

"No blood in the sink, no trace in the tap, the pipes. It reads like she came prepared, like she maybe sealed up, or changed. Like she had this in mind from the jump. I've knocked on women he's known to have dicked around with, who might be pissed off, but that's nowhere."

"Give it another push. I'll take a look at the file as soon as I get a chance. Fresh eyes."

"Appreciate that."

When he left, Eve stepped over to her desk. Her 'link indicated she had eight messages. A chunk of them, she knew, would be from media hounds. A rich guy buys it in his own home, it started the trickle that often became a flood. And the details of how would leak, she knew that, too. Nobody's finger was big enough to plug the hole in the dike when the flood was that juicy.

"All clear?" Peabody asked from the doorway.

"Yeah."

"Baxter wanted to talk about the Avenue D case? Trueheart's run some of it by me," Peabody continued. "Nothing's gelling."

"They'll go back around, work it again. What've you got for me?"

"Benedict Forrest—whose mother really was eaten by a shark. Or severely chewed on by one. He was six at the time, and living in New York under the care of a nanny and numerous servants. Mother was quite the adrenaline junkie, from what I've got. Name the life-threatening activity, she gave it a whirl. Thirty-five at TOD, twice divorced, one child. When she ended up the main course for Jaws, Anders applied for custody and guardianship and, as the biological father didn't contest, same was granted."

"How much did Anders pay him? The bio dad?"

"Five million, apparently. The guy spends most of his time cruising around hot spots in Europe, hadn't seen the kid since the divorce—four years plus before the mother died. He's been married three times since, and is currently living in the south of France. Just doesn't feel like he plays into this."

"How much of a financial interest did the mother have in the company?"

"None. She took a buyout from her father in lieu. And she was smart enough—or vindictive enough—to arrange her trust and assets so even if the father took the kid, after her death, he couldn't touch a penny of the kid's take. Anders took the kid, supported, educated, and housed him on his own nickel."

Pausing, Peabody glanced down at her notes. "Forrest came into a nice chunk of change when he turned twenty-one, another portion at twenty-five, another at thirty. He has an MBA from Harvard, where he also played baseball and lacrosse. He worked his way up the ranks at Anders from a junior exec to his current position as Chief Operating Officer."

"Any criminal?"

"Nada. Pretty regular hits for speeding, and a shitload of parking tickets, all paid up."

Eve sat back, swiveled in her desk chair. "Give me the wife."

"Ava Montgomery Anders, who I confirmed was in her hotel suite on St. Lucia when contacted about trouble at home. She booked a shuttle after the transmission. There's no record of her leaving the island by any mode prior. Born Portland,

Oregon, in 2008, upper-middle-class all the way. Previous marriage to one Dirk Bronson in 2032, ended in divorce in 2035. No offspring. Earned degrees in business and public relations from Brown—scholarship—which she put to use as the PR rep for Anders Worldwide—Chicago base, where she relocated after her divorce. Then she transferred to the New York office in 2041. She and Anders married in '44. She currently serves as the company's goodwill ambassador, serving on the board of Everybody Plays, Anders Worldwide's organization founded to provide facilities, training, and equipment for children, ah, worldwide. And serving as chairman of Moms, Too, a program that offers educational seminars, workshops, networking opportunities, and so on to mothers of kids in Everybody Plays. No criminal on her either, and she's worth about ten million in her own right."

Peabody lowered her notebook. "I could give you Greta Horowitz, but everything she told us runs true. I was about to start on Leopold Walsh, but I must find food. I can find you food, too." Peabody smiled hugely. "How about a nice sandwich?"

"How about we find out where the hell some of the reports are, and why they're not on my desk? I want—" Eve broke off as her computer signaled an incoming. "Morris comes through," she murmured.

"And while you're singing the praises of our ME, I'll go hunt and gather."

"Computer, display incoming on screen, copy to open file, and print."

Multi-task acknowledged. Working . . .

As the computer hummed, Eve scanned the toxicology report. "Well, Jesus, Tommy," she stated, "you didn't have a snowball's chance, did you?"

While it printed, she engaged her 'link to harass the sweepers for a preliminary and, because her mind was elsewhere, answered her 'link when it signaled a few minutes later.

"Dallas."

"You don't call, you don't write."

"Nadine." Eve didn't bother to curse herself as she stared into the sharp green eyes of the city's hottest reporter. The fact that they were friends made it convenient—or inconvenient, depending on the circumstances. "Gosh, I'd just love to chat, but I'm about to do lunch. Then maybe I'll have a manicure."

"That's so cute. You caught a hot one, Dallas, just the kind of case we love to spotlight on *Now*. Tomorrow night. You'll lead off, a full ten-minute segment."

"Again, gosh, but I have to have my eyes put out with a hot poker tomorrow night. Otherwise . . ."

"Thomas Anders's murder is big news, Dallas."

"We haven't determined or announced the death as murder."

"That's not what I hear. Strangled, in bed, with considerable kink attached. If not murder, was it accidental death during sex games?"

So the trickle was already a flood, Eve thought. "You know better, Nadine."

"A girl's gotta try. He was a nice guy, Dallas. I'd like to cover this right."

"You knew him?"

"I did a few features on him, his wife, his nephew over the years. That's not really knowing someone, but what I did know, I liked. Tabloid media—and a lot of other media—is going to pump up the sex, you know this. I can't avoid it, but I want to be evenhanded. So help me."

"Not this time. But I'll give you Peabody. You won't screw with her, or the investigation. And she needs to develop her media chops. So you help her."

"That's a deal. I'll have my people get in touch with her, but tell her I need her here, at the studio, by five tomorrow."

"Nadine, in five words or less, sum up your take on the relationship between Anders and his wife, and Anders and his nephew."

"With the wife, affectionate and proud. The same for the nephew, but even more so. I remember asking Anders what he considered his finest accomplishment. He turned a photo around that he kept on his desk—one of his nephew. 'You're looking at him,' is what he said. I ended the piece with it."

"Thanks." Eve clicked off, glanced over as Peabody clomped in with an armload of food.

"We got your pretend-I'm-turkey wraps, soy chips, and these cute little tubs of veggie hash. I got you a tube of Pepsi."

Eve watched while Peabody set food on her desk, tidily organizing debris to make room. "What are you angling for, Peabody?"

"Angling? Just making sure you don't forget to eat. You're always forgetting to eat, which is why you're skinny as a snake. Which looks great on you." Peabody's gaze darted up and away while she added a napkin and plastic fork. Then her breath huffed out as Eve continued to give her the fish-eye. "Okay, okay. Maybe I was hoping, if we're not on the tail of some hot lead or whatever, you could find it in your big, generous heart to—"

"Cut the crap."

"I want to leave early, take an hour's personal time. McNab and I have a date."

"You and McNab live together."

"Yeah, well, see, that's kind of the point." Peabody dragged the visitor's chair over, picked up her wrap, and chowed down. "We realized we didn't want the cohab thing to take the romance out of things. The spark. So we instituted Date Night. Tonight's the first, so I really want to get home in time to buff myself up. Special, you know? Kick him in the balls special."

"If you want to kick him in the balls—and I often want to myself—you should stay home."

"Dallas."

"Yeah, yeah, yeah. Take the hour, buff and polish, kick him in the balls."

"Thanks. We're going to this club, and not one of those bump-and-fuck joints," Peabody added, gesturing with a soy chip before popping it into her mouth to crunch. "But where you actually go to listen to music and dance with each other and stuff. I really want to look extreme, so you know, need that hour."

"Fine. You'll be making it up tomorrow. You need to report to Nadine's studio at Channel 75 at seventeen hundred."

"Whafo?" Peabody asked with a mouthful of veggie hash.

"She'll interview you on the Anders case, so make sure you're—"

"What? On the air? Me?" She choked, whistled out a breath while her eyes wheeled, then glugged down Diet Pepsi. "No."

"You'll be representing the department, and this division, so don't screw it up."

"But . . . But people watch *Now*. Practically everybody. I can't—"

"Screw it up. Exactly." It was small, it was mean, but Eve couldn't deny Peabody's reaction made the pretend turkey almost tasty. "Nadine has respect for cops, and for the process, but she's still a reporter. She's sneaky. Don't forget that. You give the facts I'll clear you to give, and the feel, your own take, but when she presses you—and she will—on investigative details, you block. Standard, I'm not at liberty."

Faintly green now, Peabody pressed a hand to her belly. "I think I'm going to be sick."

"You boot on my desk, I'll throw your gagging body out my window. You won't have to worry about going on screen."

"Can't you do it? You're used to it."

"No, I can't do it, and you need to get used to it."

"I don't know what to wear."

"Oh sweet, suffering Christ." Eve pressed her fingers against the twitching muscle beside her eye. "Window, Peabody. Headfirst."

"You couldn't fit me through that stupid window."

"Let's find out."

"Okay, okay, okay. Now my head's all screwed up."

"Unscrew it. We've got a few matters just a smidge more important than your date night and on-air debut. The vic was tranqed *twice*."

"What—who. Wait." Closing her eyes, Peabody took several deep breaths. "Anders. Okay, I'm back. Anders was tranqed?"

"Pressure syringe." Eve tapped her finger on the side of her neck. "Heavy dose of barbs, enough to knock out a horse. There were also traces of a sleep aid, standard over-the-counter. Preliminary take is this was ingested, probably three to four hours before TOD. The combo dropped him out. The killer could've performed brain surgery on him, and Anders wouldn't have noticed."

"Why not just give him a fatal dose? Why the big show?"

"Good question, and one of the reasons I haven't yet thrown you headfirst out the window. The show was as important as the murder. Disgrace? Revenge? A discarded lover who wanted him to pay? Is it smart, or is it sloppy?"

Peabody considered that over another chip. "If you wanted it to come off as it looked on the surface—accidental death due to erotic asphyxiation—you don't load him up with barbs. Maybe a mild tranq, sure, to disorient him while you do the bondage. Take your time after that, set the scene, let the tranq wear off some. If you're going to go to all that trouble, it seems like you want him to suffer. If you want him to suffer, why knock him out so he can't?"

"More good questions. You're redeeming yourself. I'm going to send the file to Dr. Mira. I'd like her profile and opinion on this. Could be the killer overdid the barbs. He had a massive dose of erectile enhancer in there, too.

"It feels personal, but let's run it through IRCCA for like crimes. We'll start trying to run down the restraints, the tranq. And we'll do a second level on financials. Forrest and the widow are the most likely to benefit financially. They've both got a solid base on their own, but who doesn't like more? And let's look for old and current lovers. Guy waits until he's well into his forties to do the marriage thing, he probably didn't say I do without banging a few prospects first."

"I can give EDD another goose, see if we've got anything there."

"I want copies of any transmissions between the vic and his wife, his nephew. Have them round up the 'links from his office."

"Lieutenant?" Trueheart, Baxter's young and studly aide, tapped lightly on the doorjamb. "Sorry to interrupt your lunch, but there's an Edmond Luce out here. He wants to talk to you regarding the Anders case. Seems pretty worked up, and . . . a lot British."

Eve dumped the remains of her wrap onto Peabody's plate, shoved her own into the recycler. "Give me a minute, then send him back."

"Yes, sir."

"Ditch this stuff, Peabody, then goose EDD, and give one to the lab while you're at it. Minimum, I want a report of any and all medications and enhancements taken from the scene."

"On that." Gathering up the rest of the remains, Peabody headed out.

"Computer, standard bio run on Luce, Edmond, British with business or personal connection to Anders, Thomas A. of Anders Worldwide. Display only."

Acknowledged. Working . . .

While she waited, Eve sent the case file and a quick memo to Dr. Charlotte Mira, the department's top profiler.

Task complete. Data displayed.

Eve scanned quickly, looking for the quick overview. Luce, London-born, was seventy-six, and served as Anders Worldwide's CEO, Great Britain. Oxford education, homes in London and in New York. Married, with one previous divorce, three children. One from first marriage.

"Copy data to file," she ordered when she heard approaching footsteps. "End display."

Acknowledged. Tasks complete.

She swiveled to face the doorway as it was filled with a big, burly bear of a man with a shock of hair the color of good sterling and eyes of nearly black that sparked off something approaching rage.

He wore khaki trousers with pleats sharp enough to draw blood and a navy vee-neck over a white shirt. Up-scale golf clothes, Eve decided. Anders missed tee time.

"You're Lieutenant Dallas?"

"That's right. Mr. Luce, what can I do for you?"

"You can tell me why the bloody hell you're smearing the reputation of a good man. Why you're spreading these salacious and scandalous lies about Tommy. The man's dead, goddamn it all, and can't defend himself against this slander."

"Mr. Luce, I can assure you I haven't as yet given any statement, officially or unofficially, to the media regarding the investigation into Mr. Anders's death. Nor have I authorized anyone to do so."

"Then why in hell is it all over the bleeding screen?"

Eve leaned back. "I'm not responsible for what the media digs out and chooses to air. It may piss me off, but I'm not responsible. You suffered a sudden and shocking loss, so I'm going to cut you a break for coming into my office and blowing off steam. Now that you have, sit down. I have some questions."

"I suggest you take your questions and—"

"Careful," Eve said with enough steel in the word to have Luce pausing, narrowing those furious eyes on her face.

"What are you going to do? Lock me up?"

Casually, Eve swiveled back and forth in her chair. "I like the word *detain* myself. Would you care to be detained, Mr. Luce, by the NYPSD for refusing to answer questions in a homicide investigation? I'd be happy to put you in holding until your attorney arrives. Otherwise, you can sit down and you can settle down. I figure you and Anders were more than business associates. You might be upset, sad, surprised by his death if that's all you were. You might be surprised again, and either shocked, fascinated or angry with the media attention. But rage and grief come from more personal associations. So this is your second, and last break. Clear enough?"

He turned and walked away, but to her window, not out the door. She said nothing as he stood there, his rigid back to her. "I can't settle down. How could I settle down? Tommy . . . we've been friends for nearly fifty years. He's godfather to my son. I stood up for him when he married Ava. He was my younger brother, in every way but blood."

"I'm very sorry, Mr. Luce, for your loss."

He glanced back at her. "How many times have you said that to someone, to strangers?"

"Too many. Entirely too many. It doesn't make it less true."

He turned now, pressed his fingers to his eyes. "We were to play golf this morning. The indoor nine at Tommy's club. He's never late, but I didn't think anything of it when he was. Traffic is so brutal, and I'd run into an acquaintance. We ended up chatting for some time, until the caddy interrupted to ask if I wanted to cancel or reschedule the tee off."

"Did you try to contact him?"

"On his mobile—his personal mobile, but it went to voice messaging. So I tried his house." He did sit now, big shoulders slumping. "Greta, the house manager, told me there'd been an accident. Told me Tommy was . . ."

"When was the last time you saw him?"

"Three weeks ago. He and Ava were in London briefly. Tommy and I had a meeting, and we all went to the theater. We played golf at my club—he loves golf—while our wives went shopping, or something. Maybe salon. I don't remember."

"When did you get into New York?"

"Yesterday afternoon. My wife and I arrived about two. Our son, Tommy's godchild, works for the New York branch. We had dinner with Harry and his family. They've just remodeled their brownstone, and wanted to show it off, of course. It's quite lovely, our daughter-in-law . . ." He trailed off, looked back at Eve. "I have no idea why I'm telling you that."

"When did you last speak to Mr. Anders?"

"On the flight over. We confirmed our golf date. The last thing I said to him, was: Brace yourself, Tommy. I'm going to clean your clock."

His face reddened, his eyes filled. For the next few moments, he sat breathing hard as he struggled for composure. "Why are they saying such horrid things about him? Isn't it enough he's gone, that a good man is gone?"

"No, it's not, and it won't be until we know why. That's my job. Who wished him harm?"

"I don't know. He could be tough in business, but he was never unfair. He watched the competition, of course, and was a competitive man. But he played by the rules. He believed in rules."

"And in his personal life? Did he play by the rules?"

The wide face reddened again, but with temper. "I won't have you implying—"

"I'm not implying anything. Obviously you know something of the circumstances of his death. If you know who had access to his home, his bedroom, I need a name. Or names."

He leaned forward, fierce as a lion. "Tommy would not cheat on Ava. On anyone."

"A great many people engage in affairs and sexual activity outside marriage. And a great many of them don't consider it cheating." She shrugged. "Just sex, means nothing. Nobody's hurt."

His mouth tightened, pure derision. "Perhaps you can live your life by those *standards*. Tommy didn't."

"Then who might want me to think he did?"

"I don't *know*. If anyone harbored such violent feelings toward him, if anyone had threatened him, he didn't tell me."

"Would he have?"

"I hope he would."

"To your knowledge, did he fire anyone, rebuff anyone?"

"By rebuff, you're speaking of a sexual proposition." Luce let out a short laugh. "I can't imagine a woman approaching Tommy that way. But I suppose . . . He was fit, charming in his way, wealthy. I suppose. But he never mentioned that sort of thing either. Of course, it's possible he didn't mention it in order to spare the other party the embarrassment and not to open the door to teasing. I would have teased him," Luce admitted, "unmercifully.

"As to firing, most terminations would be up to the individual department heads and supervisors. I don't know of any major dismissals, not recently. Ben would have a better handle on that."

"Can you tell me who benefits financially?"

"I can and I will because this wasn't about money. What was done to him . . . couldn't have been about money. Both Ava and Ben will receive Tommy's shares of Anders. Ben will hold the majority, as Tommy did after his own father's death. Ava will get the house in New York, the estate in the Hamptons, and the pied-à-terre in Paris, and all contents therein unless specifically bequested to others. Ben will inherit Tommy's yacht, a number of his personal possessions—his collection of golf clubs, but for an antique set he left specifically to me. There's a house on the coast of South Carolina that will go to him, and the London townhouse. They'll also divide, in equal shares, his portfolio, after other bequests are made."

"You know the details."

"Yes, I know the details. I witnessed the paperwork, and he insisted I read it through first. If you don't read, you don't sign—that was Tommy. Lieutenant, I visited both Ava and Ben at the house this afternoon—after . . . Believe me, they're in deep mourning. He was loved. Tommy was loved."

4 TO SATISFY HERSELF, EVE DETOURED TO THE Anders house on the way home. The traffic, as Luce had said, was brutal, but she didn't mind. The stops, starts, stalls, gave her time to think. The bad-tempered blare of horns, the occasional fist or middle finger shooting out of a window, the snarling or desperate faces of fellow drivers all reminded her why she loved New York even when it was frozen in the bitter, bitter grasp of endless winter.

Glide-cart operators, bundled up like Arctic explorers, worked with their fingerless gloves over smoking grills, and the smoke—if she cracked her window enough to catch it—smelled of chestnuts and soy dogs and grease.

Animated billboards, as they had been all winter, hyped tropical getaways where scantily clad models frolicked in the surf, or families so bright and happy they struck Eve as just a little terrifying built elaborate castles in the sand.

YOU DESERVE IT!! was the battle cry.

To Eve's mind, people all too often didn't get what they deserved.

Thomas Anders certainly hadn't after he'd tucked into bed for the last time, so it was her job to make sure he got what he deserved now. Justice. Maybe he was the paragon of decency his friend and family described, or the secret sexual perv his style of death portrayed. More likely, he'd been something in between. Wherever he landed on the human scale, he was due justice.

She hunted up a parking spot, and hoofed it the half-block crosstown to the Anders home. Since the wind bit at every inch of exposed skin, she wondered why Peabody was so juiced about getting dressed up and going back out again. Once home, Eve thought, nobody was prying her out of the warmth.

Outside, she gave the security system another gander. Palm plate, she noted, key swipe, voice recognition, full perimeter camera scans. Basic standards for a high-end system. And the code, she recalled, changed every ten days. No signs of external tampering.

When the door opened, Greta stood on the other side. "It's after one," Eve commented.

It only took Greta a moment. "Yes. Yes, it is usually my half-day. Mr. Forrest asked if I would arrange to stay through the afternoon, perhaps into the evening. Mrs. Anders needs me."

"I assume she's in."

"She is. She and Mr. Forrest are in the family parlor. If you could wait here, Lieutenant, I'll let them know."

"Fine. Greta, who else has been here today?"

"Many police."

"Other than."

"Mr. and Mrs. Edmond Luce. Ms. Plowder and Ms. Bride-West, both friends of Mrs. Anders who'd traveled to St. Lucia with her. Naturally, they cut their trip short to come back, to be here for her. There have been many calls of condolence, of course, but Mr. Ben— Mr. Forrest and I are screening those.

Several reporters attempted to gain admittance, or to contact the family. They were sent away or refused."

"Good on the last. You should keep doing that. I'll wait here."

Greta moved through the wide room off the foyer, through an archway. Alone, Eve glanced up the stairs. The master suite and some of the second level would be sealed. No one other than a cop with a master could enter the bedroom, or adjoining room by any access until Eve cleared the scene. She wondered why the widow didn't opt to stay with a friend, or even in an anonymous hotel suite until that time.

Ben came through the archway, crossed to her. Sorrow coated him, Eve thought, like oil that might stain anyone he brushed up against. Eve thought if grief had a face, his fit the bill.

"Lieutenant. Is this necessary? Ava's . . . she's having a very hard time of it."

"I understand this is difficult. I'm afraid NYPSD will be in and out of the house for some time yet, and several areas will remain sealed. You may want to try to persuade Ms. Anders to stay with friends for the next few days."

"I'm working on that. I think she feels she's deserting him somehow, if she doesn't stay here. Brigit—a friend—offered Ava her guest suite for however long she needs it. I think I've nearly convinced her to go. They called from . . . the morgue. They told us we can't have him yet."

"It takes time."

"We can go there and see him. I thought, if she's up to it, the sooner we do that, the better."

"You're probably right."

"I'd take her. She needs to . . . We both need to . . ." He trailed off, shook his head. "Do you know, can you tell me, if you know . . ."

"It's very early yet, Mr. Forrest. We're actively pursuing all lines of investigation."

"It seems like days. I know it's only been hours, but it seems like days. Sorry." He rubbed his fingers over exhausted eyes. "I looked you up. There was something familiar, but I couldn't think. I just couldn't think clearly this morning. But I looked you up. Roarke's cop."

"The NYPSD considers me their cop."

"I didn't mean—"

"It's all right."

"I mean to say, you're supposed to be the best there is. You solved the Icove case, and you caught that maniac who was kidnapping and mutilating those women. You'll find who did this to Uncle Tommy." Now, riding with grief was a plea. "You won't give up."

"I don't give up." Eve looked past him as Ava came into the room.

"Can't we have a few hours? Can't we have any time alone? Must you people be here?"

"Ava." Ben rushed to her side, took her weight when she slumped against him. "The police are doing their job. We need them to do their job."

"They've made him a joke. They've made his death a joke."

"No." Ben turned her into his arms, stroked her back. "Ssh, now."

"Take me to Brigit's, Ben. Take me away from here. I can't bear it. I can't stay here."

"All right. That's what I'll do." He glanced at Eve, who pointed to herself, then upstairs. Nodding, he led Ava away.

Though she'd have preferred an empty house, Eve walked back to the front door. She imagined the dark, the quality of it in the odd blue glow of the security lights. An efficient killer would have already sealed up, hair, hands, shoes. Extra protection, extra soundproofing with booties over the shoes. No chance of leaving any sort of print.

Directly upstairs, she thought. Down to business—priority business, she decided as she climbed the stairs. No squeaks, she noted, no creaks. Solid construction. Straight to the master bedroom, no detours. The door would be closed, as it was now. Not sealed though, she thought as she used her master to uncode the police seal.

She turned the knob, eased the door open. Again, it was soundless. Privacy shields over the windows, she recalled, and heavy blackout drapes over that. Tommy liked to sleep in his snug cave.

Pitch-black. It would be pitch-black. Even someone knowing the room intimately couldn't be sure how the victim would be positioned in the bed. A pin light would be enough, she mused. Just a thin beam to show the way.

Because she didn't want to be disturbed, she closed and locked the door behind her. "Lights on," she ordered, and took the time to arrange the room as it would have been for the killer. "Lights off," she ordered when she stood back at the door and, flipping on a pin light, used it to cross to the bed.

Syringe first. Knock him out. Did he stir? Feel that quick little nip over the skin? Count to ten—it doesn't take long—count to ten, slow and steady.

What are you thinking? she wondered. Excitement, fear? Not rage, can't be rage. He's already beyond you, you saw to that, so it's not rage.

Turn the lights back on now. No need to work in the dark. "Lights on, fire on," Eve ordered.

Did you bring the rope, or did he have that tucked away?

You brought it. Have to be sure, can't screw up now. You have to have all the tools at hand.

Was he nude already, or did you strip him? If you stripped him, where did you put the sleep clothes? A trophy?

Wrists first. Do you feel his breath, his heavy, drugged breath on your skin when you bind his wrists? They're limp, deadweight. He's already helpless, but you have a stage to set. Wrists first.

Then the ankles.

Set out the toys.

Time for the next dose. You want him hard. Slide the rings on his cock. How do you feel, fondling him when he's helpless? Enjoyment or disgust? Or neither. Is it all just the next step now?

Takes time, all this window dressing. Takes time, and effort. Have to get into bed with death now to finish it.

Eve hitched up, braced a knee on the bed. Not enough leverage, she decided, and climbed on until she knelt beside her mind picture of Anders, imagined tying the last rope, winding it around his neck. Heavy head. Secure the second end of the rope and the head falls forward. It practically does the work for you.

She eased off the bed again, smoothed out any depression. Study the work, she mused, go over your checklist. How's his breathing? Is it already changing? Is his system already sending out alarm signals his mind and body can't answer?

Pack up the light, the syringes, walk away. Leave the door open.

Unlike the killer, Eve locked and sealed it. When she walked downstairs, her mind still walking alongside the killer, she saw Greta sitting stiff-spined in a chair in the foyer.

"Mr. Forrest asked if I'd stay, in case you needed anything. He's taken Mrs. Anders to Ms. Plowder's home."

"No, I've got all I need. You should go home."

"Yes, I should go home." She put on the serviceable coat draped over her arm.

"Greta, what did Mr. Anders wear in bed?"

"I beg your pardon!"

"There were pajamas in his drawer. You supervise the laundry, correct?"

"I— Yes, of course. Mr. Anders wore sensible pajamas. A fresh pair daily, pressed. No starch."

"How many pairs did he have?"

"At last count, which would have been Monday last, Mr. Anders owned ten pairs of all-cotton pajamas."

"Ten pairs. Did Mr. Anders routinely use sleep aids?"

"I wouldn't know. I'm sorry. I have purchased them from time to time, as I do the marketing, the shopping. I can't say if either Mr. or Mrs. Anders used them, or if that was routine use."

"Okay. You've been very helpful."

Greta fit a gray hat over her head. "Being helpful is what I do."

When the door closed behind Greta, Eve stood where she was and let it settle around her. The quiet, the sensation of empty. Turning, she walked through the foyer, took the left hall. Rooms, she thought, the more money somebody had the more rooms he needed to keep the stuff he spent his money on.

And the more money and more rooms and more stuff, the more security to stop somebody from coming in and robbing you blind.

Anders's security room was off the kitchen, another locked door requiring its own keypad or code. Eve used her master, opened it. Inside were the screens for inner security, and those for outer. All ran now. Figuring security could afford a quick breach with a cop in the house, she checked the code EDD had given her, keyed it in. The current disc for the exterior front ejected.

She tapped it back in, glanced over at the empty disc file.

Load 'em up, she thought. Cover all contingencies. Go out, lock the room. Why? Just being orderly?

She strode back to the front door, took a last glance around. Stepping out, she relocked, resealed. Then looked at her wrist unit. Taking time out for the three-minute conversation with Greta, from entry to exit, the reenactment had taken just under forty minutes. Adding in time to strip the victim out of his sensible pajamas, she'd make it a comfortable forty-five minutes.

Not enough time to hunt up the security room and bypass the code, not in a house this size. Not enough to hunt up the bedroom. The killer knew the layout. Not just where the master slept, but where to find the security discs.

Closed the security room door, she thought, striding back to her car, but left the bedroom door open. Turned the lights out, but left the fire going.

In her car she ordered the heat on blast furnace, then took out her book to make some notes while they were fresh in her mind. And, only ninety minutes past the end of her shift, she bulled her way into traffic and headed home.

Speaking of a ridiculous number of rooms, she thought after driving through the big iron gates and winding up the drive. Nobody held a candle (whatever that meant) to Roarke. The house was a stunner, lording over sky and city, windows blazing hot, cold stars dripping overhead. A couple of years before she never would have believed she could live in a place so . . . spectacular, much less live there comfortably.

But she did. And pulling up in front of that vast stone beauty, leaving her cop's ride out in front where Roarke's majordomo, Summerset, would sneer at it, rated as one of the favorite parts of her day. Any day.

She climbed out of the stuffy car, jogged through cold air, and into the light- and warmth-drenched house.

He was there, of course. Lurking. The bony beanpole in a black suit who ran the house, and kept her mildly irritated like a sand-covered pebble in a shoe.

"Lieutenant," he said in a tone that scraped along the back of her neck like nails over a blackboard. "You're late, as usual."

"You're ugly, as usual. But I've learned to make allowances."

As she stripped off her coat, the fat cat Galahad gave Summerset's skinny ankle a last body rub, then padded over to Eve. She tossed her coat over the newel post, bent to give the cat a quick scratch between the ears. Duties done, she headed upstairs, with Galahad at her heels.

In the bedroom Roarke was stripped down to trousers and holding a black sweater. "Now there's timing," he said. "Maybe I shouldn't bother with this." He wagged the sweater. "And see how fast I can get you half naked instead."

Eyes narrowed, she pointed a finger at him. "How long have you been home?"

"About ten minutes, I'd think."

"See that! See!" Now she pointed a finger of both hands. "Why am *I* late according to His Boniness, but you're only minutes ahead of me and don't get sneered at."

"How do you know I wasn't sneered at?"

"Because I know. Were you?"

"I wasn't, no. But then I did have a message sent home that I'd be a bit late."

She sniffed. "Suck-up."

He smiled. "Come over here and say that."

"I'm not bouncing on you now. I've got notes to organize." She pulled off her weapon harness, draped it over the back of a chair. "Media shit's hit the public fan over how Anders died. I need to try to plug some holes."

"I made a statement myself."

"You what? A statement? What? Why? Why didn't you run it by me before—"

"I knew the man, and his corporate headquarters is in my building. I know how to make a statement, Eve. I had some experience in the process before I met you."

"Right. Right." She rubbed a spot between her eyebrows. "It's just. The whole thing smells."

"Of?"

"Overkill. I gotta . . ." She twirled a finger in the air. "Until something settles into place for me."

"You can . . ." He mimicked her gesture, "with me. I suppose you can bounce on me later, and for now we can have a meal at your desk."

"I could use the ear." She studied him as he pulled on the sweater. It was kind of a shame he needed one. "Are we supposed to date?"

"Date what?"

"Each other."

He sent her a look that combined amusement, charm, and bafflement. She wondered how he managed it. "As in I take you out, there is some form of activity, then I drop you off at the door with a long, hopeful good night kiss?"

"No." She frowned. "We never did that anyway."

"I knew I forgot something." He skimmed a finger down the cleft in her chin. "Should I ask you out on a date, darling Eve?"

"Look, I just wondered about it, that's all. Peabody started this whole thing about could she take an hour's personal to get polished up because she and McNab had this date night deal going so they wouldn't lose the juice."

"That's very sweet. Are you wondering if we're low on juice?" He took her hand, drew it to his lips.

"No." Why such a deliberately romantic gesture caused tingles straight up her arm, she didn't know. "I just wondered if that's the sort of thing you're supposed to do when you're married awhile. And you spend a lot of evenings with work."

"We like work, don't we?"

"Yeah, we do." She moved in, grabbed his hair with her fists and pulled his mouth to hers. She put some heat behind it—it was the least she could do—and felt the tingle up her arm arrow to her belly. She ended the kiss with a quick, light nip.

"Plenty of juice in reserve," she decided. She laid her hands on his cheeks a moment, then stepped back. "And I always hated dating."

Kicked back at her desk, sharing a bottle of wine and the comforting goodness of homemade chicken pot pie struck her as just about perfect. Summerset might be a pain in her ass but the man could cook.

As they ate, she rewound the facts and impressions in her head, and played them out for Roarke.

"So on one hand, you've got a guy who appears to dick around on his wife of nearly sixteen years, likes the kink, and when things go wrong, the kink partner runs. But that's bogus."

"Because he was drugged."

"That's the big one, but it's not all. Accident, even if the killer was hired sex, there would have been some attempt to revive. The very least, you take the rope away. Then there's the pajamas."

"There is?"

"Greta—who strikes me as spookily efficient as the Nazi downstairs, states the vic wore pjs. And had ten pairs. Count is nine. Where's pair number ten? I have to figure the killer took them, either for a trophy, or to dispose of them away from the scene. If he's expecting company, he either has them on so the company can undress him, or he leaves them folded in the drawer where the other nine pairs were. If he's wearing them, and it was an accident, why grab them up when you run? Doesn't follow."

"Maybe the killer worried there was DNA or other forensic evidence on them."

"The sweepers didn't find anything anywhere else in the room. Doesn't follow. Killer was sealed. Had to be sealed. The only prints in the room were Anders's, the wife's, and the housekeeper's. The few stray hairs in the bed were all his."

"Putting that aside for a moment, and given it's long odds considering what I know of Anders, there are some who get off on the idea of rape. Some who might enjoy the idea of being taken, forced, while they're unconscious. The ultimate submissive."

"People are sick in all kinds of ways," Eve commented. "But even if he was sick that way, would anyone in their right mind go into that kind of liaison without complete trust in the partner? And with that kind of trust, would the partner leave him choking to death? He was still alive when the security booted back up. I don't see it. But on the other hand . . ."

She paused to scoop up more pot pie. "The other hand is premeditated murder. Someone who's been in the house, or had access to the setup. The killer knew where Anders slept, where the security room was, knew how to override the security. I timed it, and there wasn't room for hunting around."

She walked Roarke through, step by step, as she had done. "It's cold, vindictive, ugly—you don't just want him dead, you want to mess him up after he's dead. But something's missing in that. Where's the springboard? You're that vindictive, there has to be anger or hate. If you're controlled enough to strap those down, why aren't you controlled enough to handle the details? The hefty dose of barbs—it's off. You want to humiliate him, but you don't have anything to say to him. You're alone in the house—a light tranq would be enough, give you enough to wrap him up. Don't you want him to hear why—don't you have something to say, don't you want him to *know*?

"So that's the third hand. The sham. The killer didn't care if the stage fell apart after the curtain. The killer had nothing to say to Anders. But that's missing something. Why put on the show if you can't take the bows with a captive audience? What do you gain? What's the damn point?"

"He's dead. Whatever the window dressing, mission accomplished."

"Yeah." She nodded, gesturing with her fork. "And what have I got? A devoted nephew, a loving wife, steadfast friends, the efficient housekeeper. Somebody's hiding something. That somebody knew he'd be alone in the house that night. Had to be sure of it. So . . . I dig deeper into financials—see if Anders was paying for it, or if I can find he paid for a subscription to *Bondage Weekly*. See if the wife, the nephew had any money troubles. Gambling, illegals. Sports betting's big," she considered. "Maybe Ben got in too deep."

"It won't be Ben."

"Doesn't feel like Ben. Doesn't mean it won't be connected to Ben." Eyeing him, she polished off her wine. "You want to sign on, expert consultant, civilian, and poke into some bank accounts?"

"I live for these moments."

"Take the wife. I'll take Ben. Then maybe we'll split up Anders."

"Assignments, always exciting. I've one for you. Tend to the dishes. I'll get the coffee."

It was hard to argue, especially since he'd come up with the pot pie idea. She carted the dishes, stacked them in the little washer in her office kitchen, then turned and found him studying her.

"What?"

"Awfully domestic, isn't it? A moment. Dish duty, coffee fetching, the two of us in the kitchen after a meal."

Eve glanced down to where Galahad was sniffing his bowl, obviously hoping for seconds. "That would be the three of us."

"Ah yes. Our little family." Reaching out, he brushed the tips of her choppy hair. "A nice settled moment between the business of the day and the puzzle of the evening. It occurs to me that *these* are the moments I live for."

Her heart simply melted. "I always wonder why they're enough for you."

He laid his lips on hers, soft, sweet. "You shouldn't."

The cat bumped between them, shot a leg up in the air, and began to wash his butt. With a laugh, Roarke shook his head. "And so the moment ends. Your coffee, Lieutenant," he said and handed her a mug.

She sat at her desk, and waited to settle as Roarke walked into his adjoining office. It remained an amazement, her personal miracle, that he loved her. Loved her because of or in spite of everything. In all the world, with all its misery, after all the pain, they'd found each other. He was right, of course. It was more than enough.

"Computer," she began, and ordered the next layer in the search of Anders's financials.

The rich were complicated, Eve thought, with all their many pockets inside which they tucked their booty. Stocks, bonds, trusts, tax-deferred, tax-free, liquid money, futures. Long-term, short-term. Subsets, and arms and divisions.

But under it all, somehow, someway, even the rich paid bills and bought toilet paper.

She scraped and she dug, searching for something to tie her victim to a lover or to licensed companions, running a secondary search for medications or sexual aids.

"Eve."

"What?" She looked away from the data crowding her wall screen. "I've barely started. You can't have found something already. It's not natural."

"I have, and I don't think you'll like it."

"What?"

"In Ava Anders's financials. There are regular bimonthly payments, going back for eighteen months."

"For what?" Her eyes narrowed. "To who?"

"To Charles Monroe."

"Charles." As it slapped at her out of left field, Eve dragged a hand through her hair. "Son of a bitch." This was the trouble, she thought, this was the damn problem with making friends.

It came back and bit you in the ass. "*She's* getting her pipes snaked twice a month by a licensed companion?"

"One would assume she wasn't paying for a bridge partner."

"And it just damn well has to be Charles." She sat back, let it simmer. "Why does a woman who claims to love her husband need to diddle or be diddled by an LC every two weeks?"

"You're not that naive. You know there are endless reasons for it."

"Maybe, maybe, but I'm only interested in *her* reasons." She rose, thinking she was about to be pried out of the warmth after all. "So I'll go ask him what they are."

"Now? Eve, it's after ten."

"LC's have flexible hours."

"And he's very likely to be out with a client."

"Or in with one."

"If you contact him first—"

"He'd have time to prepare. I want him off guard."

And she had a point. "I'll drive."

5

"IF HE'S IN, ISN'T WITH A CLIENT, BUT WITH Louise?" Roarke stepped into the elevator in the elegant lobby of Charles's apartment building.

Eve shrugged. "It's not like she doesn't know what he does for a living." While she didn't have any problem seeing how the smart, dedicated Dr. Dimatto fell for Charles—and he for her—she couldn't quite work out how Louise so easily accepted his work.

"Why doesn't it bother her? Seriously, it doesn't. She's not putting on a front. She's in a serious relationship with a guy who has sex with other women for a living, and it doesn't matter to her."

"I married a cop." Roarke smiled at her. "We all have our levels of acceptance. He was an LC when they met, just as she was a doctor, and one who often works in dangerous areas of the city."

She shot him the same easy smile. "So . . . if I'd been an LC when we met, you wouldn't have any problem with me banging other guys. Professionally."

"None at all, as I'd kick your ass and murder all of them. But that's just my level of acceptance."

"Yes." Pleased, she jabbed a finger into his chest. "*That* makes sense to me."

"Which is why we're suited, darling Eve, and neither of us with Charles or Louise. If Louise is here," he added when the doors opened, "would you like me to take her off somewhere for a bit?"

"Let's see how it plays."

"And if he's with a client—as I believe he only takes females—I'd be happy to engage her elsewhere while you work."

"Sure, no problem. Remembering those acceptance levels, how suited we are, and how much you like having your balls kicked up to your throat."

He put an arm around her waist for a sideways hug. "It is true love with us, isn't it?"

"Hearts and flowers, every day." She pushed the buzzer on Charles's apartment door. In less than a minute, she saw the security light blink, flicked her gaze up to the camera. The light steadied to green; the door opened.

"This is a nice surprise. Roarke. Lieutenant Sugar."

He stepped back in welcome. Charles Monroe was vid-star handsome, with a sheen of urban polish even in the casual at-home loose pants and sweater. His apartment with its strong colors, bold art, and deep cushions reflected his easy sophistication and affection for comfort. Music, what Eve thought might've been vintage jazz, flowed through the air.

"What can I get you? Some wine? Or how about some Irish coffee?" He glanced around the room as he spoke, as if checking for something he'd misplaced. "God knows it's cold enough out there."

"We're good. You alone, Charles?"

"Yes. Louise is doing a run with the medi-van tonight. These kind of temps make it rougher than usual on street people."

"No client tonight?"

Something came and went in his eyes, but his smile stayed easy. "Actually, I had a cancellation. So it's especially nice to see friends. Have a seat."

"It's police business, Charles."

"I was getting an inkling."

"About your client, Ava Anders."

"Is she all right?" Concern, and hints of alarm sounded in his voice. "She's not—"

"No, but her husband is." Eve angled her head. "It's been all over the media since this morning. You hadn't heard?"

"No." He closed his eyes a moment. "No, I hadn't. I've been busy today, and had . . . things on my mind. I haven't turned on the screen or looked at any reports. Thomas Anders is dead? Murdered since you're here. Surely you don't think Ava's responsible."

"Let's back track. Ava Anders is a client."

"Did she tell you that?"

"Her financials did."

"Then, as you have the information already, yes, she's a client."

"And the services you provide her?"

"Dallas, you know I can't. You know there has to be confidentiality between me and a client. I can't discuss the arrangement without her consent. Sit down, will you?" He said it wearily. "I'm getting a drink. Do you want anything?"

"We're fine, Charles." Roarke nudged Eve to a chair while Charles crossed to a sleek wet bar.

"How was he killed?"

"In bed, in what appears to be a sexual bondage and erotic asphyxiation accident."

"Oh Christ." Charles dropped ice into a short glass, poured whiskey over it. "Ava—"

"Wasn't there," Eve finished, and waited while he took the first sip. "It doesn't seem to surprise you—the manner of death, that his wife wasn't there. Would that be because she wasn't into the kink, or was too good at it to mess it up?"

"You'll want to ask her that. You're putting me in a position, Dallas."

"How many did you put Ava in?"

He laughed, quick and amused, and the tension in his face dissolved. "You'll have to ask her that, too."

"How about this? How did she come to be a client?"

"Referral." With the whiskey, he crossed back over, slid into a chair. "And no, I'm not going to tell you who. Not without consent. Dallas, my reputation and integrity hinge on consent, and on trust."

Eve sat back, debated different angles. "You'd be, arguably, an expert on relationships." When he laughed again, shook his head, she lifted her hands. "What? You trade in relationships. You told me once it's not only the sex, but the relationship the client pays for."

"True enough." And the strain was back on his face. "Yes, that's true enough."

"Charles, it's not my business," Roarke interrupted, "but as a friend I'll ask if everything's all right between you and Louise?"

Charles looked at Roarke. "Yes, thanks. Everything's very all right between me and Louise."

"Now that we cleared that up," Eve said, "let's try it this way. Hypothetically, why would a woman, in a long-term, ostensibly happy marriage seek the services of a licensed companion? And seek them on a regular basis."

"Hypothetically." Charles nodded. "It might be that the woman has needs, desires, even fantasies that aren't or can't be met within the marriage."

"Why?"

Now he blew out a breath. "It might be that a woman isn't comfortable seeking those needs and so on from her spouse, or the spouse isn't comfortable or able to fulfill them. It might be by satisfying those needs with a professional, safely and confidentially, the marriage partners are more content. Not every marriage, however successful, gives both partners complete emotional or sexual satisfaction."

"So what, they stay together to have conversation over dinner?"

"It might be as simple as that, but it's usually considerably more complex. The fact is sex, particularly a certain type of sex, is only one part of a relationship. I can't give you details, Dallas. Not without Ava's consent. If you get it, I'll be happy to talk to you again."

"Okay." That would have to do. "Don't contact her, Charles. If she tries to contact you, I'd appreciate it if you'd dodge until I've had a go with her on this."

"All right. I can do that."

"Good enough." Eve rose. "I'll be in touch. Hi to Louise and all that."

"I'll tell her." He stood, leaned over to kiss Eve's cheek.

I don't get it. I don't get it." Eve frowned through the windshield as Roarke drove home. "I know he's right, I know it's true, but I don't *get* it."

"Precisely what would *it* be?"

"How you can have the sex outside marriage, and that's just hunky with everybody involved? Why bother with the marriage thing?"

"Finances, companionship, habit, security, status."

"Bullshit, bullshit, bullshit."

"You really should learn to form more definite opinions."

"And the other thing, that she can't get all her jollies from within the marriage? Okay, true—I hear this all the time, especially after he kills her or vice versa, but what crap." Sheer annoyance had her slumping down in her seat. "If you didn't have the sex buzz, you shouldn't have hooked up."

"Sometimes the buzz changes frequencies for one of the partners."

"Okay. All right. Say I want to change frequencies. I decide I want you to suck your thumb and call me Mommy while I paddle your cute ass." She shifted her gaze to his profile. "What do you say?"

"I would probably suggest a reasonable compromise, such as I'd like to suck on something else, preferably something attached to you, and I'll call you whatever you like. If spanking must be involved, we'll just have to take turns there."

"See." She poked his shoulder. "That works for me."

"I sincerely hope not, but we can see."

"No." She snorted out a laugh. "I mean it works for me that you'd say let's modify a little if I came up with something weird."

"Remember that the next time I want to tie you up with your own underwear and slather your naked body with raspberry sauce."

She slid her eyes toward him again. "Was there a first time?"

"Could be."

The man, she mused, continued to surprise her. "Back to the point. I can't see a marriage staying solid if one or both partners enters into an intimate relationship elsewhere. And profession aside, the LC/client relationship is intimate." She considered, mulled, as Roarke drove through the gates. "Maybe, for instance, you're married to this guy, everything's frosty, then he turns out to be gay as an Easter basket. You got a problem. Maybe you stick it out because of those reasons you named— money, habit, whatever. And maybe you go to a professional to get off. But is that a marriage or just an arrangement?"

"Is there love? Your view on this is narrow. That's how you're built."

It didn't *feel* narrow to her. It felt right. "Marriage is a promise. That's one of the ways you talked me into it. If you break one part of the promise, it's going to crack other parts."

"Even if both parties agree?"

"I don't know." She got out of the car. "But I'm interested to hear how Ava Anders explains it."

Inside, they started upstairs together. "It seems to me," Roarke said, "that if she'd wanted to hide the payments to Charles, she'd have paid in cash. And speaking of Charles, did he seem distracted tonight? Even before he understood why we were there?"

"Yeah, something. Maybe some trouble in paradise, even though he said everything was fine."

"That would be a pity. They work together very well."

When she started to turn toward her office, he took her hand, tugged her in the opposite direction. "What? I've got work."

"We both always have work. Now, it's nearly midnight, and you've had a very long day."

"I just want to—"

"So do I. I'm thinking of ordering up some raspberry sauce."

"Funny guy. You're a funny guy. Look, I just want another hour to—"

"I have other plans for your next hour." Shifting position, he began to back her into the bedroom. "Here's that compromise. That . . . modification." He depressed the release on the weapon harness she'd strapped back on to go out.

"Maybe I'm not in the mood."

"Then . . ." He trailed a finger down her throat, flipped open the first button of her shirt. "I suppose you're going to be bored. Fire on." He opened the next button as the flames flashed in the hearth. "Lights off."

He continued to back her toward the platform, and the lake-sized bed it held, watching her eyes when her harness and then her shirt fell to the floor. "Step up," he warned when they reached the platform. "And again." Then he gave her a light shove so she fell back on the bed.

"I guess I'll just lie here and take it."

"You do that." He lifted her leg, pulled off her boot.

"Don't take it personally if I nod off."

"Of course not." He tossed the second boot aside. He ran his hands up her legs, smiling at her quiver when they stroked over her center on the way to the hook of her trousers. He drew them down her legs, let them drop.

Eve faked a yawn, tapped her hand over her mouth. "Sorry."

He cocked a brow. There wasn't another woman in the world, he thought, who could amuse, challenge, and arouse him as she did. He pulled off his sweater, tossed it aside, then sat on the side of the bed to remove his own boots. Behind him, she made exaggerated snorting sounds until he pinched her.

"Oh, sorry. Was I snoring?"

He stood, unhooked his trousers, stepped out of them. "Go back to sleep," he said as he slid onto the bed, slid onto her. "This won't take long."

She started to laugh, and the sound strangled when he closed his teeth over her breast through the thin tank she wore. "Okay then." She cleared the huskiness out of her throat. "I guess I can give you a few minutes."

"Well, now, I appreciate that." He caught her nipple, exquisite control, while he trailed a fingertip up her inner thigh, traced it at the edge of the simple cotton.

He heard her breath catch, and felt her muscles twitch, then the quiet moan when he slid just under the cotton. Slipping toward the heat and away again, teasing while her heart kicked to gallop under his relentless mouth. All that strength, all that wit, all that will melted into need beneath him.

His mouth found hers, took, as he stroked her up, still up, up to the quivering edge.

Then he rolled off. "Well, that ought to do it."

Her body all but screamed in denial.

She levered up, straddled him. He was hard as iron, and his gorgeous face covered with humor. "Funny guy," she said again. Crossing her arms, she tugged the tank up and off, then crooked both her index fingers. "Hands on, pal."

"Well, if you insist."

He cupped her breasts, brushed his thumbs over her nipples. She planted her hands on either side of his head and, leaning down, feasted on his mouth. The taste of him. She loved the taste of him, would never have her fill of it. The way his lips fit to hers, the glide of his tongue. She could spend hours, days, on his mouth alone, on the magic she found there.

With her breath quickened, her skin already hot, she flipped away, flopped onto her back. "*That* ought to do it."

They lay where they were a moment then, turning their heads, grinned at each other. And dove.

She laughed, and groaned, she gasped and giggled. The sheer fun and foolishness added bold, bright color to the deeper tones of desire. His hands were quick; her mouth avid. Together they moved recklessly over the big bed, under the cold stars gleaming through the sky window.

He drove her over, and her cry was of cheerful pleasure. This, he thought, this, the unity, the adventure of it, would always delight him. Sustain him. Even when he was inside her, when the need pounded them both, the utter joy of what they'd found, what they'd made, rushed through him. She was the happiness he'd searched for all of his life.

Her eyes, gilded by firelight, stayed on his; her lips curved. When they sprang over that shining edge together, his heart simply soared.

Under him, limp, her heart still pounding, she sighed. "Now that," she said, "should definitely do it."

In the morning, she glugged down coffee to spark her brain into handling the basic chore of getting dressed. Roarke, already dressed, alert—as was his irritating habit—scanned the stock reports while he drank his coffee in the bedroom sitting area.

"Warmer today, if you're interested."

She spoke from the depths of the closet. "Warmer than what?"

"Than a witch's teat."

Considering that, she buttoned on a plain white shirt. "I'm going to work here this morning, have Peabody meet me. Easier to go from here to the address Ava's staying at. Do you know a Brigit Plowder?"

"Socialite, married to Peter Plowder—architect. Her family builds—bridges and tunnels most particularly. She's a respected philanthropic figure. Puts her money where her cause is. Would this be where the widow's staying?"

"Yeah." Eve came out, sat down to put on her boots. Then narrowed her eyes at Roarke's long look. "What? It's a jacket. It's just a damn jacket. I don't care if it goes with the pants."

"Pity then, as it goes very well. I was thinking how stylishly professional you look, which is probably a happy accident. But nonetheless."

"Stylishly professional." She sniffed, leaned over to steal a wedge of melon from his plate. "I've got to get my stylishly professional ass to work."

"Eat."

"I'll get a bagel or whatever in my office. I need to hit those financials, since somebody interfered with police business last night."

"I should be arrested."

"Pal, that goes without saying." She leaned over to kiss him. "Later. Oh, nearly forgot. Peabody's going on *Now* tonight."

"Is she? She must be . . ." He thought of Peabody. "Terrified."

"Yeah. She'll get over it."

In her office, she tackled the financials. She remembered the bagel, then forgot it again. When she heard the clump of Peabody's winter boots, she rubbed her already blurry eyes.

"You take over here."

Peabody stopped, blinked. "Take over where?"

"These stinking financials. Give them another fifteen minutes, then we'll take Ava."

"Okay." Peabody draped a bag over the back of Eve's sleep chair.

"What's that?"

"It's an outfit. For tonight. In case I spill something on what I'm wearing, or in case what I'm wearing's stupid. McNab liked it, but he wears Day-Glo half the time." Peabody pulled off her outerwear to reveal a ruby red suit with small silver buttons running down the front. "What do you think? Does it look right?"

"Why are you asking me?"

"I don't know. I really don't know." Nerves pumping, Peabody brushed at her hair. "And I got stupid hair day going. They fix that right? They fix that sort of thing. Nadine hired Trina to do hair and makeup so . . ." Peabody trailed off, pursed her lips. "You look all good and everything today. Seriously up."

Eve shook her head. Gray pants, white shirt, navy jacket over her weapon harness. What was the *deal*? "If we've finished our fashion consultation, maybe you could spare a minute for the damn financials."

"Okay. What do you think about the earrings?"

Eve gave the silver drops a passing glance. "About you wearing them, or about me ripping them off and stuffing them up your nose?"

"Okay," Peabody said again, and hotfooted it to the desk.

"The computer hasn't popped out anything from standard searches," Eve told her. "One more shot, then I'm thinking to pass it on to Roarke. He popped something straight out of the widow's in about ten minutes last night."

"He's got the knack."

"He popped Charles out."

Peabody's head jerked up. "Our Charles?"

"In a manner of. Ava's been a regular bimonthly client of our favorite LC's for a year and a half."

"Shit. We're going to have to interview him."

"We went over there last night. He is, as expected, coy about the details. We need Ava to clear him for that. But he did tell me that she was a referral."

"If she was fooling around with a pro it might go to motive."

"It might. Hitch is she wasn't hiding it, at least not well. There were straight payments out of her personal debit account. No cover."

As she considered, Peabody played with one of the short dangles at her ear. "So, she doesn't think to hide the payments. The husband finds out, they go around about it. Fight, divorce is threatened. And she kills him, sexual overtones."

"She was out of the country."

"Right. Hired hit?"

"Too elaborate." Just too damn fussy, Eve thought. "Unless, it plays out like that, and she hired someone who tailors the hit to the client's specifications."

"Fantasy Hits R Us."

"There's a way to make money, people find it. I'm going to go over her financials and have Roarke comb them. But so far, nothing's popped there either. No suspicious withdrawals, no payments that don't jibe." She paced. "Good-looking woman. She's got style, power. The sort that could talk a lover, if he's stupid enough, into doing her dirty work for her."

"But then if she had a lover," Peabody pointed out, "why is she paying Charles five thousand a bang, twice a month?"

"Exactly, so . . ." Eve turned back. "How do you know what Charles charges a bang?"

"Ah." Peabody fussed with her hair, pulled at the silver buttons on her suit jacket. "Maybe, being curious, I looked up his rates when we were sort of dating."

"Uh-huh. Well, I can agree that if a woman's getting strange for free, she's unlikely to pay ten grand a month for a couple thrills. See what you can find."

Moving away again, Eve pulled out her 'link to schedule an appointment with Mira, and to put a hold on an interview room.

"Ladies." Roarke spoke from the doorway of their adjoining offices. "Peabody, you look ravishing."

"I do?" She nearly squealed it. "But in a screen-friendly, trustworthy, public servant kind of way?"

"Yes, indeed. The color's wonderful on you."

"Jesus," Eve said under her breath, and earned a mild stare from her husband.

"Breakfast?" he said.

Peabody watched as Eve scowled, shrugged. Then as Roarke lifted his brows with those dreamy eyes steady. Her lieutenant rolled hers, but stomped off to the kitchen.

"You guys don't even have to talk." Resting her chin on her fist, Peabody sighed. "You just know."

"It does come in handy from time to time. How was your date night?"

"It was mag. Really. Mostly because we both agreed we like noisy, crowded clubs better than grown-up, sophisticated ones. But it's good to try something new."

"Stop socializing with my partner," Eve called out from the kitchen.

"Financials," Peabody mouthed.

"Ah, yes." Casually, Roarke strolled over, gave a quick glance at the data on screen. He winked at Peabody and sent her pulse scrambling, then continued on to the kitchen where his wife was taking an annoyed bite out of a bagel.

"Breakfast," she muttered at him.

"Such as it is. Why don't I go over the financials? I can do it in considerably less time than you or Peabody, which frees you up to go out and browbeat suspects."

She frowned, chewed. "You'd have to do it straight. No unregistered, no illegal hacking."

"You underestimate the skill of an honest man."

"Yeah, but I'm talking to you." She grinned over another bite of bagel. "I could use the help, if you've got the time between schemes of universal financial domination."

"I'll work it in. Now." He brushed a crumb away from the side of her mouth, kissed her. "Go protect and serve."

"Good idea. Peabody," she said as she headed out, "with me."

"I haven't really started on—"

"The civilian's got it. Let's go take a few kicks at the grieving widow."

"That's lots more fun." Peabody jumped up, grabbed her garment bag. And because Eve was already out of earshot, turned back as Roarke came out of the kitchen. "Do you like the earrings?"

He stepped closer to give them a good study. "They're charming."

"But in a—"

"In a professional and intuitive police detective sort of way. You'll be wonderful and look the same."

"Thanks." She grabbed her coat, scarf, hat. "I—"

"Peabody! Move your damn ass!"

"Gotta go," Peabody finished on the heels of Eve's shout. And fled.

With his fresh cup of coffee, Roarke sat behind Eve's desk. He could spare twenty minutes now, he mused. "So, let's see what we have here."

6 AN ELEGANT, OLD, LOVINGLY RESTORED BUILDING on the Upper East Side housed the Plowders' apartment. The quiet, rosy brick boasted a portico entrance with wide, beveled glass doors granting passersby a peek at the polished marble lobby. A doorman, in blue and silver livery, stood guard should any of those passersby need a little move-along.

Eve noted he gave her police issue the beady eye when she pulled up to park at the carpeted curb. She didn't mind a bit. She didn't just eat bagels for breakfast, but enjoyed a good bite of doorman.

He strode across the swatch of red carpet, shook his head.

"Cop rides never get any prettier," he commented. "What house are you out of?"

She shifted her feet, and her prepared tone. "You on the job?"

"Was. Put in my papers after I did my thirty. My brother-in-law manages the place." He jerked his head toward the entrance. "Tried golf, tried fishing, tried driving the wife crazy." He flashed a smile. "Better pay, better hours on this door than doing the security guard thing. Dallas," he said, shooting a finger at her. "Lieutenant Eve."

"Yeah, that's right."

"Shoulda made you sooner. Getting rusty, I guess. I didn't hear about anybody getting murdered inside."

"Not yet." They exchanged quick cop grins. "Your tenants the Plowders have a guest I need to speak with. Ava Anders."

"Hmm. Husband got dead yesterday. Didn't know she was upstairs. She must've come in after I went off. She and the dead husband came around now and then. Her more than him, but he was friendlier."

"Was Mrs. Anders unfriendly?"

"No. Just one of the type who don't notice who opens the door for her 'cause she expects somebody to. On the snooty side, but not bitchy or anything. Him, he'd usually stop a minute going in or out, have a word, maybe ask if you caught the game—whatever the game was. Sorry to hear he got dead. I gotta call up. Worth my job if I don't."

"That's no problem. What was your house?" Eve asked as they moved to the doors.

"Did my last ten at the one-two-eight. Cold Case Unit."

"That's a tough hitch. The cold ones can haunt you."

"Yeah, they can." He pulled off his glove to offer a hand. "Frank O'Malley, formerly Detective."

"Nice to meet you, Detective."

"Peabody, Detective Delia," Peabody said when they shook. "I knew a uniform in the one-two-eight back when I was on Patrol. Hannison?"

"Sure, I knew Hannison. He's all right."

Inside the lobby with its subtly fragrant air, Frank turned to an intercom screen. "Plowder penthouse," he ordered, then waited until the screen shifted from waiting blue and the image of a woman with short brown hair swam on. "Morning, Agnes."

"Frank."

"I got a Lieutenant Dallas and Detective Peabody in the lobby. They'd like to speak to Mrs. Anders."

"I see. Hold a moment, Frank."

"That was Mrs. Plowder's personal assistant, Agnes Morelli. She's okay."

"How about the Plowders?"

"Seem like solid types to me. Not on the snooty side. Call you by name, ask after the family they got time for it. Don't skimp on the tips."

A moment later, Agnes flowed back on screen. "You can send them right up, Frank, lower parlor entrance."

"Will do. Thanks, Agnes. First elevator," he told Eve. "Thirty-nine East. That'll take you straight to the lower parlor. It's a hell of a space they got up there. Three floors, river view."

"Appreciate the help, Detective."

Inside the elevator, the hammered silver walls boasted a long, built-in bench, in case your legs got tired of riding up, or down. Since the trip took under thirty seconds, Eve couldn't imagine the bench got much use.

The doors opened straight onto a wide room in pale and pretty colors, opening to a spectacular river view through a wall of glass doors and windows. Agnes stood, in a severe black suit given unexpected charm by the full-blown red rose on the lapel.

"Good morning, I'm Agnes, Mrs. Plowder's PA. If you wouldn't mind showing me some identification. We trust Frank, of course, but—"

"No problem." Eve took out her badge, as did Peabody.

"Thank you. Please come in, have a seat. Mrs. Anders will be right down. Can I offer you some refreshment? Coffee?"

It was knee-jerk for Eve to refuse, but she decided coffee in the parlor could lend a tone of female intimacy that might be helpful. "Coffee'd be great. Black for me, coffee regular for my partner."

"Make yourselves comfortable. I'll just be a minute."

The minute they were alone, Peabody let her eyes pop wide. "Can I just say: Woot, some digs. They've got a terrace out there bigger than my entire apartment."

"I bet your apartment's a lot warmer than that terrace right now."

"Yeah, there's that." But unable to resist, Peabody started across the parlor to the glass. "It's the kind of place that makes you feel you need to glide. I don't glide very well. It must relate to my center of gravity, which would be my ass."

"It's the kind of place where birds probably splat their tiny birdbrains on the windows regular."

"That's an image, boy." And Peabody took a couple cautious steps back. "Still, it's a totally uptown view. Don't you want to see?"

"I can see fine from here." To Eve's mind, lofty heights should be left to the birdbrains. In any case, her interest centered on what and who lived in the space, not what spread outside.

A moment later, Ava made her entrance. The widow wore black in a snugly fitted, high-collared shirt with slim pants and heels. Her hair coiled at the nape of her neck, pulled tightly back from a face with shadowed, exhausted eyes. Beside her, an arm supportively around Ava's waist, Brigit Plowder conveyed boldness and challenge. She topped off at about five feet, with her tiny frame tucked neatly into a plum-colored sweater and stone-gray pants. Her hair, a pure white cap, set off laser-sharp green eyes and the arched black brows that framed them. Her mouth formed a deep bow Eve assumed could be charming when it smiled, but at the moment those lips clamped together in tight disapproval bordering on anger.

"I'm going to say this straight off." Brigit's voice was a throaty boom worthy of a woman twice her size. "This is outrageous."

"I agree. Murder is always outrageous."

A quick spark fired in those keen eyes. It might have been approval. "I understand you have a job to do, Lieutenant, and from everything I've been told about you and this one," she said with a gesture toward Peabody, "you excel at your work. That's admirable. However, bombarding Ava at such a time shows a distinct lack of sensitivity and compassion."

"It's all right, Bridge."

"It's *not* all right. Why can't you give us all a few days, just a few days to grieve?"

"Because then I give Thomas Anders's killer a few days." Eve shifted her gaze back to Ava. "I apologize for disturbing you, Mrs. Anders. The investigation requires it."

"I don't see why—"

"Look, Mrs. Plowder, I'm a murder cop, and any murder cop will tell you time's the enemy. The more time that passes, the cooler the trail. The trail goes cold, the killer can walk. When killers walk, it pisses me off. If you want to blame somebody for me being here, blame the killer. Now, the more time you stand there complaining, the more time we're going to be here."

Brigit's chin jutted out, then angled as she inclined her head. "You're absolutely right. I don't like it, don't like any of it, but you're absolutely right. Come on, Ava, let's sit down now. I'll apologize, Lieutenant, Detective," she continued as she led Ava to a thickly cushioned sofa in deep blue. "I'm rarely rude to guests in my home, even uninvited guests. I'm not altogether myself today. None of us are. Please, sit down."

As Eve and Peabody took wide-armed chairs, Agnes rolled in a tray. "I've got chamomile tea for you, Ava. You'll do better with that than coffee."

"Thank you, Agnes." Ava took the cup, stared into it.

"I'll see she drinks it this time," Brigit stated.

"Thanks." Eve accepted the coffee Agnes offered. "Since you're here, Mrs. Plowder, can you tell me when you and Mrs. Anders made your travel plans?"

"Travel? Oh. That seems like years ago already. We go away every year. Ava, Sasha—Sasha Bride-West—and myself. A week somewhere warm, a restorative at the end of winter."

"This particular restorative. When did you make the plans? The dates, the destination."

"Oh . . . Three months ago. About?" she added, turning to Agnes.

"Nearly four, actually. I booked the arrangements in November, just before Thanksgiving."

"Agnes knows all, remembers all," Brigit said, and Eve saw she'd been right. The smile was charming.

"We had such a lovely day." Ava's voice dripped like tears. "Such a lovely day on Monday. Breakfast on the terrace. Mimosas. We had mimosas, and we got just a little drunk. At breakfast, remember, Bridge?"

"Yes, honey, I remember."

"We laughed like idiots. Everything was so funny. And later, when I called Tommy later, I cut it all so short. We were going to have massages on the terrace, where we'd gotten a little bit drunk at breakfast. So I cut it all very short. 'I'll talk to you later, Tommy,' that's what I said to him. 'I'll talk to you later. I want my massage.' That's the last thing I said to him, because there wasn't any later."

"Sweetheart." Brigit brushed her fingers over Ava's cheek. "Don't do this."

"I don't know about trails going cold; I just know Tommy's dead. I saw him myself when Ben took me to him. I saw Tommy dead."

"Mrs. Anders." Peabody shifted forward. "This is a terrible time for you. We're here to help. You've lost your husband. Don't you want to know why? Don't you want to know who?"

"I don't know." Ava lifted her gaze, aimed those wet blue eyes at Peabody. "I should. I know I should. But he'll still be gone."

"He'd want you to know," Peabody said. "He'd want us to find those answers."

"I don't know them. How could I?"

"You knew him best. You were his wife. There are things you know, things you may not realize are important, are relevant. That's why we're here. We will know."

"Your husband's date book," Eve began. "Did he make the entries himself?"

"His date book? Yes."

"And the autosystem in the bedroom, the wake-up program and so on. Would he have programmed that personally?"

"Yes." Ava straightened in her seat. "He enjoyed that, hearing his first appointment of the day, being reminded of what he'd ordered for breakfast."

"The two of you must have gotten up at the same time routinely."

"Oh, if he had an early appointment, and I didn't, I'd wear earplugs. And have Greta wake me."

"Do you take sleep aids?"

"Oh, occasionally." She waved a hand. "Now and then."

"Did he?"

"Now and then. Everyone does, don't they?"

"He had very specific routines. The bedroom door always closed, the internal security cameras shut down at night, no cameras in the sleeping area of the master bedroom."

"Yes, he was very private."

"Even in hotels," Brigit put in. "We all traveled together quite a bit. Tommy always instructed housekeeping to keep the bedroom door closed, and tipped them in advance to insure they did."

"He'd have been very careful regarding home security," Eve commented.

"He had the system checked and evaluated every quarter." Ava lifted her teacup, sipped. "And upgraded whenever upgrades became available. It wasn't just security, though of course, that was the priority. But Tommy liked . . . toys, if you know what I mean."

"I do."

"He just got such a kick out of all the bells and whistles. He liked to play," she said wistfully.

And playing was the next line of questioning. "Mrs. Plowder, my partner and I need to speak with Mrs. Anders privately."

"Oh, but can't Brigit stay?" Ava fumbled for her friend's hand. "I feel so much better with her here."

"There are some sensitive questions. If after we've concluded, you opt to share them with Mrs. Plowder, that's your privilege. If you'd excuse us, Mrs. Plowder, Ms. Morelli."

"We'll be right upstairs." Brigit patted Ava's arm. "You only have to call if you want me."

As her friend left the room, Ava set down her teacup, gripped her hands together in her lap. "This is about how Tommy was found. Brigit knows. Everyone knows."

"Was your husband involved in sexual relationships outside of your marriage?"

"No."

"Was your husband aware you procured the services of a licensed professional twice-monthly for the last eighteen months?"

The prominent bones of Ava's cheeks seemed to push against her skin. Her lips trembled, even as she clamped them tightly together. When she reached for her tea again, her hand shook. "Yes. Yes. God. Do you know what people will say about him, about us if all this gets out?"

"In your previous statement you claimed to have a solid and happy marriage."

"It wasn't a claim. It's the truth."

"Yet you sought sexual gratification from a professional."

Ava closed her eyes a moment, let out a breath. When she opened them, her eyes were hard and angry. "You're very smug, aren't you? Sitting there, judging me by your lofty standards and morals."

"I'm not judging you. I'm asking you."

"Of course you're judging me, and Tommy. So will others. Even Bridge, if she knew. She's the most generous, open-hearted person I know, the most loyal of friends, but she'd never understand this. She'd never understand."

"Make me understand."

"Tommy and I loved each other. We enjoyed each other. We were devoted to each other. He used to say he made me laugh, and I made him think. Our marriage was very solid, very fulfilling to us both. A couple of years ago, a little more than that, I suppose, he felt, began to feel, he wanted more experimentation in bed." She took a long drink of tea. Embarrassment or the heat from the drink flushed color into her cheeks. "We were neither of us children. Even when we married we were mature, experienced people. My husband wanted more . . . variety in our sexual relationship, and I tried to meet that. But, I wasn't comfortable with some of his . . ."

She pressed her lips together. "In short, I wasn't able to provide him with what he wanted, and he wasn't satisfied with what I wanted in that one area of our marriage. It began to erode our relationship, to peck away at our foundation. We both felt it. Why should we allow that to destroy the rest?" she demanded. "We decided that we would take that off the table, so to speak. That sex wasn't as important as we were, what we were to each other. We would simply obtain that aspect elsewhere. Discreetly. We would use professionals, and would never engage those professionals in any of our homes."

"Did you both adhere to those terms?"

Ava looked away. "I did. Over the last few months I suspected . . . I thought Tommy might have been bringing women into the house while I was away. I found some lingerie in my drawer, another woman's lingerie Greta must have laundered and put away believing it was mine. Some of my perfume went missing. Little things."

"Did you confront him?"

"No. I was hurt, I admit it. Hurt and disappointed. Angry, too. I'd decided to take the time during this trip with my friends to decide how to handle it. He let someone into our home, and now he's dead." Her hand fisted in her lap. "I'm so angry with him, so angry with him for leaving me over this."

"Do you know the names or the agencies of the professionals he used?"

"No. We'd agreed not to bring that up. It was outside. It wasn't us. It was outside of us."

"But your payments to Charles Monroe came out of your debit account where your husband could see them."

She let out a half laugh. "Tommy never looked at my personal accounts."

"Did you look at his?"

Color rose into her face again. "Yes, I did. I did when I suspected he was bringing women home. I couldn't find anything there. I'm not sure what I'd have done if I had."

"How did you select Charles Monroe?"

"My friend Sasha recommended him. She knows. Unlike Brigit Sasha's very open. Even a little wild, by some standards. She told me he was very smooth, very skilled, and very discreet. I was a nervous wreck the first time I went to him. He put me very much at ease."

"Is he the only LC you've engaged?"

"Yes. I liked him, trusted him. I could think of our appointments as going to a therapist."

"Are you willing to give consent for Mr. Monroe to speak to us about your relationship?"

"Oh God." Ava pressed a hand to her face. "I suppose there's no place for pride or privacy any longer. Yes, I'll consent to that. In return, I need your word you'll keep as much of this private business out of the media as you can."

"You can have my word on that."

"I'll have to tell Bridge," Ava murmured. "I'm going to disappoint her."

"Mrs. Plowder strikes me as a woman who sticks," Peabody said, and Ava smiled a little.

"Yes, you're right. She is. She does. Am I to blame for this? Am I responsible? If I'd been more open, more flexible about what he wanted, Tommy would still be alive, wouldn't he? I keep asking myself that."

"The killer's responsible, Mrs. Anders. That's your answer." Eve rose. "Thank you for your time and cooperation."

When they stood inside the hammered steel of the elevator, Peabody shook her head. "Tough spot for her, the guilt on top of the grief. She can't help but ask herself is this because she has sexual hang-ups, or because he went over-the-top. Since he's the one who's dead, she's probably going to settle on door number one."

Eve only said, "Hmm." When they hit the lobby, she dug out a card. "Thanks again, Detective." She offered her hand, then the card to Frank. "You can reach me at any of those contacts, should something strike you."

"Can do." He tucked it into a pocket. "Luck, Lieutenant. Detective."

"Yeah," Eve muttered, striding to the car, "we're going to need it." She got behind the wheel. "Sounds like the vic took a hell of a turn after what, more than a dozen years of marriage."

"Happens, doesn't it? Divorce litters the land, so does adultery. And LCs do good business for a reason."

"All true." Eve danced her fingers along the steering wheel. "Marriage is mostly a sucker bet."

"Spoken by the woman with Dream Husband."

"You just said Dream Husband might take a turn down the road and decide he wants to do threesomes or—"

"Me! Me!" Peabody shot up a hand. "Pick me!"

"Yeah, I'm dying to get you between the sheets, Peabody. Keeps me up at night. The point is, you've got a dozen years in, and one night the guy comes home and says: 'Look, honey, I picked up this ball gag and anal probe on the way home. Let's go try them out."

"That would be a shocker, but I bet it was more subtle than that. Maybe he tries out a few new moves, testing the waters, and she's not receptive, and it goes from there. It's like, okay, here's a man who's got it pretty damn good. He's healthy, he doesn't have a face that scares small children. He's running a successful business, he's rich, got the good-looking, spiffed up wife who loves him. Big house, friends, a nephew who stands in as son and heir. Then he has this mid-life deal—a lot of people do—and he starts thinking yeah, he's got all this, all this is good, but what's he missing? And he's not as young or as potent as he used to be so he compensates. Instead of buying a flashy phallic-symbol vehicle, he wants to get some wild on in bed. But the wife's like: 'You want to put your what *where*?'"

"And she's more in the habit of him putting his this there." Eve nodded. "I get that. So she's just, well, okay then, you put your what where into whoever, I'll have somebody else put his there there, and we're jake?"

"There's a whole separate schism of the Free-Agers who believe in open relationships. Everybody puts their what and their this where and there. But looking at it from your POV—which I have to admit I am, too, as I'm of the opinion if he puts his what anywhere but here?" Peabody jerked a thumb at the car window. "There's the door, asshole. It didn't work for them, either. He went over the line. He couldn't keep the deal they'd made when they got married, and he couldn't keep this deal either."

"That's the pivot point," Eve agreed. "Contact Charles. Tell him we've got client consent, and we're on our way."

Louise answered the door, and put a little hitch in Eve's stride. Her blonde hair was tousled, her gray eyes sleepy. She wore winter-white lounging pants with a long-sleeved tee.

"Come on in. Charles is putting some breakfast together. I slept in—long night."

"How was it out there?" Eve asked her.

"Cold. Have a seat. I'll see if I can hunt up the coffee."

"It's okay. We just had some."

"Like that would stop you. Charles told me this is about the Anders murder."

"That's right."

"And that Anders's wife is one of Charles's clients."

"Yeah."

"Which, of course, neither of you nor Charles can discuss with me." Louise cocked up her eyebrows. "Why don't I make myself scarce?"

"We can take this somewhere else."

"That's okay, no problem. I'll have myself some breakfast in bed. That's a treat."

She walked off to the kitchen, and Peabody sent Eve a worried look. "Oh-oh."

"Yeah, something's off with them. I caught the buzz from Charles last night."

Louise came back with a pretty place setting on a silver tray. "Hi to Roarke and McNab," she said, then disappeared into the bedroom.

Charles stepped out of the kitchen looking as tired and stressed as his lover. "Dallas. Peabody." He crossed over to buss cheeks. "You got consent."

"On record." Eve took out her recorder, played back the statement.

"That'll work. So." He gestured to seats, took one of his own. "What do you want to know?"

"How did Ava Anders contact you?"

"By 'link. I have a business-only line."

"How did she strike you?"

"Nervous, and trying hard not to show it. Which is how she struck me on our first appointment."

"Where was the first appointment?"

"I looked that up after you left last night. The Blackmore Hotel, downtown. It's a busy place, which is what she wanted. She checked in, contacted me to give me the room number. This way, I could go straight up, but no one would see us together."

"Okay, this is weird, but what did she want?"

"Initially, to talk. She'd ordered lunch, and wine, which we had in the parlor of the suite. We talked—if I remember—about literature, plays, art. For some, this first interlude with a professional is very much like a first date, where you do the surface getting-to-know-you routine."

He glanced toward the bedroom where Louise, presumably, ate her breakfast in bed. "As we got to know each other over the course of time, I understood that her husband wasn't as interested in literature and so forth as he was in sports. So I could offer her that."

"Did she talk about her husband?"

"Not a great deal. It . . . spoils the mood. She might mention, usually afterward, when we were talking over a drink or coffee, that they were going on a trip, or having a dinner party, that sort of thing."

"How did she feel about him, Charles? You'd know."

"When she spoke of him, she spoke warmly, or casually, the way you do when someone's an intricate part of your life. I remember she'd been shopping once before an appointment and showed me a shirt she'd picked up for him. She said how handsome he'd look in it."

"Sexually, what was she after?"

"She liked to be tended to. She liked the lights off—a few candles were fine, but if we met during the day, which was most usual, the drapes had to be closed."

"You'd classify her as inhibited?"

"Traditional. Very. And maybe a bit self-involved. As I said, she wanted to be tended to. She wasn't as interested in touching as much as being touched. I can say that I noticed in the last few appointments something was off. She was distracted, edgy. She asked me if I ever went to clients' homes—married clients. And if I knew other LCs who did, was it unusual to pay in cash. And she asked if I had a name and address of a client, if I could find the LC hired to go there."

"What did you tell her?"

"That I only accepted home appointments from married clients if both spouses agreed, but that others have different policies in that area. Cash always works," he added with a smile. "And that it would be difficult with only a name and address to locate the LC booked. Considering the number of agencies, freelancers, levels, it wouldn't be an easy task."

"Has she tried to contact you since her husband's death?"

"No."

"When's your next appointment?"

"A week from Wednesday. She cancelled our last appointment as she was getting ready for her trip. Two o'clock, at the Blackmore again."

"Okay. If she doesn't contact to cancel, I'd like you to keep it."

He let out a sigh that had Eve's brows drawing together.

"All right."

"Problem with that?"

"No. No, no problem. I'm sorry, but if there's more, can we do it later? I actually have an appointment shortly."

"That's fine. That's it for now anyway."

"Charles," Peabody said as they got to their feet. "Is something wrong?"

"No, nothing. Just a lot on my mind. We should all have dinner soon. The six of us."

"That'd be great. You know you could tag me anytime, if you need to talk about anything."

This time when he smiled, it hit his eyes, too. "I know." He cupped Peabody's chin, lowered his lips to hers. "You tell McNab I said he's a lucky man."

Rather than climb right into the car, Peabody paced the sidewalk outside Charles's building. "Why does he seem so worried? Like something's balled up in his belly?"

"I don't know, but that's a good description."

"It can't be about the case, Dallas. It's not about Anders. If Charles knew something—"

"No, it's not about the case. I caught it from him last night before I brought up Anders."

"Maybe he's sick." Worry and distress hitched through the words. "I know how carefully LCs are screened, especially top-levels like Charles, but what if—"

"Peabody, there's nothing we can do about this. And if he was sick, Louise would know."

"You're right. You're right. It's just . . . I love him, you know? Not like *love* —McNab love, but—"

"I get it. I've got a soft spot, too. You can't know everything there is to know about a friend, or fix every problem. It's tough knowing they've got one, but . . ."

She trailed off, narrowed eyes staring at a middle distance.

"What?"

"Just thinking of friends. We've got time to drop in on the last of the mimosas-for-breakfast trio before I meet with Mira. Let's see what Sasha has to say."

Sasha Bride-West wasn't inclined to say much. She was too busy groaning through crunches under the command of the hunk of beefcake she introduced as Sven, her personal trainer.

"Ava and Tommy were going through a patch. Have you ever seen a marriage that didn't? Sven, you're killing me."

"Ten more, my warrior. You'll have abs to slay."

"I can *buy* frigging abs." When he made tsking sounds, she gritted her teeth and kept going. "Anyway, I've had three marriages. Not much smooth sailing, plenty of rough road. Seemed to work the opposite for Ava. But when she asked me to recommend a love machine, and to keep it to myself, I gave her a name—guy's a genius in bed, and damn good company out of it—and kept it to myself."

She collapsed, panting. "Water, Sven, I'm begging you."

He offered her a towel first, to mop her face. She dabbed sweat off skin the color of rich caramel cream.

"Did you follow up?"

"You mean did I ask her for the deets after?" Sasha gulped down water, paused, gulped again. "Of course I did. She wouldn't spill. And I wheedled pretty good."

Sven took the nearly empty water bottle. "It's time for your cardio."

"I hate cardio. Let's skip it and go straight to the massage."

"Sasha," said Sven, severely, and tsked again.

"All right, you sexy sadist." She pulled herself up off the floor of her home gym to climb on the cross trainer. "Give me Paris, Sven. If I'm going to hike and sprint and step, it might as well be Paris. I was going to go over and see her this afternoon," Sasha continued as the Arc de Triomphe flashed on her view screen. "But Bridge has it under control, and she's better with this kind of thing than I am. When Ava's ready for a distraction—for a trip or good drunk or retail therapy—I'm her girl. Brigit's the soft shoulder."

"How was Ava, on this last trip?"

"Good. Fine. Maybe a little tense and moody when we started out, but she chilled. Listen, I can't talk and do this torment at the same time, so is that it?"

"Yeah, that's it. Thanks. We'll see ourselves out."

As Eve turned away, she heard Sasha curse. "Sven, you bastard! There's no hills like these on the frigging Champs-Elysées."

THE MORNING INTERVIEWS GAVE EVE A LOT TO
chew on. If there'd been time, she'd have done
just that, in her office, with her boots on her
desk and her eyes on her murder board. But sessions with Mira
were gold, and not something she could afford to fluff off.

With Peabody writing up the statements and reports, Eve
strode into Mira's outer office.

"Dr. Mira is running a bit behind today," the palace guard
in the guise of admin informed her.

"How behind is a bit?"

"Only a few minutes." The woman smiled. "You're a
minute late yourself, so it won't be long."

"Fine." Turning away, Eve screwed up her face and
mouthed *You're a minute late yourself*. Then she pulled out her
'link and called her oldest friend, Mavis Freestone. Seconds
later, Mavis's happy face, surrounded by an explosion of
lavender hair, popped on screen.

"Dallas! Guess where we're going? Me and Belly
Button?"

"To hell in a handbasket?"

"To the baby doctor. Yes, we are!" Mavis said in an excited coo. "We're all clean and shiny and we're going to the baby doctor so he can look at our little dumpling butt, our magalicious baby girl ears, and our yummy tum-tummy. Isn't that right, Bellamia? Say, hi to Auntie Dallas, sugarcheeks. Say, hi."

Mavis's face was replaced by the round-cheeked (maybe it did have something to do with sugar), bright-eyed, curly-haired infant Mavis had popped out a couple months before. There were candy-striped ribbons tied in bows in the curls, drool dripping down the pudgy chin, and a huge, gummy grin. "Say hi to Bellaloca, Auntie Dallas."

"How's it going, Belle. Mavis."

"Wave bye-bye, my itsy-bitsy baby-boo. Bye-bye to Auntie Dallas. Give her a cooey-dooey—"

"Mavis!"

"What?"

"Mavis, I'm saying this for your own good. You have to stop the insanity. You sound like a moron."

"I *know*." Mavis's eyes, currently purple, rolled. "I can *hear* myself, but I can't stop. It's like a drug. So totally S. Hang on." She set down the 'link, and the screen filled with the rainbow hues of the nursery. Eve heard Mavis cooing and gooing, and assumed she was putting the kid down somewhere.

"Back. She's so beautiful. And she's *so* good. Just this morning—"

"Mavis."

"Sorry. Back." Mavis blew out a breath that fluttered the lavender bangs spiking over her eyes. "I'm kicking out to the studio later, working on a new disc. I'll be around grown-up people, lots of crazy artistic types. That'll help."

"Yeah, crazy artistic types. That's the ticket. I just have a question."

"Lay it down."

"If you and Leonardo were having problems in bed—"

"Bite your tongue in three sections and swallow it!"

"Just hear me out. If you were, and it got sticky."

"It wouldn't get sticky in bed if we were having problems there."

"Ha. Serious. If it got serious. Would you tell me?"

"Affirmative." The purple eyes registered quick worry. "You and Roarke aren't—"

"No. Second part of the question. If you started going to an LC—"

"Can it be a really frosty one? Can it be two frosty ones, with really big wanks?"

"Solid ice, mongo wanks. If you did that, you'd tell me about it."

"Dallas, if I was doing it with a pro, you couldn't shut me up. Which you'd want to because you wouldn't want to hear how they licked warm, melted chocolate off my—"

"No, I wouldn't."

"But since my big, cuddly bear already does that, and his wank is mucho mongo, I wouldn't need the LC."

"Okay." Eve turned when she heard Mira's door open. And staring, quickly ended the call. "Thanks. Later. Hey, Charles, small world."

She might have bashed him with a brick. His expression jumped from shock to disbelief and ended on flustered. "I've heard people call New York a small town," he managed. "I guess this is what they mean. I was just . . . Well."

"Eve." With a warm and welcoming smile on her pretty face, Mira stepped beside Charles. "I'm sorry I kept you waiting. Come right in. Charles, always a pleasure."

"Thank you. I'll . . ." He gestured without any of his usual style. "Let you get to work."

Over her shoulder, Eve watched him stride rapidly away as she moved into Mira's office. "What's all that about?"

"Have a seat. We'll have some tea."

While Eve frowned, Mira moved with her usual graceful efficiency between the two scoop chairs to the AutoChef to order the flowery tea she seemed to live on. Her hair, a cannily highlighted sable, swung smoothly around her patient face, setting off her calm blue eyes. Her suit, a warm and dull gold today, showed off good legs.

"Since you don't have a hair out of place, I'm guessing he didn't drop by to bang you."

Mira set delicate cups on the table between the chairs, and laughed with delight. "Wouldn't that have been interesting? Because it is, I have no intention of confirming or denying." She sat, crossed her legs smoothly, studied Eve's face. "You're annoyed because two of your friends have some private business they're not inclined to share with you."

"I'm not annoyed." Irked, Eve decided, maybe she was a little irked. "The vic's wife is one of Charles's clients, and I interviewed him regarding that this morning, so—"

"I'll tell you that what Charles and I discussed has nothing whatsoever to do with your investigation. Now, about your investigation—"

"Is he in trouble?"

Mira's eyes softened. "No, Charles isn't in trouble. He has a lot on his mind at the moment."

"So he keeps saying," Eve replied, and dropped into a chair. "People are too much damn work."

"They certainly can be."

"I could find out. It's my damn job to find things out."

"But you won't, because I've just told you he isn't in trouble, and you won't intrude."

"If these people wouldn't crisscross all the time in front of where I need to go, I wouldn't have to think about them."

Mira sipped her tea, but hiding her smile didn't hide the open amusement in her eyes. "Your life's more crowded than it used to be. And you're more contented."

"Yeah, I'm feeling real cozy right now. Forget it." She shrugged it off. Charles was a big boy. "You read the file?"

"Yes." Mira took another sip of tea as—Eve knew—she aligned her thoughts. "In my opinion, Anders knew his killer. The method used, the staging surrounding it, wasn't just personal, but intimate. Sexual, of course, but sex isn't always intimate. And there is no physical or forensic evidence that the victim engaged in sexual relations with the killer, or anyone on the night of the murder."

"Nope, he was still holding a full load. No fluids on the sheets or on the body itself. No hair, but for a few strays from the vic, skin."

"Yet it was staged to appear otherwise, and the staging's important. It took time, and planning and preparation. The killer thought about how this could and would be done for some time. There's no impulse here, no passion. A sense of the dramatic, even the theatric, but that underlying sense of order. It feels female. That may be sexist, but it doesn't feel like a same sex crime."

"If it was, he'd've staged the body differently. Given the logistics of man-on-man sex, I think a male killer would have positioned the body differently."

Mira nodded. "That's a good point."

"And even though I told Peabody not to jump to female off the get, it strikes me that if we were dealing with a man—again if sex was part of it—there'd have been more anger. If Anders was gay, he was deep in the closet. Added to it, in my interviews with the wife, she admits they'd had discussions about his sexual preferences, and she always speaks of women."

"A female killer then, one who is able to resist impulse, at least long enough to plan, and to execute that plan. One who enjoys the elaborate, the symbolic. Who had or believed she had an intimate relationship with the victim, who certainly at some point had a sexual one with him. Someone who finds sex both powerful and compelling, and demeaning."

"There are LCs like that," Eve speculated. "Who get wrapped up in it—like an addict—then burn out."

"Yes, which is why they're screened so thoroughly before licensing and thereafter to keep the license."

"Are you leaning toward pro?"

"It certainly could be—there are factors that indicate that sort of intimacy again, and distance. A professional companion must subjugate his or her own needs in order to tailor the relationship to the client's demands. The nature and the length of the relationship is completely in the client's hands."

"That's what they're paid for," Eve commented.

"Yes, and the most successful are able to consider it *as a* profession, who enjoy their work, or consider it a public service. Here, the victim was bound, was naked. He was the supplicant, the submissive. The scarfing, another symbol of who is in control, who is dominant."

And speaking of S and M, bondage, and other fringe areas of sex, Mira sipped her flowery tea. "This was a sex crime, certainly, but not one of sexual rage, or revenge. The genitals aren't destroyed or mutilated, but spotlighted."

"There's the word for it."

Mira smiled a little. "Your crime scene notes indicate he insisted the bedroom door remain closed, had black drapes, and so on. This was a private man, one who had strong feelings about bedroom privacy. So by spotlighting his most private area, his most private business, the killer demeans him. Humiliates him even after death. And yet—"

"She—since we're going with she—tranqs him halfway to a coma first. She didn't want him to feel the pain or the fear. Didn't want him to suffer the pain." And that was a particular element that stuck in Eve's craw. "It doesn't fit."

"It's a contradiction, I agree. But people can be contradictory. It may have been an accident, may have been she miscalculated the dose. And before you say it, I will: No, I don't think it was a miscalculation. Too much prep work to make such a big mistake."

Eve sat a moment, then picked up the tea and drank before she remembered it wasn't coffee. "Ah." She set it down again. "I like the wife for it."

Intrigued, Mira cocked her head. "I thought it was confirmed the wife wasn't in New York during the time of the murder."

"She wasn't."

"You suspect she hired the killing?"

"I've got nothing to support that. Nothing. Plus, I work back to why does a hire tranq him so heavily. What does a hire care if the target suffers? I'm going to have Roarke go over her financials, dig for other accounts, but it doesn't feel like a hit. At least not a pro."

"Why do you like the wife?"

"She's smart. She's a planner. She's got an answer for everything. Her responses, reactions, her demeanor, all perfect, all just right. Like she fucking studied on it. And maybe it's pushing me toward her but I can't get my head around this *arrangement* she said she and the vic had."

Pushing up to pace, Eve ran it by Mira, condensing it down to the basics.

"You don't believe her," Mira concluded. "More, you don't believe a couple inside a marriage could, or would, come to an agreement like this arrangement on sexual relationships."

"Objectively, I know people could, and would, because objectively I know people are completely screwed up. But it doesn't fit for me, it doesn't . . . It's like this one false note playing over and over in a song, and it throws me out every time. I don't know if I don't like the damn song, or if the song's bullshit."

"Objectivity is key to what you do, but so is instinct. If the note strikes you false, again and again, then you'd need to decide which note you'd play instead."

"Huh. How does it strike you?"

"I haven't heard it played from the source, and that can make a difference. But I will say that marriage partners often make arrangements and bargains that seem odd, or even wrong, to someone looking—or listening—in."

"Yeah, I keep coming back to that, too. People do the whacked all the time."

Time to let it stew, Eve decided as she hopped on a glide to start the trip back to Homicide. Time to take another look at the facts and evidence, and let the personalities and speculations simmer. With that in mind, she switched glides to detour to the Electronic Detectives Division. A face-to-face with its captain, and her old partner, might give her another angle on the security breach. She skirted by a couple of cops leaning back on the glide and jawing about basketball, wound her way around a grim-faced woman with her arms folded and piss in her eye before she ran into a logjam of bodies.

She smelled bad cologne, worse coffee, and fresh-baked goods as she snaked and elbowed her way through. Because the elevators were always worse, she stuck with the glides. As she neared EDD, the tone changed. The cops got younger, the clothes more trendy, the visible body piercings more plentiful. The smells edged toward candy and fizzy drinks. Every mother's son or daughter was hooked up—pocket 'links, ear links, headsets so the chatter jittered out, the noise of it rising through the corridor and reaching critical mass inside the squad room.

She'd never known an e-detective to be still for more than five minutes. They bopped, danced, tapped, jiggled. Eve figured it would take her less than that five minutes to go stark raving mad if she rode a desk in EDD. But it suited Feeney. He might have been old enough to have fathered most of his

detectives, and his idea of fashion ran to making sure his socks
matched, but the color and buzz of EDD fit him like one of
his wrinkled suits.

Naturally.

She turned toward his office and his open door. An
explosion of sound had her pausing, then approaching with
more caution. Feeney sat at his desk. His ginger hair with its
generous dashes of gray sat on his head like an electrified cat.
Beneath it, his comfortably droopy face was clammy and pale
if you overlooked the bright red nose that sat in the middle
like a stoplight.

The explosion of sound came again in the form of three
blasting sneezes, followed by a rattling wheeze, and a barking
curse.

"Man, you look bad."

His puffy eyes lifted. The shadows under them seemed to
droop right down to his clammy cheeks. "Got a freaking son
of a bitching cold."

"Yeah, I heard that. Maybe you should be in bed."

"I'm in bed, the wife's on me like white on tofu, how she
told me shoulda worn the muffler, and how didn't she give
me those nice earmuffs for Christmas. Damn things make me
look like I got a couple of red rats coming out of my ears.
She'll want to be pouring Christ knows into me."

He hacked, sneezed, cursed. And Eve eased back another
few inches.

"Plus, she's been taking some godforsaken class on
alternative medicine, and has it in her head colonics are the
cure for every damn thing. You think I want a colonic?"

"I really don't."

He blew his nose heroically. "You want a rundown on the
Sanders electronics."

"Anders." She could almost see the microscopic germs
dancing and mating gleefully in the air around him. "Feeney,
you gotta go home."

"I'm going to ride it out. Got inhalers, and decongestants. Don't work for shit, but I got them. I get a brain tumor, they can fix it, no problem. I get a lousy germ, and they got nothing."

"Blows, but—"

"Come on in, I'll bring up the file."

She studied him, her trainer, her mentor, her longtime partner. He was, in every way that counted, a father. And she thought of the gleeful germs banging each other all over the office. "Ah, actually, I've got to get back down. I forgot something."

"This'll only take a minute."

"Feeney, I'm not coming in there, I'm not taking one step closer without a hazmat suit. You're dog sick, you're contagious, I can actually see your germs flying around in the air having a party. You need to go home."

He lowered his head to the desk. "Stun me, will you, kid? I'm too weak to pull my own weapon and do it myself."

"Shit." She glanced back, saw McNab's cube was empty. Figured. "You." She jabbed a finger at the closest live body, even if it was clad in a banana yellow skin suit with knee-high purple airboots. "Your captain needs transportation home. Now. Arrange it. Who's next in rank?"

"Ummmm."

"Jesus. Get the transpo. I want a vehicle ready to go, and an officer at the elevator door of the garage, this sector, ground level, by the time I get there. If it's not—who are you?"

"Um, Detective Letterman."

"If it's not, Detective Letterman, I'm coming back up here and peeling you like the banana you resemble. Clear?"

"Yes, sir."

"Then do it!" Eve took several deep breaths, like a diver preparing to go under then, holding it, went into the red zone. She grabbed Feeney's coat, his hat, his scarf. "Come on, get these on."

"Wanna die at my desk," he whimpered, "not in bed like an old man."

"Jesus, stop being a baby. You're not going to die. Get your coat on. Don't breathe on me. Wear the hat. What the hell's wrong with you coming in today?"

His glassy eyes rolled up to hers. "You're turning into a woman on me, fussing and nagging."

Insulted, she yanked the hat down over his ears herself. "Watch it, pal, or I'll deck you and have a couple of your fruit baskets out there cart you out."

"That's better." He braced a hand on the desk. "You know, Dallas, I think I'm pretty fucking sick."

"That's the smartest thing you've said since I got here. Let's go." She put an arm around his waist, led him out. In the squad room, one glare cut off any questions or comments. "Call Maintenance," she ordered as she hauled Feeney out. "Have them disinfect that office."

"Sanders," Feeney wheezed.

"Anders," she corrected and called for the elevator.

"Remote was a slick one. Custom."

"Okay." When the elevator doors opened, occupants took one look at Feeney. The protests rang out immediately. "Make room or get the hell off." People scattered, deserted the ship as she pulled Feeney on. "Garage," she ordered, "ground level."

"Shut it down, booted it up the same way," Feeney continued. "No tampering with the locks. Knew the code or had a clone. Can't find any indication of cloning. Have to be slick, too."

"Okay." How *long* did it take to get to the damn garage? How soon after breeding did germs give birth to new ones?

"Nothing on the house 'links looks hinky. Got a list of 'em in the report."

"Yeah."

"Pocket 'link either. Office 'links. Going back another week on the lot, but nothing popping."

"I got it, Feeney."

"Nothing popping on his comps either." He slumped against Eve like a drunk. "Guy had a million of 'em, so it's taking awhile. Personals don't show anything off."

"You get to the wife's yet?"

"Whose wife?"

"Never mind." When the doors opened, a burly, hard-eyed uniform stepped forward. Letterman, she thought, could live.

"Captain Feeney?"

"Right here. Where's your ride?"

He gestured to a black-and-white. "Let me give you a hand. Poor bastard looks pretty sick."

"What's the closest health center?" she asked as between them they maneuvered Feeney into the backseat where he simply sprawled out facedown.

"Got a walk-in clinic on Broadway and Eighteen."

"Take him there."

"Aw, Dallas," Feeney mumbled.

"Stay with him," Eve continued. "I'll contact his wife. When she gets there, if she wants you to stay, you stay."

"Yes, sir."

"Name?"

"Klink."

"Take care of him, Officer Klink."

She slammed the door, stepped back. And watching Klink drive Feeney away wondered if she had time for a detox session.

She settled for scrubbing her hands as if her next task was to perform surgery. And tagging Feeney's wife on the move, made her way back to her own division to track down McNab. She had visions of EDD throwing an orgy of biblical proportions without Feeney in command. Just as she was about to try for McNab, she swung into her own bullpen and saw him.

His back was to her, but there was no mistaking Ian McNab. Who else had that skinny build, the long tail of blond hair flopping down the back of a shirt that resembled the view through a kaleidoscope? And who else would have his flat ass on her partner's desk?

"McNab, get your pitiful excuse for an ass off Peabody's desk and into my office."

She didn't bother to wait to see if he obeyed. She didn't doubt he would, or that he'd slip Peabody a little pinch or tickle before he did. Some things she didn't need to witness.

By the time she got coffee, he was bouncing into her office. "Hey, Dallas, I just came down to—"

"Who's the ranking officer under Feeney?"

"Ah, that would be . . . yeah, that would probably be DS Reedway. Why?"

"I just had Feeney hauled off to the health center. His—"

"Jeez." MacNab's soft green eyes clouded with worry. "Is he that bad? He looked rough this morning."

"Bad enough. Inform your detective sergeant that your captain's out sick. If he needs any information or assistance, he can contact me."

"She. DS Melodie Reedway."

"A cop named Melodie. It's just not right." She waved that off. "If your ranking officer has no objections, I'd like you as primary e-man on the Anders investigation. You're annoying, but at least I know what to expect from you."

He grinned at her. "I've been working it. I came down to give you an update."

"Feeney just gave me one on the way down to transpo—or partially. Have you started on the wife's electronics?"

"We focused on the vic's first, and he has serious boatloads. Fairly iced. Guy liked UTD—up-to-date," he translated when Eve frowned. "I can shift over to the wife's if you want. Anything special I'd be looking for?"

"Yeah, her having a conversation with the killer would be nice. You know the particulars of the case, you're a detective. You'll know when you see or hear it. Get back up there, McNab."

"Okay. Listen, I'll give Mrs. Feeney a call, let her know."

"Already done. But you could check in with an Officer Klink. He's with Feeney."

"Okay. Hey, it's mag about Peabody doing *Now* tonight. She's freaked. I was giving her a pep talk just now."

"As long as that's all you were giving her. Leave now, and don't touch my partner on the way out."

She shut the door behind him. After topping off her coffee, she sat at her desk, put her boots up on it. And studied her murder board.

Anders, Thomas A., she thought. Age sixty-one, wealthy and successful. Married, no children. Loving uncle to his only nephew, who stands as a major heir and successor. Enjoyed sports and electronic toys—and, according to his spouse, kinky sex. Staunch friend. Fair employer. Golf dates, tennis dates, season tickets to every sport known to man. Boxed seats.

Swiveling away from the murder board she brought the file up on her computer, flipped through for the crime scene photos not on the board, then studied her own record of the victim's closet/dressing room area.

Suits, sure. Looked like maybe a dozen. Two tuxes. Dress shirts, ties. Yeah, yeah. All that took up one wall of the room. The short wall. And filling the two longer walls were the casual clothes, the sports clothes. Golf pants, khakis, sports shirts, shorts, track pants, sweatshirts. And in the drawers, what had she seen when she'd opened the drawers?

Dress socks, she recalled, pulling it into her head. High-end sweaters—the cashmere, the merino wool, the alpaca. Lots of T-shirts—short- and long-sleeved. A lot with sports logos, team emblems. His own brand. Dozens of sports socks.

Boxer shorts. Plain white boxers, plain white undershirts. Tailored pajamas.

Interesting.

She added some notes to the file. After a quick knock, Peabody poked her head in. "Dallas, Ben Forrest is here. He'd like to see you."

Eve thought of the murder board, started to tell Peabody to have him wait, then thought better of it. "Send him on back."

She finished her notes, saved to the file. When the next knock sounded, she called out an absent, "Come in."

"Lieutenant, I appreciate you—" She watched Ben's face. Watched the tired eyes go wide, and the stunned horror turn them glassy. "God, oh, God."

"I'm sorry, Mr. Forrest." She stood, angled so she blocked his view of his uncle's photos. "I wasn't thinking. Let's take this outside."

"I—I . . . I know what you told me, and what they're saying in the media. How he died. But . . ."

Eve took her coat off the hook, tossed it over the board. "Sit down." She gave him a light shove to see that he did, then got him a bottle of water.

"Who would do that to him? Who would humiliate him that way? Killing him wasn't enough?" Rather than drink, Ben slapped the bottle against his palm. "It wasn't enough to take his life?"

"Who would want to humiliate him that way?"

When his gaze lifted to Eve, the fury burned. "I don't know. I swear to God, I don't know. If I did, if I even thought, maybe, maybe him or her, I'd tell you. I loved him, Lieutenant Dallas."

"I believe you. You traveled with him on occasion. On business, or pleasure. Golf trips, sports events."

"Yeah. I guess we averaged at least a trip a month."

"Ben, look at me. I believe you loved him, and I'm telling you if you hold back you're not helping him. So think before you answer me. When you traveled, just the two of you, did he ever seek out women, did he ever arrange for companionship—professional or otherwise?"

"No. Wait." He held up a hand, closed his eyes, and took a few breaths. "We nearly always shared a two-bedroom suite. We could hang out together that way. I can't swear that he was always alone in his section of the suite, or that he never went on the prowl after I was down for the night. I can't swear to it. I can only swear to you that I never saw or heard any sign of that kind of thing. I never knew him to seek out companionship. He used to ask me, to razz me sometimes, about finding a woman and settling down. Lieutenant, he was *settled*. If you're digging through the dirt somebody smeared on him, you're never going to find who did this to him. Because it's a goddamn lie."

"Okay, Ben. How about this? The two of you traveled a lot together, just the two of you. Did you ever hit any strip clubs, sex clubs? Just a boys' night out kind of thing?"

"No. That wasn't Uncle Tommy's style, and he'd've been embarrassed to go to a place like that with me. We went to games, sports bars, that kind of thing."

"All right."

He nodded, then twisted off the cap, drank the water. "They contacted Ava, and said we could have him now. I'm taking care of the arrangements. I wanted to come here to see if there's anything. Anything you can tell me."

"I can tell you that your uncle is my priority. Are you having a memorial?"

"Tomorrow." He drank again. "We didn't want to wait. Brigit's helping with the details. He'd want simple. He liked simple best."

"Who decorated the house?"

He let out a surprised laugh. "Ava. And yeah, it's not simple. Uncle Tommy liked it though, got a kick out of what he called Ava's Palace."

"I bet. The style's a lot different in his office."

"Yeah. Guy world. That's what he'd say."

"Did he take sleep aids?"

"I . . . I don't think so. I mean, maybe once in a while. I don't remember him mentioning anything like that, but I don't guess it ever came up. I know he liked the door closed, the drapes drawn when he went to bed. He said it was the only way he could get a good night's sleep. So, I guess that sort of thing was his sleep aid."

"Okay."

"Okay. Anyway, thanks." He got to his feet, and his gaze traveled back to the board covered now by Eve's coat. "I'm glad I saw that. Not the images, I'll never be glad of that. I'm glad I saw that you had that in here. That you're looking at it, that you can't turn around in this room without seeing what was done to him. It helps me know you mean it. He's your priority."

Alone, Eve turned back to the board. She lifted off her coat, tossed it over the visitor's chair. And she looked into Ava Anders's eyes.

"You're a liar," Eve stated aloud. "You're a liar, and I'm going to prove it."

8 EVE CHECKED THE TRANSMISSION HERSELF, THEN rechecked it. It was indisputable that Greta Horowitz contacted Ava Anders, the call originating from the house in New York and going to the room registered to Ava on St. Lucia. The transmission ran from 6:14 a.m. to 6:17 a.m..

With her eyes closed, Eve replayed the copy of the transmission provided by EDD. Ava had blocked video, but Eve did the same herself when calls came in while she was in bed. A pity though, a damn shame. It would've been good to see Ava's face, to read her body language. Still, the voice was pitch-perfect—every hill and valley. Sleepy annoyance, to impatience, to shock and through to grief. Every note perfectly played.

Still . . .

"Computer, send a copy of this transmission, and a copy of the recorded interview with Ava Anders today to the lab. Mark attention Chief Berenski. Memo attached: Require voice print analysis and verification ASAP. Require verification recorded voices are the same individual, and that neither sample was prerecorded or transmitted from a remote location. Dallas, Lieutenant Eve."

She added the case file name and number.

Could've worked it that way, Eve mused. Tricky, but not impossible. A voice double, a transmission bounce. She'd have EDD take another look at that possibility. But if that didn't work . . .

She did a search on private transportation, and the fastest shuttle time possible from New York to St. Lucia. The results frustrated her.

Not enough time, she admitted. There just hadn't been enough time to travel from the crime scene back to St. Lucia, back to the hotel room on the island to take the call, not even if Ava had gone off book with the transportation. Physics gave her an unimpeachable alibi.

She went back to the time line, tried to find a hole in it. Her 'link signaled, with an order to report to her commander.

To save time she squeezed herself on an elevator. She rode up partway with cops, lawyers, and a small, long-eared dog.

"Eye wit," the cop standing beside the dog told her.

"That so?"

"More like nose witness. Owner got himself mugged while he was walking Abe here. Claims Abe'll ID the guy who mugged him by smell." The cop shrugged. "We got three possibles so, what the hell."

"Yeah, good luck with that."

Eve tried to work out how they expected to convince the PA to bring charges against a suspect on the nose of a dog as she covered the rest of the distance to her commander's office.

"Go right in, Lieutenant." The admin gestured. "They're waiting for you."

Commander Whitney sat at his desk, his back to the view of the city he'd protected and served more than half of his life. His face showed the years, but Eve had always felt it showed them in a way that mattered. Showed in the lines and grooves dug into his dark skin that he'd lived those years, and remembered them.

He wore his hair short and, though she suspected his wife would have preferred it otherwise, he let the salt sprinkle liberally over the pepper. He carried his big, wide build well, and held his command with a strong hand.

"Commander," she began, then paused as the man sitting in the high-backed visitor's chair facing the desk rose. "Chief Tibble."

Not just the commander, she thought, reevaluating, but the Chief of Police.

"Lieutenant." Whitney pointed to the second chair. "Have a seat."

She obeyed, though she preferred standing, preferred giving her oral reports on her feet.

"Lieutenant." Tibble took the jump, and made her wonder why, if this was his meet, she wasn't sitting in The Tower. "I asked the commander to give me a few minutes with you here. Regarding the Anders investigation."

"Yes, sir."

He sat back. A lean man, he favored good suits, and—as she recalled—a good Scotch. Like Whitney, he'd come up through the ranks, and though he was now—essentially—a politician, the office hadn't shoved the cop out of him.

"My reason for asking is somewhat personal."

"Did you know Mr. Anders, sir?"

"No, I didn't. My wife, however, is acquainted with his widow."

Eve thought: *Crap.*

"They've served on several committees together. In any case, when my wife contacted Mrs. Anders to offer her condolences, Mrs. Anders expressed considerable concern over how the current media tone will affect not only her late husband's reputation, the business, but the charitable programs associated with Anders Worldwide. I'm in the position of asking you to assist in damping down the media."

"With all respect, Chief Tibble, how do you propose I do that? It's not Code Blue, and if it was termed such at this point, if we instigated a media blackout now, it would only feed the beast."

"I agree. Is there any area of your investigation at this point that would give them a different bone to gnaw on?"

"I believe the circumstances under which the victim was found was a setup. But if I toss that bone out, I would jeopardize the investigation, and alert the suspect to the line I'm pursuing."

"You have a suspect?"

"I do. The widow."

Tibble let out a sigh, tipped back his head and looked at the ceiling. "Hell. How—" He cut himself off. "Sorry, Jack, this is your area."

"Lieutenant, explain how a woman who was several thousand miles away at the time of the murder heads the top of your list of suspects?"

"It's not confirmed she was in St. Lucia, Commander. There was no video on the transmission from the house manager. I've sent that transmission and a sample of Mrs. Anders's voice from an interview this morning to the lab for voice print comparison. Even if that confirms her alibi, she's involved. She's part of it. She's lying, Commander. She's lying," she repeated, looking back at the chief. "She tells your wife she's concerned about the fallout from the media. The fallout revealing her husband engaged in extra-marital sex, which included bondage, scarfing, but the widow is the only person interviewed who confirms those allegations."

"Arguably," Whitney said, "the wife would know her husband's sexual proclivities while others don't."

"Yeah, and that's something she counted on. She's wrong, Commander. I don't have it solid yet, but I know she's wrong.

The staging's wrong. It's too elaborate, too . . . fussy," she said for a lack of better. "Whoever did it knew the house, the security, knew Anders's habits. There were little mistakes, but for the most part, it was well-planned. Whoever did it wanted to humiliate him, to open him to the very media frenzy that's happening. Mrs. Anders is an expert in PR. Just like she knows that if she plays this right, after the jokes about *her* die down, she'll come out golden. Who gets the sympathy, the support, the understanding? She'll be the victim, and she'll be the one squaring her shoulders and going on."

"Are you saying she did this *for* the publicity?" Whitney demanded.

"No, sir, but it's a side benefit she'd be aware of, and will find a way to exploit.

"It wasn't a stranger, Commander, it wasn't a pro, and it wasn't an accident. That leaves me with Ava Anders."

"Then prove it," Whitney told her.

"Yes, sir. I have Roarke on as expert consultant, analyzing all the financials, looking for any hidden accounts."

"If anyone could find them."

"Yes, sir," she repeated. "I intend to run a deeper background check on Mrs. Anders, and interview her first husband, as well as other friends and associates of hers and the victim's."

She rose. "Regarding the media, Chief Tibble, Detective Peabody will be appearing on *Now* this evening. I can't speak for Nadine Furst, but I do have knowledge she knew the victim and liked him. Respected him."

"Why Peabody," Whitney demanded, "and not you?"

"Because, Commander, she needs a shove into the deep end of the pool. And Nadine is very fond of Peabody. That doesn't mean she won't push or dig, but she won't eat her alive. And, in my opinion, sir, Detective Peabody can and will handle herself."

"If she fucks up, Lieutenant?" Tibble smiled. "You'll be the one dealing with my wife."

"So noted. Actually, it might be helpful for me to speak with her, if you don't object."

"Go right ahead. But fair warning. She's feeling very protective of Mrs. Anders at the moment."

Varying approaches on interviewing the wife of the Chief of Police occupied her mind all the way back to Homicide. Diplomacy could be key, and that particular key tended to go slippery in her fingers. But she'd hold it steady. Next came the trick of interviewing a cop's wife—the *top* cop's wife—without letting her suspect *you* suspected the woman she was "feeling very protective of."

Just have to pull it off, Eve thought. That's why they paid her the medium bucks.

"Lady! Yo, lady!"

It took her a minute, but she made the voice, and the small package it came from. Coffee-black skin, vivid green eyes, a curly high-top of hair. The boy hauled the same battered suitcase—approximately the size of Staten Island—he'd hauled in December when he'd been hustling the fake cashmere scarves inside it near the splatted body of a jumper on Broadway.

"Didn't I tell you before I'm not a lady."

"You're a cop. I tracked you down, and I've been waiting here, and these other cops tried hassling me about why wasn't I in school and that shit."

"Why aren't you in school and that shit?"

" 'Cause I got business." He shot a finger at her. "With you."

"I'm not buying anything."

"I gotta tip."

"Yeah? I've got one, too. Don't bite off more than you can chew."

"Why not? You can't chew it, you just spit it out anyway."

That wasn't stupid, Eve noted. "Okay, what's your tip?"

"I'll tell you, but I'm pretty thirsty." He gave her the same grin he'd flashed the previous December.

"Do I look like a mark, shortie?"

"You look like the top bitch cop in New York City. That's word on the street."

"Yeah." Maybe she could spare a minute, and the price of a Pepsi. "That is the correct word. Give me the tip, and if I like it, I'll pop for a drink."

"I know where there's suspicious activity, *and* suspicious characters. I'm gonna take you."

"Kid, you're hard-pressed to find anywhere in the city where there aren't suspicious activities and suspicious characters."

He shook his head in disgust. "You a cop or what?"

"We established that. And I've got cop work to do."

"Same guy, same place, same times. Every day for five weeks. I seen it. Maybe they see me, too, but they don't mind me 'cause I be a kid."

No, Eve thought, not stupid. Most people didn't see kids. "What does this same guy do at the same place at the same times every day for five weeks that makes him a suspicious character involved in suspicious activity?"

"He goes in with a big old shopping bag heavy the way he carries it. And a couple minutes later, *bop!* he comes out again, and he's got a different bag. It ain't heavy either." The kid adjusted the airboard slung at his back.

"Where is this den of iniquity?"

The kid's brow furrowed like an elderly grandfather's. "Ain't no den. It's a store. I'm gonna take you. It's a good tip. I oughta get an orange fizzy."

"You oughta get a kick in the ass." But she pulled out credits, passed them over, jerked a thumb at Vending. While he plugged in credits, she considered. The kid was sharp enough, and had probably seen just what he said. Meaning the store was a front—or a beard—for passing off wallets, bags, and whatever else the street thief could lift from tourists and New Yorkers foolish enough to get their pockets picked.

The kid sucked on the fizzy. "We gotta get, so you can catch them."

"Give me the location, and I'll send cops over."

"Uh-uh. I gotta show you. That's the deal."

"What deal? I didn't make any damn deal. I don't have time to go driving around, waiting for some pocket man to make his bag drop."

The boy's eyes were like glass, and just as sharp. "I guess you don't be much of a cop."

She could've stared him down, she was pretty sure of it. But he made her shoulder blades itch. "You're a pain in the ass." She checked the time, calculated. Odds were the drop spot was in Times Square where she'd had the misfortune of meeting the kid in the first place. She could swing by there on the way home. Maybe she'd get some damn work done at home without being interrupted every five minutes.

"Wait here," she ordered. "If you're not right here when I get back, I'll hunt you down like a dog and stuff you inside that suitcase. Dig?"

"I gonna show you?"

"Yeah, you're going to show me. Stay." She strode into the bullpen. "Peabody, I have to make a run, semi-personal, then I'm going to work at home."

"But—but—I have to leave for 75 in . . . in like any minute!"

"Do that, copy any new data, shoot it to my home office."

"But . . ." On a run, Peabody rushed after Eve. "You're not going with me?"

"Pull yourself together, Peabody." Eve grabbed file discs, tossed them into her bag. "You've done on-air before."

"Not like *this*. Dallas, you've gotta go with me. I can't go there by myself. I'll—"

"Jesus, how can people be *worth* all this? Take McNab. Tell his DS I cleared it." Eve dragged on her coat. "And don't fuck up."

"You're supposed to say break a leg!" Peabody called out as Eve stomped away.

"Fuck it up and I'll break your damn leg myself."

"Dallas."

"What?" She rounded on Baxter with a snarl, then remembered. "Sorry. Any new leads?"

"No. Have you—"

"No, I haven't had a chance to look at the file. Soon as I can, Baxter." A headache brought on, she knew, by sheer irritation, began to pulse behind her eyes. "Let's go, kid, and if you're stringing me you'll find out firsthand why the word is I'm top bitch cop."

In the garage the kid shook his head sorrowfully at her vehicle. He climbed in, steadied the suitcase on his lap, took a long study of the dash, then turned those Venusian green eyes on her. "This ride is crap."

"You got better?"

"I ain't got ride, but I know crap. How come top bitch cop has a crap ride?"

"This is a question I ask myself daily. You got a name?"

"You got one?"

She had the oddest feeling she amused him. "Lieutenant Dallas."

"What kinda name's Loo-tenit?"

"It's rank. It's my rank."

"I don't got no rank, don't got no ride."

"Name, kid, or the adventure stops here."

"Tiko."

"Okay, Tiko, where are we going?"

He put on what Eve supposed was his enigmatic face. "Maybe we cruise over 'round Times Square."

She drove out of the garage, wedged into traffic. "What's in the case this time?"

"I got me the cashmere scarves *and* matching caps. How

come you don't wear no cap? Heat falls out the top of your head you don't wear a cap."

"How come you're not wearing one?"

"Sold it." He grinned at her. "I'm a selling fool."

"As a selling fool, Tiko, why did you haul yourself and that case all the way down to Central to tell me about the drop?"

"I didn't drop nothing."

Not as streetwise as he appeared, she decided. "About the suspicious activities."

"I don't like suspicious activities round my yard. I got business. Somebody steals wallets and shit, then people don't have the money to buy my scarves and caps and pretty soon in good weather my one hundred percent *silk* scarves and ties."

Since it made perfect sense, Eve nodded. "Okay, why not tell one of the uniforms on the beat?"

"Why do that when I gotta line on the top bitch?"

Tough to find a hole in his logic, Eve decided. "You got digs, Tiko?"

"I got digs, don't you worry. Maybe you turn on Forty-fourth, and dump the ride there. Anybody knows anything sees this crap ride, makes it for a cop's."

Once again, he had it nailed. She cut over, shoving her way crosstown. Maybe the kid was lucky, but she scored a second level street spot between Seventh and Eighth.

"You got your weapon and shit, right?" he asked as they started to hoof it through the throng and east toward Broadway.

"I got my weapon and shit. Is this place on the west or east side of Broadway?"

"East. I got my yard on the west side, work it from Forty-second right on up to Forty-seventh. But I can stay mostly round Forty-fourth. Place is 'tween Forty-third and Forty-fourth, right on Broadway. He gonna be coming along pretty soon now."

"Here's how it's going to work. You're going to go on ahead, set up in your usual spot. I'll come along, take a look at your merchandise. You see this guy, you point him out—without pointing, get me? I'll take it from there."

Excitement danced in his eyes. "Like I'm undercover."

"Yeah, that's it. Scram."

He scrammed, short, sturdy legs pumping, huge suitcase bumping. Eve pulled out her communicator and called for a couple of uniforms. When she turned the corner onto Broadway, Tiko had his convertible case unfolded and set on its tripod legs. It didn't surprise her in the least to see he already had a couple of customers.

Broadway's perpetual party rocked with its flashing lights, sky-scraping screens, and billboards. Whole platoons of teenagers filled the sidewalks, zipping on airboards, cruising on skates, or clomping on the current trend of three-inch, gel-soled boots. On their corners, the carts did business zippily, passing out dogs, pretzels, kabobs, scoops of fries or hash, and all manner of liquid refreshment.

Tourists gawked at the colors, the ad blimps, the arcades, and the sex shops, which also did business zippily. Most of those tourists, in Eve's opinion, might have been wearing a neon sign with a blinking arrow pointing at their pockets.

PICK ME.

She sidled up to Tiko's table, and he gave her an exaggerated eyebrow wiggle. "Hundred percent cashmere. Scarves and caps. Got a special price today you buy a set."

"What's so special about it?"

He grinned. "Hundred for the set. Usually it cost you $125. Charge you five times that easy in the store. This here striped one— He's coming now." Tiko dropped his voice to a dramatic whisper, as if his words might carry through the avalanche of noise and across the street. "Red shopping bag. See him—"

"Don't point."

Eve glanced casually over her shoulder. She saw the red bag, and the tall, gangly man in a gray field jacket and black watch cap.

"You gotta go get him. Hundred dollars for the set," Tiko said to a woman who stopped to browse his stock. "Today only. You go on and get him."

Where the hell were her uniforms? "I got cops coming."

"*You* a cop."

"I'll take these," the woman said, digging out her wallet.

Tiko grabbed a clear plastic bag. "He's gonna go in!"

"I'm Homicide. Is there a dead body in there?"

"How do I know?" He managed to bag the cap and scarf, take the money, make change, and stare holes through Eve.

"Crap. You stay here. You stay *exactly* here."

To keep from drawing attention, she crossed at the light, kicked it up to a weaving sprint, ignored the curses from people she bumped aside. She kept the bagman in her crosshairs, and was less than three yards behind him when he turned into a storefront offering New York City souvenirs, including T-shirts at three for $49.95.

She pulled open the door. Short, narrow shop, she noted, evaluating quickly. One male, one female working the side counter, and the bagman heading straight back.

Goddamn uniforms, she thought.

"Help ya?" the woman said, without much interest.

"Yeah, I see something I want." Eve strode up behind the bagman, tapped his shoulder. She angled so his body was between her and the counter, in case the others got frisky, then held up her badge. "You're busted."

The woman at the counter screamed as if an axe cleaved her skull. In the split second that distracted Eve, the bagman's elbow connected with her cheekbone. Stars exploded.

"Goddamn it." Eve rammed her knee up his ass, and backhanded him into the T-shirt display. With the side of her face yipping and her weapon in her hand, she pivoted. "Lady," she warned as the woman scrambled over the counter in a bid for the front door. "One more step and I stun you stupid. On the floor. On the fucking floor, facedown, hands behind your head. You." She jerked her head toward the counterman who stood with his hands high in the air. "You're good. Stay like that. And you."

She gave the bagman an annoyed boot. "Why'd you have to go and do that? It's all worse now, isn't it?"

"I just came in here to buy a T-shirt."

"Yeah? Were you going to pay for it out of one of these?" She toed the collection of wallets and handbags that spilled out of the shopping bag.

She stared blandly at the two uniforms who rushed in from the street. "Gee, sorry, guys. Did I interrupt your coffee break? Check the back. I believe I detect suspicious activity in this establishment." She pressed her fingers lightly to her throbbing cheek. "Fucking A. And call for a bus to haul these fuckheads in. Robbery, trafficking in stolen goods—"

"Hey, Lieutenant! There's a couple hundred wallets and bags back here. And credit/debit card and ID card dupes."

"Yeah?" Eve smiled winningly at the now very sad-eyed man with his hands in the air. "Fraud, identity theft. The gift that keeps on giving."

It took another twenty minutes, but when Eve crossed the street again, Tiko stood exactly where she'd told him.

"I told them, the cops when I saw them coming." He bounced on the toes of his black skids. "I told them where."

"You did good."

"You gotta mouse coming on. You get in a fight with the suspicious character?"

"I kicked his ass. Break it down, Tiko. You're done for today."

"I can get another hour in, make up for going downtown and all."

"Not today."

"You taking those people to jail?"

"The uniforms are taking them. They don't need the top bitch cop to turn the key," she said, anticipating him. "Where are your digs, Tiko?"

He narrowed his eyes. "You don't think I got digs?"

"If you've got them, tell me where so I can take you."

"Round the corner. Apartment on the third floor, above the Greek place. Told you this was my yard."

"Yeah, you did. Break it down. Let's go."

He wasn't happy about it, she could see, but he did it. "Cost me five easy, quitting this early when I took off to go down and get you."

"I bought you a fizzy."

Because his stony stare appealed to her, she dug out some credits. Counted fifty. "That's ten percent of the five you say you lost. I figure it covers your time and your transportation."

"Solid." The credits disappeared into one of several pockets. "You stun any of those people in there?"

"No." What the hell, Eve thought. She could add some juice to the fifty. "But the woman screamed like a girl and tried to run. I told her to drop, or I'd stun her."

"Would ya?"

"Damn right. They'd stolen from a lot of people, and they were making dupe cards in the back. Looks like they were lifting IDs, too."

He shook his head in disgust. "Stealing's lazy."

Intrigued, she looked down at him. "Is it?"

"Shit, yeah. Any lazy dumbass can steal. Takes brains and some juice to *make* money. We up here." He opened a door next to a tiny gyro place. The closet-sized lobby held an elevator. On it the Out of Order sign looked about a decade old. Eve climbed the stairs with the boy. The place smelled like onions and garlic, not entirely unpleasant. The walls were dingy, the steps stained and steep.

She imagined him climbing up and down them every day, hauling his case. Yeah, it took some juice.

On the third floor, he dug out a set of keys from one of his pockets, unlatched three locks. "You can come in you want to meet my granny."

Something was cooking. Eve caught the tomatoey scent when she stepped into the tiny room, which was sparse and lace-curtain tidy.

"That my boy?" someone called through a narrow doorway.

"Yes, ma'am, Granny. I got somebody with me."

"Who you got?" The woman who stepped out of the doorway held a short-handled wooden spoon. Her hair was a white ball of fluff over a face mapped with wrinkles. But her eyes beamed that same vivid green as the boy's. She wore a baggy brown sweater and pants over her thin frame.

Fear came into those eyes, and knowledge with it. She might as well have shouted *cop!* and thrown her hands in the air like the counterman.

"There's no trouble here," Eve said.

"This is my granny. Granny, this is Loo-tenit Dallas. She's the top . . . She's a police."

"He's a good boy." The woman held out a hand so Tiko hurried to her, and she held him tight against her side.

"He's not in trouble."

"We got them, Granny, that's what we did. We got them good."

"Who? What's this about?"

Tiko tugged at her hand. " 'Member how I told you I seen those suspicious characters? You said how they was likely stealing hand over fist. And they were. I went down and told Dallas, and I took her where they were, and she went on over there and arrested them good. Ain't that the way?"

"Isn't that the way," his grandmother corrected absently.

"Tiko alerted me to suspicious activity, and assisted the NYPSD in identifying a front for street theft and identity fraud."

"Oh, my sweet Lord."

"Mrs. . . ."

"I'm so sorry. I'm so flustered, I can't hardly feel my head on my shoulders. I'm Abigail Johnson."

"Mrs. Johnson, you have a very interesting grandson, and one who went above and beyond what most people would. A lot of people owe him for it." She took out a card, searched her pockets until she came up with a pencil stub. "This is my contact information. There's a reward."

"I get a reward? Over my time and transpo?"

"A good deed is its own reward," Abigail told him.

"Yes, ma'am, that's true. However, the NYPSD would like to express its appreciation for good citizenship, and it has a program for just that. If you'll contact the person I've listed on the back of my card, they'll arrange it." She handed the card to Abigail, held out a hand to Tiko. "Nice job, kid."

"Back at cha. Sorry about the mouse."

"Not the first, won't be the last."

"Tiko, go ahead and wash up for supper now. Say goodbye to Lieutenant Dallas."

"See you around. You come on back to my yard, I'll make you a good deal." When he dashed off, Abigail drew a slow breath.

"I homeschool him two hours every evening, seven days a week. We go to church every Sunday. I make sure he's got clothes and good food. I—"

"There's no trouble here, Mrs. Johnson. If you have any, you contact me."

Eve jogged down the stairs, and back out into the cold. A good deed might be its own reward, she thought as she pressed a hand to her aching cheek. But she could sure as hell use an icebag with hers.

9

EVE WALKED INTO THE HOUSE PREPARED FOR HER daily snarkfest with Summerset, who would no doubt have something withering to say about the black eye she was brewing.

And he wasn't there.

She stood for a moment in the empty foyer almost expecting him to materialize like smoke. Puzzled, she poked her head in the front parlor. Fresh flowers, nicely simmering fire—but no Bony Ass. Mild concern jabbed its way through the puzzlement. Maybe he'd caught something like what Feeney had—and there was no possible way she was playing nurse for the resident ghoul.

Still, if he was lying unconscious somewhere in a pool of fever sweat . . . Roarke would just have to get his ass home and deal with it.

She started to turn to the house comp to run a search for him, then the top cop bitch jumped like a rabbit when Summerset's disembodied voice floated into the room.

"As I assume you might have some interest in your partner, you should be aware that Detective Peabody's appearance on *Now* begins in approximately four minutes."

"Fuck." Eve breathed out the word, scowled at the intercom. "I know what time it is." Or she did now. Annoyed, she started up the stairs, and his voice followed her.

"You'll find cold bags in the top, far right drawer of your office kitchen."

She hunched her shoulders—oh, she heard the smug satisfaction—and kept going. In her office she dumped the file bag on her desk, ordered the proper channel on screen. And because her cheek throbbed like a bitch in heat, retrieved and activated the stupid cold bag. With the blessed chill pressed against her face, she booted up her computer. Might as well deal with the next irritation on her list, she thought, and write up her report on the Times Square bust.

She'd barely begun when *Now*'s theme music boomed on. With half an ear, she listened to Nadine's intro, spared a glance at the screen where the reporter's cat's eyes stared soberly back at her. Polished and powerful was the image, Eve supposed, with the streaky blonde hair, subtle jewelry, the good legs highlighted in a sleek copper suit. Of course, most of the viewing audience hadn't seen Nadine dance half-naked at a sex club after a pitcher of zombies.

She introduced Peabody as the dedicated, decorated police officer, and cited some of the more media-worthy cases she'd helped close. When the camera panned over to her partner, Eve pursed her lips.

Trina hadn't gone freaky on her hair and face, Eve noted. She looked young, but not soft, so that was good. The suit, with its military cut, probably worked. And if you didn't know her, you wouldn't notice the utter terror in Peabody's eyes.

"Don't screw up," Eve muttered.

Nadine led her in, softballing a few, and Eve could see Peabody begin to relax. Not *too* relaxed, Eve thought. She's not your friend when you're on-air. Nobody's your friend when you're on-air.

"Damn it, now *I'm* nervous." And because of it, Eve rose and paced in front of the screen as she watched.

Handling it, handling it. Pursuing all leads, blah, blah, blah. Unable to comment on specifics, yada, yada. Peabody confirmed there had been no sign of forced entry—that was okay—and better, dropped in there were indications the security system had been compromised.

They circled around each other on the sexual nature of the murder. It was Nadine's job to dig for details and Peabody's duty to avoid giving them. Standing in front of the screen, Eve felt a quick little twist of pride. They both did nice work.

Enough got in, just enough to confirm the murder had sexual elements. But the tone, the message, transmitted clearly that Thomas A. Anders was the victim. A life had been taken.

Wrapping it up now, Eve realized. Thank Christ.

"Detective," Nadine began, "Thomas Anders was a wealthy man, a strong, visible presence in social and business circles. His prominence must bring a certain pressure onto the investigation. How does that influence your work?"

"I . . . I guess I'd say murder equalizes. When a life's taken, when another individual takes the life of another, there's no class system, no prominence. Wealth, social standing, business, those might all go to motive. But they don't change what was done, or what we as investigators do about it. We work the case the same way for Thomas Anders as we do for John Doe."

"Still, some departmental pressure would be expected when the victim has prominence."

"Actually, it's the media that plays that kind of thing up. I don't get it from my superiors. I wasn't raised to judge a person's worth by what he owns. And I was trained as a cop, as a detective, that our job is to stand for the dead—whoever they were in life."

Eve nodded, dipped her hands into her pockets as Nadine cut away to end the segment and preview the next.

"Okay, Peabody, you can live."

Ordering the screen off, Eve sat at her desk and got back to work.

There she was. Roarke stood in the office doorway, took a few enjoyable minutes to just watch her. She had such a sense of purpose, such a sense of focus on that purpose. It had appealed to him from the first instant he'd seen her, across a sea of people at a memorial for the dead. He found it compelling, the way those whiskey-colored eyes could go flat and cold as they were now. Cop's eyes. His cop's eyes.

She'd taken off her jacket, tossed it over a chair, and still wore her weapon harness. Which meant she'd come in the door and straight up. Armed and dangerous, he thought. It was a look, a fact of her, that continually aroused him. And her tireless and unwavering dedication to the dead—to the truth, to what was right—had, and always would, amaze him.

She'd set up her murder board, he noted, filling it with grisly photos, with reports, notes, names. And somewhere along the line in her day, she'd earned herself a black eye.

He'd long since resigned himself to finding the woman he loved bruised and bloody at any given time. Since she didn't look exhausted or ill, a shiner was a relatively minor event.

She sensed him. He saw the moment she did, that slight change of body language. And when her eyes shifted from her comp screen to his, the cold focus became an easy, even casual warmth.

That, he thought, just that was worth coming home for.

"Lieutenant." He crossed over, lifted her chin with his hand to study the bruising under her eye. "And so, who'd you piss off today then?"

"More like who pissed me off. He's got more than one bruise."

"Naturally. Who might that be?"

"Some mope named Clipper. I busted a snatch, switch, and drop."

"Ah." He cocked his head. "Why?"

"Good question. This kid named Tiko dragged me into it."

"This sounds like a story. Do you want some wine to go with it?"

"Maybe."

"Before you tell me the story, did you catch Peabody's appearance?"

"Yeah. Did you?"

Across the room he contemplated the wine selection, made his choice for both of them. "I wouldn't have missed it. I thought she did brilliantly."

"She didn't screw up."

He laughed, opened the bottle. "High praise, Lieutenant. It's you who trained her. The last thing she said. It's you who trained her to stand for the dead, no matter who they were in life."

"I trained her to work a case. She was already a cop."

"As you were, when Feeney trained you. So it trickles down." He walked back to hand her a glass of wine. "It's a kind of inheritance, isn't it?" With his own wine, he sat on the corner of her desk. "Now, about that eye."

He listened, by turns amused and fascinated. "How old is this Tiko?"

"I don't know. Seven, maybe eight. Short."

"He must be very persuasive as well as short and seven."

"He digs in, that's for sure. It wasn't much of a detour anyway." She shrugged. "And you had to admire his logic, pretty much down the line. They're stealing from potential customers, which cuts into his business. I'm a cop."

"Top bitch cop."

"Bet your ass. So as such I'm supposed to fix it."

"As you did." He brushed a finger over her cheek. "With minimal damage, I suppose."

"Guy had skinny arms, but they were as long as a gorilla's. Anyway, I figure the kid's got a flop—he's too clean and warmly dressed for street—probably with his gray market supplier. Couldn't've been further off there. Little apartment off Times Square with a granny cooking his supper. Great-grandmother," she added. "I ran them on the way home."

"Of course you did."

"Neither's been in any trouble. The same can't be said of Tiko's mother. Illegals busts, solicitation without a license, shoplifting that upped to petty theft that upped to grand larceny. Last couple busts were down in Florida. The granny's been guardian since he was about a year old."

"The father?"

"Unknown. She was afraid I was going to call Child Services. Afraid I was going to call them in, and she could lose the kid."

"Another cop might have."

"Then another cop would've been wrong. Kid's got a decent roof over his head, warm clothes on his back, food in his belly, and somebody who loves him. It's . . ."

"More than we had," Roarke finished.

"Yeah. I thought about that. There's no fear in this kid, and that's about all that was in me at his age. No meanness either, and you had plenty of that running your Dublin alleys. Had to have plenty of it. He's got the chance of a good life ahead of him because someone cares enough."

"From what you've said, he sounds like the kind who'll make the most of that chance."

"That's my take. And I thought about Anders. He wasn't afraid, and from everything I find, he wasn't big on the mean.

But his chance at life was taken. Because someone cared enough to end him."

"Cared enough. Interesting choice of words."

"Yeah." She looked over at her murder board, looked at Ava Anders's ID photo. "I think it fits. Listen, I couldn't get by the lab to browbeat Dickhead into running a voice print. I've got a couple samples here. It probably wouldn't take you long."

"It probably wouldn't." He considered it over a sip of wine. "I might do that for you, if you fixed my supper."

It seemed a fair trade. And if she went for one of her own personal faves—spaghetti and meatballs—he hadn't specified a choice. She continued her run on Ava Anders first, left another message on Dirk Bronson's—the first husband's—voice mail. Then she wandered into the kitchen to program the meal.

She'd only set the plates on her desk when Roarke came back in. She wondered why she even bothered with the lab.

"Good news is, it didn't take long. Bad news, from your standpoint anyway, they're a match."

"Shit. Could the St. Lucia transmission have been by remote?"

"It's not reading that way. I ran it through several types of filters. As your expert consultant, civilian, I have to tell you Ava Anders received that transmission while in the room registered to her in St. Lucia."

"She couldn't have made it back there from New York in the time frame."

"No. It's a bit too tight for that."

"Maybe the time frame's off. Anders was still alive—unconscious, dying, but still alive when the security was booted back, the doors locked again. Maybe it didn't take her as long as I calculated for the setup, and if she reactivated it all by remote, she might have been on her way back to St. Lucia earlier. It'd be tight, but maybe not too tight."

"Ground time from the crime scene to a shuttle hangar, and the same from shuttle to hotel on the island have to be added in. You're reaching, Eve."

"Damn right I'm reaching." Irritated, she scooped up some spaghetti. "I know she's in it. Okay, the vic liked electronics. Could he have a security setup that could be turned off and on by long-distance remote?"

"Not impossible. What do your e-men say?"

"Cloning remote—good shit—short-range. But they weren't looking for long. And Feeney's dog sick with a cold."

"Sorry to hear that."

"I had to practically carry him down to transpo, send him off to a health center, call his wife."

Roarke didn't bother to hide his grin. "Haven't you been the busy little scout today."

"Bite me."

"I rarely think of anything else. I can take a look at the system. As for financials, I haven't found anything off there. No suspicious withdrawals or transfers, no accounts tucked away. Not yet."

Clean, covered, Eve thought. But her gut kept adding "calculated" to that. "If she didn't do it herself and had it done, maybe she didn't use money. There are other incentives. Sex, position, blackmail. Friendship. Isn't there some saying about a real friend's the one who helps you hide the body? She's got a couple of women who strike me as real friends."

"What is it about her, Eve?"

"Things." She stabbed at a meatball. "Her clothes."

"You don't care for her fashion sense?"

"How would I know if she has any? You do." She jabbed the fork with its bite of meatball at him. "Fashion king."

"We do our best."

"So, you're dead asleep, and you get a call. Something terrible's happened, and I'm dead. What do you do?"

It took him a moment to quell the terror, to ignore the small, dark place inside him that feared getting that call every day. "Before or after I fall prostrate with grief?"

"Before, during, and after. Do you peruse your wardrobe and select a coordinating outfit—down to the footwear. Do you deal with your hair so it's perfectly groomed?"

"With my considerable skills and innate instincts that would take no time at all."

"Keep it up and I'll dump red sauce all over your fashionable smarty-pants."

"That statement is one of the countless reasons why, under the circumstances you described, I'd be lucky to remember to dress at all. But then not everyone loves the same way, Eve, or to the same levels. Or reacts the same way to hard news."

"The call for transpo went out from her hotel room six minutes after she ended the transmission with Greta. But, there's nearly a fifty-minute lag between then and her leaving the hotel. She ordered coffee, juice, fresh berries, and a croissant from her in-room AutoChef—I had the hotel look up her record. She ordered her little continental breakfast *before* she called for transpo arrangements."

"Ah. There's cold blood."

"Yeah. A little thing maybe—not evidence, but it's a thing. A lawyer would argue it's nothing. She was in shock. But it's bullshit. She was wearing perfume when she got to the house, and earrings, and a bracelet that matched her wrist unit. She didn't contact Forrest, not for hours after getting the news."

"Little things," Eve repeated. "I believe she planned it out, studied every detail, covered every track. But she can't cover who she is. She can't quite cover up her self-interest, her vanity or the calculation I see in her eyes every time I look at her."

"She didn't plan out everything. She didn't plan on you."

"I'm going to the memorial tomorrow. I'm going to talk to her again, to her friends again, to Forrest, track down this ex-husband of hers. To the housekeeper, to Charles, back to her. I'm going to annoy the living hell out of her, even if she is a friend of the chief's wife."

Idly, Roarke wound pasta on his fork. "She knows Tibble's wife? Sticky."

"Yeah." Eve blew out a breath. "It wouldn't surprise me if she'd sought out that connection as part of her outline. Get chummy with a high police official's wife. Check."

At Eve's questioning glance, Roarke nodded. "I'd agree, yes. It would be very good planning on her part. How did she make the connection?"

"Committees, charities, the usual. Next financials in line are the charitable trusts and scholarships. Maybe she siphoned off some of the money, the vic found out. She comes out better a widow than in a divorce, especially if she had any part of siphoning funds meant for the less fortunate kiddies."

"Ben would know. I should say I'd be very surprised if Ben wouldn't know about any mishandling of funds. Possibly they could have been misappropriated and replaced quickly, books cooked in a way he would miss it. But, with his uncle dead, he's majority stock holder, and acting chairman of the board. I'd imagine he's having an internal audit done to make certain the house is in order, on every level."

"She's got him snowed. That's how it looks to me. And she smears the victim with this sex dirt, automatically makes people look sideways. Could be if she played with funds, she's thought of a way to twist it so it looks like the victim did the playing."

"I can take a look."

She twirled more spaghetti onto her fork, smirked. "Aren't you going to be the busy little scout?"

"Cute. Should we go for a drive after dinner? Back to the scene of the crime?"

She studied him over a mouthful of pasta. "Here's what I like about you. Almost everything."

"So," Eve said as they stood in Anders's bedroom, "the guy's lying there, dead as Judas, and his wake-up system goes off. Good morning, Mr. Anders. Gives him the time, turns on the fireplace, starts the coffee, the shower, reminds him what he ordered for breakfast, and details his first appointment of the day."

"Who needs a wife."

Her response was a bland stare. "Anyway, it was kind of creepy. How come you don't have a system like that, ace?"

"We do, I just don't use it. It's kind of creepy. Plus I rarely need an alarm, and why would I want to order breakfast the night before or have the shower going before I was ready to take one?"

"You have habits and routines, but you're not a creature of habit and routine. He was. That was part of the weapon used against him. He was predictable. You could count on him being in bed at three in the morning, count on him programming his wake-up system, putting on his sensible pajamas. Door closed, drapes drawn. Night-night. He'd have been sleeping facing toward the door. From the angle and position of the pressure syringe mark, he'd have been sleeping on his side, facing the door. I bet he always did. She'd have known that. Checklist. Just another checklist."

She shook her head. "Go ahead and take a look at the system. We're going to have to clear the scene. I can't keep her out of the house much longer. I want another look around while I'm here."

She went through the room, this time focusing more narrowly on Ava's things. The clothes, the shoes, the lingerie. Expensive, fashionable, but on the sedate side, Eve supposed. As fit the proper woman, of a conservative bent, of her social and financial level. Nothing too flashy, everything high-end.

Eve circled the bedroom with its surplus of gilt and shine. Maybe not exactly flashy, she mused, but certainly ornate. Ava's Palace. Which was the truer reflection of the woman?

The dressing area held a salon's worth of cosmetic enhancers. Creams, lotions, rejuvenators, skin boosters lived behind shining silver doors in the bath area. Bath salts and oils filled tall clear jars arranged like art on various shelves.

Liked to pamper herself, liked to sink into the deep jet tub or stand under the sprays of the silver-walled shower and luxuriate—in an area separate from her husband's.

This is yours, this is mine.

Yet they shared a bed. Still, with a bed that size, if sex or companionship wasn't on the menu, they might as well have been sleeping in separate counties. Walking back, Eve touched one of the gold rungs on the footboard.

"This was her room," she said aloud. "Hers. He just happened to be in it. She tolerated that. Tolerated his presence, his fussy morning routine because it was hers. She *allowed* him here as long as he was useful."

Stepping out, she sealed the door again, then went down to find Roarke.

He'd pulled his hair back with a twist of leather and sat at the controls in the security area. Besides the extensive equipment built in, Roarke had one of his own handheld devices on the counter.

"It's an excellent system. One of mine," he said with a casual glance over his shoulder. "So I know it quite well. It's been extensively customized for this site. Every available option's in here. I won't say it's absolutely impossible to breach or operate by long-distance remote, but I will say if the client had ordered such a thing, he would've been advised it could compromise his system. And, if he still wanted that ability, it would've been custom-made. We'd have a paper trail. I'll check on that, but I sincerely doubt he authorized something like that."

"And the short range?"

"Every security system can be breached, and I've breached most of them myself. In my misspent youth."

"You were still misspending a couple of years ago, pal."

"Only for . . . entertainment purposes. In any case, this system's alarms and cameras were shut down by short-range. But the code was keyed in before the backup went on. That was quick work, either by someone with an excellent clone or in possession of the code. Whoever it was needed only to stand out of camera range, shut them down, along with the alarms, then walk up to the keypad and do the rest. With the right equipment, a child could have done it."

"But Ava Anders didn't. Disappointing," she admitted. "Now I have to find out who did her dirty work. Let's close up here. I want to pay a call on the way home."

"It seems to be our week for it."

They found Sasha Bride-West at home—barely. She answered the door herself, wrapped in luxurious layers of white mink. But the interruption didn't appear to trouble her in the least. Not when she leveled her gaze at Roarke and purred, "Well, hello."

"Sorry to disturb you," Eve said. "Can I have a minute?"

"You can have a minute." She aimed a sultry smile at Roarke. "How long do *you* want?"

"He's with me. Sasha Bride-West. Roarke."

"Yes, I know." She offered her hand, back up, as a woman does who hopes it'll be kissed. "We met once, briefly. I'm devastated you don't remember."

"I'll remember now."

She laughed, stepped back. "Come in. I'm on my way out to meet some friends. I'm always late anyway."

"On your way to see Mrs. Anders?" Eve asked

"Dressed like this?" Sasha tossed the white coat aside. Under it she wore riotous red, thin and snug as a layer of skin. Sven did good work. "Hardly. Ava's in seclusion until the memorial tomorrow. I do have other friends." She sent Roarke that smile again. "I always have room for more."

"For the moment, maybe we can stick to Ava."

"All right." She gestured, glided on silvery heels into a living area as bold and brash as she was. She slid into a chair. Eve wasn't sure how she managed to sit in a dress that tight and cross her legs. "What about Ava?"

"I'm just confirming some time lines, for the report. Routine stuff."

"Do you always drop by unannounced at night—and with such a gorgeous companion—for routine stuff?"

"We were out." Roarke took a seat beside Sasha, kept his tone casual. "My wife rarely leaves the cop behind."

"Poor you."

"On the morning of Mr. Anders's murder," Eve continued, "what time did Mrs. Anders wake you to tell you what had happened?"

"She didn't."

"She didn't wake you when she learned her husband was dead?"

"I don't know if she believed he was, honestly. She left a message cube. It was Bridge who woke me. About eight-thirty. A bit before nine in any case. In a state. I remember being annoyed at first as I didn't have my facial scheduled until eleven. She said Ava was gone, something had happened to Tommy. I . . ."

She let out a breath, and the brashness ebbed away. "I made some careless, callous remark, which I very much regret. Something like for Christ's sake, unless he's dropped dead on the sixth green, let me sleep. Then Bridge played the message, and it was awful. You could hear the panic and tears in Ava's voice."

"What did she say in the message?"

"I remember exactly. 'Greta called. Something's happened to Tommy. Something terrible's happened. I have to go home.' She left the message on the table in the parlor. We shared a three-bedroom suite, so she left it on the table."

"What did you do?"

"Well, we called her right away, called her 'link. She was very shaken, as you can imagine. She told us Greta had said Tommy was dead. That he was dead in his bed, but she was sure that was a mistake. That he must be ill, so she needed to get right home. She'd call us as soon as she got there, and took care of things."

"Thank you. That's very helpful." Eve waited until Sasha rose to lead them back to the door. "It's a shame she didn't wake you and Mrs. Plowder. She wouldn't have had to make that difficult trip alone."

"Brigit was furious about that, the kind of mad you get when you're incredibly worried. I don't know how many times that morning I said to her not to worry about that, how Ava must've been panicked. How she must not have been able to think of anything but getting home. It was an awful morning for all of us, Lieutenant. When Ava called to tell us Tommy was gone, we were already packed. I guess we knew she wasn't coming back. That trip, it's always the three of us, and . . . how do you mistake death? We knew she wouldn't be able to come back."

Outside Eve walked with Roarke through the crystal cold. "Panicked," she repeated, "can't think of anything but getting home. But you can think to leave a message cube. Not to wake your friends, sleeping right in the next rooms. But you can think of ordering a croissant and matching your wrist unit with a bracelet."

"She didn't want them to see her." Roarke opened the passenger door, then stood looking at Eve over it. "She didn't want them with her, didn't want to have to put on the façade on the trip back."

"No, she didn't. She wanted a little alone time, so she could sit and wallow in how fucking clever she'd been." Her eyes were flat again, cold again. "I'm going to nail her ass, Roarke. Then we'll see how clever she is."

10 UNDER THE PULSING JETS OF THE SHOWER THE next morning, Eve considered her options. She could bring Ava in, try to sweat a confession—fat chance—out of her, or just shake her confidence by letting her know she was being watched.

And she'd lawyer up in a quick, fast minute, sob to the media, and possibly Tibble's wife. Which would, most likely, alienate possible sources of information such as Forrest, Plowder, and Bride-West.

Sweating her might be satisfying, but likely unproductive at this stage.

She could continue to scrape at layers, cutting through the dirt and the bull until she found enough inconsistencies, enough probable cause to make a solid case.

But it had to be faced, she admitted, ordering the jets off to step into the drying tube. The woman was good. She'd covered her undoubtedly surgically sculpted ass in every direction. Where was the loose end? Eve asked herself as the warm air blew around her. Where was the person whose hands had secured the ropes? Where was the person who'd walked into that bedroom and done the deed Eve was flat-out sure Ava had designed?

A lover was a hard sell. The woman had a husband and a twice-monthly LC, and only so many hours in a day. Could Ava have squeezed in an affair, have juggled that many balls without anyone who knew her suspecting? Not impossible, not for someone that organized and calculating, but . . . a hard sell.

A friend? Could Plowder or Bride-West—or both—have conspired to kill Thomas Anders? What incentive could Ava have offered them to commit murder? She rolled that around while she pulled on a robe and walked into the bedroom to hunt up clothes.

Roarke sat drinking coffee and scratching Galahad between the ears. Sometime during her shower, she noted, he'd switched from stock reports to the morning news. "They've just run a brief interview with Ben on today's memorial. More of a quick statement, really, as he wouldn't answer any questions on the nature of his uncle's death or the investigation. He looked shattered."

Eve went with black because it was easiest and made it simpler to blend in during a memorial. "Let me ask you this, taking away the fact you like this guy personally. Could he have been having an affair with Ava?"

Roarke muted the screen, watching Eve as she dressed. "I can't imagine him betraying his uncle in that way—in any way, really—but particularly in that way. Even if his love for Anders was a sham, Ava isn't his type."

"Why not?"

"He tends toward younger, career-oriented, athletic types who'd be happy kicking back with a beer." He paused as she strapped on her weapon. "Good thing I snatched you up before he saw you."

"Well, now I know where to go when I'm done with you. Try this one on. The three women go off to St. Lucia. They go off somewhere together every year, so nobody thinks anything of it. But this year they have more to do than get wrapped in papaya leaves and suck down mimosas."

She shrugged into her jacket and, as Roarke observed, didn't so much as glance in the mirror as she crossed over to get coffee.

"One of them comes back to New York clandestinely, kills Tommy as per Ava's plan while Ava's ass is covered on St. Lucia. Ava's there when Greta calls, and she takes her time leaving. Giving her partner time to get back. Then she takes the shuttle home while the other two wait a reasonable amount of time, then call her to cement the story."

"Involving all three of them? Risky."

"Maybe Bride-West was still asleep, just as she said in her statement. They slip something in her martini, whatever, and . . . I'm not buying this myself, so why am I trying to sell it to you?"

He rose, placed his hands on her shoulders, kissed her brow. Then knowing she'd never think to do it herself, walked over to program some breakfast.

"It had to be someone she could trust. Absolutely. Without question. Someone who would kill for her. Her parents are divorced. One lives in Portland, one lives in Chicago. Both remarried. Nothing jumped up and bit me on the runs I did on them, and I can't find any record either of them traveling anywhere, much less New York on the night in question. She has no siblings. As far as I can determine she hasn't seen her ex-husband in about two decades. Who does she know, who does she trust to kill for her and to kill in a very specific way?"

Roarke carried back plates of bacon and eggs. Galahad feigned disinterest. "You'll have to get the coffee if you're after more. If I take my eyes off these plates for two seconds, this food will be in the cat's belly."

Eve frowned at the plates. "I was going to grab—"

"Now you're not. Get the coffee, I'm after more."

She could've argued. Thinking about the case made her want to argue, blow off the steam of it. But she wanted another hit of coffee. She got two mugs, came back and plopped down.

"I got nothing. I got nothing on her. No connection that works. And I'm talking myself into circles."

"Maybe you'll come up with something more linear when we see her at the memorial today."

The eggs were there, so she stabbed a forkful. "You're going?"

"Ben and I are friendly. Anders Worldwide is in my building. I'll pay my respects. And maybe I'll catch something you've missed. Fresh eyes."

"Fresh eyes." She picked up a piece of bacon, then swore. "Fresh eyes, damn it. I forgot. I promised Baxter I'd take a look at a case file for him. Going cold. I've been putting him off. Damn it." She bit into the bacon. "I'll have to do it this morning."

"That might be a good thing. Put your mind on that for a bit, let it rest on the other."

"Maybe. I told him some of them get by us. We can't close them all. It burns my ass to think this one could get away from me."

Galahad bellied over an inch, two inches, his bicolored eyes fixed on Roarke's plate. Roarke simply shifted his gaze, stared, and Galahad rolled onto his back to paw lazily at the air. "No one believes you're innocent," he said to the cat.

"Everyone believes she is," Eve murmured. "Hmm. What happens if somebody doesn't?" Turning that over in her mind she ate her breakfast before Galahad made his next move.

Before her shift began Eve sat in her office at Central with Baxter's murder book on the Custer case. She studied the crime scene photos first, as if coming to it fresh, without the input of the ME, the sweepers, the investigator's notes, the interviews.

Somebody, she thought, had done a quick, hard number on one Ned Custer. The room itself looked like a typical sex flop. Cheap bed, sagging mattress where Christ knew what microscopic vermin partied in a variety of body fluids. Particle board dresser, fly-spotted mirror, dull, yellowing floor, crappy paper drapes at the crappy little window. A bad joke of a bath with a rust-stained, wall-hung sink and a toilet where more vermin partied.

The cliché of sex flops, she thought.

What kind of man was Ned Custer, who needed to get his rocks off in an ugly little dump while the wife and kiddies waited at home?

A pretty damn dead one. The slash across the throat went deep, went long. Sharp blade with some muscle behind it. And some height, she mused, checking the angle. Vic topped off at five-nine. The killer . . . Eve closed her eyes, put herself in the nasty room, put herself behind Custer. Had to be at least the same height, probably an inch or two taller.

Tall for a woman then, but a lot of street whores went for high platforms and heels. Still, not a shortie.

And no one who owned a delicate stomach. It took steel-lined to hack off a guy's dick.

The blood spatters and pools told the story clearly enough. The killer stepped out of the excuse for a bathroom, attacked the victim from behind. One fast slash. No hesitation. Had to get some backsplash from that kind of blood jet. More blood from the homemade castration. With no blood in the drains, the killer either exited carting the blood—no trail, so unlikely—or came out of the bathroom sealed and protected.

Not a street whore. Not even one pumped up on illegals. Too prepared, too vicious. A whore wants to roll a mark, maybe she sticks him, but more likely she gets herself a zapper off the black market, immobilizes and cops his money and jewelry. Walks away.

Custer was dead before he walked in that room, he just didn't know it. Would anyone have done? she wondered. Or was it target specific?

She dug deeper, shooting out a message for Baxter and Trueheart to report to her when they came on shift. And she made her own notes.

She grunted at the tap on her doorjamb, then glanced up at Trueheart in his spotless uniform. "You wanted to see me, Lieutenant."

"Yeah. Where's Baxter?"

"He's not in yet. I, um, try to get in a little before shift when I can, to look over yesterday's work."

"Uh-huh." Eager beaver, she mused. Young but steady, with a good eye. And he'd lost a lot of the green he'd had on him when she'd first seen him on scooper detail. "I've been looking over the Custer murder book. You and Baxter were thorough. How many cases have you caught since?"

"Nine," he said immediately. "Two open. Plus Custer, so that's three open."

"What's your take on this one?"

"The vic led a dangerous kind of life, Lieutenant. He cruised the bars and the red lights, picked up his dates from low-level LCs. We talked to a lot of working girls and found a couple who remembered him. They, ah, said he liked it fast and rough—and ah, cheap."

"I see that. You covered the area of the crime scene, did the door to doors, hit the bars, the working girls."

"Nobody remembers who he went off with that night, other than a couple saying he might've been hooked up with a redhead. Short, straight hair—or short curly hair depending on the wit. You know how it is."

"Yeah."

"It's not the kind of area where people remember. The guy working the desk on the flop said maybe he'd seen her before, maybe not, but he's pretty sure about the hair that night. He's on the red, short, straight side."

She'd read all this in the book, but let Trueheart wind it out.

"One thing he swears on is she didn't come back down. If he didn't check them off when they came down, how could he turn the room? He gets paid on the turn. So he swears she didn't come back by the desk, and you can't get out the front without going by the desk. The fire escape was engaged. She had to go out through the window and down. And the scene, it was full of prints and DNA, fiber, hair. It's not the kind of place where housekeeping's a priority. We ran everything, interviewed everyone when we could find a match and locate the individual. Nobody stands out."

She started to speak, held off as Baxter hurried up to join his aide. "This about Custer?"

"I've reviewed the book. It's a thorough investigation so far."

"Without a single suspect."

"You're not looking at the wife."

"She's alibied up, Dallas, literally on her house 'link trying to reach the vic when he was being sliced. Trueheart and I were the ones to notify. She wasn't faking her reaction."

"No like crimes before or after, not following this pattern. It smells target specific."

"Yeah, it does."

"So who benefits?"

Baxter raked his fingers through his hair. "Okay, the wife gets rid of a guy who cheats and may be bringing home an all-you-can eat buffet of STDs, and who tunes her up when the whim strikes. She comes into a pension and life insurance policy through his employment. Not princely, but solid. But she wasn't there, that's a fact. The vic wasn't going to go into that flop with his wife when he hunted strange. And he'd've recognized her. She's three inches over five feet so she's not tall enough or strong enough to have made the cut."

"Maybe she knew somebody who was. A relative, a friend, somebody who thought she was better off with the cheating, heavy-handed husband dead. And she is."

"She's got a sister down in Arkansas, a father doing a dime on assault with intent down there, and who used to knock *his* wife around. Her mother's in New Jersey, but believe me, she couldn't have pulled this off either. As for friends, she doesn't have anybody she's tight with. Sure as hell not tight enough to slit her husband's throat for her."

"A boyfriend. The killer skews tall and strong for a female."

"Working a team." Baxter's eyes changed as he considered. "Guy's already in the bathroom, she brings the mark in . . . Then why doesn't she just go out the front? Why—"

"Lots of whys," Eve interrupted. "Who says he went up there with a woman?"

Trueheart cleared his throat. "Um, everybody, sir."

"And did everybody see the killer's plumbing? You've seen enough trannies, Baxter, to know how pretty they are when they're on the stroll. If you're not looking close enough, if you've had a few brews under your belt, a guy could find a big surprise when he reaches into the box. Everybody sees a woman, so you're looking for a woman."

"And don't I feel stupid," Baxter mumbled. "I never made the lateral move to male possibility."

"Wife's got a secret admirer, he might be man enough to dress like a woman."

"Sir? Lieutenant?" Trueheart nearly raised his hand. "It's hard to see how Mrs. Custer could've had a relationship, a boyfriend. She's got those kids, and none of her neighbors reported seeing anyone visiting her apartment regularly. We looked at that, because you have to, but we didn't find anything that indicated she had a boyfriend."

"A woman with a husband who likes to use his fists learns to be a careful woman." Eve glanced back at her own murder board. "And maybe I'm letting some of my own investigation bleed over into my thoughts on yours." She swiveled back, held out the murder book. "You've got two fresher cases open, but find time to poke at the boyfriend angle, and the doing her a favor."

"Since we'd run out of angles, I appreciate it. Come on, faithful sidekick." Baxter dropped a hand on Trueheart's shoulder. "Let's go think about men in dresses."

She toggled her mind back to her own case, checked her incomings and her messages. The lab in its better-late-than-even-more-late mode verified what Roarke had already told her. Voice print match. Rising, she added that report to her board.

"Good morning!" Bright, bouncing, and beaming, Peabody sang out the greeting and shook a pink bakery box. "I've got crullers."

"And you got through the bullpen alive?"

"I bought two boxes, tossed one at the rioting horde as I came through."

"That's not stupid."

"I would've come back before, but you were with Baxter and Trueheart, and I was collecting my kudos."

"I thought they were crullers."

With a laugh, Peabody set the box on Eve's desk. "I'm celebrating with pastries because I looked really good last night. I know how the camera's supposed to add pounds, but I didn't look tubbo. I think it was the jacket. It's slimming, and the way the buttons run and all, they trick the eye. And I was sitting on my ass, so that wasn't a problem. Jesus, I was so nervous. Completely freaked."

She dug in the box, pulled out a cruller and bit in. "Trina was great, sort of talking me down. She says you're due for a treatment, by the way."

"She's due for an ass-kicking."

"And McNab was mag, seriously mag." Peabody licked sugar off her thumb. "But you have all those people and the cameras and if you think about how many *other* people are sitting home watching, you'll throw up. Nadine was the ult, she really eased me in. But she didn't baby me, so I didn't come off like a moron. When we got home, McNab and I watched the segment like twelve times, and had lots and lots of celebration sex. Boy, I feel *great*! So what did you think when you watched it?"

"I was busy."

The bright, beaming bounce dropped hard through the trapdoor of shock. "You didn't . . . But I thought you'd—oh."

Eve let it sit for another five seconds, but even she couldn't be that mean. And there were crullers. "Jesus, Peabody, you're easy. Of course I watched. I had to know if you screwed up and I needed to kick your ass, didn't I? You didn't screw up."

The beam bounced back. "I really didn't. McNab said I sounded smart and completely on top. And I looked sexy. Did you think so?"

"I dreamed of you all night. Can we move on now?"

"One more thing. Thanks for pushing me into this. I won't be so freaky about it next time. Oh, oh, and just another thing. Mavis and Leonardo tagged us when we were on our way home from the studio, and Mavis said Belle smiled and cooed when she saw me on screen. Okay, done." She took another bite of her cruller.

"If you're ready to set your kudos aside, we're in the field. Anders Worldwide."

"The memorial's this afternoon," Peabody reminded her. "I don't think Forrest will be in. Do you want me to check?"

"No. He may not be in, but I bet his admin is. And I like the drop-in. Let's move."

Eve grabbed her coat, considered the crullers. If she left them there, out in the open, even the box would be devoured when she got back. She could hide it, but the vultures would sniff it out, which could lead them to the candy she'd stashed where—so far—the Candy Thief hadn't discovered it.

She snatched up the box on the way out. Better safe than crullerless.

Leopold Walsh had struck Eve as a man who manned his station, and guarded his prince whatever the crisis. She was right. He met them in his office—sober eyes, dark suit, and a black armband.

"I don't expect Mr. Forrest today," Leopold began. "Mr. Anders's memorial is scheduled for two this afternoon."

"We're aware of that." No offer of coffee, Eve noted, no invitation to sit. Don't like us much, do you, Leo? "Mr. Forrest and his uncle were very close, personally and professionally. Would you agree with that assessment?"

"I would."

"As you work closely with Mr. Forrest, you'd be privy to their dealings together."

"Of course."

Eve smiled. She had to admire a man who knew how to answer without saying anything. "I imagine you formed opinions regarding Thomas Anders—professionally and personally."

"I hardly see how my opinion is relevant."

"Humor me."

"In my opinion, Mr. Thomas Anders was a fair and honest man who brought that fairness and honesty into business. He trusted, correctly, that his nephew would do the same."

"The manner of Mr. Anders's death must have caused some speculation and gossip within the organization, and its accounts."

Leopold's jaw tightened. "People will talk, Lieutenant. It's human nature."

But you don't, she thought. No juicy office gossip for you. But you hear it, file it.

"What's the buzz about Mrs. Anders?"

"I don't understand what you mean."

Tighten that jaw another notch, Leo, something's going to snap. "Yes, you do."

"Mrs. Anders devoted—devotes—much of her considerable energy into the charitable and humanitarian programs sponsored by Anders Worldwide. She's very well respected."

"She puts in time around here?"

"Of course, though she most often works from home, or by attending or hostessing functions."

"You'd have been privy to her dealings with her husband, and with his nephew."

"Somewhat certainly, as Ben—as Mr. Forrest was gradually taking over his uncle's duties. Some of those duties involved the programs. I'm sorry, Lieutenant, I have a very crowded day, and a very difficult one. If that's all—"

"It's not. How would you describe the relationship between Mr. Forrest and—shit, let's simplify. How did Ben and Ava get along?"

"They were very cordial, of course. Ben admired her talent and her energy, and was certainly impressed with many of her ideas."

"Cordial. Not affectionate. He strikes me as an easy and affectionate sort, but you choose the cooler, more formal, 'cordial' to describe their relationship."

"Mrs. Anders was his uncle's wife." Leopold's tone was equally cool and formal. "Their relationship was perfectly proper."

"Proper, there's another cool term. Ben doesn't like her much, does he? Neither do you."

"I've said or implied nothing of the kind. I don't—"

"Relax. I don't like her either. So, you can keep standing there with that rod up your ass or . . ." She dropped into a chair without invitation. "Tell me why. Record off, Peabody," Eve said as she switched off her own. "Just the three of us, Leo. Off record. What about Ava sticks in your craw?"

Eve watched him debate. Propriety or the opportunity to speak his mind. Opportunity won. "She's studied, she's deliberate, and she's cold. Those aren't crimes, but personality traits. And . . ."

"Don't stop now." Eve lifted her hands, palms up in invitation.

"There's a pettiness about her. She would often circumvent Ben by making plans or decisions without consulting him or seeking his input. Her plans and decisions were always well thought out and researched. She had—has—excellent ideas. But it's been her habit to brush over Ben, a very deliberate habit. In my opinion."

"How'd Ben take that?"

"It frustrated him from time to time, though I admit, it frustrated me more."

"Did he ever complain to his uncle?"

"Not to my knowledge, and I believe I would know. He might complain to me, or use me as a sounding board. Invariably, after he had he'd say the same thing. 'Well, it's the end result that matters.' Mrs. Anders gets excellent results."

"I believe that."

"I think . . ."

"We're off record, Leo. What do you think?"

"I think she often did the same regarding Mr. Anders. That is, failed to keep him in the loop until whatever she planned was essentially a *fait accompli*. There was some office gossip, and I don't like office gossip."

"Me, I love it. How about you, Peabody?"

"Revs up the day. What kind of gossip?" Peabody asked Leo.

"There was talk that she charged certain personal expenses to program budget. Household purchases, wardrobe, salons, that sort of thing. Nothing major, you understand. That pettiness again, from my point of view. I heard Mr. Anders, I mean Mr. Reginald Anders called her on it."

"Her father-in-law? When would this be?"

"I couldn't say, exactly. He's been gone nearly two years now. I only remember the talk because they got along very well, so the reprimand—if there was one—wouldn't be expected."

Leopold shifted his stance. "I don't understand why this matters to you."

"Oh, every little thing matters to me. This reprimand, that may or may not have happened? How did they get along afterward?"

"Back to status quo. I believe she sent Mr. Reginald a box of his favorite caramel creams as an apology."

"Hmm. Mrs. Anders's position here rises with the death of her husband. The late Mr. Anders held fifty-five percent of the shares in the company, Ben came in with fifteen, and Ava held a token two percent. Is that correct?"

"I believe so."

She had his attention now, Eve noted. Big-time.

"At his death, those fifty-five shares are divided between Ben and Ava. Forty to Ben, giving him controlling interest. But fifteen added to Ava's original two brings her well up in the world. And there are twenty-eight more shares out there. A smart, resourceful woman should be able to get her fingers on a few of those, particularly when her two closest friends hold small percentages. She could bump that share up to thirty, thirty-five without breaking too much of a sweat. That's a powerful chunk of a company like this. And you know what,

Leo, now that we're just pals chatting, you don't seem shocked and surprised by what I'm implying here."

"If you're asking if I believe Mrs. Anders killed her husband, no, I don't. She was out of the country, and the nature . . . the circumstances of his death are a personal humiliation to her. She's not a woman who enjoys humiliation. If you're asking if I'm surprised you'd find her capable of killing, again, no, I'm not."

"I'm a cop. Nobody's surprised that I think anyone's capable of killing. Why do you believe she's capable?"

Leopold was either relaxed enough now, or interested enough to take a seat. "I don't like her, on a personal level. I find her ruthless, under a veneer of sophistication, under a guise of good works. The good works—this is my opinion— they didn't matter to her as much as the attention she gained from them, the media and the accolades. She resents Ben because his uncle doted on him, and I think, because people enjoy and admire Ben. She didn't love her husband."

"At last!" Eve slapped a hand on her leg. "Somebody says it. Why did you?"

Leopold's eyes widened at Eve's reaction. "I—I honestly don't know. She was invariably affectionate, even attentive. Patient. But every now and then there was a tone, or a look. I can only tell you that I don't believe she loved him, but she loved being Ava Anders. Everything I've said here is off the record. Everything I've said here I'll deny on the record."

"We're just talking here. Anything to add, Peabody?"

"You covered a lot. I was just thinking that one of the quickest and surest ways to gain sympathy and support is to be humiliated by the actions of another. A little red-face might be a reasonable trade-off for all the shoulders, all the 'isn't she braves.' It's a thought."

Leopold stared. "She was in St. Lucia."

"Yeah, she was." Eve nodded, pushed to her feet. "Still, it's interesting. You might want to mention to Ben that my partner and I came by and were asking you these interesting questions about Ava. Meanwhile, I'd like to have copies of all the files on all the projects she worked on. With Ben, or otherwise."

"All? For the last sixteen years?"

"No, all the way back to when she started at the company." She grinned at the way that previously tight jaw dropped. "Might as well be thorough."

"There will be hundreds. Hundreds of hundreds."

"Then you'd better get started."

"This will take a little time. You may want to wait in the client lounge."

"We'll come back. An hour enough time?"

"Yes, that should do."

In the elevator, Peabody turned to Eve. "How did you know he'd be the go-to guy on this?"

"He's in love with Ben. Knows it's hopeless, but he can't help what he feels. First, anything that has to do with Ben, he's going to pick up on his emotional radar. Second, I figure somebody who's got all those repressed feelings recognizes when someone else's feelings are a sham. Third? We got really lucky, pushed the right button at the right time. Contact Edmond Luce. I'm betting he and his wife are still in New York. I want another talk with him."

II LUCE AND HIS WIFE REMAINED IN NEW YORK, IN residence in one of the ritzy suites at Roarke's Palace Hotel. Linny Luce—Eve wondered how she felt about ending up with that name—opened the door and introduced herself.

She was what Eve thought of as a solid woman, well-built and compact like an efficient car designed for low maintenance and long usage. Thick brown hair with white wings framed a face more handsome than pretty. She wore a long-skirted black suit with sensible low-heeled boots and exquisite pearls. Her handshake was firm and businesslike.

"Edmond is on the 'link with London. He shouldn't be long. Please sit. I ordered up tea. It's quite good here. But I expect you know that, it being your husband's establishment."

She sat on the fat cream and white cushions of the sofa, poured out. "Milk or lemon?"

Neither was going to make Eve like tea any more than she did. "Just black, thanks."

"Detective?"

"Milk, one sugar, thanks."

"This is a difficult day for us. I hope you'll understand how I mean it when I say your call was a welcome distraction. Edmond and I . . . we can't quite fathom what to do with ourselves. After the memorial . . . Maybe it will be easier after the memorial, after we go back home."

She sighed, looking toward the wide windows that opened to the towers of New York. "Life goes on, doesn't it? It has to."

"You knew Mr. Anders a long time."

"Yes. Edmond and Tommy were friends longer, of course. But I knew Tommy over forty years. We can't think what to do with ourselves. I'm sorry, I said that, didn't I?"

"Can I ask you, Mrs. Luce, since you knew him well before his marriage, if you could tell us if he had any serious relationships before his wife?"

"Serious? I wouldn't say. He enjoyed the company of women, but he simply enjoyed the company of people. We used to tease him quite a bit about settling down. I admit I tried matchmaking a few times."

"I wonder if you could give me some names and contact information, on women you remember Mr. Anders . . . enjoying."

"Yes, I could do that." Linny looked straight into Eve's eyes. "You're asking this because of the way he was killed. That was not Tommy. I will never believe otherwise."

"When did you first meet Ava Anders?"

"Oh, she was still working for Anders—a Public Relations exec. I can't recall her title, if I ever knew. I first met her at a charity event here in New York. Ava had done the PR. A fund-raiser for one of the sports camps Tommy built. Black-tie, with dinner and dancing, a silent auction, an orchestra. Very elaborate, as I recall. She was very bright and clever. I remember watching them dancing at some point during the evening, and telling Edmond Tommy better watch out with that one."

"Watch out?"

"I suppose what I meant was, she very much had her eye on him, and seemed a woman who knew how to get what she wanted. Which proved to be true. It wasn't long after that they began to see each other socially, and whenever the four of us got together, it was obvious he was besotted by her, and she so . . . tickled by him."

"Did you like her?"

Linny's eyes widened. "Yes, of course, I did. Do. The four of us had some very lovely times together."

"Would you say he remained besotted and she tickled?"

"It's very difficult even for good friends to judge the inside of another's marriage. And marriages evolve and adjust. They remained devoted to each other, certainly."

"Friends, women friends," Peabody put in, "often discuss aspects of their marriage with each other. Dish a little on their husbands, vent their frustrations, have some laughs over the little quirks and habits."

"They do," Linny said with a smile. "Yes, they do. Ava and I aren't intimate in that way. We get along quite well, but we don't have as warm or close a relationship, you might say, as Tommy and I did. Frankly, Tommy was the glue there. I enjoy an afternoon at the football pitch, and Ava preferred the shops and galleries. I have grandchildren, and she doesn't. I'm fifteen years her senior, after all."

She glanced over as her husband strode in. "There you are, Edmond."

"Sorry for the delay. Lieutenant, Detective." He sat like a man weary to the bone. "There's to be a memorial in London, in fact, in every city around the world with an Anders base. There were details I needed to address quickly."

Linny put a hand on his knee, patted it briskly in a gesture that translated absolute unity to Eve. "You'll have some tea now."

"Mr. Luce, with Mr. Anders's death, how much influence in the company will Mrs. Anders gain?"

"Considerable, if she wants it, I suppose, but Ava's never been interested in the business per se. In the charities, the programs, the publicity, but not the mechanics of running things. That will be for Ben." He let out a long sigh. "In fact, he called just as I was finishing with London. He plans to arrange a meeting of the board and executive officers early next week. He's asked me to consider coming on as his second in command."

"Oh, Edmond."

"I know." It was his turn to pat his wife's knee. "I planned to ease back a bit. More than a bit," he admitted. "With the goal of retiring within the next two years. I hadn't told Tommy yet. In fact, I planned to broach the subject when we golfed, the day . . . the day he died. He'd want me to help Ben during the transition, Linny. I may still make that two-year goal."

"Mr. Luce, did Ben indicate he'd discussed this with Mrs. Anders?"

"No, why would he?"

"She has a seventeen percent share of the company now."

"Yes, yes, of course. I'm sorry, I'm not thinking very clearly today. In any case, as I said, Ava's never been interested in the company."

"But as the next majority share holder, as the widow of the company's president, she would be within her rights to expect a more hands-on position, a seat on the board maybe—and that goes along with that."

"Technically, yes, I suppose so. But realistically, I can't imagine it."

"You knew Reginald Anders?"

"Oh yes." Edmond's face lightened with a smile. "In fact, it was Reggie who first hired me, more than half a century ago."

"At his death, Thomas Anders inherited the majority share of the company, correct?"

"Yes. As Ben will now. Tommy considered Ben his son, and followed his own father's lead on that."

"Just so I have all the details straight. I understand Ava Anders has a small percentage of the company—well, a larger one now. But the initial share, did she come into that at her father-in-law's death?"

"I believe that's correct. Reggie was very fond of Ava."

"All right, we appreciate you seeing us at a difficult time." Her 'link signaled and, checking the display, she ordered it to answer, identify, and hold. "I need to take this. Is it possible I could use another room?"

"Of course." Linny got quickly to her feet. "Let me show you to the office. Would you like to take your tea?"

"No, that's fine." She followed her hostess into a top-flight office done with plush leather and glossy wood.

"I'll write down those names you asked for while you're taking your call. Be comfortable," Linny told her, and backing out, closed the double doors behind her.

Eve engaged her 'link. "This is Lieutenant Dallas, Mr. Bronson, thank you for holding."

"Well, well. If I'd known you were this attractive, I'd have gotten back to you sooner. What can I do for you, Lieutenant Brown Eyes?"

"First, you can cut the crap."

"Mm. I love 'em sassy." He grinned at her, the same shit-eating grin from his official ID photo. Eve figured he'd practiced and perfected that one in the mirror. "So tell me what a sassy, brown-eyed police lieutenant from New York wants with Dirk."

Dirk, she thought, was a complete asshole who had smooth, tanned cheeks that told her he'd had considerable and skilled work. Golden brows arched over eyes of Mediterranean blue like the sea she caught glimpses of behind him. His golden hair waved in the undoubtedly balmy breeze.

"You were married to an Ava Montgomery."

"Wasn't I just? A brief yet memorable episode in my past. Don't tell me Ava's in trouble." He laughed as though little could amuse him more. "What did she do? Hire the wrong caterer?"

"Her current husband was murdered a few days ago."

"Really?" His eyebrows quirked, and for a moment his face seemed to hold an expression other than smug conceit. "That's . . . inconvenient. He's a, what is it, a sporting goods king or something? I believe I own one of his tennis rackets." Then he laughed, all brassy amusement. "Do you think I killed him? After all these years, to win back the fair Ava? This is exciting."

"Why don't you tell me where you were on March eighteenth, and we'll get that little joke out of the way."

"Cruising the Aegean, as I am now—with a bevy of beauties, a number of friends, and a full crew. Would you like to come interrogate me?"

"I'll keep that in reserve. When's the last time you saw your ex-wife?"

"Which ex-wife?"

"Don't waste my time, Dirk."

"So serious. Let's see, when did Dirk last lay eyes on the lovely Ava? Ten years ago? No, longer. How time does fly. Closer to fifteen, I think. I bumped elbows with her in New York, if memory serves, at some party or premiere. Whatever. I believe she'd been recently married to the sports king."

"Why did you and Ava divorce?"

"Who remembers? I'm sure I strayed, as I do enjoy variety. Dirk is no damn good and has a selection of ex-wives and women who would be delighted to verify that."

"She didn't satisfy you sexually?"

Avid amusement shone in his eyes. "Well, aren't we nosy?"

She saw him shift, heard the rattle of ice in a glass, then watched him sip something tall and rosy. "She was—and my memory is clear on this—delightful in bed, and other interesting places. We wouldn't have gotten as far as marriage otherwise. But I have a weak will and a roving eye. In any case, I wasn't ambitious enough for her as I was—and am—content to coast and cruise. She wanted something—someone—who would provide her with opportunities for money and fame, respect. Like, I imagine, the dead sports king. I enjoy my sloth. We weren't suited."

"So she left you."

"With a tidy sum and not a backward glance. Her cold heart and steely resolve were part of her appeal to me. As I recall, she introduced me to the woman I strayed with, and gave me far too many opportunities to take advantage. But somehow, she didn't see it as her fault when advantage I took. Imagine that!"

"Imagine that. Thanks for your time."

"It's been entertaining. If you ever want to coast or cruise, be sure to look me up."

"Yeah, I'll jump right on that." She clicked off, stood for a moment absorbing. Then she went out to take leave of the Luces.

"Sounds like a big, oily ball of slime," Peabody commented after Eve filled her in.

"Yeah, he does. Polar opposite of Anders."

"Devil's advocate. A woman gets burned like that, it's reasonable she'd look for a completely different type."

"Yeah, absolutely logical, absolutely reasonable. Good plan."

"You really think plan? Like okay, sleazy ex-husband dispatched. Check. Now hook nice guy with deep pockets?"

"She introduced the ex to the woman he cheated with. Read between the lines, Peabody. If you know a kid's addicted to ice cream, do you put a big chocolate sundae in front of him and walk away? If you want out of a marriage with a tidy sum, sympathy, and no fault on you, what better way than to set up your weak-willed, roving-eyed husband? It's something she'd do. It's exactly something she'd do.

"I want to talk to Greta again. You go back, pick up the files. If you need help transporting, order it up. When you get back to Central, do a search for repeating names. Any that show multiple times in any program. Run those first."

She pulled over, spoke over the ensuing storm of horns. "Take the wheel. I'll catch a cab, then tap Roarke for a ride to the memorial."

She checked the address in her book, then decided to walk a few blocks to clear her head before engaging in the war for a cab. Since she was on foot, she pulled out her 'link to check on Feeney.

He answered, honking like a dying goose. "Man, you sound sick."

"I *am* sick. Goddamn it. You think I'm lying here in bed drinking this disgusting boiled tree bark they gave me for my health?"

She waited a beat. "Well. Yeah."

"I'm burning up. I've got hot shards of glass in my throat and ten pounds of snot in my head. And what do they do? What do they do?" His eyes bugged out like glass marbles. "They give me fucking liquid tree bark and the wife's poured so much chicken soup down me, I'm starting to cluck. I don't want to die here in this damn bed. If this is the end, I want to buy it at my desk, like a man. You gotta get me out of here, Dallas. You gotta bust me out. You can take Sheila."

His face was wildly flushed, but Eve thought that was as much from sick panic as sickness. And she wasn't altogether sure she could take Feeney's wife. "Ah, what? I can't hear you. It must be a bad 'link."

"Don't you pull that crap on me."

"Okay, okay. How about this? I've got Peabody picking up files, hundreds of them from Anders Worldwide. It's the wife, Feeney, I know it in my guts. But I've got nothing to take to the commander, much less the PA. The search and runs on these files are going to take hours. Maybe days. Peabody could fill you in, toss some to you. You could work from there."

"Best you can do is throw me a bone?" He honked again. "I'll take it."

"It's a big bone, Feeney, and I need somebody to dig out the meat."

"All right. You tell the wife."

"What? Wait!"

"You convince her you need me on this. Make it life and death."

"No! Feeney, don't—"

"Sheila!" He honked the name out, and in the lingering chill of March, Eve's hands went damp with sweat.

What people did for friendship, Eve thought, as she paid off the cab. Now *she* was responsible, according to Mrs. Feeney, if the work set back his recovery. Should've left him hacking up a lung at his desk in the first place, she told herself as she buzzed Greta Horowitz's apartment from street level.

She angled toward the view screen.

"Lieutenant Dallas?"

"Yes. Can I come up?"

"I'll open the locks."

The doors beeped clear, opened smoothly. Inside, the entryway was small, and absolutely pristine. Eve imagined Greta would tolerate no less. The elevator hummed cooperatively to the fourth floor where Greta stood in the doorway of her unit.

"Has something happened?"

"Just some follow-up questions."

"Oh. I was hoping you'd found who killed Mr. Anders. Please come in."

The apartment was as unpretentious and efficient as its occupant. Sturdy furniture, no frills, a scent of . . . clean, was the only way Eve could describe it.

"Can I get you something hot to drink?"

"No, thanks. If we could sit down for a few minutes."

"Please." Greta sat, planted her shoes on the floor and her knees together. Smoothed down the skirt of her dignified black suit.

"You're attending the memorial," Eve began.

"Yes. It's a very sad day. After, I'll go to Mrs. Plowder's, to help with the bereavement supper. Tomorrow . . ." She let out a little sigh. "Tomorrow, I am back to work. I will prepare the house so Mrs. Anders can return home."

"Prepare it?"

"It must be freshened, of course, and some marketing must be done. The bed linens . . . you understand."

"Yes."

"I'll supervise having Mr. Anders's clothes packed."

Don't waste time, do you, Ava? "Packed?"

"Mrs. Anders feels it will distress her to see them. She prefers they be removed before her return, and donated, of course, to charity."

"Of course. Mrs. Horowitz, how long did it take you to put away, give away, your husband's clothes?"

"I still have his dress uniform." She glanced over and, following, Eve saw the framed photo of the soldier Greta had loved. "People grieve in their own way."

"Mrs. Horowitz, you strike me as the sort of woman who not only knows her job, but does it very well. Who not only meets her employers' needs, but would anticipate them. To anticipate, you'd have to understand them."

"I take pride in my work. I will be glad to get back to it. I dislike being idle."

"Did you anticipate Mrs. Anders instructing you to pack away her husband's clothes?"

"No. No," she said again, more carefully. "But I was not surprised by the instructions. Mrs. Anders isn't sentimental."

"I doubt anyone would describe either of us that way, either. As sentimental. If I lost my husband . . . I'd need his things around me. I'd need to touch them, to smell them, to have them. I'd need those tangible pieces of him to get me through the pain, the shock, the sadness. You understand me?"

Gaze level on Eve's, Greta nodded. "Yes, I do."

"Would you have been surprised, if the situation were reversed, and Mr. Anders instructed you to pack up his wife's clothing?"

"Very. I would have been very surprised."

"Mrs. Horowitz, I haven't turned on my recorder. I'm just asking you for your opinions. Your opinions are very helpful to me. Did she love him?"

"I managed their house, Lieutenant, not their marriage."

"Greta," Eve said in a tone that had Greta sighing again.

"It's a difficult position. I believe honesty and cooperation with the police is an essential matter. And I believe loyalty to and discretion about an employer is not a choice, it's duty. You would understand duty, Lieutenant."

"Mr. Anders was your employer, too. Yes, I understand duty. We both have a duty to Thomas Anders."

"Yes." Greta looked at her husband's photograph again. "Yes, we do. You asked me before about their relationship, and I told you the truth. Perhaps not all shades of the truth, perhaps not my feelings on that truth."

"Will you tell me now?"

"Will you tell me first if you believe Mrs. Anders had anything to do with her husband's murder?"

"I do believe it."

Greta closed her eyes. "I had that terrible thought, not when I found him that morning, you understand. Not then. Not even that night, or the next morning. But . . . with so much time on my hands, so much time to think instead of work, I began to have those thoughts. Those terrible thoughts. To wonder."

"Why?"

"There was affection, gestures—on both sides. An indulgence on both sides. You would see this and think they are nicely married. Comfortably married, you understand?"

"Yes, I do."

"If she encouraged him to go out, play his golf or attend his games, how could you fault her? If she encouraged him to take his trips, even to extend them, it would be natural enough. Women come to prize their solitude, especially when they're long married. A little time without the man underfoot."

"The reasonable, loving, indulgent wife."

"Yes. Yes, exactly what it would seem. But, in fact, she was happier when he was gone than she was when he was home, and the longer he was gone, the happier she would be. This is my opinion," Greta hastened to add. "My sense only."

"That's what I'm after."

"I would sense an annoyance in her on the day he was scheduled to return. I could sense it even as she fussed about what meal to serve him to welcome him home. When he was gone, she would have dinner parties or cocktails with her friends. Friends of hers, you understand, that were not so much friends of his. And never with Mr. Benedict."

Greta paused, pressed her fingers to her lips for a moment, then folded her hands neatly in her lap again. "I might not be saying this to you if she hadn't instructed me to clear his clothes out of his dressing room, as she might instruct me to see that the floor were polished. Just another household task. I might not be telling you this if I didn't know she saw the disapproval I didn't hide quickly enough. And seeing it, Lieutenant, her manner changed. Her voice thickened with the tears that came into her eyes. But it was too late. I'd seen the other, heard the other, so it was too late. It was then she asked me to help at Mrs. Plowder's, and told me what she would pay for my time, which is more than it should be. It was then she told me I would have a raise in salary when I returned to work tomorrow, and that she depended on me to help her through this difficult time."

Greta looked down at the hands folded in her lap, nodded. "It was then, Lieutenant, I decided I would begin to look for other employment. Only this morning, I contacted an agency for this purpose."

"She miscalculated with you, Greta. Will you be able to go to the memorial, to the Plowders, to go back to work, for the time being, without letting her see what you think or feel?"

The faintest smile touched Greta's mouth. "I'm a domestic, Lieutenant. I'm very skilled at keeping my thoughts and feelings to myself."

"I appreciate you sharing them with me." Eve rose, held out a hand.

Getting to her feet, Greta took it, then held it. And held Eve's eyes. "We may be unfair to Mrs. Anders. But if we aren't, I trust you, Lieutenant, to make justice for Mrs. Anders."

"I'm good at my job, too."

"Yes, I believe you are."

Rather than cab it all the way back to Roarke's office, Eve flipped out her 'link as she hit the street again. The transmission bounced straight to his admin. "Hey, Caro, could—"

"Hello, Lieutenant."

"Yeah." Was she supposed to make small talk? Hadn't she done that enough already? "Well . . . sorry to interrupt. Maybe you could tell Roarke I'll meet him at the memorial."

"If you'd hold a moment, I'll put you right through to him."

"But—" Too late, she thought with a roll of her eyes as her calming blue screen saver came on.

And, as advertised, a moment later Roarke's vivid blue eyes replaced the calm. "Just called to chat?"

"Yeah, it's just talk, talk, talk with me. Listen, I just wanted to leave a message that I'll meet you at the memorial. It's still too early, so I'm going to duck into a cyber café or something, get a little work done, then cab it over."

"Where are you?"

"I'm over on Third, heading down to Fifty-fourth. So—"

"Wait there."

"Listen—" Too late, she thought again, as this time her screen went blank. "Wait there," she mumbled and jammed the 'link back in her pocket. Wait so he could drive across town to pick her up when she was perfectly capable of getting herself where she needed to go.

She could hardly call any of the women on the list Linny Luce had given her while she stood on the damn street. Those conversations would involve considerable delicacy, she imagined. And privacy.

At loose ends, she strode to the corner, swung wide of the throng waiting for the light, and studied them for a while.

Briefcases, shopping bags, baby carts—strollers, she corrected. Three people at the curb tried to out-jockey each other for position while they held up their arms to signal a cab. And the fleet of yellow streamed by, already hauling fares. Up the block a maxibus farted as it lumbered to a stop to disgorge passengers, take on more.

Some guy bopped by eating a slice and, as the scent reached out and beckoned like a lover, Eve remembered she'd not only given her ride to Peabody, but left the crullers in it.

Damn it.

She leaned back against the corner of the building while sky trams cruised overhead, traffic clogged the street, and the subway rumbled under it. Everybody going somewhere, or coming back from somewhere else.

While she waited, a couple of women already loaded like pack mules with shopping bags stopped by the display window beside her. And cooed, Eve thought, with the same over-the-top, slightly lame-brained adoration as Mavis cooing over Belle.

"Those *shoes*! They're absolutely beyond."

"Oh God! And the bag. Do you *see* the bag, Nellie? It looks positively gooshy!"

Eve tracked her gaze over. They looked like a couple of perfectly normal, perfectly sane women, she noted. And they were about to drool on the display glass over a pair of shoes and a purse. They continued to rhapsodize as they pulled the shop door open. Where, Eve assumed, they would shortly drop many hundreds of dollars for something to cart their junk around in, and many hundreds more for something that made their feet cry like babies.

She glanced away in time to spot some guy in a green army coat come flying across the street, dodging vehicles, clambering over others with a wild, happy grin plastered on his face. Happy, she assumed, because the beat cops in pursuit huffed half a block back, losing ground.

People scattered as people tended to do. Eve continued to lean back against the building, but she rolled to her toes and back as she gauged the timing. Green Coat bugled a hooting call of triumph when his combat-booted feet smacked the pavement. And flicking a glance—and his middle finger— behind him, kicked in for the dash down Fifty-fourth.

Eve simply shot out her foot.

He flew, the green coat rising like wings, and landed with what had to be a skin-scraping slide over the sidewalk. He groaned, grunted, managed a half-roll. She helped him the rest of the way to his back with a shove of her boot, which she then planted on his sternum.

"Nice take-off, bad landing." She pulled out her badge as much for the people rubbernecking as the guy under her boot.

"Shit, shit! I had it cooked and in the pan."

"Yeah? Well, now it's burnt, and so are you."

He held his hands out to show his cooperation, then used the back of one to swipe blood off his face. "What the hell're you doing standing around the damn corner?"

"Just waiting for my ride." She saw it cruise up, the mile-long black limo that actually made her stomach hurt with embarrassment. When Roarke lowered the back window, cocked his head, grinned, all she could do was scowl.

The beat cops huffed and puffed their way up to her. "We appreciate the assistance, ma'am. If you'd just—Lieutenant," the cop panted when she badged him in turn. "Lieutenant. Sir. We were in pursuit of this individual as—"

"This individual made your pursuit look like a couple of old ladies hobbling back to their rocking chairs."

"Fucking-A right," said the individual.

"Shut up. You're winded, sweating," she continued. "And this guy was fresh as a daisy until his face met the sidewalk. This embarrasses me. Now if you've got your breath back, wrap him up."

"Yes, sir. For the report, Lieutenant, the individual—"

"I don't care. He's all yours." She strode toward the limo. "Lay off the crullers," she called back, then climbed inside the shining black car.

12

"I WONDER," ROARKE SAID CONVERSATIONALLY, "HOW the city of New York and its population manage without you personally patrolling its streets."

She'd have come up with a smart remark, but he distracted her by handing her a cup of coffee. She reminded herself as she settled back that the windows were tinted. Nobody could actually see her stretched out in a limo with white rosebuds in crystal tubes while she drank coffee out of a porcelain cup.

So she did. "Why?" she asked. "Why did you pick me up in this ostentatious street yacht?"

"First, I don't find it ostentatious, but convenient. And very comfortable. Second, I had a bit of work to polish off on the way over and didn't want to drive myself. Third, *you* mentioned work, so if you need to do any, this is more comfortable than a cyber café."

"Maybe that's logical." She drank more coffee, closed her eyes a moment. And Roarke's fingers brushed her cheek.

"Did the man sprawled on the sidewalk and under your boot get any licks in?"

"No. He never saw it coming. I've just got a lot in my head."

Now he brought her hand to his lips. "Why don't you let some of it out."

She eyed him. "Was there a fourth reason we're in this boat, and was that so you could put moves on me?"

"Darling, that would be the underlying reason for all my decisions."

Because she could, she grabbed his lapel, yanked him over, and took his mouth in a kiss full of heat and promise. Then pushed him away again. "That's all you get."

"I'd prove differently, but it seems a little . . . crass as we're biding some time before attending a memorial."

He could prove differently, she knew. And the hell of it was, she enjoyed when he did. She sat a moment, trying to put her thoughts back in order. "You got any crullers on tap?"

"You want a cruller?"

"No. Damn that Peabody. Anyway—"

Roarke held up a finger, pressed the intercom. "Russ, swing by a bakery, will you, and pick up a half a dozen crullers."

"Yes, sir."

No wonder her head was screwed up, Eve thought. A couple of minutes before she'd had her boot on some idiot's chest while she dressed down a couple of lead-footed uniforms. Now she was gliding around New York drinking outrageously good coffee and getting crullers.

"You were saying?" Roarke prompted.

Might as well go with the flow. She crossed her booted ankles. "I spent the morning conducting interviews. So yeah, it's been a chatty day."

She ran it through for him, which never failed to organize her thoughts for herself. She paused only when the driver passed Roarke a bakery box, shiny white this time. She wrapped it up snacking on sugar and fat.

"It appears," Roarke said, offering her a napkin, "that when people scrape the veneer away, as you've prompted them to do, Ava Anders doesn't appear quite so smooth and glossy."

"They don't like her. What they liked, with the exception of Leopold who liked nothing about her, ever, was filtered through Anders. Tommy. With him not there as filter, the smudges are coming through. She doesn't care about being liked. Or cares only because being liked is a stepping stone to being admired. Being admired, now that's important, and it's a stepping stone to being influential."

"And Tommy. Another stepping stone."

"Yeah. People have been sleeping and/or marrying their way to the top since the first cavewoman said: 'Ugh, that one's the stronger and has the biggest club. I'll shake my mastodon-skin-covered ass at him.' "

"Ugh?"

"Or whatever cave people said. And it's not just women who do it. Cave guy goes: 'Ugh, that one catches the most fish, I'll be dragging her off to my cave now.' Ava sees Tommy and—"

"Says ugh."

"Or today's equivalent thereof. There's a rich guy, a guy people like, who has good press. A nice, easygoing sort. You can bet your ass she researched him inside out before she settled on him. Worked the transfer to New York, made sure to put herself in front of him as often as possible. Four-walls him, too. But subtly. Too aggressive, you could scare him off, too delicate he might not pick up on it. You put on the suit, the 'what Tommy likes and how Tommy likes it' suit, and you wear it like skin. And after you reel him in, you keep the suit on. Maybe a few adjustments here and there, but you keep it on. You get some power, you get the big houses, fancy life. You get some prominence, some *position*. And nudge him out of the house every chance you get so you can take the suit off and fucking breathe."

"For nearly sixteen years?"

"She could've done it for twice that. But you know what happened? His father died. I gotta look at that." She tucked it into a handy corner of her mind. "And I need to check with Charles, but I'll lay you odds her first session with Charles was only weeks after the old man went under and Tommy inherited. Boy, the stakes just went way up. 'Look at all this, and it could all be mine. How can I have it, and get out of this frigging suit.' It's gotta be itching some, and he's only got a decade on her. He could live another fifty, sixty years. It's just too much. Anyway, she's earned it. God knows, she's earned it. Divorce won't do. She could work it, sure she could work it so it was all his fault, like she did the first husband."

"But as that's already been done, it wouldn't do to repeat herself."

"You got it," she said, pleased. "And the payoff wouldn't be enough in a divorce. Not anymore, not with all the years she's put in. If he'd just die, she could be the shattered widow, the widow who picks up the pieces of her life and goes on. Why can't he just die, why can't he have a fatal accident, why . . . What if?"

"She wouldn't be the first to hook herself to wealthy then grow weary of the price," Roarke commented. "Or the first to kill over it. But the method in this case seems particularly vindictive."

"Had to be. Terrible accident, but more, one brought on by his own weakness, his own disloyalty to her. The worse he looks, the brighter her halo. And, I think, once she saw a way out, that suit got tighter and tighter until it was cutting off her blood supply. Whose fault is *that*?"

"Why his, of course."

"Oh yeah. He had to pay for that, for all the years she wore it, all the years she played the game." As she sat in the fragrant air of the limo, Eve could all but feel Ava's rage. "She hated him at the end. Whatever she felt at the start, or during, at the end she hated him."

"And the killing itself was so intimate, and so ugly," Roarke said, "because of the hate behind it."

"Bull's-eye."

"If it played out the way you think, she still has an obstacle. There's Ben."

"I bet she's got plans for Ben. She can bide her time. Unless he gets in a serious relationship, starts thinking marriage. She'd have to move faster then. Or she might consider setting it up soon. An overdose would be best. Pills, too many pills. He couldn't take the grief, couldn't take the pressure of stepping into his uncle's shoes. Opts out. There's a risk there, but if I close this case with her in the clear, as she expects, she might take it."

"Do you intend to warn him?"

"He's clear for now. Case is open, and she needs more time." Calculating it, Eve tapped her fingers on her thighs. "She needs time to lean on him, to turn to him. To present the image that he's her support now, all she has left of Tommy now. She plans, and she considers contingencies. She needs public displays of their mutual grief and dependence to establish the foundation."

"I can't say I knew Thomas Anders well, but I would have said he was a good judge of character."

"Love clouds things."

"It does, yes." Roarke danced his fingers over the ends of her hair.

She shifted to face him. "You never asked yourself, not even once, if I made a play for you because of the money?"

"You didn't make a play for me. I made the play."

"That could've been my play." She smiled at him. "And you fell heedlessly into my wiles."

"Where I landed very comfortably. The only suits you wear, darling Eve, are the ones in your closet. And then they're worn reluctantly." He laid his hand, palm down, between her breasts. "I know your heart, *a ghra.*" And drew the chain she wore under her shirt. On it winked a diamond and the metal of a saint, gifts from him. "Do you remember when I gave you this?"

He swung the chain lightly so the diamond flashed and burned.

"Sure."

"You weren't just horrified and confused, you were terrified. Fearless Lieutenant Eve Dallas, terrified by a piece of compressed carbon and what it represented."

"Love wasn't supposed to happen. Not in my what-if. Not then."

"Yet, when you finally came to me, you wore it." The diamond sparked between them. "And you wear it still. Hidden most of the time to preserve your odd cop sensibilities, but worn just there, against your heart." He slid it under her shirt again. "It was you, Lieutenant, who fell into my guile, after I gave you a bloody good shove."

"I guess we both took a fall." She glanced out the window as the limo drew to a curb behind other limos—the somber glamor of death. "Too bad Anders didn't have a better landing with his."

Photographs of Anders stood throughout the elegant double parlor. He swung a golf club or a bat, hiked a football or returned a tennis volley among the meadow of flowers on display. Sunflowers, with their deep velvet brown eyes, dominated.

"His favorite," Ben told them. "Uncle Tommy used to say if he ever retired he'd buy a little farm somewhere and grow nothing but sunflowers."

"Did he have plans for that?" Eve asked. "For retiring?"

"Not really. But he did make some noises about finding a place outside the city, taking long weekends. As long as there was a golf course handy. He was sort of toying with the idea of building a farmhouse by the sports camp upstate. A real country home, where he and Ava would eventually retire. He'd have his sunflowers, get out of the city a little more until then, and have full use of the camp facilities. Said he'd have to put in a spa for Ava, to get her to go along with it."

He smiled with grief raw in his eyes. "Anyway, he loved sunflowers. He was loved, too. We're having simultaneous memorials, all over the world. Right now, all over the world people are . . . Sorry, excuse me a minute."

He turned toward the door. Eve wondered if he'd make it out before breaking down. And she saw Leopold cross the room quickly and, laying a hand on Ben's shoulder, walk out with him.

Love, Eve thought, in sorrow and selflessness.

Then she turned to study the widow who sat pale of cheek, damp of eye in a blue velvet chair surrounded by flowers and people eager to console her. Once again, her hair was coiled at the back of her neck to show off fine bones, sharply defined features. Her widow's weeds were unrelieved black, perfectly cut to showcase her statuesque build. She wore diamonds, exquisitely, at her ears, her wrists.

"Careful," Roarke murmured, "the way you're aimed at her, the hair on the back of her neck will stand up in a minute."

Not such a bad idea, Eve thought. "Let's go offer our condolences."

Tommy had drawn a crowd, Eve thought as she moved through it. That would please the widow, that good PR the media would run with. As she approached, Ava lifted her gaze, glimmering with suppressed tears and, bracing a hand on the arm of her chair as if she needed the support, rose.

"Lieutenant. How kind of you to come. And Roarke. Tommy would be so pleased you took this time."

"He was a good man." Roarke took Ava's offered hand. "He'll be missed."

"Yes, he was, and he will be. Have you . . . have you met my friend, my dear friend Brigit Plowder?"

"I believe we have. It's nice to meet you again, Mrs. Plowder, even under such difficult circumstances."

"Sasha will be devastated you remembered me and not her." Brigit smiled at Roarke, a warm hostess to a guest. "Would you sign the mourners' book? It's an old-fashioned custom we thought Tommy would appreciate." She gestured to the narrow podium beside her, and the gilt-edged white book open on it.

"Of course." Roarke took up the gold pen to sign.

"You should have some wine." As if confused or mildly ill, Ava touched her fingers to her temple. "We're serving wine. Tommy so enjoyed a party. He wouldn't want all these tears. You should have some wine."

"I'm on duty." And for a moment, for just an instant, Eve stared into Ava's eyes and let her see. *I know you. I know what you are.*

In Ava's, behind that sheen of tears, flashed surprise. And for only a moment, for just an instant, heat flared with it. Then she swayed against her friend. "I'm sorry. I'm so sorry. I feel . . ."

"Sit now." Brigit eased Ava into the chair, stroked her cheek. "Sit back, Ava. You're taking on too much."

"How can it ever be enough? How can I . . . Where's Ben? Where's Ben?" A single tear spilled out of each brilliant eye. "I need Ben."

"I'll fetch him for you." Roarke glanced at Eve, then made his way through the crowd of mourners.

"He'll be right along," Brigit soothed. "Ben will be right along. We'll take you upstairs, sweetheart. You need some quiet. It's too warm in here, too close, with so many people. It's all too much."

"I'll give you a hand with that." Eve stepped closer. "Why don't I help you upstairs, Mrs. Anders?"

"I want Ben." Ava turned her face away to press it against Brigit. "I'll be stronger if I have Ben. He's all I have left of Tommy."

"He's coming now. He's coming, Ava."

Ben rushed through the room, the grief coated over with concern. He bent over Ava like a shield. "I'm here. I just went out for some air. I'm right here."

"Stay with me, Ben. Please, stay with me, just until we get through this."

"Let's take her upstairs."

"No, Brigit, I shouldn't leave. I need—"

"Just for a few minutes. Just a few minutes upstairs until you feel better."

"Yes, you're right. A few minutes. Ben."

"Here we are. Take my arm. You'll have to excuse us, Lieutenant."

"Sure."

So the widow, overcome, was led away to her private grief. Pitch-perfect, Eve thought. She could use some air herself, she decided, then spotted Nadine Furst across the room with Roarke.

"Personal or professional?" Eve asked when she joined them.

"Like cops, it's always both for journalists. But personal leads the way here. I liked him, very much. And Ben." She glanced toward the doorway, brushing back the sleek sweep of hair as she watched them go. "I was outside with him, having a word, when Roarke came out for him. Poor Ava, she looks so lost."

"Oh, she knows where she's going."

Nadine's eyes lit and narrowed. "What's that I hear? You don't seriously think—" She cut herself off, took a sip of the wine in her hand. "Too many ears in here. Why don't we step outside?"

"Not ready for a one-on-one."

"Peabody's better than I thought," Nadine said after a moment. "If what's going on is what I think is going on. She never dropped a crumb. Some pals you are."

"You be a pal first. Dig up those old interviews you told me about, send them to me."

"I can do that. What's in it for me?"

"That's going to depend."

"Look, Dallas—"

"Did I mention," Roarke interrupted, "how strong I found your interview with Peabody last night? You drew the best out of her, effortlessly."

"Teamwork." Nadine sulked at both of them. "I hate that."

"Get me the interviews, Nadine, then I'll give you what I can when I can. But for now, I've had enough of this place. So—shit. It's Tibble's wife. Damn it."

Not ready yet, was all Eve could think as the tall, whip-thin woman aimed toward her. Brutally short, honey brown hair crowned a strong, stunner of a face the shade of the well-steeped Irish tea Roarke occasionally enjoyed. Eve had heard the stories that once upon a time Karla Blaze Tibble made her living—and considerable sensation—as a fashion model. If she'd stalked the runways with the same purpose and panache as she crossed a mourning room, Eve decided, she would've been hard to beat.

"Lieutenant." Her voice was smoky music, her eyes tiger gold.

"Ma'am."

"Ms. Furst, Roarke, I wonder if you'll excuse us a moment? I need to speak to the lieutenant in private."

It might've been posed as a request, but there was command in the posture. Karla simply turned, and people parted for her as the Red Sea parted for Moses as she strode to the door.

"Courage." Though there was amusement in his tone, Roarke gave Eve's shoulder a supportive squeeze.

"Why do they have to have wives? Why do cops have to have wives? I'll be back in a minute." With little choice, Eve followed in Karla's wake, and joined her on the narrow, third-floor terrace.

With the traffic snarling below, Karla stood with her back to the rail. "As the primary on an open homicide, can you possibly think it's appropriate for you to speak with a reporter at the victim's memorial?"

"Excuse me, ma'am, Nadine Furst is also a personal friend."

"Friendship doesn't apply. You have a position to uphold."

Screw this, Eve thought. "Yes, I do—as do you. As the wife of the chief of police, can you possibly think it's appropriate for you to attend the memorial of the victim of an open homicide case, and speak with individuals who may be on the investigator's suspect list?"

The fury flashed, a beautiful blaze that kindled in those tiger eyes, on that amazing face. Then it banked down to an irritated simmer. "You have a point. It's very annoying that you have a point."

"I can assure you that I haven't discussed the details of the investigation with Nadine, or any other media contact."

"Yet."

"She's a useful source, and—at my discretion as primary—I may elect to use that source. As she's no pushover, I may elect to trade information for information."

"Dirt for dirt."

"If it's useful dirt, yes, ma'am."

"Oh, stop calling me 'ma'am' as if I were your third-grade teacher." She spun around to lean on the rail, facing the street this time. "I'm upset, and it set me off to see you huddled with Nadine Furst."

"I'd huddle with Jack the Ripper if it aided the investigation. I have a job to do. I understand this is upsetting to you. Your friend's husband has been murdered. You should understand that finding his murderer and building a case against that individual are my priorities."

"And I've already poked my nose in twice." Karla lifted her hands off the rail in a gesture Eve interpreted as truce. "I don't make a habit of that."

"No, you don't."

"Ava and I are friendly. We've worked closely together on several projects, and I admire her energy, her creative thinking. I liked Tommy Anders very much. He was a generous, unpretentious man, so yes, it's very difficult to accept he was murdered. And the circumstances of it, the media coverage of it. As the wife of a prominent man, I sympathize with Ava on many levels right now."

Karla turned around. "As the wife of a prominent man, so should you."

"As the primary investigator, my sympathies are with the victim."

"You're a hardcase, Lieutenant." Karla shook her head, but the fire had gone out. "Your commander considers you the best of his best. My husband believes you to be brilliant. While I generally stay out of my husband's business, I pay attention. So I know you have a reputation for getting it done. I suppose it takes a hardcase to get it done. So. I'm told you wanted to speak to me about Ava and Tommy."

"Most specifically about your work with them."

"You suspect that something within the charity work precipitated Tommy's murder."

"I need to cover all areas to conduct a thorough investigation."

"Which is cop-speak for none of your business." Karla waved a hand. "I'm not offended. Ava and I worked on a number of projects over the last couple of years. She contacted me initially to ask me to cochair and help coordinate a fashion show. Logical, given my background."

"A sports fashion show?"

"No, actually, this was geared toward the mothers of children qualified for the sports camps and associated programs. Affordable daywear, work wear, sportswear, with several of the mothers as models. Participating merchants offered generous discounts, and Anders provided each woman with a thousand-dollar wardrobe allowance. Something fun for them, as most of the emphasis is on the children. We followed up a few months later with a children's show—school clothes, athletic gear. Both were very successful. Ava was tireless."

"So I've learned."

"We've also implemented other activities. We—or Ava and some of the staff and volunteers—took the mothers to a spa resort while their children were at camp. A kind of retreat where for five days they could relax, be pampered, attend seminars, workshops, have discussion groups. It's a lovely time."

"You've attended."

"Yes, once or twice. As a den mother, so to speak. It was very rewarding to see these women who rarely have any time for themselves have an opportunity to focus on their own minds, bodies, spirits."

"They must have been incredibly grateful for that, and to Ava for providing them with a sample of a lifestyle outside of their own."

"A break from work, children, responsibilities, yes. Fun was a priority, but also education, networking, a support system. Just as in the one- or two-day retreats held in New York, or other locations throughout the year for the Moms, Too, program. A number of these women are single parents, and as such have little time to socialize, to *be* anything but a mother."

Enthusiasm for the program infused Karla's voice. Her hands moved, energetically conducting her words. "Often when a parent loses herself—or himself—in the day-to-day responsibilities and demands of raising children, they become a less effective, and less loving parent than they might be. Than they want to be. So Ava conceived of Moms, Too."

"Being together like that, at that kind of retreat or organizing a fashion show, it would be natural, wouldn't it, for you and Ava to become involved with the participants? Develop relationships."

"Yes, it's something else I've found rewarding. Tommy went beyond providing children with equipment, or even a place to use it. His idea of bringing them together, in training, in competitions, encouraging them to work and play together does so much more than put a ball glove in a child's hand. It gives them pride, friendships, an understanding of teamwork and sportsmanship. Ava's vision for the adjunct program is to give exactly that to the mothers. And to put a personal face on it, as Tommy does—did—with his active participation in the camps, in the fathers' programs, the parent-child competitions.

"And I'm going to start campaigning for funds any minute," Karla said with a laugh. "But yes, involvement is key, I think. Charity can be difficult, Lieutenant, to give or receive. These programs are designed to instill pride and self-worth."

"Outlining and executing the programs you've done with Ava must take incredible planning, an eye for details, a skill for delegation."

"Absolutely. Ava's a master at all of that."

Eve smiled. "I believe it. I appreciate you taking the time to speak to me."

"And I'm dismissed. I should get back in, say my good-byes. I hope there are no hard feelings between us."

"None on my side."

"Then I'll wish you luck with the investigation." She offered her hand again. "Oh, and, Lieutenant, a little concealer would cover up that bruise under your eye."

"Why would I want to do that?"

In the limo, Eve stretched out her legs and said, "Huh."

"As neither of you limped back inside bloody, I assume you and your chief's wife came to terms."

"Yeah, you could say. And it's funny what people say and how they say it. She's *friendly* with Ava. She liked Tommy very much. She admires Ava's energy and creative thinking. Tommy was generous and unpretentious. Mrs. Tibble's a smart woman, but she doesn't get what she just told me. That, and more." Eve shifted to Roarke.

"The other day, you gave a few bucks to a sidewalk sleeper."

He lifted his eyebrows. "Very possibly."

"No, I saw it. Outside the morgue."

"All right. And?"

"A lot of people probably tossed that guy a few that day, and a lot of other days. They don't remember him after, he doesn't remember them. But you crouched down and spoke to him eye-to-eye. Made it personal, made the connection. He'll remember you."

"He's likely to remember the twenty more."

"No, don't get cynical on me. Back when you were running the streets in Dublin, when your father beat down on you until you were half-dead. Summerset took you in, fixed you up. He offered you something—a chance, a sanctuary, an opportunity. What would you have done to pay him back? Cut out the years between then and now, and what developed between you," she added. "Then, right then, what would you have done to pay him back?"

"Whatever he'd asked."

"Yeah. Because then, he was the one with the power, with the control, with the . . . largesse. However much of a badass you were, you were vulnerable. Smaller, weaker. And he'd given you something you'd never had."

"He never asked," Roarke said.

"Because despite being a tight-assed fuckface, taking advantage of the vulnerable isn't his style. But it's Ava's."

"Where are you going with this?"

"To work. I need to see what Peabody's got so far, see if I can wheedle a quick meet with Mira. I have to get some of this organized in my head, get it down. I'll fill you in at home, then take advantage of your vulnerability of being crazy about me and curious about the case so I can put you to work."

"I'll accept that, particularly if you take advantage of me otherwise afterward."

"I'll schedule that in. I want—whoa, whoa. Wait!" She fumbled for the intercom. "Pull over. Pull over here."

"Why?" Roarke demanded as the limo swept to the curb. "We're two blocks from Central yet."

"Exactly. Do you think I want to pull up in front of my house in this thing? Jeez. I'll walk from here."

"Want the crullers?"

"Keep 'em." She grabbed the door handle with one hand, his hair with the other. One hard kiss and she was out the door. "See you."

And he watched as her long stride ate up the sidewalk, her coat billowing. Watched until she was swallowed up by distance and people.

WITH HER MIND TAPPING OUT DETAILS, EVE headed toward Homicide with the same ground-eating stride Roarke had admired outside. Not a break in the case, she thought, not yet, but damn if she didn't think she had a crack. And she was going to chisel and hammer away at that crack until it busted wide open.

Another part of her brain registered a need for caffeine, debated between supplying it hot or cold. When cold won, she stopped in front of Vending and eyed the machine with suspicion and dislike.

"Don't fuck with me," she mumbled, and plugged in credits. "Tube of Pepsi."

The machine seemed to consider, to ponder—she all but heard it whistling a taunting tune. And just as she reared back to give it a good kick, it spat out the tube along with its tedious content data. Eve snatched the tube out before it changed its mind and, turning, saw Abigail Johnson sitting on the same bench Tiko had used the day before.

Tension tightened at the back of Eve's neck as she approached the woman. "Mrs. Johnson."

"Oh, Lieutenant Dallas. I was daydreaming, didn't see you there." Shifting the box on her lap, Abigail got to her feet.

"Is there a problem?"

"No. No, indeed. The fact is, Tiko's about nagged the skin off my bones about that reward. I felt like he should understand doing what's right is enough, then, well, I started thinking it's good for a boy to get something back for doing right. And don't I punish him for doing wrong, and maybe give him some extra screen time or bake his favorite cookies when he does something especially good?"

"Works for me."

"So I contacted that number you gave me, to see about it. It was all taken care of already, they said how you'd seen to that." The bright green eyes stared into Eve's. "Why it was a *thousand* dollars, Lieutenant."

"Early estimates hit about ten thousand a day that ring was pulling in. Tiko was key in shutting it down."

"I can't get over it, that's God's truth. Fact is, I had to sit down fanning myself for a good ten minutes after that Sergeant Whittles told me how much." Abigail tipped back her head and laughed, and the sound was bright as birdsong. "Then, well, I baked you a pie." She thrust the box at a puzzled Eve.

"You baked me a pie?"

"A lemon meringue pie. I hope you like lemon meringue."

"I'd be a fool not to. Thanks."

"When they told me you weren't here, I was going to leave it for you. But I got the strong feeling there wouldn't have been anything left of it time you got back."

"You'd be right about that."

"They said how you'd be back shortly, so I just sat down to wait. They put that right through security downstairs, so they could see I wasn't bringing in anything dangerous. 'Course

I've been told my baking's dangerous to the waistline, but you don't have to fret about that."

Because it seemed to be expected, Eve opened the lid, peeked inside. The meringue looked frothy as a snowcap, with golden beads scattered over its peaks and planes. "Wow. It looks like edible art."

"Isn't that a thing to say. I know it's not much, but I wanted to give you something for what you did for my boy, for my Tiko. He told me all about it, well, about a half a dozen times he told me all about it. I wanted to say to you how it seems to me somebody like you could've brushed him off, or could've called Child Services, or a lot of other things but what you did. I've taught him to have respect for the law, and for right over wrong. But you showed him why, and you put a face on the law and on what's right that he won't forget. He won't be forgetting the reward either, but it's you he'll remember first. And so will I."

"And it seems to me, Mrs. Johnson, that a lot of boys in Tiko's position could've looked the other way—or more, tried to angle their way into a piece of what was going on. But I'll take the pie."

"I hope you enjoy it."

"I may have to knock a few of my men unconscious to get it into my office, but believe me, I will."

Eve got a good grip on the box, and put blood in her eye as she walked into the bullpen. She swore a dozen noses lifted up, at the very same instant, to scent the air. "Not a chance in hell. Peabody, my office."

After shooting a smug and evil smile at her sorrowful colleagues, Peabody breezed in behind Eve. "What kind of pie is it?"

"It's my kind of pie."

"You can't eat a whole pie by yourself. You'll get sick."

"We'll find out."

"But . . . I brought you crullers."

"Where are they?"

Peabody's mouth opened, closed on a pout as she shifted her eyes away. "Um . . ."

"Exactly." Eve set the pie box out of reach on top of her AutoChef. "What have you got besides cruller breath?"

"It's not like I ate them all personally, and you left them behind so— Okay." She deflated under Eve's icy stare. "I've got the duplicate names, and I've started running them. FYI, Mrs. Tibble's on there. She's worked on multiple projects with Ava Anders."

"I think we can take her off the list."

"Yeah. Also the mayor's wife and a number of other prominents."

"We won't discount them. Staff and volunteers go into the mix, but we're going to focus on the participants. The women Ava played Lady Bountiful with."

"I've got some with criminal, got some who were or are LCs."

"Keep them at the top. Trying to figure her. Would she go for somebody with experience, with tendencies, or somebody blank, somebody who'd run below the radar?"

She paced to the window, stared out. "She wouldn't expect us to get here, to look where we're going to look. But somebody who plans as meticulously as she does would have to consider all the possibilities. How did she weigh it?"

"Another question would be how do you convince somebody to kill for you."

"Some people bake pies. Copy all the files, shoot them here and to my home unit. And keep working it, Peabody. If somebody in there was her trigger, I bet she has plans for them, too. I just bet she has plans."

She worked it as well, formulating notes from her conversations that day, pushing through the repeated names Peabody had culled out. And she considered the logistics and man hours of interviewing literally hundreds of potential suspects.

Needle in the haystack. But sooner or later.

She pushed back, circled her head around her shoulders to loosen knots. Her incoming beeped, and it pleased her to see Nadine had sent her a file. "Copy to my home unit," she ordered.

She rubbed her tired eyes. Time to go home herself, she admitted. Take it home, pick it up again, bounce it off Roarke.

She shut down, loaded her bag, shrugged into her coat. She picked up the pie box as Mira stepped to the doorway.

"On your way out?"

"Yeah, but I've got time. They told me you were booked solid today."

"I was. And I'm late heading home. If you're leaving, why don't we walk out together, and you can tell me what's on your mind."

"That'd be good. I've got this theory," Eve began.

She briefed Mira as they took glides down to the main level, then switched to the elevator for the garage.

"The dominant personality, the benefactor or employer convinces, pressures or cajoles the subordinate or submissive to execute her will."

"Execute being the operative term," Eve commented. "But I think *cajole* is a passive term for getting someone to do murder."

"Passivity can be a weapon if used correctly. And such methods have certainly been used for gain. Anything from lying to protect the superior's mistake or misconduct, to providing sexual favors and yes, all the way up to murder. To insure continued cooperation *after* the fact, the dominant would need to continue the relationship, offer and supply reward, or threaten with exposure or harm."

To finish, Eve got off on Mira's garage level. "We're running the ones with jackets, and any LCs—currently or previously—first."

"The most logical place to start."

"The nature of the crime. You'd have to have that in you, or be so completely under Ava's thumb you couldn't so much as wiggle to see that through."

"Or utterly enthralled," Mira added. "Love comes in a lot of forms."

"Yeah, so does gratitude. And fear. I need to figure out which one of those levels she pulled. I let her see today. I let her see I know. Maybe that was a mistake, but I wanted her to sweat a little."

"It's good strategy. It gives the opponent something to worry about, and worried people make more mistakes."

"If I had a little more, just enough to bring her in, to get her in the box, I think I could trip her up. But I need to push her out of her comfort zone, isolate her from . . ." Realizing they were standing beside Mira's car, and she was down to talking out loud, Eve shrugged. "Anyway."

"If and when, I'd like to observe. I think it would be fascinating."

"I'll let you know. So . . . say hi to Mr. Mira."

"I will. Eve, don't go straight to work when you get home. Take an hour. Recharge." In a gesture that never failed to fluster Eve, Mira leaned over, kissed her cheek.

"Well. Good night."

She'd planned to go straight back to work, Mira had her there. More, she'd planned to drag Roarke into it with her. How was she supposed to hammer that crack open if she sat around for an hour doing nothing? She walked into the house with the notion of recharging later.

Summerset loomed; the cat sat and stared.

"I haven't got time for you, Flat Ass."

"Or little else, apparently, as you arrive late. Again. And have used your face as a punching bag. Again."

"That was yesterday. I offered yours, but they judged it too high on the ugly scale."

"Roarke is in the pool house, if you have any interest in your husband's whereabouts."

"I got interest." She tossed her coat over the newel post, dropped her file case at the foot of the stairs, then shoved the box she held into Summerset's hands. "I brought dessert."

That, she thought as she strolled to the elevator, confused him speechless, and was almost as satisfying as her best insult. As she rode down, she rubbed at the back of her neck. Maybe she could take time for a quick swim, stretch out some of these damn kinks she'd earned from too many hours at the comp.

Fifteen minutes, that would set her, then a big, fat burger while she played some of the data and speculations off Roarke. The man sure as hell knew about being the dominant personality.

She stepped out into the moist, fragrant warmth, into the lush green foliage and bright blooms of the tropical gardens of the pool house. Music came from the sparkling waterfall flowing down the wall—and the smooth, rhythmic strokes of the man cutting through the bold blue water of the pool.

He swam like a seal, she thought, sleek and fast, and looked like—well, if she couldn't think it, who could? He looked like a damn Irish god, with that rangy body, the ripple of muscle, the streaming black hair. When he changed up strokes, executed a surface dive, she grinned. With an ass like that, who wouldn't want to sink their teeth into it?

Maybe she could take more than fifteen minutes.

She stripped where she was, took position on the edge, and dove in. When she surfaced, he was treading water, and watching her with eyes that made the bold blue of the pool seem pale.

"It seems I've caught a mermaid."

"You haven't caught anything yet, pal. How many laps have you got in?"

"Twenty-two. I'm after thirty."

"Then I'll catch up."

She pushed off the side. He paced her awhile, which made her kick in to up the speed. Still, they hit the wall together, rolled into the turn and push. She lost him after eight, but moments later heard the rumble that told her he'd settled into the grotto corner, and its jets.

So she lost herself in the rhythm, in the water, in the effort, and somewhere in the twelfth lap, her crowded mind cleared. When she hit thirty, her muscles were loose to the point of limp, her breathing shallow, and her mind utterly relaxed.

She skimmed under the water, surfaced in the grotto beside him.

"God! *That* was a good idea."

"I have any number of them."

She let her head fall back, her eyes close. Under the water her fingers linked with his until she had her breath back. "I've got one of those coming on. Oh yeah, there it is."

She ducked under, rolled, then skimmed her way up to take him into her mouth. The water churned around her as she gripped his hips, as she felt the muscles she'd admired quiver for her. She surfaced, letting her lips run up his belly, his chest, his throat to where his mouth waited to mate with hers.

"I like your idea better than mine."

"Thought you might." She scraped her teeth over his throat. "Mira said I should recharge." Tossing her head back, she shot him a look of pure challenge. "So, recharge me."

He pulled her under with him, into that breathless, beating blue.

He'd thought himself prepared. Relaxed, comfortably aroused watching his wife burn off the day as he had. He'd imagined persuading her into wet, lazy love once she had. Instead the need for her had simply leaped into him, torn through him as a hungry animal who wanted feast and conquest.

It burned through him, a fever in the blood as he devoured her mouth, as his hands sought and took. Her gasp for air when they surfaced ended on a cry of shocked pleasure that only stoked the flames.

Her hands dug into his shoulders when he took her breast. Greedy mouth, demanding teeth. Wet and warm from the water, she trembled from the assault.

And still she said, "Yes."

"Yes," as the water closed over them again.

Her ears roared from the pound of the water, from the pound of her own blood. How could anyone survive wanting, being wanted, like this? How could anyone live without it? He set a storm inside her of feelings, sensations, of desires that throbbed toward pain. A storm that raged and blew and thundered until there was nothing left of her but a drowning, helpless love.

Rough hands pushed her back to the wall where hers gripped the edge, where her moans echoed in the heavy air as his mouth streaked up her thighs, as his tongue arrowed inside her. He tugged, shifting her so the gush of hot jets pulsed over her, inside her—hot, relentless—as his mouth worked her toward frenzy.

"I can't. I can't. God!"

The orgasm was brutal and fierce, a ripping of self from sanity.

He felt it break through her, felt the force and wonder of release. And saw when he looked into her eyes again the complete surrender to it. To him.

"Take. Take me." He drove into her, into that surrender. And lifting her hips, plunged deeper yet. As the madness pummelled him, whipped him, he heard his own voice, thick and breathless, murmuring demands and pleas in Irish she couldn't possibly understand.

And still once more, as his body battered hers, she said, "Yes."

On that single, whispered word, he surrendered.

Sprawled in the pulsing water, limbs like melted wax, Eve wasn't sure who was holding who up. She thought, vaguely, that a double drowning was a distinct possibility. But couldn't seem to care.

"Maybe it's something in the water, some sort of sex drug. You could bottle it, sell it, and make another fortune."

"Hell with that. I'm keeping it all for us. Did I hurt you at all? I'm a bit bleary."

"I can take care of myself, pal." She let her head fall like a rock onto his shoulder. "Besides. My idea."

"And a bloody good one it was."

"I was going straight up to work. Got big, fat, sticky piles of it, so I was going straight up to work. Then the gargoyle said you were down here. I thought maybe I'd take fifteen minutes for a swim, loosen up."

"Well, we sure as Christ loosened up."

"Then I saw you knifing through the water. All wet and ripply and . . . you." She tilted her head back to look at him. "I saw you, and that's all it took. Sometimes I can't breathe I love you so much."

"Eve." Emotion deepened his eyes as he kissed her, very sweetly, then he just rested his brow against hers.

"I keep thinking, well, this'll settle down. It's bound to level off and settle down. But it doesn't. Even when things are just going smooth and we're just . . . living, I can look at you, and I've got no breath left."

"Every minute with you, I'm alive. I never knew before there were pieces of me unborn, just waiting for you. I'm alive with you, Eve."

She sighed, touched his cheek. "We'd better get out of here. We're getting mush all over the pool."

It was back to murder as she pulled on the comfort of her old NYPSD sweatshirt and a pair of worn-out (just the way she liked them) jeans. While they dressed, she relayed to Roarke the conversation she'd had with Mira.

"You're worried now she'll find a way to dispose of this subordinate—as you're thinking of her, or him."

"Gotta have a plan for it. I think she *thinks* this individual wouldn't dare betray her, but she'll have a plan. She's got Brigit Plowder, who doesn't strike me as a moron, completely wrapped. Pretty much ditto on Tribble's wife. But Plowder..."

"Are you looking at her? At Brigit Plowder?"

"I look at everyone, but no, she doesn't strike me as a subordinate or... what's the word? What is it? *Supplicant*. Yeah, that's what our Ava likes. She likes having her supplicants. She bought herself plenty of them with Anders's money."

She caught a glimpse of the two of them in the mirror, paused, took a closer look. He'd put on basically the same thing she had—jeans and in his case a dark-blue sweater. But...

"How come you always look better than me?"

He glanced in the mirror as well, and smiling stepped behind her to wrap his arm around her from the back. "I can't agree with that. Eye of the beholder."

"You're still tuning from water games." She shook her head, studying them, he thought, as she might suspects in a lineup. "It's just not right. Anyway, back off, ace, we've got a load of work ahead of us and—crap, I forgot. I need to tag Charles. I need to do a follow-up there."

To amuse himself, and annoy her, he only tightened his hold.

"Hey."

"Hey, back. It'll be a working meal again, and would that make me your subordinate or your supplicant?"

"Ha-ha. You're nobody's subordinate, and you wouldn't know how to supplicate. Is that a word?"

"I'll look it up. Working meal, and you're thinking . . . burgers."

Her eyes narrowed. "What, have you gone all psychic on me?"

"Logic, and an intimate—as I've recently proven—knowledge of my wife. You missed lunch, discounting a limo cruller, and you've expended a great deal of energy in the pool, with various activities. You're hungry, which leads you to red meat. A steak won't do as you won't want the trouble of cutting anything up. So it's a burger you want."

"What am I having for dessert?"

He cocked a brow at her reflection. "Well, there you have me."

"Yeah, I got you." She turned, bit his lip. "I brought home pie."

"Really? What sort of pie?"

She only smiled, pulled out, and picked up her 'link to tag Charles.

Nervous, distracted, Charles paused outside the brownstone in the West Village and checked the display on his signaling 'link. "It's Dallas," he told Louise.

Worried, uncertain, she watched him frown at the display. "Aren't you going to answer?"

"Ah . . . no. No, I'll get back to her."

"It'll be about the Anders case. Charles, if there's something about that you haven't told her, something you're holding back because of loyalty or discretion—"

"There isn't." He slid the 'link back in his pocket. "Let's go in."

"Actually, Charles, I'm not really in the mood to socialize, especially with new people." She glanced toward the house. "I really think you and I need to talk."

The nerves already buzzing in his belly kicked up to a dull roar. "We will."

"Things haven't been—"

"Don't." He took both her hands. "Just don't. Let's go inside first. I really need to take you inside."

"All right." Inside her belly, something sank. "All right."

He led her through the iron gate, down the walk cutting through a small and lovely front garden, then up the short flight of stairs to the main level of the three-story home. But when he took out keys, she stared.

"What—"

"One minute. Just one minute." He keyed a code on the security pad, unlocked the door.

Baffled, she stepped inside.

Floors gleamed, old, rich wood providing a lovely base for the foyer, for the sturdy stairs with their glossy rail, and on to a spacious room where a fire simmered in a hearth of lapis blue.

"It's empty."

"Yes, for now."

Her footsteps echoed on the wood as she wandered into what she assumed was the living area, as she turned to look at the trio of tall windows with their carved trim.

"It's a lovely space."

"There's a lot more," he told her. "Let me show you through."

"Why?" She turned back to him. "Why are we in a beautiful and empty house in the West Village with you offering to show me through?"

"I bought it." He hadn't meant to tell her exactly that way, but she was standing there, framed by those windows, looking at him with such serious, such somber gray eyes.

"You . . . you bought this house?"

"Yes. Two weeks ago."

"Two . . . I see." She smiled. "Well, congratulations. I didn't realize you were even thinking of relocating, much less buying a home. No wonder you've been so distracted lately. So, show me the rest. These floors, Charles, they're just gorgeous. Are they all the way through? And all this space!"

She started to hurry by, but he caught her arm. "You're upset."

"No, no, just surprised. It's such a big step. Enormous."

"I've taken a couple more. I didn't tell you."

"No, you didn't tell me." Though her eyes stayed on his face, she eased back from him. "You haven't told me much of anything for weeks. So, let me be grown up and civilized about this, will you? Let me try. Is there a dining room? I bet there's a wonderful dining room, perfect for dinner parties."

"I've retired."

Though she'd pulled away to move on, that stopped her again. "What?"

"I turned in my license, the end of last week."

"Last week? I don't understand this, don't understand you. You've turned in your license, bought a house. What is this, Charles?"

"I wanted—needed to have it, to have everything in place before I told you. I applied for, and have been granted a license in psychology, specializing in sex therapy. Dr. Mira helped me there, and agreed that it was a good lateral move."

Louise stared at him with something like grief in her eyes. "You spoke with Mira, but not with me. Asked for her help, but not for mine."

"I wanted to be sure I could pull it off, Louise. She agreed to help me with the applications, the testing, the screening process. And well, talking to her throughout all this helped me be sure it was something I really wanted to do, really could do."

"As talking to me wouldn't have helped?"

"No. Yes. She's neutral, objective. And while she was helping me through it, I was dealing with buying this place. The lower level here is a good space for the office and therapy rooms. And there's . . . I'm not doing this right."

He stopped, pushed at his hair again. For a man who'd made his living, and a damn good one, he thought, on being smooth, he was bumbling this like a first-nighter. "I haven't been able to figure out how to do this. Every time I tried to work it out, I hit a wall. Louise—"

"Then let me make it easy for you. You want to change your life. A new home, a new profession. A new start then." Tears burned, but she'd be damned if she'd end this weeping and sniveling. "New relationships I'm not part of. Fine, show your gorgeous new house to her, you bastard."

"Who? No!" He had to move fast to grab her before she reached the door. "Not part of it. For Christ's sake, Louise, you're the center of it. You're the reason for it."

"How? How am I any part of any of this when you do it all without even *telling* me?"

"What would you have said to me if I told you I was going to retire because of you?"

"That's ridiculous. I've never had a problem with your work. It's your *work*. And it was your work when I met you, when I fell in love with you, damn it, Charles."

"Exactly. It never bothered you. Never made a difference in how you felt about me. But it began to bother me. It began to bother me when I just couldn't give my clients my . . . best. Because, Louise, I don't want to be with anyone but you. I don't want to touch anyone but you. I needed—for myself—I needed to lay the foundation for the new, to believe I could do this. And offer this, to you."

"Offer . . ." Her eyes widened. *"This?* This house?"

"It's closer to your clinic than either of our apartments. It's a nice neighborhood, and it's . . . it's a home, Louise. Not a place to sleep or hang clothes. It's a place to live, together, to build something together."

"I need a second." She put a hand on his chest, eased him back. "You did all this, changed your life, for me?"

"For us. I hope. If you don't like the house, we'll find another. Mira said it would probably be better to wait on the house, to consult you there. But . . . I didn't." At a loss, he lifted his hands, let them fall. "It was probably a mistake to buy it without you. But I wanted to give you something. Something solid, I guess, symbolic, and a little spectacular."

"I thought you were tired of me, that you didn't love me anymore and didn't know how to tell me." She managed a watery laugh. "You've been breaking my heart, Charles, for weeks."

"Louise." He drew her to him, kissed her damp cheeks, her lips. "It must be loving you so much, and being terrified you wouldn't want all this, that's had me screw up so badly."

"I was going to be so sophisticated and cool when you broke things off. Then I was going to gather up any of your things at my apartment and set them on fire. I'd worked it out."

"I was prepared to beg."

She tipped her head back, laid her hands on his cheeks, and smiled beautifully. "I love you, Charles. You didn't have to do this for me, or for us, but I love that you did. I love that you screwed it up. Oh! Show me the rest!" She spun away and into a circle. "Show me every inch so I can start planning how to drive you crazy with decorating ideas. I'll nag you so relentlessly over window treatments and wall colors you'll wonder why you ever wanted to cohab."

"Cohab?" He shook his head. "For two smart people who're desperately in love, we're certainly having a hard time understanding each other." He slipped a small velvet box out of his pocket, flipped the top. The diamond exploded with light and brilliance. "Marry me."

"Oh." She stared at the ring, stared into his eyes. "Oh my God."

WITH THE BURGER DEVOURED, EVE PACED IN FRONT of her wall screens. "What we have to do is divide these into categories, cross-reference. First, the people we know she had multiple contacts with. The more contact, the easier it is to establish a relationship. We put those into categories. Staff, volunteers, beneficiaries."

"She may have met any number of these people off-book," Roarke pointed out. "Private meetings. The nature of that would make the relationship more personal, more intimate."

"Yeah, can't argue. So we divide those up, too. Peabody's got a good start with the multiples, and with those we have individuals with criminals, and we have the LC angle. We need to press that."

She turned back to him. "If you were going to have someone killed—"

"Some chores a man just wants to see to himself."

She blew out a breath, scratched the back of her neck while he smiled serenely. "*If,*" she repeated. "And if you didn't want to get your manicured hands dirty, would you exploit someone with some experience in criminal behavior, someone whose past deed or deeds could also give you a lever, if necessary, or would you go with the blank slate?"

"Interesting, as both have their advantages, and their pitfalls. And it would depend, too, on what the criminal behavior consisted of."

"Yeah, we're going to do a subset there on violent knocks."

"Someone who's killed before—or has a history of violence—would bring that experience or predilection to the table." He continued to enjoy a glass of the cabernet he'd selected to go with the burgers. "Might be, one could assume, more open to bribe, pressure or reward. However, that sort may not be as trustworthy or discreet as the clean slate. Whereas, the clean slate might balk at the idea of murder, or clutch in the execution of it and botch the job."

"Maybe she did."

"The heavy tranq'ing." Roarke nodded as he was right there with her on that point. "It could indicate a delicacy of feeling, yes."

"Yeah, it takes delicacy to wrap a rope around an unconscious guy's neck so he chokes to death."

"From a distance," Roarke pointed out, "where she didn't have to see it. So it happened after she was gone."

"You're leaning toward clean slate."

"If, in my hypothetical murderous bent, I wanted to have someone eliminated—and didn't go the tried and true route of hiring a hit—I'd certainly explore that clean slate. What could I get on her, where is the pressure point or the vulnerability? What could I offer in exchange?"

"A business deal?"

He tipped his glass toward her. "Isn't it? Even blackmail is business."

"Okay. Okay. We'll divvy up this first batch. You take clean slates, I'll take the ones with jackets. And we'll divide the licensed companion connects between us."

"Aren't we the fun couple?"

"We'll dig out the party hats later. Look for any significant change in income, or anything that looks like addictions— gambling, illegals, sex, alcohol. Any debts paid off, any major purchases. They've got kids, so look at tuitions to private schools, or medical procedures. Sick kid's a big button to push. *Any* change in buying habits, income, routine in the last six months. She wouldn't want to string this out too long."

"On the staff—"

"I know what to look for, Eve. It's not my first ride on the hay cart."

"Okay, fine. But this is going to be a long ride on a really big hay cart with a tiny little needle in it somewhere."

"I walked into that one. And now," he said as he strolled toward his office, "I'm walking away."

Eve sat at her desk with coffee, with files. She spent a moment drumming her fingers and staring at her murder board. Then she shifted to begin the first of many detailed runs.

It was the kind of tedious, ass-in-the-chair work that put the knots and kinks back in no matter how thoroughly they'd been smoothed out. She felt them working up between her shoulder blades in hour one, only to lodge gleefully at the base of her neck by hour two.

"How many kids are there who need freaking hockey equipment?" she asked aloud, rubbed her neck. And zeroed in.

"Lookie here. Current data on wall screen," she ordered, then rose, stretching out as she studied the information.

Bebe Petrelli, DOB April 12, 2019. Current address 435 107th Street, Bronx. Parents Lisbeth Carmine, Anthony DeSalvo (deceased). Siblings Francis, Vincente. Married Luca Petrelli (deceased) June 10, 2047. Two children, Dominick Anthony, DOB January 18, 2048, Paul Luca, DOB July 1, 2051.

"Enough, enough, give me the damn criminal."

Working . . .

Charged with possession of illegals substance 2042.
Probation. Charged with possession with intent to distribute
illegals substance 2043, probation on first charge rescinded.
Sentenced to three to five, suspended. Licensed Companion
license revoked. Community service with mandatory
rehabilitation therapy ordered, and completed. Charged with
solicitation without a license, assault, and resisting arrest
2045. Assault charges and resisting charges dropped. Served
one year Rikers, with completion of anger management
program.

"Wonder if it worked. Computer, was subject's father
Anthony DeSalvo of the purported organized crime family?"

DeSalvo, Anthony, father of subject, alleged captain in
DeSalvo family, alleged to be Mafia-based with interests in
illegals, weapons running, protection. DeSalvo, Anthony,
garroted 2044, rival Santini family suspected of ordering his
execution. Brief gang war followed with several deaths and/
or disappearances of purported members. No arrests or
convictions made. Do you want full case files?

"Not at this time." Eve walked over to Roarke's doorway.
"I've got a hot one."

"I've got bleeding nothing. Let's see yours."

He walked in, stood as she did, studying the data with
his thumbs hooked in his front pocket. "Ah, yes, the feuding
DeSalvo/ Santini clans."

"Know any of them?"

"I've made the acquaintance of a few over the years.
They've learned to give me a wide berth."

The casual way he said it, the utter disregard in his tone, reminded Eve once more how dangerous Roarke could be. Yeah, she thought, she bet the wiser of the wise guys gave him a wide berth.

"In any case," he continued, "they're fairly small-time. Bullies and posturers and greedy hotheads. Which is why they're small-time. This family tree and the bloody roots of it would make your current subject of interest to Ava Anders, I'd think. She comes from a family that murders as part of their standard business practices. She's had her own bumps with the law, served time. How'd her husband die?"

"Good question. Computer, details on the death of Petrelli, Luca."

Working . . . Petrelli, Luca, COD fractured skull. Accompanying injuries: broken jaw, broken nose, broken fingers, both hands, broken leg, arm, shoulder. Severe facial injuries, contributory internal injuries. Body was found in the East River near Hunts Point, June 12, 2047.

"Beat the bastard to death," Eve commented. "Computer, was Petrelli known to be or suspected of being connected to organized crime?"

No connection known. Suspected due to relationship with Petrelli, Bebe. None found through surveillance or other investigative methods. Petrelli, Luca, owned and operated, with wife, Bebe's, a restaurant in Hunts Point, Bronx. No criminal record on Petrelli, Luca.

"So she marries clean," Roarke speculated. "Has a couple of kids, opens a restaurant. Not in Queens, where her family claims its contested turf, but in the Bronx. Away from that. Away from them. Then someone beats her man to death."

"And with two kids to raise, money tight, a spotted record, the blood ties, it's hard to make ends meet." Eve eased a hip down on her desk, absently stroking a hand over the cat when he bumped his head against her arm. "Hard to soldier on. You'd be grateful to someone who offered a hand, who didn't hold the past against you. Looks like Peabody and I are heading up to the Bronx in the morning. Computer, list Bebe Petrelli as a person of interest, copy all data to file. Send copy of same to Peabody, Detective Delia, home unit."

"You won't be stopping there."

"No, but that sure gave me a boost. I think it's time we took a break and had ourselves some pie."

"It's always time for pie." He glanced over as the house 'link beeped. "Yes, Summerset?"

"Dr. Dimatto and Mr. Monroe are at the gate."

"Let them in. Oh, and we'll have the pie the lieutenant brought home, with coffee for our guests. In the parlor."

"I'll see to it."

"How come people can drop by out of the blue and get pie?" Eve wondered.

"Because we're such warm and welcoming hosts."

"No, that's you. And it's my pie. Technically." She looked over at the work on her desk with the cat currently sprawled over it all. "Well, hell, I wanted to talk to Charles anyway. Computer, send a notification to Detective Peabody. Report, my home office eight-hundred—no, strike, seven-hundred-thirty hours. Dallas, Lieutenant Eve."

Acknowledged.

"Run next subject, store data." Eve shrugged. "I'll get a little jump on it while we're being warm and welcoming hosts. Anyway, Petrelli was in this fashion show Ava sponsored, attended a number of the one- and two-day Mom breaks, one of the five-day retreats just last summer, and both her kids have attended sports camps three years running."

"Solid connection," Roarke agreed as they started out of the office.

"Last year both of the kids were awarded Anders scholarships. They're in private schools now—Anders pays the freight as long as they meet academic standards and stay out of trouble. That's a lot of motive, a lot of reasons for Petrelli to keep Anders happy. A lot of reasons to be grateful."

"Use the children, particularly the children." Such things always burned in his belly. "Here's what I'll give your boys, here's how your boys can be educated, the opportunities they can have if you just do this little thing for me."

"It clicks pretty good."

"It clicks. And she would ask herself, wouldn't she, how or why anyone would connect her to Anders's murder. How would she ever be brought into it?" Roarke ran a hand down Eve's back as they descended the stairs. "Because she couldn't anticipate you. And neither, no matter how well she planned, could Ava."

Eve stopped at the parlor doorway, winced. Charles and Louise stood inside, wrapped together like pigs in a blanket, sharing a big, sloppy one in front of the parlor fire.

She slipped her hands in her pockets. "You guys need a privacy room?"

"And there's the warm welcome," Roarke murmured as the couple eased apart. And his eyebrows rose as they grinned at each other, then at their hosts like a couple of cats with bellies full of cream.

"Sorry to drop by so late," Charles began. "I got your message that you needed to speak to me, and since we were out—"

"And that's not the reason at all." With her cheeks flushed and glowing, Louise laughed and leaned against Charles. "We wanted to share our news, and used the 'link message as an excuse."

"Congratulations." Roarke crossed over to shake Charles's hand, to kiss Louise's cheek.

"We haven't told you the news yet," Louise complained.

"You don't have to, not with that rock you're wearing blinding us." Eve stood where she was, studying them both. "When did all this happen?"

"Tonight, a couple of hours ago." Louise shot out her hand with the diamond sizzling. "Look, look, look."

The woman was a doctor, Eve thought. A tough-minded, strong-spined woman with a solid core of sense. And she was bouncing like a spring over a chunk of rock. But Eve walked over, let Louise hold the ring up to her face. "Shiny," Eve said.

"It's exquisite." Roarke poked a finger into Eve's ribs. "I have all her taste in jewelry. Ah, Summerset, we'll keep the pie," he said as his man wheeled in a cart, "but we'll want to switch out the coffee for champagne. We're celebrating Charles and Louise's engagement."

"Best wishes. I'll see to it right away."

"I feel like I've already had a couple bottles. I'm so giddy!" Louise threw her arms around Eve, squeezed. "We're thinking May, late May or early June. Something small, sweet. But I'm getting ahead of it. Tell them the rest, Charles."

"We'll be moving into a house in the West Village."

"Oh, God, it's *fabulous*. One of those amazing old brownstones, wonderfully rehabbed. It even has a courtyard garden in the back. Working fireplaces, three levels. I've already earmarked a room on the third floor for my home office. And the lower level is perfect for Charles's clients."

Eve opened her mouth, slammed it back shut. But apparently some sound had snuck out before she zipped it.

"Not those clients." Charles shot Eve a look. "Part three of the news is I've retired, and am about to begin a new career in psychology, specializing in sex therapy."

"*That's* what you were doing with Mira." Eve punched his shoulder.

"Yes. Ouch. She's been an enormous help to me in the transition. A lot of LCs are married, or get married, and manage very well. I didn't want to be one of them."

"Well, good, because that's just screwy. I can say that," Eve complained when Roarke poked her again, "because he's not doing the screwy. Jeez, like you weren't thinking it."

"Excellent timing," Roarke announced when Summerset brought in the champagne. He popped the cork himself, and began to pour while Louise wandered over.

"Wow, look at that gorgeous pie. Look how beautiful the lemon is against the white meringue." She scanned over to Eve. "You'd look good in a lemony yellow."

"I'm more interested in eating the lemony yellow."

"I'm thinking wedding again—matron of honor dress. Charles and I want the two of you to stand up for us. We met through you."

"We'd be absolutely honored." The quick glance Roarke sent Eve was the equivalent of a poke. He passed around champagne, lifted his glass. "To your happiness, and the life you'll make together."

"Thank you." Charles laid a hand on Roarke's arm, then leaned over to kiss Eve, very softly on the lips. "Thank you."

"This is so . . ." Louise blinked at tears. "Everything. I'm so happy, so beyond happy. And now there's champagne and pie."

"Don't drip on it," Eve advised and made Louise laugh.

"I'm so glad you called Charles, so glad you gave us the excuse to come over. I can't think of a better way to cap off the best night of my life."

"About that," Eve began, then wondered why her brain didn't explode from the laser beam Roarke shot out of those wild blue eyes. "It can wait."

"It's all right," Charles told her. "You want to ask me something more about Ava."

Friendship, she thought, was always screwing with procedure. "Tomorrow's fine."

"It's all right," Louise echoed. "If Charles can help, we both want him to. Really," she said to Roarke. "It's another, less giddy reason we stopped in."

"I've thought about it—about Ava," Charles began. "There's been so much going on in my head it's been hard to squeeze it in. But I have thought about it."

"Ah . . . maybe we could go up to my office for a couple minutes."

"Dallas, I know you can't quite get a handle on how I can look at Charles's work—his prior work," Louise added, "as separate from our relationship. But I can. I have. It's not a problem for me. So if you have a question about the LC/client relationship, just ask it."

"I talked to her first husband. Did she ever mention him to you?"

Charles shook his head. "No. I knew she'd been married before. I do a check on any potential client. For safety, and to give myself a sense of them. A fairly early, fairly brief marriage, if I'm remembering right."

"He's an operator. Struck me that way. A womanizer with more money than morals and a really high opinion of himself. Nothing like the type I'd have put her with."

"She was young. Younger," Charles said.

"She walked away from the marriage with a nice financial settlement, after she caught him with another woman. One she'd introduced him to, and according to him, then provided him with ample opportunities to bang. She never brought that up?"

"No, she didn't."

"He also told me that Ava was enthusiastic in bed. Or good in it anyway. I tend to go with that, as his type would be more than happy to say she was a lousy lay. You indicated she was on the shy and cool side. Lights-off type."

"That's right. Sexual levels, preferences, abilities, they all can change. Inhibitions can set in for a lot of reasons."

"And women can fake enthusiasm, or lack thereof. It's tougher for a guy seeing as you wear your enthusiasm or lack thereof between your legs."

"She has such a way with words," Roarke commented. "And imagery."

"She ever fake it with you, Charles? You've been in the game long enough. You'd know. You're too professional not to."

"No, she didn't, and yes, you're right, I would've known. Clients do, occasionally, and it would be my job to determine whether to let it go, or to explore the reasons why they didn't, or couldn't orgasm." His brow knitted as he sipped champagne. "And now that you bring it up, I expected her to have some trouble there, at least the first time or two. Nerves, shyness. But she responded easily."

"You said you get a nice percentage of clients through recommendations, referrals. Did she ever send anyone to you?"

"As a matter of fact, yes. I think she sent a couple clients. One-timers. I don't remember right off, but I can look it up for you."

"Do that." She brooded a moment, trying to think if there was any angle she'd missed. "Okay. Back to pie." She took a good forkful, sampled. "Holy hell. Speaking of orgasms."

"A subject of which I never tire." Roarke took a bite himself. "Well now, this is miraculous. Where did you get it?"

"This kid's granny baked it. Talk amongst yourselves. The pie and I are busy." She got down to it, bite by tart and frothy bite. Until some bit of conversation intruded on her concentration.

"An option for you," Roarke continued. "As you consider the where and when of it."

"A wedding here? In the gardens? I don't know what to say. Charles?"

He smiled at Louise. "Bride's choice."

"Then I know exactly what to say. Yes. It's my second best yes of the night! Yes, thank you so much."

"That's fine then. Come around whenever you like to have a look around. Summerset would be a help to you there. It's a lovely spot for a wedding." Roarke looked over at Eve. "And, I think, a lucky one."

"Yeah. It's pretty damn lucky."

When the happy couple left, Eve walked back up with Roarke. "One question," she began. "Does having a wedding here mean I have to do stuff?"

"Stuff as in?"

"Screw around with caterers and florists and decorators."

"I believe Louise will want full control there."

"Thank God."

"Of course, as matron of honor, you'll have certain duties."

"What? Duties? You stand there in a fancy dress, probably holding a bunch of flowers."

He patted her shoulder as they turned into her office. "You keep thinking that, darling, for as long as it comforts you."

She scowled, pulled at her hair. "It's like Mavis having a baby, isn't it? I have to do all this stuff because they're doing all this stuff, which is completely—when you think about it—*their* stuff, but it gets to be my stuff because somehow or other *they* got to be my stuff."

"The fact I followed that clearly from point to point proves you're my stuff."

"I'm not thinking about it. I'm just not. It makes the backsides of my eyes ache. Computer, display last run."

Blowing out a breath, she dropped down at her desk to get back to murder. That was the stuff she understood.

Shortly after 1 a.m., she roused when Roarke slid an arm under her knees. "Damn it, I dropped out. Just for a minute. You don't have to . . ." But when he picked up her, she shrugged a shoulder. "Okay, what the hell. I got two more possibles. Not as strong as Petrelli, but possibles."

"Mmm." Her voice was slurry, a sign she'd not only hit the wall but slid bonelessly under it.

"Need interviews, then could run some probabilities. Gotta hammer the crack."

"Absolutely. I'll fetch you a nice big hammer first thing in the morning."

"Got hundreds left to run. Longer it takes, longer she has to patch up the damn hole. Not going to run though, no sir, not going to run."

"No, indeed." He carried her up to the bed, laid her down. As he started to unbutton her jeans, she sat up, patted his hand away.

"I can do it. You get ideas."

"Yet somehow I can resist them when my wife's all but comatose. Heroic of me."

She smiled sleepily as she wiggled out of the jeans. "Better not forget that, 'cause I'm sleeping naked." She tossed aside the sweatshirt, then climbed under the fluffy duvet. "Gonna nail it down," she murmured as she snuggled in. "It's coming around, I can feel it, and I'm going to nail it down."

"There's that hammer again." He slid in beside her, draped an arm around her waist. "Pick it up tomorrow, Lieutenant. Time to lay the tools down for the night."

"Bet she sleeps like a baby. I bet she . . . Shit!" She flopped over in bed so quickly, Roarke had to shoot down a hand to catch her knee.

"Mind the jewels then."

"He had traces of over-the-counter sleep aid in him."

"A lot of people take sleep aids routinely. In fact, on nights such as this it's a wonder I don't."

"Didn't think about them overmuch as the trace matched with what he had in his bathroom. Just a standard. But I asked Ben and the house manager, and neither of them can confirm he was a routine user. So what if she planted them there? What if she found a way to get some into him that night."

"When she was in St. Lucia."

"He took vitamins—a whole buncha vitamins regularly. He had this, ah . . . crap, my brain—"

"Is begging you to turn it off."

"It has to wait. He had this weekly dispenser deal. You fill up each day's dose, so you don't have to open a bunch of bottles or try to remember if you took the E and not the C—whatever. She could've pulled a switch."

"So he fell asleep at his desk that morning, or while putting on the third green."

"He took them at night." She smiled in the dark. "He took them at night because he thought that helped them absorb better. That's in my notes somewhere."

"All right then, she switched pills. How would you prove it, and what would you do with it should you?"

"Just another piece to poke at. I don't remember seeing any sleep aids in her bathroom, in her night table. But she said she might take a soother, or take an aid now and then."

"She was traveling," he reminded her. "She might have taken them with her."

"Yeah, I'm going to check on that. And what if—"

"Eve?"

"Yeah?"

"Remember that hammer I said I'd fetch you in the morning." She frowned in the dark. "Sort of."

"Don't make me get it now and knock you out with it." He kissed the tip of her nose. "Go to sleep."

She frowned in the dark for another minute, but her eyes began to droop. She felt his arm go around her again, drawing her in, then the muffled thud as Galahad pounced onto the foot of the bed.

As the cat arranged himself over her feet, she dropped into sleep.

IN SLEEP, SHE ARRANGED THEM. THOMAS ANDERS at the center with the others fanning out like rays. Ava, Ben, Edmond and Linny Luce, Greta Horowitz, Leopold Walsh, Brigit Plowder, Sasha Bride-West.

But no. She shifted restlessly in sleep. No, that wasn't right. He wasn't the sun, he wasn't the center. Not to her. He was only the vehicle, he was only the means.

Expendable, when the time was right. Steady, reliable, not very spectacular, predictable Tommy.

Left with a nice chunk of change. Dirk Bronson lounged in a deck chair behind Ava, sipping a frothy drink. *Not a backward glance.*

Seed money. The kickoff. The flashy lead-off batter.

Change the lineup.

In the dream, the ball field was summer green and rich brown, the white bases gleaming like marble plates. The players took that field in uniforms black as death. Brigit crouching behind the plate—catcher to Ava's pitcher—Sasha fussing with her hair at short, Edmond at first, Linny at second, Ben playing the hot corner at third with Leopold and Greta patrolling right and left fields respectively.

Short a man, Eve thought. They're short a man at center field.

I'm always the center. Ava smiled, wound up, and winged a high, fast curve. At the plate, Tommy checked his swing.

Ball one.

The crowd, in their black mourning clothes, applauded politely. *Nice call, ump.* Eve glanced back, scanned the dugout. Even in the dream it seemed strange to see Mira in a ballcap drinking tea out of a china cup. Feeney sat on the bench in his pajamas, sneezing. He's on the disabled list, she thought, but the rest of the team's here. Peabody, McNab, Whitney, even Tibble. And Roarke, of course, watching as she watched.

Ava, set, glanced over her shoulder toward third. The pitch missed, low and outside. *Ball two.*

Ava took a bow, for the crowd, for the field. *I can keep this up for years. Slow ball, fast ball, curve ball, slider. It's not a strike until I'm ready to throw one.*

She threw again, high and inside, brushing Tommy back from the plate.

Ball three.

There were mutters from the dugout, restrained hoots from the crowd. As Brigit jogged up to the mound, Ben called over to Eve, *We're playing on the wrong team. Can't you call the game? Can't you call it before it's too late?*

Not without more evidence, Whitney said from the dugout. *No cause. You need probable cause. There are rules.*

Roarke shook his head. *Far too many rules, don't you think? After all, murder doesn't play by the rules.*

Brigit jogged back, gave Tommy a pat on the cheek, then turned to Eve. *She's going to the bullpen. She needs some relief. You have to admit, it's all a little boring this way, and she'd put in a great deal of time.*

I can't stop it, Eve thought. I can only call them as I see them.

A shadow crossed the field, an indistinct form gliding over the summer grass. No, I can't stop it, Eve thought again. It has to play out. I can only make the call after the pitch.

I'm sorry, she said to Tommy, *there's nothing I can do.*

Oh well. He smiled kindly at her. *It's just a game, isn't it?*

Not anymore, Eve thought as the shadow merged with Ava, as they set, checked, wound up together. Fast ball, dead over the plate.

He lay on the rich brown dirt, the marblelike plate his headstone, and his eyes staring up at the clear blue of the sky.

On the mound, Ava laughed gaily, and took another bow for the now weeping crowd. *And he's out! Want to see the instant replay?*

It might've been a weird dream, maybe a stupid dream, Eve thought, but she rearranged her murder board in her home office the next morning.

Take a new look, she told herself. Look with fresh eyes.

Roarke came in behind her, studied the board with his hand on her shoulder. "Making patterns?"

"It's that damn dream." She'd told him about it when she'd dressed. "See, she's got her infield—the people she trusts most because she's seen to it they trust her, or have that connection to her through Anders. She's aiming to take him out. She's aimed for him from the first pitch of the first inning, but they don't see it. *He* doesn't see it, even though the batter and pitcher are in an intimate, one-on-one relationship."

"And she doesn't throw strikes."

"Exactly. No, no, not the first inning," Eve corrected. "The first was Bronson—warmed up on him, got some rhythm going on him. Maybe there were others, before Bronson, between him and Anders."

"But she struck them out, or let them get on base, then picked them off. No score, no memorable stats."

"Yeah." She glanced back at him. "For an Irish guy you get baseball pretty well."

"And still you benched me in the dugout. No batter on deck, either."

"No, no potential next batter. This ends the game. When she goes for Ben, and she will, it'll be another game, after a nice, relaxing hiatus. She pitches, she coaches, she manages. And she's the center." Eve put her fingertip on Ava's photo. "She's always the center. She didn't call in relief, she called in a shadow. Nobody sees, nobody knows. And the shadow just follows the steps. One strike, in this case, and he's out."

"And the shadow fades off, so that she—once more—remains the center. If it follows your metaphor, the late inning relief pitcher only has one job, doesn't she? Throw the strike."

"Exactly right. This pitcher doesn't have to do anything but follow orders. Doesn't have to strategize, or worry about base runners because there aren't any. Doesn't have to depend on the field, or even know them. Follow orders, throw the strike, fade away. No post-game interviews, no locker-room chat. One pitch, and out of the game. It's smart," Eve had to admit. "It's pretty damn smart."

"You're smarter, slugger." Roarke gave Eve's hair a quick tug. "It's going to piss her off when you step up to the plate and hit a grand slam."

"Right now, I'd settle for a base hit. With Bebe Petrelli."

"Ava would never have considered you'd look that deep in her lineup. And that is the end of the baseball analogies." He turned her, kissed her. "Good luck with the former Mafia princess."

Bebe Petrelli lived in a narrow row house on a quiet and neglected street in the South Bronx. Paint peeled and cracked like old dry skin over the brittle bones of the houses. Even the trees, the few left that used their ancient roots to heave up pieces of the sidewalk, slumped over the street. Along the block, some windows were boarded like blind eyes while others hid behind the rusted cages of riot bars.

Parking wasn't a problem. There couldn't have been more than a half a dozen vehicles on the entire block. Most here, Eve thought, couldn't afford the cost and ensuing maintenance of a personal ride.

"Revitalization hasn't hit here yet," Peabody commented.

"Or it took a detour."

Eve studied the Petrelli house. It looked as if it might've been painted sometime in the last decade—a leg up on most of the others—and all the windows were intact. And clean, she noted, behind their bars. Empty window boxes sat like hope at the base of the two windows flanking the front door.

"You said both her kids go to private school on Anders's nickel?"

Why the empty window boxes stirred pity inside her, Eve couldn't say. "Yeah."

"And she lives here."

"Smart," Eve replied. "It's smart. What better way to keep someone under your thumb? Give them this, hold back that. Let's go see what Anthony DeSalvo's girl, Bebe, has to say about Ava."

As they walked toward the front door, Eve saw shadows move at the windows on the houses on either side. Nosy neighbors, she thought. She loved nosy neighbors in an investigation. Rich mines to plumb.

No perimeter security, she noted. Decent locks, but no cams or electronic peeps. Locks and riot bars had to serve.

She knocked.

Bebe answered herself, through the inch-wide gap afforded by the security chain. Eve saw both the wariness and the knowledge of cop in the single brown eye.

"Ms. Petrelli, Lieutenant Dallas and Detective Peabody, NYPSD." Eve held her badge to the crack. "We'd like to come in and speak to you."

"About what?"

"Once we're in, we'll talk about it. Or you can close the door and I'll call in for a warrant that would compel you to come into Manhattan to Cop Central. Then we'll talk about it there."

"I have to be at work in another hour."

"Then you probably don't want to waste any more time."

Bebe shut the door. Eve heard the rattle of the chain through it. When it opened, Bebe stood, tired and resentful, in a red shirt, black pants, and serviceable black skids. "You're going to have to make this fast, and you're going to have to talk while I work."

With that, Bebe turned and stalked toward the back of the house.

Neat and tidy, Eve thought as she glanced at the living area. The furniture was cheap, and as serviceable as the black skids, but like the windows, clean. The air smelled fresh, with just a hint of coffee and toasted bread as they approached the kitchen.

On a small metal table sat a white plastic laundry basket. From it, Bebe took a shirt, then folded it with quick, efficient moves.

"You don't need to sit," she snapped out. "Say what you have to say."

"Ava Anders."

The hands hesitated only a second, then pulled out another shirt. "What about her?"

"You're acquainted."

"My boys are in the Anders sports programs."

"You've attended Mrs. Anders's seminars and mothers' breaks. Retreats?"

"That's right."

"And both your boys are recipients of scholarships through the Anders program."

"That's right." Bebe's eyes flashed up at that, and some of the fear, some of the anger leaked through. "They earned it. I got smart boys, good boys. They work hard."

"You must be very proud of them, Ms. Petrelli." Peabody offered a hint of a smile.

"Of course, I am."

"Their school's a clip from here," Eve commented.

"They take the bus. Have to change and take another."

"Makes a long day, for them and you, I imagine."

"They're getting a good education. They're going to be somebody."

"You had some rough times in the past."

Bebe tightened her lips, looked away from Eve and back to her laundry. "Past is past."

"The DeSalvos still have some money, some influence in certain circles." Eve glanced around the tiny kitchen. "Your brothers could help you out, you and your boys."

This time Bebe showed her teeth. "My brothers aren't getting near my boys. I haven't said word one to Frank or Vinny in years, or them to me."

"Why is that?"

"That's my business. They're my brothers, aren't they? It's not a crime if I don't want anything to do with my own brothers."

"Why does Anthony DeSalvo's only daughter hook up as an LC?"

"As a way to stick it to him, you want to know so bad. Ended up sticking it to myself, didn't I?"

A lock of graying hair fell over her brow as Bebe yanked out a boy's sports jersey to fold. "He wanted me to marry who he wanted me to marry, live the way he wanted me to live. Like my mother, looking the other way. Always looking the other way, no matter what was right in her face. So I did what

I did, and he didn't have a daughter anymore." She shrugged, but the jerkiness of the movement transmitted lingering pain to Eve. "Then they killed him. And I didn't have a father."

"You did some time, lost your license."

"You think I got shit around here, with my boys in the house? You think I'm on the shit?" Bebe shoved at the laundry basket, threw her arms wide. "Go ahead, look around. You don't need a warrant. Look the hell around."

Eve studied the flushed face, the bitter eyes. "You know how you strike me, Bebe? You strike me as nervous as you are pissed off. And I don't think it's because you're on anything."

"You cops, always looking to screw with somebody. Except when it matters. What good did you do when they killed my Luca? Where were you when they killed my Luca?"

"Not in the Bronx," Eve said evenly. "Who killed him?"

"The fucking Santinis. Who else? Fucking DeSalvos mess with them, they mess with us. Even if Luca and me, we weren't the *us.*" She gripped the basket now, as if to steady herself. And her knuckles went as white as the plastic. "We had a decent place, a decent life. He was a decent man. We had kids, we had a business. A nice family restaurant, nothing fancy, nothing important. Except to us. We worked so damn hard."

Bebe's fingers tightened on, twisted a pint-sized pair of jockies before she tossed them back in the basket. "Luca, he knew where I came from, what I'd done. It didn't matter. The past's past, that's what he always said. You've got to make the now and think about tomorrow. So that's what we did. And we built a decent life and worked hard at it. Then they killed him. They killed a good man for no good reason. Killed him and torched our place because he wouldn't pay them *protection.* Beat him to death."

She stopped to press her fingers against her eyes. "What did you cops do about that? Nothing. The past isn't the past with your kind. Luca got killed because he married a DeSalvo, and that's that."

She began to fold clothes again, but her movements were no longer efficient, and the folds no longer neat. "Now my boys don't have their father, don't have the decent place to grow up. This is the best I could do, the best of the worse. I don't own a restaurant, I work in one. I rent out a room and a bath upstairs so I can pay the goddamn rent, and so somebody's here to watch over my kids when I have to work nights. This is the life I've got now. My boys are going to have better."

"Ava Anders offered you a way to give your boys a better life."

"They earned their scholarships."

"There was a lot of competition for those scholarships," Eve said. "A lot of kids qualified, just like yours. But yours got them. Full freight, too."

"Don't you say they didn't earn what they got." She lashed toward Eve like a whip. "If you say that to me, you're going to get out of this house. You get your damn warrant, but you'll get out of my house."

"She offered a lot," Eve continued. "Little vacations, drinks by the pool. Did she single you out, Bebe?"

"I don't know what you're talking about."

"Compliment you on your boys, commiserate with you on your losses. She knew where you came from, too, and what you'd done. One little favor, just one little favor, and she'd set your boys up."

"She never asked me for a damn thing. Get the hell out of my house."

"Where were you on March eighteenth from one to five a.m.?"

"What? What? Where I am every blessed night. Here. Do I look like a party girl? Do I look like I spend my nights out on the town?"

"Just one night, Bebe. The night Thomas Anders was murdered."

She went very white, and her hand lowered to the table to brace her body. "Are you out of your *mind*? Some crazy, hyped-up LC killed him. It's all over the screen. Some . . ." Now she lowered to the chair. "God, God, you're looking at me? At me because I used to be in the life? Because I did some time? Because I got DeSalvo blood?"

"I think that's why Ava looked at you, Bebe. I think that's why she took a good, hard look. Me, I'd've asked for some of the ready, too. Get myself a nicer place, closer to the school. But you were smart not to be too greedy."

"You think I . . . How was I supposed to get to their swank place in New York? How was I supposed to get inside?"

"Ava could help you with that."

"You saying, you're standing here in my kitchen saying that Ava—Mrs. Anders—*hired* me to do her husband? I'm a goddamn hit man now? Mother of God, I cook for a restaurant, to put food in my boys' mouths and clothes on their backs. I'm going to do hits for a living, why in hell am I folding laundry?"

"Doing Ava a favor would be a way to get your kids a good education," Peabody put in. "A way to give them a chance for better."

"They *earned* it. Do you know what I had to swallow to sign my boys up for the program? To take charity, to let them know they had to take handouts? Dom wanted to play ball so bad, and Paulie wants what Dom wants. I couldn't afford the fees, the equipment, so I swallowed it and signed them up. They earned the rest. They earned the rest," she repeated as she got to her feet. "Now I got nothing more to say. You get your warrant to take me in if that's the way it is. I'm going to call Legal Aid. You get out, 'cause I've got nothing more to say."

"Shook her," Peabody said when they were back on the sidewalk.

"Yeah, it did. She relaxed some when we veered off into her family. Stayed bitchy, but relaxed. That's interesting."

"She didn't like seeing us at the door either. Most don't," Peabody admitted. "But she got the jumps the minute she made us. Guilty conscience maybe."

"Maybe. The boys are good levers, excellent buttons to push. Takes half a minute to see she'd do most anything for her sons. Ava would've seen that, factored that. Used that."

"She'd have to get from here to there and back again," Peabody considered. "I know you said Ava could've helped her with that, but I don't see Ava putting down bread crumbs by hiring personal transpo for her."

"No, neither do I. Have to be subway or bus. Take the neighbor on the right, I'll take the one on the left. Let's see what they say about the comings and goings. Then we'll go have a talk with her boarder."

"I mind my own," Cecil Blink stated the minute Eve stepped inside the musty, overheated row house. "What's she done?"

There was an avid look in his eye, and the smell of fried meat substitute in the air. "We're just making inquiries in the neighborhood. Why would you assume Ms. Petrelli had done anything?"

"Keeps to herself. That's what they say about serial killers, ain't it?" He nodded knowledgeably, and a thin storm of dandruff trickled from his scalp to the shoulders of his red checked bathrobe. "And she don't say three words to nobody if one will get her by. Don't trust a closed-mouthed female. Used to own a restaurant, before they beat the horseshit and guts out of her husband and tossed him in the river. Mafia, that's what. She's connected."

He said it as if he were giving her hot news, so Eve pasted a look of interest on her face. "You don't say?"

"I do say, and right out loud. Probably was running illegals outta that restaurant, and they killed him—rival Mafia types. That's how it's done."

"I'm going to look into that, thanks. Meanwhile, did you notice anyone in the neighborhood out very early in the morning on March eighteenth? This past Tuesday. Say four a.m.?"

"I mind my own."

Like hell. "Maybe you were restless that night, or got up for a drink of water. Maybe you noticed activity out on the street. Someone walking, or getting out of a car or cab?"

"Can't say I did." Which seemed to disappoint him. "Her next door, she comes home late—midnight maybe—three nights a week. They *say* she cooks for Fortuna's restaurant. Me, I don't go to restaurants. They charge an arm and a leg."

"Any visitors next door?"

"Boys have boys over. Probably up to no good. Woman who lives there with her—Nina Cohen—has some other biddies over every Wednesday night. *Say* they're playing bridge. Couple of the other neighborhood women got boys her boys fool with go over now and then. *Her* boys don't go to school around here. Not good enough for her. They go to *private* school. They *say* on scholarships or some such thing. More likely Mafia money, if you ask me."

"Okay. Thanks for your time."

"I'm going to be locking my doors double quick. A closed-mouth woman's a dangerous woman."

Unable to resist, Eve gave him a closed-mouthed smile, and left.

"The boys are well-behaved," Peabody reported. "She keeps a clean house. Both the neighbor and her husband were sound asleep—bedroom's at the back—on the night in question during the time line. She gives Petrelli big mother points." When Eve only nodded, and continued to sit in the car, Peabody looked around. "What are we doing now?"

"Giving Bebe a little more to think about. Unless she's going to blow off work, she should be coming out soon." Eve settled back. "You know what would be an even bigger incentive for somebody who earns mother points? You give the kids this big juicy carrot, then you threaten to yank it away. Unless."

"Get the boys in school, into the camps, give them a good taste of how it can be. Then, it's the old 'if you want them to keep this, you have to do this one little thing for me. Nobody'll ever know.' "

"It could play. There's something about her though." Eve studied those hopeful window boxes and tapped her fingers on the wheel. "But there's also something under the something. So we give her a little more to think about."

It didn't take long. Bebe came out of the house wearing a dull brown coat. Don't notice me, it said to Eve. Just getting through here, just getting by.

Her gaze flashed to the car, to Eve, and her mouth folded into a sharp, thin line. The neighbor might've given her points for motherhood, but Eve gave her points for shooting up her middle finger. It took spine to flip off a couple of cops who were dogging you for murder.

Bebe stomped up the block. Giving her a few yards, Eve eased from the curb and slowly followed. Two and a half blocks to the bus stop, Eve thought. Had to be a bitch in the worst of the winter, in the rain, in the wind. Eve slid back to the curb as Bebe stood at the stop, arms folded, eyes straight ahead.

When the bus lumbered up, Bebe stomped on. And Eve pulled out to follow. It chugged to the next stop, then the next, belching its way out of the tattered neighborhood into the next. The houses grew brighter, the sidewalks smoother, the vehicles more plentiful and newer.

"Has to be hard," Peabody said, "to come out of where you landed to work for somebody else in what you used to have."

"Slap you in the face every day." She watched Bebe get out at the next stop, shoot her a furious glare, then hurry down the block to a white-washed restaurant with a bright yellow awning.

"Peabody, see what precinct covers this area. And let's see if we can impose on a couple of our brothers from the Bronx to have Italian for lunch."

"Going to keep the pressure on."

"Yeah. She's tough, but she'll pop."

"I don't know. I think making another pair of cops is just going to piss her off, dig her in. Legal Aid lawyer's going to call us whining about harassment."

"She didn't call Legal Aid. She'll pop," Eve repeated. "Twenty says she pops before end of shift today."

"Today? With those DeSalvo genes?" Peabody snorted at the idea. "I can use twenty. You're on."

16 AT CENTRAL, EVE SIGNED ANDERS'S VITAMIN dispenser out of evidence. She set it on her desk, sat, studied it. A solid gold pill dispenser, she mused. Even Roarke didn't have one of those to her knowledge. Of course, he wasn't one for popping a bunch of pills every night of his life either.

If and when that day came, he'd probably have a platinum one, with diamond accents. Okay, no, he wouldn't. That was entirely too fussy and girly.

Which, she thought, Anders's certainly was.

More sports clothes than stylish ones. A man cave for an office.

"Bought this for him, didn't you, Ava? Planting those seeds. The poor schmuck had to use it if it was a gift from you."

Program it, she mused, turning the heavy gold box over in her hands, lift the cannily hidden tube, dump pills in. Pills tumble into proper slot. Load it up, and it tells you how many pills in each slot. Request number of any type, or any combination of types, and it dispenses, ID-ing by slot.

"Well, you liked your gadgets, Tommy, and she knew it."

She put in a call to EDD expecting to get the acting captain, and was surprised to hit Feeney.

"So. You're alive."

"Back in the saddle." He grinned at her. "Feel like a couple billion, tax-free. Whatever they gave me knocked the bastard out of me. Or the wife's chicken soup did."

"Glad to hear it. I've got this thing. Electronic pill dispenser."

"Why in hell would anybody need that?"

"Your guess is as good as. It was Thomas Anders's, and I'm working on the idea that his wife slipped a couple sleepers in here. All right if I bring it up?"

"Sure. I can send somebody down for it."

"No, I'll bring it. I want to run it by you anyway. Give me five."

She clicked off, resealed the box, initialled it, then tucked it under her arm as she headed out and up. In EDD, she veered straight away from the color and sound, and into Feeney's office.

With healthy color back in his basset hound face, Feeney sat at his desk. "I got work up the wazoo," he told her, "and already had to kick a couple asses this morning. It's good to be home."

"I spent a couple hours this morning intimidating a widowed mother of two. I love this job."

He laughed, then lifted his wiry eyebrows at the box she put on his desk. "Jesus, a *gold* pill spitter, with engraved initials?"

"For the man you want to kill who has everything."

"You said a couple of sleepers. They wouldn't do that much."

"He had traces of over-the-counter in him, but nobody can confirm he took same routinely. Ingesting one would put him out good enough to let somebody get into the bedroom, shoot him up with barbs and cock hardener. Or groggy enough so he could be bound up before he came around enough to know what was going on, because I think the barbs weren't on the order sheet. They threw the scene off from the jump. Our girl Ava isn't going to make a wrong turn like that."

"Wanted him awake for it."

"Yeah. Killer was meant to come up, truss him up, noose him—throat starts to constrict, what do you do?"

"Open your mouth and try to suck air in."

"And when he does, killer shoves the dick trick into him. The asphyxiation would get him going, then you ring the cock. Let him gasp and flop while you set the scene. If you do it right—and it wasn't done right—it's going to look like the vic was playing around on the side, dipping into the kink. Kink got out of hand. I bet part of the instructions were to loosen the scarfing after he was cooked, at least loosen it so it would appear some attempt was made to revive. Then you have your kinky cheater, a tragic, embarrassing, but fairly routine accident, and the panicked partner fleeing the scene."

"Voi-fucking-là."

"We'd look for her, sure, but we'd get nowhere. Because Anders didn't cheat, wasn't into the kink. But the scene and the evidence would read that way."

That, Eve realized—that taking his decent reputation as well as his life—gripped her guts. "But see, the killer shot him up with the dick hardener. It wasn't taken orally. Shot him up with that, I'm betting, after she shot him up with the tranq."

"You want me to see if the wife diddled with the box?"

"Yeah. If you can open it up, see if anything was taken out or added before his death. Couple of days before, probably. The wife left New York on March fifteen."

"Let me play with it." Feeney initialled the bag, unsealed it to draw the box out. "Bitch is heavy. It's got voice or manual settings. She did it manually it's going to be tougher to pin. Even if she did it by voice, a lawyer's going to argue she was his wife. She filled it or added to it at his request, even the sleeper. He's not here to say different."

"One step at a time."

She left him to it, started back down. She needed to see if Peabody had contacted Petrelli's tenant, then they needed to start working on the other possibles she'd culled from the files. Run some probabilities.

She had a feeling the computer would look favorably on Petrelli, given the data, but . . .

She paused when she spotted Benedict Forrest outside her bullpen. It was getting so she couldn't scratch her ass without coming back and finding some civilian waiting for her.

He sprang to his feet. "Lieutenant Dallas, I need to talk to you."

Since she wouldn't mind having another round with him, she gestured. "Let's take it in my office." She led the way, caught Peabody's eye as she moved through the bullpen. The gleam in it had her pointing Ben toward her office. "Go ahead in. I'll be a minute."

She skirted around desks to Peabody's. "What do you have?"

"Charles and Louise are getting *married*."

"I know. Did you—"

"I know you know because Charles just told me he told you, but you didn't tell *me*. All morning you didn't tell me."

"It wasn't the first thing on my mind."

"But this is huge." She bounced in her chair, and made Eve wonder what it was about weddings that made grown women bounce. "It's mega-mag! And he said he's turned in as LC and he's opening a practice as a therapist, and they're going to have the wedding at your house in a couple months, and—"

"Gee, Peabody, I have this connection to a murder waiting in my office. Maybe we could not take an hour later to talk about somebody else's life."

"Aw, but it's so *sweet*. And romantic."

Eve leaned down. "You do not sit here getting shiny-eyed at your desk, Detective. Not in my bullpen. Not unless you've gotten tagged by Ava Anders who gave you a full confession. Also, the words 'sweet' and 'romantic' don't come out of your mouth in my bullpen unless they are coated and dripping with sarcasm. Now suck it up."

"Spoilsport."

"Lieutenant Spoilsport to you. Nina Cohen."

"As far as she knows, Petrelli didn't leave the house on the night of the murder. But she also says Petrelli never leaves the house after midnight, so she'd assume she didn't leave." Peabody checked her watch. "Getting closer to the time you owe me twenty."

"Don't count your twenty before it crosses the road," Eve warned, and walked to her office.

Ben paced. Eve could hear the slap of his feet on her worn floor. Back and forth, back and forth. She tended to do the same herself if something was screwing with her mind.

"Sorry about that," she said as she went in. "Have a seat."

"You're looking at Ava as a suspect."

Eve closed the door behind her. It turned her office into a smaller box, but it was private. "It's a habit of mine to look at people as suspects."

"But if you're wasting time looking at someone who couldn't possibly have hurt my uncle, then you're *not* looking for the person who did." He pushed at his hair with both hands. "Leopold told me you were in asking questions about her. He's half inclined to think you're right and felt he had to warn me. As if she'd strangle me with my own belt or something. It's crazy."

"Your uncle was a wealthy man. Now she's a wealthier woman than she was when he was alive."

"So am I. Man, I mean. I'm wealthier if you want to look at the damn dollars and cents of it."

"Dollars and cents are a tried and true motive for murder."

"She wasn't even in the country. Now you're asking for files on staff and volunteers, on women with kids in the programs. Good God."

Eve eased down on the corner of her desk. "You're pretty passionate in her defense."

"I'm the only family, the only *close* family she has left." He rubbed the back of his neck as if pain lived there. "Uncle Tommy would expect me to take care of her, to support her, and damn right to defend her."

"I got the impression you and Ava weren't particularly close. Before."

"As I said—" both his voice and his handsome hazel eyes chilled "—I'm the family she has left."

"And between you, you own all but a fistful of Anders Worldwide. I guess something like that brings people closer."

Coldness flipped so quickly, so completely into shock, it surprised Eve the man didn't physically revolve with it. "That—that's a despicable thing to say."

"You're a healthy single man. She's an attractive woman."

"She's my uncle's *wife*. His widow. God, is this how you have to think? Do you make everything ugly and obscene?"

"Murder does, Mr. Forrest. Both you and Ava have tight, solid alibis. That's interesting, that both of you should be so solidly alibied."

"Interesting that she was away on a long-planned trip and that I got lucky? What's wrong with you? If you want to take shots at me, fine. But I can't have you taking them at her. Not with what she's going through."

"Does she know you're here?"

"No. As if I'd tell her what you're doing, add to her stress."

"Good. Now, take a step back. Take one back and describe your relationship with Ava before your uncle was killed." She lifted a hand before he could speak. "Don't bullshit me, Ben. Every lie I have to unknot wastes time. You want your uncle's killer caught and justice served?"

"Of course I do. Jesus, Jesus, I can hardly think of anything else. Of course I do."

"Tell me how you and Ava got along before Tuesday morning."

"All right, all right." He pressed his hand to his temple, then dropped into her visitor's chair. "We weren't particularly close. Not at odds or anything, not exactly."

"What, exactly?"

"We just . . . I guess we didn't have anything in common. Except for Uncle Tommy, and maybe we didn't always see eye-to-eye on how the programs were run or handled. But—"

"Don't but, don't qualify. Give me a picture."

He blew out a breath. "Maybe it felt, in a weird way, as if we were in competition for him. That sounds so stupid. You could say I felt the longer they were married, the less she wanted me around. Maybe the less I wanted to be around her. We just . . . But she loved him, and that's what matters. She loved Uncle Tommy. She was always buying him little gifts, or arranging for him to take a golf trip or a ski weekend, whatever."

"Uh-huh."

"Okay, maybe it would gripe me, a little, that she wouldn't always tell me until the last minute if she was planning something, then she'd blame it on Leo. Say she told Leo to tell me. That just didn't wash. Leo forgets nothing. So we'd get together, Uncle Tommy and I, at the club or the course or the game. I didn't go around the house that much. It didn't feel like his house much in the last couple years anyway."

"Why is that?"

"All that redecorating. God, you saw the place. Nowhere for a guy to put his feet up and watch some screen. He didn't mind it," Ben continued. "He said she put up with his foolishness, and he put up with hers."

He sat silent a moment, brooded. "It doesn't matter now. It's different now."

"Yeah, it is. Now tell me this. If your uncle had died of natural causes, or say in a skiing accident, would you feel this strongly, this protective of Ava?"

"How can I know something like that?"

"All she's been through, you said. You weren't just talking about his death, but about the circumstances of it. And the scandal, the embarrassment to her. So think a minute, factor that out."

"I don't know what difference it makes to—"

"Humor me," Eve interrupted.

"Well, I guess, maybe I wouldn't feel as if she needed me the way she does. What I mean to say is Ava's not generally the kind of woman who needs care." His handsome face set itself into stubborn lines. "But the circumstances are what the circumstances are."

"The circumstances are that you're sitting there feeling disloyal and crappy because you made a few minor complaints about her." A nice guy, Roarke had termed him. Eve knew some couldn't help being a nice guy, even after being kicked repeatedly in the teeth. "How'd she get along with her father-in-law?"

"With . . . fine. Great, in fact. My uncle used to joke that it was a good thing he saw her first, or she'd have hooked up with Granddad. I don't see what that—"

"Just wondering. Didn't I hear they had a little trouble shortly before his death?"

"I don't remember . . . Oh, that. Yeah, there was something, probably my fault. As I said I don't—and didn't—always like how she handles the programs. I complained to Granddad about Ava hitting the program budget for what I felt were personal expenses. He got a little hot over it, but he and Ava worked it out. Lieutenant, I understand you're doing your job, and I understand you're good at your job. But it feels wrong, just wrong, for you to look at, to think about, Ava this way. I don't want whoever killed Uncle Tommy to get away with it."

"Neither do I. I have a lot of looking at and thinking about to do, about a lot of people. Right now I'm going to ask you to put your uncle first. Don't say anything to anyone else about this conversation." She pushed off her desk. Understanding the signal, Ben rose.

"All right. I'll let you get back to work. Lieutenant, no one who knew him, really knew him, could have hurt him. It had to be a stranger. It's the only thing that makes sense."

She didn't disagree.

A couple of years, she thought as she sat back down. A couple of years ago, Anders's father died. A couple of years ago, Ava redecorated. A couple of years ago she launched her mommy programs. Short pause, and she hired Charles. Laying the groundwork, Eve mused. She thinks ahead. But, Eve wondered, just how far ahead. She called up all data on Reginald Thomas Anders.

She read official data, bios, society page squibs, interviews. He struck Eve as a tough-minded businessman who'd enjoyed his retirement, his pursuit of leisure activities. He'd suffered from and was being treated for hypertension. Slipped in the shower of his son's weekend home in the Hamptons. Reaches for something, maybe he's dizzy or just off-balance, then *whoops*, fractured skull when his head slams into the Italian marble.

Son, daughter-in-law, grandson, and several house guests in residence at the time.

What if? Eve considered, then printed out Reginald Anders's ID photo and data to add to her murder board. Back at her desk, she made a call to the Hampton investigator.

An hour later, her boots planted on her desk, she continued to study the board when Peabody came in.

"I think she did the old man," Eve said.

"Yeah, I know."

"No, the older old man. Reginald T. Anders. Maybe it was just a happy accident, one that inspired her, kicked off the rest, but she's a schemer. Petty, too, as Leo said. The older old man slapped her back for padding her expense account. She wouldn't like that one bit. And you know, I bet she already had the decorator lined up before he took his header in the shower, bumping her up to the wife of the head guy."

"What?"

Eve shook her head. "The old man had essentially retired, turning the reins over, but he still held controlling interest. That seems to be a pattern with the Anders men. Shift the controls, but hold onto the power. He dies, Tommy inherits controlling interest, at which time he transfers a little bit to his devoted wife. I bet she asked for it, too. 'Tommy, I hope it's not too much to ask, but you know how I loved Reggie. If I could have just a few shares of the company, just a reminder of him, it would mean so much to me.' Yeah, she could work that. Little sliver of the pie, just a taste while she waits for the bigger slice."

"If she wanted a big slice, why didn't she go after the old man? I mean, if she'd been able to work marrying him, she'd have cut out the middle man."

"Bet she considered it," Eve replied. "But he went for younger. About a decade younger than Ava would've been when she hooked Tommy."

"Eeuuw."

"And the *eeuuw* would be reason two. A man in his eighties marries a much younger woman, then croaks, who does everybody give the fish-eye to first?"

"The younger woman."

"Which is exactly what the investigator did, though it looked like accidental. He still took a hard look at the twenty-six-year-old aspiring actress who'd been sharing the old man's bed for a few months. He did a skim over Tommy and Ben, the main beneficiaries. He never took more than a cursory glance at Ava."

Peabody rolled it over. "If it's playing accidental anyway, she wouldn't pop out."

"I bet the party, the house party, was her idea. Yeah, I bet it was. Perfect cover. Who's going to notice if the busy hostess slips away for ten minutes? Less if she prepped it, and you can bet your ass she did."

Simple, Eve thought. Quick and easy. "All she has to do is go in, strip down. Needs to strip down so she doesn't get her clothes wet. Dad-in-law's singing in the shower. Step in, give him a shove. Step out, towel off, get dressed. Take the towel with you to your own bath. Freshen your hair and makeup, join your guests. It wouldn't take more than ten."

She dropped her feet, swiveled, sent Peabody a hard smile. "And guess who noticed first that the old man was missing. Gee, where in the world is Reggie? He's missing all the fun. Tommy, be a darling and go up and tell your father I'm making him the perfect martini."

"Cold."

"And smart. Can't do the husband the same way, not even close to the same way. People might turn that fish-eye on you. Just might. Not a household or routine accident this time, too many accidents in the Anders family. And unfortunately, I can't turn the eaten-by-a-shark incident on her."

"Switch to murder," Peabody said. "Juicy sensational murder that shines a big spotlight on it. Who's going to try to connect a bathroom accident two years ago with a sex crime now? Except you."

"It was supposed to look like kink gone wrong. An accident, technically, but yeah, a big, juicy, sensational accident. Or failing that, a sex crime. Partner gets pissed, doesn't stop at the safe word. Either way, it works for her. It makes Anders responsible for his own death. Empty house this time, with her tucked in with pals thousands of miles away. She's damn good at this. I need to . . . why are you in here?"

"Oh, I forgot with all the singing in the shower. Bronx checked in. They enjoyed spaghetti Bolognese and manicotti, respectively, while sending intimidating looks toward Petrelli in the open kitchen. She left midway through her shift. Their waitress told them she screwed up two orders, then told the owner she was feeling ill. They'd be happy to go back tomorrow, try the stuffed eggplant and lasagna."

"The sacrifices cops make. I don't think it's going to take that long. We'll keep them on tap, but meanwhile I have to review the rest of this data on the old man, write up a report, the notes, get them to Mira for her take. I've still got the Nadine interviews to watch, and I want to dig up the old man's girl toy, the rest of the house guests, and re-interview. Then . . . you know, it was a lot easier when you were the aide and I could just dump the grunt work on you."

"Aw. Besides you still dump grunt work on me."

"It's not the same. Wait a minute. Wait." Eve bolted up in her chair. "Every fucking body's got aides and admins and personal assistants."

"Except you."

"And Ava. Where's Ava's? Study and review the reports and data on the Reginald Anders death, write up notes on the new theory we just discussed. Run the list of names of house guests, start setting up interviews."

"Not that I do any grunt work."

"Out." Eve reached for her 'link, contacted Leopold. "Who does Ava use as an aide or PA?" she asked. "I don't have a name."

"Because there isn't one, officially. If she had a PA, his or her salary and benefits would come out of her pocket."

Not the Ava Eve knew. "Are you telling me she did all the drone and grunt work personally, made all the contacts, read all the files and so on?"

"No, I'm going to tell you she tapped volunteers, other staff routinely. For just quick, little favors. She used several of the mothers over the life of the program, claiming it gave them pride and training for job opportunities. She never paid any of them. Gifts, now and then." He offered a sour smile. "She likes giving gifts."

"Do you have names, specific names for people she tapped?"

"There's no list. It's unofficial, as I said. But I can probably put something together for you. I'll need to ask around, as I wasn't privy to all of who did what for her."

"I'd appreciate that."

"Lieutenant, I know Ben came to see you. I apologize. I shouldn't have said anything to him, even though you said—"

"It's no problem."

"It got in my craw, that's all I can say. It got in, and it stuck, the way she's slathering it on. Grunt and drone work? That would be his job now. She—" He cut himself off. "Obviously, it's still in my craw. I'll start putting a list together for you."

"Thanks."

She bet Petrelli was on the list. She just bet—"What!" she demanded when her in-office 'link signaled.

"Dallas, guess who's here?"

"Guess how long it's going to take me to tie your tongue into a square knot?"

"Jeez." Peabody folded said tongue safely inside her mouth. "Bebe Petrelli. And she is pissed!"

"Excellent, book an interview room, put her there."

Eve kicked back in her chair—the better to let the pissed Bebe stew a bit—and looked at the murder board. "It's starting to break, Ava. Can you feel it? Do you feel it cracking under your stylish and tasteful shoes? I'm looking forward to watching you drop through the hole. I can't quite figure out why I'm looking forward to it quite so much. But hey, I've got to get my kicks somewhere."

Eve gave it another ten minutes, then strolled out to take on Bebe in Interview.

"This is crap. This is harassment."

Eve shrugged, dropped into the chair across the little table from the very pissed off Bebe. "Call a lawyer, file a complaint. But you don't want to do that, Bebe, so let's not waste time pretending you do. You have the right to remain silent," Eve began, and recited the Revised Miranda while Bebe gaped at her.

"You're *charging* me?"

"I didn't say anything about charges—yet. I asked if you understood your rights and obligations in this matter. Do you understand them?"

"Yes, I understand them, goddamn it. I don't understand why I have any obligations. I didn't *do* anything."

"Did Ava Anders ask you to?"

"No." Bebe folded her arms tight at her waist.

"Really? She never asked you to make 'link calls for her, or maybe whip up some cannolis for a party? Run errands, take care of a little office work?"

"I thought you meant about . . ." Her arms relaxed. "Sure I helped out some. Volunteered. Anders was giving my boys a lot, and giving me a lot. So I was happy to pay Mrs. Anders back. It made it feel less like charity."

"Gave you some pride. So first, let's say, she asks you to do some little thing, then next time it's a little bit bigger thing, then bigger yet. Would you say that's the way it was, Bebe?"

"I said I helped out. I was happy to."

"Did you confide in her? Open up? You got to be tight, right? With you doing these little jobs for her. With her trusting you to do them. And you hanging out with her some at these retreats she took you on. Did you tell her how you missed your husband, how hard it was sometimes to raise your boys on your own? What your hopes and dreams for them were?"

Bebe's lips quivered before she clamped them tight. "Why shouldn't I? Part of the reason for the retreats was to share, to network and support. Why shouldn't I? There's no shame in it."

"And she was sympathetic, even intimate." To close off some of Bebe's space, Eve leaned in. "Did she open up to you,

Bebe? Did she share, so you'd know even a woman in her position, with her resources had it tough."

"It's personal. It's none of your damn business."

"It's my damn business when her husband's dead!" The rapid change of Eve's tone, from mild, even cajoling to hard and mean had Bebe jolting. "It's all my business now, so don't fuck with me. It was tit for tat, was that how she made it seem? I'll do this for you, if you do me this little favor? I can play that."

Leaning back, Eve took a casual sip from the bottle of water she'd brought in with her, and throttled down again. "You tell me what I need to know, and I'll see to it that your husband's case is reopened, reopened, Bebe, and assigned to the best available in the Bronx Homicide Division."

"They don't care about me, they don't care about Luca."

"I'll make sure they do. Peabody, can and will I make sure the Bronx cares about Luca Petrelli, and bringing his killers to justice?"

"Yes, sir, you can and will if you choose to. Bebe," Peabody added, "the lieutenant doesn't bullshit about murder. You should've figured that out by now. And after your lunch visit, you should figure she's got some pull in the Bronx."

"I'm telling you, Bebe—look at me! I'll make sure they reopen Luca's case. I'll make sure they care. I'm telling you that on record. Now. Do you want the case reopened?"

Tears shimmered and swam. Then spilled. "Yes."

"Did Ava Anders ask you to kill Thomas Anders?"

"No. No. No. She didn't. I swear on my boys, she didn't. But . . ."

"*But*. That's the sticker. The *but's* why you didn't attend the retreat six weeks ago. The *but's* why you haven't attended or served at any of the seminars or outreach programs for the last five months. Tell me about that."

Bebe swiped at tears with fingers that trembled. "I couldn't get off work. I couldn't take the time. My boys . . . She was good to me, do you *get* that? She gave us a chance, and you want me to rat her out."

"She used you, and in your gut you know it. Your father used you, your brothers used you, your dealers and your johns used you. You *know* when you're being used. What did she ask you to do?"

"She didn't ask. She . . . she told me how he abused her sexually, how he was bringing women into the house, and wanted her to . . . to participate in . . . in the kind of sex that disgusted her."

When Peabody offered her a cup of water, Bebe drank it down in one go.

"She shared that with you?" Peabody spoke gently. "Those intimate details of her marriage?"

"She said she knew I'd understand, and I did. I did understand. She said he was going to toss her out, stop the programs, cancel the scholarships, destroy everything she'd put in motion unless she gave in. It was making her sick."

"You had to feel awfully sorry for her," Peabody prompted. "And upset at the idea he'd take all that away from her. And your boys, too."

"I did. God. I didn't know what to think. I could hardly believe it. He seemed like such a nice man. But she broke down, just broke down, went to pieces. She said she'd found out he was abusing some of the kids, the girls, and she couldn't do anything about it. No one would believe her, and how he had to be stopped."

"When was this?" Eve demanded.

"Last summer. Like July. Kids were in camp, and I was doing a little work for her on a Sunday at her house."

"Just the two of you, right? Nobody else there."

"Yeah, yeah. And what set her off was she was talking to one of the women's shelters about one of the mothers who had kids in the program, about getting her job training and stuff, and when she finished, she just fell to pieces."

"Convenient."

Bebe's head snapped up at Eve's comment. "It wasn't like that. It's just, she was so upset, and it all came pouring out. He was away, her husband. He went away a lot. There was so much on her, you know? And now he's saying if she doesn't fall in line, she's out on her ass and all those kids . . . my kids. I said something about there had to be a way to stop him, to protect herself, to protect the kids. She said, the only way to stop him, a man with his kind of power, his kind of sickness, was if he was dead. How it was horrible to say, but she wished he was dead, and sometimes after he went at her, she'd lie there and think of how it could be done. How he could have an accident, if she had someone she could trust and depend on to help her. How if he had an accident, the kids would all be safe. My kids would be safe."

"What kind of accident did she suggest?"

"She didn't. She didn't because I cut her off. I cut her off because there was something in her eyes that made me think she wasn't just imagining it. I know something about that, something about that look."

As if exhausted, Bebe covered her face with her hands. "She wanted it. God, she wanted him dead, and she wanted me to help her. So I cut her off and started on about how she should talk to someone, like they were always telling us in the seminars. How she should make the break, and move on. He wouldn't really cut the programs because it would make him look bad. Stuff like that, and I got out. I got out as soon as I could, even though she backed off, told me I was right. She'd just had a bad moment, and she made me promise I wouldn't talk about what she'd said with anyone. It wouldn't be good for the programs."

Bebe heaved out a long breath. "She didn't get in touch after that to ask me to volunteer. I figured she was embarrassed. And when I went to the retreat, the last one I went to at the end of August, she avoided me. When I pinned her about it, because, I guess, I thought we were friends—sort of friends—she was really cold. Ice cold. Told me she was a very busy woman, with a lot of responsibilities, how I should remember all she'd done for my boys, and be grateful for that. How I should take care of them, and myself, concentrate on that so . . . so the scholarships didn't go away."

"Did you notice her being friendly with anyone in particular at that retreat?"

"I stayed away from her. Like you said, my father used me. My brothers. Then I put myself in the position so the johns could use me, and the dealers. I stopped letting myself be used and I met Luca."

Resentment, and some of the spit came back in her eyes. "I got it, okay? I got it, after that, she was using me. I didn't blame her so much, considering, but I wasn't going to put myself in that spot again. So I stayed away."

"Smart move."

"Is that enough? Is that want you wanted?"

"It ain't bad."

"You're going to push for them to open Luca's case? You're going to do that?"

"I did it this morning," Eve told her. "The two cops you made who had lunch in the place you work are supposed to be good, and they're picking it up. They'll be in touch with you after they review the file."

"You . . . why did you do that when I didn't give you anything for it?"

"Because your husband deserved better than he got. Because it seems to me you and your kids deserved better. And because I don't like it when a good man is killed for no good reason."

Bebe stared for another moment. Then she simply laid her head down on the table and wept.

"Record off." Rising, Eve signaled Peabody. As she left the room, she heard Peabody's voice comforting the sobbing woman.

17

EVE TAGGED FEENEY ON THE WAY FROM INTERVIEW to her office. "Give me something."

"Christ, kid, do you know how much I got piled up here from being out? I got the backlog down from my armpits to my asshole. I'll get to your box."

"Can't you just open it and see if she reprogrammed or reloaded it before . . ." She trailed off at his stony stare. He had a good one, she thought. She'd modeled hers after it. "Okay, all right. Just as soon as you can."

"If you don't interrupt me to nag, it'll be sooner."

She clicked off.

Circumstantial, she reminded herself. Even if Feeney proved that the dispenser had been reprogrammed and/or reloaded, it was circumstantial. She hated building a case on circumstantial. And that's all she had. Impressions, comments, Bebe's statement, personalities. And not a single solid piece of evidence.

Yet.

She strode back into Homicide where Baxter turned from

the AutoChef. "Dallas. The boyfriend/tranny/cross-dressing angle's not panning out. Custer case," he said when she looked blank.

"Right. Sorry, my mind's elsewhere. What's your sense, Baxter?"

"That the case is as cold as the victim. The kid and I can keep taking pokes at it when we squeeze out some time. I don't want to put it in Inactive yet. We're going to have to slap it down to the bottom of the pile, maybe give it a shake every now and then."

"Not all of them close."

"Yeah. I know. Pisser when they don't. We closed six others since we caught this one, and it's still a pisser."

She sympathized, but she had her own case to close, and needed to shuffle some of the pieces, try to see a different angle. In her office, she pulled up a couple of the possibles who'd come in below Petrelli on her list. After zeroing in on the next, gauging the time, she detailed a report on the interview with Petrelli, added notes and speculations.

"Computer, run probability. Given the data, the statements, what is the probability Ava Anders is a big, fat liar?"

Your question is not properly structured and cannot be answered on a probability scale. Please rephrase.

"Seemed straightforward to me. Try this. Run probability given the data and statements included in the Anders, Thomas A., homicide that Anders, Ava, has lied to the primary and/ or to other individuals who gave an account of conversations with subject."

Working . . .

Eve rose, programmed coffee. Stared out the window.

Task complete. Conflicting statements given regarding conversations with subject indicate a 97.3 percent probability

Anders, Ava, has given false statements. Probability cannot
determine which statements are false and which are factual.

"I think I can figure that out. Run second probability.
Given the data, and assuming the statement just logged by
Petrelli, Bebe, is factual, what is the probability that Anders,
Ava, arranged, devised or is involved in the murder of Anders,
Thomas A."

Working . . .

"Yeah, chew on that. Circumstantial, more circumstantial.
But probabilities have some weight. Enough weight, somebody
sinks. Who else did you set up the way you set up Bebe, Ava?
Who else did you have on the line?"

Task complete. Factoring Petrelli statement as a factual account,
the probability is 50.2 percent that Anders, Ava, arranged,
devised or is involved in the murder of Anders, Thomas A.

"Bollocks to that," Eve stated, pulling out one of Roarke's
phrases. "Fifty doesn't add weight. It's a wash. I need another.
I need one of the other fish on the line to flip."

"Dallas." Peabody gave the doorjamb a quick rap. "I
arranged transpo for Petrelli. Didn't want her having to deal
with the bus or the subway. She was pretty wrecked."

"Fine." Eve turned, held out a hand, rubbed her fingers
and thumb together.

Peabody shoved her hands in her pockets. "I don't have
twenty on me. Isn't it enough reward that you got her to spill
it on Ava?"

In answer Eve simply wiggled the fingers of her outstretched
hand.

"Okay, okay, man." She snatched up a memo cube from Eve's
desk. "This is going to have to come out of my Roarke fund."

"You have a fund for Roarke? To donate to him, or to try to buy him?"

"I wish—on the buying part. It'd be a skim for McNab. We have a deal where we both got to pick one person, and if we ever got the chance to . . ." She closed her fist, pumped it while she wiggled her eyebrows. "With said person, the other of us would understand. A one-shot deal. I picked Roarke."

"Well, he's a superior lay, so you'd have that before I peeled the skin off your still quivering body, roasted it on an open fire, then force-fed it to you."

"Okay then. So . . ." Clearing her throat, Peabody turned the cube on record. "I owe Dallas, Lieutenant Meaniepants Eve, twenty dollars to be paid out of my hard-earned, under-appreciated detective's salary next payday. Peabody, Detective Churchmouse Delia."

She tossed the memo cube. Eve caught it one handed, slid it into her pocket. "What's the Roarke fund?"

"Oh, I'm earmarking a little every payday and socking it away. When I get a decent amount I'm going to have him invest it for me. He said he would. It's not a superior lay, but hey, could be a nice bang."

"Never known him to misfire. Start on the interviews on old man Anders. Plowder and Bride-West are on there. Don't hit them. Start with out-of-towners. Start with the ones Ava isn't tight with. The girl toy, any of the staff who were there, particularly any temps or staff who've been fired or have resigned. Low-key it, just following up on additional information that's come to light. Just reconfirming, blah blah. I'm heading into the field shortly, then I'm working from home."

"You're going solo?"

"Actually, I'm going to call in a superior lay, who also looks like a superior lay. He could be handy in my next interview."

"Okay, but if you get laid in the field, I expect to read the details thereof in your report. All the details."

"Keep that up and you'll usurp Jenkinson's Sick Bastard title."

"That's a personal goal of mine. Dallas, are we getting anywhere? I mean, we know what we know. But are we getting anywhere toward bringing her down for it?"

"She won't think so. And that's why we're getting somewhere. Get started on the interviews, full reports on all of them."

"How many house guests?"

"Sixteen house guests, eight staff."

"Twenty-four interviews? It'll take hours."

"Then I'd get started. Out."

Eve picked up her 'link, and considered it a good omen when Roarke answered personally. "Lieutenant. What can I do for you?"

"I was wondering how you'd feel about meeting me at a sex club."

"How odd. I was just thinking what we might do this evening, and that was top of my list."

"Bang She Bang, downtown on Spring. Does an hour from now work for you?"

"I can make it work considering the incentive."

A stray thought brought on a scowl. "You don't own it, do you?"

He cocked a brow. "I don't believe I own any establishment with that name. I could probably pick it up within the hour if that would help."

She'd bet more than Peabody's twenty he could do just that. "No, thanks. I'll just use the Power of Roarke to my advantage on this one."

"I thought it was the Fear of Roarke."

"Depends on the situation. I'm thinking power will squeeze more juice out of this one than fear."

"Either are at your disposal. In an hour, Lieutenant."

After he clicked off she made a few calls, scribbled a few

notes, imagined sitting on her hands to keep herself from nagging Feeney.

Peabody hailed her as Eve started out. "I talked to the girl toy—Angel Scarlett. She got all choked up when I mentioned the old man. I don't think she's going to be winning any awards as an actress. Her rundown was consistent with her earlier statement, but not so exact it felt practiced."

Peabody did a left-to-right swivel in her chair. "She and the old man had taken a nap—which she made sure I knew was a euphemism for boinking, then she went down to take a swim. She was in the pool with some of the other guests—and that's consistent with their original statements—when the old man went down in the shower."

Peabody glanced down at her notes. "Cocktails and canapes were being served out there. I asked casually about her hostess, and she was offhand about that. Ava was flitting around somewhere, like always. You were off on the martini. It was a gin and tonic, which was the old man's summer drink of choice. Ava was mixing gin and tonics herself, and commented that the old man wasn't down. Wouldn't Tommy go up and tell his father they were all having cocktails. A few minutes later, he ran out on the terrace, up outside the old man's room, yelled for help. He'd already called nine-one-one, already moved the body in an attempt to revive. That's all in the reports. But I did get something new."

"Stun me."

"It probably won't stun you that Angel wasn't, and isn't, Ava's biggest fan. Cold, snobbish, self-righteous—and those were the compliments. And she said she thought things were a little chilly between Ava and the old man that weekend."

"Why?"

"Didn't know. Her 'big white bear' as she called him never talked business with her, and never gossiped about family. He didn't care for it when she complained about Ava's attitude toward her, so she kept it to herself. But she noticed they weren't all chummy, as usual. Didn't have coffee together by the pool that morning, and that was a habit of theirs. She suspected they'd had a little spat, but since she didn't know, kept that to herself, too."

"Write it up, log it in. I may have a line to tug on that. Later."

The trip down to Spring, an exercise in tedium on the best days, became a pitched battle due to an overturned glide-cart and the stalled Rapid Cab that had crashed into its grill. Even from ten cars back, Eve could see it would only get worse as the cab driver and the cart operator were currently beating the snot out of each other.

Eve called it in, snapping out an order for a black-and-white or patrol droids. Pissed, she slammed out of her vehicle, whipping out her badge as she strode forward. Mostly, she noted, the two men were just rolling around on raw soy fries and dogs, bapping each other on the back.

"Break it up! NYPSD, and I said break it up." She gave both of their shins a sharp rap with her boot. "Break it up or I'm hauling you both in. And as God is my witness, if any piece of either one of you makes contact with any piece of me, you're serving the full pop on assaulting an officer."

Both men lifted bloodied faces to hers, and began to shout complaints and accusations.

"Zip it! And you people! Go and find something else to do. Show's over here. You, cab guy, what's your story?"

"I'm cruising for a fare." His voice was musical, a tropical island song that contrasted sharply with the bleeding mouth and swollen eye. "Guy's hailing half a block down, and I gonna pick him up. And this one, this one, he *shoves* the cart out in the street. In front of me!"

"Fuck I did! Why'd I wanna do that? Wreck my cart thataway?"

" 'Cause you crazy man!"

Eve pointed at Cab Guy to shut him down.

"Your cart's in the street, pal." A scrapper, Eve noted, about half the size of Cab Guy, with New York as pugnacious in his tone and attitude as his bloody nose.

"Yeah, it's in the ever-fucking street, but I didn't shove it there. Goddamn kids did. Damn kids, they come along, and one's ordering a dog and fries so I'm on him, you know? And another one of 'em musta flipped off my brakes. Next I know the bunch of 'em are shoving my cart off the corner. Laughing like hyenas. Look what they done to my cart." He spread his arms wide as blood dribbled out of his nose. "What they want to do that for? I'm just trying to make a living here."

"Can you ID them?"

"I don't know. Maybe. Look at my cart, wouldja? Look at my stuff."

"I see these boys!" Cab Guy waved a hand in the air. "I see them go flying across the street. Airboards."

"Yeah, yeah." Cart Guy bobbed his head. "They had airboards. Couple of them riding tandem. I didn't see which way they went. I was trying to grab the cart, get to the brake, but the cab . . ." He shoved back his hair. "Man. Sorry about your cab."

"Not your fault. I see the kids. I can help identify." Cab Guy offered a unifying smile with bloodied teeth. "Sorry about your cart, man."

Eve turned the situation over to a black-and-white and a couple of beat droids. Cab and Cart Guy were now enjoying solidarity. They'd be neighborhood kids, she assumed. And they'd likely roll another cart or two before the day was done. But damned if she was going to help track them down.

She was ten minutes over the hour already.

It came to a total of twenty minutes behind before she could park, flip her On Duty, and hit the sidewalk. She'd already seen him—her expert consultant, her superior lay. He leaned against the wall of the graffiti-scrawled, post-Urban War rattrap that held Bang She Bang, wearing a dark suit with the thinnest of pinstripes with a spring-weight overcoat billowing a bit as he worked on his handheld.

His wrist unit was likely worth more than the building against which he braced. In this neighborhood with its funky junkies, chemi-heads, grifters, shifters, and spine crackers, a man's life was at risk for his shoes. From her vantage point, she saw what Tiko would've called a suspicious character swagger in Roarke's direction, his hand in his pocket and his fingers very likely closed over a sticker.

Roarke simply flicked his gaze up, over, locked them on. And suspicious character kept on swaggering by.

"You." Eve jabbed a finger at one of the grunts loitering in a doorway.

"Fuck you," he called back, and added his middle finger in case English wasn't her first language.

Eve flipped out her badge as she crossed the sidewalk. The badge itself didn't mean much here. It was all about what she put behind it. "That's Lieutenant, as in: Fuck you, Lieutenant."

Beside the grunt, his gap-toothed companion sniggered.

"Here's what I could do," Eve supposed. "I could slap your head against that wall, while I'm kicking your balls into your belly," she added to the companion. "And after that, I can have you in restraints while I turn out your pockets. You're carrying illegals."

"Fuck you know. You can't rouse without probable."

"I see the illegals. I've got X-ray vision.'

"No shit?" The companion grinned at her, wide-eyed. "That is frosty, complete."

"Ain't it? But I'm not going to do that. I'm not going to do runs on both of you, then come around to your flops and turn them upside down and inside out. I'm not going to personally see to it that you spend the next several days in a cage. I'm not going to do that because you're both going to stand right here until I come back, and you're going to watch my ride there as if it were your own beloved child. I come out, and my official police vehicle's exactly where I left it, in exactly the condition I left it, we part friends. Otherwise, I'm going to be paying you a visit later. Got it?"

The first guy shrugged. "I got nothing better to do."

"That's handy, because I do. You got ten now," she said and pulled out the bribe. "You get another when I come back. I bet your name's John Smith," she said to the companion.

"Hell, no. Clipper Plink."

"That's what I said. You're Clipper Plink."

"How do you *know* this stuff?" He eyed her as if she were the Second Coming. "You got superpowers, bitch?"

"Damn right."

"Jesus, Clip," she heard the grunt say as she strode toward Roarke, "can you be any fucking dumber?"

He loved to watch her work, Roarke thought. It never failed to fascinate and entertain him. So he'd done just that, relaxed against the wall while she'd taken aim at the pair of street toughs. Well, one and a half toughs, he supposed was more accurate. They hadn't stood a chance against her when she'd tossed on the badass cop as she did her coat.

Now she strode to him, the faintest hint of a smile on her face. "How many street thieves, muggers, and spine crackers did you flick off with one 'Try it, boy-o, and you'll be pissing blood for sometime to come' stare?"

"I didn't count. I don't believe this is a very safe neighborhood. I'm relieved I have a cop nearby."

"Yeah, like you need one."

"Only you, darling. Night and day. Boy-o?"

"That particular stare has the boy-o in it. Don't tell me you came down here in a ride as fancy as the suit?"

"Then I won't. Why don't you tell me why we're heading in to this sex dive on an evening that makes me almost believe spring may come again?"

"One of the strippers, LC for club work, also happens to be one of Ava's mommies. I'll fill you in on the rest later, figure you can follow along as we go. But I want to take her now. She's only on about another hour."

"Let's not waste time then." He pulled open the door.

They walked out of the almost spring evening and into the sharp, bright world of sex for sale.

It smelled of sweat, cum, smoke from a variety of illegal substances, and the cheapest of alcoholic liquids. A great many of those unattractive substances splattered the floor. Men and women with hard eyes, glassy eyes, crazed eyes, bored eyes hunched at tables or squatted at a short, stained bar on backless stools while two servers—one male, one female—carted drinks or empties on trays. Both were naked, unless you counted tats and piercings, their skin pulsing faintly red in the ugly light.

On a small, raised stage, two women—it would be absurd to term them dancers—humped long silver poles while what only the deaf could mistake for music blasted. Each wore a sparkling band at the waist, with a few bills tucked in. Neither, Roarke noted, had pulled in much for this particular number.

He walked to the bar with Eve. The man running the stick had skin so white it nearly glowed. The faint pink around his eyes usually indicated funky-junkie, but Roarke noted the eyes were the palest of blues—water blue—and just as clear.

The albino slapped a short glass of something the color and consistency of coal oil on the bar in front of a customer before moving down to them. "Stand at the bar, you order one drink minimum. Table runs two."

"Cassie Gordon?"

"Stand at the bar, one drink minimum."

Even those pale eyes should've made her for a cop, Roarke thought. Roarke pulled out a ten, covering them both, even as she pulled her badge. "Keep the drinks," Roarke told him. "I've a fondness for my stomach lining."

Eve slapped the badge down. "Cassie Gordon."

"We got a license." The albino gestured behind him where it was displayed, as per city ordinance. "Up to date."

"I didn't ask for your license. Cassie Gordon."

The bartender plucked up Roarke's bill, slid it into his own pocket. "She's up with a private. Got another five minutes on his roll. Then she's on in twenty, you can catch her between, wait till she's done. No matter to me. You take a table, cost another ten."

"Pal, I wouldn't sit at one of those tables if I was decked out in a hazmat suit. What you're going to do is show us a clean private room—not one of the sex rooms—and you're going to send Cassie there. You're going to signal her to cut it short, and come down. If you don't, my partner and I are going to make your life really unhappy."

"This isn't a cop." The bartender jerked his head at Roarke. "Cops don't dress like that."

"I'm not, no," Roarke said in what seemed like the most pleasant of tones, if you were deaf and didn't hear the jagged threat under it. "And that's why I'll hurt you more, and enjoy it more. Where's the owner's peep?"

"Got no reason to cause trouble." The bartender reached under the bar. Even as Eve braced, she heard a faint buzz. A door behind the bar slid open.

"That'll do nicely then. I'll be matching that first ten when we're done." Roarke's terrifyingly pleasant tone never altered. "Unless you do something to annoy me or my partner here. That happens, I'll be having the first ten back along with a chunk of you."

Eve said nothing until they were inside the peep—a small, relatively clean room holding a couple of chairs, a little desk, and boasting a wall of screens that surveyed the club.

"I've got the badge. I get to do the intimidating and make the threats."

"Why'd you ask me for this romantic date if you weren't aiming to let me play, too?"

"I wanted to scare the albino bartender in the sex club."

He laughed, tapped his finger on the dent in her chin. "Aw, darling, I promise you can scare the next one."

"Yeah, because the city's loaded with them. We've probably got a couple minutes. So lightning-round version."

She zipped through the salients on Bebe Petrelli, skimmed over her theory about the senior Anders to give Roarke a taste, and ended with her supposition Ava might have approached Cassie Gordon.

"She made a mistake with Petrelli," Roarke pointed out. "Do you think she made another?"

"Won't know until I ask. Gordon's done strip and sex work for eight years. A woman makes it through eight years doing that, she probably knows how to read people. She's got a daughter. Ten-year-old daughter, in the program. Ice skater. No father in the picture. Kid didn't cop a scholarship, but Anders is paying for her rink time. She's got a private coach. On paper, Gordon's paying her." Eve nodded to the screen. "Do you figure she makes enough in a dive like this to pay for a private coach?"

"Not in a thousand rides on the pole, not here."

"She's going to tell us where she's getting the money for the coach, how many favors she's done for Ava. And I'm going to know if one of those favors was killing him."

"There she is."

Roarke looked away from Eve's fierce eyes to the screen where a tall blonde in a short green robe swayed through the tables on glossy, high-platform heels. As she passed, one of the men at a table for three reached out, stuck his hand under her robe.

The blonde backhanded him, knocking him out of the chair without breaking stride.

"Well now, there's another woman who can take care of herself." He smiled at Eve. "That sort never fails to appeal to me."

IT WAS CERTAINLY INTERESTING, TO ROARKE'S mind, sharing a small room with the outsized personalities of two women. Cassie Gordon shoved herself into the room, a provocatively dressed Amazon with annoyed eyes the same hard brown as her roots. The eyes latched on Eve, and the wide, mobile mouth curled.

"You got ten minutes. I'm on in twenty. I don't dance, I don't get paid, so unless the freaking NYPSD plans on compensating me for my . . ."

Her gaze tracked over to Roarke, zeroed in. Annoyance one-eightied to pleasure; the lips rearranged themselves from curl to curve. "Well, hello, Officer Incredible. Are you here to search and manhandle me? I hope."

Roarke didn't have time to decide if he felt amusement or insult at being mistaken for a cop before Eve stepped into Cassie's face. "You're going to want to talk to me."

"I'd rather talk, and lots and lots of other things with him." But she shrugged, dropped into a chair, crossed her long, bare legs. "What's the beef?"

"Let's start off with your whereabouts between one and five a.m. on the morning of March eighteenth. Tuesday morning."

"Home." She skimmed back her hair, gave Roarke what he considered a rather masterful eye-fuck. "In my big, lonely bed."

"Cut the crap, Cassie, or we'll be having this conversation at Central."

"What's your twist? That time of night I'm home. I work days."

"A lot of people in your profession put in overtime. You were acquainted with Thomas Anders."

"Not especially. I know who he is—was," she corrected. "My little girl's in the Anders sports program. She's a figure skater. She's a champion. But I didn't hob with the nob."

"Ever been to the Anders's home?"

"Are you fucking kidding me?" Cassie reared back her head and laughed. "Is she fucking kidding me?" she said to Roarke.

"She's not, no. Why is the question so amusing?"

"I take my clothes off and turn tricks for a living. Not the kind of dinner party guest I expect the Anderses entertain regular."

"But Mrs. Anders did indeed entertain you," Roarke continued. "At retreats, spas, hotels."

"That's different. Those things were for mothers of kids in the programs. I'm a goddamn good mother," she snapped, pointing at her own partially concealed breasts. "Nobody can say different."

"No one is," Roarke said smoothly as Eve appeared to be giving him the line. "But you did socialize with Ava Anders."

The sound she made combined snort with Bronx cheer. "If you can call it that."

"What would you call it?"

"Same kind of arrangement I just concluded upstairs."

"She fuck you, Cassie?" Eve asked.

"Not literally. I got no problem doing the girl-on-girl if the fee's right, but I don't think she's into that." A shrug shifted the robe so her right breast peeked out coyly. "She wanted something, I gave it, and I got paid. That's how I look at it."

"What did she want?"

"I figure I got the invite so she could show how—what's the word—democratic she is. And I figure that's bull. But my kid? She's a freaking jewel, so I can take the bull or anything else gets thrown at me if it's for her."

"What did Ava throw at you?"

"Look, I gotta get in costume. It's my last round this shift, and I can't afford—"

"You'll be compensated." Roarke remained relaxed, answered his wife's stony stare with the mildest of glances while Cassie studied them both.

"I can earn five hundred on the last round."

"Talk about bull," Eve began.

"You'll be compensated," Roarke repeated. "Answer the lieutenant, stop playing it out, and you'll get the five."

Those hard eyes narrowed. "You ain't no cop."

"A fact for which I give thanks daily. You can answer the question the cop asks and get the five or, well, you'll be answering them anyway in less comfortable surroundings and get nothing. And since you'll be squeezing in the round after we leave in any case, you've a chance at five clear in your pocket."

"Not a cop, but not stupid." Another shrug, but Cassie followed this one with an absent tug that closed the front of her robe again. Or nearly. "Okay, it's like this. I take Gracie, my kid, to the ice rink in the park. Been doing that since she was about three. Even I can see she's got a knack for it, and she freaking loves it. I can't afford rink time, or not much of it, so she only got to skate in the winter. And good skates, good lessons, they're out of orbit. I applied for the Anders program, and she got in. Man, it was like I'd given her the world. I'd do anything to make sure she keeps it."

"Anything Ava asked?"

"Look, bitch wants to know how I handle tricks, I'm not going to get razzed about it. She wants to get a peek into the dirty, no skin off mine. She figures I owe her volunteer time, I work it in. My kid gets good skates, nice skating clothes, solid rink time. She wants to pretend her old man's interested in the dirty, what's it to me?"

"Pretend."

Smiling, Cassie ran a finger tip up and down the front of her robe. "I know when I'm being played. These little *chats* were for her benefit. Maybe she wanted to try some shit out with her old man. Couldn't hurt, right? Except he's dead, right? Died doing the dirty. She do him?"

"She was out of the country at the time."

"Lucky for her, I guess."

"You don't like her one bit," Roarke commented.

"Not one small bit." Cassie held up her thumb and forefinger a fraction apart, then slapped them closed. "She lords it over—or ladyies it over you. Covers it up with the 'we're all part of the big happy Anders family,' but she expects you to do plenty of bowing and scraping. I can give a fat asshole a bj upstairs, I can bow and scrape. I get compensated."

"Did she share information about her sex life with you?"

"She said her old man was into the dirty and the strange and she wasn't, but more subtle than that. Feeling me out was my sense. I half-expected her to hire me to do him so she could watch and get pointers. Thing is, I don't think she liked me any more than I liked her and we both knew it. Both knew we were shoveling the shit."

"What did you have to do for her to earn the private coach?"

"I pay for the coach." Cassie tapped her thumb between her breasts. "I pay."

"You don't earn enough juice working here to cover private coaching."

"I get a lot of tips."

"What's that I hear?" Eve cocked her head. "Oh yeah, that's the sound of five hundred sucking down the drain."

"Goddamn it." Cassie pushed to her feet, stared hard at Eve. "This is about the murder, right? That's big-time. You're big-time. Christ knows you are," she said to Roarke. "I need some assurance you're not going to shake me down over small-time."

"If you're working off book, I'm not interested in rousting you for it."

Cassie took a moment to stare, to study, then apparently satisfied by what she read on Eve's face, nodded. "I do some private. I'm not licensed for private. And I do the coach's father for free, every week. It's like a barter, cuts down on the fee. He's a nice guy, actually. Can't get out much 'cause he busted himself up bad about thirty years ago. He's gimpy, got scars. Even if Anders offered coaching, I'd keep it how it is, because it's working. And I gotta have a part in providing for my kid. If you've got some cop idea that I was doing Anders, and screwed up the deal so he kicked, that's off, way off. I'm home nights. I don't leave my kid home alone. Not ever. You ask anybody. You want to look at somebody, you ought to take another look at the wife. Make damn double sure *she* wasn't there."

"Why is that?"

"Bitch got stones. She's got cold, hard stones."

They were done. Roarke knew Eve's rhythm well enough to know she'd written Cassie off. But he was curious. "Why are you working here? You could make more in a classier place."

"I can't dance worth shit." She said it cheerfully. "Classier places expect classier strippers. I got this." She opened her robe, revealing a curvy body that showed some wear. "It's good, but it ain't great. I go more upscale," she continued, absently tying the robe again, "they'd want me to get the shifting parts put back in place. Here, they don't care about that, long as you put in your rounds and pull in your quota of bjs and handjobs upstairs.

"I can work days, and be home at night with my girl. Not a lot of places going to let me call that shot. And I don't work weekends, because I'm with my kid. It's a trade-off. It's worth it. She's worth it. You're going to see her take gold in the Olympics one day. She's a freaking champion."

"Gracie Gordon. I'll remember. Appreciate the time." Eve took a step toward the door, and Roarke slipped a money clip out of his pocket, peeled off bills.

"Shit a brick, you carry like that?" Sheer shock covered Cassie's face. "In this neighborhood?"

"I carry as I please. There's the five, and one extra. For the champion."

Cassie stared at the six hundreds in her hand. "You're all right, Blue Eyes." She lifted her head to look into them. "You're all right, down the line. You ever want a free bang, you got one coming."

"It would, no doubt be a memorable bang. But my wife is fiercely jealous and territorial." He grinned over at a very cold-eyed Eve.

"Her? You? That's a kick in the ass."

"Every damn day," Eve muttered, and strode out.

She kept striding, out of the club, back into the comparatively fresh air of the city street. And fisted her hands on her hips as she spun to him. "Did you *have* to do the 'my wife' crap?"

His grin remained, and only widened. "I did, yes. I felt a desperate need for your protection. I believe that woman had designs on me."

"I'll put a design on you that won't come off in the shower."

"See, now I'm excited." Reaching out, he toyed with the lapel of her coat. "What have you got in mind?"

"And you gave her six fucking hundred dollars."

"Looks like you'll be buying dinner tonight."

She made a sound, a kind of grinding grunt as she fisted her hands in her hair and yanked. No wonder she got headaches, he mused.

"Look, King of the World, you've got no business giving some stripper who's also a suspect six bills."

"Isn't that the Power of Roarke?" he countered. "And I didn't give her the six for the very intriguing flash. *And*," he continued, giving her a quick poke, "she stopped being a suspect, a serious one, the minute you saw her backhand that drunk degenerate in the club."

Before she could argue, the grunt in the doorway yelled out. "Hey, cop. You gonna move this crap ride or leave it here all damn night?"

She only turned her head, burned him to silence with one stare. "If she makes six bills in six rounds in that dump *I'll* go up and dance on a pole."

"As much as I'd enjoy seeing that—in fact, am in my head at this moment—I'm forced to agree. But it's neither here nor there. She named the five, I agreed to it. The sixth was for the child, and she'll see the child gets it. I admire and respect a woman who does the necessary, whatever it might be, for her child."

She let out a breath, and it was the wind coming out of her sails. He'd thought of his mother, of course, Eve realized. Of what she'd suffered and sacrificed. Of what she'd died for. "Still," she said because she couldn't think of anything else. "And why did I take her off the list when she knocked that jerk out of his chair?"

"Because you saw, as I did, a direct woman who handles business in a straightforward manner. She might have killed Anders if her reasons were strong enough, but she'd never have left him to choke to death."

"You should've been a cop."

"You're just saying that to get back at me for the 'my wife' comment. We'll consider ourselves even."

She considered. "I'm not buying dinner because I'm tapped, and we can get it free at home. Give Sulky and his friend Stupid another ten, will you?"

When he joined her in the car, she gave him a smirk. "Bet you didn't give them a tip."

"Actually, I did. It was that if they ever saw this particular crap ride in the neighborhood again, they should remember the pair of tenners, and your considerable wrath. Now why should you be tapped?"

"What? Oh. I don't know. Because people keep wanting money for stuff. Buy a damn Pepsi, they expect some coin. Bastards."

"How much shagging Pepsi do you drink?"

"I don't know. Plus there's, you know, stuff that comes up. Weasels to pay off."

"Weaseling is departmentally covered in your budget."

Her lips curled. "Yeah, and by the time I get the kick back from that I'll be retired and taking hula lessons in Maui. What is this, an inquisition?"

"I don't understand why—and yes, I'm saying it, so suck it up—my wife is walking around tapped. Make a bloody withdrawal from your account, or ask me for a bit of the ready."

"Ask you for . . . ." Fortunately, the light turned red, forcing her to stop. It was marginally safer to swing around and glare at him while stopped. "I'll be damned if I'll ask you for money."

"You just asked me for ten to pay your street thug."

"That's different."

"How?"

"Because . . . It wasn't for me, it was for him. I'll put in a chit for it, pay you back."

"While we're taking those hula lessons, possibly eating poi. Don't be an idiot."

"Call me an idiot again, all you'll be able to eat is poi, seeing as you'll be missing most of your teeth."

"I didn't call you an idiot, I told you not to be one," he snapped back. "And if you don't drive this bleeding car we'll have a riot on our hands."

She supposed the explosions going on in her head had blocked out the blaring horns. She zipped through the light, steamed up the next few blocks, then swung back when she hit the next red. "I've been handling my own ready all my life and I don't need a freaking allowance from my daddy. I do just fine."

"Obviously, since you're walking about with empty pockets."

"I got the plastic, don't I?"

The look he gave her would have withered stone. "How things must've changed since I was running the streets. I never accepted the plastic."

He had her there. "So I didn't get around to pulling out a little cash the last few days. So what? I don't know why you're so pissed about it."

"You don't, no. Quite obviously, you don't."

The fact that he didn't add to that, said nothing at all as she fought and maneuvered her way uptown told her he wasn't just pissed, he was over the line into furious.

She didn't get it, didn't get it, didn't get it. How had they gone from perfectly fine to taking a few acceptable pokes at each other to furious?

So now he sat there, ignoring her, working with his PPC again. Probably prying into her bank account to see what an idiot she was in his gazillionaire opinion. Snapping and slapping at her because she'd run a little short between paydays.

So the fuck what?

She picked at it, gnawed at it, brooded over it the rest of the way. When she stopped in front of the house, when they got out of opposite sides of the car, she stood with the car between them. "Look—"

"No, you're going to need to look, Eve. We'll go inside so that you do."

Since he strode away, she had little choice but to follow. *Don't need this now,* she thought. *Don't need some marital knot to unravel when I've got work.* She always had work, a little voice reminded her, and did nothing but make her feel guilty.

When he stepped inside, Roarke simply held up a finger. Eve watched, with surprise and envy, as Summerset slipped back out of the foyer without a word. With the path effortlessly cleared, she trudged up the steps after Roarke.

She expected him to head to one of their offices or their bedroom. Instead he walked into one of the quiet and beautiful sitting rooms. A banquet of blooming plants charmed a trio of windows. A pair of curved settees in muted stripes faced each other across a slim, glossy table. After shrugging out of his coat, Roarke tossed it over one of the pretty fabric chairs.

"I'll have a drink with this."

It didn't surprise her to see the wine fridge when he crossed over, opened a panel. When he'd drawn the cork, he took two glasses from another panel, poured.

"Why don't you sit?"

"I feel like I'm about to get dressed down by an annoyed parent because I blew my spending money on candy. I don't like it, Roarke."

"I'm not your father, and I don't give a damn what you spend your money on. There, better?"

"No."

"Well then, that's a pity. Myself, I'm going to sit down, drink this wine, and continue to resist the urge to rap your head against the handiest solid surface."

When he sat, when he sipped, she continued to stand. "You can't be this mad because I ran short before payday."

"You'd be wrong about that."

She'd have preferred the heat, a good fiery blast of it. And she knew he understood that, *knew* it, as he gave her rigid ice. "Jesus, what's the big deal? I had some unforeseens. I had to flip a couple to a weasel last week, and I don't know, other stuff. There was that kid, and—"

"I've just said I don't care how you spend your money. I care that you'd rather walk around without any in your pocket than ask me for a bit of cash. Or get it for yourself as you know the combination of the damn safes around here."

"I'm not going into one of your safes for—"

"And there it is." He set the wine glass down in a gesture so careful, so deliberate, she understood he'd barely resisted heaving it. "You won't go into *my* safes. And you can't see how insulting that is to me? To us?"

To give herself a moment, she took off her coat, tossed it over with his. Then she sat, picked up the wine. Studied it. "You think it should be easy, that it should be smooth because we're married for me to hit you up—"

"There it is again. How the hell is it hitting me up?"

"Christ." Despite the fact that her head throbbed, she took a good slug of wine. "Because that's how it would feel. Do you know how long it's taken me to get used to living here—well, almost used to it—to feel, really, feel that it is my home? Not yours, not even ours, those were easier. But mine? Your money came down in the minus column for me. I fell for you in spite of it. If that makes me an idiot, too damn bad."

"I came from nothing, and built this. I've pride in that, and so I understand yours. Your pride. I also know the money means little to nothing to you. So why then, can't you take a bit of what means so little rather than running on empty when it's so ridiculously unnecessary?"

Not so pissed now, she noted with some relief. Baffled, maybe even a little hurt, but no longer furious. "I didn't think about it. I didn't notice I was so light until I pulled out the ten.

I've had other things on my mind besides . . . And all that's true, but all that's an evasion."

She drank again to ease the tightness in her throat. "I can't. I'm sorry, really, that it hurts or upsets you. I can't hold out my hand to you, not for money. I just can't. So it's going to have to piss you off or insult you or whatever it does. I just can't do it, Roarke."

He picked up his glass again, said nothing for several moments as he sat, as he sipped. "You could if we were on more even ground, as you see it?"

"No. It's not how much, it's at all."

He searched her face. "That's hardheaded, short-sighted, and tight-assed. But, all right then."

"All right then?" Flabbergasted, she gaped at him. "All right? That's it?"

"Those may be three of your qualities that land in the minus column for me," he said with a hint of a smile. "I fell for you despite them." He pulled out his money clip, and that finger came up, silencing her as effectively as it had Summerset. He set fifty on the table between them. "You'll do me a favor and take that as a loan so you don't walk out of here with nothing but your hard head and tight ass in the morning. That'll make sixty you owe me come payday, counting the previous ten."

"Okay." She took the fifty, stuffed it in her pocket. "Did we just compromise?"

"I believe we did."

"Good." She took another sip of wine, looked around. "So. This is a nice room."

"It is, yes. It's just been redecorated. Came out well, I think."

"Get out. Really? When?"

"Just after the holidays." He smiled fully now. "I believe I mentioned something to you about it, in case you wanted any input on the colors and fabrics and so on."

"Oh. Yeah. I guess I remember something about that. You probably did better without me."

"I never have, never will."

She sighed, sunk into love with him. "Maybe we could have dinner in here tonight."

"Is that another compromise?"

"I was thinking of it more like interest on the sixty."

He laughed. "Well then, I charge high rates. You'll have to get the meal to work that off."

"No problem." She stood up. "And in the spirit of compromise, it's going to be pizza." She looked around again. "Where the hell's the AutoChef in here?"

They sat together on one of the curved settees, the mood mellow as they shared pizza and wine. And if the conversation turned to murder, it suited both of them.

"So Feeney's got the pill dispenser thing. If I'd known he was going to dick around with it, I'd've brought it home and shoved it on you."

"If it was played with, he'll find out soon enough. In any case, even if it was, it wouldn't prove she'd done it. He could have reprogrammed it himself. That wouldn't work for you in court."

"It's another weight. Even small weights add up. It goes to opportunity. Conversely, she can't prove he routinely took sleep aids, or ever took them for that matter. There's only her word he had sidepieces, brought them home. I spoke with three of his former romantic interests. Every one of them describes him as a shy sort of lover—sweet, not very adventurous. Gentle. Every one of them."

"More weight, certainly, but Ava planted seeds that this was a relatively recent change."

"A guy goes from sweet, shy, and gentle in bed to a raging perv who molests minors? She's going to have a hard time convincing a jury there. And, her diddling with Charles is documented, while there isn't any documentation Anders diddled. That'll work against her instead of covering her ass like she planned. I've got Petrelli's statement. It would've fit in nicely for me if Cassie Gordon's had run parallel. I have to figure Ava saw she wasn't going to be able to use Gordon, not that way. So there's at least one more. The one she worked well enough to kill for her."

"You have another candidate there?"

"Yeah, we'll go into those possibilities tomorrow. But I need to spread it out. Maybe it's not a repeater on the mommy breaks. Or somebody with some smears and smudges. She goes for clean, say—the way you liked it—and keeps her away from the group. Makes her more a personal pet.

"So many damn names," she complained. "It'll take weeks to get through them. Chasing my tail. Pisses me off."

"I'll give you a hand with it. You'd eliminate anyone with a husband or cohab, I'd assume. As she wouldn't have wanted to risk her surrogate telling her mate. Single parents would be highest probability. Ones without any close family—but for the children—or friends, for that matter. Someone smart enough to follow directions, and also weak enough or frightened enough to follow them."

"See, you should've been a cop."

He only sighed. "Why would you want to start another fight when we've just made up?"

"We have to have sex to really make up."

"Well then."

"Not now, ace." She gave him a light shove back. "Work first, makeup sex later." Rising, she wondered if she'd regret scarfing down that last slice of pizza. "I need to take another hard look at the case file on the old man's death. Her father-in-law. Pick it apart, find the chinks. People don't commit perfect murders, and she sure as hell didn't pull off every last detail twice. If I can find the cracks there, they could lead to the cracks here. Or vice versa."

"I guess you'll be wanting that hammer again."

She grinned at him. "Sex, sex, sex. That's all it is with you."

"That's my one-track mind." He stood, pulled her close and took her in a kiss that had her eyes rolling to the back of her head. "Just collecting my down payment," he told her.

She glanced back at the room as they walked out together. "Redecorating, redecorating. How much lead time did you need to get somebody in to do the room?"

"Essentially none, but I do own the firm who did the job."

"Yeah, you being you. How much for normal people?"

"It would depend on the size of the job, the demands of the client, and how much money the client was willing to throw at the decorating team."

"I bet your people could find out easy who Ava used, and when she had her first consult."

"I bet they could. I'll make a call." He gave her ass a friendly pat. "I'll be in shortly. I want to change out of this suit."

She kept going, then turned, walked backward. "Roarke?"

He glanced back. "Hmm?"

"I'd have fallen for you even if you had twice as much money, which is virtually impossible. But still."

"I'd have fallen for you even if your head was twice as hard, again virtually impossible. And still."

"We're good," she said, then continued on to her office.

19 WHEN HE CAME IN, SHE SAT AT HER DESK, HER jacket tossed on the back of her sleep chair. The jacket, he knew, would bother her while she worked. The weapon she still wore? Its weight wouldn't register any more than the weight of her own arms.

Steam rose out of the mug on her desk. Coffee, he thought, nearly equalled the weapon as part of her essential makeup.

She hadn't yet worked herself into exhaustion on this one. He'd seen her work, worry, wrangle with a case until her system simply collapsed from neglect. But this one, he realized, was different. She was juiced.

"It's a competition."

She glanced over, brows knit. "What?"

"You're as involved and determined as you are, always. You've made the victim yours, as you always do. But you're not suffering this time around."

"Suffering? I don't suffer."

"Oh, but you do, darling Eve. Murder infuriates you, insults you, and the victims haunt you. Every one. But for this, for this particular one, it's challenged you above all else. She challenges you—and your attitude toward her, which strikes me as a personal level of dislike, kicks that up a notch. You're damned if you aren't going to beat her."

"Maybe. Whatever works. Whatever gets the job done. So, the efficient Leopold came through. I've got his incoming here, the list of parents Ava tapped for grunt work. The ones he had some record of or remembered, anyway. We'll split those if you're up for it."

"Shoot my share to my unit."

"Okay. We'll divide by alpha. We should . . . I don't like her," Eve said suddenly. "Didn't like her pretty much from the jump. Didn't like her when I stood watching her on the security screen as she walked into the house the morning of."

"With her well-groomed hair and coordinating wardrobe," Roarke remembered.

"Yeah. It was . . ." Eve snapped her fingers. "But that screws objectivity, so I pushed it back. Thing is, it kept pushing back in again. It took me awhile—well, not that much while, but some—to figure out why."

Since he sensed something there, he sat on the corner of her desk. "All right. Tell me why."

"Don't get bent over it."

He angled his head. "Why would I?"

"She reminds me of Magdelana."

He said nothing for a moment, just watched her face then, rising, he walked over to the murder board to study Ava's.

"Not just the high-class blonde thing," Eve began.

"No," he said quietly, "not just." He thought of Magdelana, the woman he'd once cared for. The woman who'd betrayed him, and on the return trip had done everything in her power to hurt Eve and chip away at their marriage.

"Not just," he repeated. "They're both users, aren't they? Manipulators with a wholly selfish core polished over with sophistication and style. Very much the same type. You're right about that."

"Okay."

Hearing the relief in her voice, he looked over at her. "Did you think I'd be annoyed or upset by the comparison?"

"Maybe some, maybe more if I'd finished it out and said that because she reminds me of Magdabitch, I'm going to experience a tingly, even orgasmic satisfaction by bringing her down."

"I see. Revenge by proxy."

"She deserves the cage on her own merits or lack thereof. But yeah, maybe some element of revenge by proxy."

Walking back, he leaned down, kissed the top of Eve's head. "Whatever works. And now that you've pointed it out, I'll enjoy some of that tingly satisfaction as well. Thanks for that."

"It's small, petty, and probably inappropriate of us."

"Which will make it all the more orgasmic. Send over the file. I'll just cop some of your coffee, then get started."

Whatever works, Eve thought again as he strolled into the kitchen. What really worked, was them.

She ordered her unit to copy and send Roarke's unit the names on file beginning with N surnames. Then she opened the first half of the file, took a quick scan.

Plenty of little slaves and servants to pick from, she thought. A nice wide field of the vulnerable, the needy, the grateful. The bitch just had to keep circling until . . .

"Wait. Whoa. Wait."

With coffee in hand, Roarke stepped back in. "That was fast."

"Wait, wait, wait." Scooping back her hair, Eve launched to her feet. "Computer, display on screen, data for Custer, Suzanne."

"Who might that be?" Roarke wondered.

"Wait, wait. Computer, display on second screen, data on Custer, Ned."

Roarke did wait, studied both photos, the basic identification data. "Husband and wife, and he's deceased. Recently."

"He's Baxter's." She dropped back down into the chair. "I didn't keep the damn file. I need the damn case file on this guy."

"Move," Roarke ordered. "Get up. Give me a moment."

"Don't hack into Baxter's police unit. I'll tag him and—"

"And I'll have it for you a great deal quicker. It's hardly hacking, as it's ridiculously easy. And you're authorized in any case." He gave her shoulder a light, but purposeful shove. "Give me the chair a minute."

"All right, all right." In any case, it gave her time to pace and think. She stared at the woman on screen—pretty in a toned-down, tired-eyed kind of way. Couple of kids, professional mother's stipend, philandering, heavy-handed husband.

"Coincidence, my ass."

"Quiet," Roarke muttered. "Half a minute more here. Ah, and there we are. What do you need from this?"

"Take down the data on screen, put that up. We'll scroll through." She felt it, felt it in her bones. But . . . "I want your take here without any of my input first."

He read, as she did, of the quick and nasty death of one Ned Custer by person or persons unknown. Cheap sex flop, slit throat attack from behind—castration, no trace or DNA, no witnesses. No trail.

"So the wife was well-alibied, I see."

"Solid. They ran the 'link calls, confirmed the source. She was in her apartment when he got sliced. No boyfriends, no close relatives or friends. Baxter and Trueheart are thorough, and they didn't pop anything on this."

"She's one of Ava's mothers."

"Yep."

"*Strangers on a Train.*"

"Huh?" Her head swiveled back toward him. "What train? Nobody was on a train."

"I haven't run that vid for you, have I?" Coolly, he continued to study the screen, continued to read data. "It's a good one. Early twentieth-century, Hitchcock film. You've enjoyed Hitchcock."

"Yeah, yeah, so?"

"Briefly, two men—strangers—meet on a train, and the conversation turns to how each wishes to be rid of a certain individual in his life. And how it could be done without the police suspecting them if each did in the other's. Very clever, as there's no real connection between the two men. It was a book first, come to think of it."

"Strangers," Eve repeated.

"In this case, the one who wanted his wife done didn't take the other—an unstable sort, who wanted his father done—seriously. But, the wife was dispatched, and the unstable sort pressured the sudden widower to complete the bargain. It's twisty and complex. You'll have to watch it."

"The exchange is what clicked for me," Eve told him. "The possibility of that. You do mine, I do yours. We're both alibied, and who'd look at either of us for the other's? Why would Baxter look at Ava Anders in the murder of this guy? She doesn't know him, and even if you note that Suzanne Custer's in the Anders program, it doesn't pop. It doesn't mean a thing."

"Until you look at Anders's murder, won't let it slide as an accident, and dig deep enough to see this. And wonder."

"Probability scan's going to bottom out." Already annoyed by that, Eve hissed out a breath. "It'll bottom out until I can plug in more. What about you? Do you buy it?"

"The stronger personality, the more powerful one, hatches the plan, draws the weaker one in. And does the job first, to add pressure and obligation. Even threat. When the weaker follows through, it's not quite as clean and tidy. Yes, I'd buy it."

"It's easier to pry open the weaker one. We pull Suzanne Custer in, we work her." Pacing, Eve circled the murder board. "Work her right, work her hard enough, she'll flip on Ava. Need more first. You move."

He pushed back from the desk. "Do you still want runs on the other names?"

"I'll put a drone on that. This is the money shot here, this is the one. I've got a tingly."

"Save it for me, will you?"

"Ha. I need everything I can get on her. Baxter's got a solid murder book. We just have to look at the data from a different angle now. Suzanne didn't kill her husband. She killed Ava's."

"There had to be contact between the two murderers," Roarke pointed out. "Confirming the first, setting up the second."

"Where did Custer get the murder weapon, the drug, the enhancer? That's a place to pick at. Ava had to give her the security code, the layout." As she spoke, Eve scrawled down names, connections, questions. "They changed the code every ten days, so there had to be a way to pass that on. We pick at Ava at the same time. She's not going to be alibied so damn tight for the night of Ned Custer's murder. She fits," Eve added. "She's the right height for the angle of the killing strike. The right personality to have planned it without leaving a trace behind, the right personality to use someone else to get what she wanted."

"Baxter would have had EDD check all Custer's 'links, her comp for communication and activity before her husband's murder, and—I assume—for a week or so after it."

"Yeah, but not for before Anders." Eve planted a finger on Thomas Anders's name on her notes. "No point. She wasn't a suspect, not with her alibi, in her husband's. You look, you check, but Baxter didn't feel it. Because it wasn't there to feel. We'll pull them now, all of them. Anders's, too. We'll go back to before the Custer murder on them."

She drummed her fingers. "Asshole like Custer, I bet he kept cock enhancers around. The barbs, now . . . where's a nice mom of two like Suzanne going to get her hand on them? They came from her. That part wasn't in Ava's plan."

"A terrible thing when your husband's murdered that way," Roarke commented. "I'll bet a kindly doctor would prescribe tranquilizers for the widow. Put them all together instead of doling them out for yourself . . ."

"Good. That's good. A medical won't want to give us that information, not without a warrant, but we start with her financials, see if she paid a doctor, paid a pharmacy between the murders. Close to the second murder, yeah, close, I bet. Got cold feet as it got toward the sticking point."

She engaged her 'link, put through to Baxter's home. When she hit voice mail, she ordered a transfer to his mobile.

She heard music first, something low and bluesy that said sexual foreplay to her. Baxter's face came on with dim lighting in the background.

"This better be damn good."

"My home office, tomorrow eight-hundred hours."

"I'm not on the roll till Monday. I've got—"

"You are now. Tag your boy, too."

"Give me a break, Dallas. I've got a clear field and a hot brunette on tap."

"Then you'd better turn her on full tonight, because you're here at eight. How much do you want to close the Custer case, Baxter?"

The irritated scowl vanished. "You got something there?"

"Hotter than any brunette who'd give you a clear field. Eight-hundred. If you've got any personal notes not in the murder book, bring them."

"Give me a goddamn hint, will you?"

"*Strangers on a Train*. Look it up." She clicked off, contacted Peabody, then Feeney.

"Sounds like we'll need the standard cop breakfast buffet," Roarke decided. "And a Saturday one at that."

"You don't have to feed them. I want Mira, too," she

considered. "I'd like her take on the suspect profiles." She glanced at her wrist unit. "It's not really all that late."

"While you're interrupting the Miras' evening, send me the file. I'll poke into the financials."

She frowned at him. "It's still open and active. Yeah, you could do that. And I can order the full search on the electronics. When you do the financials, see if anything pops back aways that points toward Suzanne Custer buying the sex aids."

After copying and sending the file, Eve stared at her 'link. It wasn't really that late, she reminded herself. But she had sex aids on the brain, and that nudged her into thinking how the Miras might be spending their night together. "Jesus, way to wig myself out."

She hedged, and ordered the transmission to go straight to voice mail. "Dr. Mira, I didn't want to disturb your evening. I've got something on the Anders case, a strong possibility of a connection with a previous homicide that's still open and active. I realize tomorrow's Saturday—" Or she did now that Roarke had mentioned it. "—I have a team meeting at my home office tomorrow at eight—"

"Eve?"

"Oh, hey." There was music again. It wasn't porn vid music, thank God, but it spoke of an intimate evening at home to Eve. "Sorry to bother you when you're . . . whatever. I have something I'd like to pull you in on. I've set a meeting at my home office in the morning, if your schedule—"

"What time?"

"Eight-hundred."

"I can make that. I'll be there. Do you want me to study anything in the meantime?"

"I'd actually like you to come into this fresh."

"Fine." Mira glanced away, laughed as she sent a warm look off screen. "Dennis sends his best. I'll see you in the morning."

"Thanks."

Eve swiveled away from the 'link, pressed her fingers to her eyes. "They're going to do it," she mumbled. "If not now, soon. I wish I didn't have to know that."

To clear the image, and the thought, out of her head, she turned back to Baxter's file, and started digging.

At some point the cat wandered in to leap on her desk. When he got nothing but, "Don't sit on my stuff," he leaped back down to stalk into Roarke's domain.

She started a new file listing the correlations, the connections —actual and possible—the time lines. Using the backside of her murder board, she arranged photos, notes, reports. Stood back, studied it.

She could see it, actually see it. The steps, the stages, the moves, the mistakes. Not enough, she admitted, not for an arrest, not for a conviction. But there would be.

Lock and key, that's how she saw it. The Anders case the lock, the Custer case the key. Once she fit them together, turned it just right, it would open. Then she'd reach in and grab Ava by the throat.

She turned to Roarke's office. He sat at his desk, the cat draped over his lap. "Find anything?"

"Custer's financials don't allow her much wiggle room. From what I can see, the husband ran the show there previously. Most of the withdrawals, debits are in his name. There are several in one particular sex shop—Just Sex—in the six months before his untimely. As it wouldn't have surprised me to find certain items you had interest in—"

"Hopefully you mean professional interest."

He only smiled. "As, and so forth, I entertained myself and did a bit of searching at the vendor's . . ."

"You hacked."

"You say that in such a disapproving tone. I explored. You'll certainly do so yourself, legally and tediously, but I like having my curiosity satisfied."

He said nothing more, only picked up the bottle of water on his desk and drank. And his eyes laughed at her over the bottle.

"Crap. Yes, I'll get the data by fully legal means, but what did you find?"

"Multiple purchases of what's delightfully marketed as Hard-on. It comes in a phallic-shaped bottle."

"Check one."

"Purchases of various sexual aids and toys. Cock rings, probes, textured condoms, vibrators."

"Check two."

"Nothing on the ropes, I'm afraid."

"But they carry them. We checked venues for that type of rope, and they carry them. Did Suzanne pay a visit there?"

"No record of that, no. They do take cash. She did, however, visit a clinic two weeks before Anders's death. She saw a Dr. Yin there according to the records—"

"Which you hacked into?"

"Which I explored," he said mildly. "And she incurred a debit at the attached pharmacy, filling a prescription for a box of home pressure syringes, and a liquid form of lotrominaphine—a barbiturate used to aid sleep and nervous conditions."

"Big, fat, red check. I have to get all this data through channels, get it all lined up. Then I'm going to knock her down with it."

"Where are you going?"

"It's never too late to call an APA," she said as she hurried back to her desk. "I'm going to contact Reo, do the fast talk and get the paperwork started on warrants for the data you just gave me."

"And after we dropped it all nicely tied in a bow into her lap," Roarke said to the cat. "That's a cop for you."

He heard her giving her pitch to Cher Reo, then arguing with the soft-voiced, tough-minded APA. He busied himself for the next few minutes studying and analyzing the last weeks of Suzanne Custer's financials.

"Find another spot," Roarke told Galahad, and hauled the limp mass of cat up, dropped him lightly on the floor. When he walked into Eve's office, she sat at her desk, keying in more notes.

"She's getting them. Whined about it, but she's getting them."

"Whined, perhaps, because you contacted her at very close to midnight."

"Mostly. You can put them together like that." Eve lifted her hands, fingers open and pointed toward each other, then slid them together. "Like teeth. Like gears. You just have to see the big picture. It's a nearly perfect, well, machine, to stick with the teeth and gears. Clean and efficient. The problem is the operators. She made her mistake selecting this operator."

He eased back down on her desk. "Why was this particular operator a mistake?"

"Look at her." Eve gestured toward the screen. "Look at her background data, look at her face. Ava looks and she sees somebody weak, easily manipulated, easily cowed because she stayed with a cheating, abusing husband. She sees ordinary, a woman nobody's going to look at twice. A woman who *owes* her."

"What do you see?"

"That, all that. But I also see a woman who takes the time and trouble to find something better for her kids, something that makes them happy. One who, according to the statements in Baxter's knock-on-doors, kept those kids and herself clean and out of trouble. She never crossed the line before this. When you push somebody like that across the line, or seduce them over it, sooner or later they look back and regret it. I'm going to make her regret sooner."

"You can get started on that in just under eight hours."

"Why . . . Oh."

"There's nothing more you can do tonight."

"Not really." She saved, copied, shut down. "Probably better to let it cook anyway."

He took her hand, tugged her along when she looked back at the murder board. "You should be interested that Suzanne Custer's better off financially with a dead husband than she was with a live one."

"Little life insurance, decent pension."

"More than that. On a quick analysis of their financials for the past twelve months, he spent approximately forty-six percent of their combined incomes on his personal needs, wants, and pursuits. Leaving the fifty-four to cover housing, food, medical, clothing, transportation, educational supplies for the children, and so on. She has his life insurance payment now, and—as a widowed professional mother, with the pension from his employment—nearly the same income as before. About eight percent less."

"With forty-six percent less outlay. So she's actually—why do I have to do math at midnight?"

"Thirty-eight percent to the good—using that table, and one year as an example."

"Good enough for me. It's not the megabucks Ava reaps, but it's solid. It's . . . proportionate, if you think about it. And it's another button to push when we get Custer into Interview. Thanks."

She mulled it over as she undressed. "Some of the seminars Anders offered are on budgeting, financial planning. What do you bet Ava talked to Suzanne about her money situation and how it could get a lot brighter?"

"A basic strategy would be to list all advantages. And push home all the disadvantages of the status quo. I imagine some of those seminars dealt with being proactive, with empowerment, making tough choices to improve your family situation. Any and all could be twisted by a clever woman to seduce, as you said, a vulnerable one."

"So many mind games," Eve mused, "so little hard evidence."

"It's cooking until morning," he reminded her. "And speaking of seductions." He gripped her hips. "I believe we have to finish making up."

"Oh yeah. I guess I could work that in now." Bracing her hands on his shoulders, she pushed off the balls of her feet, rising up with his helpful boost to wrap her legs around his waist. "How mad were we?"

"Furious."

"It didn't seem that bad, looking back."

"It was a pitched battle that nearly shook the foundation of our marriage."

"My ass."

"Yes, it is." He gave it a squeeze before tumbling to the bed with her. He laughed down at her, then kissed her lightly. "It's a good day when it ends like this."

She laid a hand on his cheek. "They're pretty much all good days for me now, even the bad ones."

All good, she thought, *with him.* When her mouth lifted to his, they both sank in.

So it was to be slow and easy, quiet and sweet. And so married, Eve thought, with one anticipating the other. A rise, a fall, a turn, a glide. A thrill, yes, it would always and ever be a thrill—the feel of him, the taste of him. But comfort twined with it, a velvet ribbon through the silver blade.

Her pulse quickened, and muscles, tight from a long, long day, relaxed.

He felt her give, that slow, fluid yielding to him. To herself. She warmed his blood, steadied his heart even as its beat went fast and thick. He drank her in, there, just there under the line of her jaw where the skin was so amazingly sweet. Pleasure slid through him as her hands stroked, gripped, whispered over him.

It was she who took him in, opened and asked and took, guiding him into the heat. Surrounding him with it so that each long, slow thrust pulsed and pumped through them both.

Slow, beautifully slow, drawing out and out and out every drop of pleasure. She stared into his eyes, her fingers locked with his now, clamped together as they held each other to that lazy, that torturous pace. She held, even when her breath came short, her head arched back.

He pressed his lips to the curve of her throat. Skimmed up the scrambling pulse, once again along that sweet spot under her jaw. His mouth found hers, and with that final link, let himself go.

20 EVE SET UP EARLY THE NEXT MORNING, LINING up the data she'd already accumulated and organized. For now, she set aside the results of Roarke's *explorations*. The warrants would pull that information in soon enough.

She decided to say nothing about the buffet table, the extra seating, that had found its way into her office. What would be the point? She skimmed over her notes, took a last round with her murder boards.

Baxter surprised her by walking in just before eight.

"Guess the brunette wasn't so hot after all."

"She was smoking. I left her warm and cozy in . . . that's food. Hot damn!"

Eve watched him bullet over to the buffet, lift the lid of the first warmer. "Yo, that is pig meat." He plucked out a slice of bacon, bit in.

"Just help yourself," Eve said dryly.

"Gonna." Bearing no shame, Baxter grabbed a plate. "While I do you can tell me what you've got that has me here eating meat of pig—and hey!—egg of actual chicken at eight-hundred on a Saturday."

"You'll get it when the team gets here."

"We've got a team now?" He surfed the warmers, began to pile the plate with food while he studied Eve and the buffet offerings. It seemed to her it was a tough toss-up which interested him more.

"We've got a team now. Where's Trueheart?"

"On the way. Peabody?"

"The same. I've called in Feeney and Mira and . . . the civilian," she said as Roarke walked in.

"Baxter."

"Primo pig. Thanks."

"My pleasure." Roarke poured himself a cup of coffee, lifted his eyebrows at Eve. "Lieutenant?"

"Yeah, yeah, why not? We'll see if we can work in the briefing between courses."

"Woohoo, breakfast!" Peabody all but skipped into the room, just ahead of McNab.

"I told you not to feed the puppies," Eve scolded.

"But they're so cute." Roarke handed her the coffee.

"Sorry, am I late?" Trueheart hurried in. "I missed the . . . Wow." His young hero face went bright as a birthday candle at the sight of the buffet.

"Grab some pig, kid," Baxter told him. "Team feed. Hey, Feeney, Dr. Mira."

"Good morning. Isn't that lovely!" Mira shot a smile at Eve, beamed at Roarke. "And so considerate."

"Don't eat all the damn bacon, McNab." Feeney muscled him aside to claim his own.

"There's ham, too," McNab told him with his mouth full of it.

"When you all finish stuffing food in your faces, maybe you could listen up."

"I got no problem listening while I'm stuffing." Feeney glanced around. "You?"

"Well, damn it, everybody just fill it up and sit down with it somewhere." Cops and food, she thought. Put them in the same room, invite chaos. "This is a goddamn official briefing not an all-you-can-eat."

"Here you are then." Roarke handed her a plate of bacon and eggs. "You won't be so cross if you have a bit of breakfast."

"This is your fault."

"It is, isn't it?" He grinned without an ounce of remorse. "Go on then, shovel some in."

She did, as everyone else was. "Some of you vultures . . . sorry," Eve said to Mira, "no offense."

Mira took a neat bite of creamy eggs. "None taken."

"Some of you may be aware that Detective Pig-Eater there and his aide, Officer Danish, caught a homicide a couple months back. Baxter, quick overview."

"Custer, Ned," he began, and reeled off the basic facts.

When he'd finished, Eve flipped Suzanne Custer's ID and data on screen. "The widow's alibi holds," she said. "The 'link to 'link transmissions she made originated in her apartment, and EDD analysis verifies they were live trans, not recorded. Suzanne Custer didn't slit her husband's throat. She not only wasn't there, but lacked the physicality for the killing blow."

"Too short, too slight," Baxter confirmed between shovels.

"The extensive and thorough investigation by the gluttonous primary and his aide unearthed no sidepiece, no relative, no friend who might have killed Custer on the wife's behalf," Eve continued. "Said investigation found no financial payment, or other bartering tool that may have been used by the wife to hire the hit. The widow does, however, benefit financially from Custer's death, and as the vic had a documented history of spousal abuse, adultery, and kept his fist closed over the purse strings, the widow also benefits on emotional, physical, and practical levels from his death."

"Dallas, we can't pin her." Baxter lifted his hands, one of them holding a chunk of grilled ham speared on a fork. "We dead-ended on every angle we played with her connected to the murder."

"She went white." Trueheart shifted in his seat as Eve turned her gaze on him. "When Detective Baxter and I went to inform her, she didn't seem all that surprised to find cops at the door. More tired, resigned. She said how she didn't have money for bail. And when we told her he was dead, she went white. It didn't feel faked, I guess I want to say. It rang true."

"It probably was true. Let's switch over to the Anders case. Peabody and I caught this one."

Baxter rose to get more coffee as Eve laid out the salients. "Are you looking for a connect?" he asked. "Because both vics appear to have been killed by an LC, or a sex partner?"

"That's an interesting connection, isn't it? And one of the mistakes made. Ava Anders." Eve ordered Ava's ID photo and data split screen with Suzanne's. "Also solidly alibied at the time of her husband's murder. While she apparently has more friends, certainly more influence and resources than Suzanne, no evidence leads to murder for hire. Her circle of friends don't play in. She also gains financially, and when you scrape away at the surface of her claims of a happy marriage to the lies and manipulations underneath, she gains on several other levels."

She turned to study the screen. "These women have a great deal in common, under the surface. And they're connected. Another mistake. Suzanne Custer's two kids are part of the Anders sports programs. Suzanne's attended several of Ava's seminars and mommy retreats. She's done some volunteering, too."

"Huh." It was all Feeney said, but Eve glanced at him, and saw it had clicked.

"You think the Anders woman got the idea to off her husband from what happened to Custer?" Baxter's brows drew together as he stared hard at the screen. "Little Suzanne caught a lucky break, why can't I? Maybe she talks an LC into doing her the favor, pays her off through the program or the company, then . . ."

"Simpler than that," Feeney commented and enjoyed another scoop of hash browns. "Simpler's best."

Baxter frowned, then . . . "Well, Christ."

It hit, Eve noted, hard enough for Baxter to forget his coffee and pig meat. "Give me a hand, will you," she said to Roarke.

Together they turned Eve's murder board so the second side faced the room. "Ava Anders to Bebe Petrelli and Cassie Gordon. They didn't pan out for her, but she tested waters there. Ava Anders to Charles Monroe. Professional LC, clean record, sterling rep. Use him to build her claim that her husband liked the kink, and she didn't. That she loved him regardless. Ava to Brigit Plowder and Sasha Bride-West. Alibis. Girlfriends, tight circle."

As she outlined, Eve tapped each photo, each connection.

"Ava to Edmond and Linny Luce—friends of vic who would, in turn, testify as to the comfortable and happy marriage. Except they don't like her—under the surface, they don't like her a bit. She didn't count on that. She didn't count on any real connection being made between her—lady of the manor, lady bountiful—with the less fortunate women in the program she oversees."

Now she pinned her finger to Ned Custer's photo. "She sure as hell didn't count on any connection between the murder of a philandering, blue-collar asshole and the murder of her renowned philanthropist husband. Murders committed months apart, with different MOs, in different parts of the city."

"It could work," Peabody said under her breath. "It could really work."

"It did work," Eve corrected. "Two men are dead."

"You think they *traded* murders. Fuck me," Baxter added.

"I know they did. Ava's been planning this a long time. At least two years, since I believe she killed her father-in-law.

But probably longer than that. Once the father-in-law was out of the picture—" Eve tapped Reginald Anders's photo on the board. "Lots more at stake. More money, more power, more control. That skin she was wearing, boy, that really had to start to tighten up on her. Every single day, to have to look at this guy she'd married, play the contented wife, listen to him drone on and on about his sports, his business, his programs. Planning the murders, that would help her get through it. That light at the end of the tunnel."

"Yes," Mira agreed when Eve turned to her. "For a goal-oriented personality, one who sees the big picture, the planning is part of the reward. For one who's skilled in long-term role-playing, there would be considerable satisfaction in the success of that role. But you're talking years, Eve. Any actor, even one so amoral and self-serving, would require breaks."

"The vic traveled a lot, she encouraged it. And she would often entertain during those trips, leaving out the vic's nephew and closer friends. Her parties, her way. And Charles. He added to her cover, to the picture, but let's not discount the release of good sex—especially when you're in the driver's seat. The client holds the power with an LC."

"If she did Custer, she must've stalked him," McNab put in. "The wife couldn't know what bar he'd troll in the night of. And Anders couldn't have pulled it off on impulse. She had to be set."

"Exactly right. We'll canvass his haunts again, and show Ava's photo, and the photo of her with red hair I'm having Yancy generate. She picked the flop, had to. Her type wouldn't leave that to chance."

"Agreed," Mira said.

"We find a connection between her and the flop. Show her photo there. She's not going to be alibied for the night of Custer's murder, but we're going to get that solid. She bought the wig, she bought the clothes. We're going to find out where. We're going to go over the case file from the father-in-law's death and find her mistakes. And we're going to bring her in. We're going to sew her up, and we're going to take her down for two counts of murder, and one count of conspiracy to commit."

"Suzanne Custer," Baxter murmured.

"Yeah, she's the needle in the haystack *and* the needle for the thread. She trusts you."

"Yeah." Baxter sighed it. "Yeah, she does."

"We'll use that. We're going to break her down, Baxter, you and me. We'll break her because she's not built like Ava."

"She got nervous." Trueheart shifted his attention to Baxter. "When we went back to talk to her, a few days after the murder, she was jumpy and nervous. She didn't want to talk to us. You smoothed her down."

"Yeah, yeah. It set off a little buzz, but there was nothing to tie her. Nothing. So I put it down to regular nerves and the situation. She had me, goddamn it."

"Now we've got her," Eve reminded him. "Dr. Mira, can you give us a personality profile on Suzanne Custer?"

"From Detective Baxter's overview, I'd say she's a woman who accepts or perhaps expects her own victimization. She accepted, or certainly lived with, her husband's behavior. While it appears she sought more for her children, she failed to take advantage of programs offered for abused women. It's possible she didn't see herself as such. She doesn't control, or seek control. At this point, until further study, my opinion would be she fears and seeks those with authority over her."

"A woman who does what she's told."

"So it would seem," Mira said, "from the data I have at this point. I'd like to look at her background, her childhood."

"I'd appreciate if you could do that ASAP. Feeney, McNab, I need a search on electronic purchases. Look for the wig, costumes re Ava. Dig in. She may have picked them up a year ago, two years. Hell, she might've had them for a decade. Look for all communications between her and Suzanne Custer and her personal 'links, and any at Anders. I've got warrants to check all communication devices owned by Plowder and Bride-West."

"On it," Feeney told her, and kept eating.

"Trueheart, you're with Peabody. Check for Suzanne's purchases at a smut shop called Just Sex. Her husband shopped there, so odds are if she needed anything for the job, that's where she'd go. Get the medicals on her from her health clinic—a Dr. Yin and prescriptions from its pharmacy. Tap the Transit Authority. She had to get from her apartment to the Anders house and back. Mother of two, I bet she uses the subway routinely, and a fare card."

"Lieutenant." Trueheart raised his hand and lowered it again as Baxter elbowed him. "I don't think she'd leave the kids alone. I don't think she'd have gone out and left her kids unattended. She's just not the type for it."

"Okay. Then let's find out if she got a sitter, or where her kids were on the night of. If the civilian has time . . ."

"The civilian can probably carve out a few minutes here and there," Roarke commented.

"A remote was used to shut down the security at the Anders house. A high-end and illegal remote. Where did it come from and which one of our killers obtained it? I haven't picked up a hot one there. You find out."

"Not as entertaining as a visit to a smut shop," Roarke considered, "but the black market has some appeal."

"Good luck." Feeney saluted him. "Coulda been any of a couple dozen types—or versions of types—picked up any time within the last couple years. Coulda been homemade for that matter, you had any snap for it."

Roarke smiled at him. "Adds to the fun, doesn't it?"

"Let's all go out and have fun. Baxter," Eve said, "with me."

"I wouldn't have pegged her." Baxter brooded out the side window as Eve drove. "She snowed me right from the get."

"You didn't peg her because she didn't do it."

"Same thing as doing it, and I didn't get a whiff. The boy did. When we went back and she was nervy, he caught the whiff. and I blew it off, explained it away. I didn't see it, didn't smell it, didn't hear it."

"Guess you'd better turn in your papers then. I hear private security's a good gig for washed-out cops."

"To borrow a phrase, bite me." But it didn't seem he could work up any steam. "She's soft, Dallas. Mira'll come up with her psycho-whatever, but it comes down to her being a soft sort, a little wounded, a lot tired. Mousy, if you get me. Right now, with all you worked out, I'm trying to see her going into that house, pumping Anders full of tranqs and setting him up like a kink kill, and I can't see it."

"You like her. You feel sorry for her."

Irritation tightened his face. "I like lots of people, and feel sorry for some. That doesn't stop me from seeing a stone killer when she's in my damn face."

"You're taking it personal, Baxter."

"Damn right I am." There was steam now as he jerked toward Eve. "And don't give me any of that objectivity crap. You wouldn't be so fucking good at the job if you didn't take it personal."

Eve gave him a minute to stew. "You want me to tell you you screwed up? You missed it? You didn't see what you should've seen? Nothing I'd like better because it makes my day to ream out a smart-ass pig-eater like you. But I can't do it. You didn't screw up. You can't miss what's not in play, and can't see what isn't there."

"You saw Ava Anders."

"I didn't like her goddamn face—and yeah, some of it was personal. I wouldn't have seen the how if you hadn't nagged my *ass* off about Custer. So reschedule your pity party, Baxter. We don't have time for it now."

"Assuming we're playing to our strengths, you'll be taking bad cop."

"And you'd be the cop with the soft spot for the tragic, little widow."

"Yeah." He hissed out a breath. "Fucking A. I feel played, so I'll be picking up the hats and balloons for the pity party later."

"Don't forget the cake." She scouted out a parking spot as she neared Suzanne's address. "It's going to spook her, seeing me instead of Trueheart. Having to go into Central. If she's thought about any of this happening, she may have thought about lawyers. You need to reassure her. Routine, tying things up."

"I know how to play good cop." He got out, waited for Eve on the sidewalk. "I need to take the lead with her, initially, keep her steady, make her think I'm a little ticked that you're insisting on the official routine."

"I know how to play bad cop," Eve countered.

It was a miserable post-Urban War building. One of the structures tossed up from the rubble and never intended to last. Its concrete gray walls were blackened with age and weather, scored with graceless graffiti and misspelled obscenities.

They walked into a narrow, frigid entryway and took the rusted metal stairs up to the third floor. Everything echoed, Eve noted. Their feet on the treads, the sounds leaking out of doors and walls as they passed by, the noises from the street outside.

But none of the early spring warmth pushed in to boost the chilly air.

Baxter positioned himself at the door, knocked. The over-bright sound of kids and Saturday morning screen whooped on the other side. One of those odd and somehow creepy morning cartoon deals that had the kids yammering and squealing, Eve imagined.

Who made those things?

A high-pitched girly voice called out for mommy so clearly, the door itself might've been made of paper.

The locks thunked, and the door scraped and groaned as it opened.

She'd been pretty once, Eve thought at her first in-person study of Suzanne Custer. She might be pretty again, given decent nutrition, reasonable sleep, a break from stress. As Eve didn't see those elements in her future, she thought Suzanne's pretty days were long over.

She looked exhausted, pale, too thin, as if the meat under her skin had been gnawed away. Her dull, listless hair had been pulled back, leaving her tired face defenseless. A small, round-eyed kid of the male variety (probably) stood at her side.

"Detective Baxter."

"Mrs. Custer. Hey there, Todd!" Baxter flashed a grin, shot the boy with his finger.

"We're watching 'toons."

"So I hear. Hi, Maizie."

The little girl had a year or two on her brother, and the soft prettiness that had once been her mother's. She sent Baxter a big, beaming smile.

"I'm sorry." Suzanne shoved at her hair, then reached down to wrap her arm around her son's shoulders. "We're a little disorganized this morning. I was . . . just cleaning up after breakfast, before I take the kids to practice. Is this . . . do you have any . . . Can this wait until later?"

"I'm afraid it can't, Mrs. Custer." Eve edged Baxter aside, and all but felt his annoyed frown. "We have a number of things to clear up, and we'll need to handle this at Central."

"At Central? But—"

"I'm sorry, Mrs. Custer." Baxter's voice poured warm cream over quiet apology. "This is my lieutenant. As we've been unable to close your husband's case in a timely manner, Lieutenant Dallas needs to see to some procedural matters."

"At Central," Eve said, clipping the words.

"But, my kids."

"I don't—"

"Lieutenant, please." Baxter interrupted Eve, then eased forward toward Suzanne. "I can arrange to have them taken to practice, or you can bring them with you and we'll see they're supervised while we finish this up. Whichever you want."

"I don't know. I—"

"I can't miss practice." Cartoons forgotten, Maizie jumped up. "I just *can't*. Mom, please!"

"Why don't I take care of their transportation?" Baxter suggested. "And have a couple of officers stay with them. Then when we're done, we'll make sure you get to the field. Okay, LT?"

Eve only shrugged, as if she didn't give a damn. "Make it fast. You've put enough time and department resources into this. I'll wait outside."

"Sorry about that," Eve heard Baxter say as she walked away. "The lieutenant's a stickler for procedure. I'll try to fast-walk all this through."

On the street, Eve checked in with Peabody. "Status?"

"Wallowing in smut. I had no idea there were so many devices designed to be inserted in orifices. Many are sold in variety and party packs. You can select one of forty-dollar value with any body piercing."

"That's a deal."

"Well, it's kind of tempting. McNab would wig in a completely excellent way. But seeing as I'm on duty . . ."

"Seeing as. But keep jabbering, Peabody, and I'll give you a completely free piercing back at Central."

"We have a clerk who recognized Suzanne Custer," Peabody said quickly. "Made her right off. Said she remembered because she—Suzanne—looked so off the rails. She bought several of the items that match those on the Anders scene. The clerk didn't want to bother checking on it, but she's flirting with Trueheart."

"Trueheart's flirting with a smut shop clerk? What has Baxter done to that kid?"

"No, no, *she's* doing the flirt thing. He's turned all shades of red, but that's worked for us." Peabody grinned. "It is pretty damn cute. So she checked, and we're getting the paperwork. Suzanne didn't buy the rope here. But, she asked about it. They were out of the velvet bondage set. It's a popular item, as we learned when we did the initial search."

"Check the shops closest to your current location. And if you come back with any piercings, they better not be visible."

"Ouch," Peabody said as Eve clicked off.

Once she had Suzanne at Central, Eve left her in Interview to sweat for fifteen minutes and watched through the observation window.

"She's terrified," Baxter said.

"Good. It probably won't take very long to break her down. You go in first, make your apologies for the mean old LT." She glanced over as Mira stepped in.

"She looks worn down. Eaten up." Her face impassive, Mira stepped closer to the glass. "Guilt would be a viable weapon on her. And her children, they'd be a vulnerable area. She'll fear you the most," she said to Eve. "The capable, powerful female—everything she's not. The authority figure. As, I suspect, Ava Anders is to her. She's accustomed to violence. It won't frighten her overmuch. Nor will threats to her person, as she's accustomed to those as well. She's also used to being isolated, cut off from any support. So offers of friendship, understanding, support draw her in. Her children are her one accomplishment. She would sacrifice a great deal for them."

"I need to make her flip on Ava."

"She'll need to believe you're more powerful, and more dangerous than Ava."

"I am, so she will. Go," Eve told Baxter.

"The friendship offered by Ava," Mira continued as Baxter stepped out, "the support, the bargain struck—if indeed one was—weigh heavily on Ava's side. The power Ava has over her now is tremendous."

"I know how to play her." When Mira said nothing, Eve watched Baxter enter Interview, listened to him speak reassuringly to Suzanne. "I know what it's like to be knocked around regular, isolated, held down so you believe it's the only way. And I know how far you'll go to make it stop."

"She's nothing like you, and neither are her circumstances."

"No. But I know how to play her. Baxter, he feels for her. Decent men tend to feel for women like her."

"But you don't."

"No, I don't. She could've walked. Any time. Packed up, grabbed the kids and walked." Studying Suzanne through the glass, Eve felt not a single twinge of sympathy. "You said she'd sacrifice for her kids, but what has she given them? What kind of life has she opened them to by letting them see, every day, that she's so weak she'll let their father slap her around, come and go as he pleases, spend his money on tricks instead of food. You don't offset that with sports programs, Dr. Mira. That woman took the life of a stranger, the life of a good man, the man who offered her children hope. She did that rather than walk away.

"So yeah, I guess I do feel for her. I feel disgust. I've got no qualms about putting her away. I just want to make damn sure I put Ava Anders away with her."

"Eve." Mira put a hand on Eve's arm as Eve started to step out. "There's a difference between weak and evil."

"Yeah, but there's sure a lot of overlap."

Eve entered Interview. "Record on. Dallas, Lieutenant Eve, and Baxter, Detective David, in Interview with Custer, Suzanne, in the matter of the murder of Custer, Ned, case number HC-20913, and any and all related events or crimes. Detective, have you read Mrs. Custer her rights?"

"No, Lieutenant."

"Do so. For the record."

He sighed. "Yes, sir. It's a formality, Mrs. Custer. You have the right to remain silent."

Fear widened Suzanne's eyes, quickened her breath as Baxter recited the Revised Miranda. Eve took a seat at the table, slumped back. "Do you understand your rights and obligations in this matter?" she demanded.

"Yes, but—"

"Here's something that strikes me, Suzanne. It just seems so damn handy that you'd be sitting at home trying to tag your cheating shitbag of a husband on his 'link while some unidentified hooker's slitting his throat. What, were you going to ask him to bring home a jug of soy milk?"

"No. He was late. I just wanted to—"

"He was late a lot, wasn't he? Did you whine on his voice mail every time he was late?"

"No, but—he promised. He promised he wouldn't be. I said I'd leave him if he didn't stop."

"You were never going to leave him." Eve allowed some of the disgust to eke into her voice. "You didn't have the guts for that. And now you don't have to. Instead he's gone, and you've got that nice life insurance policy, the pension."

"Come on, Lieutenant, ease off a little."

She scorched Baxter with a look. "You've eased off plenty for both of us. Did you find some sap like the detective here to do it for you, Suzanne? Cozy yourself up to some guy who doesn't slap you around, feels sorry for you. So he does this—" Eve pulled out a crime scene photo, tossed it onto the table. "So you can be free."

"No." Suzanne closed her eyes rather than look at the photo. "I didn't want another man. I just wanted my husband to be a good man, a good father. My kids deserve a good home, a good father."

"The money you've got coming in now, you can get them out of that rattrap. Where are you taking them, Suzanne?"

"I don't know. I thought, I think, maybe south, maybe down to Arkansas with my sister. Out of the city. Away. I can't think about it yet. Somewhere else, for a fresh start. There's nothing wrong with that." She looked imploringly at Baxter. "Nothing wrong with wanting a fresh start with my kids."

"Of course not. It's been rough on you here. Rough for a long time. It'd be good for the kids to get out of the city, somewhere with a lot of green. Anders has sports programs all over the country."

She winced at the Anders name, looked away. "If I could get them in a good school, down south somewhere, the schools have teams. They have sports."

"Are you going to give up the freebies?" Eve demanded. "The free equipment, camps, programs, the mom retreats. It's been a pretty good deal for you, hasn't it?" Eve flipped open a file. "You had a few nice vacations here, on the Anders's dime, didn't you?"

"Seminars, and—and support groups."

"Yeah, Thomas Anders gave you and your kids plenty. Too bad about him, huh?" Eve tossed another photo down, one of Thomas Anders dead in his bed.

Suzanne jerked away, dropped her head between her knees and gagged.

"Jesus, Lieutenant! Hey, hey," Baxter laid a hand on Suzanne's back. "Take it easy. Take it slow. Let me get you some water."

"Let her puke." Eve shoved out of her chair, then dropped down, pushing Suzanne's head back until their eyes met. "Did it make you sick to do it? Did it curdle your guts to strip off his nice, neat pajamas, tie his hands and feet? Did your hands shake like they are now when you wrapped the rope around his neck? He didn't give you any trouble, you saw to that. Put him under so you wouldn't have to see the look in his eyes when he choked."

"No." Her eyes wheeled like an animal's with its leg snapped in a trap. "I don't want to be here. I don't know what you're talking about."

"You still screwed it up. You didn't tie the rope tight enough, so it took him a long time to die. You didn't do it the way she told you. She was so specific, but you couldn't pull it off. Not like she did with Ned. Quick, clean, done. You got messy, you got weak. It looks like she'll walk, and you'll spend the rest of your life in a cage. An off-planet cage. You'll never see your kids again."

"I don't know what you're talking about. Detective Baxter, please make her stop."

"For God's sake, Dallas, let her breathe. Suzanne. Suzanne." He eased down to sit on the edge of the table, took Suzanne's trembling hand, looked into her eyes. "We know it was Ava's idea. All of it. We know she planned it. If you tell us everything, all of it, maybe I can help you."

"No, no. You're trying to trick me. You're trying to make me say things. She said you'd—"

"She said we'd try to block you in?" Eve finished. "She was right about that. But she told you we'd try to block you in on Ned's murder and you were clear there. Nothing to worry about there. She didn't figure this, did she? Neither of you figured this. I know what you did."

Eve shoved Baxter aside, shoved her face into Suzanne's. "I know you killed Thomas A. Anders. The man who paid for the equipment your kids are wearing right now. You selfish, heartless bitch."

"That's crazy. I didn't even know him. A person doesn't kill someone she doesn't even know."

"That's what she told you? They'll never suspect. She was wrong again, wasn't she? Her mistakes, all her mistakes, and I'm going to make you pay for every one of them. I'm going to put you in a cage, Suzanne. Look at me!"

With one violent yank, she dragged Suzanne's chair around.

"I'm going to put you in, and she can't stop me. She won't try because you're useless to her now. She'll cry for the cameras and laugh behind closed doors because you're too stupid to help yourself. And your kids? It'll be strangers raising them now."

"No. Please. God."

"Lieutenant, come on. Give her a second. Suzanne. You need to tell us everything. If you cooperate, I can help you. I'll talk to the PA." Baxter reached down, squeezed her hand. "Maybe she pressured you or threatened you. Blackmailed you. Maybe you felt you didn't have a choice."

"I'm compiling evidence against her right now," Eve broke in. "When I have enough, she'll be in here. She'll be the one turning on you. If she flips first, she'll get the deal. Personally, I want both of you to live the rest of your miserable lives in an off-planet cage. You've got one minute. One to change my mind. After that, I'm done. You're booked, murder in the first, and your kids are gone."

"Please don't, please! You don't understand."

"No, you don't understand, you weak, pathetic excuse for a human being. I know what you did. I know how you did it. I know why you did it. And you've got one shot to put it out your way or I'll personally toss you in that cage and lock it."

"Lieutenant, Lieutenant, give her a chance. Give her a minute. Help us understand," Baxter said to Suzanne. "I want to understand, so I can help you."

"I didn't think it was going to be real!" Suzanne burst out. "I didn't think it was real. And then it was. I didn't know what else to do. She said I had to."

"Spit it out," Eve snapped. "Who said you had to what?"

Suzanne closed her eyes again. "Ava said I had to kill her husband because she'd killed mine. Just like we agreed." Suzanne laid her head down on the table. "I'm so tired. I'm so tired now."

21 EVE STEPPED OUT TO CALL CHER REO, AND TO give Baxter a few moments to help Suzanne compose herself. She flicked a glance over as Mira slipped out of Observation. Mira walked by, stopped at Vending, and ordered three waters, and a Pepsi for Eve.

After finishing her conversation, Eve tucked her 'link back in her pocket, took the tube. "Thanks. PA's willing to deal for the bigger fish. Ava's a much bigger fish. A big, splashy one."

"And Suzanne is nothing and no one, comparatively. She killed, Eve, there's no disputing it. But she was used."

"The choice was there; she made it." Eve drank. "But I'm willing to deal, too."

"I'll be watching the rest. When she gets a lawyer, there will be a demand for a psychiatric evaluation."

"She can have her head shrunk by a platoon of doctors, after I get my confession. And yeah, I'm perfectly aware I'm using her, too. I've got no problem with that."

"You shouldn't have, but—"

"She's soft," Eve interrupted. "That's what you're seeing, and you've got some sympathy for her. Go ahead. But I see Thomas Aurelious Anders."

With a nod, Mira went back into Observation.

Eve stepped back into Interview. "Lieutenant Dallas re-entering Interview," she said for the record. "Here's the deal, Suzanne. Are you listening?"

"Yes, I'm listening."

"The PA will drop the charges down from one count of Murder One, one count of Conspiracy to Murder to one count of Murder Two. That keeps you on-planet, with visitation access to your kids."

Tears dripped, as if Suzanne's eyes were leaking faucets. "How long?"

"Fifteen to twenty."

"Fifteen. Oh God. God. They'll be grown."

"You'll be eligible for parole in seven," Baxter told her.

"If you don't cooperate, if this goes to trial, the charges bounce back. You're looking at the probability of two life sentences, running consecutively. Off-planet." Eve sat. "Your choice."

"My kids. I . . . I have a sister. Can my kids go to my sister?"

"I'll look into that. Personally." Baxter nodded. "I'll talk to your sister, to Child Services."

"They'll be better off with her. I should've taken them and gone to my sister years ago." She swiped at the tears with the tissues Baxter gave her. "Everything would be different if I'd done that. But I didn't. I thought, Ned's their father and they should be with their father. I thought, I'm his wife, and I'm supposed to make the home. If I did better, everything would work out. But I didn't do better, and it just got worse and worse. And then . . ."

"You met Ava Anders," Eve prompted.

"Yes." Suzanne closed her eyes for a moment, took several breaths. "She was so good to us, to everyone. She made me feel like I could do better. Be better. Ned didn't care about the program, but he didn't mind. Got the kids out from underfoot, he said. But sometimes, just sometimes, he'd go to a practice or a game. And that was good. He'd even take us out for pizza after sometimes. It was better when he did. And the last time, after the last time he hit me, he promised he wouldn't do it again. And he didn't this time. He didn't hit me for weeks, and he was around more. I thought, this is going to be all right. But then he started coming home late again, and smelling of sex."

"You talked to Ava about that?" Baxter asked.

"What? No . . . Before, we talked before. Months ago. Just before the kids went back to school. When they were at camp and I went to the retreat, the end of August. God, Ned was so angry that I went, but it was good to be there. To have that time away. We'd talked before—Ava, I mean."

Taking the cup of water, she sipped, paused, sipped again. "She was so nice to me. She'd sit with me late at night and talk and talk. She understood how hard it was with Ned that way because her husband hurt her, too. She never told anyone but me. He hurt her, and he made her do things. And he did things with girls—girls who were too young to be hurt that way.

"Everyone thinks he was so good." Tears streamed out of Suzanne's eyes, soaking the tissues as she mopped. "But he was a monster."

"That's what she told you?"

"She was afraid of him. I know what that's like. We cried together. She couldn't stand what he was doing to her, and more, to the children. She said he and Ned were alike. One day, Ned would hurt my babies. One day he could . . . with Maizie."

She closed her eyes, shuddered. "He'd never—he'd never touched Maizie like that, but he hit the kids sometimes. When they were bad, or when he'd had too much to drink. I thought, what would I do if he tried to do to Maizie what Mr. Anders did with young girls? I said, I think I said, I'd kill him if he touched her that way."

Her voice cracked, and began to waver and jump as she continued. "It would be too late then, Ava said, like she was afraid it was too late for her. She said she'd help me. We could help each other. We didn't have to live like this anymore, or risk the children."

Suzanne reached for the water, then simply rubbed the cup over her forehead. "She said it was just like in the seminars and groups, where we talked about being proactive, about being strong. Taking action to make a difference. She'd stop Ned and I'd stop Mr. Anders. No one would ever know."

"Stop?" Eve qualified.

Her shoulders hunched, Suzanne stared at the table. "Kill. We would kill them. No one would know—how could they—because each of us would be innocent of the crime that connected to us. She'd go first, to show good faith. We'd wait a few months and we'd be careful about contacting each other between. Then she'd stop Ned."

She heaved a breath, looked up at Eve again. "She said stop, not kill. I knew what she meant, I did, but it seemed right when she said it. She'd stop Ned before he hurt my children, stop him from hurting me. And then, we'd wait again, two or three months, and I'd stop Mr. Anders."

"Did she tell you how you'd stop him?"

Suzanne shook her head. Her eyes continued to flood, but they were empty behind the tears. Beaten, Eve thought. Broken.

"She said she thought she knew a way, so it would look like an accident. And so when they found him they'd know the kind of man he was. She knew I was strong, deep down, and good, a good mother, a good friend. She knew I'd save her, and she'd save me and my kids. We gave each other our word. We recorded it."

"Recorded?"

"She had a recorder, and we each recorded our intention, our promise. I said my name and that I promised on the lives of my children to kill the monster Thomas A. Anders. That I would kill him with my own hands, and in a way that was symbolic and just. She said the same, except Ned's name, and she swore on the lives of all the children of the world."

"Dramatic."

Little spots of color bloomed on Suzanne's white cheeks. "It *meant* something. It was important. I felt important. I never felt like that before."

"What did she do with the recording?"

"She said she was going to put it in a bank box. For safety. After we stopped Ned and Mr. Anders, we'd destroy it together. We didn't talk much after that. Not for a while. She's very busy. And when I got home, and everything was the way it is at home, I thought, none of that was real. It was just like a session. Or maybe I wanted to think that."

She bowed her head, then shoved at the hair that fell over her face. "I don't know anymore. But I put it away. I forgot about it. Almost all the time. Then things got a little better for a while with Ned. I saw Ava at the offices one day, and I told her how things were better. She smiled at me, and she said they'd get better yet." On a choked sob, Suzanne pressed a hand to her mouth. "I swear, I didn't think, didn't really think about what we'd said that night. I didn't think of any of that, and Ned started staying out again, and we started fighting again. I told myself I was going to leave him this time, that I was stronger now. Because of Ava."

Her breath came in two quick hitches. "I felt stronger, because of Ava, and what she'd given me. How she'd made me feel about myself. And then Detective Baxter came with Officer Trueheart, and they said Ned was dead. They said he'd gone into a hotel room with an LC, and he was dead. I never thought about Ava and what we'd said that night, way back in August. I thought it was just as they'd told me. He'd picked up the wrong kind of woman."

"When did she contact you after that?"

"A few days later." Suzanne pressed her fingers to her eyes. "That's when everything fell apart. The kids were in school. I was going to do the marketing. I always do the marketing on Monday morning, so I was walking to the market, and she came up beside me. She said: 'Keep walking, Suzanne. Keep walking and don't say anything yet.' We walked another three blocks, I think, then we crossed and walked another two or three. She had a car, and we got in. When I asked where we were going, she said somewhere we could talk. I told her I had to do the marketing, and she started to drive. And she started to tell me."

As Suzanne's breath began to wheeze, Baxter nudged the water toward her. "What did she tell you, Suzanne?"

"She said she'd fulfilled the part of the bargain we'd made, and asked how I felt now that I was free. I couldn't even talk for a minute. She was different—um, I don't know how to explain. She laughed, but it was different from before. It scared me. She scared me. I started to cry."

What else is new, Eve thought, you weak, whiny, *worthless* excuse for a human being.

"I started to say I hadn't meant any of it. Not really. But it was too late—that's what she said. It was too late for any second thoughts, any regrets. It was done. Now it was my turn. She kept driving, not even looking at me. She told me how she'd killed Ned."

Eve waited while Suzanne drank, and mopped more useless tears. "I need the details."

"Oh, God." Blubbering, Suzanne covered her face. "Oh, God. I can't."

Brutally cold in face, voice, manner, Eve shoved Suzanne's hands down. "You will. Here's one thing Ava's right about. It's too late. Give me the details."

Staring at Eve, trembling, Suzanne began. "She—she watched him for a few nights. Followed him into bars, watched him drink, watched him pick up women. Studied him is what she said, learned his habits and routines—his territory. She said his territory. And—and she rented rooms in a couple of the places he used for sex, and mapped them out. Preparation, she said. Preparation was key. She said she made herself look like a whore because that's what he liked. That's what most men liked. Please, can I have some more water?"

Baxter rose to fill the cup.

"She stalked him," Eve prompted.

"I guess. I guess. She said she went up to him while he was drinking, told him he looked like he knew how to party. She sat with him awhile—not too long, she said because she didn't want anyone to pay attention to her. She put her hand between his legs, rubbed. She said he came along with her like an idiot dog. That's what she called him."

The water in the cup Baxter gave her sloshed, dripped over the rim as Suzanne lifted it to drink. "They went to one of the places she'd mapped out. And when they were upstairs, he grabbed at her breasts, and she let him, let him touch her. But she told him she needed the bathroom first. And in the bathroom she put on a suit like doctors wear, and she sealed her hands, too, then got the knife. She called out for Ned to turn around. Turn around and close your eyes, she said to him. She had a big surprise for him.

"I'm sorry, I—I spilled water on the table."

"Finish it," Eve ordered.

"God." As if to hold herself in place, Suzanne crossed her arms tight over her own torso. "She said he did what she told him, like a good boy, and she came out, came out and she used the knife. She said he made the funniest noises, and grabbed at his throat like he had an itch there. How his eyes got so big, how he tried to talk. How he fell, and the way the blood just gushed out. How he just lay there and she . . . God. She cut it off, cut his penis off. A sym—a symbol. She put everything back in the bag she had, and when she knew he was good and dead, she went out by the fire escape. She walked for blocks and blocks. She said she felt like she could've flown, but she walked to where she'd left her car."

"What did she do with the bag, Suzanne?" Eve asked. "Did she tell you?"

"The bag?"

"With the knife in it."

"I feel sick."

"What did she do with the bag?"

Suzanne cringed. "In a recycler."

"Where?"

"I don't know. While she was walking to her car."

"Where was her car?"

"I don't know. Blocks away. Uptown, I think she said. Blocks away from where she killed Ned because the cops weren't going to look for a street whore so far away. She drove home, and she took a long bath with a glass of cognac, and she slept like a baby."

Her face gray now, Suzanne looked back at Eve. "I haven't slept. I don't think I've had an hour's real sleep since that day. She'd stopped the car. A rest stop off the Turnpike. We were in New Jersey now. I don't remember how we got there. I wasn't crying anymore. I got sick. It made her mad, but I couldn't help it. She let me open the door, and I threw up in the parking lot.

"I'm so tired now."

"Dallas," Baxter began, "maybe we should—"

Eve only shook her head to cut him off. "What did Ava do after you were sick?"

"After, she drove away from there, around the back where the big trucks are, and she told me what had to happen next. What I had to do. I said I couldn't, but she said if I didn't, she'd do to me what she'd done to Ned, and then she'd do it to my kids. My kids. No one would believe me if I told them. Who did I think I was? I was nobody, and she was an important and respected woman. They'd lock me up if I tried to tell them, unless she killed me first. She knew where my kids went to school, where they played, where they slept. I'd better remember that."

There was a dreamy quality in Suzanne's voice now, as if the reliving of it had put her into a trance.

"And I was better off, she said. Couldn't I see how much better off I was now? What she'd done for me? She said I had to wait. A couple of months would be best. She would get me a remote, and the passcode. She would explain exactly what I had to do and how I had to do it. She gave me a 'link. I wasn't to use it for anything. She would contact me on it when it was time. And she'd be watching me. And my kids. She told me what I was going to do, how easy it would be. If I messed it up, she had the recording, and she'd send it to the police. Or maybe I'd just have a tragic accident one day, me and the kids. She told me I should be grateful. She'd given me a fresh start. Now I had to pay for it. I had to stick to my part of the deal."

"Take us through it."

"It had to be late at night. After midnight, but before one. I'd use the remote to shut down the security, then I'd use the passcode and go inside. I—I had to seal up first. Straight up the stairs, to the bedroom. The door would be closed, and he'd be sleeping facing the door. He'd have taken a sleeping pill because she'd replaced his nightly vitamins with them. I had to . . . I had to take off his pajamas, use the rope—the rope she told me to buy—on his wrists and his ankles. I was supposed to give him a dose of male sex enhancer, and . . . God, put the rings on him, and some of the lotion. Set out the toys. He'd wake up some, and that was good. I'd see what it was like. It would make it better for all of us. Then I was to put the rope around his neck, tighten it. Watch, watch until I knew he was dead."

She drank again, three small sips. "I was supposed to take it off after, the rope, but leave it there. Then go down, through the house, through the kitchen, and take the security tapes. That would make it look like I'd been there before, that it was all an accident—like it was his own fault. I was supposed to walk out, turn everything back on—the security, then walk all the way to the subway on Fifth."

"What about the 'link, the discs?"

"She was to contact me on it at two. It was supposed to be done by two, but it wasn't. I couldn't . . . Then she called, and she was so angry. So I did it. I did what she said, except I couldn't stand the idea of him knowing, and I used the medication I'd gotten from the doctor to help me sleep, and I couldn't watch him die, so I ran out."

"Where's the 'link, the discs, the remote?"

"I was supposed to put them in a recycler on Fifth. But I forgot. I can't even remember getting on the subway, but I must have because I was home. I didn't remember about them until the next day, after my kids came home from school. They stayed at a friend's the night before, because I couldn't leave them alone. And I guess I always knew I'd do what she told me. I was afraid to put them in a recycler near the house. I was afraid to keep them in the house. I didn't know what to do. I shoved the bag in the closet because I couldn't *think*."

"Do you still have them?"

"I was going to take them to the park today, where the kids practice. I was going to put them in the recycler there. But you came."

Eve signaled Baxter, who rose and strode out of the room. "Detective Baxter has left Interview. Has she contacted you again, Suzanne?"

"No, not since that night—that morning. It's like a dream. I was walking, walking—after—and she called on the 'link. She said: 'Well?' And I said I'd done it. And she said, 'Good girl.' That's all. 'Good girl,' like I'd finished my chores. I killed him. I know he was a monster, but I think she's one, too."

"You think?"

"What's going to happen now? Can you tell me what's going to happen now?"

"We're going to go back over the details. What kind of vehicle did she drive?"

"A black one."

"Do better."

"It was black and shiny. Expensive. I don't know about cars. I've never had a car."

"When you were walking with her, the day you were going to the market, did you see anyone you know?"

"I don't know many people. Ned didn't like—"

"Stop it," Eve said sharply, and Suzanne jerked straight. "You know your neighbors, at least by sight, the people who run the market, your children's friends, their parents."

"I guess I do. I don't remember. I was so surprised to see her, and Ned had just . . ."

"No one spoke to you?"

"Just Ava. It was really cold, and I was looking down—the way you do."

The way *you* do, Eve thought. "Was the car on the street or in a lot?"

"A lot. An auto lot."

"Which way did you walk?"

"Ah, um . . . West because we went right by the market, and then we crossed after a few blocks, and walked north. I think maybe on Seventh. Maybe. I'm not sure."

"Which rest stop did she use?"

"I don't know, I don't know. They all look the same, don't they? I was sick."

"How long were you gone? No, don't give me that 'I don't know shit,' Suzanne. What time did you leave for the market?"

"About nine-thirty."

"What time did you get home?"

"It was almost noon. I had to take the bus. She dropped me at the transpo center across from the tunnel, and gave me bus fare. I had to take the bus back."

"How long did you wait for the bus?"

"Only a few minutes. I got lucky. I got off and walked back to the market. Mr. Isaacs said how he thought I wasn't coming in that day."

"Mr. Isaacs?"

"He runs the market, and I always go on Mondays, before ten. He said how I looked tired, how I should try to get some rest, and he gave me pop treats for the kids. I forgot that. He gave me treats for the kids. He's a nice man. He and his wife run the market. I went home, and I put everything away, and I thought, 'None of this is happening. It's not real.' Then I got sick again, because it was. I have to tell my kids. I don't know how."

"When you were at the retreat and made your bargain, where were you?"

"In Ava's suite. She told me to come up after the last seminar, but not to tell anyone. People get jealous. She just wanted to relax with a friend." Tears spurted again. Eve wondered how the woman had any more in her. "She said we were friends."

"You had drinks. Did she order them?"

"There was a bottle of wine and a pretty platter of fruit and cheese. Everything was so pretty."

"Did anyone call or come by while you were there?"

"No. She had the Do Not Disturb on the door and the links. So we could relax, she said."

Eve pressed a little more, then judged she'd wrung Suzanne dry. For now. "You're going to be booked, and you're going to be remanded. The court's going to assign an attorney to you. You've got the best deal you're going to get. Don't expect any more."

She rose as Baxter came back in. "Detective Baxter re-entering Interview." When she crossed to him, he spoke quietly.

"Got the search warrant. Do you want me to take that?"

"No. Walk her through Booking. She's tapped out for now."

"I contacted the sister while I waited for the warrant to come through. She's confused and shocked, like you'd expect. She's making arrangements to come up for the kids. CS cleared that."

"You pushed some buttons."

"The kids are going to have it hard enough. Not their fault."

"Walk her through," Eve repeated. "I'll have Peabody and Trueheart exercise the warrant. I need a couple hours to sort through all this. We need to keep this arrest off the radar."

With a nod, Baxter walked to Suzanne. "You need to come with me now."

Eve waited until he'd led Suzanne through the door. "Interview end." Then she dragged her hands through her hair. "Christ. Jesus Christ."

When she stepped out, Mira was there. "I don't want to hear about her emotional trauma, her fear of authority figures or her goddamn remorse. Thomas Anders died by her hand."

"Yes, he did. That doesn't make her less pitiable. A year in prison, twenty years, Suzanne Custer's life is essentially over. It was over the minute Ava Anders targeted her."

"Tell me this: Did Suzanne Custer know what she was doing when she put that rope around Thomas Anders's neck? Was she legally, mentally—and I'll even go one more—morally aware of right and wrong?"

"Yes, she was. She is culpable for her act, and should pay for what she did. Are there extenuating circumstances, would I—or any other psychiatrist—consider diminished capacity? Yes. But she killed Thomas Anders fully aware of her actions."

"That's good enough for me."

"Eve. You're so angry."

"Damn right I am. Sorry, I don't have time to comb through my own psyche. I've got work." She turned and, pulling out her communicator, strode away.

In her office, she hit the AutoChef for coffee before sitting down at her desk to begin the calculations for the most likely lots Ava had used, and the rest stop where she'd taken Suzanne. Little bits, she thought. Little bits and pieces. While the computer worked, she wrote her report on the interview, made notes, added to her time lines.

When the computer spit out its most probables, she studied the map, gauged the distances, the locations, simmered them with her understanding of Ava.

"I think we've got that. Yeah, I think we do," she muttered. And only grunted at the knock on her door.

"Hello, Lieutenant."

She barely glanced at Roarke. "She doesn't go far—just far enough. But she's not as fucking smart as she thinks she is. Doesn't know people as well as she believes."

"I'm sure you're right." He sat on the corner of her desk. "A moment?"

"I don't have much of a moment. Suzanne copped to it all. Jesus, it was like flipping a switch on a dike or a dam, whatever, and having it all gush out. Ava went for the weak, the runt of the litter you could say. Miscalculated. Makes Suzanne easy to manipulate."

"And that was the miscalculation," he said with a nod. "Because you're very good at manipulating."

"She counted on the power of her personality, of the pecking order to push Suzanne into doing the job. But she read her partner wrong. Way wrong. My take? She believed Suzanne would be flattered and happy to hook up with her, believed Suzanne would be grateful to be rid of her lousy husband, and do exactly what she was told. She had contingency plans, sure—she's always got herself a Plan B, C or D, but she didn't see that under it, Suzanne's a major fuckup."

"That's harsh."

"She deserves harsh." The anger roiled inside her. "At any point, any fucking point, she could've stopped. Back in August when Ava proposed the plan, she could've stopped. When Ava told her how she'd killed her husband, she could've stopped. Any time over the last two months, she could've stopped. In the hour she was in the house with Anders, she could've stopped. And now it's all, gee, I'm sorry? Boo-hoo? I feel sick? Screw that."

"Does she enrage you for what she did, or that she was weak enough to do it?"

"Both. And I'm happy to be a part of making her pay. Making both of them pay. Ava got what she wanted, but she had to push too hard. And she used the wrong sort of manipulation in the end. Smarter, much smarter to have appealed to Suzanne's soft side. 'Please help me. You're the only one I trust, the only one I can depend on. I've done this for you, just as I promised. Please don't turn your back on me now.' Instead, she was so revved from the murder she played hardball, and cracked her tool. All I had to do was give it a few good knocks."

She pushed away from the desk, crossed over to stare out the window.

Roarke gave her a moment of silence for her own thoughts. "What troubles you about it, Eve? Under your anger?"

"It's personal. I can deal with that, but it's the way it's personal that gnaws a little. Mira's already poking at me about it, and that's irritating."

"Because she sees that you look at Suzanne and think of yourself. The child you were. Battered, trapped, helpless. And the choice you made to save yourself."

Eve glanced back. "It shows? That's irritating, too."

"To me, and to Mira. But you wear your armor well, Lieutenant."

"She wasn't a child, Roarke. She wasn't helpless, or didn't have to be. She chose to kill, to obey another bidding to kill, rather than deal."

That, he knew, would eat at her. The uselessness of it. "And it pisses you off. She lay down and took it, when there were so many options. She took the life of a man she didn't know because someone told her to. Her husband's dead because she stayed with him rather than walk away. And now her children are, essentially, orphaned."

"She said she thought her children should have their father. That it was her responsibility to stay."

"Ah."

Having said it, Eve realized some of the knots in her belly had slackened. "Yeah, I thought of your mother, and how she'd thought the same. How she'd died for that. But goddamn it, Roarke, your mother was so young, and I can't believe she'd have stayed for years. I can't look at you and believe that. Can't think of the family you found and believe that. She'd have taken you and walked, if she'd had another chance."

"I think of that. Aye, sometimes I think of that. And that's why I believe as well. But in God's truth, I don't know if it's a comfort or a curse to believe it."

"It's a comfort to me," she said, and watched his eyes warm.

"Then it will be to me as well. Thanks."

"Suzanne Custer sat and made a bargain over wine and cheese. Some part of her knew it was real, however much she denies it. However much she can't face it. She agreed to Ava's terms. She didn't try to back out until after her own husband's throat was slit. She didn't go to Ava the next morning, or the next week and tell her, 'Deal's off. No can do.' She let it ride. Ned Custer was a son of a bitch, and he may have deserved to have his balls kicked black and blue, might've deserved some time in a cage for spousal abuse, but he didn't deserve having his throat slit and his dick sawed off. But the wife who claims she wanted her children to have their father set him up for just that. So I don't feel for her. I'm damned if I will."

Roarke rose and went to her, laid his hands on her shoulders, his lips on her brow. "It's useless to be angry with yourself because you do feel something. Just that thin edge of pity around the disgust."

"She doesn't deserve my pity." And Eve sighed. "Or any more of my time slapping at myself for that thin edge of it I do feel. I need to get in the field."

He gave her shoulders a brisk rub. "Here I've come by as I did my job so well and so quickly; now you're tossing me aside."

"You pinned the remote? Already?"

"I did, yes. I'll have some coffee."

"How the hell—"

"Are you going to get me some coffee or not?"

"Crap." She programmed it. "Spill."

"Assuming you don't mean the coffee—as what would be the point—I've just come from a chat with an old . . . acquaintance. He happens to specialize in electronics that aren't legal in the strictest sense of the word."

"He sells illegal jammers and bypasses on the black market."

"To put a fine point on it, yes. He manufactures them, most usually for specific clients at quite a hefty markup. He's very good at it. In fact, perhaps the best in New York." He waited a significant beat. "Now."

"Now that you aren't in the same market."

"Aren't you clever? I started at the top of the chain, as I assume Ava would want someone talented, efficient, and reliable—also with a reputation for being discreet. She went for Charles, after all, who has those qualities in his former profession. I'll admit I didn't expect to hit straight off the mark. But that's precisely what I did."

"This guy, this acquaintance designed and sold the remote to Ava."

"Three months ago, he received a package at his legitimate place of business."

"His front."

"You're so picky. The package contained an order for a very specifically designed device. It contained the specs for the security system the device was to bypass. He tells me he was impressed with the research the potential client had done. And," Roarke added with a smile, "with the considerable amount of cash as downpayment. Another payment would be made on delivery, and the final sent if and when the client deemed the device satisfactory."

"Is that how he usually does business?"

"That would be telling." Roarke stroked a finger down the dent in her chin. "But I can say this arrangement was a bit unusual. The offered fee was more than his usual as well. So he took the job."

"He never saw her. Never had direct contact with her."

"No. He made the device, and as instructed left it in a drop box, which contained the second payment."

"A guy could get stung that way," Eve commented.

"Not this guy, or not easily. He's a nose for cops, and the setup. He also believes in knowing who he's dealing with, so he had an underling stake out the box."

Eve's lips spread in a grin. "I might like this guy."

"Actually, I believe you would. In any case, the woman who picked it up didn't match Ava's description, but she delivered it, along with some dry cleaning, to the Anders's home. The third payment was made, as promised. And my acquaintance thought little of the matter until he heard of Thomas Anders's murder. This put him in a bit of a sticky situation."

"Yeah, accessory before the fact's pretty sticky. Will he testify?"

"That would depend on several issues. Immunity, anonymity—the man does have a business to protect—and a reasonable payment."

"I'll set it up. We may not need him, but I'll put it in play." Eve took his coffee, drank some herself. "You're useful."

"And always eager to be used."

"I've got Peabody out on something else. Why don't you ride over to New Jersey with me?"

"Being used across state lines. How could I resist?"

22

"YEAH, WE GET YOUR ILLEGALS DROPS, YOUR VANDALS, your vehicle boosters, rapists, muggers." The NJTP security tech, with VINCE embroidered over his shirt pocket, shrugged. "Get plenty of action, mostly between midnight and six. Me, I work the days. I got seniority."

"It's days I'm interested in," Eve reminded him. "A specific day a couple of months ago."

"We got security cams covering all the lots, the grounds, the vending. Can't use 'em in the johns, so that's where we get the most action." He pulled at his nose, swiveled on his high-backed stool. "But we roll 'em over every seventy-two hours. We got nothing goes back two months."

"Do you go back two months, Vince?"

"Sure. I've been here twelve years come June."

"Two women in a high-end black car, with one of them puking out the passenger door."

He shot her a quick and sour grin. "Jesus, New York, you know how many people we got puking in the lots, in the johns? Every damn-where?"

"I bet you don't have that many booting it between ten and eleven on a weekday, non-holiday morning." She pulled out a photo. "This would be the puker."

He took the photo, scratched his ass, scratched his head. "She don't ring for me. Looks like mostly anyone."

"What about this one?"

There was more scratching as Vince studied Ava's photo. "Looks like somebody. This one's driving, right? Nice, black Mercedes—new model, two-door sedan."

"You remember that?"

"Yeah, now that I'm thinking about it. Blondie here didn't look like the road-trip sort, and they never got out to use the john. Women hardly ever pass up a trip to the john, they pull into a rest area. The other one tosses it out the door, and I think: 'There goes breakfast.' I remember 'cause I expected they'd go into the john, clean up the sick one. But the blonde, she just drives around to the truck lot, parks again. I let maintenance know they had a cleanup, got me some coffee. Can't say I noticed how long they sat there or when they left."

Back in the car, Roarke stretched his legs. "Are you going to pass up a trip to the john?"

"Ha-ha. I can put her here with Suzanne. Right here in the Alexander Hamilton rest area off the Turnpike. Who the hell was Alexander Hamilton, and why is there a rest area off the Turnpike named after him?"

"Ah . . ."

"Never mind. There's a new model Mercedes sedan, black, registered to Ava Anders. This little chat with Vince confirms the day, the time—and I'll back that up because I'll betcha that big, black Mercedes has a pass scanner for the toll. Can't confirm what was said, but it puts Ava with Suzanne here. How's she going to explain that one?"

"She'll have something. Hamilton was one of America's Founding Fathers, and its first Secretary of the Treasury."

"Who? Huh?"

"You asked," Roarke said, pocketing his PPC again. "Where to now?"

Eve frowned at him a moment. "Is that what you're doing, playing with that thing all the time? Looking up trivia?"

"Among other things. Something else you'd like to know?"

"Whole bunches of things. Right now, we're going to go to the market to find out a few." She answered her dash 'link. "Dallas."

"We got it. Bag was in the closet," Peabody said, "as advertised. A disposable 'link, several security discs, and a very rocking bypass remote—along with a pair of light blue men's pajamas, the pressure syringes, and the meds."

"Get them in, log them. I want chain of evidence pristine. Have Feeney and McNab start on the contents. I'm in the field, got a couple more stops to make."

"It's falling apart on her," Roarke commented.

"She's going to hire a big, fat, sneaky lawyer. A fucking fleet of big, fat, sneaky lawyers. The type who get shit suppressed, tossed out, who pump in reasonable doubt. I don't have enough. I can put her with Suzanne in Jersey a few days after Custer's murder. Proves nothing. What Peabody just picked up only proves Suzanne was in the Anders's house, and pretty much sews up she killed him. We've got her confession already. She's locked. Your acquaintance can state that the device was taken to the Anders residence. He can't put it in Ava's hands. I've got her lies, her association with an LC, I've got her father-in-law's death, which I wheedled the local cops into opening again. Disposable 'link. Batt's going to be dead, and when the battery dies on those, it wipes the transmissions. I need more."

The chubby and cheerful Mr. Isaac gave her a bit more.

"Right after her husband was killed, yes? I remember very well. Terrible thing. She comes in on Mondays, about nine-thirty on Monday mornings, poor Mrs. Custer. But this day, a few days after I hear her husband's dead, I see her go right by carrying her market bag."

"Was she alone?"

"No. I started to go outside, call out to her, thinking she'd forgotten where she was going. Being upset about her husband. But then I saw she was with someone. She was with a very fancy lady. Beautiful coat with fur on the collar," Isaacs added, brushing his fingers down the front of his apron to demonstrate. "Long black coat, brown fur trim. Very nice. I think I've seen the fancy lady once or twice before, but not that coat."

"You saw the woman before that day?"

"Once or twice. I know my neighborhood, I know my people."

"Is this the woman?" Eve offered Ava's photo.

"Yes, yes, this is the woman poor Mrs. Custer was with that morning. Such pretty hair she has. I remember, it was a very sunny day, and the sunshine seemed to bounce off her pretty hair. She wore shades. As I said, it was a very bright day, but she's very striking. I'm sure this is the same woman. They walked right by. Mrs. Custer looked so sad and tired. She came back, by herself, a couple hours later. Maybe more, we were busy. I thought, 'Poor little thing—Mrs. Custer—she's been crying.' I gave her some pop treats for the children."

She hit the lot next, a small, overpriced two-decker.

"This sort of lot won't have security discs for two months ago," Roarke reminded her. "And their records won't include license number, make or model. It's just the time in and out, the fee, the slot."

"They'd have tag number, make, and model for reserved parking. No way Ava would cruise around looking for a parking spot. Not someone who plans, who researches. She'd book one. Scanner reads reservation number, and to reserve you need to verify tag number."

"Well now, you're right about that."

"She'd've done the same thing for the Custer stalking and hit. She'd be thinking of her own convenience, and never seriously consider we'd get here. I put her vehicle here, I put it there, it adds weight. You've got a new assignment.'

"I'm going to be talking to auto lot owners. With her vehicle number I could find it quicker myself."

"Channels. Pristine chain. We take the long way. I'll drive. You get started."

She closed herself off for twenty minutes back at Central. She shut her door, closed everyone out while she sat, feet up, eyes closed to walk herself through the steps, the stages, the routes.

With a glance at the time, she made another call. "Mrs. Horowitz, Lieutenant Dallas. I have a couple of questions."

"Of course."

"Mrs. Anders attends a lot of functions—balls, parties, and so on. Does she ever attend costume types—masked balls, fancy dress, that sort of thing?"

"There's a fancy-dress gala in October every year."

"Where does she keep her wigs?"

"All the costume pieces she has made or purchased are kept in storage on the third floor."

"Does she own a red wig?"

"I believe she owns a few, in different shades and styles. I haven't been in the storage area for some time."

"Thanks."

Eve ended transmission, and placed another to APA Reo. Then she called in the team.

In the conference room, Eve paced while Baxter brooded into his coffee and Roarke passed the time on his PPC. Peabody, with no new visible piercings, huddled together with Trueheart. EDD had yet to arrive. Cher Reo entered next, the pretty blonde with the Southern drawl and the raptor claws in court.

"Hello, gang." She nodded at Eve. "Let's hear the pitch."

"We're not all here. Feeney—" Eve narrowed a stare at him as he strolled in with McNab. "You're late."

"You want it fast or you want it right?"

"I just want it. Status, EDD first."

Feeney took out his notebook. "Pill dispenser, vic's, opened and reprogrammed the morning Ava Anders left for St. Lucia. None of her prints inside or out. Office 'links, Anders Worldwide. No transmissions to or from Suzanne Custer during the last six months. Same for the home and personal 'links we were given access to. Security discs recovered from Custer apartment show no unusual activity. Remote recovered from Custer apartment is extreme. Custom job, specific for the system at Anders's residence. We found two uses. One use six weeks ago, and one the morning of the Anders murder."

"Ava test drove it."

"Be my take. Disposable 'link, dead as disco. Those type don't hold transmissions much over twenty-four anyway. If they do that. And this one's cheap shit."

"You're telling me you got zip?"

"I didn't say zip." He stretched out his legs, crossed them at the ankles. "Every electronic byte leaves an imprint. A smudge anyway. You go in right, and you can finesse. We got what you could call echoes. 'Link's a piece of crap, but crap can be manipulated. We need to process the echoes, tune them up, sort them out. Something's there. Give us a day or two, and we'll pull it out."

"Good. Peabody?"

"Adult toy items matching those at the Anders crime scene were purchased by Suzanne Custer, or earlier by Ned Custer. All but the ropes were obtained by her at Just Sex. She purchased the ropes, with cash, at Bondage Baby. Custer also obtained, by doctor's prescription, lotrominaphine, the medication found in Thomas Anders, as well as six pressure syringes. Four syringes were also found in the bag recovered from the Custer apartment, as was the partially used prescription of the tranq. She's wrapped."

"And yet," Reo commented, "Murder Two."

"It'll be worth it," Eve told her. "In Interview, Suzanne Custer stated that at Ava Anders's suggestion the two women entered into a bargain to kill each other's husbands. Reportedly, Anders recorded their promise."

"That's dumbass," McNab put in. "Why incriminate yourself on record?"

"If Ava ever recorded her own statement, she's long since wiped it. But I'll bet she's got Suzanne's tucked away for leverage."

McNab nodded. "Not so dumbass."

"Three days after the Custer murder, Anders waylaid Custer on Custer's way to her usual Monday morning marketing. Custer and Anders were seen together, and today identified by Isaacs, Jerome, the market's owner." Eve pointed a finger at McNab before he could speak.

"Yes, dumbass, but we're dealing with a woman who never believed we'd have any reason to tie her and Suzanne Custer together. And if we asked? She could easily claim she'd dropped by to pay her condolences.

"So moving on. Custer further stated that Anders informed her Anders had killed Ned Custer—and gave all details to same. And it would soon be time to complete the bargain. According to Custer's statement, Anders used threats and duress to obtain her agreement, while Anders drove into New Jersey, to a rest area. A security tech at same has identified Anders and her vehicle, corroborating Custer's statement. At that time, Anders gave Custer the disposable 'link, and described how Thomas Anders was to be killed."

"You're going to get a lot of she said/she said here, Dallas," Reo commented.

"Yeah, so we'll need to make what Custer said stick. We need those echoes cleared, Feeney. Custer did not, as Anders instructed, dispose of the 'link, the remote, the discs. Anders lied about her husband's sexual proclivities."

"Prove it," Reo demanded.

"Your job. But, she told both Custer and one Petrelli, Bebe, that Thomas Anders was a sexual deviate, and a pedophile. She indicated same to a Gordon, Cassie. There is no evidence this was true. In fact, there is weighty evidence it was not. Ava engaged a licensed companion for several months. There is no evidence Thomas Anders used LCs or engaged in extra-marital affairs, as Ava claims. Let *her* prove it," Eve added.

"After receiving the news that her husband was dead," Eve continued, "Ava ordered a tasty breakfast, ate same, dressed, and groomed meticulously. She didn't wake her friends, but took a shuttle home alone."

"I just don't like her." Reo examined her nails. "I don't like Ava one little bit."

"Get in line. Rewind two months. Custer, Ned, was last seen with a tall woman, a redhead, taken to be a pro. She went from a bar to a flop with the victim, and did not exit by the door. Ava told Suzanne that after slitting Custer's throat, and whacking him off in a permanent manner, she exited via the fire escape. She owns several red wigs."

"Get me something physical," Reo insisted. "It's a good circumstantial case, but—"

"The vehicle registered to Ava Anders was parked eight blocks north and one east of the Custer murder scene," Roarke put in without looking up. "The vehicle had reserved parking for that slot, in that lot, for a period of two weeks. It was used three times, the last on the night of the murder, clocking in at 10:12 p.m., clocking out at 2:08 a.m."

"Okay, that's interesting." Something lit in Reo's eyes. "How do we prove she drove it there?"

"Because she fucking did," Eve snapped. "Because on that night and the ten days prior, Thomas Anders was out of town, and she could come and go as she pleased. Look at the time line. She kills her father-in-law, and that's the turn."

"Reginald Anders's death was deemed accidental." Reo tossed up a hand. "Don't bite my head off, that's the face. You've got the case re-opened, and I'm inclined to agree she killed him because I don't like her. But at this point, we've got an old man slipping in the shower."

"We won't end with that. She hired a decorator the week before Reginald Anders took the fall. Shortly after it's reported she and the old man had a private talk in his office about her charging personal expenses to program budgets. She didn't walk out happy. And according to the housekeeper, decorating talk began two weeks after the father-in-law's death, though she'd already contracted with one.

"You're going to say some spouses sneak in something like that—the decorating crap," Eve said, anticipating Reo. "Why would she? Every statement we've taken on their marriage, on Anders, describes him as indulgent. He wouldn't have given a shit about that."

"Then why wait to tell him?" Reo asked. "Picky, I know, but defense attorneys are, as a rule."

"It was her congratulations present to herself. She didn't bring it out until after she'd done the old man. Until that was behind her. Weeks after that, she hires Charles Monroe, telling one of her friends—out of the goddamn blue—that she and her husband are sexually incompatible. She revs up the mommy retreat program, and starts to scope. Here, she approaches Petrelli, whose family has ties to organized crime. She *suggests* Petrelli might find a way to dispose of Anders, who she claims is a pervert. That craps out. She approaches Gordon, an LC who is also in the program, and asks for details about kink. And finally, she finds her mark here, with Custer."

"Suzanne was prime bait," Baxter put in.

"Detective Yancy executed a composite of Ava with the style and color of hair witnesses reported re Ned Custer," Eve added. "We're going to find somebody who'll put her in the bar, in the flop."

"Do it, because I'd love to bring her down." Reo closed her notebook. "Can you get me a confession?"

"That's the plan. I need to get her out of the house so we can go in and cop the wig without her being aware. Feeney, I need you to mock me up a disposable 'link exactly like that one. We've got her statements on record. I want to hear her voice come out of it. Baxter, talk to Suzanne again, make sure she's clear on exactly what Ava said the morning Anders was murdered. Peabody, put a couple of the men in soft clothes on the sleazy side. Roarke, see if your *acquaintance* will come down. He's not going to have to say a thing. Reo will give him immunity and I'll authorize two bills."

"What am I giving immunity for?"

"We'll get to that. I want Petrelli and Gordon in here, and the night clerk from the flop. Trueheart I'm going to be sending you to bring Ava in."

He blinked as if something had flown into his eyes. "Sending me?"

"You won't worry her. You're too young and pretty, and you're going to apologize. If she cries lawyer, she cries lawyer, but I don't think she will. Not right off. Take another uniform. A young, green one. I'll tell you when to go, and how to handle her. What are you smiling at?" she asked Roarke.

"It's such an interesting show you're planning."

"Yeah, so let's work out the song and the dance."

I t wasn't a stretch for Trueheart to appear apologetic and accommodating. Even with seasoning a la Baxter, he remained a sweet-natured, happy-to-help kind of guy. Young and fresh, and—to the careless or cynical eye—not all that smart. What Ava saw were two young, handsome, somewhat bumbling cops who seemed embarrassed with their current duty.

"I'm awfully sorry, ma'am." Trueheart added a pained smile. "I know it's an inconvenience, especially at such a difficult time, but the lieutenant—"

"Yes, it's very inconvenient, and a very difficult time. I fail to see why I should have to go downtown. Why doesn't the lieutenant come to me?"

"Um, she would, ma'am, but she's in this meeting with the commander and the chief, about the, ah . . . the, ah, media problem in regards to the case."

"Taking some licks for it." The second uniform delivered his first scripted line on cue.

"Come on." Trueheart frowned him down. "And I believe Chief Tibble would like to personally apologize to you about the media stuff. So we were sent to transport you down to Central."

"Young man, I understand you're just following orders, but you can't possibly expect to bundle me in the back of a police car, to add that kind of mortification on top of everything else."

"Ah, well, um . . ." Trueheart glanced at his companion, who only shrugged helplessly. "If you wanted to call a cab, I guess—I don't know. Maybe I could call in and ask—"

"Nonsense, that's just nonsense. I'll take my own car. I'm free to come and go as I please, aren't I? I'm not under arrest, am I?"

"Oh gosh, no, ma'am. I mean, yes, ma'am on the first part. We could follow you in. I'm sure that's okay, and I could arrange a parking permit in the VIP visitor lot. Would that be all right?"

"I'd think it's the least you could do, and thank you. Now, I'll have to ask you to wait outside while I—"

"You didn't do the RM." The second cop delivered his next line, and Trueheart flushed and shifted his feet.

"I don't know that we're supposed to—"

"My sergeant kicked my ass—pardon me, ma'am—for not just yesterday. I don't want to screw up again."

"Okay, okay. I'm awful sorry, Mrs. Anders, but we're just going to read you the Revised Miranda before we go, since you're going to be talking to the lieutenant about the investigation. A formality thing." Trueheart added an earnest, and nervous smile. "Is that all right with you?"

"Fine, fine, fine." Ava waved him on. "Hurry it up. I don't want a police car outside my house all afternoon."

"Yes, ma'am. Well. You have the right to remain silent." To add to the picture, Trueheart pulled out a small card with the warning printed on it, and read it with intense concentration. He hoped it wasn't overplayed. "Um. Do you understand your—"

"Am I an idiot?" Ava snapped. "Of course I understand. Now, shoo, I'll be out in a few minutes."

"Yes, ma'am. Thank you, ma'am." After the door shut in his face, Trueheart walked back to the police car with his companion. "Dallas is a solid genius," he stated, then engaged his communicator. "It's Trueheart, Lieutenant."

At Central, Eve fueled up on coffee. "Trueheart's follow- ing her in. I want the sweepers on that car the minute it's parked."

"You, like, read her mind," Peabody said. "You knew she'd drive in."

"She wouldn't turn down an opportunity to have the Chief of Police grovel to her, and lord it over me. And she wouldn't get in a black-and-white unless she was cuffed and carried. Besides, if she left the car at home, the sweepers could process it there. Reo's warrant covers us. I want this to run like clockwork. Everyone in place." Even as she went over the details in her head, Eve turned to her partner. "I need to take her one-on-one, Peabody. You get that?"

"Yeah. And I know my cue. We've got two men in place to swing in, execute the warrant on the house and bring in the wigs. It's like a sting, isn't it, and nearly as juicy as a battering-ram-slamming, blaster-bursting takedown. Without the potential for fatal injuries. It's all: *Psyche!*"

"We twist her, and we twist her. We twist her right, and she snaps." Eve stared at her murder board. The steps and stages, the bits and pieces. Now it was time to put them all together.

"Lieutenant." Roarke studied her from the doorway.

"I'll go check on stuff," Peabody said and eased out.

"She's on her way. Bringing the car in."

"You called that one. Your diverse cast of characters appears to be in place. You know you're risking those big, fat lawyers with this stage you've set."

"Yeah. She's smart enough to lawyer, but I'm betting she's too arrogant to squeal for one right off. At the end she will. At the end she'll be screaming for a lawyer." And for once, Eve admitted, the sound of that would be like music to her ears. "But first she'll be shaken, shaken enough to *have* to put me in my place."

"As Magdelana tried to."

There was no point denying it. "To her eventual disappointment . . . and fat lip. I'm not hanging onto that, if that's worrying you." When he stepped in, those blue eyes level on hers, and traced a fingertip along the shallow dent in her chin, she sighed, then shrugged. "Okay, maybe a little. But I'm not pissed at you about that, about her."

He leaned down, kissed her very softly.

"Much. You didn't see her, at least not until what she was doing was shoved in your face. Must be a guy thing when it comes to a certain kind of female. Thomas Anders didn't see it in Ava, for years and years. He lived with her, and he didn't see her. Not who she really is. I'm not pissed at him about it. He loved her. I'm pissed she used that, and him. Used anyone who came to hand, with absolutely no conscience. For game and profit. She killed him for that. For game and profit."

"And you imagine, if I hadn't had certain things shoved in my face, hadn't seen, if some circumstances had been different, Maggie would have eventually done for me."

"Why share the majority of the known universe if you can have it all for yourself?"

"Right you are. And, yes, she would have tried to end me at some point. Fortunately, I'm married to the top bitch cop in the city, and well-protected."

"Fortunately, you can take care of yourself. Tommy Anders couldn't." She turned back to the board, to the ID photo of Anders's smiling, easygoing face.

"It hits me. Some of them do, and it hits me because he was a nice man who loved his wife and used his money and position to do good things. He's dead, lives are ruined or at best forever changed, all because she wanted all the marbles. So . . . I'm going to squash her like the ugly spider she is."

"Lieutenant." Peabody poked in. "She's just pulled into the lot."

"Curtain up," Roarke said.

23

TO ROARKE'S MIND, COP SHOPS TENDED TOWARD
the loud, the confused, and the crowded. One
such as Cop Central twisted and twined, rose
and fell, in a serpentine labyrinth where cops, suspects, victims,
lawyers, techs all bumped and burrowed amid constant clatter
and movement.

And still, through all that, the choreography Eve had
staged moved seamlessly. Perhaps as so many of the players
were unaware of their role, their actions and reactions fell as
natural as rainwater.

He watched on screens in an observation room with
Feeney and the director herself as Trueheart and his fellow
uniform—both looking as wholesome and harmless as apple
pie—escorted Ava onto the elevator, then off again.

"It'll be quicker and less crowded," Trueheart explained
in his polite tone, "if we take the glides from here, Mrs.
Anders."

As they rode up, others rode down. On the down, a man
in a stained T-shirt and dingy dreads who Roarke would have

made for a cop at six blocks, swiveled, pointed. "Hey, hey! That's the one there. That's the broad left with Cuss. Hey!"

Ava angled away toward Trueheart's agreeable face. "Sorry," he said. "We get all kinds through here."

He led her off the glide, across a short span of floor, just as a female officer walked Bebe Petrelli toward the down. The reaction of both civilians struck Roarke as priceless. Shock on both faces, distress following on Petrelli's, fury darkening Ava's, even as the cop quickly hustled Petrelli to the left and away.

Little fissures in the mask, Roarke noted. And up the next glide they went. This time Baxter brought Cassie Gordon on just below. Cassie's gaze tracked up, latched. "Well, hey. Hey, Ava!" A sharp and deadly amusement colored Cassie's voice. "What're you doing here?"

Ava glanced back, skimmed her cold eyes over Cassie. "I'm sorry. Do I know you?"

"Sure, but then I'm just one of the horde. How's it going?"

"You'll have to excuse me. I'm pressed for time. Can we get this done?" she demanded of Trueheart.

"Yes, ma'am, we're nearly there. This way." Deliberately, he walked her by Homicide where the night clerk from the sex flop sat on a bench outside, flanked by two cops. He stared at her as she approached. The fissures widened as color flooded Ava's face.

"Right in here." Trueheart opened the door of Interview A. "I'll make sure the lieutenant knows you're here. Can I get you something to drink? Coffee maybe."

"I'd prefer something sweet and cold. Ginger ale in a glass."

"Yes, ma'am."

In Observation, Eve hooked her thumbs in her pockets. "Putting her game face on. Knows we're watching. Anybody with a brain, and brains she's got, knows how Interview works."

"Spooked her some."

"Yeah, but pissed her off more. That's what's going to hang her. Well, time to go kick her ass."

"Want me to kiss your head?"

"Want me to mention your sick day pajamas?"

"That's mean. You make me proud. Go skin your fish."

Eve didn't want to keep Ava waiting long. Keep the temper up, those little edges of fear. She walked into Interview carrying plenty of files and attitude. "Mrs. Anders."

"Lieutenant. I've had about enough of your incompetence, and your callousness. I demand to see your chief."

"We'll get to that. Record on. Dallas, Lieutenant Eve, in interview with Anders, Ava, regarding case number HA-32003, Anders, Thomas A., and all related events and crimes." Eve dropped into a chair. "We've got a lot to clear up, Ava."

"Mrs. Anders. I'd like to clear up the way you and this department have handled the media."

Eve only smiled. "It's been an interesting couple of days for me. How about you?" At Ava's stony stare, Eve's smile widened. "I don't catch many like these, and I've got to hand it to you: You damn near pulled it off. I bet you're wondering how I'm going to get you for murder."

"What a hideous thing to say to me! A slanderous thing to say. I didn't kill Tommy. I loved my husband. I was out of the country when he died, and you know that very well."

"Save the shiny eyes and tear-choked voice. I know you." Eve leaned forward. "I knew you the minute I saw you. You're a grasping, greedy, self-important excuse for a human being. But you've got brains, Ava, and you've got patience. So what it comes down to is how you want to play this part of it. Let me give you something to think about. Suzanne Custer."

"Is that name supposed to mean something to me?"

"Think about it. Think about the fact that when we bring her in, we'll give her a chance to slip and slide. She'll have the opportunity to wheel and deal. Personally, I think she's going to grab it like a lifeline."

"Lieutenant Dallas, I have no idea what you're trying to do here, unless it's generate more media frenzy than you've already managed. And that you're somehow blaming me for that, and the fact you've been reprimanded for mishandling it. It's been established, without any doubt, that I was in St. Lucia when my Tommy was killed."

"You weren't in St. Lucia when Ned Custer's throat was slit."

"I don't know anyone by that name. What does that have to do with me?"

"Are you going to deny you know Suzanne Custer?"

"I know a great many people." She paused, offered a considering frown. "Suzanne? Yes, of course. I know her slightly. She's one of our mothers."

"The same Suzanne Custer whose husband was murdered in a sex flop in Alphabet City a couple of months ago."

"How horrible." Ava pressed a hand to her own throat. "Poor Suzanne. I try not to follow media reports on violence. I'm so terribly sorry to hear about this, but I don't know what it has to do with me, or with my Tommy."

"Makes you wonder what Suzanne might say if she gets a chance to address that."

Peabody entered with a red wig inside an evidence bag. She nodded at Eve, slipped out. "Lookie here. Pretty." Eve held up the bag. "Familiar?"

"I assume it's one of mine, as I have one like it. Or did. I attend costume galas from time to time. I'd like to know how it came to be in your possession."

"By duly executed warrant. Let me just mention Ned Custer again, a bar pickup and sex flop. Give you another shot here, Ava. You're a striking woman. Tall and well-turned-out." Opening the file, she withdrew a photo she'd had the police artist compose. It appeared dim, even dingy, just as she'd ordered.

"You even turn out pretty well as a cheap redhead in a crappy security cam still. Maybe not suitable for framing," she added as Ava stared down at it. "But a picture tells a story. Here's a story I like. You pick up Custer in the bar, take him to the flop, slit his throat, carve off his works, and boogie on. Why? You're just going to have to help me out there. Why does a woman like you slum it with a man like Custer, and end up killing him?"

"I can hardly help you as there *is* no why. It's insane."

"Maybe things didn't go the way you figured. He's not a smoothie like Charles Monroe. Maybe you were trying to get your kicks on seeing as your husband leaned that way. Help me out here. Gotcha, Ava." Eve tapped the photo. "I've got you in the bar, with Custer. In the flop, with Custer. You can help me, and help yourself, or I let Suzanne pick up the story from here."

"It's not what you think. Not at all what you think."

Trueheart came in with a plastic glass filled with ice and ginger ale. "Excuse me. I'm sorry it took so long."

Eve waited while Trueheart stepped out, while Ava sipped. *Yeah, you think,* Eve mused. *Think how to play it. Bet I know how you will.*

"Suzanne . . . I felt sorry for her. I wanted to help her."

"By offing her lousy husband? Man, who couldn't use a pal like you?"

"Good God, no." Ava pressed a hand to her heart. In lieu of the not-currently-in-fashion wedding ring, a blood-red ruby glowed. "I took an interest in her, and it was frustrating that she refused to help herself. I know it was foolish of me, I know that, but to prove a point, I arranged a kind of intervention between her and her husband."

"What kind of intervention would that be? The kind that involves castration?"

"Don't be so horrible and crude! I wanted to *help.* Why would I conceive the mothers' programs unless I wanted to help these women?"

"What did you do? To help?"

"I went to the bar that he frequented and lured him—you could say I lured him—to that horrible hotel room. Suzanne was there. It was a way to catch him in the act, to make him face what he was doing. I left immediately after she came in, to give them privacy."

She pressed her fingers to her eyes. "I haven't spoken to her since. She hasn't contacted me, and didn't take my few attempts to reach her. I assumed things didn't work out as we'd hoped. But I had no idea . . . If she killed him, Lieutenant, if that's what happened, it had to be in self-defense. It had to be."

"Let me just compact all this. You dressed up like a hooker, went to the bar, to the flop with Ned Custer, as a favor to his wife?"

Ava lifted her chin. "I don't appreciate your implications, or your attitude."

"Gee, pardon the hell right out of me."

"Lieutenant, it's so easy to become involved with the lives of these women, to *feel* for them. Suzanne was desperate to save her marriage, her family. She was so certain that if he was caught that way, he'd agree to counseling. And, well, I admit, it seemed exciting. We're very hands-on at Anders. Tommy and I believed in *involvement*. I made a terrible mistake. And now a man's dead." She covered her face with her hands.

"Okay, let's clarify for the record. You state that you met Ned Custer in the bar on the night of January twenty of this year, that you went with him to the flop."

"Yes, yes, to meet Suzanne. He was angry, of course, but she asked me to go. To leave them alone so they could talk it out. I should never have left. I see that now." As if in a plea for understanding, Ava held out her hands to Eve. "How could I know she'd kill him? She said she wanted to save her marriage, how could I know she'd kill him?"

"That's a tough one. You couldn't know."

"I feel terrible about it. Sick about it. But Suzanne, my God, she must've been—"

This time it was Baxter who stepped in, carrying several evidence bags. He murmured as he leaned down to Eve. "Custer's en route."

"Thanks. And look what we have now. Black market bypass remote. And these security discs taken from your home." Eve lifted the disposable 'link. "Cheap-ass piece of crap. Pressure syringes, cock thickener, tranq. All confiscated from Suzanne Custer's apartment."

"My God, my God, is that . . . is that the device used to circumvent our security?" Ava's voice dropped down to a strained whisper. "When Tommy . . . Suzanne? Oh my God, did Suzanne kill Tommy?"

"Bet she did."

"But, but, *why*? Why? Her children were in the program. Tommy and I . . . No. No. No." With her hands pressed to her temples, Ava shook her head from side to side in what Eve considered overacting. "Not because of what happened with her husband. Not because of what I did that night! Please, not because of that."

"Yeah, because of that."

"How can I ever forgive myself?" She wept then, harsh, angry sobs. "It's my fault. It's all my fault. Oh, Tommy. Tommy."

"Do you need a minute, Ava?" Eve reached over, patted her hand. "This is rough. I'm sorry I was so hard on you at the start of the interview. I had to get the motive."

"It doesn't matter, none of it matters. It's my fault. If I hadn't agreed to that foolish business with Suzanne's husband, if I'd never gone to that horrible room with him, Tommy would be alive."

"You're right about that. But here's the thing. You listening, Ava? Can you compose yourself? Okay?"

"Yes. I'm sorry. I'll try, I'll try. This is all such a shock."

"Here's another. Suzanne Custer was never in that flop with you and her husband."

"Of course she was. I saw her. I spoke with her."

"She was in her apartment, blocks away, leaving messages on her husband's 'link while you were slitting his throat. While you came out of the bathroom, sealed up with a six-inch serrated blade and raked it across his throat, she was home, pacing the floor, trying to reach him while you watched him bleed out, while you hacked off his dick, then climbed out the window. While you *practically flew* ten blocks to the auto lot where you had parked your Mercedes, New York plate A AVA in the slot you'd reserved."

It *was* tingly, Eve realized. It was downright tingly to watch Ava's face.

"I got the time in, I got the time out. Time out comes twenty-one minutes after time of death. Here's something else. You sealed up, but you didn't think about how dirty the windows are in those flops, how nasty the sills are, how that crud might latch on to the bottom of your fuck-me shoes. We'll be processing your shoes, Ava, and I'm betting on them."

Eve shrugged. "Not really important though, since you've admitted—on record—that you were there."

"And I told you why, and that the man was alive when I left. What possible reason would I have to kill him? To—to mutilate him afterward? I didn't even know him."

"You've already said why. If Custer hadn't been killed, Tommy would be alive. See this?" She tapped the 'link. "Piece of crap, as I said. Most people think these crappy disposables can't hold transmission history. But those EDD geeks? They're freaking magicians."

Eve leaned forward, smiled brilliantly. "*Good girl.* Do you remember saying that to Suzanne—from the balmy shores of St. Lucia, when she reported she'd done the job? Wanna hear for yourself?" Eve pressed a button on the link, and Ava's voice buzzed out.

Good girl.

"They'll clean that up some, but I wanted you to hear it as soon as it was ready. Nice of you to give Suzanne that little pat on the head."

"This is ridiculous, and you're pathetic. It's obvious Suzanne killed her husband and mine. She must be horribly sick. As far as that 'link goes, I spoke with her any number of times over the last months."

"From St. Lucia? They triangulate these transmissions really well."

"I don't recall. I might have."

And more tingles, Eve thought, as she saw the pulse in Ava's throat start to pound. "Previous statement: You haven't spoken or had contact with Suzanne Custer since the night her husband was murdered."

"I might have been mistaken about that."

"No, you lied about that. It's the lies that tripped you up. It was a pretty solid plan, I'll give that to you. But you couldn't keep it simple. You had to elaborate, make yourself more of a stoic, loyal, and loving wife by painting your husband as so much less than he was. You had to make him pay for all those years you played the loving wife. He never hired LCs, never had affairs, never demanded kink from you."

"You can't prove or disprove what happens between people in the privacy of their bedroom."

"Yeah, that was your thinking on it. It's not bad. But I can prove no one who ever knew him or had business with him can corroborate your claim. I can prove you substituted a sleep aid for his nightly vitamin the morning before you left for St. Lucia. I can prove you conspired with Suzanne Custer in a scheme where each of you agreed to murder the other's spouse. I can prove you approached at least two other women, fishing the idea before you settled on Suzanne."

"It means nothing, none of it means—"

"Not done," Eve commented. "I can prove your father-in-law—whose murder I'm also going to hang on you given a little more time—was annoyed with the way you were allocating funds earmarked for the program."

"Ridiculous." But her body jumped. "Insane."

"You keep thinking that," Eve invited. "Reginald Anders's murder opened the door to your long-term plans. I can prove you not only spoke with, not only contacted Suzanne after Custer's murder, but drove to a lot several blocks from her home—reserved slot again—and met her on the street where you were seen by witnesses. Black coat, fur trim. We've got that in evidence now, too. I can prove you drove her to a rest stop off the Turnpike, where you were seen by witnesses."

"She was blackmailing me."

"Oh please."

"After she killed her husband, she blackmailed me. She said she'd call the police, that she'd tell them I was having an affair with her husband, and that she knew he was meeting me that night. I was terrified. I met her that day, outside her building, to give her the last payment. I drove out of the city to that rest area, and I gave her the last payment. I told her it had to be the last, and she was angry. That must be why she killed Tommy."

"How much she sting you for? Quick, quick," Eve said when Ava hesitated. "How much?"

"Two hundred thousand dollars."

"See, you should've lowballed it. That's too much for her to hide, too much for you to skim without leaving crumbs."

"I sold some jewelry."

"No, Ava, no." Heaving a sigh, Eve leaned in. "Now you're disappointing me. I gave you more credit. We can check that. First, going back, Suzanne doesn't have the brains or the balls to blackmail anyone. Going further back, not only wasn't she in the room when Ned bought it, but she's too short to have executed the killing blow. This is basic forensics, and juries are pretty savvy there. Got you cold on that one. Witnesses, forensics, your own statement putting you there."

"She didn't come. She didn't come as arranged, and he attacked me."

"Who? Let's be specific since we've got such a winding road here."

Ava picked up her cup again, drank. "Suzanne's husband."

"Ned Custer attacked you?"

"Yes. He wanted sex, and I told him Suzanne was coming, and he was furious, and attacked me. I was terrified; you have to understand. He was going to rape me, so I grabbed the knife."

"From where?"

"From . . ."

"Quick!" Eve snapped and had Ava jolting again. "Where'd you get the knife?"

"From him. He had the knife. He threatened me with it, and we struggled. I lashed out, in fear for my life."

"You killed Ned Custer."

"Yes, yes, but in self-defense. He was a mad man, waving the knife, shouting. He tore at my clothes. I was terrified."

"I'll take the admission of guilt, but not the plea. And neither will a jury. Basic forensics again, Ava. You took him out from behind."

"We were struggling."

"With one, clean slice. No defensive wounds, no signs of struggle on him or in the room. You did a damn good job of it."

"I want a lawyer. Now."

"Sure. While we're taking care of that," Eve said as she began to gather the evidence bags and files, "I'll go have a little chat with Suzanne. She should be here by now."

"It was her idea."

"I'm sorry, Ava, you've invoked your right to counsel. I can't take any further statements from you until such time as—"

"Fuck the lawyer. I don't want a damn lawyer. I need your help. Aren't you a public servant? Isn't it your duty to help someone in trouble? Isn't that what I *pay* you for?"

"So I'm told. For the record, you're again waiving your right to counsel?"

"Yes, yes, yes. It was her idea. I was upset with Tommy for some silly thing, and I'd been drinking. She came to my room, at the retreat, and we started to talk."

Ava's breath came fast. Eve imagined her thoughts came even faster.

"She said we'd both be better off without our husbands. I was in a mood, I agreed. Then she hatched this idea about how each of us would kill the other's. It was foolishness, or so I believed. We talked and talked, plotting it out. Laughing about it. It was just a *joke*. I was awfully drunk, just feeling blue and ridiculous, and it made me laugh to speculate on how we'd do it.

"But then weeks later, she came to me and told me it was time. I was horrified, of course. I told her she had to be out of her mind to think I'd do such a thing. Out of her mind to believe I actually wanted my Tommy dead. She was . . . fierce. If I didn't do what we'd agreed, she *would* kill Tommy. I wouldn't know when or how, but she would kill him. She meant it. The more I argued, pleaded, protested, the more vicious she became. I did it to save my husband, I did it to save his life."

"You're scraping bottom now, but thanks for the 'I did it.' And the confession of the initial plot."

"Hers! Hers! It was her plot."

"She couldn't plot her way out of her own apartment. Look at this." Eve tapped the evidence bags. "Didn't you *tell* her to get rid of this stuff? But no, she hauls it home and stuffs it in her closet. You picked a moron for a partner, Ava—or a patsy, depending on your view of it. But you screwed up plenty. Both of your husbands killed in sex-related murders? I'm not the moron here. You're too stupid to pull it off, too hyped on giving your own enough juice to put you into media spotlight. It's that PR training. Any story's a good story. You fucked this up, all the way back to your father-in-law."

"You'll never prove it. None of it. Everything you have is speculation."

"Oh, lots more than. And there's the little matter of your confessions."

"You twisted my words around. You tricked me, put words in my mouth. And you didn't advise me of my rights before the interview."

"Officer Trueheart did—on record. Covers us both, Ava." Eve smiled broadly. "Oh, and you may not have recognized the guy talking to Roarke outside. But he's the kind of businessman who takes precautions. You had one of your volunteers pick up the remote—but I've got a solid witness who followed her all the way to your house, where it was delivered. It's just icing on my cake. But, upside for you? You're going to get hours and hours of screen time over this."

Eve shook her head, picked up her files and bags. "You stupid, pitiful murderer."

Ava came up like a tidal wave, heaving the table aside. That tight skin she'd worn for years was split into shreds now, Eve noted.

"Stupid? We'll see who's stupid at the end of the day, you *bitch*. Nobody's going to believe any of this. I have friends. Powerful friends and between us we'll eat you and your ridiculous *interview* to bits."

"Lady, you've got no one. You did have. You had a good, decent man who loved you."

"What do you know about it? What do you know? Sixteen years of my life invested in a man who obsessed about golf and box scores, and children that weren't his own. I earned everything I have."

"Marrying it isn't earning it."

"You married money. Who are you to talk?"

"I married a man. The man. You'll never get that. Your kind isn't capable of it. On the door."

When it opened, she passed out the files and bags to the officer outside, then turned back. "Ava Anders, you're under arrest for the murder of Ned Custer, and for conspiracy to murder Thomas A. Anders. Other charges include—"

"Get me a fucking lawyer. Get the Prosecuting Attorney in here. Now, goddamn it. He'll make a deal for my testimony against that twit."

"You can have the lawyer, but the PA already made a deal with Suzanne Custer this morning." Eve grinned. *"Psych."*

She saw it coming. God, she'd been praying for it all through the interview. Anticipating it so that the cop on the door, and those in Observation stayed back, as she'd ordered, when Ava charged her.

She turned away from the nail swipe so those long, pretty nails barely broke the skin under her jaw. And she took the first shove that bashed her into the wall.

The rest would look better on the record that way. Eve stomped on Ava's instep, plowed an elbow into her gut, then finished with a solid uppercut.

She studied the woman sprawled unconscious at her feet. "Guess we'll get into those other charges when you wake up. On the door." Eve stepped over Ava. "You and another officer take her down through Booking when she regains consciousness. She wants a lawyer, see that she's allowed to contact one."

"Yes, sir. Lieutenant, you're bleeding some."

"Yeah." Eve brushed her fingertips over the nail marks. "All in a day's. Interview end."

Reo was the first out of Observation. "Good enough for you?" Eve asked her.

"And then some. I'm going to make her lawyers cry like babies. Fun for me now. You've had yours."

"Showed?"

"To those of us who know and love you. You should've decked her before she scratched you."

Eve angled her head, tapped just below the marks. "Jury's going to love it, if it goes that far. Wrap her up, Reo. I want to take a moment out of my day now and then to think about her rotting in a cement cage off-planet."

"Anything for a pal. I'd better get to it."

"Peabody, get the paperwork on this, will you?"

"Sure, it was fun to watch so writing it up's fair as the price of admission."

She started by, but Baxter stepped in her path. And held

out a hand. A bit baffled she took it, shook. "It's a good day," he said, and she nodded.

"Yeah, it's a good day. You're back off the roll until Monday."

"I'll see this through, then I'm off."

She cut through to her office for a quick boost of coffee. Thinking of Tibble—and more important, his wife—she decided she'd contact Commander Whitney, give her oral. And let him pass it on. Just in case.

"Sit," Roarke ordered as he walked in with a small first-aid kit.

"Look, Nurse Studly—"

"We'll play Nurse Studly and Patient Sexy later. Now sit so I can doctor those scratches. Nasty cats like that have nasty germs."

"She is pretty nasty." Eve sat, tipped up her head. "I should've just knocked her back. If I get slapped for knocking her out, I've got it coming."

"I don't think so."

"The instep was for Suzanne's kids, the elbow in the gut was for me. The knockout, that was for Tommy Anders."

As he cleaned and medicated the scratches, Roarke met her eyes. "She deserved each, and the rest you've seen to she'll get. You strung it out quite a bit."

"Yeah, that was indulgent. But I liked how she kept twisting herself up, changing her story. And all the tinglies were tough to resist. She's good at planning, but she's crappy at thinking on her feet. Makes it tougher for her lawyers when she gives so many conflicting statements in one interview. Plus, she's not going to be able to afford a bunch of fat lawyers now."

"Oh?"

"She can't use anything coming from the death of her spouse, as she's charged with conspiring to murder same. That cuts it back. And if I can pin down the Hampton case, she'll lose what she got from the father-in-law's death. She's going to have a lot less to spend on fancy lawyers. Anyway."

"Anyway." He leaned down, brushed his lips to hers. "You're done." He set the first-aid kit on her desk. "Any thoughts to going home?"

"Yeah, as soon as I contact Whitney and run it for him. And I figure I'll give Nadine a heads-up. Maybe you can buy me a fat, juicy steak."

"Maybe I could."

"Roarke."

"Eve."

It made her smile, but her eyes stayed serious on his. "What she said about me marrying for money?"

"You answered it, and quite well."

"Yeah, but we know some people think that."

"Eve—"

"Some people think it sometimes, some people think they know it all the time. You and me, we know different."

"We do, yes." He drew her to her feet, and this time the kiss was long and deep and just a little dark. "We both know you married me for the sex."

"Well, yeah, which is why I don't mind if some people think it was the money, because that's less personal. Thanks for the first aid."

"I'd say anytime, but it so often is."

She grinned, then sat down to contact her commander.

Roarke settled in her visitor's chair. He took out his PPC and amused himself by checking the stock reports on Anders. He thought it might be quite fitting to buy up the shares formerly owed by Ava Anders.

And put them in Eve Dallas's name.